STENDHAL

is the pseudonym made illustrious by
Marie Henri Beyle (1783-1842), one of the
world's greatest writers.

Born and educated at Grenoble, Stendhal
distinguished himself as a soldier under
Napoleon. He spent most of his adult
life in the French foreign service,
peculiarly suitable to him since he was a man
of the world who enjoyed and understood
the most complex and sophisticated society.

Stendhal was a lion in the Paris literary
salons, but Italy was the beloved country
of his choice. Journals he kept while
living in Milan provided material
for his greatest novel,
THE CHARTERHOUSE OF PARMA.

Stendhal even composed his famous epitaph
in his adopted language, Italian:
"Visse, scrisse, amò."
"He lived, he wrote, he loved."

A BANTAM CLASSIC

THE CHARTERHOUSE
OF PARMA

by

STENDHAL
(Marie Henri Beyle)

The definitive modern translation

by

LOWELL BAIR

With an introduction by
HARRY LEVIN

THE CHARTERHOUSE OF PARMA

Published as a Bantam Classic July 1960

Library of Congress Catalog Card Number: 60-7376

INTRODUCTION

BY HARRY LEVIN

The happy few, to whom this book is dedicated on its final page, must have been multiplying in recent years. In 1943 the sole available English translation, that of C. K. Scott-Moncrieff, was dropped from a popular list of reprints because it had not proved popular enough to reward its publishers. Since then not only has it come back into print, but it has been accompanied by many of Stendhal's other and lesser works, some of them translated for the first time. Now Mr. Bair has given us at last an American *Charterhouse of Parma*, well designed for a wide circulation, which succeeds in catching the rapid pace and dynamic immediacy of its unique original. Scott-Moncrieff's version, like everything else he touched, had its literary qualities; yet it sometimes carried them to the point of mannerism or pedantry. Too often it rendered colloquial phrases by Anglicisms confusing to non-English readers. It also went out of its way to Italianize French words which might more pertinently have been Englished. The net impression is that of a British tourist determined to be our guide through Italy—whereas the author's personal rhythm and confidential tone should invite us directly, as they do here, to a complete absorption in his story.

He would not himself have been surprised at this increasing measure of public acceptance. He had learned to accept his own career as a rather ineffectual man of the world, with a highly developed taste for travel, for the arts, and for the feminine sex, who had seen youthful service in the Napoleonic campaigns and was eking out his middle age at a minor consular post. The tangible fruit of his leisure, the outcome of so much scattered observation and accumulated experience, was his voluminous writing. Though it gained little recognition for him among his contemporaries, he does not seem to have minded. Addressing himself to posterity, he cultivated the special candor and the sharp penetration which it takes to reach that ultimate audience. Correctly he predicted that he would be rediscovered a generation after his death, and that he might not be fully appreciated until the middle years of the twentieth century. That he would ever find a following in the United States—a republic which he admired in principle and distrusted in practice—probably went beyond his expectations. Yet he would like us better today because we enjoy the opera; while we, in welcoming a new edition of his masterpiece, may congratulate ourselves upon our maturing appreciation.

It is not hard to understand why earlier editions lapsed, or why—with the exception of Balzac—the book attracted scant notice from contemporary critics. Balzac, in his enthusiastic review, declared that it ought to be read primarily by diplomats, statesmen, publicists, social leaders, the most distinguished artists, the twelve or fifteen hundred personalities dominating European life. Through this generous but somewhat intimidating overstatement, he evidently wanted to single out the particular charm it has for those who share its worldly wisdom; who recognize, from their own responsibilities and involvements, how subtly and shrewdly Stendhal has retraced the varying patterns of human interrelationship. Worldliness of this kind is more frequently conveyed by memoirs, aphorisms, or comedies than it is by the more subjective novel; and indeed there are elements of those other forms in *The Charterhouse of Parma*. When Balzac retitled it *The Modern Prince*, he implied that it might hold a further appeal for the less sophisticated, as a Machiavellian handbook introducing them to the ways of the world. But maturity is the password to Stendhal's domain; to the reader who lacks it, he will seem cold and cynical, as will Jane Austen, Congreve, Voltaire, and Montaigne.

In that respect Stendhal's previous major novel, *The Red and the Black*, has proved more appealing to younger sensibilities. It prepared the way for later fictional studies of the adolescent ego, of the ambition to become a superman, and of protest or revolt against an established system. Hence we could compare it with Dostoevsky's *Crime and Punishment*, Dreiser's *American Tragedy*, or Jean Genet's *Our Lady of the Flowers*. On the other hand, *The Charterhouse of Parma* is quite incomparable. No one but Stendhal could have written anything like it. Not that it is autobiographical, like so many of his other writings. Rather, it may be regarded as a testament of his last years, a consummation of all his strivings and strayings, the crystallization—to use a characteristic term—of his peculiar responses to a sequence of epoch-making circumstances. This may help to explain the remarkable feat of its composition, during the fifty-two days between

November 4 and December 26, 1838. Dictation, though it may have led to a number of trivial inconsistencies, enabled Stendhal to sustain the note of improvisation, the conversational spontaneity of his style at its best. Its apparent effortlessness was grounded, as he might have claimed with Whistler, upon a lifetime's effort of artistic preparation.

Stendhal liked to base his fiction on actual documents, and he was particularly interested in first-hand anecdotes of the Italian Renaissance. In the present instance he was following an account of the grand courtesan, Vandozza Farnese: how her noble house had owed its rise to her notorious affair with Cardinal Borgia, who became Pope Alexander VI, and how her nephew Alessandro had survived intrigue and imprisonment to ascend the papal throne as Paul III. Here, with certain strategic differences, was an outline for Stendhal's narration. His focal point would still be the duchy of Parma; but he transposed the time from the sixteenth century to his own day, more than a hundred years after the long rule of the Farnese dynasty. The tale begins in 1796, about one year before the hero's birth, and ends shortly after his death, just before the pretended date of writing in 1830. The foreword misleadingly states that the place of writing was far away from Paris; actually Stendhal dictated the narrative, while he was home on leave from his consulate at Civitavecchia, in his apartment on the Rue Caumartin. The plains of Lombardy, the banks of the River Po, and the waters of Lake Como seem all the sunnier for having been evoked through the mist and chill of a Parisian winter.

The allure of "delightful places" is made explicit in the quotation from Ariosto that heads the first volume. Stendhal's idyllic vision of Italy, as he makes clear by frequent cross-reference, is a critique of the France he knew—which, in turn, was the beginning of the France we know, in its moods of calculation and restlessness. His autobiography, *The Life of Henri Brulard*, culminates with the mood of liberation he felt as a sublieutenant in Napoleon's Italian campaign of 1800. These emotions, transferred to Lieutenant Robert, charge the opening atmosphere of *The Charterhouse of Parma;* and Robert, destined to be a general at Waterloo, plays more than a walk-on part; for it is discreetly hinted that the hero, Fabrice, nominally the second son of the Marquis del Dongo, was really the offspring of the Frenchman's romantic *liaison* with the Marquise. Milan in the brief days of the French occupation, as capital of the Cisalpine

Republic, represented a cultural fulfilment which meant so much to Stendhal that he had the word "Milanese" inscribed on his tombstone in the Montmartre Cemetery. It meant, along with more intimate recollections, a convergence of the new ideas set in motion by the French Revolution with those ardors and energies which for him were uniquely personified by the Italian character.

However, this euphoric possibility was cut off by the fall of Napoleon, and that is why the turning-point of Waterloo forms the precipitating episode in the adventures of Fabrice. Under the wave of European reaction associated with the time-serving policies of Metternich, the Italian city-states were squeezed between the Austrian Empire and the temporal might of the Papacy. Their ill-starred régimes made repressive attempts to turn back the clock of history, which to Stendhal were as anachronistic as the powdered hair of his Metternichian politician, Count Mosca. Stendhal believed in enlightenment, and continued to hope for progress; but, amid the revolutions and reactions of his epoch, he had lost his illusions about reforming human nature; and his Liberals, when they come to power, behave as ignobly as his Ultras. In effect, he possesses that rare insight which Lionel Trilling would call "the liberal imagination." Moreover, he has that even rarer talent, a liberal sense of humor. Instead of sketching his ideal state, he caricatures a utopia in reverse, a comic-opera principality depicted upon a scale which reduces its stateliest annals to absurdity. Well might he mockingly wish for an epic pen; for in Parma he created a realm which is ruled by the mock-epic spirit.

Such a setting presupposes a residue of disappointed heroism somewhere in the background. Its touchstone, for Stendhal, is the cult of Napoleon; and its most expressive reverberation is his treatment of Waterloo. This was the first time that the discomforting realities of modern warfare, as experienced by the befuddled participant, had been adequately presented in literature—as subsequent writers, from Tolstoy to Hemingway, have warmly acknowledged. The contrast between the heroic and the anticlimactic, between Fabrice's poetic anticipations and the newspapers after the battle, is Stendhal's refinement upon the technique originated by Cervantes and employed by all realists. That preliminary disillusionment serves as prologue to the grandiose anticlimax of Parma, its hypocritical court, and its reversal of values. Curbing his naive idealism, Fabrice must strictly conform to outmoded standards of conduct and opinion. He must learn to play the game of careerism, which his mentors liken to the game of whist; and he learns so well that, before too long, he finds himself playing whist at the Prince's table. Still more appropriate is the recurrent metaphor of acting. Characters and situations are described as actors and performances; significant encounters take place at the theater; courtiers indulge in *commedia dell' arte;* hero and heroine communicate, at a crucial moment, by *recitative.*

The Charterhouse of Parma is not a historical novel, though it is framed by a hypothetical set of consequences to historic events. Despite its panoramic scope, it concentrates on the psychological sphere; it registers the impact and growth of awareness in the basic experiences of war, politics, love, and religion. Stendhal's novels characteristically follow the fortunes of some neophyte, who is initiated by his elders into the difficult problems of getting along in the world. Stendhal seems to identify emotionally with Julien Sorel, the self-made protagonist of *The Red and the Black,* in his quarrel against society. But toward the aristocratic conformist, Fabrice del Dongo, the author's attitude seems more detached, more closely to be identified with the young protegé's older sponsors. Like Homeric gods, they wangle his destinies; whereas Julien was both conspired against and conspiring, their conspiracies work on Fabrice's behalf. Count Mosca, the local Machiavelli, gives him the benefit of avuncular counsel because he himself is the lover of Fabrice's aunt, the incomparable Duchess of Sanseverina. She is approaching her forties, alas, while Mosca has entered his fifties, during a period when Fabrice—who was in his seventeenth year at Waterloo—is hardly more than twenty-three.

The shift of vantage-point seems to accord with a growing consciousness of the difference between generations as the nineteenth century matured. Slight of stature, prone to tears, Fabrice is taken in hand by a series of motherly women, such as the jailor's wife and the *vivandière.* The dominant figure is, of course, the Sanseverina, a woman whose glamor seems to transcend the limits of merely literary creation. She is a Helen of Troy who, from the walls, directs the strategies of Trojans and Greeks alike; a Cleopatra who beguiles Pompey and Caesar and Antony, not in succession but simultaneously. Stendhal's reminiscence of his mother, who died in his infancy, was distinctly erotic; reciprocally, the Duchess is more than maternal in affectionate surveillance of her nephew. The irony is that, since her brother was not Fabrice's father, in-

ix

cest does not bar a romance between them. She is torn by jealousy when Fabrice, after many casual affairs, falls in love with his jailer's daughter, Clelia Conti; and Mosca, whose relation to his mistress is an adultery of convenience, repeats the pattern by becoming jealous of Fabrice. The single person who understands Gina Sanseverina is the doctor-poet Ferrante Palla, conscientious highwayman and self-nominated tribune of the people, whose entrance into the scene precipitates further reversals.

Overt theatricality masks an underlying sincerity on the part of such Stendhalian figures, which comes to the surface in desperate monologues or capricious gestures. They go through the polite motions, they keep up with courtly gossip: who's in, who's out. They are capable, in self-defense, of blackmail, double-crossing, most of the crimes that Stendhal takes pains to deplore. Sooner or later the moment is bound to come when their repressed passions erupt in public, like— as Stendhal repeatedly said of politics—a pistol-shot at a concert. Gina backs a revolution in Parma which Palla leads; and, though it fails, their fine Italian hands are to be detected in the Prince's assassination. Fabrice rather passively savors the fruits of nepotism, breaking out in an occasional duel or abduction; and yet his decisive acts are prompted by ardent and idealistic motives. Each of his successive initiations, military, political, and amatory, leads him—through a wayward sort of justice, pre-shadowed by numerous omens— to prison. He is incarcerated for his escapades in the brooding citadel of Parma, an imaginary landmark which resembles the Castle of Sant' Angelo at Rome. It casts its shadow over the book as the Spielberg, the fortress that symbolized Austrian repression, menacingly brooded over Stendhal's Italy.

Ideologically, then, the citadel is a monument to the constraining forces of despotism, a house of correction for Parma's invisible cohort of free-thinkers. Yet, psychologically, it is not so repellent a symbol as that view of it might suggest. Its paradoxical fascination lures us, as we are lured by the prisons of Piranesi, not so much downward into the dark underground as upward to an emanation of light. Fabrice's clearest omen was manifested when Father Blanès hid him in the belfry from which he could gaze down upon his native landscape. His feeling of ecstatic detachment prefigured the felicity he would experience in looking out from his tower at the Parmesan sky. True enough, his happiness is dependent upon the proximity of the charming Clelia, and their telegraphic courtship seems to have been predestined from their chance meeting several years before. Small wonder if, like the prisoner of Chillon, he regains his freedom with a sigh. And it is not without significance that his incarceration has lasted nine months, as if it were a regression to the womb. He makes a dashing escape, again prearranged through the intervention of Gina, who has her own mixed reasons for seeing him rescued from the confinement of Clelia's orbit. Inevitably, voluntarily, soon he returns to his blissful durance.

No compunction is wasted over his crime. Morally it is treated as the merest peccadillo, though it is politically exploited to embarrass the government with crises. Nor does anyone seem to be shocked at the fact that this callow rake is technically one of the religious. His novitiate, contrasted with his baptism of fire on the battlefield, seems to be no more than a matter of form, plus the proper clerical opinions. Though he sincerely prays whenever his mundane affairs need divine assistance, it never occurs to him that his way of life taints him daily with the sin of simony. With the collusion of the snobbish Archbishop, he is hastily promoted to the top of the ecclesiastical hierarchy. He uses his position, along with certain histrionic gifts, in order to become a famous preacher. His sermons are theatrical attractions which draw the crowds from the rival *matinée*, and ultimately accomplish their amorous purpose: Clelia, now married to another, is persuaded to break her vow that she never will see Fabrice. She reverts to it, with practised equivocation, by arranging for trysts with him in the darkness. The child of their illicit union becomes, through an apt fatality, the secret object of competing affections and deceptions; less fortunate than his father, he does not survive them.

Thus love, when finally attained by Fabrice, is alloyed with unhappiness; while the Sanseverina, passionate creature that she has been, has been successively thwarted by three loveless marriages. War, as Stendhal's impulsive novice had dabbled in it, had turned out to be wholly bereft of heroics. Religion, which he has yet to take seriously, he has professed as if it were a branch of politics. Each of his initiations has left him in a deeper stage of disillusion. What next? What retreat but the somber institution which has lent the novel its name, and which does not appear in it until the concluding page? The Charterhouse is far less central than the citadel; its function is to stand apart from the story. Stendhal seems to have conceived his work in three volumes, to have completed two of them in detail, and then—at the last-minute behest of his publisher—to have rounded things off with a few abrupt and crowded paragraphs. Yet the shock of a tragic ending after the comedy, the prospect of solitude after so much society, is the logical solution. The gesture of withdrawal operates to restore the values that have been reversed; Stendhal's lovers, after all, have souls to think about; and though they may comply with the courtly hypocrisies, their determining choices are unworldly.

The Charterhouse means incarceration, for Fabrice, with a vengeance. Deliberately he has chosen the most austere and isolated of monastic disciplines—a decision stimulated, perhaps, by Stendhal's memories of the Grande Chartreuse near his birthplace, Grenoble. No Clelia will brighten the view from Fabrice's cell; no Sanseverina will preside over his fate; no Mosca will plot for his well-being. He will die young, within a year after taking his Carthusian vows, preceded by Clelia and followed by the Duchess. But he will doubtless have had the opportunity to review, in monkish contemplation, what he has lived through in passionate action. Stendhal has drawn a curtain across his penance, and he is remembered for his debonaire moments. Yet his world would be incomplete if he did not end by renouncing it, by rushing from the extreme of gay abandonment to the extreme of melancholy rigor. Between those extremes a vast distance is traversed and put into perspective, so that—from the Stendhalian heights—the scenery is magnificent and the overview exhilarating. As for the aftertaste, Stendhal himself summed it up in his favorite critical label, *sec*. That dryness is not of the dry-as-dust academy, nor is it the drouth of an esoteric wasteland. It is the bittersweet ebullition of sparkling wine.

FOREWORD

This novel was written in the winter of 1830, and at a distance of three hundred leagues from Paris; it therefore contains no allusions to the events of 1839.

Long before 1830, in the days when our armies were over-running Europe, I happened to be billeted in a canon's house. This was in Padua, a charming Italian city. As my stay lengthened, the canon and I became friends.

Passing through Padua again toward the end of 1830, I hurried to the good canon's house. He was no longer living, and I knew it, but I wanted to revisit the drawing room where we had spent the many pleasant evenings which I have missed so often ever since. I found the canon's nephew and his wife, who welcomed me as an old friend. A few people came in, and we did not separate until very late that night. The nephew sent out for an excellent *zabaione* from the Caffè Pedrocchi. What kept us up more than anything else was the story of Duchess Sanseverina, to which someone alluded, and which the nephew was kind enough to relate fully, in my honor.

"In the country to which I'm going," I said to my friends, "I won't find many evenings like this, so, to while away the long hours of darkness there, I'll make a novel of your story."

"In that case," said the nephew, "I'll give you my uncle's chronicles. Under the heading of Parma, he mentions some of the intrigues at that court in the days when the duchess held sway over it. But be careful! The story is anything but moral, and now that you pride yourselves on your evangelical purity in France, it may earn you a criminal reputation."

I am publishing this novel without changing anything in the manuscript of 1830. This may have two drawbacks:

The first one concerns the reader: the characters, being Italians, will perhaps interest him less, since hearts in Italy are quite different from French hearts. The Italians are sincere, straightforward people who, unabashed, say what they think. They have only spasmodic outbursts of vanity; it then becomes a passion and takes the name of *puntiglio*. And to them, poverty is not a subject of ridicule.

The second drawback has to do with the author.

I confess that I have had the temerity not to smooth out the rough spots in the characters; but, on the other hand, I state emphatically that I cast the strongest moral censure on many of their acts. What would be the use of giving them the lofty morality and social graces which distinguish the character of the French, who love money above all else and almost never sin from hatred or love? The Italians in this novel are more or less the opposite. Furthermore, it seems to me that each time we move two hundred leagues northward from the South, a new novel is called for, as different as the landscape. The canon's niece had known and even loved Duchess Sanseverina, and she has begged me to alter nothing in her adventures, which are reprehensible.

January 23, 1839

BOOK ONE

Gia mi fur dolci inviti a empir le carte
I luoghi ameni.

— ARIOSTO, SAT. IV

CHAPTER ONE

Milan in 1796

On May 15, 1796, General Bonaparte made his entry into
Milan at the head of that young army which had just crossed
the Bridge of Lodi and taught the world that, after so many
centuries, Caesar and Alexander now had a successor. The
miracles of valor and genius which Italy witnessed in the
space of a few months aroused a slumbering people. Only a
week before the arrival of the French, the Milanese still
regarded them as nothing but a mob of brigands who invariably fled before the troops of His Imperial and Royal Highness—this, at least, was what was repeated to them three
times a week by a little newspaper no bigger than your hand,
printed on dirty paper.

In the Middle Ages, the republicans of Lombardy had
shown valor equal to that of the French, and it had earned
them the privilege of seeing their city razed to the ground by
the German emperors. Since becoming "loyal subjects," their
chief concern had been printing sonnets on little handkerchiefs
of pink taffeta each time there was a wedding of some young
lady belonging to a rich or noble family. Two or three years
after this great period of her life, the young lady would take
an attendant gallant; sometimes the name of the *cicisbeo*
chosen by the husband's family occupied an honorable place
in the marriage contract. It was a far cry from these effeminate
ways to the deep emotions aroused by the unexpected arrival
of the French army. A new and passionate way of life soon
sprang into being. An entire people realized, on May 15,

1

1796, that everything they had respected till then was supremely ridiculous and sometimes odious. The departure of the last Austrian regiment marked the downfall of the old ideas. Risking one's life became fashionable; people saw that, in order to be happy after centuries of insipid feelings, they had to love their country with genuine love, and seek heroic actions. They had been plunged into profound darkness by the long, vigilant despotism of Charles V and Philip II; they overturned these tyrants' statues and suddenly found themselves flooded with light. For the past fifty years, as Voltaire and the *Encyclopédie* became increasingly influential in France, the monks had been loudly proclaiming to the good people of Milan that learning to read or acquiring any knowledge of the world was an utter waste of time, and that if they scrupulously paid their tithes to the parish priest and faithfully related all their little sins to him, they were almost sure to have a fine place in heaven. To complete the enervation of this people once so violent and contentious, Austria had sold them, at a low price, the privilege of not having to furnish any recruits for her army.

In 1796, the Milanese army was composed of twenty-four worthless rascals in red uniforms who guarded the city in conjunction with four magnificent regiments of Hungarian grenadiers. Morals were extremely lax, but passion was very rare. Besides the annoyance of having to tell the parish priest everything, under penalty of being ruined even in this world, the good people of Milan were also subjected to certain little monarchical restrictions that were constantly irritating. For example, the archduke, who resided in Milan and ruled in the name of the emperor, his cousin, had conceived the lucrative idea of engaging in the grain trade. As a result, the peasants were foribdden to sell their grain until His Highness had filled his granaries.

In May, 1796, three days after the arrival of the French, a young and slightly mad miniature-painter by the name of Gros, later famous, who had come with the army, heard someone in the great Caffè dei Servi (which was then in fashion) describing the exploits of the archduke, who, besides everything else, was enormously fat. He picked up the list of ices printed on one side of a sheet of ugly yellow paper, and on the back of it he drew a picture of the fat archduke: a French soldier was thrusting a bayonet into his stomach, and, instead of blood, an incredible quantity of grain was pouring out. Anything resembling what is called a lampoon or a caricature was unknown in that country of wary despotism. The drawing, left by Gros on the table of the Caffè dei Servi, appeared to be a miracle descended from heaven; it was printed during the night, and the next day twenty thousand copies of it were sold.

That same day, notices were posted to announce a levy of six million lire, imposed for the needs of the French army, which, having just won six battles and conquered twenty provinces, lacked only shoes, trousers, coats and hats.

The mass of happiness and pleasure that burst into Lombardy with these shabby Frenchmen was so great that only the priests and a few noblemen felt the burden of this levy of six million lire, which was soon followed by many others. The French soldiers laughed and sang all day long; they were all under twenty-five years of age, and their commanding general, who was twenty-seven, was known as the oldest man in his army. Their gaiety, youthfulness and carefree behavior provided an amusing answer to the furious preaching of the monks, who for the past six months had been announcing from their pulpits that the French were monsters, that they were obliged, under penalty of death, to burn everything and cut off everyone's head. For this purpose, each regiment marched with a guillotine in the lead.

In the countryside, French soldiers could be seen in cottage doorways, dandling the housewife's baby, and nearly every evening some drummer, playing a fiddle, would improvise a ball. Since their quadrilles proved to be so difficult and intricate that the soldiers, who, moreover, scarcely knew them themselves, could not teach them to the women of the country, it was the women who taught the young Frenchmen the *monteferrina*, the *saltarello* and other Italian dances.

The officers had been lodged, as far as possible, in the houses of rich families; they had great need to renew their strength. For example, a lieutenant named Robert was billeted in the palace of the Marquise del Dongo. When this officer, a young conscript of rather free and easy morals, entered the palace, his entire fortune consisted of a single scudo worth six francs which he had received at Piacenza. After the crossing of the Bridge of Lodi, he had taken a magnificent pair of brand-new nankeen trousers from a handsome Austrian officer who had been killed by a cannon ball. No garment has ever come at a more opportune moment. His epaulettes were of wool, and the cloth of his coat was sewn to the lining of his sleeves to hold the pieces together. But there was an even sadder detail: the soles of his shoes were made of pieces of hats which he had also picked up on the battlefield, on the other side of the Bridge of Lodi. These makeshift soles were attached by strings that were clearly visible on the uppers of his shoes, so that when the major-domo of the house came into his room to invite him to dine with the marquise, the young officer was overcome with embarrassment. He and his orderly spent the two hours that separated them from that fateful dinner in trying to patch up his coat a little, and in dyeing the wretched strings on his shoes with black ink. Finally the terrible moment arrived.

"I've never felt more ill at ease in my life," Lieutenant Robert said to me later. "The ladies thought I was going to frighten them, but I was trembling more than they were. I kept looking down at my shoes, and I didn't know how to walk gracefully. The Marquise del Dongo was then in the full bloom of her beauty: you saw her yourself, with her beautiful eyes, full of angelic sweetness, and the lovely auburn hair that framed her charming oval face so attractively. In my room there was a *Herodias* by Leonardo da Vinci that looked like a portrait of her. By God's grace, I was so overcome by her supernatural beauty that I forgot about my clothes. For the past two years I'd seen nothing but ugly and miserable things in the mountains around Genoa. I took the liberty of saying a few words to her about my delight.

"But I had sense enough not to spend much time making compliments. As I was delivering my pretty phrases, I looked into a dining room made entirely of marble and saw a dozen footmen and lackeys dressed in what then seemed to me the height of splendor. Imagine—the rascals had not only good shoes, but silver buckles as well! Out of the corner of my eye, I could see them staring stupidly at my coat, and perhaps at my shoes too, and it cut me to the quick. I could have frightened them all with a word, but how could I have put them in their place without running the risk of alarming the ladies? For the marquise, to give herself a little courage, as she told me many times afterward, had sent for her husband's sister, Gina del Dongo, who later became the charming Countess Pietranera, from the convent school where she was then a boarder. In prosperity, no one ever surpassed her in gaiety and gracious wit, just as, in adversity, no one ever surpassed her in courage and serenity of soul.

"Gina, who was about thirteen at that time, but looked eighteen, a lively, forthright girl, as you know, was so afraid of bursting out laughing at the sight of my costume that she didn't dare to eat. The marquise, however, showered me with polite, constrained attentions; she could clearly see glimmers of impatience in my eyes. In short, I was cutting a sorry figure. I was swallowing contempt, something that's said to be impossible for a Frenchman. Finally a heaven-sent idea illuminated my mind: I began telling the ladies about my poverty, about what we had suffered for two years in the mountains around Genoa, where we'd been retained by idiotic old generals. There, I said, we were given paper money which wasn't legal tender in that region, and three ounces of bread a day. I hadn't been speaking two minutes before there were tears in the good marquise's eyes and Gina had become serious.

" 'What, lieutenant,' said Gina, 'three ounces of bread?'

" 'That's right, signorina; but I must add that three times a week there was no ration at all, and that, since the peasants we lived with were even poorer than ourselves, we used to give them a little of our bread.'

"When we left the table, I offered the marquise my arm and accompanied her to the door of the drawing room, then I hurried back and gave the servant who'd waited on me at table the single scudo on which I'd built so many castles in Spain as I planned how to spend it.

"A week later, when it was well established that the French weren't guillotining anyone, the Marquis del Dongo came back from his castle of Grianta, on Lake Como, where he had gallantly taken refuge at the approach of the army, abandoning his beautiful young wife and his sister to the hazards of war. His hatred of us was equal to his fear, that is, it was immeasurable. His fat, pale, sanctimonious face was comical to see when he greeted me politely. On the day after his return to Milan, I received three and a half yards of cloth and two hundred lire from the levy of six million. I fitted myself out with new clothes and became the ladies' cavalier, for the season of balls was beginning."

Lieutenant Robert's story is essentially the same as that of every other Frenchman; instead of making fun of those brave soldiers' poverty, the people took pity on them and loved them.

This period of unexpected happiness and excitement lasted only two short years. The jubilation was so frenzied and widespread that it is impossible for me to give any idea of it, except by this profound historical observation: these people had been bored for a hundred years.

The love of pleasure natural to southern countries had once reigned at the court of the Viscontis and the Sforzas, those famous Dukes of Milan. But since 1635, when the Spaniards seized the Duchy of Milan and began ruling it as taciturn, suspicious and haughty masters, always in fear of revolt, all gaiety had fled. The people, adopting the ways of their masters, thought more of avenging the slightest insult with a dagger than of enjoying the present moment.

Wild joy, gaiety, sensuality and forgetfulness of all sad or even reasonable feelings were carried to such a point between May 15, 1796, when the French entered Milan, and April, 1799, when they were driven from it by the Battle of Cassano, that it was possible to cite old millionaire merchants, usurers and notaries who, during this interval, forgot to be morose and preoccupied with making money.

At most it would have been possible to count a few families belonging to the higher nobility who had withdrawn to their country mansions, as though to sulk against the general exultation and lightheartedness. It is also true that these rich and noble families had been unpleasantly singled out in the imposition of levies for the French army.

The Marquis del Dongo, annoyed by the sight of so much gaiety, was one of the first to withdraw. He returned to his magnificent castle of Grianta, beyond Como, and the ladies took Lieutenant Robert there. This castle, standing in a position that is perhaps unique in the world, on a plateau a hundred and fifty feet above that sublime lake, with a view of a large part of it, had once been a fortress. The del Dongo family had built it in the fifteenth century, as was everywhere evident from the marble statues and ornaments bearing their coat of arms. There were still drawbridges and deep moats. The moats no longer contained water, it is true, but with its walls eighty feet high and six feet thick, the castle was safe from sudden attack, and that was what made it dear to the heart of the suspicious marquis. Surrounded by twenty-five or thirty servants whom he assumed to be devoted to him, apparently because he never spoke to them without insulting them, he was less tormented by fear there than in Milan.

His fear was not entirely unwarranted: he was in active communication with a spy whom the Austrians had posted on the Swiss border, three leagues from Grianta, to aid the escape of prisoners taken on the battlefield, and this might have been taken seriously by the French generals.

The marquis had left his young wife in Milan, where she directed the affairs of the family. She had the responsibility of meeting the levies imposed on the Casa del Dongo, as they say in Italy. She tried to have them diminished, which forced

6

her to visit those noblemen who had accepted public office, and even a few influential commoners.

A great event took place in the family. The marquis had made arrangements for a marriage between his younger sister, Gina, and a very rich man of the highest birth. But he powdered his hair; for this reason, Gina always received him with shouts of laughter, and before long she committed the folly of marrying Count Pietranera. He was, to be sure, a very worthy and handsome gentleman, but his family fortune had been lost before his birth, and, to complete his disgrace, he was a passionate supporter of the new ideas. Pietranera was a second lieutenant in the Italian Legion, a further source of despair for the marquis.

After those two years of wild excitement and happiness, the Directory in Paris, behaving like a well-established sovereign, began to show deadly hatred of anything that was not mediocre. The incompetent generals it assigned to the Army of Italy lost a series of battles on those same plains of Verona which, two years before, had witnessed the prodigious feats of Arcole and Lonato. The Austrians moved closer to Milan. Lieutenant Robert, who was now a major and had been wounded in the Battle of Cassano, came to lodge for the last time in the house of his friend the Marquise del Dongo. Their farewells were sad. He left with Count Pietranera, who was following the French in their retreat toward Novi. The young countess, whose brother had refused to give her the share of the family estate to which she was entitled, followed the army in a cart.

Then began that period of reaction and return to old ideas which the Milanese call *i tredici mesi* (the thirteen months), since it was their good fortune that this return to stupidity lasted only thirteen months, until Marengo. All that was old, sanctimonious and morose reappeared at the head of affairs and resumed leadership of society; those who had remained faithful to respectable doctrines soon spread the news in the villages that Napoleon had been hanged by the Mamelukes in Egypt, as he deserved to be for so many reasons.

Among those who had gone off to their country estates to sulk, and had now come back athirst for vengeance, the Marquis del Dongo distinguished himself by his fury; his fanaticism naturally led him to the head of his party. These gentlemen, who were quite decent when they were not afraid, but who were still trembling, succeeded in beguiling the Austrian general. Although normally a rather kind man, he let himself be persuaded that severity was a farsighted

7

policy: he ordered the arrest of a hundred and fifty patriots who were the best men in Italy at the time.

They were soon deported to the Gulf of Kotor, and, when they had been thrown into underground caves, the dampness and especially the lack of food meted out quick and proper justice to all those scoundrels.

The Marquis del Dongo was given a high position, and since he numbered sordid avarice among his many other fine qualities, he publicly boasted of not sending a single scudo to his sister, Countess Pietranera. Still madly in love, she refused to leave her husband and was now starving with him in France. The good marquise was in despair; finally she managed to pilfer a few small diamonds from her own jewel case, which her husband took away from her every evening in order to lock it up in an iron strongbox under his bed. She had brought him a dowry of eight hundred thousand lire, and he gave her eighty lire a month for her personal expenses. During the thirteen months when the French were out of Milan, that timid woman found pretexts for always wearing black.

We must now confess that, following the example of many solemn authors, we have begun our hero's story a year before his birth. This essential personage is none other than Fabrizio Valserra, Marchesino* del Dongo, as they say in Italy. He had just taken the trouble to be born when the French were driven out, and, by the accident of birth, he found himself the second son of that Marquis del Dongo who was such a great lord, and with whose fat, pasty face, false smile and unbounded hatred of the new ideas you are already acquainted. The whole family fortune was entailed to the elder son, Ascanio del Dongo, the worthy image of his father. He was eight years old, and Fabrizio two, when General Bonaparte, whom all wellborn people thought of as having been long since hanged, suddenly swooped down from the Saint Bernard Pass. He entered Milan; that moment is perhaps unique in history: imagine a whole people madly in love! A few days later, Napoleon won the Battle of Marengo.

It would be useless to tell the rest. The joy of the Milanese was unrestrained, but this time it was mingled with thoughts of vengeance: those good people had been taught to hate. They soon witnessed the arrival of all that remained of the patriots who had been deported to the Gulf of Kotor; their

* Pronounced "markayseena." The local custom, borrowed from Germany, is to give this title to every son of a marquis, *contine* to every son of a count, *contessina* to every daughter of a count, etc.

8

return was celebrated with national rejoicing. Their pale faces, wide, astonished eyes and emaciated limbs formed a strange contrast with the joy that burst forth on all sides. Their arrival was the signal for the departure of the families who had most seriously compromised themselves. The Marquis del Dongo was among the first to flee: he went back to his castle of Grianta. The leaders of the great families were filled with hatred and fear; but their wives and daughters, remembering the joys of the first stay of the French, regretted leaving Milan and missing the gay balls that were given in the Casa Tanza immediately after Marengo. A few days after the victory, the French general whose duty was to maintain order in Lombardy noticed that all the tenant farmers of the nobility, and all the old women in the countryside, far from still thinking about that amazing victory at Marengo, which had changed the whole destiny of Italy and reconquered thirteen fortresses in one day, were entirely preoccupied with a prophecy of San Giovita, the patron saint of Brescia. According to those holy words, the success of the French and of Napoleon was to cease exactly thirteen weeks after Marengo.

There is one thing which slightly excuses the Marquis del Dongo and the other noblemen sulking in the country: without any pretense, they really believed in the prophecy. Not one of them had read more than four books in his life. They openly made preparations to return to Milan at the end of thirteen weeks; but, as time went by, there were new triumphs for the cause of the French. On his return to Paris, Napoleon, by wise decrees, saved the revolution at home, just as he had saved it from foreign powers at Marengo. The Lombard noblemen, sheltered in their castles, then discovered that they had at first misunderstood the prediction made by the patron saint of Brescia: it was not a question of thirteen weeks, but of thirteen months. The thirteen months went by, and the success of the French seemed to be increasing every day.

We shall skip over ten years of progress and happiness, from 1800 to 1810. Fabrizio spent the early part of this period in the castle of Grianta, giving and receiving many beatings among the peasant boys of the village, and learning nothing, not even how to read. Later he was sent to the Jesuit school in Milan. His father the marquis demanded that he be shown Latin, not in the works of those old authors who were always talking about republics, but in a magnificent volume illustrated with more than a hundred engravings, a masterpiece of seventeenth-century art: it was the Latin genealogy of the Valserra family and all its members who had held the title of Marquis del Dongo, published in 1650 by Fabrizio del Dongo, Archbishop of Parma. Since the fortunes of the Valserras had been chiefly military, the engravings depicted a great many battles, and there was always some hero named Valserra wielding his sword mightily. This book delighted young Fabrizio. His mother, who adored him, occasionally obtained permission to go to see him in Milan. Since her husband never gave her any money for these journeys, her sister-in-law, the charming Countess Pietranera, always lent her what she needed. After the return of the French, the countess had become one of the most distinguished women at the court of Prince Eugene, Viceroy of Italy.

When Fabrizio had made his First Communion, she obtained permission from the marquis, still in voluntary exile, to take him out of his school from time to time. She found him strange, intelligent and very serious, but he was also a handsome boy who was not too much out of place in a fashionable lady's drawing room; otherwise, he was as ignorant as anyone could wish, and scarcely able to write. The countess, who brought her enthusiastic character into everything, promised her patronage to the head of the school if her nephew Fabrizio made astonishing progress and received many prizes at the end of the year. To give him the means of earning them, she sent for him every Saturday evening and often did not return him to his masters until Wednesday or Thursday. Although the Jesuits were tenderly cherished by the viceroy, the laws of the kingdom had ordered them expelled from Italy, so the rector of the school, a shrewd man, was fully aware of the advantages to be gained from his association with a woman who was all-powerful at court. He was careful not to complain about Fabrizio's absences, and, although more ignorant than ever, the boy was awarded five first prizes at the end of the year. On that condition, the distinguished Countess Pietranera, accompanied by her husband, the general in command of one of the divisions of the Guard, and five or six of the most important personages of the viceroy's court, came to witness the awarding of the prizes in the Jesuit school. The rector was complimented by his superiors.

The countess took her nephew to all those brilliant festivities which marked the too short reign of the charming Prince Eugene. Acting on her own authority, she had made him an officer in the hussars, and Fabrizio, at the age of twelve, wore that uniform. One day, enchanted by his handsome appearance, the countess asked the prince to give him a position at court as a page, which implied that the del Dongo family was ready to join the party in power. The next day, she had to use all her influence to make the viceroy agree to forget her request; nothing was lacking but the consent of the future page's father, and that consent would have been resoundingly refused. After this folly, which made the sulky marquis shudder, he found a pretext for summoning young Fabrizio back to Grianta. The countess had utter contempt for her brother; she regarded him as a wretched fool who would be malicious if it were ever within his power. But she was passionately fond of Fabrizio, so, after ten years of silence, she wrote the marquis a letter begging him to send her nephew back to her. She received no reply.

When he returned to that formidable castle, built by the most bellicose of his ancestors, Fabrizio knew nothing in the world except how to perform military drills and ride a horse. Count Pietranera, whose doting fondness for the boy was equal to his wife's, had often given him a horse to ride and taken him with him on parade.

On his arrival at the castle of Grianta, Fabrizio, his eyes still red from the tears he had shed over having to leave his aunt's beautiful drawing rooms, found only the warm caresses of his mother and his sisters. The marquis was enclosed in his study with his elder son, the Marchesino Ascanio. They spent their time there concocting letters in code which had the honor of being sent to Vienna; father and son appeared only at mealtimes. The marquis kept repeating with affectation that he was teaching his natural successor to keep double-entry accounts of the yield of each one of his estates. Actually, however, he was too jealous of his power to discuss such things with the son who would inevitably inherit all those entailed estates. He employed him in coding the dispatches, fifteen to twenty pages in length, which, two or three times a week, he had taken into Switzerland, from where they were forwarded to Vienna. The marquis claimed to be keeping his lawful sovereigns informed about internal conditions in the Kingdom of Italy, about which he himself knew nothing, and yet his letters won him great esteem; here is why: he posted a reliable agent on the highway to count the number of soldiers in any French or Italian regiment that was moving to a new station, and when he reported the fact to the court at Vienna, he was always careful to diminish the number of soldiers by at least a quarter. His letters, otherwise ridiculous, had the merit of contradicting others that were more accurate; they were therefore received with pleasure. And so, shortly before Fabrizio's arrival at the castle, the marquis had received the star of a famous Order, the fifth to adorn his chamberlain's coat. To tell the truth, he suffered from the fact that he did not dare to display this coat outside his study, but he never allowed himself to dictate a dispatch without first putting on his embroidered costume, bedecked with all his Orders. He would have felt that he was showing disrespect if he had done otherwise.

The marquise was amazed by her son's charming personality. But she had maintained the habit of writing two or three times a year to General Count d'A——, which was now Lieutenant Robert's name. She had a horror of lying to people she loved; she questioned her son and was appalled by his ignorance.

"I myself know nothing," she thought, "so if it seems to me that he's learned very little, Robert, who knows so much, would regard his education as a total failure; and nowadays a man must have ability." She was almost equally amazed by another discovery: Fabrizio had taken seriously all the religious doctrines the Jesuits had taught him. Although she herself was quite religious, the boy's fanaticism made her shudder. "If the marquis is clever enough to see that means of influencing him," she thought, "he'll rob me of my son's love." She shed many tears, and they increased her passion for Fabrizio.

Life in that castle, peopled by thirty or forty servants, was extremely dull. Fabrizio therefore spent all his days hunting or gliding over the lake in a boat. He was soon on close terms with the coachmen and stablemen; they were all enthusiastic partisans of the French, and openly made fun of the pious valets in the personal service of the marquis or his elder son. The great subject of ridicule with regard to those solemn personages was that, following the example of their masters, they powdered their hair.

CHAPTER TWO

. . . Alors que Vesper vient embrunir nos yeux,
Tout épris d'avenir, je contemple les cieux,
En qui Dieu nous escrit, par notes non obscures,
Les sorts et les destins de toutes créatures.
Car lui, du fond des cieux regardant un humain,
Parfois mû de pitié, lui montre le chemin;
Par les astres du ciel qui sont ses caractères,
Les choses nous prédit et bonnes et contraires;
Mais les hommes chargés de terre et de trépas,
*Méprisent tel écrit, et ne le lisent pas.**

—RONSARD

The marquis professed a vigorous hatred of enlightenment. "Ideas have been the ruin of Italy," he would say. He did not quite know how to reconcile this holy horror of learning with his desire to see his son Fabrizio perfect the education so brilliantly begun in the Jesuit school. To run as little risk as possible, he placed the continuation of Fabrizio's Latin studies in the hands of the good Father Blanès, parish priest of Grianta. For this the priest should have known Latin himself, but it was an object of scorn to him; his knowledge of it was limited to the ability to recite the prayers in his missal and give his flock an approximate idea of their meaning. He was nevertheless highly respected and even feared in the canton. He always said that it was not in thirteen weeks, or even in thirteen months, that the world would witness the fulfillment of the famous prophecy of San Giovita, patron saint of Brescia. He would add, when speaking to trusted friends, that the number thirteen had to be interpreted in a way that would surprise many people if he were free to tell everything (1813).

The fact is that Father Blanès, a man of *primitive* honesty

---

* When evening comes to darken our eyes, smitten with the future, I contemplate the heavens, in which God clearly writes the fates and destinies of all creatures. For sometimes, moved to pity as He looks down from the heavens at a human being, He shows him the path; by the stars that are His signs, He foretells both good and evil things to us. But men, burdened with earthly matters and death, despise these writings and do not read them.

13

and virtue, and an intelligent man as well, spent every night in his belfry: he was madly devoted to astrology. After using up all his days in calculating the conjunctions and positions of various stars, he would employ the better part of his nights in following them in the sky. Because of his poverty, his only instrument was a long telescope with cardboard tubes. It is not difficult to imagine the contempt in which the study of languages was held by a man who spent all his time discovering the precise dates of the fall of empires and the revolutions that change the face of the world. "What more do I know about a horse," he would say to Fabrizio, "when I've been taught that in Latin it's called an *equus?*"

The peasants feared Father Blanès as a great magician; for his part, with the aid of the terror aroused in them by the long hours he spent in the belfry, he kept them from stealing. His colleagues, the priests of the neighboring parishes, were bitterly jealous of his influence and hated him; the Marquis del Dongo merely despised him, because he reasoned too much for a man of such low condition. Fabrizio worshiped him: to please him, he sometimes spent whole evenings making enormous additions or multiplications. Then he would go up to the belfry; this was a great favor, one which Father Blanès had never granted to anyone else; but he loved the boy for his candor. "If you don't become a hypocrite," he would say to him, "you may become a man."

Two or three times a year, Fabrizio, reckless and impetuous in his pleasures, would come close to drowning himself in the lake. He was the leader of all the great expeditions undertaken by the peasant boys of Grianta and Cadenabbia. These children had obtained several small keys, and on very dark nights they would try to open the padlocks of the chains with which boats were attached to trees or big stones near the water's edge. It must be explained that the professional fishermen of Lake Como place trawl lines at a great distance from shore. The upper end of each hanging line is fastened to a small plank covered with cork, and stuck into this plank is a very flexible hazel twig supporting a little bell that tinkles whenever a fish becomes caught and jerks the line.

The great object of the nocturnal expeditions led by Fabrizio was to go out and inspect the trawl lines before the fishermen had heard the warning given by the little bells. The boys chose stormy weather for their perilous ventures, and they embarked early in the morning, an hour before dawn. When they climbed into their boats, these children thought they were plunging into the greatest danger; this was the noble side of their action. Following the example of their fathers, they would devoutly recite an *Ave Maria*. Now it sometimes happened that just as they were about to leave, immediately after the *Ave Maria*, Fabrizio would be struck by a premonition. This was the fruit he had gathered from his astrological studies with his friend Father Blanès, whose predictions he did not believe in. According to his young imagination, this premonition would infallibly announce a good or bad outcome; and since he was more resolute than any of his companions, the whole band gradually became so accustomed to omens that if, as they were about to embark, they spotted a priest on the shore, or saw a crow flying to their left, they would quickly put the padlock back on the chain of the boat and all go home to bed. Thus, while Father Blanès had not imparted his rather difficult science to Fabrizio, he had, without knowing it, infected him with boundless confidence in signs that could foretell the future.

The marquis felt that any mishap with regard to his coded correspondence might place him at his sister's mercy, so every year at the time of the feast of Saint Angela, Countess Pietranera's patron saint, Fabrizio was given permission to go to Milan for a week. He spent the whole year either looking forward to this week or regretting its passing. On that great occasion the marquis presented him with four scudi for his diplomatic journey and, according to his custom, gave nothing to his wife, who went with her son. But one of the cooks, six footmen and a coachman with two horses always left for Como the day before, and every day in Milan the marquise had a carriage at her disposal, and a dinner for twelve people.

The sulky kind of life led by the Marquis del Dongo was certainly not very entertaining, but it had the advantage of permanently enriching the families who were righteous enough to maintain it. The marquis had an income of over two hundred thousand lire a year, and he spent less than a quarter of it; he lived on hope. During the thirteen years between 1800 and 1813, he believed constantly and firmly that Napoleon would be overthrown within six months. It is easy to imagine his delight when, at the beginning of 1813, he learned of the disasters of the Berezina! The taking of Paris and the fall of Napoleon almost made him lose his head; he allowed himself to make remarks that were extremely insulting to his wife and sister. At last, after fourteen years of waiting, he had the ineffable joy of seeing Austrian troops march back into Milan. Following orders from Vienna, the Austrian general received the Marquis del Dongo with a consideration bordering on respect; he was quickly offered one of the most important posts in the government, and he accepted it as the payment of a debt. His elder son was given a lieutenancy in one of the finest regiments of the monarchy, but his second son steadfastly refused to accept the rank of cadet that was offered to him. This triumph, which the marquis enjoyed with rare insolence, lasted only a few months, and was followed by a humiliating setback. He had never had any talent for public affairs, and fourteen years spent in the country with his servants, his notary and his doctor, added to the irascibility of the old age that had overtaken him, had turned him into a totally incompetent man.

Now it is not possible to keep an important position in an Austrian country without having the kind of ability required by the slow and complicated, but extremely reasonable administration of that old monarchy. The Marquis del Dongo's blunders scandalized his staff and even halted the course of administrative business. His ultra-monarchistic statements irritated the populace, which the government wished to plunge into the slumber of apathy. One fine day he learned that His Majesty had graciously deigned to accept his submitted resignation from his administrative post, and was at the same time conferring on him the office of "Second Grand Major-Domo Major of the Lombardo-Venetian Kingdom." The marquis was indignant over the atrocious injustice of which he was a victim. He, who abhorred freedom of the press, published an open letter to a friend. Finally he wrote to the emperor that his ministers were betraying him, that they were all Jacobins. Having done these things, he sadly returned to his castle of Grianta.

He had one consolation. After the fall of Napoleon, certain powerful individuals in Milan had Count Prina, a former minister of the King of Italy and a man of the highest merit, attacked in the street. Count Pietranera risked his life to save that of the minister, who was beaten to death with umbrellas, and whose agony lasted five hours. A priest, the Marquis del Dongo's confessor, could have saved Prina by opening the gate of the San Giovanni church, in front of which the unfortunate minister was dragged and even abandoned for a while in the gutter in the middle of the street; but he derisively refused to open his gate, and six months later the marquis had the happiness of securing a fine promotion for him.

He detested Count Pietranera, his brother-in-law, who, with an income of less than a thousand lire, dared to be quite content, ventured to show his loyalty to what he had loved all his life, and had the insolence to extol that spirit of justice without respect of persons which the marquis called a kind of infamous Jacobinism. The count had refused to serve in Austria; much was made of this refusal, and several months after Prina's death the same individuals who had paid the assassins succeeded in having General Pietranera thrown into prison. Thereupon the countess, his wife, took out a passport and ordered post horses for a journey to Vienna, where she intended to tell the emperor the truth. The assassins became frightened, and one of them, a cousin of the countess, came to her at midnight, an hour before her departure for Vienna, with an order for her husband's release. The next day the Austrian general called in Count Pietranera, received him with all possible courtesy and assured him that his retirement pension would soon be paid to him on the most advantageous terms. The good General Bubna, a man with a keen mind and a warm heart, seemed deeply ashamed of Prina's murder and the count's imprisonment.

After this brief storm, quelled by the countess's firm character, she and her husband lived as best they could on his retirement pension, which, thanks to General Bubna's recommendation, was paid without delay.

Fortunately, it happened that for the past five or six years the countess had been on extremely friendly terms with a very rich young man who was also a close friend of the count; he did not fail to place at their disposal the finest team of English horses in Milan, his box at La Scala, and his house in the country. But the count had a noble heart and a sense of his own courage; he was easily carried away, and would then make rash remarks. One day when he was out hunting with some young men, one of them, who had not served under the same flags as the count, began making jokes about the bravery of the soldiers of the cisalpine republic. The count slapped him, they fought on the spot and the count, who stood alone in his opinions among all those young men, was killed. There was a great deal of talk about this "duel," and those who were present when it happened decided to take a trip to Switzerland.

That ridiculous courage known as resignation, the courage of a fool who lets himself be hanged without saying a word, was not in the countess's character. Furious over her husband's death, she wished that Limercati, the rich young man who was her intimate friend, would also take it into his head

17

to journey to Switzerland, and there either shoot or slap Count Pietranera's murderer.

Limercati found this plan utterly ridiculous, and the countess realized that contempt had killed her love for him. She redoubled her attentions to him; she wanted to stir up his love, then cast him aside and drive him to despair. To make this scheme of vengeance intelligible to French readers, I must explain that in Milan, which is in a country far away from ours, people are still driven to despair by love. The countess, who, in her mourning clothes, far outshone all her rivals, flirted with the young men who held the highest ranks in society, and one of them, Count N——, who had always said that he found Limercati's virtues a little too heavy and stiff for a woman of such wit and intelligence, fell madly in love with her. She wrote to Limercati:

> Will you please, for once, act like an intelligent man? Pretend that you have never met me.
> I am, with perhaps a touch of contempt, your very humble servant,
>
> Gina Pietranera

After reading this note, Limercati went off to one of his country estates; his love rose to fever pitch, he lost his reason and spoke of shooting himself, which is quite uncommon in countries whose people believe in hell. The day after his arrival in the country, he wrote to the countess to offer her his hand and his income of two hundred thousand lire. She sent his letter back to him, unopened, by Count N——'s groom. Whereupon Limercati spent three years on his estates, returning to Milan every month, but without ever having the courage to stay there, boring all his friends with descriptions of his passionate love for the countess and detailed accounts of the favors she had once bestowed on him. In the beginning, he would add that she was ruining herself with Count N——, and that such a relationship dishonored her.

The fact is that the countess had not the slightest love for Count N——, and she told him so when she was completely sure of Limercati's despair. The count, who was a man of the world, begged her not to divulge the sad truth she had confided to him. "If you will have the extreme indulgence," he added, "to go on receiving me with all the outward marks of favor granted to an acknowledged lover, I may find a suitable position for myself."

After this heroic declaration, the countess wanted nothing

more to do with Count N——'s horses or his box at the opera. But for fifteen years she had been accustomed to a life of the utmost elegance; she now had to solve this difficult, or, to speak more accurately, impossible problem: how to live in Milan on a pension of fifteen hundred lire. She gave up her palace, rented two sixth-floor rooms and dismissed all her servants, even her maid, whom she replaced with a poor old woman who did housework for several different people. This sacrifice was actually less heroic and painful than it seems to us: in Milan, poverty is not a subject of ridicule, and therefore does not appear to timorous souls as the greatest of all evils. After several months of this noble poverty, during which she was constantly besieged by letters from Limercati and even from Count N——, who also wanted to marry her, it happened that the Marquis del Dongo, normally a man of abominable stinginess, reflected that his enemies might gloat over his sister's wretched circumstances. What! A del Dongo reduced to living on the pension that the court of Vienna, which had given him so much cause for complaint, granted to the widows of its generals!

He wrote to her that an apartment and an allowance worthy of his sister were waiting for her in the castle of Grianta. The countess's impulsive soul enthusiastically embraced the idea of this new way of life. It had been twenty years since she had lived in that venerable castle, rising majestically amid old chestnut trees planted in the days of the Sforzas. "There," she said to herself, "I'll find rest, and, at my age, isn't that happiness?" (Since she was now thirty-one, she regarded herself as having reached the age of retirement.) "A happy and peaceful life is waiting for me at last, on the shore of that sublime lake where I was born."

I do not know whether she was mistaken, but one thing is certain: that passionate woman, who had just refused so lightly the offer of two enormous fortunes, brought happiness into the castle of Grianta. Her two nieces were overjoyed.

"You've given me back the wonderful days of my youth," the marquise said to her as she embraced her. "The day before you arrived, I was a hundred years old."

The countess began revisiting, with Fabrizio, all the enchanting spots in the vicinity of Grianta which have been so highly celebrated by travelers: the Villa Melzi, which stands opposite the castle, on the other side of the lake, and provides it with a striking view; higher up, the sacred woods of the Sfondrata, and the bold promontory which separates two arms of the lake, that of Como, so voluptuous, and the one

19

that stretches out toward Lecco, full of severity—sublime and delightful spectacles which the most renowned site in the world, the Bay of Naples, equals but does not surpass.

It was with exaltation that the countess recaptured the memories of her early youth and compared them with her present sensations. "Lake Como," she thought, "isn't surrounded, like Lake Geneva, by large fields thoroughly fenced and cultivated according to the best methods, which remind you of money and speculation. Here, on all sides, I see hills of uneven height covered with clumps of trees planted by chance, and which the hand of man hasn't yet spoiled and forced to 'yield a profit.' Among these beautifully shaped hills that run down to the lake in such strange slopes, I can keep all the illusions of Tasso's and Ariosto's descriptions. Everything is noble and tender, everything speaks of love, nothing recalls the ugly aspects of civilization. The villages halfway up the slopes are hidden by big trees, and the charming architecture of lovely steeples rises above the treetops. If, here and there, some little field, fifty paces wide, interrupts the clumps of chestnut and wild cherry trees, my satisfied eyes see plants growing in it that are happier and more vigorous than elsewhere. Beyond those hills, whose summits offer hermitages, all of which one would like to live in, my astonished eyes perceive the peaks of the Alps, always covered with snow, and their stern austerity recalls enough of the sorrows of life to increase my present rapture. The imagination is touched by the distant sound of church bells from some little village hidden beneath the trees; these sounds, softened as they float over the water, take on a tone of gentle melancholy and resignation, and seem to say to man, 'Life is fleeting, so don't reject the happiness that's offered to you; hasten to enjoy it.'"

The language of these delightful spots, whose like cannot be found anywhere else in the world, gave her back the heart she had had at sixteen. She could not understand how she had been able to spend so many years without seeing the lake again. "Can it be," she thought, "that happiness has taken refuge at the beginning of old age?" She bought a boat which she, Fabrizio and the marquise decorated with their own hands, for they lacked money for everything, even though they lived in a house that was maintained in the greatest splendor: since falling out of favor with the government, the Marquis del Dongo had redoubled his aristocratic ostentation. For example, to reclaim ten paces of land from the lake, near the famous avenue of plane trees in the direction of

Cadenabbia, he was having a dike built whose estimated cost would be eighty thousand lire. At the end of the dike, a chapel was being constructed from plans drawn up by the famous Marquis Cagnola. It was made entirely of enormous blocks of granite, and inside it Marchesi, the sculptor then in vogue in Milan, was building a tomb for him on which numerous bas-reliefs were to depict the noble deeds of his ancestors.

Fabrizio's elder brother, the Marchesino Ascanio, decided to join the ladies on their outings; but his aunt threw water on his powdered hair, and every day she found some new practical joke with which to assail his solemnity. Finally he relieved the joyous group, who had not dared to laugh in his presence, by delivering them from the sight of his fat, pasty face. They believed him to be a spy for his father, the marquis, and they had to humor that stern despot, who had been in a constant rage ever since his forced resignation.

Ascanio swore to take vengeance on Fabrizio.

There was a storm in which they were exposed to danger; although they had very little money, they paid the boatmen generously to say nothing to the marquis, who was already showing great irritation over their taking his two daughters with them. They ran into another storm; the storms are violent and unpredictable on this beautiful lake: gusts of wind unexpectedly rush out of two mountain gorges on opposite shores and clash above the water. The countess insisted on landing in the midst of the thunder and the howling wind; she said that if she could stand on a certain rock isolated in the middle of the lake, about the size of a small bedroom, she would witness an extraordinary spectacle: she would see herself assailed on all sides by furious waves. But when she leapt out of the boat she fell into the water. Fabrizio dived in to save her, and they were both swept a considerable distance away. Drowning is no doubt undesirable, but boredom, taken by surprise, was banished from the feudal castle.

The countess had become fascinated by Father Blanès's astrology and primitive character. The little money she had left after acquiring the boat had been spent on a small telescope bought at a bargain price, and nearly every evening, with her nieces and Fabrizio, she would install herself on the platform of one of the Gothic towers of the castle. Fabrizio was the learned member of the group. They would spend several hours there, gaily, far from all spies.

It must be admitted that there were days when the countess did not say a word to anyone. She would be seen strolling beneath the tall chestnut trees, lost in somber reverie: she was too intelligent not to feel occasionally the boredom that comes from not being able to exchange ideas with anyone. But the next day she would laugh as she had done the day before. It was the lamentations of her sister-in-law, the marquise, which produced those gloomy impressions on her naturally active mind.

"Are we going to spend all that's left of our youth in this dreary castle?" the marquise would cry out.

Before the countess's arrival, she had not even had the courage to feel these regrets.

They lived in this manner through the winter of 1814 to 1815. Twice, despite her poverty, the countess went to spend a few days in Milan; her purpose was to see a sublime ballet by Vigano, performed at La Scala, and the marquis did not forbid his wife to accompany her sister-in-law. They went to draw the quarterly payments of the countess's meager pension, and it was the poor widow of the cisalpine general who lent a few sequins to the enormously rich Marquise del Dongo. These expeditions were delightful. They invited some old friends to dinner and consoled themselves by laughing at everything, like real children. This Italian gaiety, full of verve and unexpectedness, made them forget the heavy gloom which the gazes of the marquis and his elder son spread around them at Grianta. Fabrizio, barely sixteen, admirably acted the part of head of the household.

On March 7, 1815, the ladies had been back for two days from a delightful little trip to Milan; they were strolling along the lovely avenue of plane trees which had recently been extended to the very edge of the lake. A boat appeared, coming from the direction of Como, and began making strange signals. One of the marquis' agents leapt up on the dike: Napoleon had just landed at Cannes. Europe was guileless enough to be surprised by this event, which did not surprise the Marquis del Dongo. He wrote his sovereign a letter full of effusive emotion; he offered him his abilities and several million lire, and repeated to him that his ministers were Jacobins in league with the Paris ringleaders.

On March 8, at six o'clock in the morning, the marquis, wearing all his decorations, had his elder son dictate to him the first draft of a third political dispatch. While he was solemnly occupied in transcribing it in his fine, careful handwriting, on paper watermarked with an image of the sovereign, Fabrizio was having himself announced to Countess Pietranera in her room.

"I'm leaving," he said to her. "I'm going to join the emperor, who is also King of Italy; he showed so much friendship to your husband! I'll go by way of Switzerland. Last night in Menaggio, my friend Vasi, the barometer merchant, gave me his passport. Now I'd like you to give me a few napoleons, because I have only two of my own. But I'll go on foot if necessary."

The countess wept with joy and anguish. "Good heavens!" she exclaimed, seizing Fabrizio's hands. "Why did you have to take that idea into your head?"

She stood up, went over to her linen closet and took out a little purse, decorated with pearls, which she had carefully hidden there: it was all she possessed in the world.

"Take it," she said to Fabrizio, "but in the name of God, don't get yourself killed! What would your poor mother and I have left if you were taken from us? As for Napoleon's succeeding, it's impossible, my poor friend: our gentlemen will manage to destroy him. A week ago in Milan, didn't you hear the story of the twenty-three well-organized assassination plots that he escaped from only by a miracle? And at that time he was all-powerful. And you've seen for yourself that the will to ruin him isn't lacking in our enemies; France was nothing at all after his departure."

It was in a tone of the keenest emotion that the countess spoke to Fabrizio about Napoleon's future destiny. "In allowing you to join him," she said, "I'm sacrificing to him what is dearest to me in all the world." Fabrizio's eyes became wet, he shed tears as he embraced her, but his determination to leave was not shaken for an instant. He effusively explained to his dear friend the reasons that had decided him to leave, and which we take the liberty of finding quite amusing.

"As you know, last evening at seven minutes to six we were walking southward on the shore of the lake, along the avenue of plane trees below the Casa Sommariva. There, for the first time, I saw in the distance the boat coming from Como with the great news. As I watched it without thinking of the emperor, with nothing in my mind except envy of those who are able to travel, I was suddenly seized with profound emotion. The boat landed, the agent spoke to my father in an undertone, my father's face changed color and he took us aside to announce the 'terrible news' to us. I turned toward the lake for no other purpose than to hide the tears that were flooding my eyes.

"Suddenly, high in the air, to my right, I saw an eagle, the bird of Napoleon. It was flying majestically toward Switzerland, and therefore toward Paris. 'And I too,' I said to myself immediately, 'will cross Switzerland with the swiftness of an eagle, and go to offer that great man something which, though of little value, is all that I can offer: the aid of my feeble arm. He tried to give us a fatherland, and he loved my uncle.' Then, while the eagle was still in sight, for some strange reason my tears abruptly stopped. And the proof that this idea was sent from heaven is that at the same moment, without hesitation, I made my decision and saw the means of making the journey. In the twinkling of an eye, all the sorrows which, as you know, poison my life, especially on Sundays, were swept away, as though by the breath of God. I saw the great figure of Italy raising herself from the mire in which the Germans kept her plunged;* she stretched forth her lacerated arms, still half laden with chains, toward her king and liberator. 'And I,' I said to myself, 'a still unknown son of that unfortunate mother, will go off to die or conquer with that man marked by destiny, the man who tried to cleanse us of the scorn heaped on us by even the vilest and most slavish inhabitants of Europe.'

"You know," he added, lowering his voice, moving closer to the countess and looking at her intently with fiery eyes, "you know that young chestnut tree my mother planted with her own hands, during the winter in which I was born, beside the big spring in our forest, two leagues from here: I decided to go and see it before doing anything else. 'Springtime isn't too far advanced,' I said to myself, 'so if my tree has leaves, that will be a sign for me. I too must emerge from the torpor in which I'm languishing in this cold, gloomy castle.' Don't you feel that these old, blackened walls, now symbols of despotism and once its instruments, are a true image of dreary winter? They are to me what winter is to my tree.

"Would you believe it, Gina? Last evening, at half-past seven, I reached my tree: it had leaves, pretty little leaves that were already quite big! I kissed them without harming them. I respectfully dug the earth around my beloved tree. Then, filled with new emotion, I went over the mountain to Menaggio: I needed a passport to enter Switzerland. Time had flown; it was already one o'clock in the morning when I arrived in front of Vasi's door. I thought I'd have to knock for a long time to wake him, but he was still up, with three of his friends. As soon as he heard my first few words he

---

* The speaker has a passionate nature; he is rendering in prose a few lines by the famous Monti.

cried out, 'You're going to join Napoleon!' and threw his arms around my neck. And the others embraced me enthusiastically. 'Why am I married!' said one of them."

Countess Pietranera had grown thoughtful; she felt she ought to bring forward a few objections. If Fabrizio had had the slightest experience, he would have seen clearly that she herself did not believe in the sensible arguments she hastened to give him. But, lacking experience, he had determination; he did not deign even to listen to them. She was soon reduced to making him promise that he would at least tell his mother about his plans.

"She'll tell my sisters, and those women will betray me without knowing it!" cried Fabrizio with a kind of heroic disdain.

"Speak more respectfully," said the countess, smiling through her tears, "of the sex that will make your fortune, because men will always be antagonistic to you: you're too fiery for prosaic souls."

The marquise burst into tears when she learned of her son's strange plan; she did not feel its heroism, and did everything she could to hold him back. When she was convinced that nothing in the world except the walls of a prison could stop him from leaving, she gave him the little money she possessed. Then she recalled that, since the day before, she had nine or ten small diamonds, worth perhaps ten thousand lire, which the marquis had entrusted to her with instructions to take them to Milan to have them set. Fabrizio's sisters came into their mother's room while the countess was sewing these diamonds into our hero's coat; he gave the poor women back their paltry napoleons. His sisters were so enthusiastic over his plan, and they embraced him with such tumultuous joy, that he picked up the few diamonds that still remained to be hidden and decided to leave at that very moment.

"You'd betray me without knowing it," he said to his sisters. "Since I have so much money, there's no use taking clothes with me; I can buy them anywhere."

He embraced those people who were so dear to him and left at once, without even going into his room. He walked so swiftly, always afraid of being pursued by horsemen, that he reached Lugano that same evening. By God's grace he was now in a Swiss town, and no longer in fear of being overpowered on the lonely road by soldiers in his father's pay. From Lugano he wrote him a noble letter, a piece of childish weakness which gave substance to the marquis' anger. Fabrizio took the stagecoach through the Saint Gotthard Pass. He traveled rapidly and entered France by way of Pontarlier.

The emperor was in Paris, and there Fabrizio's troubles began. He had left with the firm intention of speaking to the emperor, and it had never occurred to him that this might be difficult. In Milan, he had seen Prince Eugene ten times a day, and could have spoken to him if he had wished. In Paris, he went every morning to the courtyard of the Tuileries to watch the military reviews held by Napoleon, but he was never able to approach the emperor. Our hero believed all Frenchmen to be as deeply concerned as himself over the extreme dangers to which the country was exposed. At the table of the hotel in which he was staying, he made no mystery of his plans or his devotion; he met some young men who were friendly, kind and even more enthusiastic than he, and who, within a few days, did not fail to rob him of all the money he possessed. Fortunately, out of pure modesty, he had not mentioned the diamonds his mother had given him. On the morning when, after an orgy the night before, he found that he had been thoroughly robbed, he bought two fine horses, engaged one of the horse-dealer's grooms, a former soldier, as his servant, and, filled with contempt for the glib-tongued young men of Paris, set out to join the army. He knew nothing except that it was assembling near Maubeuge.

As soon as he reached the frontier, he decided it would be ridiculous for him to stay in a house, warming himself in front of a good fire, while there were soldiers camping in the open. Despite everything his servant, who was not lacking in common sense, could say, he rashly hurried off to join the bivouacs at the extreme frontier, on the road to Belgium. No sooner had he reached the first battalion stationed beside the road than the soldiers began staring at that young civilian whose clothes bore no resemblance to a uniform. Night was falling and a cold wind was blowing. Fabrizio walked over to a fire and asked for hospitality, offering to pay for it. The soldiers looked at each other, amazed above all by the idea of payment, and obligingly gave him a place beside the fire while his servant made a shelter for him. An hour later, however, the regimental sergeant-major passed within sight of the bivouac and the soldiers went to tell him about the arrival of this foreigner who spoke bad French. The sergeant-major questioned Fabrizio, who spoke to him in a very suspicious tone about his passionate devotion to the emperor, whereupon the sergeant-major asked him to go with him to the colonel, who had established himself on a nearby farm. Fabrizio's servant came up with the two horses. The sight of them apparently made such a deep impression on the sergeant-major that he immediately changed his mind and began questioning the servant also. The latter, a former soldier, instantly guessed his questioner's plan of action; he spoke of the powerful protection his master enjoyed, and added that surely no one would steal his fine horses from him. A soldier summoned by the sergeant-major immediately seized the servant by the collar, another soldier took charge of the horses and the sergeant-major sternly ordered Fabrizio to go with him without argument.

After making him walk a good league through the darkness seemingly made more intense by the fires of the bivouacs that lit up the horizon on all sides, the sergeant-major turned Fabrizio over to a provost marshal who solemnly asked to see his papers. Fabrizio showed him his passport, which described him as a barometer merchant, "carrying his merchandise."

"How stupid they are!" exclaimed the provost marshal. "This time they've gone too far!"

He questioned our hero, who spoke of the emperor and of freedom with the keenest enthusiasm, whereupon the provost marshal was overcome with a fit of laughter.

"My God!" he cried. "You're not very bright! They've got their nerve, sending us simple-minded young fools like you!" And, despite everything Fabrizio said, despite his frenzied efforts to explain that he was actually not a barometer merchant, the provost marshal sent him to the prison at B——, a small town nearby, where our hero arrived at three o'clock in the morning, beside himself with rage and dying of fatigue.

First astonished, then furious, understanding absolutely nothing of what was happening to him, Fabrizio spent thirty-three long days in that wretched prison. He wrote letter after letter to the local commander, and it was the jailer's wife, a handsome Flemish woman of thirty-six, who undertook to have them delivered. But since she had no desire to have such a good-looking young man shot, and since, furthermore, he paid her well, she regularly threw his letters into the fire. Late in the evening, she would deign to come and listen to the prisoner's laments; she had told her husband that the young simpleton had money, whereupon the prudent jailer had given her a free hand. Making use of his authorization, she obtained a few gold napoleons, for the sergeant-major

27

had taken only the two horses and the provost marshal had confiscated nothing at all.

One afternoon in June, Fabrizio heard the sound of heavy gunfire in the distance. They were fighting at last! His heart leapt with impatience. He also heard a great deal of noise in the town: a large movement of troops was being carried out, and three divisions were passing through B——. When the jailer's wife came to share his sorrows at eleven o'clock that evening, Fabrizio was even friendlier to her than usual; then he took both her hands and said, "Let me get out of here and I swear on my honor that I'll come back to the prison as soon as the fighting is over."

"Don't talk nonsense! Do you have the wherewithal?"

He looked upset; he did not understand the word "wherewithal." Seeing his reaction, the jailer's wife concluded that his funds were at a low ebb, so, rather than speaking of gold napoleons as she had decided to do, she spoke only of francs.

"Listen," she said, "if you can let me have a hundred francs, I'll put a double napoleon over each eye of the corporal who'll come to relieve the guard during the night, so he won't be able to see you leaving the prison. If his regiment is going to march tomorrow, he'll agree."

The bargain was quickly concluded. The jailer's wife even consented to hide Fabrizio in her bedroom, from where he could more easily make his escape in the morning.

The next day, before dawn, she said to him affectionately, "My dear boy, you're still very young to take up this miserable trade. Take my advice, never come back to it again!"

"What!" exclaimed Fabrizio. "Is it a crime to want to defend the fatherland?"

"Never mind. Always remember that I saved your life. Your case was cut and dried: you'd have been shot. But don't tell anyone about it, because you'd get my husband and me thrown out of here. And whatever you do, don't repeat your silly story about being a gentleman from Milan disguised as a barometer merchant, it's too stupid. Listen to me carefully: I'm going to give you the uniform of a hussar who died in the prison day before yesterday; open your mouth as little as possible, but if a sergeant or an officer should question you in such a way that you're forced to answer, tell him you've been lying sick in the house of a peasant who took you in out of charity when he found you trembling with fever in a ditch beside the road. If he's not satisfied with that answer, tell him you're on your way to rejoin your regiment.

You may be arrested because of your accent; if so, say you were born in Piedmont, that you're a conscript who stayed in France last year, and so on."

For the first time, after thirty-three days of rage, Fabrizio realized what lay behind everything that had happened to him. They thought he was a spy. He argued with the jailer's wife, who was feeling affectionate that morning. Finally, while she was plying her needle, taking in the hussar's uniform to fit him, he told the astonished woman his story in very clear terms. For a moment she believed him: he seemed so candid, and he looked so handsome dressed as a hussar!

"Since you're so eager to fight," she said to him at length, still half-convinced, "you should have enlisted in a regiment when you came to Paris. All you'd have had to do was buy a sergeant a drink and the whole thing would have been settled!" She added much good advice for the future, and finally, at daybreak, she put Fabrizio out of the house after making him swear over and over again that he would never mention her name, no matter what happened.

As soon as he was outside the little town, boldly striding along with the hussar's saber under his arm, he began to have misgivings. "Here I am," he said to himself, "with the uniform and the marching orders of a hussar who died in prison, where he was sent, I'm told, for having stolen a cow and a few pieces of silverware. I've inherited his identity, so to speak . . . and without wishing it or expecting it in any way! Beware of prison! The omen is clear: prisons will cause me great suffering!"

Less than an hour after Fabrizio had left his benefactress, it began raining so heavily that the new hussar could scarcely walk, encumbered by a pair of unwieldly boots that had not been made for him. He met a peasant riding a wretched horse; he bought it, making himself understood by signs, since the jailer's wife had urged him to speak as little as possible, because of his accent.

That day the army, which had just won the Battle of Ligny, was marching straight toward Brussels. It was the day before the Battle of Waterloo. At noon, with the torrential rain still falling, Fabrizio heard the sound of cannon fire; his happiness made him completely forget the horrible despair into which he had been plunged by his unjust imprisonment. He rode on until a very late hour; then, since he was beginning to have a little common sense, he went to ask for a night's lodging in a peasant's house far off the road. This peasant wept and claimed that everything had been taken from him. Fabrizio gave him three francs and he found some oats. "My horse is no beauty," thought Fabrizio, "but some sergeant-major might take a liking to him just the same," and he lay down beside him in the stable.

The next morning, an hour before dawn, Fabrizio was on the road again, and he had managed to caress his horse into a trot. By five o'clock he could hear cannon fire: it was the prelude to Waterloo.

CHAPTER THREE

Fabrizio soon came across some *vivandières*,* and the deep gratitude he felt toward the jailer's wife at B—— drove him to speak to them; he asked one of them where he could find the Fourth Regiment of Hussars, to which he belonged.

"You'd do just as well as not to be in such a hurry, soldier boy," said the *vivandière*, touched by his pallor and beautiful eyes. "Your grip isn't strong enough yet for the saber fighting that will go on today. If you had a musket I wouldn't say anything, because you could fire your bullet as well as anyone else."

This advice displeased Fabrizio. But no matter how much he urged on his horse, he could go no faster than the *vivandière's* cart. Now and then the gunfire seemed to come closer, and it prevented them from hearing each other; for Fabrizio, beside himself with enthusiasm and happiness, had resumed the conversation. Each word she spoke increased his happiness by making him understand it. Except for his real name and his flight from prison, he eventually told everything to that woman who seemed so kind. She was amazed and understood nothing of what the handsome young soldier was telling her.

"Now I see what's behind it all!" she finally exclaimed triumphantly. "You're a young civilian in love with the wife of some captain in the Fourth Hussars. Your sweetheart made you a present of the uniform you're wearing, and you're running after her. As sure as there's a God in heaven, you've never been a soldier! But, like the fine boy you are, since your regiment's under fire you want to go to it, so nobody can call you a coward."

* Women who followed the army to sell food, drink and supplies to the soldiers.—L.B.

Fabrizio agreed to everything: it was his only means of getting good advice. "I know nothing about the ways of these Frenchmen," he thought. "If I'm not guided by someone I'll manage to get myself thrown in prison again, and they'll steal my horse."

"First of all, my boy," said the *vivandière*, who was becoming more and more his friend, "admit that you're under twenty-one. I wouldn't put you past seventeen, at the very most."

It was the truth, and Fabrizio admitted it with good grace.

"So you're not even a conscript—it's only because of your lady's pretty eyes that you're going off to get your bones broken. My God, she doesn't ask for much! If you've still got some of that gold she gave you, you'd better buy yourself another horse before you do anything else: just look at the way your old nag pricks up his ears whenever a cannon booms from a little closer up! He's a peasant horse, and he'll get you killed as soon as you're in the line. You see that white smoke there, above the hedge? That's musket fire, my boy! So get ready for a good scare when you start hearing bullets whistle past. You'd better eat something while there's still time."

Fabrizio followed her advice; handing her a napoleon, he asked her to take out of it what he owed her.

"It hurts me to see him!" cried the woman. "The poor boy doesn't even know how to spend his money! It would serve you right if I grabbed your napoleon and whipped Cocotte into a fast trot—that old nag of yours would never catch me! What would you do, you poor simpleton, if you saw me leave you in the dust? Get this into your head: when the cannons are growling, never show your gold. . . . Here's eighteen francs and fifty centimes, so your breakfast has cost you thirty sous. Now we'll soon have some horses for sale. If there's a small one, give ten francs for it, and don't give more than twenty francs for any horse, even if it's the one that carried all four Aymon brothers at the same time."

When breakfast was over, the *vivandière*, who was still holding forth, was interrupted by a woman who had been cutting across the fields and had now reached the road.

"Margot! Margot!" shouted the woman. "Your Sixth Light Infantry is over there, to the right!"

"I'll have to leave you, my boy," said the *vivandière* to our hero, "but I still feel sorry for you. You don't know anything about anything, and you're going to get yourself blown to

31

pieces, as sure as I'm standing here! Come to the Sixth Light Infantry with me."

"I realize I don't know anything," said Fabrizio, "but I want to fight and I'm determined to go over there toward that white smoke."

"Look at the way your horse is twitching his ears! He may not be very strong, but he'll get out of hand as soon as you're there: he'll start galloping, and God only knows where he'll take you. Take my advice, will you? As soon as you're with the soldiers, pick up a musket and a cartridge pouch, get down beside them and do exactly what they do. But my God, I'll bet you don't even know how to bite open a cartridge!"

Fabrizio was stung to the quick, but he nevertheless admitted to his new friend that she had guessed correctly.

"Poor boy! He's going to be killed right away, as sure as there's a God in heaven! It won't take long. You *must* come with me," concluded the *vivandière* in a tone of authority.

"But I want to fight."

"Oh, you'll fight, don't worry! The Sixth Light is a tough regiment, and today there's enough fighting for everybody."

"But how long will it take us to get to your regiment?"

"No more than a quarter of an hour."

"If I'm recommended by this good woman," thought Fabrizio, "my ignorance of everything won't make them take me for a spy, and I'll be able to fight." Just then the cannon fire redoubled, one shot coming immediately after another. "It's like a rosary," said Fabrizio.

"You can hear the muskets now," said the *vivandière*, giving a flick of her whip to her little horse, which seemed excited by the gunfire.

She turned to the right and took a road that cut across the fields. It was covered wtih mud a foot deep, and the little cart nearly became stuck. Fabrizio pushed it along. His horse fell twice. The road soon became drier and was nothing but a path through the grass. Fabrizio had not gone five hundred paces when his nag stopped short: lying across the path was a corpse which terrified both the horse and its rider.

Fabrizio's face, naturally pale, took on a marked greenish tinge. After looking at the dead man, the *vivandière* said, as though talking to herself, "He's not from our division." Then, looking up at our hero, she burst out laughing. "Ha, ha, my boy!" she cried. "Here's something for you!"

Fabrizio remained frozen. He was struck above all by the dirty feet of the corpse, which had already been stripped of its shoes and left with nothing but a wretched pair of blood-stained trousers.

"Come closer," said the *vivandière*, "get off your horse: you'll have to get used to this. Look," she cried, "he got it through the head!"

A bullet had entered beside the nose and gone out through the opposite temple, disfiguring the corpse in a hideous manner and leaving it with one open eye.

"Come on, my boy," said the *vivandière*, "get off your horse and give him a handshake, to see if he'll return it."

Without hesitation, though ready to give up the ghost from disgust, Fabrizio leapt off his horse, firmly gripped the corpse's hand and shook it. Then he stood motionless, as though drained of all life; he felt that he did not have the strength to remount his horse. What horrified him most of all was that open eye.

"She's going to think I'm a coward," he said to himself bitterly, but he felt that it was impossible for him to move: he would have fallen. It was a terrible moment; he was on the verge of fainting. The *vivandière* saw this, jumped lightly down from her little cart and, without a word, handed him a glass of brandy which he drank in one swallow; he was able to climb back onto his nag, and he rode on without saying anything. The *vivandière* looked at him now and then out of the corner of her eye.

"You'll fight tomorrow," she said to him at length, "but today you'll stay with me. You can see for yourself that you'll have to learn the trade of soldiering."

"No, I want to fight right away!" cried our hero with a somber air which struck the *vivandière* as a good omen. The cannon fire was increasing, and seemed to be coming closer. The shots were beginning to form a kind of figured bass; there was no interval between one shot and the next, and above this figured bass, which resembled the roar of a distant torrent, the sound of musket fire was clearly distinguishable.

At this point the road plunged into a little forest; the *vivandière* saw three or four French soldiers running toward her at full speed; she quickly jumped down from her cart and ran to hide herself fifteen to twenty paces from the road. She crouched in the hole left by a big tree that had been uprooted a short time before.

"Now I'll see whether I'm a coward!" thought Fabrizio. He stopped beside the little cart abandoned by the *vivandière* and drew his saber. The soldiers passed without paying any attention to him, running alongside the trees, to the left of the road.

"They're ours," said the *vivandière* calmly as she returned, out of breath, to her little cart. "If your horse could gallop, I'd tell you to ride on ahead to the end of the woods, to see if there's anyone on the plain."

Fabrizio did not wait to be told twice: he broke off a poplar branch, stripped it of its leaves and began beating his horse with all his might; the nag broke into a gallop for an instant, then resumed its customary little trot. The *vivandière* had brought her horse to a gallop. "Stop! Stop!" she cried to Fabrizio. Soon they were both outside the woods. When they reached the edge of the plain they heard a terrifying uproar: cannons and muskets were thundering on all sides, to the left, to the right, behind them. And since the woods they had just left occupied a hillock nine or ten feet above the plain, they had a rather good view of one corner of the battle. But there was no one in the meadow beyond the woods. This meadow was bordered, about a thousand paces away, by a long row of thick willow trees; above the willows they could see white smoke which occasionally spiraled up into the sky.

"If only I knew where the regiment is!" said the *vivandière*, perplexed. "We mustn't cross this big, flat meadow. By the way, if you see an enemy soldier, stick him with the point of your saber, don't amuse yourself by slashing at him."

Just then she caught sight of the four soldiers we have already mentioned: they were entering the plain from the woods, to the left of the road. One of them was on horseback. "Here's your chance," she said to Fabrizio. "Hello there!" she shouted to the soldier on horseback. "Come here and have a glass of brandy." The soldiers all came toward her. "Where's the Sixth Light Infantry?" she asked.

"Over there, five minutes from here, across the canal that runs alongside the willows. Colonel Macon has just been killed."

"Do you want five francs for your horse?"

"Five francs! That's very funny! Five francs for an officer's horse that I'm going to sell for five napoleons within a quarter of an hour!"

"Give me one of your napoleons," said the *vivandière* to Fabrizio. Then, walking up to the soldier on horseback: "Get off right now, here's your napoleon."

The soldier dismounted. Fabrizio gaily leapt into the saddle and the *vivandière* unstrapped the small saddlebag that was on his nag.

34

"Come on, give me a hand!" she said to the soldiers. "Do you always stand around and watch a lady work?"

But as soon as the captured horse felt the saddlebag on his back he began to rear, and Fabrizio, who was a very good rider, needed all his strength to control him.

"That's a good sign!" said the *vivandière*. "The gentleman isn't used to being tickled by a saddlebag!"

"A general's horse!" cried the man who had sold him. "A horse that's worth ten napoleons if he's worth a sou!"

"Here's twenty francs," said Fabrizio, overjoyed at feeling himself astride a spirited horse.

Just then a cannon ball plowed into the line of willows, striking them from an angle, and Fabrizio saw the curious spectacle of all the little branches flying in either direction as though cut off by a scythe.

"Looks like the cannon's moving in a little," the soldier said to him, taking his twenty francs.

Fabrizio was still under the spell of this curious spectacle when a group of generals, followed by a score of hussars, galloped across one corner of the broad field at the edge of which he had stopped. His horse whinnied, reared two or three times in succession, then jerked his head violently against the bridle that was holding him back. "All right, then, so be it!" Fabrizio said to himself.

The horse, suddenly released, dashed forward at full speed and caught up with the escort following the generals. Fabrizio counted four gold-braided hats. A quarter of an hour later, from a few words spoken by a hussar riding near him, Fabrizio understood that one of these generals was the famous Marshal Ney. His happiness knew no bounds. He could not guess, however, which one of the generals was Marshal Ney; he would have given anything in the world to know, but he remembered that he must not speak. The escort stopped to cross a wide ditch filled with water from the rain of the day before. It was bordered by tall trees, and its left bank ended the field at whose far edge Fabrizio had bought his horse. Nearly all the hussars dismounted. The side of the ditch was nearly vertical and very slippery, and the surface of the water was three or four feet below the level of the field. Fabrizio, distracted by his joy, was thinking more about Marshal Ney and glory than about his horse, which, being high-spirited, jumped into the ditch, splashing the water to a considerable height. One of the generals was thoroughly drenched and swore loudly: "God damn the stupid ass!" Fabrizio felt deeply

35

wounded by this insult. "Can I demand satisfaction?" he wondered.

Meanwhile, to prove that he was not really so awkward, he tried to ride his horse up the opposite side of the ditch. But it was very steep and five or six feet high. He had to give up. He then rode upstream, with the water up to his horse's head, until he came to a watering place; he easily rode up this gentle slope and into the field on the other side of the ditch. He was the first man of the escort to reach it. He began trotting proudly along the bank. The hussars were floundering around in the ditch, having a rather difficult time of it, for in many places the water was five feet deep. Two or three horses became frightened and tried to swim, which caused a terrible splashing of muddy water. A sergeant noticed the maneuver that had just been carried out by the unmilitary-looking young recruit.

"Head upstream, there's a watering place on the left!" he called out, and gradually they all crossed over.

On reaching the other bank, Fabrizio had found the generals there alone. The sound of cannon fire seemed to redouble, and he scarcely heard one of the generals, the same one he had splattered so well, when he shouted into his ear, "Where did you get that horse?"

Fabrizio was so agitated that he answered in Italian: "*L'ho comprato poco fa.*" ("I bought him just now.")

"What did you say?" shouted the general.

But the uproar became so loud just then that Fabrizio could not answer him. We must confess that our hero was not very heroic at that moment. His fear, however, was only of secondary importance: he was, above all, outraged by the noise that was hurting his ears. The escort broke into a gallop; they were crossing a large plowed field that lay on the other side of the ditch, and the ground was strewn with corpses.

"Redcoats! Redcoats!" the hussars of the escort shouted joyfully. At first Fabrizio did not understand, then he noticed that, true enough, nearly all the corpses were dressed in red. One detail made him shudder: he saw that many of the unfortunate redcoats were still alive; they were obviously calling for help, but no one stopped to give it to them. Our hero, extremely humane, took infinite pains to make sure that his horse did not step on any redcoats. The escort stopped; Fabrizio, who was not paying enough attention to his duty as a soldier, went on galloping, staring at one of the poor wounded men.

"Stop, you idiot!" the sergeant shouted at him. Fabrizio

saw that he was twenty paces to the right and in front of the generals, and precisely in the direction in which they were looking through their field glasses. When he came back to take his place behind the other hussars, who had remained a few paces in the rear, he saw that the stoutest of the generals was speaking to the man beside him, also a general, in a tone of authority and almost of reprimand; he was swearing. Fabrizio could not restrain his curiosity; despite the advice not to speak which his friend the jailer's wife had given him, he formulated a short sentence in good, correct French and said to the man beside him, "Who's the general that's 'dressing down' the one next to him?"

"Why, that's the marshal!"

"What marshal?"

"Marshal Ney, you fool! Where have you been serving?"

Fabrizio, though extremely touchy, had no thought of resenting the insult: lost in childish admiration, he was contemplating the famous Prince de la Moskova, the "bravest of the brave."

Suddenly they all set off at a fast gallop. A short time later Fabrizio saw, twenty paces ahead of him, a plowed field that was being stirred up in a singular fashion. The bottoms of the furrows were filled with water, and the damp earth that formed the ridges of these furrows was flying around in little black lumps thrown three or four feet into the air. He noticed this odd phenomenon as he passed, then his thoughts returned to the marshal's glory. He heard a sharp cry beside him: two hussars were falling, struck by cannon balls, and when he looked at them they were already twenty paces behind the escort. What seemed horrible to him was a bloody horse that was thrashing around on the plowed earth, entangling its hooves in its own entrails as it tried to get up and follow the others; its blood was flowing into the mud.

"Ah, now I'm under fire at last!" thought Fabrizio. "I've been in battle," he told himself several times with satisfaction. "Now I'm a real soldier." The escort was galloping at breakneck speed, and our hero realized it was cannon balls that were making the earth fly up all around him. He vainly looked in the direction from which the balls were coming: he saw only the white smoke of the battery an enormous distance away, and amid the steady rumble of the cannons he seemed to hear volleys being fired from much closer up; he understood absolutely nothing about what was going on.

Just then the generals and the escort rode down onto a

narrow road that ran five feet below the level of the plain and was covered with water.

The marshal stopped and looked through his field glasses again. This time Fabrizio was able to study him at leisure: he saw that he had light blond hair and a big, red face. "We have no faces like that in Italy," he said to himself. "With my pale skin and my brown hair," he added sadly, "I'll never look like that." To him, these words meant: "I'll never be a hero."

He looked at the hussars: with only one exception, they all had yellow mustaches. And while he was looking at them, they all looked at him. Their stares made him blush; to end his embarrassment, he turned his head toward the enemy. He saw widely extended lines of men in red, but what greatly astonished him was that these men seemed extremely small to him. Their long files, which were regiments or divisions, appeared to be no higher than the hedges. A line of red-coated cavalry was trotting toward the sunken road along which the marshal and the escort were riding slowly, floundering in the mud. The smoke made it impossible for them to distinguish anything in the direction in which they were advancing; occasionally men riding at a gallop could be seen against the background of this white smoke.

Fabrizio suddenly saw four men riding toward him at full speed from the direction of the enemy. "Ah, we're being attacked!" he said to himself; then he saw two of the men speak to the marshal. One of the generals of the marshal's staff galloped off toward the enemy, followed by two hussars from the escort and the four men who had just arrived.

After they had all crossed a little canal, Fabrizio found himself beside a sergeant who seemed to be quite good-natured. "I must talk to this one," he thought, "then maybe they'll stop looking at me." He meditated for a long time.

"Sir, this is the first time I've ever been in battle," he said at length to the sergeant. "But is this a real battle?"

"It'll do till a real battle comes along. But who are you?"

"I'm the brother of a captain's wife."

"And what's your captain's name?"

Our hero was terribly embarrassed: he had not foreseen this question. Fortunately the marshal and the escort again set off at a gallop. "What French name shall I say?" thought Fabrizio. Finally he remembered the name of the owner of the hotel in which he had stayed in Paris. He brought his horse close to the sergeant's and shouted to him at the top of his lungs: "Captain Meunier!"

The sergeant, having misunderstood because of the roar of the cannons, replied, "Ah, Captain Teulier! Well, he's been killed!"

"Good!" thought Fabrizio. "Captain Teulier. I must pretend to be grief-stricken." He took on a piteous expression and cried out, "Oh, my God!"

They had left the sunken road and were now dashing across a little meadow. Cannon balls were again falling around them. The marshal headed toward a cavalry division. There were dead and wounded men on all sides, but this sight had already ceased to make such a deep impression on our hero: he had other things to think about.

While the escort was halted, he caught sight of the little cart of a *vivandière*; his tender feelings for those worthy women prevailed over everything else: he galloped toward the cart.

"Come back here, you jackass!" shouted the sergeant.

"What can he do to me here?" thought Fabrizio, and he went on galloping toward the *vivandière*. When he spurred his horse, he had had some hope that she might be the kind *vivandière* he had met that morning. The horse and the little cart were very much like hers, but their owner proved to be quite different, and our hero found that she looked extremely disagreeable. As he approached her he heard her say, "And he was such a handsome man, too!" An ugly sight awaited the new soldier: the leg of a cuirassier, a handsome young man five feet ten inches tall, was being cut off at the thigh. Fabrizio closed his eyes and drank four glasses of brandy, one after the other.

"You're really gulping it down, my boy!" exclaimed the *vivandière*.

The brandy gave him an idea: "I must buy the good will of my companions in the escort."

"Give me the rest of the bottle," he said to the *vivandière*.

"But do you realize," she answered, "that the rest of that bottle costs ten francs, on a day like this?"

When he galloped back to the escort, the sergeant called out, "Ah, you're bringing us something to drink! Is that why you deserted? Give it to me."

The bottle made the rounds; the last man to take it threw it away after drinking from it and said to Fabrizio, "Thanks, comrade!" They all looked at him with good will in their eyes. Their glances took a hundred-pound weight from his heart: it was one of those hearts of overly delicate construction which need the friendship of everyone around them. At last he was no longer spurned by his companions, there was a bond between them! He took a deep breath, then calmly said to the sergeant:

"And if Captain Teulier has been killed, where can I find my sister?" He regarded himself as a little Machiavelli for having said "Teulier" so naturally instead of "Meunier."

"You'll find out this evening," replied the sergeant.

The escort set off again and headed toward some infantry divisions. Fabrizio felt completely drunk: he had downed too much brandy and was swaying slightly in the saddle. He appropriately recalled a remark his mother's coachman used to make: "When you've been bending your elbow, keep looking between the ears of your horse and do what the man beside you does." The marshal stopped for a long time with a number of cavalry units which he ordered to charge; but for an hour or two our hero was scarcely conscious of what was happening around him. He felt profoundly weary, and whenever his horse galloped he bounded heavily in the saddle, like a lump of lead.

Suddenly the sergeant shouted to his men, "Don't you see the emperor, you fools?" The escort immediately began crying out, "Long live the emperor!" Our hero stared till his eyes bulged from their sockets, as can well be imagined, but all he saw was a group of generals riding at a gallop, followed by another escort. The long horsehair plumes on the helmets of the dragoons prevented him from distinguishing any faces. "So I've been unable to see the emperor on a battlefield because of those damned glasses of brandy!" This reflection roused him completely.

They again went down into a road filled with water: the horses wanted to drink.

"Was that really the emperor who just rode past?" he asked the man beside him.

"Of course! He was the one without any braid on his coat. How could you have missed him?" replied his companion in a kindly tone. Fabrizio felt a strong desire to gallop after the emperor's escort and attach himself to it. What a joy it would be really to fight the war in the train of that hero! That was why he had come to France. "I'm perfectly free to do it," he thought, "because, after all, I have no reason for serving where I am, except the will of my horse, which started galloping after these generals."

What made him decide to stay was the fact that his new comrades, the hussars, were treating him pleasantly; he was beginning to regard himself as a close friend of all the soldiers with whom he had been riding for several hours. He saw between them and himself that noble friendship of the heroes of Tasso and Ariosto. If he attached himself to the emperor's escort, he would have to get acquainted all over again; the other cavalrymen might even be hostile to him because they were dragoons and he was wearing a hussar's uniform, like all the others who were following the marshal. Our hero was overjoyed by the way they now looked at him. He would have done anything in the world for his comrades; his soul and his mind were in the clouds. Everything seemed to have taken on a new aspect, now that he was among friends. He was dying to ask questions. "But I'm still a little drunk," he said to himself. "I must remember the jailer's wife." When they left the sunken road he noticed that the escort was no longer with Marshal Ney; the general they were following was tall and thin, with a hard face and fiery eyes.

This general was none other than Count d'A——, the Lieutenant Robert of May 15, 1796. How happy he would have been to meet Fabrizio del Dongo!

Fabrizio had long since ceased to see the earth flying up in little black clods from the impact of cannon balls. They rode up behind a regiment of cuirassiers; he distinctly heard grapeshot striking against their breastplates, and he saw several men fall.

The sun was already very low in the sky, and it was about to set when the escort left a sunken road, ascended a little slope three or four feet high and entered a plowed field. Fabrizio heard a strange little noise quite close to him. He turned his head: four men had fallen with their horses. The general himself had been thrown to the ground, but was now standing up, covered with blood. Fabrizio looked at the fallen hussars: three of them were still making a few convulsive movements and the fourth was shouting, "Pull me out!" The sergeant and two or three of his men had dismounted to assist the general, who, leaning on his aide-de-camp, was trying to take a few steps away from his horse, which lay struggling on its back, lashing out furiously with its hooves.

The sergeant walked over to Fabrizio. At that moment, our hero heard someone behind him say quite close to his ear, "It's the only one that can still gallop." He felt someone seize his feet and raise them, and at the same time someone else took hold of him under the arms. He was lifted over his horse's rump, then allowed to slip to the ground, where he landed in a sitting position.

The aide-de-camp took Fabrizio's horse by the bridle. The

general, with the help of the sergeant, mounted it and galloped away. He was quickly followed by the six remaining men. Fabrizio, furious, got to his feet and ran after them, shouting, "*Ladri! Ladri!*" ("Thieves! Thieves!") It was comical to be running after thieves in the middle of a battlefield.

The escort and the general, Count d'A——, soon disappeared behind a row of willows. Fabrizio, demented with rage, also came to this line of willows and found himself at the edge of a very deep ditch. He crossed it; then, having reached the other side, began swearing once more when he again saw, but at a very great distance, the general and the escort, who were now vanishing among the trees. "Thieves! Thieves!" he shouted, this time in French. In despair, much less from the loss of his horse than from the treachery of which he had been a victim, he sank down on the ground beside the ditch, exhausted and dying of hunger. If his fine horse had been taken away from him by the enemy, he would have given it no further thought, but he had been betrayed and robbed by that sergeant he had liked so much, and by those hussars he had regarded as brothers! That was what broke his heart. He could find no consolation for such infamy.

Leaning his back against a willow, he began to weep bitterly. He destroyed one by one all his dreams of chivalrous and sublime friendship, like that of the heroes of *Jerusalem Delivered*. Watching the approach of death was nothing if you were surrounded by heroic, sensitive souls, by noble friends who clasped your hand as you breathed your last! But how could anyone keep his enthusiasm when surrounded by base scoundrels? Like all indignant men, Fabrizio was exaggerating.

After pitying himself for a quarter of an hour, he noticed that the cannon balls were beginning to reach the row of trees beneath which he was meditating. He stood up and tried to get his bearings. He looked at the meadows bordered by a wide ditch, and at the row of thick willows; he thought he knew where he was. He saw an infantry unit crossing the ditch and entering the meadows, a quarter of a league in front of him. "I was about to fall asleep," he thought. "I must avoid being taken prisoner." And he began walking, very swiftly. As he advanced, he was reassured, for he recognized the uniforms of the regiments by which he had been afraid of being intercepted: they were French. He shifted his course to the right to catch up with them.

After the moral pain of having been so infamously betrayed

and robbed, there was another pain which was now making itself felt more keenly every moment: he was starving. It was therefore with great joy that after walking, or rather running, for ten minutes, he saw that the infantry unit, which had also been moving very swiftly, was now stopping as though to take up a position. A few minutes later he arrived among the first soldiers.

"Comrades, could you sell me a piece of bread?"

"Listen to him! He thinks we're bakers!"

Fabrizio was crushed by this harsh remark and the general outburst of unpleasant laughter that followed it. So war was no longer that surge of noble emotion which united all souls enamored of glory, as he had imagined it to be from Napoleon's proclamations! He sat down, or rather let himself fall on the grass; he turned very pale. The soldier who had spoken to him, and who had stopped ten paces away to clean the lock of his musket with his handkerchief, walked up to him and tossed him a piece of bread; then, seeing that he had not picked it up, he put some of it into his mouth. Fabrizio opened his eyes and ate the bread. He did not have the strength to speak.

When he finally looked around for the soldier, so that he could pay him, he found himself alone: the nearest soldiers were a hundred paces from him, and walking away. He stood up mechanically and followed them. He entered a forest. Ready to drop from exhaustion, he was already looking for a comfortable resting place when, to his inexpressible joy, he recognized first the horse, then the cart, then finally the *vivandière* he had met that morning! She ran over to him and was alarmed by his appearance.

"Keep walking, my boy," she said to him. "Have you been wounded? And where's your fine horse?" So saying, she led him to her cart and helped him climb into it, holding him under the arms. No sooner was he in the cart than our hero, overwhelmed by fatigue, fell fast asleep.*

CHAPTER FOUR

Nothing could wake him, neither the musket shots fired near the little cart, nor the trotting of the horse which the *vivandière* was whipping with all her might. The regiment,

* See page 432.

having been unexpectedly attacked by swarms of Prussian cavalry after believing all day that victory was assured, was now retreating, or rather fleeing in the direction of France.

The colonel, a handsome, smartly dressed young man who had just succeeded Macon, was cut down by a saber. The major who took his place, an old man with white hair, ordered the regiment to halt. "God damn it," he shouted to the soldiers, "in the days of the Republic, we didn't run away till the enemy forced us to! . . . Defend every inch of ground with your lives," he said, swearing. "Now it's the soil of our country that those Prussians are trying to invade!"

The little cart stopped; Fabrizio abruptly woke up. The sun had set a long time before, and he was amazed to see that it was almost dark. The soldiers were running in all directions in a confusion that greatly astonished our hero; they looked shamefaced to him.

"What's going on?" he asked the *vivandière*.

"Oh, nothing. It's just that we're done for, my boy. The Prussian cavalry is cutting us to pieces, that's all. At first that fatheaded general thought they were our men. Come on, hurry, help me fix Cocotte's trace, it's broken."

A few musket shots went off ten paces away. Our hero, now fresh as a daisy, said to himself, "I haven't actually done any fighting all day long: all I've done is escort a general."

"I must fight," he said to the *vivandière*.

"Don't worry, you'll fight, and more than you want to! We're done for."

"Aubry, my boy," she shouted to a corporal who was passing by, "take a look at the cart every once in a while to see how it's coming along."

"Are you going to fight?" said Fabrizio to Aubry.

"No, I'm about to put on my dancing shoes and go to a ball!"

"I'll follow you."

"Take good care of that little hussar," shouted the *vivandière*. "He's a brave young man."

Corporal Aubry walked along without saying a word. Nine or ten soldiers ran up to him. He led them behind a big oak tree surrounded by brambles, then posted them at the edge of the woods, still without saying a word, in a widely extended line, at least ten paces apart. "Now listen," he said to them, speaking for the first time, "don't start shooting before you hear the order: remember that you've got only three cartridges apiece."

"But what's going on?" wondered Fabrizio. Finally, when

he found himself alone with the corporal, he said to him, "I don't have a gun."

"Keep quiet! Go out there, fifty paces in front of the woods, and you'll find one of the poor soldiers who have just been sabered: take his cartridge pouch and his musket. But don't rob a wounded man. Take a musket and a cartridge pouch from a man who's good and dead, and hurry, or you'll get yourself shot by our own soldiers."

Fabrizio ran off and quickly came back with a musket and a cartridge pouch.

"Load your musket and get over there behind that tree. And whatever you do, don't fire till I give you the order— Good God!" said the corporal, interrupting himself, "he doesn't even know how to load his musket!" He continued his speech as he helped Fabrizio: "If an enemy cavalryman gallops toward you to saber you, stay behind your tree and don't fire till he's at point-blank range, no more than three paces away—your bayonet must be almost touching his uniform. . . . And get rid of that big saber! Do you want it to trip you? My God, just look at the kind of soldiers they're sending us now!" As he said this, he took the saber himself and angrily threw it away. "Now wipe off the flint of your musket with your handkerchief. But have you ever fired a musket?"

"I've done a lot of hunting."

"Thank God for that!" said the corporal with a loud sigh. "Now remember: don't fire till I give you the order." And he walked away.

Fabrizio was overjoyed. "At last I'm going to do some real fighting!" he said to himself. "I'm going to kill an enemy! This morning they were shooting cannon balls at us, and I wasn't doing anything but exposing myself to the danger of being killed—a fool's game!"

He looked all around with extreme curiosity. Some time later he heard seven or eight musket shots go off quite near him. But since he had not received the order to fire, he stood still behind his tree. It was almost night; he felt as though he were lying in wait during a bear hunt in the mountains of Tremezzina, above Grianta. A hunter's trick occurred to him: he took a cartridge from his pouch and removed the bullet. "If I see him," he thought, "I mustn't miss him." And he slipped this second bullet into the barrel of his musket. He heard two shots close beside his tree, and at the same time he saw a horseman dressed in blue galloping past in front of him, from his right to his left. "He's not within three paces,"

45

he thought, "but at that distance I'm sure to hit him." He carefully followed the cavalryman with the end of his barrel and finally pulled the trigger; the rider fell from his horse.

Our hero thought he was on a hunting party: he joyfully ran toward the game he had just brought down. He was already touching the man, who seemed to be dying, when two Prussian cavalrymen bore down on him with incredible speed to saber him. Fabrizio ran for the woods as fast as his legs could carry him, dropping his musket to increase his speed. The Prussian horsemen were only three paces behind him when he reached some young oak trees, perfectly erect and no bigger than his arm, which had been recently planted along the edge of the woods. These little oaks stopped the horsemen for a moment, but then they passed through them and continued to pursue Fabrizio across a clearing. They were again about to catch him when he darted in among seven or eight big trees. At that moment his face was nearly burned by the flames of five or six muskets that were fired in front of him. He ducked his head; when he raised it again he found himself facing the corporal.

"Did you kill your man?" Corporal Aubry asked him.

"Yes, but I lost my gun."

"There's no shortage of muskets. You're a damned good soldier. You may look stupid, but you've done a good day's work. These men just missed the two horsemen who were chasing you and coming straight toward them. I didn't see them. Right now we've got to get out of here in a hurry. The regiment must be an eighth of a league away by now, and on top of that, there's a little meadow where we may be attacked by surprise."

As he spoke, the corporal swiftly led his ten men away. Two hundred paces further on, when they entered the little meadow he had mentioned, they came across a wounded general who was being carried by his aide-de-camp and an orderly.

"Give me four of your men," he said to the corporal in a faint voice, "I've got to be carried to the field hospital: one of my legs has been shattered."

"Go to hell," replied the corporal, "you and all the other generals! You've betrayed the emperor today!"

"What!" said the general. "Are you disobeying my orders? Do you know that I'm General Count B——, in command of your division," etc., etc. He made a speech. His aide-de-camp rushed at the soldiers. The corporal jabbed him in the arm with his bayonet, then hurried off with his men. "I wish

46

they were all like you, with their arms and legs broken!" he said, swearing. "They're nothing but a bunch of miserable idiots! They've all sold out to the Bourbons and betrayed the emperor!" Fabrizio was shocked as he listened to this terrible accusation.

Toward ten o'clock at night, the little band caught up with the regiment on the outskirts of a large village with several narrow streets, but Fabrizio noticed that Corporal Aubry avoided speaking to any of the officers.

"It's impossible to go forward!" said the corporal. The streets were all jammed with infantry, horsemen and, above all, caissons and supply wagons. The corporal turned into three of these streets: he had to stop each time after taking a score of steps. Everyone was swearing and losing his temper.

"There's another traitor in command here!" he shouted. "If the enemy has sense enough to surround the village, we'll all be caught like rats in a trap. Follow me, men!"

Fabrizio saw that there were now only six soldiers with the corporal. Through a big open gate they entered a spacious farmyard. From there they went into a stable whose little door led them into a garden. They became lost in it for a few moments, wandering in all directions. But finally they went through a hedge and found themselves in a vast field of buckwheat. In less than half an hour, guided by the shouts and confused noises, they reached the highway on the other side of the village. The ditches along this road were filled with abandoned muskets; Fabrizio picked up one of them. The road was quite wide, but it was so densely packed with carts and fleeing soldiers that the corporal and Fabrizio had advanced no more than five hundred paces at the end of half an hour. They were told that the road led to Charleroi. When the village clock struck eleven the corporal said, "Let's cut across the fields again."

The little band was now composed of only three privates, the corporal and Fabrizio. When they were a quarter of a league away from the road, one of the privates said, "I'm exhausted."

"So am I," said another.

"Do you think that's news to me?" said the corporal. "We're all in the same boat. But just obey my orders and you'll come out all right." He saw five or six trees growing along a ditch in the middle of an enormous grainfield. "Head for those trees!" he said to his men. "Lie down, there," he added when they had reached them, "and be careful not to make any noise. But before we go to sleep, who's got some bread?"

"I have," said one of the soldiers.

"Hand it over," said the corporal authoritatively. He divided the bread into five pieces and took the smallest one for himself.

"A few minutes before dawn," he said as he ate, "we're going to have the enemy cavalry on top of us. We mustn't let ourselves be sabered. In these big plains, a man by himself is done for if cavalrymen come at him, but five men can save themselves. Stick close together with me, fire only at point-blank range, and I'll try to get you to Charleroi by tomorrow night."

The corporal woke them an hour before dawn and made them reload their muskets. The tumult on the highway was still going on, and had not stopped all night: it was like the sound of a torrent heard in the distance.

"They look like sheep running away," Fabrizio said to the corporal innocently.

"Shut up, you little fool!" said the corporal indignantly; and three soldiers who, along with Fabrizio, made up his entire army, glared angrily at the young Italian, as though he had just uttered a blasphemy. He had insulted their nation.

"That's going too far!" thought our hero. "I've noticed this before, at the viceroy's palace in Milan. They never run away, oh, no! With these Frenchmen, you're not allowed to tell the truth if it offends their vanity. But their ferocious looks don't impress me one bit, and I must let them know it."

They continued walking five hundred paces away from the torrent of fugitives that covered the highway. A league further on, the corporal and his little band crossed a narrow road which joined the highway, and on which there were many soldiers lying. Fabrizio bought a rather good horse for forty francs and carefully selected a big, straight saber from among the swords that had been thrown away here and there. "Since I've been told that you're supposed to jab with the point of your saber," he thought, "this is the best one." Thus equipped, he brought his horse to a gallop and soon caught up with the corporal, who had gone on ahead. He steadied himself in his stirrups, took the scabbard of his straight saber in his left hand and said to the four Frenchmen:

"Those people fleeing along the highway look like a flock of sheep. . . . They're running like frightened sheep. . . ."

The stress he laid on the word "sheep" was useless: his companions no longer remembered that it had angered them an hour before. Here we see one of the contrasts between the Italian and French characters. The French character is no doubt the happier of the two: it slides over the events of life and holds no grudges.

We shall not hide the fact that Fabrizio was greatly pleased with himself after he had spoken about "sheep." They continued on their way, making light conversation. Two leagues further on, the corporal, still amazed at not having seen any enemy horsemen, said to Fabrizio, "Since you're our cavalry, gallop over to the farm on that little hill and ask the peasant if he'll 'sell' us some lunch. Tell him there are only five of us. If he hesitates, give him five francs of your money in advance, but don't worry: we'll take it back after lunch."

Fabrizio looked at the corporal; he saw an imperturbable gravity in him, and an air of genuine moral superiority. He obeyed. Everything took place as the commander-in-chief had anticipated, except that Fabrizio insisted that they should not take back the five francs he had given the peasant.

"It's my money," he said to his companions, "and I'm not paying for your food: I'm paying for the oats he gave my horse."

He spoke French so badly that they thought they detected a tone of superiority in his words. They were deeply offended, and from then on they began making preparations in their mind for a duel at the end of the day. They found him very different from themselves, which offended them. Fabrizio, on the other hand, was beginning to feel a great deal of friendship for them.

They had been walking for two hours without saying a word when the corporal, looking at the highway, cried out joyfully, "There's the regiment!" They were soon on the road, but, alas, there were fewer than two hundred men around the eagle. Fabrizio soon caught sight of the *vivandière*. She was traveling on foot, her eyes were red, and she wept from time to time. He looked in vain for the little cart and Cocotte.

"Pillaged, plundered, robbed!" cried the *vivandière* in answer to our hero's gaze. He dismounted from his horse without a word, took it by the bridle and said to her, "Get on." She did not wait to be told twice.

"Shorten the stirrups for me," she said.

Once she was comfortably settled on the horse, she began to tell Fabrizio about all the disasters of the night. After a narrative of endless length, but avidly listened to by our hero, who, to tell the truth, understood nothing of what she was saying, although he felt tender friendship for her, she added, "And to think that it was Frenchmen who robbed me, beat me, ruined me!"

"What! It wasn't the enemy?" said Fabrizio with an air of innocence that gave charm to his pale, handsome, serious face.

"You're so foolish, my poor boy!" said the *vivandière*, smiling through her tears. "But even so, you're very nice."

"And just the way he is, he brought down his Prussian very well," said Corporal Aubry, who, amid the disorderly throng on the road, happened to be walking on the other side of the horse which the *vivandière* was riding. "But he's proud," continued the corporal. (Fabrizio started.) "And what's your name? After all, if there's a report I'd like to mention you."

"My name is Vasi," replied Fabrizio, with a singular expression, "I mean Boulot," he added, quickly catching his mistake.

Boulot had been the name of the possessor of the marching orders given to him by the jailer's wife at B——. He had carefully studied them two days before, for he was beginning to reflect a little and was no longer so surprised by things. Besides the marching orders of the hussar, Boulot, he was also carefully keeping the Italian passport according to which he could claim the noble name of Vasi, barometer merchant. When the corporal reproached him for being proud, he had almost answered, "I, proud? I, Fabrizio Valserra, Marchesino del Dongo, who consent to bear the name of a Vasi, barometer merchant?"

While he was making these reflections and saying to himself, "I must remember that my name is Boulot, or beware of the imprisonment that fate has threatened me with," the corporal and the *vivandière* had exchanged a few words about him.

"Don't accuse me of being nosy," the *vivandière* said to him in a less familiar tone than usual, "because I'm asking you questions for your own good. Who are you, really?"

Fabrizio did not answer at first; he was considering that he could never find more devoted friends to ask for advice, and he was in urgent need of advice. "We'll soon be coming to a fortified town," he thought. "The commanding officer will want to know who I am, and look out for prison if my answers let him see that I don't know anyone in the Fourth Regiment of Hussars, whose uniform I'm wearing!" As a subject of Austria, Fabrizio was aware of all the importance that must be attached to a passport. The members of his family, although noble and devout, and although they be-

50

longed to the victorious party, had been bothered more than a score of times with regard to their passports; he was therefore not in the least offended by the *vivandière*'s question. But while he was seeking the clearest French words in which to formulate his answer, the *vivandière*, goaded by keen curiosity, added, to prompt him to speak, "Corporal Aubry and I will give you some good advice to guide you."

"I'm sure you will," replied Fabrizio. "My name is Vasi and I'm from Genoa. My sister, who's famous for her beauty, is married to a captain. Since I'm only seventeen, she asked me to come and stay with her so that she could show me something of France and educate me a little. She wasn't in Paris when I arrived, and I knew she was with this army, so I came here and looked all over for her, but I couldn't find her. The soldiers were surprised by my accent and had me arrested. I had money then, so I gave some to the provost marshal. He gave me a set of marching orders and a uniform and said to me, 'Get out of here, fast, and swear you'll never mention my name.'"

"What was his name?" asked the *vivandière*.

"I gave him my word," replied Fabrizio.

"He's right," said the corporal. "The provost marshal is a dirty rat, but our friend here mustn't tell his name. But what's the name of your captain, your sister's husband? If we know his name, we can try to find him."

"Teulier, a captain in the Fourth Hussars," answered our hero.

"So," said the corporal rather shrewdly, "because of your foreign accent, the soldiers thought you were a spy?"

"That's the infamous word!" cried Fabrizio, his eyes flashing. "I who have such love for the emperor and the French. That was the insult that offended me most."

"There was no insult, that's where you're wrong," said Corporal Aubry gravely. "The soldiers' mistake was perfectly natural." He then explained with great pedantry that in the army a man must belong to a definite unit and wear a uniform, otherwise he will obviously be taken for a spy. "The enemy sends us a lot of them," he said. "Everybody's a traitor in this war." The scales fell from Fabrizio's eyes; he realized for the first time that he had been wrong about everything that had been happening to him for the past two months.

"But the boy must tell us his whole story," said the *vivandière*, whose curiosity was becoming more and more aroused. Fabrizio obeyed. When he had finished, she said solemnly to the corporal, "This boy actually isn't a soldier at all. We're going to have an ugly kind of war, now that we've been beaten and betrayed. Why should he get his bones broken for no good reason?"

"And he doesn't even know how to load his musket," said the corporal, "either by the numbers or at will. I'm the one who put in the bullet that brought down the Prussian."

"And that's not all: he shows his money to everybody," added the *vivandière*. "He'll be robbed of everything he's got as soon as he's no longer with us."

"The first cavalry sergeant he meets," said the corporal, "will arrest him so that he'll bribe him to let him go, and he may even force him to fight for the enemy, because everyone's a traitor now. The first man who comes along will order him to follow him, and he'll obey; he'd do better to join our regiment."

"I'd rather not, if you don't mind, corporal!" Fabrizio quickly exclaimed. "It's more comfortable to go on horseback. Besides, I don't know how to load a musket, and you've seen for yourself that I'm a good rider."

Fabrizio was very proud of this little speech. We shall not report the long discussion about his future destiny that took place between the corporal and the *vivandière*. Fabrizio noticed that, in their discussion, they repeated three or four times all the details of his story: the soldiers' suspicions, the provost marshal who had sold him a uniform and a set of marching orders, how he had found himself a member of the marshal's escort the day before, how he had seen the emperor galloping past, how the general's horse had been killed, and so on.

With feminine curiosity, the *vivandière* kept harking back to the way he had been dispossessed of the good horse she had made him buy: "You felt someone grab you by the feet, then they lifted you gently over your horse's tail and set you down on the ground!"

"Why does she keep repeating something all three of us know perfectly well already?" wondered Fabrizio. He did not yet know that, in France, this is how the common people go in search of ideas.

"How much money do you have?" the *vivandière* asked him abruptly. He did not hesitate to answer. He was aware of the nobility of her soul: this is the bright side of France.

"Altogether, I may have thirty gold napoleons left, and nine or ten five-franc coins."

"In that case, you have a clear field!" exclaimed the *vivandière*. "Get away from this army that's fallen apart. Turn off from the direction it's moving in, take the first beaten track you come to, over there, to your right, make your horse keep up a good pace and keep heading away from the army. Buy yourself some civilian clothes the first chance you get. When you're nine or ten leagues away from here and you don't see any more soldiers, take a stagecoach to some nice, quiet town and rest and eat beefsteaks for a week. Never tell anyone you were in the army: the gendarmes would pick you up as a deserter. You're a very nice boy, but you're not sharp enough yet to answer the questions they'd ask you. As soon as you've got civilian clothes on your back, tear your marching orders into a thousand pieces and start using your real name again: say that you're Vasi. . . . And where should he say he's coming from?" she asked the corporal.

"From Cambrai on the Schelde. Listen: it's a nice little town, with a cathedral, and Fénelon."

"That's it," said the *vivandière*, "never say you were in the battle, don't breathe a word about B——, or the provost marshal who sold you the marching orders. When you're ready to go back to Paris, go to Versailles first and come through the gates of Paris from that direction, leisurely and on foot, as though you were just taking a stroll. Sew your napoleons into your trousers, and when you have to pay for something be careful to show only the exact amount you need. What makes me sad is that people are going to take you in, you're going to be robbed of everything you've got. And what will you do when you're out of money? You don't know how to take care of yourself . . ." etc., etc.

The good *vivandière* went on talking for a long time. The corporal upheld her views by nodding his head, unable to get in a single word. Suddenly the crowd of people that covered the highway quickened their pace, then, in the twinkling of an eye, they all crossed the little ditch that ran along the left side of the road and began fleeing as fast as their legs could carry them. From all sides there were shouts of, "The Cossacks! The Cossacks!"

"Take back your horse!" cried the *vivandière*.

"I'll do no such thing!" said Fabrizio. "Gallop away! Hurry! I'm giving him to you. Do you want enough money to buy another little cart? Half of what I have is yours."

"Take back your horse, I mean it!" cried the *vivandière* angrily; and she prepared to dismount. Fabrizio drew his saber, shouted "Hold tight!" and slapped the horse several times with the flat of the blade. The startled animal galloped off in the direction taken by the fugitives.

Our hero looked at the highway. Only a few moments before, three or four thousand people had been hurrying along it, packed together like peasants in a procession. After the word "Cossacks," he saw exactly no one. The fugitives had abandoned shakos, muskets, sabers, etc. Fabrizio, astonished, climbed up to a field that lay twenty or thirty feet above the right side of the road. He looked up and down the highway, but saw no trace of Cossacks. "Strange people, these French," he thought. "Since I'm supposed to go to the right, I may as well start moving without delay. Those people may have some reason for running away that I don't know about." He picked up a musket, made sure it was loaded, stirred the powder of the priming charge, cleaned the flint, then selected a well-filled cartridge pouch and looked around again in all directions: he was completely alone in the middle of that plain which had been so densely covered with people a short time before. In the far distance he could see fugitives who were beginning to vanish behind the trees, still running. "It's all very odd!" he thought, and, remembering the maneuver employed by the corporal the night before, he walked over and sat down in the middle of a grainfield. He went no further, because he wanted to see his good friends again, the *vivandière* and Corporal Aubry.

In the grainfield he found that he had only eighteen napoleons left, not thirty as he had thought; but he still had the small diamonds he had placed in the lining of his hussar boots in the bedroom of the jailer's wife at B——. He hid his napoleons as well as he could, pondering deeply over the sudden disappearance of the others. "Is it a bad omen for me?" he wondered. His chief sorrow was that he had not asked Corporal Aubry this question: "Have I really been in a battle?" It seemed to him that he had, and he would have been blissfully happy if he had been certain of it.

"However," he thought, "I went into battle under a prisoner's name, I had a prisoner's marching orders in my pocket, and, worse still, I was wearing a prisoner's uniform! It's an unlucky sign for the future. What would Father Blanès say about it? And that miserable Boulot died in prison! The whole thing is sinister; fate will lead me into prison." He would have given anything in the world to know whether the hussar, Boulot, had been really guilty. When he reviewed his memories, it seemed to him that the jailer's wife at B—— had told him that the hussar had been arrested not only for stealing silverware, but also for stealing a peasant's cow and beating the peasant unmercifully. Fabrizio had no doubt that he would some day be imprisoned for a crime that would bear some relation to Boulot's. He thought of his friend, Father Blanès; what would he not have given to be able to consult him!

Then he recalled that he had not written to his aunt since leaving Paris. "Poor Gina!" he thought, and there were tears in his eyes when suddenly he heard a little noise close by: it was a soldier with three horses which looked as though they were starving. He had unfastened their bridles and was holding them by their bridoons, allowing them to eat the grain. Fabrizio started up like a partridge; the soldier was frightened. Our hero noticed this and yielded to the pleasure of acting the part of a hussar for a moment.

"One of those horses belongs to me, by God!" he cried. "But I'm willing to give you five francs for the trouble you've taken to bring him to me."

"Are you trying to make a fool of me?" said the soldier.

Fabrizio aimed his musket at him from a distance of six paces.

"Give me that horse or I'll blow your brains out!"

The soldier's musket was slung over his shoulder; his hand moved toward it.

"If you make the slightest movement, you're dead!" cried Fabrizio, rushing at him.

"All right, then, give me the five francs and take one of the horses," said the soldier, disconcerted, after casting a regretful glance at the highway, which was completely deserted. Holding his musket with his left hand, Fabrizio tossed him three five-franc coins with his right.

"Get down or I'll shoot. . . . Bridle the black one and take the two others away from here. I'll put a bullet into you if you make one false move."

The soldier obeyed sullenly. Fabrizio went up to the horse and put his left arm through the bridle without taking his eyes off the soldier, who was slowly moving away. When he was at a distance of fifty paces, Fabrizio leapt nimbly onto the horse. He was scarcely in the saddle, still feeling for the right stirrup with his foot, when he heard a bullet whistle past, just missing him: the soldier had shot at him. Fabrizio, beside himself with rage, began galloping toward the soldier, who ran as fast as his legs could carry him, and soon Fabrizio saw him mounted on one of the two horses, galloping away. "Good, now he's out of range," he said to himself.

The horse he had just bought was a magnificent animal, but he seemed to be dying of hunger. Fabrizio returned to the highway, where there was still not a living soul. He crossed it and began trotting toward a little rise in the ground to the left, where he hoped to find the *vivandière* again; but when he reached the top of it he saw nothing but a few isolated soldiers, over a league away. "I'm fated never to see that good, kind woman again!" he said to himself with a sigh. He rode to a farm which he had seen in the distance, to the right of the road. Without dismounting, and after paying in advance, he had some oats given to his poor horse, which was so famished that it bit the manger. An hour later, Fabrizio was trotting along the highway, still hoping vaguely to find the *vivandière*, or at least Corporal Aubry.

After riding for some time, constantly looking in all directions, he came to a marshy stream crossed by a rather narrow wooden bridge. On the near side of the bridge, to the right of the road, stood an isolated house bearing the sign of the White Horse. "I'll have dinner there," thought Fabrizio. At the head of the bridge there was a cavalry officer with his arm in a sling; he was on horseback and looked very sad. Ten paces away from him, three cavalrymen on foot were filling their pipes.

"Here are some people," thought Fabrizio, "who look to me as though they'd like to buy my horse for even less than it cost me." The wounded officer and the three men on foot were watching him approach and seemed to be waiting for him. "I really shouldn't cross the bridge, I ought to follow the bank of the stream to the right: that's what the *vivandière* would advise me to do, to stay out of trouble. . . . Yes, but if I run away, tomorrow I'll feel miserably ashamed. Besides, my horse has good legs, and the officer's horse is probably tired: if he tries to dismount me, I'll gallop away from him." Reasoning thus, Fabrizio prepared his horse for action and rode forward as slowly as possible.

"Come on, hussar, advance!" shouted the officer in a tone of authority.

Fabrizio advanced a few more paces, then stopped.

"Do you want to take my horse away from me?" he called out.

"Not at all. Come forward."

Fabrizio looked at the officer: he had a white mustache and an extremely honest face. The handkerchief supporting his left arm was soaked with blood, and his right hand was also wrapped in a piece of bloody cloth. "It's the men on foot who are going to grab the bridle of my horse," thought

Fabrizio; but when he looked at them more closely he saw that they were wounded too.

"In the name of honor," said the officer, who wore the epaulettes of a colonel, "stay here as a mounted sentry and tell all the dragoons, light cavalrymen and hussars you see that Colonel Le Baron is in that inn over there, and that I order them to join me."

The old colonel seemed overcome with sorrow. With his first words he had completely won over our hero, who sensibly replied, "I'm very young, sir, for anyone to listen to: I'd better have a written order from you."

"He's right," said the colonel, looking at him attentively. "You can still use your right hand, La Rose: write out the order."

Without a word, La Rose took a little parchment notebook from his pocket, wrote a few lines, tore out the page and handed it to Fabrizio, to whom the colonel repeated the order, adding that after two hours of duty he would, of course, be relieved by one of the three wounded cavalrymen who were with him. Having said this, he went into the inn with his men. Fabrizio watched them walk away and remained motionless at the head of his wooden bridge, deeply impressed by their dismal, silent grief. "They're like enchanted genies," he said to himself. Finally he unfolded the sheet of paper and read the order, which was worded as follows:

Colonel Le Baron, of the 6th Dragoons, Commanding Officer of the 2nd Brigade of the 1st Cavalry Division of the 14th Corps, hereby orders all troopers, dragoons, light cavalrymen and hussars not to cross the bridge, and to join him in the White Horse Inn, near the bridge, where his headquarters are located.

Headquarters, near La Sainte Bridge,
June 19, 1815. For Colonel Le Baron,
wounded in the right arm, and by his order.
—Sergeant La Rose

Fabrizio had been standing guard at the bridge for no more than half an hour when he saw six light cavalrymen coming toward him on horseback, and three others on foot. He told them of the colonel's orders.

"We'll be back," said four of the mounted cavalrymen, and they crossed the bridge at a fast trot. Fabrizio then began speaking with the two others. During their discussion, which became animated, the three men on foot crossed the bridge. One of the two mounted cavalrymen who still remained finally asked to see the order again and rode off with it say, saying, "I'm going to take it to my friends. They'll be sure to come back, wait right here for them." He galloped away, and his companion followed him. It had all taken place in the twinkling of an eye.

Fabrizio, furious, called one of the wounded soldiers, who appeared at a window of the White Horse Inn. This soldier, on whom Fabrizio saw a sergeant's stripes, came downstairs and shouted to him as he approached, "Hold your saber in your hand! You're on guard duty!"

Fabrizio obeyed, then said to him, "They took the order with them."

"They're in a bad mood after yesterday's business," said the sergeant gloomily. "I'm going to give you one of my pistols: if anyone tries to force his way past you, fire a shot into the air and I'll come out, or the colonel himself will appear."

Fabrizio had clearly seen the sergeant's gesture of surprise when he heard that the order had been taken away from him; he realized that he had received a personal insult, and he promised himself he would not let it happen again.

Armed with the sergeant's horse pistol, Fabrizio had proudly resumed his guard duty when he saw seven hussars riding toward him. He had placed himself in a position to block the bridge. He told them of the colonel's orders, they all looked greatly annoyed, and the boldest one tried to cross the bridge. Fabrizio, following the wise advice of his friend the *vivandière* who, the morning before, had told him to thrust rather than slash, lowered the point of his big, straight saber and threatened to plunge it into the man who was trying to force his way past him.

"Ah, the little toy soldier wants to kill us!" shouted one of the hussars. "As though we hadn't been killed enough yesterday!" They all drew their sabers at once and rushed at Fabrizio; he thought he was about to die, but he remembered the sergeant's surprise and was determined not to be despised again. Moving backward onto the bridge, he tried to defend himself with the point of his sword. But he looked so ludicrous as he wielded his big, straight, heavy-cavalry saber, which was much too heavy for him, that the hussars soon saw whom they were dealing with; from then on they tried, not to wound him, but to cut his clothes off his body. He thus received three or four little saber cuts on his arm.

Meanwhile, still faithful to the *vivandière*'s instructions, he kept thrusting his saber forward with all his might. Unfortunately, one of these thrusts struck a hussar in the hand; enraged at having been wounded by such a soldier, he countered with a vigorous thrust which caught Fabrizio at the top of the thigh. The damage was increased by the fact that our hero's horse, far from fleeing the fight, seemed to take pleasure in it, and lunged toward the assailants. Seeing Fabrizio's blood flowing down his leg, they were afraid they might have carried the game too far; they pushed him toward the left parapet of the bridge and galloped away. At his first free moment, Fabrizio shot his pistol into the air to notify the colonel.

Four hussars on horseback and two on foot, from the same regiment as the others, were coming toward the bridge when the shot went off. They had been attentively watching what was happening on the bridge. Thinking that Fabrizio had fired at their comrades, the four mounted men galloped toward him with sabers raised: it was a veritable charge. Colonel Le Baron, alerted by the pistol shot, opened the door of the inn, rushed out onto the bridge just as the galloping hussars reached it, and personally ordered them to halt.

"There are no more colonels here!" cried one of them, and urged his horse forward. The exasperated colonel broke off the reprimand he had been giving him and seized the right rein of the horse with his wounded right hand.

"Halt, you poor excuse for a soldier!" he said to the hussar. "I know you: you're from Captain Henriet's company."

"Well, then, let the captain give me the order himself! Captain Henriet was killed yesterday," he added with an unpleasant laugh, "and you can go to hell!"

So saying, he tried to force his way past; he pushed the old colonel, who fell on the bridge in a sitting position. Fabrizio, who was two paces further out on the bridge, but facing toward the inn, spurred his horse, and when the breast of the assailant's horse knocked down the colonel, who kept his grip on the right rein, Fabrizio, indignant, thrust his sword at the hussar with all his might. Fortunately, the hussar's horse, feeling itself drawn downward by the bridle to which the colonel was still clinging, made a lateral movement, so that the long blade of Fabrizio's heavy-cavalry saber slid along the hussar's vest and its entire length passed before his eyes. Furious, the hussar whirled around and violently slashed at Fabrizio with his sword. It cut through his sleeve and made a deep gash in his arm; our hero fell.

One of the dismounted hussars, seeing the two defenders of the bridge on the ground, seized the opportunity and leapt on Fabrizio's horse, hoping to make off with it by galloping across the bridge.

As he ran out of the inn, the sergeant had seen his colonel fall, and thought he was gravely wounded. He ran after Fabrizio's horse and plunged the point of his saber into the back of the thief, who fell. The hussars, seeing that there was no longer anyone on the bridge except the sergeant on foot, galloped across it and swiftly rode away. The one without a horse ran off across the fields.

The sergeant came up to the wounded men. Fabrizio had already stood up; he was not in great pain, but he was bleeding heavily. The colonel got to his feet more slowly. He was still dazed by his fall, but he had not been wounded.

"I'm not in any pain, except from that old wound in my hand," he said to the sergeant.

The hussar whom the sergeant had wounded was dying.

"May the devil take him!" cried the colonel. "But," he said to the sergeant and the two other cavalrymen who came running up, "take care of this boy I foolishly exposed to danger. I'll stay on the bridge myself and try to stop those madmen. Take the boy to the inn and bandage his arm—use one of my shirts."

CHAPTER FIVE

This whole adventure had taken place in less than a minute. Fabrizio's wounds were nothing; his arm was bandaged with strips of cloth cut from the colonel's shirt. He was offered a bed on the second floor of the inn.

"But while I'm being pampered on the second floor," he said, "my horse will get bored all by himself in the stable and go off with another master."

"Not bad for a conscript!" said the sergeant, and Fabrizio was installed on a bed of fresh straw in the same manger to which his horse had been tied.

Then, since Fabrizio felt very weak, the sergeant brought him a bowl of mulled wine and made a little conversation with him. A few compliments included in this conversation carried our hero into seventh heaven.

Fabrizio did not wake up till dawn the following morning.

The horses were whinnying loudly and making a terrible uproar; the stable was becoming filled with smoke. At first Fabrizio was bewildered by all the noise and did not even know where he was; finally, half suffocated by the smoke, he had the idea that the house was on fire. In the twinkling of an eye he was out of the stable and on his horse. He looked up: smoke was pouring from the two windows above the stable, and the roof was covered with swirling black smoke. During the night, a hundred fugitives had come to the White Horse Inn; they were all shouting and swearing. The five or six whom Fabrizio could see from close up seemed to be completely drunk; one of them tried to stop him and shouted at him, "Where are you taking my horse?"

When Fabrizio was a quarter of a league away, he looked back: no one was following him, and the house was in flames. He recognized the bridge, thought of his wound and felt his arm tightly wrapped in the bandages, and very hot. "I wonder what's become of the old colonel," he thought. "He gave his shirt to bandage my arm." Our hero was the coolest, most dispassionate man in the world that morning; the quantity of blood he had lost had delivered him of the whole romantic component of his character.

"Let's turn to the right and get out of here," he said to himself. He calmly began following the course of the stream, which, after passing under the bridge, flowed to the right of the road. He recalled the good *vivandière*'s advice. "What friendship!" he thought. "What an open character!"

After riding for an hour he found himself very weak. "What now? Am I going to faint?" he wondered. "If I faint, my horse will be stolen, and maybe my clothes, and my diamonds along with my clothes." He did not have the strength to guide his horse. He was trying to keep his balance in the saddle when a peasant, who had been digging in a field beside the highway, noticed his pallor and came over to offer him a glass of beer and some bread.

"When I saw how pale you were, I thought you must be one of the wounded men from the big battle," said the peasant. Never did help come at a more opportune moment. As Fabrizio was chewing the piece of black bread, his eyes began to hurt when he looked straight ahead. When he felt a little better he expressed his thanks. "And where am I?" he asked. The peasant told him that three-quarters of a league further on there was a small market town by the name of Zonders, where he would be well taken care of.

Fabrizio reached this town, not knowing too clearly what

61

he was doing, and thinking only of keeping himself from falling off his horse with every step. He saw a big gate standing open and rode through it: he was in the courtyard of the Currycomb Inn. The good mistress of the house, an enormous woman, ran up to him and called for help in a voice that quavered with pity. Two young girls helped him to dismount; as soon as he was off his horse he fainted. They called in a surgeon, who bled him. For the rest of that day, and for several days afterward, Fabrizio did not know too well what was being done to him; he slept almost constantly.

The saber wound in his thigh threatened to form a dangerous abscess. When his mind was clear again, he insisted that his horse be taken care of, and repeated often that he would pay well, which offended the good mistress of the inn and her daughters.

He had received two weeks of admirable care, and was beginning to collect his thoughts a little, when he noticed one evening that his hostess seemed to be deeply troubled. A short time later, a German officer walked into his room. They answered him in a language Fabrizio did not understand, but he saw that they were obviously talking about him; he pretended to be asleep. He waited for some time, then, when he thought the officer must be gone, he called his hostesses and asked, "That officer came to put my name on a list and make me a prisoner, didn't he?" The hostess assented with tears in her eyes. "Well, there's some money in my dolman!" he cried, sitting up in bed. "Buy me some civilian clothes and I'll ride away tonight. You've already saved my life once by taking me in just as I was about to fall dying in the street; save me again by making it possible for me to go back to my mother."

At this moment, the hostess's daughters burst into tears; they were trembling with fear for Fabrizio, and since they scarcely understood French, they came up beside his bed to question him. They discussed the situation with their mother in Flemish, but their compassionate eyes kept turning back to our hero. He thought he could make out that his escape might get them into serious trouble, but that they were willing to take the risk. He thanked them effusively, clasping his hands. A Jew of the district supplied a complete outfit; but when he brought it, toward ten o'clock that night, the young ladies saw, after comparing it with Fabrizio's dolman, that it would have to be taken in considerably. They immediately set to work; there was no time to lose. He indicated where there were a few napoleons hidden in his uniform and asked his hostesses to sew them into the clothes they had just bought for him. A fine pair of new boots had also been delivered. He did not hesitate to ask the worthy girls to slit open his hussar boots at the place he pointed out to them, and they hid his small diamonds in the lining of his new boots.

As a strange result of his loss of blood and the weakness that had ensued, Fabrizio had almost completely forgotten his French. He spoke Italian to his hostesses, who spoke a Flemish dialect, so that they made themselves understood almost entirely by signs. When the girls, who were perfectly disinterested, saw his diamonds, their enthusiasm for him knew no bounds: they thought he must be a prince in disguise. As for Fabrizio, he found them charming, and toward midnight, when the surgeon had told him he could drink a little wine, because of the journey he was about to undertake, he felt almost disinclined to go. "Where could I be better off than here?" he said. However, at about two in the morning he got dressed. Just as he was leaving his room, the good hostess informed him that his horse had been taken away by the officer who had come to search the house several hours earlier.

"Oh, the swine!" cried Fabrizio, swearing. "He's robbed a wounded man!" Our young Italian was not philosophical enough to recall the price at which he himself had acquired the horse.

Aniken told him, weeping, that they had rented a horse for him; she would have preferred him to stay; their farewells were tender. Two tall young men, relatives of the good hostess, lifted Fabrizio into the saddle. During the journey they held him on the horse while a third young man, walking a few hundred paces in front of the little convoy, made sure there were no suspicious patrols on the road. After traveling for two hours, they stopped at the house of a cousin of the hostess of the Currycomb Inn. Despite anything Fabrizio could say to them, the young men accompanying him refused to leave him; they claimed to know the passages through the woods better than anyone else.

"But tomorrow morning," said Fabrizio, "when my escape becomes known and you're not seen anywhere in the region, your absence may make trouble for you."

They set off again. Fortunately, when daylight appeared, the plain was covered by a thick fog. Toward eight in the morning, they came near a little town. One of the young men went on ahead to find out if the post horses had been stolen.

The postmaster had had time to hide them and round up some wretched nags with which he had stocked his stables. Someone was sent to bring two horses from the marsh in which they were hidden, and three hours later Fabrizio got into a little cabriolet that was in a sad state of disrepair, but drawn by two good post horses. He had regained some of his strength. His parting with the young men, the hostess's relatives, was extremely emotional; no matter what friendly pretexts he managed to think of, they steadfastly refused to take any money. "In your condition, you need it more than we do," these worthy young men always replied.

Finally they left, carrying the letters in which Fabrizio, somewhat invigorated by the agitation of the journey, had tried to express to his hostesses everything he felt for them. He had written with tears in his eyes, and there was certainly some love in the letter addressed to little Aniken.

The rest of the journey was uneventful. By the time he reached Amiens, he was suffering a great deal from the saber wound in his thigh. The country surgeon had not thought to incise the wound, and, despite the bloodlettings, an abscess had formed. During the two weeks that Fabrizio spent in the inn at Amiens, kept by an obsequious and greedy family, the Allies were invading France, and he made so many profound reflections on the things that had just happened to him that he became another man. He remained childish on one point only: Was what he had seen a battle? And, if so, was it the Battle of Waterloo? For the first time in his life, he found pleasure in reading: he kept hoping to find in the newspapers, or in accounts of the battle, some description that would enable him to identify the places where he had ridden with Marshal Ney's escort, and later with the other general. During his stay in Amiens, he wrote nearly every day to his good friends at the Currycomb Inn.

As soon as he was well he went to Paris. At his old hotel, he found a score of letters from his mother and his aunt, begging him to come home as soon as possible. Countess Pietranera's last letter had a certain enigmatic quality which made him extremely uneasy and destroyed all his tender daydreams. His character was such that a single word was enough to make him easily foresee the greatest misfortunes, and his imagination would then undertake to depict them in horrible detail.

"Be careful not to sign the letters you send us to give us news of yourself," the countess had written. "When you return, you must not come directly to Lake Como: stop at Lugano, in Swiss territory." He was to arrive in that little town under the name of Cavi. At the main inn he would find the countess's manservant, who would tell him what to do. His aunt ended her letters with these words: "Conceal your mad escapade by all possible means, and be sure not to keep any printed or written papers on you; in Switzerland you will be surrounded by friends of Santa Margherita.* If I have enough money, I will send someone to the Hôtel des Balances in Geneva, and you will be given all the details which I cannot put down in writing, but which you must know before you arrive. But, in the name of God, not one more day in Paris! You would be recognized by our spies there."

Fabrizio's imagination began conjuring up the wildest ideas, and he was incapable of any pleasure other than that of trying to guess what it was his aunt had to tell him that was so extraordinary. He was arrested twice during his journey across France, but managed to get away each time. He owed these unpleasant difficulties to his Italian passport, and to his odd profession of barometer merchant, which was scarcely in keeping with his young face and his arm in a sling.

Finally, in Geneva, he met a man in the countess's service who told him on her behalf that he, Fabrizio, had been denounced to the police of Milan as having gone to inform Napoleon of certain proposals drawn up by a vast conspiracy organized in the late Kingdom of Italy. If such had not been the object of his journey, the denunciation stated, what was the use of traveling under an assumed name? His mother would try to prove the truth, namely, that he had never gone beyond Switzerland, and that he had hastily left the castle as the result of a quarrel with his elder brother.

On hearing this story, Fabrizio felt a surge of pride. "So they think I was a kind of ambassador to Napoleon!" he said to himself. "They think I had the honor of speaking to that great man! Would to God that I had!" He remembered that his ancestor seven generations back, a grandson of the one who had come to Milan as a member of Sforza's retinue, had had the honor of being beheaded by the duke's enemies, who surprised him as he was on his way to Switzerland to recruit

* Signor Pellico has made this name known all over Europe: it is that of the street in Milan on which the headquarters and prisons of the police are located.

soldiers and convey proposals to the praiseworthy cantons. In his mind's eye he saw the engraving in the family genealogy relating to this event. When he questioned the manservant, Fabrizio learned that he was outraged by one detail which he finally blurted out, despite the countess's strict and repeated orders to keep silent about it. It was Ascanio, Fabrizio's elder brother, who had denounced him to the police of Milan. This cruel news nearly drove our hero into a fit of madness.

To go to Italy from Geneva, one must pass through Lausanne. Fabrizio decided to set off on foot immediately and travel ten or twelve leagues in this manner, even though the stagecoach from Geneva to Lausanne was scheduled to depart in two hours. Before leaving Geneva he got into a quarrel in one of the dreary local cafés, with a young man who, he said, was looking at him in an odd way. Nothing could have been truer. The young Genevan, phlegmatic, sensible and concerned with nothing but money, thought him mad: on entering the café, Fabrizio had cast furious glances in all directions, then upset the cup of coffee that was brought to him, spilling it on his trousers. In this quarrel, Fabrizio's impulse was entirely in keeping with the sixteenth century: instead of discussing a duel with the young Genevan, he took out his dagger and rushed at him to stab him. In that moment of passion, he forgot everything he had learned about the code of honor and reverted to instinct, or, to speak more accurately, to his earliest childhood memories.

The confidential agent he found in Lugano increased his fury by giving him new details. Since Fabrizio was well liked in Grianta, if it had not been for his brother's kind deed no one would have said anything about him, everyone would have pretended to believe he was in Milan, and the attention of the police in that city would never have been drawn to his absence.

"The customs officials have no doubt been given your description," his aunt's messenger said to him, "and if we follow the highway, you'll be arrested at the border of the Lombardo-Venetian kingdom."

Fabrizio and his men knew every mountain path between Lugano and Lake Como; they disguised themselves as hunters—that is, as smugglers—and since there were three of them and they all looked rather determined, the customs officers they met had no desire to do anything but greet them. Fabrizio regulated his pace so that he did not reach the castle till midnight; by then his father and all the menservants with powdered hair had been in bed for a long time.

He climbed down into the deep moat without difficulty and entered the castle through the little window of a cellar: this was where his mother and his aunt were waiting for him, and soon his sisters came running in too. For a long time there were alternate outbursts of tears and transports of tenderness, and they had scarcely begun to talk reasonably when the first glow of dawn came to warn those people who regarded themselves as unfortunate that time was flying.

"I hope your brother hasn't suspected your arrival," said Countess Pietranera. "I've hardly spoken to him at all since his noble gesture, and his vanity has done me the honor of being offended by it. Tonight at supper I deigned to speak to him; I needed to find some excuse to hide my wild joy, which might have made him suspicious. Then, when I saw that he was filled with pride over what he thought was our reconciliation, I took advantage of his joy to make him drink recklessly, so I'm sure he's had no thought of lying in wait to carry on his trade of spying."

"We'll have to hide our hussar in your apartment," said the marquise. "He can't leave right away, because we haven't yet recovered enough control over our reason, and we still have to decide on the best way to throw the terrible Milanese police off the scent."

This plan was adopted; but the marquis and his elder son noticed the next day that the marquise was constantly in her sister-in-law's room. We shall not try to depict the transports of tenderness and joy which continued to move those happy people that day. Italian hearts are much more tormented than ours by the wild ideas presented to them by a burning imagination, but, on the other hand, their joys are much more intense and last longer. The countess and the marquise were totally deprived of their reason that day; Fabrizio had to keep repeating all his stories. Finally the prospect of continuing to elude the vigilance of the marquis and his son Ascanio seemed so difficult to them that they decided to go and hide their common joy in Milan.

They went as far as Como in the boat usually used by the household; to do otherwise would have aroused a thousand suspicions. But when they reached the harbor of Como, the marquise remembered that she had left some papers of the utmost importance in Grianta. She quickly sent the boatmen back for them; these men were therefore unable to make any remarks about the way the two ladies spent their time at Como. As soon as they arrived, they hired at random one of those carriages which wait for customers near the high medieval tower that rises above the Milan Gate. They left immediately, before the driver had time to speak to anyone. When they were a quarter of a league outside the town, they met a young hunter with whom they were both acquainted, and who, since they had no man with them, was kind enough to act as their escort as far as the gates of Milan, where he had been going already, hunting along the way.

Everything was going well, and the two ladies were engaged in lighthearted conversation with the young traveler, when, at a bend which the road makes to curve around the charming hill and wood of San Giovanni, three constables in plain clothes leapt out and grabbed the horses' bridles. "Oh! My husband has betrayed us!" cried the marquise, and fainted. A sergeant who had remained some distance behind walked up to the carriage and said in a voice suggestive of the tavern, "I'm sorry I have to carry out this mission, but I hereby arrest you, General Fabio Conti."

Fabrizio thought the sergeant was ridiculing him by calling him a general. "You'll pay for that!" he thought. He looked at the constables in plain clothes and watched for a favorable moment to leap out of the carriage and run away.

The countess smiled—as a precautionary measure, I believe—then said to the sergeant, "But my dear sergeant, do you really think this child of sixteen is General Conti?"

"Aren't you the general's daughter?" asked the sergeant.

"Take a look at my father," said the countess, pointing to Fabrizio. The constables burst into uncontrollable laughter.

"Show me your passports and don't argue," said the sergeant, nettled by the general merriment.

"These ladies never take passports to go to Milan," said the driver with a cold, philosophical air. "They're coming from their castle at Grianta. This is Countess Pietranera and the other lady is the Marquise del Dongo."

The sergeant, disconcerted, walked to the heads of the horses and consulted with his men there. The conference had been going on for a good five minutes when Countess Pietranera asked these gentlemen to allow the carriage to be driven forward a few paces into the shade; the heat was overwhelming, even though it was only eleven o'clock in the morning. As he was gazing attentively in all directions, looking for a way of escape, Fabrizio saw a young girl of fourteen or fifteen step onto the dusty highway from a little path that intersected it. Weeping timorously into her handkerchief, she was walking between two constables in uniform, and three paces behind her, also between two constables, walked a tall, gaunt man who affected an air of dignity, like a prefect marching in a procession.

"Where did you find them?" said the sergeant, now feeling thoroughly drunk.

"Running across the fields, with no trace of a passport."

The sergeant appeared to lose his head completely; he now had five prisoners before him, instead of the two he needed. He walked a short distance away, leaving only one man to guard the male prisoner who was putting on majestic airs, and another to prevent the horses from moving forward.

"Stay here," said the countess to Fabrizio, who had already leapt out of the carriage, "everything's going to be all right."

They heard a constable exclaim, "What's the difference? They don't have passports, so they're fair game anyway!" The sergeant did not appear to be quite so certain. The name of Countess Pietranera made him feel uneasy; he had once known General Pietranera and was unaware of his death. "The general isn't the kind of man who wouldn't get revenge on me if I arrested his wife without good reason," he thought.

During these deliberations, which were long, the countess had entered into conversation with the young girl who was standing beside the open carriage on the dusty road; she had been struck by her beauty.

"The sun is going to hurt you," she said to her. "This good soldier," she added, turning to the constable who had been assigned to hold the heads of the horses, "will surely allow you to sit in our carriage."

Fabrizio, who had been wandering around the carriage, walked up to the girl to help her climb in. She had her foot on the step and was already raising herself, with Fabrizio supporting her by the arm, when the imposing man, who was standing six paces behind the carriage, called out in a voice made gruff by his desire to maintain his dignity, "Stay on the road: don't get into a carriage that doesn't belong to you."

Fabrizio did not hear this order. Instead of getting into the carriage, the girl tried to climb back down, and since he continued to support her, she fell into his arms. He smiled, she blushed deeply; they stood looking at each other for a moment after she had disengaged herself from his arms.

"She'd be a charming prison companion," thought Fabrizio. "What profound thoughts lie behind that forehead! She would know how to love."

The sergeant came up to them with an air of authority and said, "Which of these ladies is named Clelia Conti?"

"I am," said the girl.

"And I," cried the elderly man, "am General Fabio Conti, Chamberlain to His Most Serene Highness the Prince of Parma! I consider it an outrage that a man like myself should be hunted down like a thief!"

"Day before yesterday, when the police inspector asked to see your passport as you were leaving the port of Como, didn't you tell him to mind his own business? Well, today he's stopping you from minding yours."

"My boat was already moving away from shore, I was in a hurry and there was a storm coming up. A man not in uniform shouted to me from the quay to come back to port; I told him my name and continued on my way."

"And this morning you slipped out of Como, didn't you?"

"A man like myself doesn't take a passport to go from Milan to see the lake. This morning, at Como, I was told I'd be arrested at the gate, so I left the town on foot with my daughter. I was hoping to find some carriage on the road that would take me to Milan, and I assure you that the first thing I do when I get there will be to go to the general in command of the province and register my complaints with him."

A heavy load seemed to have been taken from the sergeant's shoulders.

"Well, general, you're under arrest, and I'm going to take you to Milan. . . . And who are you?" he said to Fabrizio.

"This is my son," said the countess, "Ascanio, son of Lieutenant General Pietranera."

"Is he without a passport, countess?" asked the sergeant, now in a much calmer state of mind.

"At his age, he's never taken one out; he never travels alone, he's always with me."

During this conversation, General Conti was putting on a greater and greater display of offended dignity with the constables.

"Not so much talk!" said one of them. "You're under arrest, that's all there is to say."

"You'll be lucky," said the sergeant, "if we let you rent a horse from some peasant, because otherwise, in spite of the dust, the heat, and your rank of Chamberlain of Parma, you'll walk to Milan with our horses beside you."

The general began to swear.

"Shut up!" said the constable. "Where's your general's uniform? Anyone can say he's a general!"

The general flew into a rage.

70

Meanwhile, things were going much better in the carriage. The countess had taken command of the constables as though they were her servants. She had given one of them a scudo to go get some wine and cool water from a little cottage that could be seen two hundred paces away. She had found time to calm Fabrizio, who had been determined at all costs to escape into the woods that covered the hill. "I have two good pistols," he had said.

She persuaded the enraged general to let his daughter get into the carriage. The general, who loved to talk about himself and his family, took this opportunity to tell the ladies that his daughter was only twelve years old, having been born in 1803, on October 27, although everyone assumed her to be fourteen or fifteen, because her mind was so highly developed.

"A thoroughly common man," said the countess's eyes to the marquise.

Thanks to the countess, everything was satisfactorily settled after an hour's discussion. A constable discovered that he had some business to attend to in a nearby village and rented his horse to General Conti after the countess had said to him, "You'll get ten lire." The sergeant went off alone with the general; his men stayed behind under a tree in the company of four enoromus bottles of wine, almost like small demijohns, which the constable who had been sent to the cottage had brought back with the help of a peasant. Clelia Conti was authorized by the worthy chamberlain to accept a place in the ladies' carriage for the trip back to Milan, and no one dreamed of arresting the son of that gallant general, Count Pietranera.

After the first few moments given over to an exchange of courtesies and comments on the little incident that had just ended, Clelia Conti noticed the touch of enthusiastic warmth with which the beautiful countess spoke to Fabrizio; she was surely not his mother. Her interest was especially aroused by repeated allusions to something supremely heroic, bold and dangerous which he had done a short time before, but despite all her intelligence she was unable to discover what they were referring to.

She looked with astonishment at the young hero whose eyes seemed to be still aglow with all the fire of action. As for him, he was somewhat dumbfounded by the extraordinary beauty of that girl of twelve, and his glances made her blush.

When they were one league from Milan, Fabrizio said he was going to visit his uncle and took leave of the ladies.

"If I ever get out of my difficulties," he said to Clelia, "I'll go to see the beautiful pictures in Parma, and then will you be so kind as to remember this name: Fabrizio del Dongo?"

"Good!" said the countess. "Now we know how skillful you are at concealing your identity! Signorina, be so kind as to remember that this young rascal is my son, and that his name is Pietranera, not del Dongo."

Late that night, Fabrizio entered Milan by the Renza Gate, which leads to a fashionable promenade. Sending two servants to Switzerland had exhausted the extremely meager savings of the marquise and her sister-in-law. Fortunately, Fabrizio still had a few napoleons left, and one of the diamonds, which they decided to sell.

The ladies were well liked and knew everyone in the city. The most important personages in the Austrian and pious party went to speak in Fabrizio's favor to Baron Binder, the Chief of Police. These gentlemen could not understand, they said, how anyone could take seriously the foolish escapade of a sixteen-year-old boy who had quarreled with his elder brother and run away from home.

"My business is to take everything seriously," gently replied Baron Binder, a wise and melancholy man. He was at that time engaged in organizing the famous police force of Milan, and had undertaken to forestall a revolution like the one which had driven the Austrians from Genoa in 1746. This police force, later made so famous by the adventures of Pellico and Andryane, was not exactly cruel: it carried out harsh laws in a rational and merciless manner. Emperor Francis II wanted to strike terror into those bold Italian imaginations.

"Give me," repeated Baron Binder to all of Fabrizio's protectors, "a *proven* day-by-day account of the young Marchesino del Dongo's activities; describe everything he did from the time he left Grianta, on March 8, until his arrival last night in this city, where he's hiding in one of the bedrooms of his mother's apartment, and I'm prepared to treat him as the most charming and mischievous young man in Milan. But if you can't supply me with his itinerary during all the days following his departure from Grianta, then, no matter how exalted his birth may be, and no matter how much respect I may have for the friends of his family, isn't it my duty to have him arrested? Isn't it my duty to keep him in prison until he's given me proof that he didn't go to deliver a message to Napoleon from the few malcontents who may exist in Lombardy among the subjects of His Imperial and Royal Highness? Note further, gentlemen, that if young del Dongo succeeds in justifying himself on this point, he will still be guilty of having gone abroad without a properly issued passport, and of having taken a false name and knowingly made use of a passport issued to a common workman, that is, to a man belonging to a class far below his own."

This declaration, cruelly logical, was accompanied by all the marks of deference and respect which the Chief of Police owed to the high position of the Marquise del Dongo and the important personages who had come to intercede in her behalf.

The marquise was in despair when she learned of Baron Binder's reply.

"Fabrizio is going to be arrested," she cried, weeping, "and once he's in prison, heaven only knows when he'll get out! His father will disown him!"

Countess Pietranera and her sister-in-law consulted with two or three close friends, and despite anything they could say, the marquise was absolutely determined to send her son away that night.

"But you can see quite clearly," the countess said to her, "that Baron Binder knows your son is here; he's not a malicious man."

"No, but he wants to please Emperor Francis."

"But if he thought it would help his career to throw Fabrizio in prison, he'd be there already. And you'd be showing an insulting mistrust of the baron if you made Fabrizio run away."

"But in admitting to us that he knows where Fabrizio is, he's as good as said to us, 'Send him away!' No, I'll never be able to breathe freely as long as I can say to myself, 'In a quarter of an hour my son will be within prison walls!' No matter what Baron Binder's ambitions may be, he regards it as useful to his personal position in this country to make a show of consideration for a man of my husband's rank, and I see proof of that in the strange openheartedness with which he's admitted that he knows where to find my son. Furthermore, he's obligingly described the two offenses Fabrizio is accused of in his unworthy brother's denunciation, and explained that both of those offenses entail imprisonment: isn't that the same as telling us that if we prefer exile the choice is ours to make?"

"If you choose exile," the countess kept repeating, "we'll never see him again for the rest of our lives."

Fabrizio, who was present during the whole conversation,

along with one of the marquise's old friends, now a counselor of the tribunal formed by Austria, was definitely in favor of running away. And so he left the palace that very night, hidden in the carriage that was taking his mother and his aunt to La Scala. The coachman, whom they mistrusted, went to wait in a tavern as usual, and while the footman, in whom they had complete confidence, kept watch over the horses, Fabrizio, disguised as a peasant, slipped out of the carriage and left the city. The next morning he crossed the border with the same good luck, and a few hours later he was installed on an estate his mother owned in Piedmont, near Novara, at Romagnano, to be precise, where Bayard was killed.

It can well be imagined how attentively the ladies listened to the performance when they were in their box at La Scala. They had gone there only to be able to consult with some of their friends who belonged to the liberal party, and whose appearance at the del Dongo palace might have been given a bad interpretation by the police. In the box, it was decided to approach Baron Binder in a different manner. It was out of the question to offer money to that perfectly honest magistrate, and anyway, the ladies were extremely poor; they had forced Fabrizio to take with him all the money that remained from the sale of the diamond.

It was very important, however, to know the baron's final word on the matter. The countess's friends reminded her of a certain Canon Borda, an amiable young man who had once made advances to her, and in a rather ignoble way; unable to succeed, he had reported her intimacy with Limercati to General Pietranera, whereupon he had been banished as a contemptible wretch. This canon now went to play tarots with Baroness Binder every evening, and was naturally a close friend of her husband. The countess made up her mind to take the horribly painful step of going to see the canon. Early the next morning, before he left home, she had herself announced to him.

When his only servant pronounced the name of Countess Pietranera, the canon was so overcome with emotion that he could hardly speak; he did not try to repair the disorder of his very simple dressing gown.

"Show her in, then leave us alone," he said in a faltering voice. The countess came in; Borda fell to his knees.

"This is the position in which a wretched madman ought to receive your orders," he said to the countess, who, in her simple morning dress which almost amounted to a disguise was irresistibly attractive that day. Her deep sorrow over Fabrizio's exile, the violence she was doing to her feelings in coming to the house of a man who had behaved so treacherously with her—everything combined to give incredible brilliance to her eyes.

"This is the position in which I want to receive your orders," cried the canon, "because it's obvious that you have some favor to ask of me, otherwise you wouldn't have honored with your presence the house of a wretched madman who, carried away by love and jealousy, once behaved abominably toward you, when he saw that he had no hope of winning your favor."

These words were sincere, and they were all the more admirable because the canon was now in a position of great power. The countess was moved to tears by them; her heart had been chilled by humiliation and fear, which had now been replaced in an instant by compassion and a little hope. In the twinkling of an eye, she passed from a state of extreme misery to what was almost happiness.

"Kiss my hand," she said to the canon, holding it out to him, "and stand up." (She addressed him in the second person singular, but it must be pointed out that in Italy this form is used to indicate frank, open friendship as well as more tender feelings.) "I've come to ask you to obtain a pardon for my nephew Fabrizio. Here's the whole truth, without the slightest dissimulation, as one tells it to an old friend. At the age of sixteen and a half, he's done an incredibly foolish thing. We were in the castle of Grianta, on Lake Como; one evening at seven o'clock a boat coming from Como brought us the news that the emperor had landed at Cannes. The next morning, Fabrizio left for France, after borrowing the passport of a working-class friend, a barometer merchant by the name of Vasi. Since he doesn't exactly look like a barometer merchant, he hadn't gone ten leagues into France before his handsome appearance got him arrested; his outbursts of enthusiasm in bad French seemed suspicious. Some time later, he escaped and managed to reach Geneva. We sent someone to meet him in Lugano—"

"You mean Geneva," said the canon, smiling.

The countess finished the story.

"I'll do everything for you that's humanly possible," said the canon effectively. "I place myself entirely at your orders. I'll even commit imprudent acts. Tell me, what shall I do as soon as this poor drawing room is deprived of this celestial apparition, which marks an epoch in the story of my life?"

"You must go to Baron Binder and tell him you've always loved Fabrizio, that you were already visiting our house at the time of his birth, and that, in the name of the friendship the baron has shown for you, you beg him to use all his spies to find out whether, before leaving for Switzerland, Fabrizio had the slightest contact with any of those liberals he keeps under supervision. If the baron's agents serve him at all well, he'll see that nothing more than a foolish youthful escapade is involved. As you know, in my lovely apartment in the Dugnani palace I had some engravings representing the battles won by Napoleon: it was from the captions of those engravings that my nephew learned to read. By the time he was five, my husband was explaining the battles to him. We used to put my husband's helmet on his head, and the boy would drag his big saber around. Well, one fine day he learned that my husband's god, the emperor, was back in France. He set off to join him, like a young hothead, but he didn't succeed. Ask your baron what punishment he wants to inflict on him for that moment of madness."

"I was forgetting one thing," said the canon: "you'll see that I'm not completely unworthy of the pardon you're granting me. Here," he said, rummaging through the papers on his desk, "is the denunciation by that infamous *col-torto* [hypocrite]. Look, it's signed 'Ascanio Valserra del Dongo,' and he's the one who started the whole affair. I took it from police headquarters last night, and I went to La Scala in the hope of finding someone who usually goes to your box, so that I could communicate it to you through him. A copy of this document has been in Vienna for a long time. Here's the enemy we have to fight."

The cannon and the countess read the denunication together. He told her he would send her a copy of it by some trustworthy person before the day was over. She returned to the del Dongo palace with joy in her heart.

"No one could be a more gallant man than that former scoundrel," she said to the marquise. "Tonight at La Scala, at a quarter to eleven by the theater clock, we'll send everyone out of our box, put out the candles and close the door; then, at eleven o'clock, the canon himself will come and tell us what he's been able to do. We decided that would be the best way for him to avoid compromising himself."

The canon was a very intelligent man; he was careful to keep the appointment, and he showed that perfect generosity and unreserved openheartedness which are almost never found except in countries where vanity does not dominate all other feelings. His denunciation of the countess to her husband, General Pietranera, was one of the great regrets of his life, and he had now found a way to free himself of his remorse.

That morning, when the countess had left his house, "Now she's having an affair with her nephew," he had said to himself, for he was not cured. "Proud as she is, she's still come to see me! ... When poor Pietranera, she rejected with horror all my offers to help her, even though they were perfectly courteous and well presented to her by Colonel Scotti, her former lover. The beautiful Countess Pietranera living on fifteen hundred lire a year—what an idea!" exclaimed the canon, pacing vigorously up and down his bedroom. "Then going off to live in the castle of Grianta with an abominable *seccatore*, that Marquis del Dongo! ... But now everything's clear! It's true that young Fabrizio is charming, tall, handsome, always smiling ... and, even better, he has a certain look of gentle sensuality in his eyes ... a face like a Correggio painting," he added bitterly.

"The difference in age ... not too great. Fabrizio was born right after the arrival of the French, about '98, if I remember correctly. The countess must be about twenty-seven or twenty-eight, and no one could be prettier or more adorable; in this country fertile in beauties, she outshines them all: Marini, Gherardi, Ruga, Aresi, Pietragrua, she surpasses all those women. ... They were living happily together, hidden on the shores of that beautiful Lake Como, when the young man decided to join Napoleon's army. ... There are still noble hearts in Italy! Despite everything that's been done! Dear fatherland! ... No," continued that heart inflamed by jealousy, "there's no other possible explanation for her resignation to a life of vegetating in the country, with the disgust of seeing every day, at every meal, that horrible face of the Marquis del Dongo, plus that repulsive, pasty countenance of the Marchesino Ascanio, who's going to be worse than his father! ... Well, I'll serve her loyally anyway. At least I'll have the pleasure of seeing her otherwise than through my opera glasses."

Canon Borda explained the matter quite clearly to the two ladies. Actually, the baron was as well disposed as anyone could wish. He was delighted that Fabrizio had run away before any orders could arrive from Vienna, for Binder had no power to decide anything: he was awaiting orders in this matter as in all others. Every day he sent to Vienna exact copies of all his reports, then he waited.

During his exile at Romagnano, it was necessary, first of all, that Fabrizio should go to Mass every day, choose as his confessor an intelligent man devoted to the cause of the monarchy, and admit only the most irreproachable sentiments to him in the confessional. Secondly, he must not associate with anyone regarded as having an independent mind, and on occasion he must speak of rebellion with horror, and as something that was never permissible. Thirdly, he must never let himself be seen in a café, never read any newspapers other than the official gazettes of Turin and Milan, show a distaste for reading in general, and, above all, never read any book published after 1720, with the possible exception of the novels of Sir Walter Scott. "And finally," added the canon with a touch of malice, "he must be sure to pay court openly to one of the pretty women of the region, a woman of noble birth, naturally. That will show that he doesn't have the somber and dissatisfied spirit of a budding conspirator."

Before going to bed, the countess and the marquise wrote Fabrizio two endless letters in which they explained, with charming anxiety, all the advice that Borda had given them.

Fabrizio had no desire to be a conspirator: he loved Napoleon, and, as a member of the nobility, felt that he was made to be happier than others and considered the middle class ridiculous. He had never opened a book since leaving school, where he had read only books adapted by the Jesuits. He established himself at some distance from Romagnano, in a magnificent palace, one of the masterpieces of the famous architect Sanmicheli; but it had been uninhabited for thirty years, so that the rain came into every room and not one window could be closed. He took possession of the steward's horses and rode them all day long without ceremony. He seldom spoke to anyone; he was absorbed in thought. The advice to take a mistress belonging to some ultra-monarchist family was quite agreeable to him, and he followed it to the letter. He chose as his confessor a scheming young priest who wanted to become a bishop (like the confessor of the Spielberg[*]); but he would travel three leagues on foot, wrapped in what he believed to be impenetrable mystery, to read the *Constitutionnel*, which he thought sublime. "It's as noble as Alfieri and Dante!" he often exclaimed.

Fabrizio had one point in common with a typical young Frenchman: he was much more seriously concerned with

[*] See M. Andryane's curious memoirs, which are as entertaining as a novel, and will be as lasting as Tacitus.

his horse and his newspaper than with his orthodox-minded mistress. But there was still no room for any concern with imitating others in that guileless and resolute soul, and he made no friends among the society of the large market town of Romagnano. His simplicity was taken for haughtiness; no one knew what to make of his character. "He's a younger son dissatisfied because he's not the elder," said the parish priest.

CHAPTER SIX

We will frankly admit that Canon Borda's jealousy was not entirely groundless. On his return from France, Fabrizio had appeared in Countess Pietranera's eyes as a handsome stranger whom she had once known well. If he had spoken of love, she would have loved him; did she not already have a passionate and, so to speak, boundless admiration for his conduct and his person? But he embraced her with such an effusion of innocent gratitude and straightforward friendship that she would have been horrified with herself if she had looked for any other feeling in that almost filial affection. "Actually," she thought, "a few friends who knew me six years ago, at Prince Eugene's court, may find me still pretty and even young, but to him I'm a respectable lady . . . and, if everything must be said without regard for my vanity, an elderly woman." (The countess deluded herself about the period of life she had reached, but not in the manner of ordinary women.) "Besides, a boy his age always exaggerates the ravages of time to some extent, whereas a man who's further along in years. . ."

The countess, who was pacing back and forth in her drawing room, stopped in front of a mirror, then smiled. It must be pointed out that for several months her heart had been under attack by a singular individual. Shortly before Fabrizio's departure, the countess, who, without completely admitting it to herself, was already beginning to think about him a great deal of the time, had fallen into deep melancholy. All her occupations seemed pleasureless and, if we may use the word, tasteless. She told herself that Napoleon, wishing to attach the Italian people to himself, would make Fabrizio his aide-de-camp. "He's lost to me!" she exclaimed, weeping. "I'll never see him again! He'll write to me, but what will I be to him ten years from now?"

It was in this frame of mind that she took a trip to Milan. She hoped to get more direct news of Napoleon there, and—who knows?—perhaps also some news of Fabrizio as a consequence. She had not yet admitted it to herself, but her active nature was beginning to grow extremely weary of the monotonous life she was leading in the country. "It's not living," she thought, "it's only keeping oneself from dying." Every day she had to look at the powdered heads of her brother, her nephew Ascanio, and their servants! What would outings on the lake be like without Fabrizio? She drew her only consolation from the friendship that united her with the marquise. But for some time now this intimacy with Fabrizio's mother, who was older than herself and had lost all hope in life, was beginning to be less pleasant to her.

Such was Countess Pietranera's singular position: with Fabrizio gone, she had little hope for the future; her heart needed consolation and the distraction of novelty. In Milan she developed a passion for the opera; she would go to La Scala and shut herself up alone for long hours in the box of her old friend General Scotti. The men she sought to meet in order to get news of Napoleon and his army seemed coarse and vulgar to her. When she came home, she would improvise on her piano till three in the morning.

One evening at La Scala, in the box of one of her friends, to which she occasionally went in search of news from France, she was introduced to Count Mosca, a minister in the government of Parma. He was a pleasant man who spoke of France and Napoleon in such a way as to give her heart new reasons for hope or fear. She returned to that box the next evening; the same intelligent man was there again, and she talked to him with pleasure during the whole performance. She had not spent such an animated evening since Fabrizio's departure. This man she found so entertaining, Count Mosca della Rovere Sorezana, was at that time Minister of War, of Police and of Finance to that famous Prince of Parma, Ernesto IV, renowned for his severity, which the liberals of Milan called cruelty. Mosca was in his early forties. He had strongly marked features, no trace of self-importance, and a simple, lighthearted manner which disposed people in his favor. And he would have been quite handsome if an odd whim on the part of his prince had not forced him to powder his hair as a token of his sound political sentiments. Since Italians have little fear of offending anyone's vanity, they are quick to adopt a tone of intimacy and make personal remarks. The remedy for this practice is not to see each other again if one's feelings have been hurt.

"Why do you powder your hair, count?" asked the countess, the third time they met. "Powdered hair on a man like you! A charming man, still young, who fought on our side in Spain!"

"It's because I didn't steal anything in Spain, and therefore have to earn a living. I was mad for glory; a flattering word from the French general who was commanding us, Gouvion-Saint-Cyr, meant everything to me then. After the fall of Napoleon I learned that while I was using up my fortune in his service, my father, a man of imagination who already saw me as a general, had been building a palace for me in Parma. In 1813 I found myself with a fortune consisting entirely of a large unfinished palace and a pension."

"A pension? Thirty-five hundred lire, like my husband's?"

"Count Pietranera was a lieutenant general. As a lowly major, my pension was only eight hundred, and even that was never paid to me until I became Minister of Finance."

Since there was no one else in the box except the lady of extremely liberal opinions to whom it belonged, the conversation continued with the same frankness. When questioned, Count Mosca spoke of his life in Parma. "In Spain," he said, "under General Saint-Cyr, I braved bullets to earn a decoration and then a little glory; now I dress up like a character in a comedy to earn an impressive establishment and a few thousand lire. As soon as I entered this kind of chess game, the arrogance of my superiors offended me and I became determined to occupy one of the highest positions. I've succeeded in doing so, but my happiest days are always the ones I spend in Milan now and then. Here, it seems to me, the heart of your Army of Italy is still alive."

The countess's curiosity was stimulated by the frankness, the *disinvoltura* with which the minister of such a dreaded prince expressed himself. From his title, she had expected to find a pretentious, self-important personage, but what she saw was a man who was ashamed of the loftiness of his position. He had promised to give her all the news from France that he could gather. This was a great indiscretion in Milan during the month that preceded Waterloo. The issue for Italy at that time was to be or not to be, and everyone in Milan was in a fever, either of hope or of fear. In the midst of this universal agitation, the countess made inquiries about this man who spoke so lightly about a position that was so widely envied, and which was his only means of livelihood.

Curious and interestingly strange things were reported to her: "Count Mosca della Rovere Sorenza," she was told, "is about to become the Prime Minister and acknowledged favorite of Ranuccio-Ernesto IV, the absolute ruler of Parma and, furthermore, one of the richest princes in Europe. The count would already have attained that supreme position if he'd been willing to adopt a more solemn demeanor; they say the prince often lectures him on that point. 'What do my manners matter to Your Highness,' he answers freely, 'as long as I handle your affairs well?' This favorite's good fortune is not without thorns, however. He must please a sovereign who's no doubt a man of intelligence and good sense, but who, since taking his place on an absolute throne, seems to have lost his head, and shows, for example, suspicions worthy of a silly woman.

"Ernesto IV is brave only in war. On the battlefield, he's been seen a score of times leading a column to the attack as a valiant general should. But after the death of his father, Ernesto III, when he returned to his dominions, where he unfortunately wields unlimited power, he began to lash out wildly against the liberals and liberty. He soon began to feel that he was hated, and finally, in a moment of ill temper, he had two liberals hanged who may not have been very guilty, on the advice of a wretched scoundrel by the name of Rassi, a kind of Minister of Justice.

"From that fatal moment, the prince's life was changed. He's now tormented by the strangest suspicions. He's not yet fifty, but fear has so diminished him, if I may use that word, that whenever he talks about the Jacobins and the plans of the central committee in Paris, his face becomes that of an old man of eighty; he reverts to the fantastic fears of early childhood. His favorite, Rassi, the Chief Justice (or First Magistrate) owes all his influence to his master's fear, so whenever he's afraid his favor may be declining he hastens to discover some black, fantastic plot. If thirty rash men gather to read the *Constitutionnel*, Rassi declares them to be conspirators and sends them to prison in that famous citadel of Parma, the terror of all Lombardy. Since it's very high— a hundred and eighty feet, they say—it can be seen from a great distance in the middle of the vast plain, and the physical form of that prison, about which horrible things are told, makes it, through fear, the queen of the whole plain that stretches from Milan to Bologna."

"It's hard to believe," another traveler said to the countess, "but at night, on the fourth floor of his palace, guarded by eighty sentinels who shout whole sentences every quarter of an hour, Ernesto IV trembles in his bedroom. With all the doors secured by ten bolts, and all the neighboring rooms, above and below, filled with soldiers, he's afraid of the Jacobins. If a floorboard happens to creak, he grabs his pistols and thinks there's a liberal hiding under his bed. All the bells in the castle are immediately set in motion, and an aide-de-camp goes to wake up Count Mosca. When he arrives in the castle, the Minister of Police doesn't deny that there's a plot, quite the contrary. Alone with the prince, and armed to the teeth, he inspects every corner of the room, looks under the bed, and, in short, goes through all sorts of ridiculous actions worthy of an old woman.

"All these precautions would have seemed degrading to the prince in the happy days when he was waging war and had never killed anyone except with bullets. Since he's a highly intelligent man, he's ashamed of these precautions; they seem ridiculous to him, even while he's taking them, and the source of Count Mosca's enormous influence is that he uses all his skill in making sure that the prince will never have to blush in his presence. It's he, Mosca, who, in his capacity as Minister of Police, insists on looking under the furniture and even inside the contrabass cases, or so they say in Parma. It's the prince who objects to this and makes fun of his minister for his excessive punctiliousness. 'We musn't take any chances,' answers Count Mosca. 'Think of the satirical sonnets with which the Jacobins would overwhelm us if we let you be killed. It's not only your life we're defending, it's also our honor.'

"But apparently the prince is only half taken in by this, because if anyone in the city should take it into his head to say that a sleepless night has been spent in the castle, Chief Justice Rassi sends the malicious humorist to the citadel, and once a man is a prisoner in that lofty abode rising in 'fresh air,' as they say in Parma, it takes a miracle for anyone to remember his existence. It's because he's a soldier, and because in Spain he saved himself from surprise attacks a score of times with his pistol in his hand, that the prince prefers Count Mosca to Rassi, who's much more pliant and servile. Those poor prisoners in the citadel are kept in rigorous solitary confinement, and all sorts of stories are told about them. The liberals claim that, in accordance with one of Rassi's ideas, the jailers and confessors are under orders to convince them that one of them is taken out and executed every month or so. On those days, the prisoners are allowed to go up on the platform of the enormous tower, a hundred and eighty feet above the ground, and from there they see a procession marching past, with a spy playing the part of a poor devil who's going to his death."

These stories, and a dozen others of the same type and of equal authenticity, keenly interested Countess Pietranera. The next day, she asked Count Mosca for details and teased him vigorously. She found him amusing and told him he was a monster without knowing it. One day, as he was going back to his inn, the count said to himself, "Not only is that Countess Pietranera a charming woman, but when I spend the evening in her box I manage to forget certain things in Parma which it stabs my heart to remember." *This minister, despite his lighthearted air and his sparkling manner, did not have a soul like that of a Frenchman: he could not "forget" the things that pained him. When there was a thorn in his pillow, he had to break it off and wear it down, pricking his quivering limbs in the process.* (I apologize for this passage, translated from the Italian.)

The day after this discovery, the count found that, despite the affairs that had brought him to Milan, the hours went by with exasperating slowness. He was so restless that he could not stay in one place, and he exhausted his carriage horses. Toward six o'clock he mounted his saddle horse and rode to the Corso, where he had some hope of meeting Countess Pietranera. Having failed to find her there, he recalled that La Scala opened at eight o'clock; he went there, but saw no more than ten people in the immense auditorium. He felt somewhat sheepish about being there. "How is it possible," he thought, "that, having passed the age of forty-five, I'm abandoning myself to follies that would make a second lieutenant blush? Fortunately, no one suspects them." He hurried outside and tried to while away the time by strolling through those pretty streets that surround La Scala. They are lined with cafés which, at that hour, are overflowing with people. Before each of these cafés there are crowds of curious onlookers sitting on chairs in the middle of the street, eating ices and criticizing the passers-by. The count was an outstanding passer-by, so he had the pleasure of being recognized and accosted. Three or four obtrusive individuals of the kind who cannot be abruptly dismissed seized this opportunity to obtain an audience with the powerful minister. Two of them handed him petitions; a third contented himself with giving him endless advice on his political conduct.

"A man of my intelligence," he thought, "shouldn't let himself be caught napping; a man of my power shouldn't take a stroll in public." He returned to La Scala and decided to take a box in the third tier; from there he could look down, without being seen by anyone, into the box in the second tier where he hoped to see the countess arrive. Two full hours of waiting did not seem too long to this man in love; sure of not being observed, he happily abandoned himself to his folly. "Doesn't old age," he thought, "consist above all in no longer being capable of such delightful childishness?"

At last the countess appeared. Armed with his opera glasses, he examined her with rapture. "Young, sparkling, light as a bird," he thought. "She doesn't look twenty-five. Her beauty is the least of her charms: where else can you find a soul like hers, a soul that's always sincere, that never acts 'with prudence,' that abandons itself entirely to the impression of the moment, that asks only to be carried away by some new object? I can understand Count Nani's follies."

The count gave himself excellent reasons for being mad, as long as he was thinking only of conquering the happiness he saw before his eyes. He no longer found such good ones when he began to consider the concerns, sometimes extremely dismal, that filled his life. "A man of ability," he thought, "whose intelligence has been paralyzed by fear, gives me an elegant life and a great deal of money for being his minister; but if he should dismiss me tomorrow, I'd be left old and poor, in other words, the most despised kind of man in the world—what a wonderful person to offer the countess!"

These thoughts were too gloomy, so he turned his attention back to Countess Pietranera herself; he never tired of looking at her. To be able to think about her better, he did not go down to her box. "I've just been told that she took Nani only to get back at that idiot Limercati, who refused to run his sword through her husband's murderer, or have him stabbed by someone else. I'd fight a dozen duels for her!" cried the count ecstatically. He kept consulting the theater clock, whose brightly illuminated figures, standing out against a black background, notified the audience every five minutes of the approaching hour when it would be permissible to visit a friend's box. He said to himself, "I can spend only half an hour in her box, at the very most, since I'm such a recent acquaintance. If I stay any longer, I'll be calling attention to myself, and thanks to my age, and still more to this damned

85

powdered hair of mine, I'll give the attractive impression of being an old fool."

But one reflection abruptly decided him: "If she should leave her box to pay a visit, I'd be well rewarded for the avarice with which I've been saving up my pleasure." He stood up to go down to the box in which he saw the countess; suddenly he lost nearly all desire to present himself there. "Ah, this is charming!" he exclaimed, laughing to himself and stopping on the stairs. "It's a surge of real shyness! It's been a good twenty-five years since such a thing happened to me!"

He almost had to force himself to enter the box, and, being an intelligent man, he took advantage of the accident that was happening to him: he made no effort to appear at ease or display his wit by plunging into some amusing story; he had the courage to be shy, and he used his intelligence in letting his agitation reveal itself without making him look ridiculous. "If she takes it amiss," he thought, "I'll be lost forever. What! Shy, with powdered hair whose grayness would be visible if it weren't for the help of the powder! But after all, the feeling is genuine, so it can be ridiculous only if I exaggerate it or make a deliberate display of it." The countess had so often been bored in the castle of Grianta, opposite the powdered heads of her brother, her nephew, and a few other right-thinking bores of the vicinity, that it never occurred to her to give any thought to the way her new admirer wore his hair.

Since her mind was shielded against laughter when he came in, she was attentive only to the news from France which he always gave her in private, when he came into her box; he no doubt invented some of the details. As she discussed them with him that evening, she noticed that his eyes were handsome and kind.

"I imagine," she said to him, "that in Parma, amid your slaves, you don't have such a pleasant look in your eyes: it would spoil everything and give them some hope of not being hanged."

The total absence of self-importance in the man who was known as the leading diplomat in Italy seemed extraordinary to the countess; she even felt that he had a certain charm. And since he spoke well and with ardor, she was not offended by his having seen fit to play the part of a zealous suitor for one evening, without consequences.

This was a great step forward, and quite dangerous. Fortunately for the minister, who never met with any serious

86

resistance from the ladies of Parma, the countess had arrived from Grianta only a few days before, so her mind was still dulled by the boredom of life in the country. She had almost forgotten the art of witty conversation, and everything connected with an elegant and lighthearted way of life had taken on, in her eyes, a slight tinge of novelty which made it sacred. She was in no mood to make fun of anything, not even an amorous admirer who was forty-five and shy. A week earlier, the count's temerity might have been given a very different kind of reception.

At La Scala, it is customary to limit to twenty minutes or so those little visits paid to other boxes; the count spent the whole evening in the box in which he had had the good fortune to meet Countess Pietranera. "She's a woman," he said to himself, "who brings back all the madness of my youth!" But he was well aware of the danger. "Will my position as an all-powerful pasha forty leagues away from here be enough to make me be forgiven for this foolishness? I'm so bored in Parma!" Every quarter of an hour, however, he promised himself he would leave.

"I must admit," he said to the countess, laughing, "that I'm bored to tears in Parma, so I ought to be allowed to intoxicate myself with pleasure whenever I come across it. Allow me, therefore, without consequences and for only one evening, to play the part of a zealous suitor. Alas, in a few days I'll be far away from this box, which makes me forget all sorrow, and even, you will say, all decorum."

A week after this inordinately long visit in the box at La Scala, and as a result of several little incidents whose description would perhaps seem tedious, Count Mosca was head over heels in love, and the countess was already thinking that his age ought not to be an objection if she found him attractive in every other way. Their thoughts had reached this point when Mosca was recalled by a messenger from Parma. His prince seemed to be afraid when he was left alone. The countess returned to Grianta; since her imagination had ceased to embellish that lovely place, it seemed barren to her. "Have I become attached to that man?" she wondered. Mosca wrote to her and had nothing to pretend, for absence had taken away the source of all his thoughts. His letters were amusing. He had an unusual little idea which was not badly received: to avoid comments on the part of the Marquis del Dongo, who did not like to pay for the delivery of mail, he had couriers bring his letters to the post offices of Como, Lecco, Varese and other charming towns in the vicinity of the lake. Another purpose of this was to have the couriers bring back answers to him; he achieved his goal.

The days on which the couriers arrived soon became great events in the countess's life. These couriers brought flowers, fruit and little presents which had no value in themselves, but which amused her, as well as her sister-in-law. Her memory of the count was mingled with the idea of his great power. She had become interested in everything that was said about him; even the liberals paid tribute to his abilities.

The chief reasons for the count's evil reputation were, first, that he was regarded as the head of the ultra-monarchist party at Parma, and second, that the liberal party had as its leader a scheming woman who was capable of anything, even success: the enormously wealthy Marquise Raversi. The prince was careful not to discourage the party that was not in power; he knew very well that he would always be the master, even with ministers chosen from among the men who frequented the Marquise Raversi's drawing room. Countless details of these intrigues were reported at Grianta. The absence of Mosca, whom everyone described as a minister of the greatest ability and a man of action, made it possible to forget about his powdered hair, the symbol of everything heavy and dull; it was an unimportant detail, one of the obligations of the court in which he was playing such a brilliant part. "A court is ridiculous," the countess said to the marquise, "but it's amusing. It's an interesting game, but one whose rules must be accepted. Who ever thought of complaining about the ridiculousness of the rules of whist? And yet, once you're used to the rules, it's pleasant to defeat your opponent with a grand slam."

The countess often thought about the author of all those delightful letters. The days when she received them were pleasant to her; she would take her boat and go off to read them in one of the lovely spots near the lake, such as La Pliniana, Bellano or the Sfondrata woods. These letters seemed to console her a little for Fabrizio's absence. In any case, she could not forbid the count to be deeply in love with her. Before a month had gone by, she was thinking of him with tender affection. For his part, Count Mosca was almost sincere when he offered to hand in his resignation, leave the ministry and come to spend the rest of his life with her in Milan or anywhere else. "I have 400,000 lire," he wrote, "which will always give us an income of 15,000 a year." And the countess thought, "A box at the theater again, and horses, and all the rest!" It was a delightful dream. The sublime

beauties of the different aspects of Lake Como were beginning to cast their spell on her again. She often went to its
shores to dream of this return to an elegant and interesting
life which, against all likelihood, was now becoming possible
for her again. She saw herself on the Corso, in Milan, happy
and gay as she had been in the days of the viceroy. "Youth,"
she thought, "or at least an active life, would begin again
for me!"

Sometimes her ardent imagination concealed things from
her, but she never had any of those voluntary illusions which
arise from cowardice. She was above all a woman who was
honest with herself. "I may be a little too old to do wild and
foolish things," she thought, "but envy, which deludes itself
the same as love, could still poison my life in Milan. After
my husband's death, my noble poverty was quite a success,
and so was my refusal of two great fortunes. My poor little
Count Mosca doesn't have one twentieth of the wealth laid
at my feet by those two fools, Limercati and Nani. My meager
widow's pension, obtained with great difficulty, the dismissal
of my servants, which caused a sensation, my little sixth-floor
room, which brought carriages in front of the door—all that
once formed a remarkable spectacle. But no matter how
skillfully I go about it I'll still have some disagreeable moments if, still having only my widow's pension as my entire
fortune, I go back to Milan to live in the modest middle-class
comfort we can expect from the income of fifteen thousand
lire that Mosca will have left after his resignation. One
powerful objection, which envy will use as a terrible weapon,
is the fact that, although he's been separated from his wife
for a long time, he's still married. His separation is known in
Parma, but it will be news in Milan and I'll be accused of
causing it. So farewell to my beautiful La Scala, farewell to
my divine Lake Como, farewell!"

Despite these predictions, if the countess had had any
money of her own she would have accepted Mosca's offer to
hand in his resignation. She regarded herself as a middle-
aged woman, and the court frightened her. But what will
seem utterly implausible on this side of the Alps is that the
count would have been glad to resign. This was at least what
he succeeded in making the countess believe. In all his letters
he begged, with ever-increasing desperation, for a second
meeting with her in Milan. She finally granted it to him.
"If I swore I had a mad passion for you," she said to him
one day in Milan, "I'd be lying. I'd be all too happy, now
that I'm past thirty, to love the way I once did at twenty-

89

two. But I've seen the end of so many things that I thought would last forever! I have the most tender affection for you, I trust you without reserve, and I prefer you to all other men in the world." She thought she was being perfectly sincere, and yet, toward the end, this declaration contained a little falsehood. If Fabrizio had wanted to, he might have been able to prevail over everyone else in her heart. But Fabrizio was only a child in the eyes of Count Mosca, who had arrived in Milan three days after the young hothead's departure for Novara and hastened to speak to Baron Binder in his favor. The count had decided that nothing could be done to end Fabrizio's exile.

He had not come to Milan alone: in his carriage was Duke Sanseverina-Taxis, a handsome little old man of sixty-eight with dapple-gray hair, very urbane, very well-dressed, enormously rich, but not of sufficiently noble birth. It was his grandfather only who had amassed millions in the office of farmer-general of the revenues of the State of Parma. His father had gotten himself appointed as ambassador of the Prince of Parma to the court of — by the following argument: "Your Highness gives thirty thousand lire a year to his ambassador at the court of —, who cuts a rather sorry figure there. If Your Highness will deign to give me that post, I will accept a salary of six thousand lire. My expenditures at the court of — will never be under a hundred thousand lire a year, and my steward will remit twenty thousand to the treasury of the Ministry of Foreign Affairs in Parma every year. That sum may be used to pay the salary of any embassy secretary it may be desired to place in my service, and I will show no curiosity whatever about diplomatic secrets, if there are any. My object is to give distinction to my family, which is still a new one, and to make it illustrious with one of the high offices of the realm."

The present duke, son of this ambassador, had made the awkward mistake of showing himself to be a semi-liberal, and for the past two years he had been in despair. During the time of Napoleon, he had lost two or three million lire by his obstinacy in remaining abroad, and yet, ever since the re-establishment of order in Europe, he had been unable to obtain a certain Grand Cordon which adorned his portrait, and its absence was making him waste away in sorrow.

At the stage of intimacy which follows love in Italy, there was no longer any objection of vanity between the two lovers. It was therefore with perfect simplicity that Mosca said to the woman he adored, "I have two or there plans of action to offer you, all rather well devised; I've been thinking about nothing else for the past three months. First: I hand in my resignation and we lead a good middle-class life in Milan, Florence, Naples or anywhere else you like. We'll have an income of fifteen thousand lire, not counting the prince's bounties, which will continue more or less. Second: you condescend to live within the territory where I have some power. You buy a property: Sacca, for example, a charming house in the middle of a forest, overlooking the Po; you can have the deed signed within a week from now. The prince will attach you to his court.

"But here we come to an enormous difficulty. You'll be well received at court: no one would dare show any disapproval in my presence. Besides, the princess considers herself unhappy, and I've just rendered her a few services with you in mind. But this is the supremely important difficulty: the prince is a very pious man, and, as you know, I have the misfortune to be married, which is bound to give rise to countless little annoyances. You're a widow: it's a fine title which ought to be exchanged for another, and that's the object of my third proposal.

"It would be possible to find a new husband who wouldn't be bothersome. But first of all he would have to be a very elderly man, because why should you refuse me the hope of replacing him some day? Well, I've come to an agreement on this singular arrangement with Duke Sanseverina-Taxis, who, of course, doesn't know the name of his future duchess. He knows only that she'll make him an ambassador and give him the Grand Cordon which his father had, and whose lack makes him the unhappiest of mortals. Aside from that, the duke isn't too idiotic; he has his clothes and wigs sent from Paris. He's not at all the kind of man who would ever do anything malicious, thought out in advance. He seriously believes that honor consists in having a cordon, and he's ashamed of his wealth. A year ago he came to me and suggested founding a hospital in order to get his cordon. I laughed at him then, but he didn't laugh when I suggested a marriage to him. My first condition was, of course, that he should never set foot in Parma."

"But do you realize that what you're proposing to me is extremely immoral?" said the countess.

"No more immoral than everything that's done at our court and a dozen others. One of the conveniences of absolute power is that it sanctifies everything in the eyes of the people; and how can something be ridiculous if no one notices it? Our policy for the next twenty years will consist in trembling with fear of the Jacobins, and what fear! Each year, we'll believe ourselves to be on the eve of '93. You'll hear, I hope, the fine speeches I make on that subject at my receptions! They're beautiful! Anything that can diminish that fear will be 'supremely moral' in the eyes of the noble and the pious. And in Parma, everyone who isn't noble or pious is either in prison already or packing up to go there. You can be sure that no one in Parma will see anything odd about your marriage until the day when I fall out of favor. It's an arrangement that involves no dishonesty toward anyone, and that's the main thing, it seems to me. The prince, whose favor is our bread and butter, has placed only one condition on his consent: that the future duchess must be of noble birth. Last year my position brought me a hundred and seven thousand lire, all told, and my total income must have come to a hundred and twenty-two thousand. I invested twenty thousand at Lyons.

"So here are your choices: either a life of luxury based on having a hundred and twenty-two thousand lire to spend, which in Parma is the equivalent of at least four hundred thousand in Milan, but with a marriage that will give you the name of a decent man whom you will never see except at the altar; or else a modest middle-class life with fifteen thousand lire a year in Florence or Naples—because I agree with you that you've been admired too much in Milan: we'd be persecuted by envy, and it might succeed in making us bitter. The life of luxury in Parma would have, I hope, a few touches of novelty, even in your eyes, which have seen the court of Prince Eugene; it would be wise to learn something about it before shutting the door on it. Don't think I'm trying to influence your decision. As for me, I've definitely made up my mind: I'd rather live in a fifth-floor apartment with you than go on leading that life of luxury by myself."

The possibility of this strange marriage was debated by the two lovers every day. The countess saw Duke Sanseverina-Taxis at the Scala ball, and he seemed quite presentable to her. In one of their final conversations, Mosca summed up his proposal as follows: "We must take decisive action if we want to spend the rest of our lives in an enjoyable manner and avoid growing old before our time. The prince has given his approval. Sanseverina is a man whose good points outweigh his bad ones; he has the finest palace in Parma and an unlimited fortune; he's sixty-eight years old and has a mad passion for the Grand Cordon. But his life is marred by one great blemish: he once paid ten thousand lire for a bust of Napoleon by Canova. His second sin, which will bring on his death if you don't come to his rescue, is that he once lent twenty-five napoleons to Ferrante Palla, a madman from Parma, but also something of a genius, whom we later sentenced to death—*in absentia*, fortunately. This Ferrante has written two hundred lines of poetry in his life, and nothing can equal them. I'll recite them to you some day, they're as good as anything in Dante. The prince will send Sanseverina to the court of ——, he'll marry you on the day of his departure, and in the second year of his stay abroad, which he'll call a diplomatic mission, he'll receive that Cordon of —— which he can't live without. You'll have in him a brother who won't be at all disagreeable to you. He'll sign in advance all the papers I want him to sign, and besides, you'll see him either seldom or never, whichever you prefer. He would like nothing better than never to show his face in Parma, where he's embarrassed by his grandfather the farmer-general and his alleged liberalism. Rassi, our hangman, claims that the duke secretly subscribed to the *Constitutionnel* through Ferrante Palla, the poet, and for a long time this slander was a serious obstacle to the prince's consent."

If a historian faithfully reports all the details of a story that has been told to him, why should he be held responsible for them? Is it his fault if the characters, seduced by passions which, unfortunately for him, he does not share, descend to actions that are profoundly immoral? It is true that such things are no longer done in a country where the only passion that has survived all others is the love of money, a means of satisfying vanity.

Three months after the events we have just related, Duchess Sanseverina-Taxis astonished the court of Parma by her easy graciousness and the noble serenity of her mind, and her house was beyond all comparison the most pleasant one in the city. This was what Count Mosca had promised his master. Ranuccio-Ernesto IV, the reigning prince, and his wife the princess, to whom the duchess was presented by two of the greatest ladies in Parma, gave her a most distinguished welcome.

She was curious to see the prince who controlled the destiny of the man she loved; she wanted to please him, and she succeeded too well. She found a man who was tall but rather stout; his hair, mustache and enormous side whiskers were strikingly blond, according to his courtiers; anywhere else, their faded hue would have earned the ignoble description of "tow-colored." In the middle of his plump face a small, almost feminine nose was tilted slightly upward. But the duchess noticed that, in order to distinguish all these elements of ugliness, she had to try to see each of his features separately. On the whole, he looked like a man of intelligence and firm character. His manner and bearing were not without majesty, but he often tried to impress the person with whom he was talking, and he would then become awkward and fall into an almost constant swaying back and forth from one leg to the other. However, he had a penetrating and commanding gaze, there was a certain nobility in the gestures of his arms, and his speech was both measured and concise.

Mosca had already told the duchess that, in the large room where he gave audiences, the prince had a full-length portrait of Louis XIV and a beautiful *scagliola* table from Florence. She found the imitation striking: he obviously sought to achieve the expression and noble speech of Louis XIV, and he leaned on the *scagliola* table in such a way as to give himself the appearance of Joseph II. He sat down immediately after the first few words he addressed to the duchess, in order to give her a chance to make use of the stool to which her rank now entitled her. At that court, duchesses, princesses and the wives of Spanish grandees may sit down without invitation; all other ladies must wait to be invited by the prince or the princess, and, to mark the difference in rank, those august personages were always careful to allow a short interval to elapse before they bade the ladies who were not duchesses to be seated. The duchess found that at certain moments the prince's imitation of Louis XIV was a little too strongly marked: in the way he tilted back his head with a kindly smile, for example.

Ernesto IV wore a fashionable dress coat from Paris; each month a dress coat, a frock coat and a hat were sent to him from that city, which he abhorred. But on the day when he received the duchess he was wearing an oddly mixed costume: red knee breeches, silk stockings and high shoes whose model can be found in the portraits of Joseph II.

He gave Duchess Sanseverina a gracious reception. He said perceptive and witty things to her, but she saw quite clearly that there was nothing excessive about his welcome. "Do you know why?" Count Mosca said to her when the audience was over. "It's because Milan is a larger and more beautiful city than Parma. If he'd given you the reception I was expecting, and which he led me to hope for, he would have been afraid of seeming like a provincial gentleman enraptured by the graces of a beautiful lady who'd just arrived from the capital. Also, he's probably upset by something I hesitate to tell you: he sees no woman in his court who can rival you in beauty. When he went to bed last night, that was the sole subject of his conversation with Pernice, his chief valet, who renders me certain services. I foresee a minor revolution in etiquette. My greatest enemy at this court is a fool who goes by the name of General Fabio Conti. Imagine an eccentric individual who's been in battle perhaps one day in his life, and who starts out from that point to imitate the bearing of Frederick the Great. Furthermore, he also does his best to reproduce the noble affability of General Lafayette, because he's the head of the liberal party here (God knows what liberals!)."

"I already know your Fabio Conti," said the duchess. "I had a glimpse of him near Como: he was arguing with the police." And she related the little incident which the reader will perhaps remember.

"Some day," said the count, "if your mind ever succeeds in penetrating the depths of our etiquette, you will learn that young ladies do not appear at court here until after they're married. And yet the prince has such patriotic ardor for the superiority of his city of Parma over all others that I'm willing to bet that he'll find some way to have young Clelia Conti, our Lafayette's daughter, presented to him. She's quite charming, there can be no doubt about it, and up till last week she was still regarded as the greatest beauty in the prince's dominions.

"I don't know whether the horrible things the prince's enemies have circulated about him have reached the castle of Grianta: he's been depicted as a monster, an ogre. The fact is that Ernesto IV was once full of nice little virtues, and it can be added that if he'd been as invulnerable as Achilles he would have continued to be a model potentate. But in a moment of boredom and anger, and also a little in imitation of Louis XIV, who beheaded a hero of the Fronde when he was discovered living peacefully and insolently on an estate near Versailles, fifty years after the Fronde, Ernesto IV had two liberals hanged one day. It appears that those rash gentlemen used to meet regularly to speak ill of the prince and earnestly pray that a plague would descend on Parma and rid them of the tyrant. Their use of the word 'tyrant' was proved. Rassi called that a conspiracy. He had them sentenced to death, and the execution of one of them, Count ——, was atrocious. This happened before my time.

"Since that fatal day," the count added, lowering his voice, "the prince has been subject to fits of fear that are 'unworthy of a man,' but which are the sole source of the favor I enjoy. If it weren't for his overwhelming fear, my merit would be found too blunt, too harsh, for this court where imbeciles abound. Would you believe that the prince looks under all the beds in his apartment before going to sleep at night, and spends a million lire, which in Parma is the equivalent of four million in Milan, to maintain a good police force? And you see before you, duchess, the chief of that terrible police. By means of the police—in other words, through fear—I've become Minister of War and of Finance; and since the Minister of the Interior is my nominal superior, insofar as the police force lies within his authority, I've had that office given to Count Zurla-Contarini, a hard-working idiot who gives himself the pleasure of writing eighty letters a day. Only this morning I received one on which Count Zurla-Contarini had had the satisfaction of writing the number 20,715 with his own hand."

Duchess Sanseverina was presented to the sorrowful Princess of Parma, Clara-Paolina, who, because her husband had a mistress (a rather pretty woman, the Marquise Balbi), considered herself the unhappiest person alive, which had perhaps made her the most boring one. The duchess found her to be a tall, very thin woman who was not yet thirty-six and looked fifty. If she had not completely neglected herself, her face, with its regular and noble features, might have been regarded as beautiful, although it was somewhat marred by her big, round, dim-sighted eyes. She received the duchess with such obvious timidity that certain courtiers, enemies of Count Mosca, dared to say that the princess looked like the woman being presented, while the duchess looked like the sovereign. The duchess, surprised and almost disconcerted, was unable to find words that would place her in a position inferior to the one in which the princess had placed herself. To give a little self-assurance to the poor princess, who was basically not lacking in intelligence, the princess could think of nothing better than to launch into a long dissertation on botany. The princess was really quite learned on this subject: she had some excellent greenhouses and a great many tropical plants. In merely trying to extricate herself from an embarrassing situation, the duchess acquired the lifelong devotion of Princess Clara-Paolina, who, shy and almost speechless at the beginning of the audience, found herself so much at ease toward the end of it that, contrary to all the rules of court etiquette, this first audience lasted no less than an hour and a quarter. The next day, the duchess bought some exotic plants and let it be known that she was a great lover of botany.

The princess spent all her time with the venerable Father Landriani, Archbishop of Parma. He was a man of learning and even of intelligence, and his honor was unquestionable, but he offered a strange sight when he was seated in his crimson velvet chair (a privilege of his position), opposite the armchair in which the princess sat surrounded by her ladies-in-waiting and her two "lady companions." The old prelate, with his long white hair, was even shyer, if that were possible, than the princess; they saw each other every day, and every audience began with a silence that lasted a good quarter of an hour. It was such a distressing problem that Countess Alvizi, one of the lady companions, had become a kind of favorite because she had the knack of encouraging them to talk to each other and break the silence.

To terminate the series of presentations, the duchess was admitted to the presence of His Most Serene Highness the crown prince, a young man slightly taller than his father and shyer than his mother. He had an excellent knowledge of mineralogy and was sixteen years old. He blushed violently when he saw the duchess enter, and was so perturbed that he was totally unable to think of anything to say to that beautiful lady. He was a handsome young man who spent all his time in the woods with a hammer in his hand. Just as the duchess was standing up to bring this silent audience to an end, the crown prince cried out, "My God, how pretty you are!" She did not consider this to be in too bad taste.

Two or three years before Duchess Sanseverina's arrival in Parma, the Marquise Balbi, a young woman of twenty-five, was able to pass for the most perfect example of "Italian prettiness." She still had the most beautiful eyes in the world, and the most winsome little expressions, but, seen from close up, her skin was covered with countless fine little wrinkles that made her look like a youthful old woman. Viewed from a certain distance—in her box in the theater, for example—she was still a beauty, and the people in the orchestra seats felt that the prince had very good taste. He spent every evening in her house, but often without ever opening his mouth. His obvious boredom had made the poor woman worry herself into a state of extraordinary thinness. She laid claim to infinite shrewdness, and always smiled with malice. Having the loveliest teeth in the world but very little sense, she would smile slyly at random, hoping to give a totally different meaning to what she was saying. Count Mosca maintained that it was her constant smiling, accompanied by inner yawns, that had given her all her wrinkles. She had a finger in every pie, and there was never a government transaction involving more than a hundred thousand lire without a little "remembrance" (this was the polite word in Parma) for the marquise. There was a widespread rumor that she had invested six million lire in England, but her fortune, of very recent origin, actually did not exceed a million and a half. It was to protect himself from her wiles, and to have her under his thumb, that Count Mosca had made himself Minister of Finance. Her only passion was fear disguised as sordid avarice. "I'll die in abject poverty," she sometimes said to the prince, who was always offended by the remark. The duchess noticed that the lavishly gilded anteroom of the Marquise Balbi's palace was lighted by only one candle which stood dripping onto a precious marble table, and that the doors of her drawing room had been blackened by the fingers of her footmen.

"She received me," the duchess said to Count Mosca, "as though she expected me to give her a gratuity of fifty lire."

The course of the duchess's triumphs was slightly interrupted by the reception she was given by the most astute woman at court, the renowned Marquise Raversi, a consummate schemer who was the leader of the faction opposed to that of Count Mosca. She was determined to overthrow him, especially in the past few months, since she was Duke Sanseverina's niece and was afraid her inheritance might be jeopardized by the charms of the new duchess. "That Raversi is not a woman to be despised," the count said to the duchess. "I consider her capable of anything—so much so that I separated from my wife only because she insisted on taking one of the Marquise Raversi's friends, Cavaliere Bentivoglio, as her lover."

The marquise, a tall virago with jet-black hair, remarkable for the diamonds she wore all day and the rouge with which she covered her cheeks, had declared herself the duchess's enemy in advance. She set about opening the hostilities as soon as she received her in her house. In the letters he wrote from ——, Duke Sanseverina seemed so delighted with his embassy, and above all with his hope of receiving the Grand Cordon, that his family was afraid he might leave part of his fortune to his wife, whom he kept showering with little presents. The Marquise Raversi, though thoroughly ugly, had as her lover Count Balbi, the handsomest man at court. In general, she succeeded in everything she undertook.

The duchess maintained a majestic establishment. The Sanseverina palace had always been one of the most magnificent in the city of Parma, and the duke, in view of his embassy and his future Grand Cordon, was spending vast sums of money to embellish it still more; the duchess supervised the alterations.

The count had guessed correctly: a few days after the duchess's presentation, young Clelia Conti came to court. She had been made a canoness. To parry the blow which this favor might seem to strike at the count's influence, the duchess gave a party on the pretext of inaugurating the garden of her palace, and, with her usual gracious charm, she made Clelia, whom she called her young friend from Lake Como, the queen of the evening. Her monogram appeared as though by chance on the principal illuminated decorations. Although somewhat pensive, young Clelia talked engagingly about the little incident near the lake, and about her deep gratitude. She was said to be very pious and very fond of solitude. "I'm willing to bet," said the count, "that she's intelligent enough to be ashamed of her father." The duchess made the girl her friend and felt attracted to her. Not wishing to appear jealous, she included her in all her pleasure parties. In short, her plan was to try to diminish the hatreds directed against the count.

Everything was pleasing to the duchess. She was amused by that court existence in which there is always the danger of a storm; it seemed to her that she was starting her life anew. She was fondly attached to the count, who was ecstatically happy. This delightful situation had given him perfect self-possession with regard to everything that concerned only his interests and ambitions. Thus, scarcely two months after the duchess's arrival, he obtained the post of Prime Minister and the honors that went with it, honors which came very close to those accorded to the sovereign himself. The count had complete control of his master's mind, and one proof of this which occurred in Parma made a deep impression on everyone.

To the southeast, ten minutes away from the city, rises that famous citadel, so renowned in Italy, whose massive tower is a hundred and eighty feet high and can be seen from such a great distance. This tower, built on the model of

Hadrian's tomb in Rome by the Farnese, grandsons of Paul III, early in the sixteenth century, is so thick that on the platform with which it ends it has been possible to build a residence for the governor of the citadel and a new prison known as the Farnese Tower. This prison, constructed in honor of the eldest son of Ranuccio-Ernesto II, who had become his stepmother's lover, is regarded in the region as beautiful and remarkable. The duchess was curious to see it. On the day of her visit, the heat was overwhelming in Parma. High up in the tower she found cool air, which delighted her so much that she spent several hours there. Her hosts obligingly opened the rooms of the Farnese Tower to her.

On the platform of the great tower she met a poor imprisoned liberal who had come out to enjoy the half-hour walk he was allowed to take every third day. On her return to Parma, not yet having the discretion necessary in the court of an absolute ruler, she talked about this man, who had told her his whole story. The Marquise Raversi's faction seized on her remarks and repeated them everywhere, strongly hoping they would offend the prince. Ernesto IV often said that the essential thing was to impress people's imaginations. " 'Forever' is an impressive word," he would say, "and more terrible in Italy than elsewhere." Consequently, he had never granted a pardon in his life. A week after her visit to the fortress, the duchess received a letter granting a commutation of sentence, signed by the prince and the minister, with the name left blank. The prisoner whose name she wrote was to have his property restored to him and be allowed to go and spend the rest of his life in America. She wrote in the name of the man who had spoken to her. Unfortunately this man proved to be a semi-scoundrel, a weak character; it was on the basis of his confessions that the famous Ferrante Palla had been sentenced to death.

The singularity of this pardon raised Duchess Sanseverina's position to new heights of felicity. Count Mosca was ecstatically happy. He was enjoying one of the most splendid periods of his life, and it had a decisive influence on Fabrizio's destiny. Fabrizio was still at Romagnano, going to confession, hunting, not reading, and paying court to a noble lady, in accordance with his instructions. The duchess was still a little upset by this last necessity. Another sign that boded no good for the count was that, while she spoke to him with utter frankness about everyone else, and thought aloud in his presence, she never mentioned Fabrizio to him without carefully formulating her remarks in advance.

"If you like," the count said to her one day, "I'll write to that charming brother of yours on Lake Como, and with a little effort on my part and that of my friends at ——, I'll force the Marquis del Dongo to request a pardon for your charming Fabrizio. If it's true, and I certainly won't doubt it, that Fabrizio is a cut above the young men who ride their English horses through the streets of Milan, what a life for him, at eighteen, to be doing nothing, with no prospect of ever doing anything! If heaven had endowed him with a genuine passion for anything, even fishing, I'd respect it; but what will he do in Milan, even after he's obtained his pardon? At a certain hour of the day, he'll ride a horse he's had brought from England, then, at another hour, for lack of anything better to do, he'll go to see his mistress, whom he'll love less than his horse . . . But if you order me to, I'll try to procure that kind of life for your nephew."

"I'd like him to be an officer," said the duchess.

"Would you advise a sovereign to entrust a post which, on a given day, might take on a certain importance, to a young man who, first of all, is subject to enthusiasm, and, secondly, has already shown enthusiasm for Napoleon to the point of going off to join him at Waterloo? Think what would have become of us all if Napoleon had won at Waterloo! We'd have no liberals to fear, it's true, but sovereigns from ancient families would be able to rule only by marrying daughters of his marshals. So, for Fabrizio, a military career would be like the life of a squirrel in a revolving cage: a great deal of movement to go nowhere. He'd have the sorrow of seeing himself surpassed by all sorts of devoted plebeians. The most important quality in a young man today, and perhaps for the next fifty years, as long as we live in fear and religion hasn't been re-established, is not to be subject to enthusiasm and to have no mind of his own.

"I've thought of one thing, but it's going to make you cry out in protest at first, and it will give me infinite trouble for more than one day; it's an act of folly that I'm willing to commit for you. But tell me, if you can, what folly I wouldn't commit to win a smile from you!"

"Well?" said the duchess.

"Well, three members of your family have been Archbishop of Parma: Ascanio del Dongo, who wrote some time in the seventeenth century, Fabrizio in 1699, and another Ascanio in 1740. If Fabrizio is willing to become a prelate and distinguish himself by virtues of the highest order, I'll make him a bishop somewhere, then an archbishop here—provided my influence lasts that long. The real objection is this: will I remain a minister long enough to carry out that fine plan, which will require several years? The prince may die, or he may have the bad taste to dismiss me. But in any case it's the only way I have of doing something for Fabrizio that will be worthy of you."

They had a long discussion; the idea was extremely repugnant to the duchess.

"Prove to me again," she said to the count, "that no other career is possible for Fabrizio." The count proved it.

"You'll miss the brilliant uniform," he added, "but I know of nothing I can do about that."

At the end of the month which the duchess had requested in order to think the matter over, she yielded with a sigh to the wise views of the minister. "He can either ride stiffly on an English horse through the streets of some large city," he had said repeatedly, "or he can enter a calling that's not out of keeping with his birth; I see no middle course. Unfortunately, a nobleman can't become a doctor or a lawyer, and this is the era of lawyers. Always remember that you'll be giving your nephew, in the streets of Milan, the same fate as the young men of his age who are regarded as the most fortunate. Once his pardon is obtained, you'll give him twenty, thirty thousand lira, it doesn't matter; neither of us has any intention of saving money."

The duchess was sensitive to the idea of glory; she did not want Fabrizio to be an ordinary spendthrift. She returned to her lover's plan.

"I want to make one thing clear," he said to her: "my idea is not to turn Fabrizio into a model priest, like so many of those you see. No, he's a great nobleman before all else; he can remain perfectly ignorant if he sees fit, and he'll become a bishop and an archbishop just the same, if the prince continues to consider me useful.

"If, by your orders, you deign to change my proposal into an immutable decree, Parma must not see our protégé in a humble position. His rapid rise will offend people if they've seen him here as an ordinary priest; he must not appear in Parma until he's wearing purple stockings* and has every-

---

* In Italy, a young man who has an influential protector or a well-developed mind may become a *monsignore* and a *prelato*, which does not mean bishop; he then wears purple stockings. He is not required to take any vows to become a *monsignore*: he may take off his purple stockings and get married.

thing befitting his rank. Everyone will then guess that he's going to become a bishop, and no one will be offended.

"If you take my advice, you'll send him to study theology for three years in Naples. If he likes, during the vacations of the Ecclesiastical Academy he can go to see Paris and London; but he must never show himself in Parma." This last remark made the duchess shudder.

She sent a courier to her nephew to ask him to meet her at Piacenza. Need it be said that this courier was supplied with all the necessary money and passports?

Having been the first to arrive in Piacenza, Fabrizio ran forward to meet the duchess and embraced her with transports of joy which made her burst into tears. She was glad the count was not present; it was the first time she had had this feeling since the beginning of their love affair.

Fabrizio was deeply touched, then distressed by the plans she had made for him. It had always been his hope that, once that affair of Waterloo was settled, he would finally become a soldier. The duchess was struck by one thing which strengthened the romantic opinion she had formed of her nephew: he absolutely refused to lead the life of a café idler in one of the large cities of Italy.

"Can't you see yourself on the Corso in Florence or Naples," she said, "with thoroughbred horses? For the evenings, a carriage, an attractive apartment . . ." and so on. She insisted with delight on this commonplace happiness which she saw Fabrizio reject with disdain. "He's a hero," she thought.

"And after ten years of that pleasant life, what will I have done?" said Fabrizio. "What will I be? A 'mature' young man who will have to give way to any handsome adolescent making his entry in the world, also riding an English horse."

At first he refused even to consider a career in the Church. He spoke of going to New York, of becoming a republican soldier and citizen in America.

"How mistaken you are!" replied the duchess. "You'll have no war, and you'll fall back into the life of the cafés, only without elegance, without music, without love affairs. Believe me, life in America would be as dreary for you as it would be for me." She explained to him the cult of the "Almighty Dollar," and the respect that must be shown for ordinary workmen, who decide everything by their votes. They returned to the idea of a career in the Church.

"Before you rise up in arms," said the duchess, "try to understand what the count is asking of you: there's no question of your becoming a poor priest, more or less exemplary and virtuous, like Father Blanès. Remember what your uncles, the Archbishops of Parma, were like; reread the accounts of their lives in the supplement to the genealogy. Above all, it's fitting for a man of your name to be a great lord, noble, generous, an upholder of justice, destined to become the head of his order . . . and a man who, in his whole life, commits only one unscrupulous act, but a very useful one."

"So all my illusions are gone with the wind!" said Fabrizio, sighing deeply. "It's a cruel sacrifice! I admit I hadn't given any thought to the horror of enthusiasm and intelligence, even when used to their own advantage, which from now on is going to reign among absolute sovereigns."

"You must realize that a proclamation, or a caprice of the heart, can suddenly drive an enthusiast into the party opposed to the one he's served all his life!"

"I, an enthusiast?" said Fabrizio. "What a strange accusation! I can't even fall in love!"

"What!" exclaimed the duchess.

"When I have the honor of paying court to a beauty, even one of noble birth and pious sentiments, I can think of her only when I see her."

This confession made a strange impression on the duchess.

"I ask you for a month," said Fabrizio, "in which to take leave of Signora C—— of Novara, and, something that's still more difficult, to say good-by to the daydreams of my whole life. I'll write to my mother, who'll be kind enough to come to see me at Belgirate, on the Piedmontese side of Lake Maggiore, and thirty-one days from now I'll be in Parma, incognito."

"No, you mustn't do that!" cried the duchess. She did not want Count Mosca to see her speaking to Fabrizio.

The same two people met again at Piacenza. This time the duchess was extremely agitated; a storm had arisen at court: the Marquise Raversi's faction was within sight of victory. It was possible that Count Mosca would be replaced by General Fabio Conti, leader of what was known in Parma as the "liberal party." Except for the name of the rival who was growing in the prince's favor, the duchess told Fabrizio everything. She again discussed the possibilities of his future, even with the prospect of lacking the count's all-powerful protection.

"I'm going to spend three years at the Ecclesiastical Academy in Naples," said Fabrizio, "but since I must be above all a young nobleman, and since you won't require me to lead the strict life of a virtuous seminary student, that stay in Naples doesn't frighten me at all. My life there will be at least as enjoyable as my life in Romagnano, where the members of good society were beginning to regard me as a Jacobin. During my exile I discovered that I know nothing, not even Latin, not even how to spell. I was planning to begin my education all over again at Novara, and I'll be glad to study theology in Naples; it's a complicated subject."

The duchess was delighted. "If we're driven away from court," she said, "we'll come to see you in Naples. But since you've accepted, until further orders, the idea of wearing purple stockings, the count, who's well acquainted with the Italy of today, has given me some instructions for you. Believe or don't believe the things that are taught to you, *but never raise any objections.* Imagine that you're being taught the rules of whist—would you raise any objections to the rules of whist? I told the count you were a believer, and he was glad to hear it; it's useful in this world and in the next. But if you are a believer, don't descend to the vulgarity of speaking with horror of Voltaire, Diderot, Raynal and all those other harebrained Frenchmen who were the forerunners of bicameral government. Let those names pass your lips as seldom as possible; but, when you must, speak of those gentlemen with calm irony: their ideas have long since been refuted, and their attacks no longer have any importance. Believe blindly everything you're told at the Academy. Remember that there are people who will faithfully take note of your slightest objections. You'll be forgiven for a little amorous intrigue, if you handle it well, but not for a doubt: with age, amorous intrigues cease and doubt increases. Act on this principle when you go to confession. You'll have a letter of introduction to a bishop who's the factotum of the Cardinal Archbishop of Naples: to him alone you must admit your escapade in France and your presence in the vicinity of Waterloo on June 18. But abridge your story a great deal, diminish your adventure, admit it only to avoid the reproach of concealing it—you were so young at the time!

"The count's second piece of advice to you is this: If a brilliant argument occurs to you, a triumphant retort that would change the course of the conversation, don't give in to the temptation to shine, remain silent; perceptive people will see your intelligence in your eyes. It will be time to display your wit when you're a bishop."

Fabrizio made his debut in Naples with a modest carriage and four good Milanese servants whom his aunt had sent to him. After a year of study, no one described him as having a brilliant mind. He was regarded as a great nobleman, hard-working and very generous, but something of a libertine.

That year, rather amusing for Fabrizio, was terrible for the duchess. The count was three or four times within a hairs-breadth of ruin. The prince, more fearful than ever because he was ill that year, believed that by dismissing him he would rid himself of the odium attached to the executions that had been carried out before the count became a minister. Rassi was the intimate favorite he was determined to keep at all costs. The count's perils made the duchess passionately devoted to him; she no longer thought about Fabrizio. To provide a pretext for their possible withdrawal, it was discovered that the air of Parma, which actually is a little damp, as in all of Lombardy, was not at all good for her health.

Finally, after periods of disfavor during which the count, even though Prime Minister, went as long as twenty days without ever seeing his master in private, he emerged victorious. He had General Fabio Conti, the alleged liberal, appointed governor of the citadel in which the liberals sentenced by Rassi were imprisoned. "If Conti is lenient to his prisoners," Mosca said to his mistress, "he'll be dismissed from favor as a Jacobin whose political ideas made him forget his duty as a general; if he shows himself stern and merciless, and I think that's the direction in which he'll be inclined, he'll cease to be the leader of his party, and he'll alienate every family that has one of its members in the citadel. The poor man knows how to take on an air of infinite respect whenever the prince comes near him, he changes clothes four times a day if necessary, and he's able to discuss questions of court etiquette, but he doesn't have a mind capable of following the difficult path which is his only means of escape. And in any case, I'll be here."

On the day after General Fabio Conti's appointment, which ended the ministerial crisis, it was learned that Parma was going to have an ultra-monarchist newspaper.

"What quarrels that newspaper will give rise to!" said the duchess.

"The idea of founding it," replied the count, laughing, "may well be my masterpiece. Little by little, I'll let it be taken away from me, against my will, by the most rabid monarchists. I've had attractive salaries attached to the editorial posts. Those posts will be solicited from all directions. The whole affair will carry us through a month or two, and the dangers I've just been exposed to will be forgotten. Two solemn gentlemen, P— and D—, have already put themselves forward as candidates."

"But that newspaper will be revoltingly absurd!"

"I'm counting on that. The prince will read it every morning and admire the doctrines of its founder: myself. In questions of detail, he'll either approve or be offended; and two of his working hours will be taken up. The newspaper will stir up opposition, but by the time serious complaints begin coming in, eight or ten months from now, it will be entirely in the hands of the rabid monarchists. It will be that party, which is bothersome to me, that will have to answer the complaints, and I'll make a few myself. I prefer a hundred absurdities to one hanging. Who remembers an absurdity two years after the issue of the official newspaper in which it appeared? But if a man is hanged, his sons and relatives will have a hatred of me that will last as long as my life, and possibly shorten it."

The duchess, always passionately interested in something, always active, never idle, had more intelligence than the whole court of Parma; but she lacked the patience and impassivity required for success in intrigue. She had, however, managed to follow with keen attention the interests of the various cliques, and she was even beginning to have some personal influence with the prince. Clara-Paolina, the princess consort, surrounded with honors but imprisoned in the most antiquated kind of court etiquette, considered herself the most unfortunate of women. Duchess Sanseverina paid court to her and undertook to prove to her that she was not so unfortunate as she thought.

It must be pointed out that the prince saw his wife only during dinner: this meal lasted thirty minutes, and he sometimes went for weeks on end without saying a word to her. The duchess tried to change all that. She amused the prince, especially since she had been able to preserve all her independence. Even if she had wanted to, she could not have succeeded in never hurting the feelings of any of the fools who infested that court in droves. It was this utter candor of hers that made her detested by the common run of the courtiers, all counts or marquis with incomes averaging five thousand lire a year. She became aware of this misfortune after the first few days and devoted herself exclusively to pleasing the sovereign and his wife, the latter of whom had absolute control over the crown prince. The duchess knew how to amuse the sovereign, and she took advantage of the extreme attention he paid to her every word to make remarks that cast ridicule on the courtiers who hated her. Since the foolish acts that Rassi had made him commit, and foolish acts involving bloodshed cannot be rectified, the prince had been sometimes afraid and often bored. This had led him to wretched envy: he felt that there was little enjoyment in his life, and he became gloomy whenever he thought he saw others enjoying themselves; the sight of happiness made him furious. "We must hide our love," the duchess said to her lover, and she allowed the prince to conclude that she was only moderately enamored of the count, although she still regarded him as a man worthy of the highest esteem.

This discovery had given His Highness a happy day. The duchess occasionally let fall a few words about her plans to devote several months each year to visiting the parts of Italy with which she was not yet acquainted, such as Naples, Florence and Rome. Now nothing in the world could have been more distressing to the prince than an apparent desertion of this sort; it was one of his most pronounced weaknesses: he was cut to the quick by anything that might be interpreted as showing scorn for his capital city. He felt that he had no way of retaining Duchess Sanseverina, and she was by far the most celebrated woman in Parma. She had achieved an unprecedented triumph over Italian laziness: people came in from the surrounding countryside to attend her "Thursdays," which were veritable festivals during which she nearly always presented something new and exciting. The prince was dying to see one of them, but how could he go about it? Visit the house of an ordinary private individual? That was something neither he nor his father had ever done!

One Thursday it was cold and rainy. All through the evening, the prince kept hearing carriages rumbling over the pavement of the square in front of the palace, on their way to Duchess Sanseverina's house. He felt a surge of impatience: other people were enjoying themselves, while he, a sovereign prince, an absolute ruler, who ought to enjoy himself more than anyone else, was bored! He rang for his aide-de-camp.

He had to wait while a dozen trustworthy men were posted along the street that ran from his palace to the duchess's. At last, after an hour that had seemed to him a century, and during which he had been tempted a score of times to brave the daggers and go out without any precautions, he appeared in the first of Duchess Sanseverina's drawing rooms. There would have been less surprise in that drawing room if it had been struck by lightning. In the twinkling of an eye, a stupefied silence fell over each of the gay, noisy rooms as the prince entered it; everyone stared at him with wide-open eyes. The courtiers looked bewildered; the duchess alone showed no surprise. When they finally recovered enough strength to speak, their prime concern was to answer this great question: Had the duchess been notified of the prince's visit, or had she been taken by surprise like everyone else?

The prince enjoyed himself, and the reader will now be able to judge the duchess's impulsive character, and the unlimited power which her vague remarks about a departure, skillfully dropped in the prince's presence, had enabled her to assume.

As she was showing the prince to the door and listening to the gallant things he was saying to her, she suddenly conceived a singular idea which she dared to express to him quite simply, as though it were perfectly commonplace:

"Your Highness, if you would address to the princess three or four of the gracious remarks you've been lavishing on me, you would be making my happiness far more certain than by coming here and telling me that I'm pretty, because not for anything in the world would I have the princess take a hostile view of the outstanding mark of favor with which you have just honored me."

The prince stared at her and replied curtly, "I believe I'm free to go wherever I please."

The duchess blushed. "I only wanted," she said quickly, "to avoid exposing Your Highness to the risk of a useless trip, because this Thursday will be the last: I'm going off to spend a few days in Bologna and Florence."

When she returned to her drawing rooms, everyone believed her to be at the highest peak of favor. She had just hazarded something which no one within living memory had ever dared to do. She motioned to the count, who left the whist table and followed her into a small room that was lighted but empty.

"What you've done was very bold," he said, "and I would never have advised you to do it. But in a smitten heart," he added, laughing, "happiness increases love, and if you leave tomorrow morning, I'll follow you tomorrow night. I'll be delayed only by the drudgery that goes with the office of Minister of Finance, with which I was foolish enough to burden myself, but in four hours of well-employed time it's possible to hand in a great many accounts. Let's go back inside, my dear, and put on an act of ministerial self-satisfaction in all freedom, and without reserve: it may be our last performance in this city. If he thinks he's being defied, the man is capable of anything: he'll call it 'making an example.' When these people are all gone, we'll decide on the best way to barricade you for the night. The best thing might be to leave without delay for your house at Sacca, near the Po, which has the advantage of being only half an hour away from Austrian territory."

It was a delightful moment for the duchess's love and self-esteem. She looked at the count, and her eyes filled with tears. He was a powerful minister, surrounded by a crowd of courtiers who showered him with homages equal to those they paid to the prince himself, and yet he was willing to give up everything for her sake, and without the slightest hesitation!

When she went back into the drawing room she was beside herself with joy. Everyone bowed down before her.

"How good fortune changes the duchess!" the courtiers said on all sides. "You'd hardly recognize her. At last that Roman soul, so far above everything, has deigned to appreciate the inordinate favor the sovereign has bestowed on her!"

Toward the end of the evening, the count came up to her and said, "I must tell you some news." Those standing near her immediately walked away.

"When the prince returned to the palace," said the count, "he paid a visit to his wife in her bedroom. Think what a surprise that was! 'I've come to tell you,' he said to her, 'about the delightful evening I've just spent in Duchess Sanseverina's house. She asked me to give you a detailed account of the way she's remodeled that grimy old palace.' He then sat down and described each one of your drawing rooms to her. He stayed with her for over twenty-five minutes. She was weeping with joy. Despite her intelligence, she couldn't think of anything to say that would carry on the conversation in the light tone His Majesty chose to give it."

This prince was not a malicious man, no matter what the liberals of Italy might say about him. He had imprisoned a rather large number of them, it is true, but he had acted from fear, and he sometimes said to himself, as though to console himself for certain memories, "It's better to kill the devil than to let him kill you." On the day following the evening we have just described, he was filled with joy, for he had done two good deeds: going to the duchess's "Thursday," and speaking to his wife. At dinner he spoke to her again. In short, that "Thursday" of Duchess Sanseverina's brought about a domestic revolution which had repercussions all over

Parma. The Marquise Raversi was thrown into consternation, and the duchess had a double joy: she had been able to be useful to her lover, and had found him more in love with her than ever.

"All that because of a rash idea that suddenly came into my mind!" she said to the count. "I'd no doubt have more freedom in Rome or Naples, but would I find such a fascinating game there? No, certainly not, my dear count, and I owe all my happiness to you."

CHAPTER SEVEN

It is with little details of court life as insignificant as those we have just related that the story of the next four years would have to be filled. Every spring the marquise and her daughters came to spend two months either in the Sanseverina palace or at Sacca, on the bank of the Po. There were some very pleasant moments, and they talked about Fabrizio, but the count would never allow him a single visit to Parma. He and the duchess had to rectify a few rash and foolish actions, it is true, but in general Fabrizio followed the line of conduct that had been laid down for him: that of a great nobleman who is studying theology and does not rely entirely on his virtue to assure his advancement. In Naples, he had developed a keen interest in the study of antiquity and begun to carry out excavations; this passion had almost replaced his passion for horses. He had sold his English horses in order to continue his excavations at Miseno, where he had found a bust of Tiberius as a young man which had taken its place among the finest relics of antiquity. The discovery of this bust was almost the keenest pleasure he had experienced in Naples. He had too proud a heart to seek to imitate other young men, to wish, for example, to play the part of a lover with a certain seriousness. He had no lack of mistresses, but they were of no importance to him, and despite his age it could be said of him that he was unacquainted with love; he was loved all the more because of it. There was nothing to prevent him from acting with the finest self-assurance, because for him one young and pretty woman was the equal of another, although the one he had met most recently seemed the most exciting. One of the most greatly admired ladies in Naples had behaved foolishly in his honor during the last year of his stay there. This had amused him at first, then finally bored him so overwhelmingly that one of the joys of his departure was his deliverance from the attentions of the charming Duchess of A——.

It was in 1821, after he had passed all his examinations with fair success, that his director of studies, or tutor, received a decoration and a present, and he, Fabrizio, set out to see at last that city of Parma about which he had dreamed so often. He was now a *Monsignore* and had four horses hitched to his carriage. At the post house before Parma he took only two horses, and when he entered the city he stopped at the San Giovanni church, which contained the ornate tomb of Archbishop Ascanio del Dongo, his great-great-uncle, author of the Latin genealogy. He prayed beside this tomb, then walked to the duchess's palace. She had been expecting him to arrive several days later. Her drawing room was filled with people, but soon she was left alone with Fabrizio.

"Well, are you satisfied with me?" he said to her, throwing himself in her arms. "Thanks to you, I've spent four rather happy years in Naples, instead of living in boredom at Novara, with my mistress authorized by the police."

The duchess could not get over her astonishment: she would not have recognized him if she had met him in the street. She found that he was really one of the handsomest men in Italy; he had, above all, a charming face. When she had sent him to Naples he had the appearance of a reckless daredevil; the riding crop he always carried in those days had seemed an inherent part of his being. Now he had the noblest and most restrained manner in the presence of strangers, and in private she found that he still had all the fire of his early youth. He was a diamond that had lost nothing by being polished.

He had not been there an hour when Count Mosca came in, a little too soon. The young man spoke to him so graciously about the Cross of Parma that had been awarded to his tutor, and he showed such perfect discretion in expressing his deep gratitude for certain other benefits which he did not dare to mention so openly, that the minister passed favorable judgment on him at first sight. "This nephew of yours," he whispered to the duchess, "is well fitted to grace any of the high offices to which you may wish to raise him in the future."

So far, everything had been going wonderfully well, but when the count, thoroughly satisfied with Fabrizio and till then attentive only to his conduct, glanced at the duchess, he saw an odd look in her eyes. "This young man is going to make an extraordinary impression here," he said to himself. It was a bitter reflection; the count had reached his fifties, a cruel word whose full repercussions can perhaps be felt only by a man who is desperately in love. Setting aside his severities as a minister, he was extremely kind and quite worthy of being loved. But to him the cruel word "fifties" cast a black shadow over his whole life and might have been capable of making him cruel on his own account. In the five years since he had persuaded the duchess to come to Parma, she had often aroused his jealousy, especially at first, but she had never given him any real grounds for complaint. He even believed, and rightly, that it was for the purpose of more firmly attaching his heart that she had resorted to those apparent marks of favor shown to several fashionable young men of the court. He was sure, for example, that she had rejected the advances of the prince, who had made an instructive remark at the time.

"But if I accepted Your Highness's devotion," she had said to him, "how would I ever dare to face the count again?"

"I'd be almost as embarrassed as you. The dear count! My friend! But it's a difficulty that could be quite easily surmounted. I've already given some thought to it: the count would be put in the citadel for the rest of his life."

At the time of Fabrizio's arrival, the duchess was so carried away with happiness that she gave no thought at all to the ideas which her eyes might suggest to the count. The effect was profound and his suspicions were irremediable.

Fabrizio was received by the prince two hours after his arrival. The duchess, foreseeing the good effect this audience would have on the public, had been soliciting it for the past two months. This favor placed Fabrizio in an outstanding position from the start. The pretext for it had been that he was only passing through Parma on his way to visit his mother in Piedmont. At the moment when a charming little note from the duchess came to tell the prince that Fabrizio was awaiting his orders, His Highness was bored. "I'm going to see," he told himself, "a silly little saint, with either a dull or a crafty face." The Town Major had already reported Fabrizio's visit to the tomb of his uncle the archbishop. When he entered, the prince saw a tall young man whom he would have taken for some young officer if it had not been for his purple stockings.

This little surprise drove away his boredom. "Here's a lusty young man," he thought, "for whom I'm going to be asked God knows what favors: everything that's within my power.

He's just arrived, so he must be nervous. I'll give him some Jacobin politics and we'll see how he answers."

After his first few gracious words, the prince said to Fabrizio, "Well, *Monsignore*, are the people of Naples happy? Is the king loved?"

"Your Serene Highness," replied Fabrizio without a moment's hesitation, "when I passed through the streets I always admired the excellent bearing of the soldiers in the various regiments of His Majesty the King. The better classes are respectful toward their masters, as they ought to be, but I confess that never in my life have I allowed the people of the lower classes to speak to me about anything except the work for which I pay them."

"What a crafty hawk he is!" thought the prince. "Here's a well-trained bird with the duchess's shrewdness behind him!" Rising to the challenge, he employed great skill in making Fabrizio speak on this perilous subject. Stimulated by the danger, the young man was fortunate enough to find admirable answers. "It's almost insolent to make a display of love for one's king," he said. "It's blind obedience that one owes to him." In the face of such prudence, the prince almost became irritated. "Here, apparently," he thought, "is a man of keen intelligence who's come to us from Naples, and I don't like that breed. A man of keen intelligence may follow the best principles, and he may even believe in them, but on one side or another he's always a first cousin of Voltaire and Rousseau."

The prince almost felt as though he were being defied by such impeccable conduct and unassailable answers on the part of a young man just out of school; what he had expected had not happened. He abruptly assumed a good-natured tone and, going back in a few words to the great principles of society and government, he quoted, adapting them to the circumstances, a few phrases from Fénelon which he had been made to learn by heart when he was a child, to be used in public audiences.

"These principles surprise you, young man," he said to Fabrizio (he had called him *Monsignore* at the beginning of the audience and he intended to call him *Monsignore* again when he dismissed him, but he felt that in the course of the conversation it would be more adroit, more favorable to emotional turns of speech, to address him in familiar and friendly terms). "I admit that they bear little resemblance to the long-winded rigmarole on absolutism" (this was his expression) "that can be read every day in my official news-

114

paper. . . . But good heavens, why am I telling you about that? The men who write for my newspaper are totally unknown to you."

"I beg Your Serene Highness's pardon: not only do I read the Parma newspaper, which seems to me rather well written, but I also agree with it in maintaining that everything that has been done since the death of Louis XIV, in 1715, has been both criminal and foolish. Man's greatest interest is his own salvation, there can be no two ways of looking at the matter, and it's a happiness that will last forever. The words 'liberty,' 'justice' and 'the greatest happiness of the greatest number' are infamous and criminal; they form the habit of argument and mistrust in people's minds. A Chamber of Deputies 'mistrusts' what those men call 'the Ministry.' Once that fatal habit of *mistrust* has been contracted, human weakness applies it to everything; man comes to mistrust the Bible, the commands of the Church, tradition, and so on. As soon as that happens, he is lost. Even if—and this is horribly false and criminal to say—this mistrust of the authority of rulers established by God were to bring happiness during the twenty or thirty years of life which each of us may expect, what is half a century, or a whole century, compared to an eternity of torment?" And so on.

From the way Fabrizio was speaking, it could be seen that he was trying to organize his ideas to make them as easily understandable as possible to his listeners; it was clear that he was not reciting a lesson.

The prince soon lost all desire to match wits with this young man whose grave and simple manner made him feel ill at ease.

"Good-by, *Monsignore*," he said to him abruptly. "I see that they give an excellent education at the Ecclesiastical Academy in Naples, and it's quite natural that when such good precepts fall on such a distinguished mind, the results are brilliant. Good-by." And he turned his back on him.

"I haven't made a good impression on that pompous ass," thought Fabrizio.

"Now it remains to be seen," thought the prince as soon as he was alone, "whether that handsome young man is capable of a passion for anything; if so, he's a perfect example of his kind. . . . Could anyone have repeated more intelligently the lessons he learned from his aunt? It seemed to me I could hear her speaking. If there should be a revolution here, it would be she who would edit the *Monitor*, as the Marquise San Felice did in Naples! But in spite of her twenty-

115

five years and her beauty, the Marquise San Felice managed to get herself hanged! A warning to women who are too clever for their own good."

The prince was mistaken in believing Fabrizio to be his aunt's pupil. Intelligent people who are born to the throne, or near it, soon lose all delicacy of perception; they banish freedom of speech, which strikes them as vulgarity, from their presence; they refuse to see anything but masks, yet claim to judge the beauty of complexions. The amusing part of it is that they believe themselves to be highly perceptive. In this case, for example, Fabrizio believed nearly everything we have heard him say, although it is true that he never thought more than twice a month about all those great principles. He had keen desires, he had intelligence, but he had faith.

The desire for freedom, and the fashion and cult of "the greatest happiness of the greatest number," with which the nineteenth century has become infatuated, were nothing in his eyes but a heresy that would pass away like all others, but after killing many souls, just as a plague kills many bodies during its reign over a given region. And in spite of all this, he read the French newspapers with delight, and even exposed himself to danger to get them.

When Fabrizio returned, still bristling from his audience in the palace, and told his aunt about the prince's various attacks, she said to him, "You must go to see Father Landriani, our excellent archbishop, without delay. Go there on foot, climb the stairs softly, and make as little noise as you can in the anterooms. If you're kept waiting, so much the better, a thousand times better! In short, be *apostolic!*"

"I understand," said Fabrizio: "our man is a pious hypocrite."

"Not at all, he's virtue personified."

"Even after what he did when Count Palanza was executed?" said Fabrizio, astonished.

"Yes, my friend, even after what he did then: our archbishop's father was a clerk in the Ministry of Finance, a humble commoner; that explains everything. Monsignor Landriani is a man of keen, far-reaching and profound intelligence. He's sincere and he loves virtue. I'm convinced that if another Emperor Decius were to come into the world, he would undergo martyrdom like the Polyeuctus in the opera that was performed here last week. That's the good side of the picture; now here's the other side: as soon as he's in the presence of the sovereign, or even the Prime Minister, he

116

becomes agitated, he blushes, and it's physically impossible for him to say no. That's why he's done the things that have given him his cruel reputation all over Italy. But what most people don't know is that when public opinion enlightened him on the trial of Count Palanza he set himself the penance of living on bread and water for thirteen weeks, as many weeks as there are letters in the name Davide Palanza. We have at this court an infinitely clever scoundrel by the name of Rassi, the First Magistrate, or Chief Justice, who cast a spell over Father Landriani at the time of Count Palanza's death. During his thirteen-week penance, Count Mosca, out of pity and also a little out of mischievousness, invited him to dinner once or even twice a week, and, to avoid showing any disrespect, the good archbishop dined like everyone else. He would have felt that there was a certain rebelliousness and Jacobinism in openly displaying the penance he had imposed on himself for an action approved by his sovereign. But it was known that for each dinner at which his duty as a faithful subject had forced him to eat like everyone else, he increased his penance by two more days of living on bread and water.

"Archbishop Landriani is a man of superior mind, and a first-rate scholar. He has only one weakness: *he wants to be loved.* So you must show affection when you look at him, and on your third visit you must love him without reserve. That, combined with your noble birth, will make him adore you right away. Don't show any surprise if he accompanies you to the stairs, act as though you're accustomed to such manners; he's a man who was born on his knees before the nobility. Aside from that, be simple and apostolic; no wit, no brilliance, no quick repartee. If you don't alarm him, he'll enjoy your company. Remember that he must make you his vicar-general of his own free will. The count and I will be surprised and even annoyed by such an excessively rapid promotion: it's essential that we give the prince that impression."

Fabrizio hurried to the archbishop's palace. By a singular stroke of luck, the good prelate's servant, somewhat deaf, did not hear the name "del Dongo" and announced a young priest named Fabrizio. The archbishop was with a priest whose morals were far from exemplary. He had summoned him in order to scold him, and was now delivering his reprimand. Since this was a painful thing for him to do and he did not want it weighing on his heart any longer, he kept the grandnephew of the great Archbishop Ascanio del Dongo waiting for three-quarters of an hour.

How can we depict his apologies and his despair when, after conducting the priest to the second waiting room and, on his way back, having asked the man who was waiting there "what he could do for him," he noticed the purple stockings and heard the name of Fabrizio del Dongo? The incident seemed so amusing to our hero that on this first visit he ventured to kiss the holy prelate's hand in a transport of affection. It was touching to hear the archbishop repeating in despair, "A del Dongo kept waiting in my anteroom!" He felt himself obliged, by way of apology, to tell him the whole story of the priest, his misdeeds, his answers, etc.

"Is it possible," Fabrizio thought on his way back to the Sanseverina palace, "that this is the same man who hastened the execution of poor Count Palanza?"

"And what does Your Excellency think now?" Count Mosca asked him, laughing, when he saw him enter the duchess's palace. (The count did not want Fabrizio to call him "Your Excellency.")

"I'm thunderstruck. I know nothing about human nature. If I hadn't known that man's name, I'd have been willing to bet that he couldn't bear the sight of a chicken being bled."

"And you'd have won your bet," said the count. "But when he's in front of the prince, or even in front of me, he can't say no. Actually, in order to produce my full effect on him, I must be wearing my yellow Grand Cordon on my coat. He'd contradict me if I were wearing ordinary clothes, so I always put on a uniform before receiving him. It's not for us to destroy the prestige of power: the French newspapers are demolishing it fast enough. I'm not sure the 'mania of respect' will last as long as we do, and you, my nephew, will outlive respect. Some day you'll be an ordinary man!"

Fabrizio greatly enjoyed the count's company: he was the first man of superior mind and character who had ever deigned to speak to him without pretense. Furthermore, they had a common interest in excavations and relics of antiquity. For his part, the count was flattered by the extreme attention with which the young man listened to him, but there was one grave objection: Fabrizio occupied an apartment in the Sanseverina palace, spent all his time with the duchess, and innocently let it be seen that this intimacy was the source of all his happiness; and his eyes and complexion had a freshness that drove the count to despair.

For a long time Ranuccio-Ernesto IV, whose amorous desires were seldom thwarted, had been nettled by the fact that the duchess's virtue, well known at court, had not made an exception in his favor. As we have seen, Fabrizio's intelligence and presence of mind had offended him from the start. He was displeased by the great affection which Fabrizio and his aunt recklessly showed for each other; he listened with extreme attention to the courtiers' remarks, which were endless. The young man's arrival and the extraordinary audience he had obtained were the news and astonishment of the court for a month. This gave the prince an idea.

Among his palace guards there was a soldier who could hold his wine in an admirable manner. He spent all his time in the taverns and made direct reports to his sovereign concerning the morale of the troops. Carlone lacked education, otherwise he would long since have been promoted. He had a standing order to be in front of the palace every day when the great clock struck noon. One day, a little before noon, the prince himself went to arrange in a certain way the shutters of a room located between two floors and connected with his dressing room. He returned to this room shortly after the clock had struck noon and found the soldier there. The prince had a sheet of paper and writing materials in his pocket; he dictated the following letter to the soldier:

Your Excellency, you are no doubt highly intelligent, and it is thanks to your profound sagacity that this State is so well governed. But, my dear count, such great success never fails to arouse a little envy, and I am very much afraid that people will soon be laughing at your expense if your sagacity does not grasp the fact that a certain handsome young man has had the good fortune to inspire, perhaps involuntarily, a most singular love. This happy mortal is said to be only twenty-three, and what complicates the matter, my dear count, is that you and I are much more than twice that old. In the evening and from a certain distance, you are a charming, scintillating, witty and gracious as anyone could be; but in the morning and in private, the newcomer may, all things rightly considered, be more attractive. We women set great value on the freshness of youth, especially when we are past thirty. Is there not already talk of attaching that delightful adolescent to our court by giving him some fine position? And who is the person who discusses it with you most often?

119

The prince took the letter and gave the soldier two scudi. "This is in addition to your regular pay," he said gloomily. "Don't breathe a word of this to anyone, or you'll find yourself in the dampest dungeon of the citadel."

In his office the prince had a collection of envelopes addressed to most of the people at his court in the handwriting of this same soldier, who was thought to be unable to write and never even wrote his police reports. The prince took out the envelope he needed.

A few hours later, Count Mosca received a letter through the post. The time of arrival had been calculated, and just as the postman, who had been seen entering with a little letter in his hand, was leaving the ministerial palace, Mosca was summoned to His Highness's presence. Never had the favorite appeared to be overwhelmed by blacker sadness; to enjoy it more fully, the prince called out to him as soon as he saw him, "I need to relax a little by having a chat with my friend, instead of working with my minister. I have a splitting headache this evening, and furthermore my mind is filled with gloomy thoughts."

Is it necessary to describe the terrible irritation that was enraging the Prime Minister, Count Mosca della Rovere, by the time he was allowed to leave his august master? Ranuccio-Ernesto IV was highly skilled in the art of torturing a heart, and at this point I might, without being too unjust, make the comparison of a tiger that likes to toy with its prey.

The count had himself driven home at a gallop. As he hurried into his house he called out that not one living soul was to be allowed to come upstairs, had the ministerial clerk on duty told that he was free to leave (the idea of knowing that a human being was within range of his voice was odious to him), and rushed to shut himself up in his great picture gallery. There at last he was able to abandon himself to all his fury. He spent the whole evening there without a light, pacing aimlessly up and down, like a man who has lost his reason. He was trying to impose silence on his heart, so that he could concentrate all his strength and attention on the problem of what course of action he ought to take. Plunged into a state of anguish that would have moved his cruelest enemy to pity, he said to himself, "The man I abhor lives in the duchess's house and spends all his time with her. Should I try to make one of her maids speak? Nothing could be more dangerous: she's so kind, she pays them so well! And they adore her! (And who, in the name of God, doesn't adore her!)

"Here's the question," he went on angrily, "should I let her guess the jealousy that's consuming me, or should I say nothing about it? If I remain silent, she won't hide anything from me. I know Gina: she's a woman who always acts on her first impulse. Her behavior is unpredictable, even to herself. If she tries to work out a plan in advance, she gets tangled up in it. When it's time to act, she always gets some new idea which she follows joyfully, as though it were the finest idea in the world, and then it ruins everything.

"If I say nothing about my martyrdom, she won't hide anything from me and I'll see everything that may happen. . . .

"Yes, but by speaking I'll create other circumstances, I'll make her reflect, I'll forestall many of those horrible things that may happen. . . . Perhaps she'll send him away." (The count sighed.) "In that case, I'll be almost victorious; even if she's a little annoyed at the time, I'll calm her. . . . And what could be more natural than her annoyance? She's loved him as a son for fifteen years. There lies all my hope: *as a son.* . . . But she hadn't seen him since his flight to Waterloo, and now that he's returned from Naples he's another man, especially for her. *Another man,*" he repeated angrily, "and that man is charming! Above all, he has that guileless, tender air and those smiling eyes which promise so much happiness! And she must not be accustomed to seeing eyes like that at our court. . . . Their place is taken here by gloomy or sardonic looks. I myself, harassed by government affairs, reigning only through my influence over a man who would like to make me appear ridiculous—what kind of a look must *I* often have in my eyes! Ah, no matter how careful I am, my eyes must be the oldest thing about me! Doesn't my gaiety always border on irony? . . .

"I'll go further, since I must be honest here: doesn't my gaiety always give a glimpse of something that's closely allied with it: absolute power . . . and malice? Don't I sometimes say to myself, especially when someone is irritating me, 'I can do whatever I like'? And I even add a foolish reflection: 'I ought to be happier than other people, because I possess what others lack: sovereign power in three-quarters of all situations.' Well, let's be just: the habit of making that reflection must spoil my smile . . . must give me a look of selfishness . . . and self-satisfaction. . . . And how charming *his* smile is! It breathes the easy happiness of early youth, and gives rise to it in others."

Unfortunately for the count, the weather that evening was hot and sultry, with the approach of a storm in the air; in short, it was the kind of weather which, in that part of the world, leads people to make extreme resolutions. How could I describe all the lines of reasoning, all the ways of looking at what was happening to him, which tortured that passionate man for three deadly hours? Finally the counsel of prudence prevailed, solely as a result of this reflection: "I'm probably out of my mind, I think I'm reasoning, but I'm not: I'm only turning around, trying to find a less painful position, passing some decisive argument without seeing it. Since I'm blinded by excessive grief, I'd better follow the rule which all sensible people recommend, and which they call 'prudence.' Besides, once I've uttered the fatal word 'jealousy,' my role is established forever. On the other hand, if I say nothing today, I can speak tomorrow, I'll remain in control of the whole situation."

The crisis had been too violent; the count would have gone mad if it had lasted much longer. He was relieved for a few moments, and his attention returned to the anonymous letter. Who could have sent it? Then followed a search for names, and a judgment with regard to each one of them. This provided a diversion. Finally he recalled the flash of malice that had appeared in the prince's eyes when he had said, toward the end of the audience, "Yes, my friend, we must both admit that the pleasures and cares of the most successful ambition, and even those of unlimited power, are nothing compared to the intimate happiness given by relations of tenderness and love. I'm a man before I'm a prince, and when I have the good fortune to be in love, my mistress speaks to the man, not to the prince." The count compared this moment of malicious glee with the following sentence from the letter: "It is thanks to your profound sagacity that this State is so well governed."

"The prince composed that sentence!" he exclaimed. "For a courtier, it would be gratuitous rashness. The letter came from His Highness."

With this problem solved, the little joy caused by the pleasure of having unmasked the sender of the letter was soon effaced by the cruel vision of Fabrizio's charming graces, which came into his mind again. It was like an enormous weight falling back down on the poor man's heart. "What does it matter who sent the anonymous letter?" he cried out furiously. "Is the fact it reports to me any less real? This caprice of hers may change my whole life," he said, as though to excuse himself for being so distraught. "At the first opportunity, if she loves him in a certain way, she'll go off with him to Belgirate, to Switzerland, to any corner of the world. She's rich, and besides, even if she had to live on very little money, what would it matter to her? Didn't she admit to me, less than a week ago, that her palace, so magnificent and so well arranged, bored her? Her youthful heart must have something new! And with what simplicity this new happiness presents itself to her! She'll be carried away before she's given any thought to the danger, before she's given any thought to pitying me! And yet I'm so miserable!" cried the count, bursting into tears.

He had sworn that he would not go to see the duchess that evening, but he could not restrain himself; never before had his eyes been so thirsty to look at her. He arrived at her house toward midnight. He found her alone with her nephew: at ten o'clock she had sent everyone else away and given orders that no more visitors were to be admitted.

At the sight of the tender intimacy that reigned between those two people, and of the duchess's artless joy, a frightful difficulty rose up before the count's eyes, and unexpectedly! It had not occurred to him during his long deliberation in the picture gallery: how was he to conceal his jealousy?

Not knowing what pretext to resort to, he claimed that he had found the prince extremely ill-disposed toward him that evening, that he had contradicted everything he said, and so on. He had the pain of seeing the duchess scarcely listening to him and paying no attention to details which, only two days before, would have set her off on an endless line of reasoning. He looked at Fabrizio: never had that handsome Lombard face appeared to him so simple and so noble! Fabrizio was paying no more attention than the duchess to the difficulties he was relating.

"Really," thought the count, "his face combines extreme kindness with a certain expression of artless, tender joy that's irresistible. It seems to be saying, 'Love and the happiness it gives are the only serious things in the world.' And yet if you mention some matter in which intelligence is required, his eyes light up and amaze you, and you remain disconcerted. Everything is simple to him, because he sees everything from above. My God, how can I fight such an enemy! And what would life be without Gina's love? With what rapture she seems to be listening to the sallies of that young mind which, to a woman, must seem absolutely unique!"

A horrible idea seized the count like a cramp: "Shall I stab him here, in front of her, then kill myself?"

He walked around the room, scarcely able to remain on his

feet, but with his hand convulsively clutching the handle of his dagger. Neither the duchess nor Fabrizio paid any attention to what he was doing. He told them he was going to give an order to his servant, but they did not even hear him; the duchess was laughing affectionately at something Fabrizio had just said to her. The count walked up to a lamp in the first drawing room and looked to see whether the point of his dagger was well sharpened. "I must be gracious and perfectly polite to that young man," he said to himself as he went back to rejoin them.

He was losing his reason; it seemed to him that they had leaned toward each other and were kissing, there, before his eyes. "That's impossible in my presence," he thought, "my mind is becoming unhinged. I must calm myself. If I behave boorishly she's capable, out of pure spite from wounded vanity, of going off to Belgirate with him, and there, or during the trip, chance may bring about a remark that will give a name to what they feel for each other, then all the consequences will follow in a moment.

"Solitude will make that word decisive, and anyway, once she's no longer with me, what will become of me? And if, after overcoming all sorts of difficulties created by the prince, I go to show my old, careworn face in Belgirate, what role will I play in the presence of those two deliriously happy people? Even here, what am I but the *terzo incomodo*?" (The beautiful Italian language is made for love! *Terzo incomodo*, a bothersome third person!) "How painful it is for an intelligent man to realize that he's playing that detestable role, yet be unable to get up and go away!"

The count was on the verge of losing all self-control, or at least of betraying his pain by the discomposure of his features. When he found himself near the door as he was walking around the room, he abruptly fled, calling out in a warm, friendly tone, "Good-by, you two!" And to himself he said, "I must avoid bloodshed."

On the day following this horrible evening, after a night spent in alternation between detailed consideration of Fabrizio's advantages and excruciating outbursts of the cruelest jealousy, the count had the idea of summoning a certain young servant he had in his employ. This man was courting a young girl by the name of Cecchina, the duchess's favorite maid. He was fortunately very steady, even miserly, in his conduct, and hoped to find a position as porter in one of the public institutions of Parma. The count ordered him to go and bring his sweetheart Cecchina immediately. He obeyed, and an hour later the count suddenly appeared in the room where the girl was waiting with her fiancé. He alarmed them both by the quantity of gold he gave them, then he addressed these few words to the trembling Cecchina, looking her straight in the face: "Does the duchess make love with *Monsignore?*"

"No," replied the girl, making up her mind after a moment of silence, "no . . . *not yet,* but he often kisses her hands, laughing, it's true, but with great emotion."

This testimony was completed by dozens of answers to as many frenzied questions from the count. His anxious passion made the two poor people fully earn the money he had thrown to them. He finally believed what he was told and became less unhappy. "If the duchess ever has any suspicion of this conversation," he said to Cecchina, "I'll send your fiancé to spend twenty years in the fortress, and you won't see him again until his hair has turned white."

A few days went by, during which Fabrizio also lost all his gaiety.

"I assure you," he said to the duchess, "that Count Mosca has a certain antipathy to me."

"So much the worse for His Excellency," she replied somewhat irritably.

This was not the real source of the anxiety that had made Fabrizio's gaiety vanish. "Chance has placed me in an untenable position," he said to himself. "I'm sure she'll never say anything: she'd be as horrified by a too significant word as she would be by an act of incest. But if some evening, after a rash and unrestrained day, she begins to examine her conscience and decides that I may have guessed the inclination she seems to have for me, what role will I play in her eyes? Precisely that of the *casto Giuseppe!*" (An Italian saying which alludes to the ridiculous role played by Joseph with the wife of the eunuch Potiphar.)

"Shall I nobly confide in her in such a way as to give her to understand that I'm incapable of serious love? I don't have enough control over my mind to be able to set forth that idea without making it absolutely indistinguishable from a piece of impertinence. My only alternative is to claim to have left a great passion in Naples. In that case, I could go back there for twenty-four hours. It would be a safe course to follow, but what good would it do? There's still the possibility of an affair with some woman of humble rank in Parma. It might displease her, but anything is preferable to the horrible role of the man who refuses to see the truth. It might jeopardize my future, too; I'd have to lessen the danger by exercising caution and buying discretion."

In the midst of all these thoughts, the cruel truth was that Fabrizio really loved the duchess far more than anyone else in the world. "It takes a terribly clumsy man," he told himself angrily, "to have such dread of not being able to convince someone of something that's so true!" Lacking the skill to extricate himself from his position, he became somber and sorrowful. "My God! What will become of me if I quarrel with the only person in the world to whom I'm passionately attached?" On the other hand, he could not bring himself to spoil such delightful happiness by an indiscreet word. His position had so many charms! The intimate friendship of such a pretty and gracious woman was so sweet! As far as the more commonplace aspects of life were concerned, her patronage gave him a very pleasant position at that court whose great intrigues, thanks to her explanations of them, were as amusing to him as a comedy.

"But I may be awakened by a thunderbolt at any moment!" he thought. "If those gay and tender evenings, spent almost entirely in private with such an exciting woman, should lead to something better, she'll think she's found a real lover in me. She'll expect transports of rapture and madness, and I'll still have nothing to offer her except the most wholehearted friendship, but without love; nature has excluded me from that kind of sublime madness. How many reproaches I've already had to endure on that account! I can still hear the Duchess of A——, and I cared nothing for her! The duchess will think I lack love for her, when it's actually love that's lacking in me; she'll never be willing to understand. Often after she's related to me, with all her unique grace and exuberance, some court anecdote that's necessary to my education, I kiss her hands and sometimes her cheek. What will become of me if her hand ever presses mine in a certain way?"

Fabrizio appeared every day in the most highly respected and least amusing houses in Parma. Guided by the duchess's shrewd advice, he ingratiated himself with the two princes, father and son, with Princess Clara-Paolina, and with the archbishop. He achieved a number of successes, but they did not console him for his mortal fear of becoming estranged from the duchess.

CHAPTER EIGHT

And so, less than a month after his arrival at court, Fabrizio had all the chagrins of a courtier, and the intimate friendship that gave him all his happiness was poisoned. One evening, tormented by these thoughts, he left the duchess's drawing room, where he now gave too strong an impression of being a reigning lover. Wandering aimlessly through the city, he saw a theater lighted up and went inside. It was a gratuitous imprudence for a man of his calling, and one he had firmly promised himself to avoid in Parma, which, after all, is only a small town of forty thousand inhabitants. It is true that after the first few days he had freed himself of his official costume; in the evening, unless he were going to some gathering of the very highest society, he was always dressed simply in black, like a man in mourning.

At the theater he took a box in the third tier, to avoid being seen. Goldoni's *La Locandiera* was being performed that evening. Fabrizio looked at the architecture of the auditorium, seldom turning his eyes to the stage. But the large audience kept bursting into laughter at every moment. He glanced at the young actress who was playing the part of the hostess and found her amusing. Then he looked at her more attentively: she seemed quite winsome to him, and, above all, perfectly natural. She was an artless young girl who was the first to laugh at the delightful things Goldoni put in her mouth, and she seemed amazed to hear herself saying them. He asked what her name was. "Marietta Valserra," he was told.

"Ah," he thought, "she's taken my name! That's odd." Despite his plans, he did not leave the theater until the end of the play. He came back the next evening, and three days later he knew Marietta Valserra's address.

On the very evening of the day when he had obtained this address, with considerable difficulty, he noticed that the count was behaving quite amiably toward him. The poor jealous lover, who had to make superhuman efforts to remain within the bounds of prudence, had put spies on the young man's trail and was pleased by his theater escapade. And imagine the count's joy when, on the day following the evening during which he had managed to be friendly to Fabrizio, he learned that the latter, only half disguised by a long blue frock coat, had gone up to the wretched apartment which Marietta Valserra occupied on the fifth floor of an old house behind the theater! His joy redoubled when he found out that Fabrizio had presented himself under a false name, and had had the honor of arousing the jealousy of a scoundrel by the name of Giletti, who in town played minor servants' parts, and in the villages danced on a tightrope. This noble lover of Marietta's was lavish in his abuse of Fabrizio and said he wanted to kill him.

Opera companies are formed by an *impresario* who engages, here and there, the performers he can pay, or whom he finds unemployed, and the company thus collected at random remains together for one season, or two at the most. It is not the same with theatrical troupes: although they move from town to town, changing their residence every two or three months, they form what might be called families, whose members all love or hate each other. Within each troupe there are established couples which the fashionable seducers of the towns where the troupe performs sometimes have great difficulty in separating. This was precisely the case with our hero: little Marietta was quite fond of him, but she was terrified of Giletti, who was determined to be her sole master and kept close watch on her. He proclaimed everywhere that he would kill the *Monsignore*, for he had followed Fabrizio and succeeded in discovering his name.

This Giletti was the ugliest man in the world, and the last fit for love: he was inordinately tall, terribly thin, thoroughly pockmarked and a little cross-eyed. Moreover, filled with the graces of his profession, it was his custom to enter the wings where his colleagues were gathered by turning cartwheels or performing some other pleasing feat. He triumphed in roles in which the actor, his face whitened with flour, must give or receive an endless number of blows with a stick. This worthy rival of Fabrizio's had a salary of thirty-two lire a month and considered himself rich.

It seemed to Count Mosca that he had returned from the gates of death when his observers gave him full certainty of all these details. His gracious manner reappeared; he seemed gayer and more urbane than ever in the duchess's drawing room, and he carefully refrained from telling her anything about the little adventure that had restored him to life. He even took precautions to make sure that she would be informed as late as possible of everything that was going on. Finally he had the courage to listen to the voice of reason, which for the past month had been crying out to him in vain that whenever a lover's ascendancy begins to decline, he must travel.

An important affair called him to Bologna. Twice a day, couriers from the ministry brought him not so much the official papers from his offices as news of little Marietta's love affairs, the terrible Giletti's anger, and Fabrizio's various ventures.

One of the count's agents asked several times for a performance of *Harlequin, Skeleton and Pie,* one of Giletti's triumphs (he popped out of the pie just as his rival Brighella was cutting into it and gave him a beating). This was only a pretext for giving him a hundred lire. Giletti, who was up to his ears in debt, was careful to say nothing about this windfall, but he became amazingly arrogant.

Fabrizio's whim had changed into a matter of defending his vanity (at his age, his cares had already reduced him to having *whims!*). Vanity led him to the theater. Marietta performed with great gaiety and amused him; on leaving the theater, he was in love for an hour. The count returned to Parma when he heard that Fabrizio was in real danger: Giletti, who had been a soldier in the fine regiment of Napoleon Dragoons, was speaking seriously of killing him, and was already making preparations to flee to Romagna afterward. If the reader is very young, he will be shocked by our admiration for this fine act of virtue. It required, however, no small effort of heroism on the count's part to return from Bologna; after all, his face often showed marks of fatigue in the morning, and Fabrizio had such freshness, such serenity! Who would ever have dreamed of reproaching him for Fabrizio's death if it had occurred in his absence and for such a foolish reason? But he had one of those rare souls that harbor eternal remorse for a noble action which could have been done but was not; furthermore, he could not bear the idea of seeing the duchess sad, and through his fault.

He found her taciturn and gloomy when he returned. Here is what had happened: her young maid, Cecchina, tormented by remorse and judging the gravity of her misdeed by the size of the enormous sum of money she had received for committing it, had fallen ill. One evening the duchess, who was quite fond of her, went up to her room. The young girl could not hold out against this show of kindness: she burst into tears, tried to give her mistress what was left of the money she had taken, and finally had the courage to confess the questions the count had asked her and what she had replied to them. The duchess ran over to the lamp and put it out, then told Cecchina that she forgave her, but on condition that she would never say a word about that strange scene to anyone. "The poor count," she added lightheartedly, "is afraid of ridicule; all men are like that."

The duchess hurried down to her bedroom. As soon as she had shut herself up inside it, she burst into tears. To her there was something horrible about the idea of making love with Fabrizio, whom she had known as a baby; and yet what was the meaning of her conduct?

Such was the cause of the black melancholy in which the count had found her plunged. As soon as he arrived she began having fits of impatience with him, and almost with Fabrizio; she wished she could never see either of them again. She was angered by what was to her the ridiculous part Fabrizio was playing with regard to young Marietta; for, as a true lover unable to keep a secret, the count had told her everything. She could not resign herself to this disaster: her idol had a flaw. Finally, in a surge of genuine friendship, she asked the count for advice. It was an exquisite moment for him, and a handsome reward for the honorable impulse that had brought him back to Parma.

"What could be simpler?" he said, laughing. "Young men want to have every woman they see, then by the next day they've forgotten all about it. Isn't he supposed to go to Belgirate to see the Marquise del Dongo? Well then, let him go! During his absence, I'll ask the theatrical troupe to take their talents elsewhere, and I'll pay their traveling expenses. But before long he'll be in love again with the first pretty woman that chance brings his way. It's perfectly natural, and I wouldn't want to see him otherwise. . . . If necessary, have the marquise write to him."

This idea, expressed with an air of complete indifference, was a flash of light to the duchess; she was afraid of Giletti. That evening the count announced, as though by chance, that there was a courier who would pass through Milan on his way to Vienna; three days later, Fabrizio received a letter from his mother. He left, greatly annoyed at not yet having been able, thanks to Giletti's jealousy, to take advantage of the excellent intentions which Marietta had communicated to him through her *mammacia*, an old woman who served as her mother.

Fabrizio found his mother and one of his sisters at Belgirate, a large Piedmontese village on the western shore of Lake Maggiore; the eastern shore belongs to the Milanese, and consequently to Austria. This lake, parallel to Lake Como and also running north and south, lies about ten leagues further to the west. The mountain air, the calm, majestic aspect of that superb lake, which reminded him of the one on whose shores he had spent his childhood—everything combined to change Fabrizio's chagrin, bordering on anger, into gentle melancholy. It was with infinite tenderness that the memory of the duchess now presented itself to him. It seemed to him that, from a distance, he was beginning to feel for her that love which he had never felt for any woman. Nothing would have been more painful to him than to be separated from her forever, and, while he was in this frame of mind, if she had deigned to resort to the slightest coquetry, such as, for example, opposing a rival to him, she would have conquered his heart. But, far from taking such decisive measures, she bitterly reproached herself when she found her thoughts constantly following in the young traveler's footsteps. She reproached herself for what she still called a caprice, as though it were something abominable. She became twice as attentive and obliging to the count, who, entranced by so much charm, did not listen to the sane voice of reason which prescribed a second journey to Bologna.

The Marquise del Dongo, busy with preparations for the wedding of her elder daughter, whom she was marrying to a Milanese duke, had only three days to give to her beloved son. Never before had she found such tender affection in him. In the midst of the melancholy that was progressively taking possession of his soul, a strange and even ridiculous idea had occurred to him, and he suddenly decided to act on it. Dare we say that he wanted to consult Father Blanès? This worthy old man was totally incapable of understanding the sorrows of a heart torn between puerile passions of nearly equal strength, and furthermore it would have taken Fabrizio a week to give him even a glimpse of all the interests he had to treat with careful consideration in Parma, but when he thought of consulting him he recaptured the freshness of his feelings at the age of sixteen. It may be difficult to believe, but it was not merely as a wise man or a completely devoted friend that Fabrizio wanted to speak with him; the object of his expedition, and the feelings that agitated him during the fifty hours it lasted, are so absurd that, in the interests of our story, it would no doubt have been better to pass over them in silence. I fear that his credulity may deprive him of the reader's sympathy, but after all, such was his nature, so why should I flatter him more than anyone else? I have not flattered Count Mosca or the prince.

Fabrizio, then, since the whole truth must be told, accompanied his mother to the port of Laveno, on the eastern shore of Lake Maggiore, the Austrian side, where she landed at about eight o'clock in the evening. (The lake is regarded as neutral territory, and no passport is required of anyone who does not set foot on shore.) But scarcely had night fallen when he disembarked on that same Austrian shore, in the middle of a little wood that juts out into the water. He had rented a *sediola*, a kind of swift, rustic tilbury, which enabled him to follow his mother's carriage at a distance of five hundred paces. He was disguised as a servant of the Casa del Dongo, and none of the many policemen and customs officials ever thought of asking to see his passport. A quarter of a league from Como, where the marquise and her daughter were to stop for the night, he took a path to the left which, after skirting the small town of Vico, joins a narrow road recently built along the extreme edge of the lake. It was midnight, so he could reasonably hope not to encounter any policemen. The road ran through a little forest whose trees projected the black outlines of their foliage against a sky that was filled with stars but veiled by a light mist. The water and the sky were profoundly peaceful; Fabrizio's soul could not resist that sublime beauty: he stopped and sat down on a rock that jutted out into the lake, forming a little promontory. The universal silence was broken only, at regular intervals, by the gentle ripples of the lake as they came in to expire on the shore.

Fabrizio had an Italian heart, and I ask that he be excused for it; this defect, which will make him less likable, consisted chiefly in the fact that he had only spasmodic outbursts of vanity, and that the mere sight of sublime beauty moved him deeply and took away the sharp, bitter sting of his sorrows. As he sat on his isolated rock, no longer having any need to be on his guard against the police, protected by the deep night and the vast silence, tears came to his eyes and he experienced there, at little cost, the happiest moments he had known for a long time.

He resolved never to lie to the duchess, and it was because he loved her to the point of adoration at that moment that he swore to himself that he would never tell her he loved her; never would he utter the word "love" in her presence, since the passion that went by that name was foreign to his heart. In the fervor of generosity and virtue that had brought on his momentary bliss, he decided to tell her everything at the first opportunity: his heart had never known love. Once he had firmly resolved to carry out this courageous plan, he felt as though an enormous weight had been lifted from his shoulders. "Perhaps she'll have a few words to say to me about Marietta," he thought. "Well then, I'll never see little Marietta again!" he replied to hmiself gaily.

A morning breeze was beginning to temper the overwhelming heat that had reigned during the day. The faint white glow of dawn was already outlining the peaks of the Alps that rise to the north and east of Lake Como. Their massive shapes, snowcapped even in June, stood out against the azure of a sky which is always clear at those immense altitudes. A spur of the Alps reaching southward into happy Italy separates the shores of Lake Como from those of Lake Garda. Fabrizio cast his eyes over all the spurs of those sublime mountains. As the dawn grew brighter, it revealed the valleys that separated them, illuminating the fine mist rising from the bottoms of the gorges.

He began walking again. After passing the hill that forms the peninsula of Durini, he at last saw the belfry of the village of Grianta, from which he had so often observed the stars with Father Blanès. "How ignorant I was in those days!" he thought. "I couldn't even understand the ridiculous Latin of those astrological treatises my teacher used to consult. I think I respected him mainly because, understanding only a few words here and there, my imagination took over the task of giving meaning to them, and gave them the most romantic meaning possible."

Little by little his thoughts took another course. "Could there be something real in that science?" he wondered. "Why should it be different from the others? Let's say that a certain number of imbeciles and crafty people agree among themselves that they know the Mexican language, for example; with that qualification they impose themselves on society, which respects them, and on the government, which pays them. They're showered with favors precisely because they have no intelligence, and because those in power need have no fear that they'll rouse the people to revolt and make grandiloquent speeches filled with noble sentiments! Take Father Bari, for instance: Ernesto IV recently awarded him a pension of four thousand lire and the Cross of his Order for having reconstituted nineteen lines of a Greek dithyramb!

"But my God, do I have a right to regard such things as ridiculous? Am I in any position to complain?" he said to himself abruptly, coming to a standstill. "Wasn't that same decoration given to my tutor in Naples?" He had a feeling of deep uneasiness; the fine fervor of virtue which had made his heart beat proudly a short time before was now changing into the base pleasure of having gotten a good share for himself in a robbery. "Well," he thought at length, with the lackluster eyes of a man who is dissatisfied with himself, "since my birth gives me the right to profit from those abuses, it would be abysmally stupid of me not to get my share; but I must never let myself speak against them in public." This line of reasoning was not unsound, but he had fallen a long way from the heights of sublime happiness to which he had been transported an hour before. The thought of privilege had withered that plant, always so delicate, which is known as happiness.

"If we mustn't believe in astrology," he went on, trying to distract himself, "if that science, like three-quarters of the non-mathematical sciences, is nothing but a collection of enthusiastic fools and cunning hypocrites who are paid by those they serve, why is it that I think so often and with such emotion about the details of one fateful incident? I got out of the prison at B——, but with the uniform and the marching orders of a soldier who'd been imprisoned for good reason."

Fabrizio's reasoning was never able to penetrate any further; he moved around the difficulty in a hundred different ways without succeeding in surmounting it. He was still too young; in his moments of leisure, he delighted in savoring the sensations produced by the romantic circumstances with which his imagination was always ready to supply him. He was far from employing his time in patiently observing the real characteristics of things in order to discover their causes. Reality still seemed dull and sordid to him. I can understand that one might not like to look at it, but in that case one ought not to reason about it. And one certainly ought not to raise objections with the various components of one's ignorance.

Thus, while he did not lack intelligence, Fabrizio failed to see that his half-belief in omens was for him a religion, a profound impression received at the beginning of his life. To think about that belief was to feel; it was happiness. And he stubbornly persisted in trying to find out how it might be real, a *proven* science, in the same category as geometry, for example. He zealously searched his memory for all the instances in which omens he had observed had not been followed by the fortunate or unfortunate events they seemed to announce. But while he believed himself to be reasoning and advancing toward the truth, his attention lingered happily over the cases in which the omen had been clearly followed by the predicted event. His soul was filled with respect and deep emotion, and he would have felt invincible repugnance for anyone who denied the validity of omens, especially if the denial had been made with irony.

Fabrizio had been walking without realizing the distance he was covering, and he had reached this point in his futile reasoning when he looked up and saw the wall of his father's garden. This wall, which supported a beautiful terrace, rose more than forty feet above the road, to his right. A string-course of hewn stone at the top, near the balustrade, gave it a monumental aspect. "Not bad," Fabrizio said to himself coldly. "It's good architecture, almost in the Roman style." He was applying his new knowledge of antiquity. Then he turned his head away in disgust: his father's severities, and especially his brother Ascanio's denunciation of him after his return from France, had come back into his mind.

"That infamous denunciation was the cause of my present life," he thought. "I may hate it, I may despise it, but it did change my destiny. What would have become of me once I'd been sent off to Novara, scarcely even tolerated by my father's business agent, if my aunt hadn't made love with a powerful minister? Or if that aunt had happened to have only a cold, commonplace heart instead of the warm, passionate heart that loves me with a kind of fervor which astonishes me? Where would I be now if she had a heart like her brother's?"

Overwhelmed by these cruel memories, Fabrizio was now walking with faltering steps. He reached the edge of the moat exactly opposite the magnificent façade of the castle. He hardly cast a glance at that great edifice blackened by time. The noble language of architecture found him insensitive; the memory of his father and his brother had closed his soul to all sensations of beauty, all his attention was concentrated on keeping himself alert in the presence of hypocritical and dangerous enemies. For a moment he looked with marked disgust at the little window of the fourth-floor bedroom he had occupied before 1815. His father's character had robbed his childhood memories of all charm. "I haven't gone in there," he thought, "since March 7, at eight o'clock in the evening. I came out to go and get Vasi's passport, and the next day my fear of spies made me hasten my departure.

When I came back from France, I didn't have time to go up there, not even to look at my engravings again, thanks to my brother's denunciation."

He turned his head away in horror. "Father Blanès is eighty-three now," he said to himself sadly. "My sister says he almost never comes to the castle any more; the infirmities of old age have had their effect. That firm, noble heart has been chilled by time. God only knows how long ago he stopped going up to his belfry! I'll hide in the cellar, under the vats or the wine press, until he wakes up; I won't disturb the kindly old man's sleep. He's probably forgotten my face: six years makes a great difference at his age! I'll find nothing but the tomb of a friend! And it's really childish of me to have come here to confront the disgust my father's castle arouses in me."

He was now entering the little square in front of the church. It was with an astonishment bordering on delirium that he saw, on the third floor of the ancient belfry, the long, narrow window illuminated by Father Blanès' little lantern. The priest was in the habit of placing it there when he went up to the cage of planks that formed his observatory, so that its light would not prevent him from reading his planisphere. This map of the heavens was stretched over a large earthenware vase which had once held one of the orange trees of the castle. In the opening of the bottom of the vase burned the tiniest of lamps. Its smoke escaped through a little tin pipe whose shadow marked north on the map. The memory of these simple things flooded Fabrizio's soul with emotions and filled it with happiness.

Almost without thinking, he used both hands to make the short, low whistle that had formerly been his signal for admission. He immediately heard several tugs given to the rope which opened the latch of the belfry door from the top of the observatory. He ran up the stairs in a state of frenzied excitement. He found the priest sitting in his wooden armchair, in his usual place, with his eye glued to the sight of a mural quadrant. With his left hand, he motioned Fabrizio not to interrupt his observation. A moment later he wrote down a figure on a playing card, then, turning around in his chair, he opened his arms to our hero, who rushed into them with tears in his eyes. Father Blanès was his true father.

"I was expecting you," said the priest after the first effusive words of affection. Was he merely speaking as he thought a learned man ought to, or, since he often thought of Fabrizio, had some astrological sign, by pure chance, announced his return?

"My death is now drawing near," said Father Blanès.

"What!" cried Fabrizio, deeply perturbed.

"Yes," continued the priest in a tone that was serious but not at all sad, "five and a half or six and a half months after I've seen you again, my life, having found its full complement of happiness, will be extinguished. *'Come face al mancar dell'alimento.'*" ("Like a little lamp when its oil runs dry.") "Before the supreme moment, I shall probably go for a month or two without speaking, and after that I shall be received into the bosom of our Heavenly Father—provided He finds that I have fulfilled my duty in the post in which He has placed me as a sentinel.

"You're now overcome with fatigue, and your great emotion has made you ready for sleep. Ever since I began expecting you, I've kept a loaf of bread and a bottle of brandy in the big chest that contains my instruments. Give your life that sustenance and try to regain enough strength to listen to me for a while longer. It's within my power to tell you several things before this night has completely given way to day; I now see them much more clearly than I may see them tomorrow. For we are always weak, my child, and we must always take our weakness into account. Tomorrow, perhaps, the old man, the earthly man, will be occupied with preparations for death, and you will have to leave me tomorrow night at nine o'clock."

When Fabrizio had obeyed him in silence, as was his wont, the old priest went on: "So it's true, then, that when you tried to see Waterloo you found nothing at first except a prison?"

"Yes, Father," replied Fabrizio in amazement.

"Well, that was a rare stroke of good fortune, because now, warned by my voice, your soul can prepare itself for another prison which will be far more harsh, far more terrible! You will probably leave it only through a crime, but, thank heaven, that crime will not be committed by you. Never fall into crime, no matter how strongly you may be tempted. I seem to see that it will be a question of killing an innocent man who, without knowing it, has usurped your rights. If you resist the violent temptation that will seem justified by the laws of honor, your life will be very happy in the eyes of men . . . and reasonably happy in the eyes of the sage," he added, after a moment of reflection. "You will die like me, my son, sitting on a wooden seat, far from all luxury,

137

cured of all illusions about luxury, and, like me, without having any serious reproach to make to yourself.

"And now, all discussion of things that lie in the future is ended between us; I could add nothing of any great importance. I have tried in vain to see how long your imprisonment will last; will it be six months, a year, ten years? I have been unable to discover anything. Apparently I have committed some transgression and heaven has seen fit to punish me by the distress of my uncertainty. I have seen only that after your imprisonment, although I do not know whether it will be at the very moment when you leave the prison, there will be what I have called a crime, but fortunately I feel sure that it will not be committed by you. If you are weak enough to let yourself become involved in that crime, the rest of my calculations will be nothing but one long error. In that case, you will not die with peace in your soul, on a wooden seat, and dressed in white." As he spoke these words, Father Blanès tried to stand up.

It was only then that Fabrizio observed the ravages of time: he took nearly a minute to stand up and turn toward Fabrizio, who stood watching him, motionless and silent. The priest then threw himself in his arms, embracing him with great affection. Then he went on, with all his old cheerfulness: "Try to arrange yourself among my instruments so as to be able to sleep with a little comfort. Take my fur-lined coats, you'll find several very valuable ones which Duchess Sanseverina sent me four years ago. She asked me for a prediction concerning you; I didn't send it to her, but I kept her fur-lined coats and her excellent quadrant. Every announcement of the future is an infraction of the rule, and it has this danger: it may alter the event, in which case the whole science collapses like a house of cards. Furthermore, there were some harsh things to be said to that duchess, who is still so pretty.

"By the way, don't be frightened in your sleep by the bells that will make a terrible uproar near your ear when they're rung for the seven o'clock Mass. Later, the great bell that shakes all my instruments will be rung on the floor below. Today is the feast of San Giovita, martyr and soldier. As you know, the little village of Grianta has the same patron saint as the city of Brescia, a fact which, incidentally, was responsible for an amusing mistake on the part of my illustrious master, Giacomo Marini of Ravenna. He informed me several times that I would have a rather distinguished ecclesiastical career. He thought I would be the rector of the magnificent San Giovita church in Brescia; instead, I have been the parish priest of a little village of seven hundred and fifty homes! But everything has been for the best. Less than ten years ago I saw that if I had been a priest in Brescia my destiny would have been to be cast into a prison on a hill in Moravia: the Spielberg.

"Tomorrow, I'll bring you all sorts of delicacies stolen from the great dinner I'm going to give for all the priests of the vicinity who come to take part in my High Mass. I'll bring them to the first floor, but don't try to see me, don't come down to get them until you've heard me leave. You must not see me again *in daylight*, and, since the sun will set tomorrow at twenty-seven minutes past seven, I won't come to embrace you until about eight. And you must leave while the hours are still counted by nine, that is, before the clock has struck ten. Be careful not to let yourself be seen at the windows of the belfry: the police have your description, and they're to some extent under the command of your brother, who's a first-rate tyrant. The Marquis del Dongo is growing weaker," added Blanès sadly, "and if he saw you again he might give you some of his wealth without a written act. But such benefits, tainted with fraud, do not befit a man like you, whose strength will some day lie in his conscience. The marquis abhors his son Ascanio, and it is that son who will inherit the five or six million lire he possesses. That is just. As for you, at his death you will be given a pension of four thousand lire a year, and fifty ells of black cloth for your servants' mourning clothes."

CHAPTER NINE

Fabrizio had been roused to a state of feverish excitement by the old man's discourse, his own concentrated attention, and his extreme fatigue. He had great difficulty in going to sleep, and his sleep was troubled by dreams that were perhaps portents of the future. He was awakened at ten o'clock in the morning by tremors that shook the whole belfry; a terrible noise seemed to be coming from outside. He got up in bewilderment, first thinking that the end of the world had come, then believing himself to be in prison. It took him some time to recognize the sound of the great bell, which forty peasants were ringing in honor of San Giovita; ten would have been enough.

Fabrizio looked around for a place from which he could see without being seen. He discovered that from that great height he could look down into the gardens and even the inner courtyard of his father's castle. He had forgotten this. The idea of that father drawing near the end of his life changed all his feelings. He could see even the sparrows that were looking for crumbs of bread on the large balcony of the dining room. "They're the descendants of the ones I used to tame," he thought. This balcony, like all the other balconies of the castle, was laden with a great number of orange trees in large earthenware vases. He was moved by the sight of them. The whole inner courtyard, thus adorned, with its shadows darkened and sharply defined by the dazzling sunlight, had a truly majestic appearance.

His father's failing health returned to his mind. "But it's really very strange," he thought. "My father is only thirty-five years older than I am; thirty-five and twenty-three make only fifty-eight!" His eyes, fixed on the windows of the bedroom of that stern man who had never loved him, became filled with tears. He shuddered, and a sudden chill ran through his veins when he thought he recognized his father crossing a terrace planted with orange trees which was on the same level as his bedroom; but it was only a servant.

Immediately below the belfry, a number of young girls, dressed in white and divided into groups, were engaged in making patterns of red, blue and yellow flowers on the surface of the street along which the procession was to pass. But there was another sight which spoke more ardently to Fabrizio's soul: from the belfry he could look out over the two branches of the lake for a distance of several leagues, and this sublime view soon made him forget all others, awakening in him the loftiest of feelings. All the memories of his childhood thronged back to besiege his mind; and that day spent imprisoned in a belfry was perhaps one of the happiest of his life.

His happiness carried him to heights of thought that were rather foreign to his character; he considered the various events of life, he, so young, as though he had already reached its furthest limits. "I must admit," he finally said to himself, after several hours of delightful revery, "that since my arrival in Parma I've never known the serene and perfect joy I found in Naples when I galloped along the roads of Vomero or wandered on the shores of Miseno. All the complicated interests of that petty little court have made me petty too. . . . I take no pleasure at all in hating; I even think it would be a sad happiness for me to humiliate my enemies, if I had any. . . . But I have no enemies . . . Just a moment!" he suddenly exclaimed. "I do have an enemy: Giletti. . . . How strange: the pleasure it would give me to see that ugly man go to hell has outlived the very slight fancy I had for Marietta. She's far inferior to the Duchess of A——, whom I was obliged to make love with in Naples because I'd told her I was in love with her. Good God! How often I was bored during those long meetings granted me by that beautiful duchess! I never went through anything like that in the shabby bedroom, which also served as a kitchen, where Marietta received me twice, and for only a few minutes each time.

"My God, what do those people eat! It's pitiful! I should have given her and her *mammacia* a pension of three beefsteaks payable daily. . . . Marietta used to distract me from the petty thoughts which that court put into my mind.

"I might have done well to choose the life of the cafés, as the duchess says; she seemed inclined in that direction, and she's much more intelligent than I am. With her patronage, or even with only the pension of four thousand lire and the capital of forty thousand invested in Lyons, which my mother intends for me, I'd always have a horse and a few scudi to spend on excavations and a collection of ancient relics. Since I seem fated never to know love, such things will always be my great source of happiness. Before I die, I'd like to return to the battlefield of Waterloo and try to identify the meadow where I was so gaily lifted off my horse and seated on the ground. After that pilgrimage, I'd come back often to this sublime lake; nothing so beautiful can be seen anywhere else in the world, for my heart at least. What's the use of going so far to seek happiness when it's right here before my eyes!

"Ah, there's one objection: the police will drive me away from Lake Como. But I'm younger than those who control the actions of the police. Here," he added, laughing, "I'd find no Duchess of A——, but I *would* find one of those girls down there arranging flowers on the pavement, and, to tell the truth, I'd love her just as much. Hypocrisy chills me, even in love, and our great ladies aim at effects that are too sublime. Napoleon has given them ideas about proper conduct and fidelity.

"Good God!" he suddenly exclaimed, drawing his head back from the window, as though afraid of being recognized in spite of the shadow cast by enormous shutters which protected the bells from rain. "Here comes a troop of constables in full uniform!" Ten constables, including four non-commissioned officers, had indeed appeared at the end of the main street of the village. The sergeant in command was posting them at intervals of a hundred paces along the route of the procession. "Everyone knows me here; if I'm seen, I'll go straight from Lake Como to the Spielberg, where they'll put a chain weighing a hundred and ten pounds on each of my legs—and what a painful blow that would be to the duchess!"

It took Fabrizio two or three minutes to recall that, first of all, he was over eighty feet above the ground, that he was standing in a comparatively dark place, that the bright sunlight would shine in the eyes of anyone who might look up in his direction, and that, finally, the people were walking with wide-eyed stares through streets whose houses had all been freshly whitewashed in honor of the feast of San Giovita. Despite this clear reasoning, his Italian soul would have been incapable of any pleasure from then on if he had not shielded himself from the constables' gaze by nailing a tattered piece of cloth over the window after cutting two holes in it for his eyes.

The bells had been making the air quiver for the past ten minutes, the procession was coming out of the church, and the *mortaretti* had begun to go off. Fabrizio turned his head and recognized the little esplanade with a parapet overlooking the lake where in his childhood he had so often exposed himself to the danger of having the *mortaretti* go off between his legs, with the result that his mother liked to have him at her side on the morning of holidays.

It must be explained that *mortaretti* (or little mortars) are nothing but musket barrels sawed off to a length of only four inches; that is why the peasants eagerly gather the musket barrels which, since 1796, European politics has sown so abundantly in the plains of Lombardy. When they have been reduced to a length of four inches, these little guns are loaded up to the muzzle and placed on the ground in a vertical position, then connected with each other by a trail of gunpowder. They are lined up in three ranks like a battalion, numbering two or three hundred in all, somewhere near the route of the procession. When the Blessed Sacrament approaches, the trail of powder is ignited, and then begins a running fire of sharp explosions, thoroughly irregular and ridiculous; the women are always intoxicated with joy. Nothing is so gay as the sound of these *mortaretti* heard from a distance across the lake, and softened by the rippling of the water. This curious sound, which had so often delighted him in his childhood, drove away the somewhat too serious thoughts that had been assailing our hero. He took out the priest's big astronomical telescope and recognized most of the men and women who were taking part in the procession. Many of the charming little girls who had been only eleven or twelve when he left were now magnificent women in the full flower of vigorous youth. They revived his courage; he would gladly have braved the constables in order to speak to them.

After the procession had passed and gone back into the church through a side door which Fabrizio could not see, the heat soon became extreme, even at the top of the belfry. The people went home, and deep silence fell over the whole village. Several boats took on a load of peasants returning to Bellagio, Menaggio and other villages on the lake. Fabrizio could hear the sound of each stroke of the oars, and this simple detail enraptured him; his present joy was composed of all the unhappiness and constraint he had found in the complicated life of a court. How happy he would have been at that moment to glide for a league over the surface of that serene, beautiful lake which reflected so well the depths of the sky!

He heard someone open the downstairs door of the belfry: it was Father Blanès' old maidservant bringing a large basket. It was almost more than he could do to keep from speaking to her. "She has almost as much friendship for me as her master does," he thought, "and besides, I'm leaving at nine o'clock tonight: wouldn't she keep a sworn secret for only a few hours? But I'd displease my friend! I might get him into trouble with the police!" And he let Ghita go without speaking to her. He ate an excellent dinner, then lay down to sleep for a few minutes. He did not awaken till half-past eight in the evening; Father Blanès was shaking his arm, and it was dark.

Blanès was extremely tired; he seemed to have aged fifty years since the night before. He no longer spoke of serious things. "Embrace me," he said to Fabrizio, sitting in his wooden armchair. He clasped him in his arms several times. "The death," he said at length, "which will end this long life of mine will have nothing about it so painful as this separation. I have a purse which I will leave with Ghita, with orders to draw on it for her needs, but to give you whatever is left in it if you should ever come to ask for it. I know her: after those instructions, she's capable, to save money for you,

143

of not buying meat more than four times a year, unless you give her very precise orders. You yourself may be reduced to poverty, and your old friend's pittance may be of use to you. Expect nothing from your brother except atrocious behavior, and try to earn money by some kind of work that will make you useful to society. I foresee strange storms; perhaps in fifty years idlers will no longer be tolerated. You may lose your mother and your aunt, your sisters will have to obey their husbands. . . . Now go, go! Hurry!" cried Blanès urgently. He had just heard a little sound in the clock which indicated that it was about to strike ten; he would not even let Fabrizio embrace him one last time.

'Hurry, hurry!" he cried. "It will take you at least a minute to go down the stairs! Be careful not to fall: that would be a terrible omen!" Fabrizio rushed down the stairs and began running as soon as he reached the square in front of the church. He was just in front of his father's castle when the clock struck ten. Each stroke reverberated in his chest and filled it with strange agitation. He stopped to reflect, or rather to abandon himself to the passionate feelings inspired in him by the contemplation of that majestic edifice which he had judged so coldly the night before.

He was roused from his revery by the sound of footsteps; he looked up and found himself in the midst of four constables. He had two excellent pistols whose priming he had just renewed during dinner. The slight sound he made in cocking them attracted the attention of one of the constables and nearly got him arrested. He saw the danger he was in and considered firing the first shot; it was his right to do so, for it was the only way he had of resisting four well-armed men. Fortunately the constables, who were making their rounds to clear out the taverns, had not shown themselves entirely unresponsive to the courtesies that had been extended to them in several of those friendly establishments; they did not make up their minds quickly enough to do their duty. Fabrizio ran away as fast as his legs could carry him. The constables ran after him a few paces, shouting, "Stop! Stop!" Then all became silent again. After running three hundred yards or so, Fabrizio stopped to catch his breath. "The sound of my pistols nearly got me arrested," he thought. "The duchess would certainly have had good reason to tell me, if I'd ever been allowed to see her lovely eyes again, that my mind takes pleasure in contemplating what will happen in ten years, but forgets to notice what's happening right under my nose."

Fabrizio shuddered as he thought of the danger he had

just escaped. He quickened his pace, but soon he could not restrain himself from running again, which was not too prudent, for it attracted the attention of several peasants who were on their way home. He could not bring himself to stop until he was in the mountains, over a league away from Grianta, and even after he had stopped he broke into a cold sweat at the thought of the Spielberg.

"I'm wild with fear!" he said to himself. Hearing this word, he was almost tempted to feel ashamed. "But isn't my aunt always telling me that what I need most is to learn to forgive myself? I always compare myself with a perfect model which can't exist. All right, I'll forgive myself for my fear, because it's also true that I was quite ready to defend my freedom, and certainly all four of them wouldn't have been left standing to take me off to prison. What I'm doing now is unmilitary: instead of withdrawing rapidly, after having achieved my objective and perhaps given the alarm to my enemies, I'm amusing myself with a whim that's more ridiculous, perhaps, than all the good priest's predictions."

For instead of taking the shortest course and going to the shore of Lake Maggiore, where his boat was now waiting for him, he was making an enormous detour to go and see "his tree." The reader may recall the love Fabrizio bore for a chestnut tree planted by his mother twenty-three years earlier. "It would be worthy of my brother," he thought, "to have had that tree cut down. But people like him are incapable of delicate feelings: I'm sure it's never occurred to him. Besides," he added firmly, "that would not be a bad omen." Two hours later his face took on a look of consternation when he saw that some malicious person, or a storm, had broken one of the young tree's main branches, which was now hanging down, withered. He respectfully severed it with his dagger and carefully smoothed over the cut so that water could not get inside the trunk. Then, although time was very precious to him, since day was about to break, he spent a good hour turning up the soil around his beloved tree. When all these foolish acts had been accomplished, he swiftly headed back toward Lake Maggiore. On the whole, he was not at all sad: the tree had grown well and was sturdier than ever. It had almost doubled its size in the past five years. The broken branch was only an accident of no consequence. Now that he had cut it off, it was no longer harmful to the tree, which would grow even taller, since its branches began further up.

Fabrizio had not gone a league when a bright band of

white light in the east outlined the peaks of the Resegone di Lecco, a famous mountain of the region. The road he was following was becoming covered with peasants, but, instead of having military ideas, he let himself be moved by the sublime or touching aspects of those forests in the vicinity of Lake Como. They are perhaps the finest in the world; I do not mean that they are the forests which bring in the most "shiny francs," as the Swiss say, but that they are those which speak most eloquently to the soul. In Fabrizio's position, honored as he was by the attentions of the Lombardo-Venetian police, listening to the language of the forest was a piece of childish folly. "I'm half a league from the border," he finally said to himself. "I'm going to encounter customs officers and constables making their morning rounds: the fine cloth of my coat will arouse their suspicions, and they'll ask to see my passport. A name meant for prison is clearly spelled out on that passport, so I'm under the pleasant obligation to commit murder. If, as usual, the constables are patrolling in pairs, I can't just stand and wait till one of them grabs me by the collar before I shoot. If he holds onto me for even a few moments as he falls, I'll find myself in the Spielberg."

Horrified above all by this necessity of being the first to shoot, perhaps at an old soldier who had once served under his uncle, Count Pietranera, Fabrizio ran to hide himself in the hollow trunk of a big chestnut tree. He was renewing the priming of his pistols when he heard a man coming toward him through the forest, singing very well an aria by Mercadante, who was in vogue at that time in Lombardy.

"Here's a good omen!" thought Fabrizio. The aria, to which he was listening attentively, took away the little touch of anger that had begun to mingle with his reasoning. He carefully looked up and down the road and saw no one. "The singer must be coming along some side road," he thought. Almost at the same instant he saw a manservant, very neatly dressed in the English style, riding slowly toward him on a mediocre horse, leading a fine thoroughbred that was perhaps a little too lean.

"Ah," thought Fabrizio, "if I reasoned like Count Mosca when he tells me that the danger to which a man exposes himself is always the measure of his rights over his fellow man, I'd shoot that servant through the head, and once I was riding that lean horse, I wouldn't care about all the constables in the world. As soon as I got back to Parma I'd send some money to the man, or his widow. . . . But that would be an atrocity!"

146

CHAPTER TEN

While he was thus moralizing with himself, Fabrizio leapt out onto the highway which runs from Lombardy into Switzerland; at that spot, it is a good four or five feet below the level of the forest. "If my man is frightened," he thought, "he'll gallop away and leave me standing here like a fool." By now he was within ten feet of the servant, who was no longer singing. He could see in his eyes that he was afraid; he was perhaps about to turn his horses around. Without having yet decided on anything, Fabrizio leapt forward and seized the bridle of the lean horse.

"My friend," he said to the servant, "I'm not an ordinary robber, because I'm going to begin by giving you twenty lire, but I'm forced to borrow your horse from you because I'll be killed if I don't get out of here right away. The four Riva brothers are after me; you probably know them: they're great hunters. They just caught me in their sister's bedroom. I jumped out the window and here I am. They've come into the forest after me, with their dogs and guns. I hid in that big hollow chestnut tree because I saw one of them cross the road. Their dogs will soon track me down! I'm going to get on your horse and gallop a league beyond Como, then I'll go to Milan and throw myself at the viceroy's feet. I'll leave your horse at the post house with forty lire for you, if you consent with good grace. If you make the slightest resistance, I'll kill you with these pistols. If, after I'm gone, you put the police on my trail, my cousin, the brave Count Alari, Equerry to the Emperor, will make sure your bones are broken."

Fabrizio was inventing this speech as he went along, speaking in a perfectly peaceful tone.

"And my name is no secret," he said, laughing. "I'm the Marchesino Ascanio del Dongo. My castle is near here, at Grianta. . . . Let go of that horse, damn you!" he said, raising his voice. The servant, stupefied, did not say a word. Fabrizio transferred his pistol to his left hand and took the bridle with his right; the servant let go. Fabrizio leapt onto the horse and set off at a canter. When he had gone three hundred paces or so, he realized that had forgotten to give the man the twenty lire he had promised him. He stopped. There was no one on the road except the servant, who was following

147

him at a gallop. He signaled him with his handkerchief to continue riding toward him, and when he was within fifty paces of him he tossed a handful of coins on the road, then set off again. Far behind him, he saw the servant picking up the money. "There's a truly reasonable man," he said to himself, laughing. "Not one useless word!" He rode swiftly southward, stopped at an isolated house, then set off again several hours later. By two o'clock in the morning he had reached Lake Maggiore. He soon saw his boat floating offshore; at a pre-arranged signal, it came toward him. Seeing no peasant to whom he could hand over the horse, he set the noble animal free.

Three hours later he was in Belgirate. There, in friendly territory, he took a little rest. He was filled with joy: he had succeeded perfectly. Dare we indicate the real causes of his joy? His tree had grown splendidly, and his soul had been refreshed by the deep and tender emotion he had felt in Father Blanès' arms. "Does he really believe," he wondered, "in all those predictions he made to me, or, since my brother has given me the reputation of being a Jacobin, a totally unscrupulous man who will stop at nothing, was he only trying to prevent me from yielding to the temptation to shoot some scoundrel who's done me a bad turn?"

Two days later, Fabrizio was back in Parma, where he greatly amused the duchess and the count by relating to them with the utmost exactitude, as he always did, the whole story of his journey.

On his arrival, he found the porter and all the servants of the Sanseverina palace dressed in mourning.

"Whom have we lost?" he asked the duchess.

"The excellent man who was known as my husband has just died in Baden. He left me this palace. That had already been agreed upon, but as a token of friendship he added a legacy of three hundred thousand lire, which has posed a serious problem for me: I don't want to give it up in favor of his niece, the Marquise Raversi, who plays abominable tricks on me every day. You're an art-lover: find me a good sculptor and I'll erect a tomb for the duke that will cost three hundred thousand lire."

The count began telling anecdotes about the marquise.

"I've tried in vain to win her over by doing favors for her," said the duchess. "As for the duke's nephews, I've made them all colonels or generals. In return, they send me disgusting anonymous letters at least once a month. I've been forced to engage a secretary to read letters of that kind."

"And those anonymous letters are the least of their sins," said Count Mosca. "They manufacture infamous denunciations at an amazing rate. I could have brought that whole clique before the lawcourts a dozen times, and Your Excellency may well imagine," he added, addressing Fabrizio, "whether my good judges would have convicted them."

"There, that's what spoils everything else for me," replied Fabrizio with an artlessness that was amusing to find at a court. "I'd have preferred to see them convicted by magistrates judging according to their conscience."

"Since you travel to develop your knowledge of the world, you'll do me a great favor by giving me the names and addresses of a few judges like that: I'll write to them before I go to bed."

"If I were a minister, that lack of honest judges would offend my self-esteem."

"But it seems to me," replied the count, "that Your Excellency, who has such great love for the French, and who once lent them the support of his invincible arm, is now forgetting one of their great maxims: It's better to kill the devil than to let the devil kill you. I'd like to see how you'd govern these ardent souls, who read the history of the French Revolution all day long, with judges who would acquit the people I accuse. They'd soon reach the point of not convicting even the most obviously guilty scoundrels, and each one of them would regard himself as a Brutus. But I have a bone to pick with you: doesn't your delicate soul feel any remorse over that handsome though slightly lean horse which you just abandoned on the shore of Lake Maggiore?"

"I fully intend," said Fabrizio with great seriousness, "to reimburse the owner of that horse for the advertisements and any other expenses he may incur in getting it back from the peasants who will find it. I'm going to read the Milan newspaper carefully to find a notice of a lost horse; I know the description of this one very well."

"He's really *primitive!*" said the count to the duchess. "And what would have become of Your Excellency," he went on, laughing, "if, while you were galloping at full speed on that borrowed horse, it had decided to stumble? You'd have found yourself in the Spielberg, my dear young nephew, and all my influence would scarcely have been enough to have thirty pounds taken off the weight of the chains attached to your legs. You'd have spent ten years or so in that pleasure resort. Your legs might have become swollen and gangrenous, in which case they'd have been neatly cut off for you. . . ."

"Oh, please!" cried the duchess with tears in her eyes. "Don't carry your gloomy story any further! He's come back to us. . . ."

"And I'm even happier about it than you are, believe me," said the count with great seriousness. "But why didn't this troublesome boy ask me for a passport bearing a suitable name, since he was going into Lombardy? At the first news of his arrest, I'd have gone to Milan, and my friends there would have been willing to close their eyes and assume that their police had arrested a subject of the Prince of Parma. The story of your expedition is charming and amusing, I readily agree," he went on in a less sinister tone. "I like the way you leapt out from the forest onto the highway, but, between you and me, since that servant held your life in his hands, you had a right to take his. We're going to arrange a brilliant career for Your Excellency, at least that's what the duchess has ordered me to do, and I don't think even my worst enemies could accuse me of ever having disobeyed her commands. What a terrible blow it would have been to her and to me if that lean horse had stumbled during the steeple-chase you just ran. It would almost have been better if the horse had broken your neck."

"You're in a very tragic mood this evening, my friend," said the duchess, deeply moved.

"It's because we're surrounded by tragic events," replied the count, also with emotion. "We're not in France, where everything ends with a song or a year or two in prison, and it's really wrong of me to talk about all these things to you in a lighthearted way. . . . And now, my young nephew, suppose I find a way to make you a bishop—because frankly I can't begin by making you Archbishop of Parma, as Her Grace the Duchess, here present, sensibly wants me to do. Once you're in your bishop's palace, where you'll be far away from our wise advice, what will your policy be, more or less?"

"To kill the devil rather than let him kill me, as my friends the French put it so well," replied Fabrizio, his eyes glowing. "To keep by all possible means, including pistol shots, the position you will have secured for me. In the genealogy of the del Dongo family, I've read the story of our ancestor who built the castle of Grianta. Toward the end of his life, his good friend Galeazzo Sforza, Duke of Milan, sent him to visit a fortified castle on our lake: there was fear of another invasion by the Swiss. Just before he left, the Duke of Milan said to him, 'I must at least write a few words of greeting to the governor.' He wrote a short letter and handed it to him, then asked him to give it back so that he could seal it. 'That will be more polite,' he said. Vespasiano del Dongo left, but as he was sailing across the lake he remembered an old Greek tale, for he was a learned man. He opened his master's letter and found that it contained an order, addressed to the governor, to put him to death as soon as he arrived. Sforza, too preoccupied with the trick he was playing on our ancestor, had left a space between his signature and the last line of the letter. In that space, Vespasiano del Dongo wrote an order stating that he was to be recognized as governor-general of all the fortresses on the lake, then destroyed the top of the letter. His authority was duly acknowledged when he arrived at the fortress. He then threw the governor down a well, declared war against Sforza, and after a few years exchanged his fortress for those vast estates which have made the fortune of every branch of our family, and which will some day give me an income of four thousand lire a year."

"You talk like an academician!" exclaimed the count, laughing. "That was a fine stroke of genius you just told us about, but it's only once every ten years that a man has the amusing opportunity to do exciting things like that. A man who's half idiotic, but attentive and prudent every day, can very often enjoy the pleasure of triumphing over men of imagination. It was through a foolish flight of imagination that Napoleon surrendered himself to the prudent 'John Bull' instead of trying to escape to America. John Bull, in his countinghouse, had a good laugh at that letter in which he refers to Themistocles. In all ages, the base Sancho Panzas of this world have won out over the sublime Don Quixotes in the long run. If you're willing not to do anything extraordinary, I have no doubt that you will be a highly respected if not highly respectable bishop. However, my remark still holds good: Your Excellency acted recklessly in that affair of the horse, and came within a hairsbreadth of lifelong imprisonment."

These last words made Fabrizio shudder, and he was overcome with deep amazement. "Was that the imprisonment I was threatened with?" he wondered. "Was that the crime I was not to commit?" Blanès' predictions, which he had made light of as prophecies, now assumed in his eyes all the importance of genuine omens.

"What's the matter with you?" the duchess asked him in surprise. "The count has given you gloomy ideas."

"I've been enlightened by a new truth, and instead of rebelling against it, my mind has adopted it. It's true, I came very close to an endless imprisonment! But that servant looked so neat and trim in his English coat! What a shame it would have been to kill him!"

The count was delighted by his little air of virtue.

"He's excellent in every way," he said, looking at the duchess. "Let me tell you, my friend, that you've made a conquest, and the most desirable on of all, perhaps."

"Ah," thought Fabrizio, "here comes a joke about little Marietta!" He was mistaken; the count went on:

"Your *evangelical* simplicity has won the heart of our venerable archbishop, Father Landriani. One of these days we'll make a vicar-general of you, and the delightful part of the jest is that the three present vicars-general, all hard-working, capable men, two of whom, I believe, were vicars-general before you were born, will write a fine letter to their archbishop requesting that you be given the highest rank among them. They will base their attitude on your virtues, first of all, and then on the fact that you're the grand-nephew of the celebrated Archbishop Ascanio del Dongo. When I learned of the respect in which your virtues were held, I immediately promoted the senior vicar-general's nephew to the rank of captain; he'd been a lieutenant ever since the siege of Tarragona by Marshal Suchet."

"Go right now, dressed just as you are, to pay an affectionate visit to your archbishop!" cried the duchess. "Tell him about your sister's marriage; when he learns that she's going to be a duchess, he'll find you more 'apostolic' than ever. But remember: you know nothing of what the count has just told you about your future appointment."

Fabrizio hurried to the archbishop's palace. His conduct there was simple and modest; this was a manner he could assume all too easily, whereas he had to make an effort to play the part of a great nobleman. As he listened to Archbishop Landriani's rather lengthy stories, he said to himself, "Should I have shot the servant who was leading that lean horse?" His reason said yes, but his heart could not accustom itself to the bloody image of the handsome young man falling disfigured from his horse.

"I wonder if the prison that would have swallowed me up if my horse had stumbled was the same prison with which I'm threatened by so many omens."

This question was of the utmost importance to him, and the archbishop was pleased by his air of profound attention.

CHAPTER ELEVEN

On leaving the archbishop's palace, Fabrizio hurried to the house in which Marietta lived. From a distance he heard the loud voice of Giletti, who had sent out for wine and was regaling himself with his friends the candle-snuffers and the prompter. Marietta's *mammacia*, who acted as her mother, came out alone in answer to Fabrizio's signal.

"Things have been happening since the last time you were here!" she said. "Some of our actors have been accused of celebrating the great Napoleon's name-day with an orgy, so we've all been called Jacobins, and our poor little troupe has been ordered to leave the State of Parma, and long live Napoleon! But they say the minister shelled out some money. Anyway, one thing is sure: Giletti has money. I don't know how much, but I've seen him with a handful of scudi. Our manager has given Marietta five scudi for her traveling expenses to Mantua and Venice, and he's given me one. She's still very much in love with you, but she's afraid of Giletti. Three days ago, after our last performance, he was determined to kill her. He gave her two tremendous slaps, but that's not the worst of it: he tore her blue shawl, too. It would be very nice of you if you'd give her another blue shawl. We'd say we won it in a lottery. The drum major of the carabineers is putting on a fencing match tomorrow, you'll find the time posted on every street corner. Come to see us: if Giletti has gone to the fencing match and it looks as though he'll be gone for a long time, I'll stand at the window and give you a signal to come up. Try to bring us something nice, and Marietta will be madly in love with you."

As he descended the winding stairs of that squalid, dilapidated house, Fabrizio was filled with compunction. "I haven't changed," he thought. "All those fine resolutions I made on the shore of our lake, when I was looking at life so philosophically, have flown away. My mind wasn't in its usual state; the whole thing was a dream, and it's vanished in the face of stern reality."

When he entered the Sanseverina palace at eleven o'clock that evening, he said to himself, "Now's the time to act." But it was in vain that he sought in his heart the courage to speak with sublime sincerity, which had seemed so easy

153

to him during the night he had spent on the shore of Lake Como. "I'm going to offend the person I love most in all the world; if I speak, I'll sound like a bad actor. I'm not really worth anything except in certain moments of exaltation."

"The count has been wonderfully kind to me," he said to the duchess after he had told her about his visit to the archbishop. "I appreciate it all the more because I have the impression that he has only a very moderate liking for me, so my conduct toward him must be perfectly correct. He has his excavations at Sanguigna, which he's still passionately interested in, judging from the trip he made day before yesterday, at least: he galloped twelve league to spend two hours with his workmen. If they find fragments of statues in the ancient temple whose foundations have just been uncovered, he's afraid they'll steal them from him. I have a mind to offer to spend thirty-six hours at Sanguigna. I'm going to see the archbishop again tomorrow at five o'clock; I can leave in the evening and make the trip during the coolness of the night."

At first the duchess made no reply.

"You seem to be looking for excuses to stay away from me," she said at length, with great affection. "You've just come back from Belgirate, and already you've found a reason for leaving again."

"Here's a good chance to speak to her," thought Fabrizio. "But on the lake I was a little mad: in my enthusiasm for sincerity, I didn't see that my compliment ends in a piece of impertinence. I'd say to her, 'I love you with the most devoted affection, and so on, but my heart is incapable of real love,' and doesn't that amount to saying, 'I can see that you're in love with me, but I must warn you that I can't pay you back in the same coin'? If she's in love with me, she may be angry at me for having discovered it, and if she feels nothing but friendship for me, she'll be revolted by my impudence. . . . And that's the kind of offense that's never forgiven."

As he was pondering these important ideas, Fabrizio, unaware of what he was doing, was pacing up and down the drawing room with the grave and lofty air of a man who sees disaster staring him in the face.

The duchess watched him with admiration. He was no longer the boy she had known as a baby, no longer the nephew who was always ready to obey her: he was a serious, dignified man whom it would be delightful to be loved by. She stood up from the ottoman on which she had been sitting, threw herself in his arms with great emotion and said, "Do you really want to run away from me?"

"No," he replied with the air of a Roman emperor, "but I want to act wisely."

This answer was capable of various interpretations; he did not have the courage to go any further and run the risk of offending that admirable woman. He was too young, too susceptible to emotion; his mind supplied him with no gracious expressions in which to convey the meaning of what he wanted to say. In a spontaneous outburst of feeling, and despite all his reasoning, he took that charming woman in his arms and covered her with kisses. Just then they heard the sound of the count's carriage entering the courtyard, and the count himself came into the drawing room immediately afterward. He seemed deeply moved.

"You've aroused some singular passions," he said to Fabrizio, who was almost stunned by the remark. "This evening," he went on, "the archbishop had the audience which His Serene Highness grants him every Thursday. The prince has just told me that the archbishop seemed deeply perturbed; he began with an erudite speech that he'd learned by heart, and which was totally incomprehensible to the prince at first. He ended by declaring that it was important for the Church of Parma that *Monsignore* Fabrizio del Dongo be appointed as his chief vicar-general, and that later, after completing his twenty-fourth year, he should be appointed as his coadjutor, *with the right of future succession.* I was alarmed to hear this, I admit. It seemed to me that the archbishop was rushing things a little, and I was afraid of an angry outburst from the prince. But he looked at me and laughed, then said to me in French, 'That was your doing, monsieur.'

"'I swear before God and Your Highness,' I cried out with all possible earnestness, 'that I had absolutely no knowledge of the words "future succession."' Then I told him the truth, what we were saying in this very room only a few hours ago. I added, with feeling, that I'd regard myself as overwhelmed with favor by His Highness if he would eventually deign to grant me a minor bishopric to begin with. He must have believed me, because he saw fit to be gracious. He said to me, with all possible simplicity, 'This is an official matter between the archbishop and myself; you're not involved in any way. The good prelate delivered a long, boring report to me, and then he made an official proposal. I answered coldly that the man in question was very young and, more important, very new at my court, and that it would almost seem as though I were paying a draft drawn on me by the emperor if I were to give the prospect of such a lofty position to the son of one of the high officials of his Lombardo-Venetian kingdom. The archbishop protested that no such recommendation had been made. It was a stupid thing to say to *me*, and I was surprised to hear it from a man of his shrewdness. But he's always disconcerted when he speaks to me, and this evening he was more upset than usual, which gave me the idea that he was especially eager to have his request granted. I told him I knew better than he did that there had been no recommendation in del Dongo's favor from any high quarter, that no one at my court denied his ability, that his moral reputation was not too bad, but that I was afraid he might be susceptible to *enthusiasm*, and that I'd promised myself never to give important positions to any madmen of that species, with whom a prince can never be sure of anything.

" 'Then I had to endure a grandiloquent speech that was almost as long as the first one: the archbishop sang the praises of the enthusiasm of the House of God. "You clumsy fool," I thought, "you're going astray, you're endangering the appointment, which was almost granted; you should have stopped short and thanked me effusively." But no: he continued his homily with ridiculous intrepidity. I tried to think of an answer that wouldn't be too unfavorable to young del Dongo. I found one, and a rather good one, too, as you can judge for yourself: "Pious VII was a great pope and a great saint," I said to him. "He alone, among all sovereigns, dared to say no to the tyrant who saw all Europe at his feet. He was susceptible to enthusiasm, and that was what had led him, when he was Bishop of Imola, to write his famous *Pastoral Letter of Citizen Cardinal Chiaramonti*, in support of the cisalpine republic."

" 'My poor archbishop was stupefied. To complete his stupefaction, I said to him very seriously, "Good-by, Monsignor. I shall take twenty-four hours to reflect on your proposal." The poor man added a few supplications, badly worded and rather inopportune after I'd said the word "good-by." And now, Count Mosca della Rovere, I charge you to tell the duchess that I will not postpone for twenty-four hours an action which may be agreeable to her; sit down there and write the archbishop the letter of approval that will settle the whole matter.'

"I wrote the letter," concluded the count, "and he signed it. Then he said to me, 'Take it to the duchess without delay.

Here it is; it has provided me with a pretext for giving myself the pleasure of seeing you again this evening."

The duchess read the letter with ecstatic joy. During the count's long story, Fabrizio had had time to regain his composure. He showed no surprise at what had happened, he took it like a true nobleman who had always assumed that he was entitled to those extraordinary advancements, to those strokes of good fortune which would make a commoner lose his reason. He expressed his gratitude, but in measured terms, and ended by saying to the count, "A good courtier should flatter the dominant passions of his superiors. Yesterday you expressed a fear that your workmen at Sanguigna would steal any fragments of ancient statues they might discover. I, too, am very fond of excavations, so, with your permission, I'll go and see the workmen. Tomorrow evening, after properly expressing my thanks to the prince and the archbishop, I'll leave for Sanguigna."

"But," said the duchess to the count, "can you guess the cause of the good archbishop's sudden devotion to Fabrizio?"

"I don't need to guess. The vicar-general whose brother is a captain said to me yesterday, 'Father Landriani goes on the sound principle that an archbishop is superior to his coadjutor. He's overjoyed to have done a favor for a del Dongo, and to have him under his authority. Everything that calls attention to Fabrizio's high birth adds to the archbishop's happiness: he has a man like that as his assistant! In the second place, he's taken a liking to *Monsignore* Fabrizio; he doesn't feel at all shy in his presence. And finally, for the past ten years he's been nourishing a vigorous hatred of the Bishop of Piacenza, who openly proclaims his intention of succeeding him as Archbishop of Parma, and who, furthermore, is a miller's son. It's with a view to this future succession that the Bishop of Piacenza has established close relations with the Marquise Raversi, and those relations are now making the archbishop tremble for the success of his favorite scheme: to have a del Dongo on his staff, and give him orders.'"

Two days later, early in the morning, Fabrizio was directing the work of excavation at Sanguigna, opposite Colorno (which is the Versailles of the Princes of Parma). The excavations extended into the plain near the highway that runs from Parma to the bridge of Casalmaggiore, the first town in Austrian territory. The workmen were digging a long trench across the plain, eight feet deep and as narrow as possible. They were seeking, along the ancient Roman road, the ruins of a second temple which, it was said in the region,

157

had still been in existence in the Middle Ages. Despite the prince's orders, several peasants were not without envy as they watched those long trenches crossing their property. No matter what was said to them, they persisted in believing that a search was being made for some treasure. Fabrizio's presence was especially valuable in preventing disturbances. He was not bored; he followed the work with passionate interest. Now and then the workmen would turn up some medal or other, and he did not want to give them time to make arrangements among themselves for hiding it and carrying it away.

The weather was beautiful; it was about six o'clock in the morning. He had borrowed an old single-barreled gun. He shot a few larks. One of them fell on the highway, wounded. On his way to pick it up, he saw a carriage in the distance, coming from Parma and heading toward the frontier at Casalmaggiore. He had just reloaded his gun when he recognized Marietta in the dilapidated carriage, which was approaching him at a very slow pace. Beside her sat the tall, lanky Giletti and the old woman she passed off as her mother.

Giletti imagined that Fabrizio was standing in the middle of the road, with a gun in his hand, to insult him and perhaps even to take Marietta away from him. Being a man of valor, he leapt out of the carriage. In his left hand he held a big, rusty pistol, and in his right a sword still in its scabbard, which he used when the needs of the troupe made it necessary for him to play the part of a marquis.

"Bandit!" he shouted. "I'm glad to see you here a league away from the border! I'm going to take care of you right now—your purple stockings won't protect you here!"

Fabrizio was making eyes at Marietta and paying little attention to Giletti's jealous cries when suddenly he saw the barrel of the rusty pistol only three feet from his chest. He barely had time to knock it aside, using his gun as a club. The pistol went off, but hit no one.

"Stop, damn you!" Giletti shouted at the driver of the carriage. At the same time, he had enough presence of mind to seize the end of his adversary's gun and hold it away from himself. He and Fabrizio began tugging at it with all their might. Giletti, much stronger, began advancing steadily by placing one hand in front of the other, and he was about to take complete possession of the gun when Fabrizio fired it to prevent him from using it. He had clearly seen that the end of the barrel was more than three inches above Giletti's shoulder; the shot went off near his ear. He was slightly stunned for a moment, but he quickly recovered.

"Oh, so you want to blow my brains out, you dirty coward! I'll show you!"

Giletti threw off the scabbard from his marquis' sword and rushed at Fabrizio with admirable speed. Having no weapon, Fabrizio gave himself up for lost.

He fled toward the carriage, which had stopped a dozen paces behind Giletti. He passed to the left of it, grabbed its springs with one hand, quickly swung around and passed near the door on the right side, which was open. Giletti, running after him on his long legs, did not think to check his motion by grabbing the springs of the carriage and went on for a few paces in his original direction before he could stop. As Fabrizio passed by the open door, he heard Marietta say to him softly, "Be careful, he'll kill you! Here!"

At the same moment, he saw a big hunting knife fall from the carriage door. He bent down to pick it up, but just then he was struck on the shoulder by Giletti's sword. When he stood up he found himself only six inches away from Giletti, who struck him a furious blow with the pommel of his sword. The blow was so powerful that it completely dazed him; at that moment, he was on the verge of being killed. Fortunately for him, Giletti was still too close to him to be able to thrust the point of his sword into him. When he regained his senses, Fabrizio ran away as fast as he could. He threw off the sheath of the hunting knife as he ran, then quickly turned around and found himself three paces away from Giletti, who was pursuing him. Fabrizio stabbed him as he hurtled toward him. Giletti had time to deflect the knife a little with his sword, but the blade plunged into his left cheek. He passed close by Fabrizio, who felt a sharp pain in his thigh: Giletti had taken out his own knife and stabbed him with it. Fabrizio leapt to his right and turned around. The two adversaries were now at last within proper fighting distance of each other.

Giletti was swearing like a soul in hell. "I'll slit your throat, you damned priest!" he kept repeating. Fabrizio was completely out of breath and unable to speak; the blow on the face from the pommel of Giletti's sword was causing him great pain, and his nose was bleeding abundantly. He parried several thrusts with his hunting knife and made several lunges without knowing too clearly what he was doing; he had a vague impression that he was in a public fencing match. This idea had been suggested to him by the twenty-five to thirty workmen who had formed a circle around the two combatants, though at a respectful distance from them, for they were constantly running and lunging at each other.

The fight seemed to be slackening a little, and the blows were no longer following one another with the same speed, when Fabrizio said to himself, "Judging from the pain I feel in my face, he must have disfigured me." Filled with rage by this idea, he leapt at his enemy with the point of his knife held outward. It entered the right side of Giletti's chest and came out near the left shoulder. At the same moment, Giletti's sword plunged to the hilt through Fabrizio's upper arm, but the wound was not serious, for the blade merely slipped under the skin.

Giletti had fallen; as Fabrizio moved toward him, looking at the knife in his left hand, this hand opened mechanically and let the weapon drop to the ground.

"The scoundrel is dead," thought Fabrizio. He looked at Giletti's face: blood was streaming from his mouth. He ran to the carriage.

"Do you have a mirror?" he cried out to Marietta. She looked at him, deathly pale, and did not answer. With great composure, the old woman opened a green sewing bag and gave Fabrizio a little mirror with a handle no longer than his hand. He looked at himself in it and felt his face all over. "My eyes are undamaged," he thought. "That's one important thing I don't have to worry about." He looked at his teeth: they had not been broken. "Then why am I in such pain?" he said to himself, half aloud.

The old woman answered him: "It's because the top of your cheek was crushed between the pommel of Giletti's sword and the bone underneath. Your cheek is terribly swollen and bruised. Put some leeches on it right away and it won't be anything serious."

"Ah, leeches right away!" said Fabrizio, laughing; and he recovered all his self-possession. He saw that the workmen were standing around Giletti, looking at him without daring to touch him.

"Don't just stare at him, help him!" he shouted to them. "Take off his coat...." He was going to continue, but when he looked up he saw five or six men three hundred paces away on the highway, walking steadily toward the scene of the fight.

"They're constables!" he thought. "Since a man has been killed, they'll arrest me and I'll have the honor of making a formal entry into the city of Parma. What a story for the courtiers who are friendly with the Marquise Raversi and hate my aunt!"

Immediately, with lightning speed, he threw the gaping workmen all the money he had in his pockets and leapt into the carriage.

"Stop the constables from following me," he shouted to the workmen, "and I'll make your fortunes. Tell them I'm innocent, that the man *attacked me and tried to kill me!*

"And you," he said to the driver, "whip your horses into a gallop! You'll have four gold napoleons if you cross the Po before those men can catch me."

"All right," said the driver, "but don't be afraid: those men are on foot, so all my little horses have to do is trot to leave them far behind." So saying, he set off at a gallop.

Our hero was offended by the driver's use of the word "afraid," because he had actually been terribly afraid after being struck on the face by the pommel of Giletti's sword.

"We may meet some men on horseback coming toward us," said the prudent driver, thinking of the four napoleons, "and the men behind them may shout to them to stop us." By this he meant, "Reload your guns. . . ."

"Oh, you're so brave, my little *monsignore!*" cried Marietta, kissing Fabrizio. The old woman was looking out the window of the carriage; after a time she drew back her head and calmly said to Fabrizio, "There's nobody following you, sir, and there's nobody on the road ahead of us. You know how strict the Austrian police are: if they see you galloping like this along the bank of the Po, they'll arrest you, that's one thing you can be sure of."

Fabrizio looked out the window and said to the driver, "Slow down to a trot." Then he asked the old woman, "What kind of a passport do you have?"

"Three instead of one," she answered, "and each one of them cost us four lire: isn't that an outrage for poor dramatic artists who have to travel all year round? Here's the passport of Signor Giletti, dramatic artist: that will be you. And here are our two passports, Marietta's and mine. But Giletti had all our money in his pocket—what's to become of us?"

"How much did he have?" asked Fabrizio.

"Forty beautiful scudi," said the old woman.

"She means six, plus some small change," said Marietta, laughing. "I won't let my little *monsignore* be cheated!"

"Isn't it only natural, sir," said the old woman calmly, "that I should try to get thirty-four scudi out of you? What's thirty-four scudi to you? And we've lost our protector! Now

161

who's going to find lodgings for us, and argue about prices with the drivers when we travel, and make everybody afraid? Giletti wasn't handsome, but he was useful, and if Marietta here hadn't been such a fool as to fall in love with you right away, he'd never have noticed anything, and you'd have given us a lot of money. We're very poor now, believe me."

Fabrizio was touched; he took out his purse and gave the old woman a few napoleons.

"As you can see for yourself," he said to her, "I have only fifteen left, so there's no use playing any more tricks on me."

Marietta threw her arms around his neck and the old woman kissed his hands. The carriage was still moving along at a slow trot.

When they saw in the distance the yellow barriers with black stripes which indicate the beginning of Austrian territory, the old woman said to Fabrizio, "You'd better go through on foot with Giletti's passport in your pocket. We'll stop awhile, with the excuse of making ourselves look more presentable. Besides, the customs officials will inspect our baggage. If you take my advice, you'll stroll casually through Casalmaggiore. You'll even go into a café and drink a glass of brandy. Then, as soon as you're outside the town, go like the wind! The police are devilishly sharp in Austrian territory; they'll soon know there's been a man killed. You're traveling with a passport that isn't yours, and that's enough to get you two years in prison all by itself. Turn right when you leave the town and go on to the Po. When you get there, hire a boatman to take you to Ravenna or Ferrara. Get out of the Austrian States as fast as you can. You can buy another passport from some customs official for forty lire. The one you have now would be fatal. Don't forget: you've killed a man."

As he walked toward the pontoon bridge of Casalmaggiore, Fabrizio carefully read Giletti's passport. Our hero was terribly afraid; he recalled vividly everything Count Mosca had told him about how dangerous it would be for him to return to the Austrian States. And now, two hundred paces ahead, he saw the fateful bridge that was going to bring him into those states, whose capital, in his eyes, was the Spielberg. But how could he do otherwise? The Duchy of Modena, which borders the State of Parma to the south, returned its fugitives in accordance with a special agreement, and the border of the state lying in the mountains in the direction of Genoa was too far away. His misadventure would be known in Parma long before he could reach those mountains. He therefore had no choice but to enter the Austrian states on the left bank of the Po. It would probably take thirty-six to forty-eight hours before a message could reach the Austrian authorities asking them to arrest him. After careful reflection, he set fire to his passport with his lighted cigar: in Austrian territory, it was better for him to be a vagabond than Fabrizio del Dongo, and it was possible that he might be searched.

Aside from the perfectly natural repugnance he felt at the idea of entrusting his life to the passport of the unfortunate Giletti, this document presented certain material difficulties: Fabrizio's height was five feet five at the most, not five feet ten, as was indicated on the passport; he was nearly twenty-four years old and looked younger, while Giletti had been thirty-nine. We must admit that our hero spent a good half-hour pacing up and down an embankment that ran beside the Po, near the pontoon bridge, before he made up his mind to come down to it.

"What advice would I give to someone else in my place?" he asked himself at length. "To go across, obviously, because it's dangerous to stay in the State of Parma: a constable may have been sent in pursuit of the man who killed another man, even if it was in self-defense." He went through his pockets, tore up all his papers and kept nothing except his handkerchief and his cigar case; it was important for him to shorten the examination he would have to undergo. He thought of one formidable objection which might be raised, and to which he could find only unsatisfactory answers: he was going to say that his name was Giletti, but all his linen was marked with the initials "F.D."

As can be seen, Fabrizio was one of those unfortunate people who are tormented by their imaginations; it is a rather common fault among intelligent people in Italy. A French soldier of equal or even inferior courage would have walked across the bridge immediately, without thinking of any difficulty in advance. But he would also have exercised all his cool-headedness, and Fabrizio was far from cool-headed when, at the end of the bridge, a little man dressed in gray said to him, "Come into the police office to have your passport checked."

The office had dingy walls studded with nails from which the officials' pipes and dirty hats were hanging. The big pine desk behind which these officials were ensconced was spotted with ink and wine. Two or three thick registers with green leather bindings bore stains of all colors, and the edges of their pages had been blackened by the touch of many hands.

Piled up on top of the registers were three magnificent laurel wreaths which had been used two days earlier for one of the emperor's festivals.

Fabrizio was struck by all these details and they gripped his heart: this was the price he had to pay for the magnificent, immaculate luxury that shone in his charming apartment in the Sanseverina palace. He was forced to enter that dirty office and appear in it as an inferior. He was about to undergo an interrogation.

The official who put out his yellow hand to take Fabrizio's passport was a short, swarthy man with a brass ornament on his tie. "He's an irritable commoner," thought Fabrizio. The official seemed greatly surprised when he read the passport. He studied it for a good five minutes.

"You've had an accident," he said to the stranger, glancing at his cheek.

"Our driver overturned the carriage at the foot of the embankment of the Po."

Then silence fell again, and the official cast fierce glances at the traveler.

"I know what he's going to do," thought Fabrizio: "he's going to say he's sorry to have to tell me such bad news, but that I'm under arrest." All sorts of wild ideas ran through our hero's mind, which was not very logical at that moment. For example, he thought of running out through the office door, which had been left open. "I'll take off my coat and jump into the Po, I can probably swim across it. Anything is better than the Spielberg." The police official was staring at him as he calculated his chances of succeeding in this desperate attempt. Their faces were both interesting to see. The presence of danger gives genius to the sensible man: it raises him, so to speak, above himself; in the man of imagination, it inspires dramatic fancies, bold, it is true, but often absurd.

Our hero's indignant face made a striking sight as he underwent the scrutiny of the police official decked out with his brass ornaments. "If I killed him," thought Fabrizio, "I'd be convicted of murder and sentenced to twenty years at hard labor, or to death, which would be much less horrible than the Spielberg, with a hundred-and-twenty-pound chain on each leg and nothing to eat but eight ounces of bread a day, and that lasts for twenty years, so I wouldn't get out till I was forty-four." His logic was overlooking the fact that, since he had burned his own passport, there was nothing to indicate to the police official that he was the rebel Fabrizio del Dongo.

Our hero was already sufficiently afraid, as we have seen; his fear would have been much greater if he had known the thoughts that were going through the official's mind. This man was a friend of Giletti's, so it is easy to imagine his surprise when he saw his passport in the hands of someone else. His first impulse was to have the stranger arrested, but then it occurred to him that Giletti might well have sold his passport to this handsome young man, who had apparently committed some crime in Parma. "If I arrest him," he thought, "Giletti will be in trouble, because it will be easily discovered that he's sold his passport; on the other hand, what will my superiors say when they find out that I, a friend of Giletti's, have stamped a visa on his passport when it was handed to me by someone else?" He stood up, yawning, and said to Fabrizio, "Just a minute, sir." Then, obeying a policeman's habit, he added, "A difficulty has come up." Fabrizio said to himself, "My escape is going to come up."

The official left the office, leaving the door open, and the passport remained on the pine desk. "The danger is obvious," thought Fabrizio. "I'll take my passport and slowly walk back across the bridge. If the constable questions me, I'll say I've forgotten to have my passport stamped by the police chief of the last village in the State of Parma." He already had the passport in his hand when, to his inexpressible astonishment, he heard the official with the brass ornaments say, "I can't go on, this heat is stifling me! I'm going to the café for a cup of coffee. Go into the office when you've finished your pipe, there's a passport to be stamped; the foreigner is already there."

Fabrizio, who was tiptoeing out of the office, found himself face to face with a handsome young man who was saying to himself with a singsong intonation, "All right, let's stamp that passport, and I'll put my flourish on it."

"Where do you wish to go, sir?"

"To Mantua, Venice and Ferrara."

"Ferrara it is," replied the official, whistling. He picked up a stamp, printed the visa on the passport in blue ink and quickly wrote the words "Mantua, Venice and Ferrara" in the space left blank by the stamp. Then he waved his hand in the air several times, signed his name and dipped his pen again for the flourish, which he made slowly and with infinite care. Fabrizio followed every movement of his pen. The official looked at his flourish with satisfaction, added five or six dots to it and finally handed the passport back to Fabrizio, saying in a lighthearted tone, "Have a good trip, sir."

Fabrizio was walking away at a pace whose swiftness he was trying to conceal when he felt someone seize his left arm. He instinctively clutched the handle of his dagger, and if he had not seen that he was surrounded by buildings he might have done something rash. Seeing his alarm, the man who was holding his arm said to him by way of apology, "But I called you three times, sir, and you didn't answer. Do you have anything to declare to the customs?"

"I have nothing on me but my handkerchief. I'm going to do some hunting with one of my relatives who lives near here."

He would have been at a loss if he had been asked to name this relative. Because of the heat and his emotions, he was as wet as if he had fallen into the Po. "I don't lack courage when I'm dealing with actors," he thought, "but officials with brass ornaments throw me into a panic. I'll write a comic sonnet on that theme for the duchess."

As soon as he entered Casalmaggiore, he turned right and walked along a dingy street which leads down to the Po. "I have great need of the help of Bacchus and Ceres," he said to himself, and he entered a shop in front of which hung a gray dishcloth attached to a stick. The word *"Trattoria"* was written on this cloth. A tattered bedsheet, supported by two thin wooden hoops and hanging down to within three feet of the ground, sheltered the doorway of the *trattoria* from the direct rays of the sun. Inside, a half-naked and very pretty woman received our hero with respect, which gave him great pleasure. He hastened to tell her that he was starving. While she was preparing a meal for him, a man of about thirty came in without greeting anyone. Suddenly he stoop up from the bench on which he had casually thrown himself down and said to Fabrizio, *"Eccellenza, la riverisco."* ("I salute Your Excellency.") Fabrizio was in a very cheerful mood by now; instead of forming sinister plans, he answered, laughing, "And how the devil do you know My Excellency?"

"What! Your Excellency doesn't recognize Ludovico, one of Duchess Sanseverina's coachmen? We used to go to Sacca ever year, but I always caught a fever there, so I asked the duchess for a pension and retired. And now I'm rich: instead of twelve scudi a year, which was the most I had a right to expect, the duchess told me she was going to give me a pension of twenty-four scudi so that I'd have time to write sonnets, because I'm a poet in my dialect, and the count told me that if I ever had any troubles, all I had to do was come and talk to him. I had the honor of driving you for a stage,

166

Monsignore, when you went to make your retreat, like a good Christian, at the Charterhouse of Velleia."

Fabrizio looked at the man and recognized him vaguely. He had been one of the most carefully dressed coachmen of the Sanseverina palace. Now that he was rich, he said, his only clothes were a coarse, torn shirt and a pair of canvas breeches, once dyed black, which hardly came down to his knees; a pair of shoes and a battered hat completed his outfit. Furthermore, he had not shaved for two weeks. As he ate his omelet, Fabrizio spoke with him exactly as though their conversation were between equals. He gathered that Ludovico was the hostess's lover. He quickly finished his meal, then said to him softly, "I have something to discuss with you."

"You can speak freely in front of her, Your Excellency, she's really a very good woman," said Ludovico in an affectionate tone.

"Well, my friends," said Fabrizio without hesitation, "I'm in trouble and I need your help. First of all, let me tell you that there's nothing political about my case: it's just that I've killed a man who tried to murder me because I spoke to his mistress."

"Poor young man!" said the hostess.

"You can count on me, Your Excellency!" cried the coachman, his eyes aflame with the most ardent devotion. "Where do you wish to go?"

"To Ferrara. I have a passport, but I'd prefer not to speak to the police: they may have heard about what I've done."

"When did you kill that man?"

"At six o'clock this morning."

"Is there any blood on your clothes, Your Excellency?" asked the hostess.

"I was thinking of that," said the coachman, "and besides, the cloth of his clothes is too fine: you don't see anything like it very often in our countryside, and it would attract attention. I'll go and buy some clothes from the Jew. You're about my height, Your Excellency, but more slender."

"Please stop calling me 'Your Excellency,' it may attract attention."

"All right, Your Excellency," replied the coachman, leaving the tavern.

"Just a minute!" cried Fabrizio. "What about money? Come back!"

"Don't worry about money!" said the hostess. "He has sixty-seven scudi and they're all at your service. And I," she

167

added, lowering her voice, "have about forty scudi which I'm happy to offer you; we don't always have money on us when accidents like that happen."

Because of the heat, Fabrizio had taken off his coat when he first entered the *trattoria*.

"That vest you're wearing may make trouble for us if someone comes in—anyone would notice its fine 'English cloth' right away." She gave our fugitive a black vest belonging to her husband. A tall young man, dressed with a certain elegance, came into the tavern through an inside door.

"This is my husband," said the hostess. "Pietro Antonio," she said to him, "this gentleman is a friend of Ludovico's. He had an accident this morning on the other side of the river, and he wants to escape to Ferrara."

"Well then, we'll take him there," said her husband very politely. "We have Carlo Giuseppe's boat."

Owing to another weakness of our hero, which we shall admit as naturally as we have described his fear in the police office at the end of the bridge, he had tears in his eyes: he was deeply touched by the perfect devotion he had found in these peasants. He was also thinking of his aunt's characteristic kindness. He wished he were able to make these people's fortunes. Ludovico came back, carrying a bundle.

"Well, good-by," the husband said to him in a friendly tone.

"No, not yet!" said Ludovico, greatly alarmed. "People are beginning to talk about you, Your Excellency. They noticed that you hesitated before turning into our *vicolo*, and that you left the main street like a man who wanted to hide."

"Hurry upstairs to the bedroom," said the husband.

This bedroom was big and beautiful; the two windows were covered with gray cloth instead of glass, and there were four beds, each six feet wide and five feet high.

"Hurry, hurry!" said Ludovico. "There's a conceited ass of a constable who came here not long ago. He tried to make love to the pretty woman downstairs, and I told him he might run into a bullet some day when he's out on the road. If that miserable dog hears any talk about you, he'll want to play a dirty trick on us: he'll try to arrest you here, to give Teodolinda's *trattoria* a bad name.

"What!" Ludovico exclaimed, seeing Fabrizio's bloodstained shirt, and his wounds bandaged with handkerchiefs. "So the *porco* defended himself! This is a hundred times more than you need to get yourself arrested. I didn't buy a shirt for you." He opened the husband's wardrobe without ceremony and gave of his shirts to Fabrizio, who was soon dressed like a rich country commoner. Ludovico took down a net that was hanging on the wall, placed Fabrizio's clothes in the basket where the fish are put, ran downstairs and quickly went outside through a back door; Fabrizio followed him.

"Teodolinda," he called out as he passed the *trattoria*, "hide what's upstairs. We're going to wait in the willows. And you, Pietro Antonio, send us a boat right away, the pay will be good."

Ludovico led Fabrizio across more than twenty ditches. The widest of them were spanned by long, limber planks which served as bridges. Ludovico withdrew each plank after they had walked across it. When they came to the last ditch, he quickly pulled away the plank and said, "We can catch our breath now: that dog of a constable will have to go more than two leagues to catch you. . . . You're all pale. I remembered to bring a little bottle of brandy."

"I can certainly use it. I'm beginning to feel the wound in my thigh, and I had a terrible fright in the police office at the end of the bridge."

"I can well imagine, with a bloodsoaked shirt like the one you were wearing then," said Ludovico. "The only thing I can't imagine is how you ever dared to go into such a place. As for your wounds, I know what to do about that. I'm going to put you in a nice cool place where you can sleep for an hour. The boat will come to pick us up there, if there's any way of getting one; otherwise, when you've had a little rest, we'll go on two short leagues further and I'll take you to a mill where I'll rent a boat myself. You have much more knowledge than I, Your Excellency; the duchess will be in despair when she learns of the accident: she'll be told that you've been mortally wounded, perhaps even that you killed the other man treacherously. The Marquise Raversi will be sure to spread every kind of evil gossip that can hurt the duchess. You might write to her, Your Excellency."

"And how could I get the letter to her?"

"The workmen of the mill where we're going earn twelve soldi a day. In a day and a half they can be in Parma, so let's say four lire for the journey, and two for the wear and tear on their shoes. If the errand were for a poor man like myself, it would be six lire; since it's for a noble lord, I'll give twelve."

When they came to the resting place, in a cool, leafy clump of alders and willows, Ludovico walked on alone for over an hour to get some ink and paper. "My God, how good I feel here!" thought Fabrizio. "Good-by, fortune! I'll never be an archbishop!"

On his return, Ludovico found him sound asleep and did not want to awaken him. The boat did not arrive until sunset. As soon as Ludovico saw it appear in the distance, he called Fabrizio, who wrote two letters.

"You have much more knowledge than I, Your Excellency," said Ludovico with a pained expression, "and I'm afraid I may displease you at the bottom of your heart, no matter what you may say, if I make a certain suggestion."

"I'm not as simple-minded as you think," replied Fabrizio. "Whatever you say, to me you'll always be a faithful servant of my aunt, and a man who's done everything in his power to get me out of a nasty situation."

It took many more protestations to convince Ludovico to speak, and when he had finally made up his mind to do so, he began with a preface that lasted a good five minutes. Fabrizio became impatient, but then he said to himself, "Whose fault is it? It's because of our vanity, which this man has seen quite clearly from his driver's seat as a coachman." Ludovico's devotion finally led him to run the risk of speaking plainly.

"What wouldn't the Marquise Raversi give to the messenger you'll send to Parma to get hold of those two letters! They're in your handwriting, so they could be used as legal evidence against you. You will no doubt regard me as inquisitive and indiscreet, Your Excellency, and furthermore you may be ashamed to place the wretched handwriting of a coachman before the duchess's eyes, but my concern for your safety forces me to speak, even though you may consider me impertinent. Couldn't you dictate those two letters to me? If you do, I'll be the only one who's compromised, and very slightly at that. If necessary, I could say you came up to me in the middle of a field, with an inkhorn in one hand and a pistol in the other, and ordered me to write."

"Give me your hand, my dear Ludovico!" cried Fabrizio. "And to prove to you that I don't want to keep anything secret from a friend like you, copy these two letters just as they are."

Ludovico realized the full significance of this mark of confidence and was deeply moved by it, but after he had written a few lines, noticing that the boat was moving swiftly toward them along the river, he said to Fabrizio, "The letters will be finished more quickly if Your Excellency will take the trouble to dictate them to me." When the letters had been written, Fabrizio added an A and a B to the last lines, then, on a little slip of paper which he afterward crumpled, he wrote in French, "Believe A and B." The messenger was to carry this crumpled piece of paper in his clothing.

When the boat came within range of his voice, Ludovico called the boatmen by names that were not theirs. Without answering, they brought the boat to the bank a thousand paces further on, looking in all directions to make sure they had not been seen by some customs official.

"I'm at your orders," Ludovico said to Fabrizio. "Do you want me to take the letters to Parma myself? Do you want me to go with you to Ferrara?"

"Going to Ferrara with me is a service I hardly dared to ask of you. We'll have to land and try to enter the town without showing my passport. I hate the idea of traveling under the name of Giletti, and I don't know of anyone but you who could buy me another passport."

"Why didn't you say so at Casalmaggiore! I know a spy who would have sold me an excellent passport, and at a good price, no more than forty or fifty lire."

One of the boatmen, who had been born on the right bank of the Po and therefore had no need of a foreign passport to go to Parma, agreed to deliver the letters. Ludovico, who knew how to handle an oar, undertook to row the boat with the other man.

"Further on down the river," he said, "we'll find several armed police boats; I'll manage to avoid them."

They were forced to hide a dozen times among little islands nearly flush with the water and covered with willows. Three times they went ashore to let the boat drift empty past the police craft. Ludovico took advantage of these long moments of leisure to recite several of his sonnets to Fabrizio. The sentiments they contained were genuine enough, but they were so blunted by their expression that they were not worth writing down. The strange part of it was that the ex-coachman had emotions and ways of seeing things that were vivid and picturesque, but he became cold and commonplace as soon as he began to write. "It's just the opposite in fashionable society," thought Fabrizio. "People now know how to express everything gracefully, but their hearts have nothing to say." He realized that the greatest pleasure he could give to that faithful servant would be to correct the spelling mistakes in his sonnets.

"People laugh at me when I show them my notebook," said Ludovico, "but if Your Excellency will be so kind as to dictate the spelling of the words to me letter by letter, those envious people will have nothing to say: spelling doesn't make a genius."

It was not until two nights later that Fabrizio was able to land safely in a clump of alders a league before Pontelagoscuro. He remained hidden in a field of hemp all through the next day, and Ludovico went on to Ferrara, where he rented a small lodging in the house of a poor Jew who immediately understood that there was money to be earned if he knew how to keep silent. That evening, at nightfall, Fabrizio rode into Ferrara on a little horse. He was in great need of assistance, for he had been weakened by the heat on the river, and the knife wound in his thigh, along with the sword wound Giletti had given him at the beginning of their fight, had become inflamed and were giving him a fever.

CHAPTER TWELVE

The Jew who owned the house sent for a discreet surgeon who, also realizing that there was money to be earned, told Ludovico that his "conscience" required him to make a report to the police on the wounds of the young man whom he, Ludovico, called his brother.

"The law is clear," he said. "It's obvious that your brother didn't wound himself, as he maintains, by falling off a ladder while holding an open knife in his hand."

Ludovico replied coldly to this honest surgeon that if he should decide to yield to the urgings of his conscience, before leaving Ferrara he would have the honor of falling on him in the same way: with an open knife in his hand. Fabrizio strongly reprimanded him when he told him about this incident, but there was no time to be lost in getting away. Ludovico told the Jew he wanted to try letting his brother have some fresh air; he went off to get a carriage, and our friends left the house, never to return. The reader is no doubt becoming rather bored with this account of all the measures which the lack of a passport makes necessary; this kind of preoccupation no longer exists in France, but in Italy, and especially in the vicinity of the Po, everyone is constantly talking about passports.

Once they had left Ferrara without difficulty, as though they were merely going out for a drive, Ludovico sent the carriage away, re-entered the town through another gate and came back to pick up Fabrizio in a *sediola* which he had rented for a journey of twelve leagues. When they were near Bologna, our friends had themselves driven across the fields until they came to the road which enters the city from the direction of Florence. They spent the night in the most wretched inn they could find, and the next day, since Fabrizio felt strong enough to walk a little, they entered Bologna as though they were taking a stroll. They had burned Giletti's passport: his death must have become known by now, and there would be less danger in being arrested as men without passports than as bearers of the passport of a man who had been killed.

Ludovico knew several servants in great houses in Bologna; it was agreed that he would go and make contact with them. He told them that, while traveling from Florence with his younger brother, the latter, feeling a need to sleep, had let him go on alone an hour before sunrise. He was to rejoin him at the village where he, Ludovico, would stop to spend the hottest part of the day. But when his brother did not arrive, Ludovico had decided to turn back. He had found him wounded by a blow from a stone and several knife thrusts, and the men who had picked a quarrel with him had also robbed him. This brother was a handsome boy who knew how to groom and drive horses, read and write, and would be glad to find a position in some good house. Ludovico avoided mentioning, until the occasion should arise, that when Fabrizio had fallen the robbers had run off with the little bag containing their linen and their passports.

When he arrived in Bologna, Fabrizio, feeling extremely tired and not daring to go to an inn without a passport, entered the immense church of San Petronio. He found it delightfully cool inside, and he soon felt completely revived. "What an ingrate I am!" he suddenly said to himself. "I go into a church just to sit down, as though it were a café!" He fell to his knees and effusively thanked God for the protection with which he had obviously been surrounded ever since he had had the misfortune to kill Giletti. The danger which still made him shudder was that of being recognized in the police office at Casalmaggiore. "How can it be," he wondered, "that an official whose eyes showed so much suspicion, and who read my passport at least three times, didn't notice that I'm not five feet ten inches tall, that I'm not thirty-eight years old, and that I'm not pockmarked? What thanks I owe to you, dear God! And how long I waited to lay my unworthy soul at your feet! My pride wanted to

173

believe that it was to vain human prudence that I owed the good fortune of escaping from the Spielberg when its jaws were already opening to swallow me!"

Fabrizio spent over an hour in this state of extreme emotion, in the presence of the vast goodness of God. Ludovico came in unnoticed and stood in front of him. Fabrizio, who had buried his face in his hands, looked up, and his faithful servant saw tears streaming down his cheeks.

"Come back in an hour," Fabrizio said to him rather sternly.

Ludovico forgave his tone because of his piety. Fabrizio recited several times the Seven Penitential Psalms, which he knew by heart, lingering over the verses that had some bearing on his present situation.

Fabrizio asked God to forgive him for many things, but it is remarkable that it never occurred to him to number among his sins his plans to become an archbishop solely because Count Mosca was Prime Minister and regarded that position and the majestic life that went with it as suitable for the duchess's nephew. He had desired it without passion, it is true, but he had still thought about it, exactly as he would have thought about becoming a minister or a general. It had never entered his mind that his conscience might be involved in that plan of the duchess's. This is a remarkable feature of the religion he owed to the teachings of the Milanese Jesuits. This religion *takes away the courage to think about unaccustomed things* and particularly forbids *personal judgment* as the most monstrous of sins, for it is a step toward Protestantism. To know what one is guilty of, one must question one's priest, or read the list of sins printed in the books entitled *"Preparation for the Sacrament of Penitence."*

Fabrizio knew by heart the list of sins, drawn up in Latin, which he had learned at the Ecclesiastical Academy in Naples. Thus, when he came to the sin of murder in his recital of this list, he forcefully accused himself before God of having killed a man, but in self-defense. He passed rapidly, without paying the slightest attention, over the various articles relating to the sin of *simony* (the procuring of ecclesiastical offices for money). If someone had suggested that he pay two thousand lire to become the chief vicar-general of the Archbishop of Parma, he would have rejected the idea with horror; but, although he did not lack intelligence and, above all, the ability to reason logically, it never once occurred to him that the use of Count Mosca's influence in his favor might be a form of simony. Such is the triumph of a Jesuit education: it inculcates the habit of ignoring things which are as plain as day. A Frenchman, brought up amid the self-interest and irony of Paris, might, without dishonesty, have accused Fabrizio of hypocrisy at the very moment when our hero was opening his heart to God with utter sincerity and deep emotion.

Fabrizio did not leave the church until he had prepared the confession he planned to make the next day. He found Ludovico sitting on the steps of the enormous stone peristyle which rises from the spacious square in front of the façade of San Petronio. Just as the air is purer after a great storm, so Fabrizio's soul was now serene, happy and refreshed.

"I feel quite well now, my wounds are hardly bothering me at all," he said to Ludovico when he came up to him. "But first of all I must ask you to forgive me: I answered you crossly when you came to speak to me in the church; I was examining my conscience. . . . And now, tell me how things are going for us."

"They're going very well: I've rented lodgings—quite unworthy of Your Excellency, I must say—in the house of the wife of one of my friends. She's a very pretty woman, and furthermore she's on intimate terms with one of the most important agents of the police. Tomorrow I'll go and report how our passports were stolen. My report will be well received; but I'll pay for the delivery of the letter which the police will write to Casalmaggiore to find out whether in that commune there's a man by the name of Ludovico San Micheli who has a brother named Fabrizio who's in the service of Duchess Sanseverina in Parma. It's all settled, *siamo a cavallo*." (An Italian saying: "We're saved.")

Fabrizio had suddenly taken on a very serious expression; he asked Ludovico to wait a moment, then went back into the church, almost running. As soon as he was inside he fell to his knees again and humbly kissed the stone floor. "It's a miracle, Lord!" he cried out with tears in his eyes. "When you saw that my soul was willing to return to the path of duty, you saved me. Almighty God, it's possible that some day I may be killed in a quarrel: at the time of my death, please remember the state of my soul at this moment." And he again recited the Seven Penitential Psalms, with transports of intense joy. Before leaving the church he went up to an old woman who was sitting in front of a large Madonna and beside an iron triangle placed vertically on an iron stand. The edges of this triangle bristled with many spikes designed to hold the little candles lighted by pious worshipers before the celebrated Madonna of Cimabue. Only seven candles were burning when Fabrizio approached; he registered this fact in his memory with the intention of later reflecting on it at leisure.

"How much do those candles cost?" he asked the old woman.

"Two baiocchi apiece."

They were, in fact, no thicker than a quill pen, and less than a foot long.

"How many candles can be put on your triangle?"

"Sixty-three, since there are seven lighted ones on it now."

"Ah," thought Fabrizio, "sixty-three and seven make seventy: that's something else to be noted." He paid for the candles, placed and lighted the first seven of them himself, then knelt to present his offering and said to the old woman when he stood up, "It's 'for grace received.'"

"I'm starving," he said to Ludovico when he rejoined him.

"Let's go to our lodgings instead of a tavern: the mistress of the house will go out and buy some food for us. She'll rob you of twenty soldi or so, and that will make her all the more devoted to you."

"It would also make me starve for an hour longer," said Fabrizio, laughing with the serenity of a child, and he entered a tavern near San Petronio. To his great surprise he saw Peppe, his aunt's servant, the same one who had come to meet him at Geneva, sitting at a nearby table. Fabrizio motioned him to say nothing. After eating rapidly, he stood up and walked out with a smile of happiness playing over his lips. Peppe followed him, and our hero entered San Petonio for the third time. Ludovico discreetly remained outside, strolling around the square.

"Oh, *Monsignore*! How are your wounds? The duchess is terribly worried: for a whole day she thought you were dead and abandoned on some island in the Po. I'll send a messenger to her right away. I've been trying to find you for the last six days. I spent three days in Ferrara, looking in all the inns."

"Do you have a passport for me?"

"I have three different ones: one with Your Excellency's full name and title, another with your name only, and a third with a false name, Giuseppe Bossi. There are two copies of each passport, according to whether you wish to arrive from Florence or from Modena. All you have to do is go for a stroll outside the town. The count would be glad to have you lodge in the Albergo del Pellegrino, whose owner is a friend of his."

With apparent casualness, Fabrizio walked along the right aisle of the church until he came to the place where his candles were burning. He fixed his eyes on the Madonna of Cimabue, then said to Peppe as he knelt, "I must give thanks for a moment." Peppe followed his example. As they left the church, Peppe noticed that Fabrizio gave a twenty-lire coin to the first beggar who asked him for alms; this beggar uttered cries of gratitude which attracted the swarms of poor people of every description who usually adorn the square in front of San Petronio. They all wanted their share of the twenty lire. The women, despairing of making their way through the tumultuous crowd, pounced on Fabrizio, shouting at him to say whether it was not true that he had given his money to be divided among all of God's poor people. Peppe, brandishing his gold-headed cane, ordered them to leave His Excellency alone.

"Oh, Your Excellency," the women all began to shriek, "you must give twenty lire for us too!" Fabrizio quickened his pace, the women followed him, still shrieking, and a large number of poor men, running in from all the different streets, created a kind of minor riot. This whole horribly dirty and energetic crowd kept shouting, "Your Excellency!" Fabrizio had great difficulty in freeing himself from the mob. This incident brought his imagination back down to earth. "I've gotten only what I deserved," he thought, "for letting myself become involved with the rabble."

Two women followed him to the Saragossa Gate, through which he left the town. Peppe stopped them by threatening them seriously with his cane, and by tossing them some small change. Fabrizio climbed the charming hill of San Michele in Bosco, walked around part of the town outside the walls, took a path which led him to a point five hundred paces out on the road from Florence, then came back into Bologna and solemnly handed the police official a passport on which his description was noted in precise detail. This passport gave him the name of Giuseppe Bossi, theology student. He noticed a little blot of red ink which had been dropped, as though by accident, near the lower right-hand corner of the page. Two hours later he had a spy at his heels, because of the title of "Your Excellency" given to him by his companion in front of the beggars of San Petronio, whereas his passport bore none of the titles which give a man the right to have himself addressed as "Your Excellency" by his servants.

Fabrizio saw the spy and merely laughed at him; he had ceased to give any thought to passports or the police, and was childishly amused by everything. Peppe had been ordered to stay with him, but, seeing how satisfied he was with Ludovico, he decided that he would prefer to go back to the duchess and bring her the good news himself. Fabrizio wrote long letters to the two people who were dear to him, then he had the idea of writing a third to the venerable Archbishop Landriani.

This letter produced a marvelous effect; it contained a precise account of Fabrizio's fight with Giletti. The good archbishop, deeply moved, did not fail to go and read the letter to the prince, who was quite willing to listen to it, being rather curious to see how that young *monsignore* would go about excusing such an appalling murder. Thanks to the Marquise Raversi's numerous friends, the prince, along with everyone else in Parma, believed that Fabrizio had enlisted the aid of twenty or thirty peasants to overpower an insignificant actor who had had the insolence to try to stop him for taking little Marietta. At a despotic court, the first clever schemer controls the "truth," just as fashion controls it in Paris.

"What the devil's wrong with him?" the prince said to the archbishop. "One can have things like that done by someone else, but it's not good form to do them oneself. Besides, one doesn't kill an actor like Giletti, one buys him off."

Fabrizio did not have the slightest suspicion of what was going on in Parma. The fact was that it remained to be seen whether the death of that actor, who while he was alive had earned thirty-two lire a month, would bring on the downfall of the ultra-monarchist ministry and its leader, Count Mosca.

On learning of Giletti's death, the prince, annoyed by the independent airs which the duchess had been giving herself, had ordered Chief Justice Rassi to deal with the case as though it involved a liberal. For his part, Fabrizio believed that a man of his rank was above the law; he failed to realize that in countries where members of great families are never punished, intrigue can do anything, even against them. He often spoke to Ludovico about his complete innocence and said that it would soon be publicly announced; his great argument was that he was not guilty. Whereupon Ludovico said to him one day, "I don't understand why Your Excellency, who has so much intelligence and education, should bother to say such things to me, his devoted servant. You take too many precautions: those are the kind of things that ought to be said in public, or in a law court."

"This man thinks I'm a murderer, but he doesn't love me

any less because of it," thought Fabrizio, lost in amazement.

Three days after Peppe's departure, Fabrizio was surprised to receive an enormous letter tied with a silken thread, as in the days of Louis XIV, and addressed to "His Most Reverend Excellency Monsignore Fabrizio del Dongo, Chief Vicar-General of the Diocese of Parma, Canon," etc.

"But am I still all that?" he said to himself, laughing. Archbishop Landriani's epistle was a masterpiece of logic and clarity; it filled no less than nineteen large pages, and it gave an excellent account of everything that had happened in Parma on the occasion of Giletti's death.

A French army, commanded by Marshal Ney and marching on the city, would not have produced a greater effect [wrote the good archbishop]. With the exception of the duchess and myself, everyone here believes that you wantonly killed the actor Giletti. Even if such a misfortune had actually occurred, it would have been the kind of thing which can usually be smoothed over with a few thousand lire and a six months' absence; but the Marquise Raversi wants to use the incident to overthrow Count Mosca. It is not for the terrible sin of murder that the public condemns you, it is only for your "awkwardness," or rather your insolence in scorning to resort to a *bulo*. [An inferior kind of hired cutthroat.] I am translating for you in plain terms the talk I hear all around me, for since that everlastingly deplorable misfortune I have been going every day to three of the most important houses in the city in order to have an opportunity to vindicate you. And never have I felt that I was making a more righteous use of what little eloquence Heaven has deigned to grant me.

The scales fell from Fabrizio's eyes. The duchess's many letters, filled with outbursts of affection, never condescended to tell him the facts. She swore to him that she would leave Parma forever if he did not return there in triumph.

The count will do everything humanly possible for you [she wrote to him in the letter that accompanied the archbishop's]. As for me, my character has been changed by your noble escapade: I have become as miserly as the banker Tombone. I have dismissed all my workmen. Furthermore, I have dictated an inventory of my fortune to the count, and it has proved to be much less sizable

179

than I thought. After the excellent Count Pietranera's death—which, incidentally, you would have done much better to avenge, rather than risking your life against a creature like Giletti—I was left with an income of twelve hundred lire and debts amounting to five thousand. I remember, among other things, that I had two and a half dozen pairs of white satin slippers from Paris, and only one pair of shoes to wear in the street. I have almost made up my mind to take the three hundred thousand lire left to me by the duke, which I intended to use in erecting a magnificent tomb for him. Moreover, it is the Marquise Raversi who is your principal enemy, that is to say, mine. If you are bored all by yourself in Bologna, you have only to say the word and I will come to join you there. I am sending you four more bills of exchange. . . .

The duchess said nothing to Fabrizio about the opinion which people in Parma had of his affair; she wanted above all to comfort him, and, in any case, the death of a ridiculous creature like Giletti did not seem to her the kind of thing for which a del Dongo could be seriously reproached. "How many Gilettis have our ancestors sent into the next world," she said to the count, "without anyone ever thinking of reproaching them for it!"

Fabrizio, overcome with astonishment, and glimpsing the true state of affairs for the first time, began to study the archbishop's letter. Unfortunately, the archbishop himself believed him to be better informed than he actually was. Fabrizio gathered that the main cause of the Marquise Raversi's triumph was the fact that it was impossible to find any eyewitnesses of the fatal combat. The servant who first brought news of it to Parma had been at the inn of the village of Sanguigna when it took place; Marietta and the old woman who acted as her mother had disappeared, and the marquise had bribed the driver of the carriage to make an infamous deposition.

Although the proceedings are wrapped in deepest mystery [wrote the good archbishop in his Ciceronian style], and directed by Chief Justice Rassi, of whom Christian charity alone can prevent me from speaking ill, but who has made his fortune by relentlessly hounding unfortunate people accused of crimes, like a hunting dog pursuing hares; although this Rassi, I say, whose

180

baseness and venality your imagination could not exaggerate, has been placed in charge of the case by the angry prince, I have been able to read the driver's three depositions. By a remarkable stroke of good fortune, the scoundrel contradicts himself. And I will add, since I am writing to my vicar-general, the man who, after myself, is to have charge of this diocese, that I have sent for the priest of the parish in which that misguided sinner lives. I will tell you, my dear son, that this priest already knows, through the driver's wife, the number of scudi he has received from the Marquise Raversi; I will not go so far as to affirm that the marquise has demanded that he slander you, but it is possible. The scudi were delivered to him by a wretched priest who performs rather inglorious functions for the marquise, and whom I have been forced to forbid, for the second time, to say Mass. I will not tire you with an account of the various other steps which you may expect me to have taken, and which, furthermore, were part of my duty. A canon, one of your colleagues in the cathedral, a man who is sometimes too keenly aware of the influence bestowed on him by his family's fortune, to which, by divine permission, he has become the sole heir, ventured to say in the house of Count Zurla, Minister of the Interior, that he regarded that peccadillo (he was referring to the murder of the unfortunate Giletti) as proved against you. I summoned him to appear before me, and there, in the presence of my three other vicars-general, my almoner, and two parish priests who happened to be in the waiting room, I asked him to describe to us, his brothers, the evidence for the complete conviction he claimed to have acquired against one of his colleagues in the cathedral. The wretched man was able to articulate only a few inconclusive reasons. Everyone spoke up against him, and, even though I did not feel it necessary to add more than a few words, he burst into tears and made us the witnesses of a full confession of his complete error, whereupon I promised him secrecy, in my own name and in the name of everyone who had been present during the interview, but on condition that he would use all his zeal in correcting any false impressions that might have been created by the remarks he had been making for the past two weeks.

I shall not repeat to you, my dear son, what you have no doubt known already for a long time, namely, that of the thirty-four peasants employed in the excavations undertaken by Count Mosca, and whom the Marquise Raversi claims to have been paid by you to assist you in a crime, thirty-two were at the bottom of their trench, busy with their work, when you seized the hunting knife and used it to defend your life against the man who had attacked you. Two of them were outside the trench; they shouted to the others, "*Monsignore* is being murdered!" This cry alone is striking proof of your innocence. But Chief Justice Rassi claims that those two men have disappeared! Eight of the men who were at the bottom of the trench have been found. The first time they were questioned, six of them declared that they had heard the cry, "*Monsignore* is being murdered!" I know, through indirect channels, that during their fifth questioning, which took place last night, five of them declared that they did not remember clearly whether they had actually heard the cry or had only been told of it by one of their companions. Orders have been given to inform me of where these laborers live, and their parish priests will make them understand that they will be damning themselves if they allow themselves to alter the truth in order to earn a few scudi.

The good archbishop went into endless details, as can be judged from those we have just reported. Then he continued, in Latin:

This affair is nothing less than an attempt to overthrow the present ministry. If you are sentenced, it can only be to hard labor or to death, in which case I will intervene by declaring from my archiepiscopal throne that I know you are innocent, that you merely defended your life against a bandit, and that I have forbidden you to return to Parma as long as your enemies are triumphant here. I even propose to stigmatize the Chief Justice as he deserves; hatred of that man is as common as esteem for his character is rare. But on the eve of the day when the Chief Justice is to pronounce his unjust judgment, Duchess Sanseverina will leave the city, and perhaps even the State of Parma; in that case, no one has any doubt that the count will hand in his resignation. Then, in all probability, General Fabio Conti will come into the ministry and the Marquise Raversi will triumph. The great disadvantage of your case is that no capable man has been appointed to direct the actions necessary to bring your innocence to light and foil the attempts being made to suborn witnesses. The count believes he is fulfilling this role, but he is too great a nobleman to descend to certain details; furthermore, in his capacity as Minister of Police, he was obliged from the beginning to issue the sternest orders against you. Finally—dare I tell you?—our sovereign believes you to be guilty, or at least pretends to believe it, and has brought a certain bitterness into the affair.

(The words corresponding to "our sovereign" and "pretends to believe it" were in Greek, and Fabrizio was infinitely grateful to the archbishop for having dared to write them. He cut out this line with his penknife and destroyed it on the spot.)

Fabrizio stopped a score of times as he read this letter; he was stirred by surges of deepest gratitude. He immediately wrote an eight-page letter in reply. He was often obliged to raise his head to keep his tears from falling on the paper. The next day, as he was about to seal this letter, he decided that its tone was too worldly. "I'll write it in Latin," he thought. "That will make it seem more proper to the worthy archbishop." But as he sought to construct fine Latin sentences of great length, carefully patterned after Cicero, he recalled that one day when the archbishop was speaking to him about Napoleon he had made a point of calling him "Buonaparte"; all the emotion that had moved him to tears the day before instantly vanished. "O King of Italy," he cried, "I will preserve after your death the loyalty which so many others swore to you while you were alive! . . . The archbishop is fond of me, no doubt, but it's because I'm a del Dongo and he's the son of a commoner." In order that his fine letter in Italian would not be wasted, he made a few necessary changes in it and sent it to Count Mosca.

That same day, Fabrizio came across little Marietta in the street; she blushed with joy and motioned him to follow her without speaking to her. She quickly walked to a deserted porch. There, to avoid being recognized, she pulled down the black lace which she was wearing on her head in accordance with local custom. Then she turned around sharply and said to Fabrizio, "Why is it that you're walking so freely in the street?"

He told her his story.

"Good heavens!" she said. "You've been to Ferrara! And I

looked all over for you there! I've quarreled with the old woman because she wanted to take me to Venice and I knew you'd never go there, since you're on the Austrian blacklist. I sold my gold necklace to come to Bologna—something told me I'd have the good luck to meet you here. The old woman came here two days later, so I won't ask you to come and see us: she'd make more of those horrible demands for money that makes me feel so ashamed. We've lived quite well since that terrible day, and we've spent less than a quarter of what you gave her. I'd rather not visit you in the Albergo del Pellegrino; it would attract too much attention. Try to rent a little room on a quiet street, and at the *Ave Maria* [nightfall] I'll be back here, under this same porch." Having said this, she fled.

CHAPTER THIRTEEN

The charming young girl's unexpected appearance made Fabrizio forget all serious ideas. He began living in Bologna with a feeling of joy and security. His guileless tendency to draw happiness from everything that filled his life showed through in the letters he wrote to the duchess, so much so that it began to irritate her. He scarcely noticed this, although he did write in abbreviations on the face of his watch, "When writing to the d., never say, 'when I was a prelate, when I was a churchman;' it makes her angry." He had bought two small horses with which he was highly pleased. He would harness them to a rented barouche whenever Marietta wanted to go to see one of those delightful scenic spots in the vicinity of Bologna. He took her to the Reno Falls nearly every evening. On the way back, he would stop by to see the kindly Crescentini, who vaguely regarded himself as Marietta's father.

"Well, if this is the café life that seemed so ridiculous to me for a man of any worth," thought Fabrizio, "I was wrong to scorn it." He was forgetting that he never went into a café except to read the *Constitutionnel*, and that, since he was totally unknown to the fashionable society of Bologna, the joys of vanity had nothing to do with his present happiness. When he was not with Marietta, he was at the Observatory, where he was taking a course in astronomy. The professor had developed a great fondness for him, and Fabrizio lent him his horses on Sundays, so that he could cut a fine figure with his wife on the Corso della Montagnola.

He had a horror of making anyone unhappy, no matter how unworthy of respect he might be. Marietta was determined that he should not see the old woman, but one day while she was in church he went up to visit her *mammacia*, whose face flushed with anger when she saw him come in. "Now's the time to play the del Dongo," he told himself.

"How much does Marietta earn in a month when she has an engagement?" he asked, with the air of a self-respecting young man entering the balcony of the Italian Opera in Paris.

"Fifty scudi."

"You're lying, as usual. Tell me the truth, or by God you won't get a single centesimo!"

"Well, she was earning twenty-two scudi in our company in Parma, when we had the bad luck to meet you. I was earning twelve scudi, and we each gave Giletti, our protector, a third of our earnings. Out of that, Giletti gave Marietta a present every month or so; it was usually worth about two scudi."

"You're still lying: you got only four scudi. But if you're good to Marietta, I'll engage you as though I were an impresario. You'll receive twelve scudi a month for yourself, and twenty-two for her; but if I ever see her with red eyes, I'll stop my payments."

"You're acting high and mighty, but the fact is that your fine generosity will ruin us!" replied the old woman furiously. "We'll lose our *avviamento* [connections]. When we have the enormous misfortune to be deprived of Your Excellency's protection, we'll no longer be known by any of the troupes, they'll all be full. We won't find any engagements, and because of you we'll starve to death."

"Go to the devil," said Fabrizio, leaving.

"I won't go to the devil, you ungodly rascal! I'll merely go to the police and tell them you're a *monsignore* who's thrown his frock away, and that your name is no more Giuseppe Bossi than mine is."

Fabrizio had already gone a little way down the stairs; he came back.

"First of all, the police know my real name better than you do; but if you take it into your head to denounce me, if you're ignoble enough to do that," he said to her with great seriousness, "Ludovico will have a talk with you, and your old carcass won't be stabbed six times, but two dozen, enough to keep you in the hospital for six months, and without snuff."

The old woman turned pale, seized Fabrizio's hand and tried to kiss it.

"I gratefully accept the offer you've made for Marietta and myself. You look so kind that I mistook you for a fool. Think about it: other people may make the same mistake. I advise you to make a habit of looking like a noble lord." Then she added, with admirable impudence, "Think over that good advice, and since winter isn't far off, make Marietta and me a present of two good coats of the fine English cloth sold by that big merchant on the Piazza San Petronio."

Pretty Marietta's love offered him all the charms of the sweetest friendship; this made him think about the happiness of the same kind which he might have found with the duchess.

"But isn't it amusing," he sometimes said to himself, "that I'm immune to that exclusive, passionate obsession known as love? Among all the affairs that chance brought my way in Novara or Naples, did I ever meet a woman whose presence, even during the first few days, I preferred to a ride on a fine horse I'd never ridden before? Could it be that what's known as love is only another lie? I feel love, of course, just as I feel hunger at six o'clock! Could it be that liars have taken that rather vulgar propensity and turned it into the love of Othello, of Tancred? Or should I believe that I'm made differently from other men? Is my soul lacking in one passion? Why should it be? That would be a strange fate!"

In Naples, especially toward the end of his stay there, Fabrizio had met women who, proud of their rank, their beauty and the social position of the admirers they had sacrificed to him, had set out to dominate him. As soon as he became aware of their plans, he had broken off with them in the quickest and most scandalous manner. "Now," he thought, "if I ever let myself be carried away by the pleasure, which is certainly great, of being on intimate terms with that pretty woman known as Duchess Sanseverina, I'll be exactly like that foolish Frenchman who one day killed the goose that laid the golden eggs. It's to the duchess that I owe the only happiness I've ever experienced through tender feelings. My affection for her is my whole life, and besides, what would I be without her? A poor exile reduced to living from hand to mouth in a dilapidated country house outside Novara. I remember that during the heavy autumn

186

rains I had to put an umbrella over the canopy of my bed at night, for fear of an accident. I used to ride the steward's horses; he was willing to tolerate it out of respect for my blue blood, but my stay was beginning to seem a little long to him. My father had given me an allowance of twelve hundred lire, and thought himself damned for keeping a Jacobin alive. My poor mother and my sisters did without new dresses to make it possible for me to give a few little presents to my mistresses. That way of being generous pierced my heart. Furthermore, people were beginning to suspect my poverty, and the young noblemen of the region were about to pity me. Sooner or later, some conceited ass would have shown his contempt for a poor Jacobin who had failed in his plans, because that's exactly what I was in those people's eyes. I'd have fought a duel that would have either put me in the Fenestrelle fortress or forced me to take refuge in Switzerland again, still living on my allowance of twelve hundred lire. I have the good fortune to be indebted to the duchess for the absence of all those evils; and furthermore, it's she who feels for me the impassioned affection that I ought to feel for her.

"Instead of leading that ridiculous, wretched life which would have turned me into a sad animal, a fool, for the past four years I've lived in a big city and I have an excellent carriage; that has kept me from knowing envy and all the other base feelings of the provinces. My overindulgent aunt always scolds me for not drawing enough money from the banker. Do I want to ruin that admirable position forever? Do I want to lose the only friend I have in the world? I have only to tell a lie, to say 'I love you' to a charming woman who may be unique in the world, and for whom I feel the warmest friendship. But I don't know what it means to be in love! She'd be constantly reproaching me for the lack of that ardent emotion which is unknown to me. Marietta, on the other hand, who doesn't see into my heart and regards a caress as a rapture of the soul, thinks I'm madly in love with her and considers herself the most fortunate of women.

"Actually, the only time I've ever had even an inkling of that tender obsession which, I believe, is called 'love' was when I was with that young girl Aniken in the inn at Zonders, near the Belgian border."

It is with regret that we are going to record here one of Fabrizio's worst actions; in the midst of this tranquil life a wretched fit of vanity took possession of his heart, which was still rebellious to love, and led him far astray. In Bologna at the same time as himself, there happened to be the famous Fausta F——, unquestionably one of the finest singers of our time, and perhaps the most capricious woman who ever lived. The excellent poet Burati, of Venice, had written that famous satirical sonnet about her which was then on the lips of princes as well as the humblest street urchins:

> Wishing and not wishing, adoring and detesting in the same day, finding satisfaction only in inconstancy, despising what the world worships, while the world worships her: Fausta has these faults and many more. Therefore never look upon that serpent. If you are rash enough to look upon her, you will forget her caprices. If you have the good fortune to hear her, you will forget yourself, and love will make of you, in an instant, what Circe long ago made of Ulysses' companions.

For the moment, this miracle of beauty was under the spell of the enormous side-whiskers and lofty insolence of the young Count M——, so much so that she was not revolted by his abominable jealousy. Fabrizio saw this count in the streets of Bologna and was offended by the air of superiority with which he occupied the pavement and deigned to display his graces to the public. He was an extremely rich young man who considered himself privileged to do anything he pleased, and since his arrogance had given rise to threats against him, he never went out without being surrounded by nine or ten *buli* (a kind of hired assassin) who wore his livery and had been brought from his estates near Brescia. Fabrizio's eyes had once or twice met those of the terrible count when he happened to hear Fausta sing. He was amazed by the angelic sweetness of her voice; he had never imagined anything like it, and it gave him sensations of supreme bliss which contrasted sharply with the placidity of the life he was now leading. "Could this be love at last?" he wondered. Consumed with curiosity to experience this feeling, and, furthermore, amused by the thought of defying Count M——, whose expression was more fearsome than that of any drum-major, our hero indulged in the childish project of passing much too often in front of the Tanari palace, which Count M—— had rented for Fausta.

Late one afternoon, as Fabrizio was trying to make himself seen by Fausta, he was greeted by very loud laughter from the count's *buli*, who were standing near the door of the Tanari palace. He hurried home, took some good weapons and passed in front of the palace again. Fausta, hidden behind the blinds, had been waiting for his return, and she set it down to his credit. M——, jealous of everyone on earth, became especially jealous of Signor Giuseppe Bossi and angrily made a number of ridiculous remarks, whereupon our hero sent him a letter every morning which contained only these words: "Signor Giuseppe Bossi destroys undesirable insects and lives at the Pellegrino, 79 Via Larga."

Count M——, accustomed to the respect which his enormous fortune, his "blue blood" and the boldness of his thirty servants assured him everywhere, refused to understand the language of these little notes.

Fabrizio wrote others to Fausta. M—— placed spies around this rival, whose attentions were perhaps not received with displeasure. First he learned his real name, then the fact that, for the moment, he could not show himself in Parma. A few days later, Count M——, his *buli*, his magnificent horses and Fausta left for Parma.

Fabrizio, caught up in the game, followed them the next day. Ludovico's dramatic remonstrances were in vain; Fabrizio sent him about his business, and Ludovico, very brave himself, admired him; besides, the journey would bring him closer to his pretty mistress at Casalmaggiore. Through Ludovico's efforts, nine or ten veterans of Napoleon's regiments were engaged as servants by Signor Giuseppe Bossi. "Provided I have no communication with the Minister of Police, Count Mosca, or with the duchess," thought Fabrizio in the midst of his foolhardy pursuit of Fausta, "I'll be endangering no one but myself. I'll tell my aunt later that I was going off in search of love, that beautiful thing which I've never encountered. The fact is that I think about Fausta when I don't see her. . . . But is it the memory of her voice that I love, or Fausta herself?"

Having given up all thought of an ecclesiastical career, Fabrizio had grown a mustache and side-whiskers that were almost as awesome as those of Count M——, and this disguised him a little. He established his headquarters, not in Parma—that would have been too rash—but in a nearby village in the middle of the forest, on the road to Sacca, where his aunt had a country house. Following Ludovico's advice, he announced himself in this village as the valet of a powerful and eccentric English lord who spent a hundred thousand lire a year to give himself the pleasures of hunting, and who would soon arrive from Lake Como, where he was at present detained by the trout-fishing.

Fortunately, the attractive house which Count M—— had rented for the fair Fausta was located at the southern end of the city of Parma, precisely on the road to Sacca, and her windows overlooked the beautiful lanes bordered by high trees which extend beneath the high tower of the citadel. Fabrizio was not known in this unfrequented quarter. He had Count M—— followed, and one day when the latter had just left the admirable singer's house, Fabrizio had the audacity to appear in the street in broad daylight; it is true, however, that he was mounted on an excellent horse, and well armed. Some musicians, of the kind that roam the streets in Italy and are sometimes very skillful, came and planted their double-basses beneath Fausta's windows. After a prelude they sang, rather well, a cantata in her honor. She came to a window and easily noticed a gracious young man who had stopped his horse in the middle of the street; he saluted her, then began giving her looks whose meaning was unmistakable. Despite the exaggeratedly English costume which Fabrizio had adopted, she soon recognized him as the author of the passionate letters that had been the cause of her departure from Bologna. "Here's a very unusual man," she thought. "It seems to me that I'm going to fall in love with him. I have two thousand lire in cash, so I can well afford to rid myself of that terrible Count M——. Actually, he lacks wit and he's completely predictable; the only thing that makes him even slightly amusing is the horrible appearance of his servants."

The next day, having learned that at eleven o'clock every morning Fausta went to the center of town to attend Mass in the same church of San Giovanni that contained the tomb of his ancestor, Archbishop Ascanio del Dongo, Fabrizio ventured to follow her there. Ludovico had, it is true, procured a fine English wig for him, with beautiful red hair. In reference to the color of this hair, which was that of the flames burning his heart, he wrote a sonnet which Fausta found charming. This little war lasted for a full week, but Fabrizio found that, despite all his efforts, he was making no real progress: Fausta refused to receive him. He was overdoing his eccentric effects; she said later that she had been afraid of him. He was no longer sustained by anything except the faint remaining hope of succeeding in feeling what is known as "love," but he was often bored.

"Let's leave, sir," Ludovico kept saying to him. "You're not in love: I can see that you're hopelessly cool-headed and sensible. Besides, you're not getting anywhere. Shame alone should be enough to send us on our way." Fabrizio was about to leave in his first moment of ill-humor when he learned that Fausta was going to sing in Duchess Sanseverina's palace. "Perhaps her sublime voice will finish setting my heart on fire," he thought, and he had the temerity to go, undisguised, into that palace where he was known to every eye. It is not difficult to imagine the duchess's emotion when, toward the very end of the concert, she noticed a man dressed as a footman standing near the door of the main drawing room; his appearance reminded her of someone. She sought out Count Mosca, and it was only then that he told her of Fabrizio's monumental and truly incredible folly. The count took it extremely well. He was greatly pleased by Fabrizio's love of a woman other than the duchess. Being a perfectly gallant man outside of politics, he acted on the principle that he could find happiness only if the duchess was happy. "I'll save him from himself," he said to her. "Imagine how delighted our enemies would be if he were arrested in this palace! I therefore have over a hundred of my men here, and that's why I sent to ask you for the keys to the great water tower. He acts as though he were madly in love with Fausta, and so far he hasn't been able to take her away from Count M——, who makes it possible for that madwoman to live the life of a queen." The duchess's face betrayed sharp pain: so Fabrizio was nothing but a libertine, completely incapable of tender, serious feelings!

"And he didn't come to see us!" she said at length. "I'll never be able to forgive him for that! And I've been writing to him every day in Bologna!"

"I greatly admire his self-restraint," replied the count. "He doesn't want to compromise us with his escapade. It would be amusing to hear him tell about it."

Fausta was too impetuous to keep silent about anything that was on her mind. The day after the concert, during which her eyes had addressed every aria to the tall young man dressed as a footman, she spoke to Count M—— about an unknown admirer.

"Where do you see him?" asked the count furiously.

"In the streets, in church," replied Fausta, taken aback. She immediately tried to repair the damage done by her imprudence, or at least to lead the count away from anything that might remind him of Fabrizio: she launched into an endless description of a tall young man with red hair and blue eyes; he was no doubt some very rich and awkward Englishman, or a prince. At this last word Count M——, who was not noted for the keenness of his perception, conceived the idea, delightful to his vanity, that his rival was none other than the Crown Prince of Parma. This poor melancholy young man, guarded by five or six tutors, assistant tutors, perceptors, etc., etc., who never let him go out until they had held a conference on the matter, cast strange glances at every passably pretty woman he was allowed to approach. At the duchess's concert, his rank had placed him in front of the rest of the audience, in an isolated armchair three paces from the fair Fausta, and the way he looked at her had deeply offended Count M——. This insane idea inspired by his vanity—that he had a prince as a rival—greatly amused Fausta, and she took delight in confirming it with a hundred artlessly given details.

"Is your family," she asked, "as old as the Farnese family, to which that young man belongs?"

"What do you mean, as old? There's no bastardy* in *my* family!"

As luck would have it, Count M—— was unable to see his supposed rival at leisure; this confirmed him in the idea that he had a prince as his adversary. The fact was that, when the interests of his project did not call him to Parma, Fabrizio remained in the forest near Sacco and the banks of the Po. Count M—— had become much prouder, but also much more cautious, since he had begun to believe that he was in a position to contend against a prince for Fausta's heart: he begged her very seriously to show great reserve in everything she did. After throwing himself at her feet like a jealous and passionate lover, he told her quite bluntly that it was important to her honor that she should not allow herself to be taken in by the young prince.

"Excuse me, but I wouldn't be taken in by him if I loved him: I've never seen a prince at my feet."

"If you yield," he said with a haughty look, "I may not be able to take vengeance on the prince, but I will certainly take vengeance." And he left, slamming the doors. If Fabrizio had presented himself at that moment, he would have won his suit.

"If you value your life," Count M—— said to her that evening as he took leave of her after the performance, "make sure I never find out that the young prince has entered your

---

* Pier Luigi, the first sovereign of the Farnese family, so renowned for his virtues, was, as is well known, the natural son of His Holiness Pope Paul III.

house. There's nothing I can do to him, damn it, but don't make me remember that I can do anything I please to you!"

"Ah, my little Fabrizio," thought Fausta, "if only I knew where to find you!"

A rich young man who has been surrounded by flatterers since birth can be led far by wounded vanity. The very real passion which Count M—— had once felt for Fausta was now violently reawakened. He was not stopped by the dangerous prospect of coming into conflict with the only son of the sovereign in whose territory he was now residing, just as he did not have the good sense to try to see this prince, or at least have him followed. Unable to attack him otherwise, M—— dared to think of making him look ridiculous. "I'll be banished forever from the State of Parma," he said to himself. "Well, what do I care about that?" If he had tried to reconnoiter the enemy's position, he would have learned that the poor young prince never went out without being accompanied by three or four old men, stodgy guardians of etiquette, and that the only pleasure of his choice allowed to him in this world was mineralogy.

Fausta's house, where the best society of Parma congregated, was surrounded day and night by observers. M—— knew hour by hour what she was doing and, above all, what was being done around her. There is one thing to be praised in the jealous lover's precautions: that capricious woman at first had no idea of his increased surveillance. The reports of all his agents informed Count M—— that a very young man, wearing a red wig, often appeared beneath Fausta's windows, but always in a new disguise. "It's obviously the young prince," he thought, "otherwise why should he disguise himself? Well, by God, I'm not the kind of man to give in to him! If it weren't for the usurpations of the Venetian Republic, I'd be a sovereign prince myself."

On San Stefano's Day, his spies' reports took on a darker tone: they seemed to indicate that Fausta was beginning to respond to the ardent attentions of her unknown admirer. "I could leave with her immediately," thought M——. "But no! In Bologna I fled from del Dongo, here I'd be fleeing from a prince! What would that young man say? He might think he'd succeeded in frightening me! And my family is as good as his, by God!" M—— was furious, but, to complete his misery, his main concern was to avoid letting Fausta, whom he knew to be fond of mockery, see him in the ridiculous role of a jealous lover. And so, on San Stefano's Day, he spent an hour with her, after she had given him a warm welcome which seemed to him the height of insincerity, and left her shortly before eleven o'clock as she was getting dressed to go to Mass in the church of San Giovanni.

He went home, put on the shabby black coat of a young theology student and hurried to San Giovanni. He sat down behind one of the tombs which adorn the third chapel on the right. He could see everything that went on in the church from beneath the arm of a cardinal who is represented kneeling on his own tomb; this statue cut off the light from the back of the chapel and hid him sufficiently. He soon saw Fausta come in looking more beautiful than ever; she was wearing her finest clothes, and was escorted by a score of admirers belonging to the highest society. There was a radiant smile on her lips, and joy shone from her eyes. "It's obvious," thought the jealous wretch, "that she expects to meet here the man she loves, whom she may not have been able to see for a long time, thanks to me." The keen happiness in Fausta's eyes suddenly seemed to redouble. "My rival is here," thought M——, and the fury of his vanity knew no bounds. "What kind of a figure am I cutting here, forming a pair with a young prince in disguise?" But no matter what he did, he was never able to discover his rival, whom his eyes sought avidly in all directions.

Every few moments, after looking all around the church, Fausta would fix her eyes, filled with love and happiness, on the dark corner in which M—— was hiding. In an impassioned heart, love is apt to exaggerate the lightest shades of meaning and draw absurd conclusions from them: poor M—— finally convinced himself that Fausta had seen him, that, having perceived his deadly jealousy in spite of all his efforts, she now wanted to reproach him for it and, at the same time, console him for it with her tender glances.

The cardinal's tomb, behind which M—— had taken up his post of observation, was raised four or five feet above the marble floor of the church. When the fashionable Mass was over, toward one o'clock, most of the worshipers left, and Fausta dismissed her admirers on the pretext that she wished to pray. She remained kneeling on her chair, and her eyes, now brighter and more tender than ever, were fixed on M——. As soon as there were only a few people left in the church, she had stopped taking the trouble to glance all around it before happily bringing her eyes to rest on the statue of the cardinal. "What delicacy!" thought Count M——, believing the she was looking at him. At last she stood up and abruptly walked out, after making a few strange movements with her hands.

M——, intoxicated with love and almost completely cured of his mad jealousy, had left his place, intending to hurry to his mistress's house and thank her a thousand times, when, as he was passing in front of the cardinal's tomb, he noticed a young man dressed entirely in black: the baneful creature had been kneeling against the epitaph of the tomb in such a way that the jealous lover's searching gaze had passed over his head without seeing him.

The young man stood up, quickly walked away, and was instantly surrounded by seven or eight rather awkward and odd-looking men who seemed to be in his service. M—— rushed after him, but, without any particularly noticeable efforts, he was stopped in the narrow wooden passage at the entrance by the awkward men who were protecting his rival. When he finally reached the street, all he was able to see was someone closing the door of a shabby carriage which, by a strange contrast, was drawn by two excellent horses. In a moment it was out of sight.

He went home panting with rage. His spies soon arrived and calmly reported that the mysterious admirer, disguised as a priest, had been piously kneeling against a tomb that stood at the entrance of a dark chapel in the church of San Giovanni. Fausta had remained in the church until it was nearly deserted, then she had rapidly exchanged certain signals with the unknown man: she had made what appeared to be crosses with her hands. M—— hurried off to see his faithless mistress. For the first time, she was unable to hide her agitation; she told him, with the lying candor of a passionate woman, that she had gone to the church of San Giovanni as usual, but that she had not seen the man who was persecuting her. At these words, M——, beside himself, insulted her vehemently and told her what he had seen with his own eyes. The boldness of her lies increased the violence of his accusations; he finally drew his dagger and rushed toward her.

"All right," she said to him with great self-possession, "everything you've complained about is perfectly true, but I tried to hide it from you to avoid driving you into rash, senseless plans for vengeance which might ruin us both, because you must know this once and for all: if I've guessed correctly, the man who's pursuing me is not likely to meet with any opposition to his wishes, not in this country, at least." After adroitly reminding M—— that, after all, he had no authority over her, she ended by saying that she would probably stop going to the church of San Giovanni. M—— was head over heels in love; a touch of coquetry may have been mingled with prudence in her heart; he felt himself disarmed. He thought of leaving Parma. The young prince, however powerful he might be, could not follow him, or, if he did, would then become no more than his equal. But his pride told him once again that his departure would still seem to be a retreat, and he forbade himself to consider it.

"He doesn't even suspect that my little Fabrizio is here," Fausta thought with delight. "Now we can make fun of him in a priceless way!"

Fabrizio had no inkling of his good fortune. The next day, when he found the singer's windows tightly closed and did not see her anywhere, it began to seem to him that his escapade had lasted long enough. He felt remorse. "In what kind of a position am I placing poor Count Mosca?" he thought. "After all, he's the Minister of Police! He'll be regarded as my accomplice, and the only thing I'll have achieved by coming here will be the destruction of his career! But if I abandon the project I've pursued so long, what will the duchess say when I tell her about my attempts at love?"

One evening when, ready to give up the whole enterprise, he was lecturing himself in this manner, as he was strolling beneath the tall trees that separated Fausta's house from the citadel he noticed that he was being followed by a spy of very small height. He vainly tried to get rid of him by walking through several different streets; the microscopic creature seemed glued to his heels. Exasperated, he darted into a lonely street that ran along the Parma River, where his men were lying in wait. At a signal from him, they leapt on the poor little spy, who fell at their knees: it was Bettina, Fausta's maid. After three days of boredom and seclusion, she had disguised herself as a man to escape the dagger of Count M——, of whom she and her mistress were terribly afraid, and set out to find Fabrizio to tell him that Fausta loved him passionately and was burning to see him, but that she could no longer go to the church of San Giovanni.

"It was about time!" thought Fabrizio. "Hurray for persistence!"

The little maid was very pretty, a fact which roused him from his moral musings. She informed him that the promenade and all the streets through which he had passed that evening were carefully though unobtrusively watched by M——'s spies. They had rented rooms on the first or second floors of various houses from which, silently hiding behind the blinds, they observed everything that went on in the apparently unfrequented streets and heard everything that was said there.

"If those spies had recognized my voice," said Bettina, "I'd have certainly been stabbed as soon as I went home, and my poor mistress might have been stabbed with me." Her terror made her charming to Fabrizio. "Count M—— is furious," she went on, "and my mistress knows he'll stop at nothing. . . . She told me to tell you that she'd like to be a hundred leagues away from here with you!"

She then told him of the scene that had taken place on San Stefano's Day, and of M——'s fury: he had not missed a single one of the amorous glances and signs which Fausta had addressed to Fabrizio, with whom she had been madly in love that day. M—— had drawn his dagger and seized her by the hair; if it had not been for her presence of mind, she would have been lost.

Fabrizio took the pretty Bettina up to a little apartment he had rented nearby. He told her that he was from Turin, and that his father was an important personage who happened to be in Parma for the moment, which forced him to take a great many precautions. Bettina replied, laughing, that he was a much greater nobleman than he wished to appear. It took our hero some time to realize that the charming girl took him for no less a personage than the crown prince himself. Fausta was falling in love with Fabrizio, and at the same time she was beginning to be frightened, so she had decided to speak to her maid about the prince and not mention Fabrizio's name to her. Fabrizio finally confessed to the pretty girl that she had guessed correctly. "But if my identity ever becomes known," he added, "despite the great passion of which I've given your mistress so many proofs, I'll be forced to stop seeing her, and my father's ministers, those malicious scoundrels whom I'll some day dismiss from office, will immediately order her to leave the country which she has been adorning with her presence."

Toward morning, Fabrizio arranged with the little maid several plans by which he hoped to succeed in obtaining a rendezvous with Fausta. He sent for Ludovico and another of his servants, a very resourceful man. They worked out an agreement with Bettina while he wrote a wildly extravagant letter to Fausta; all the exaggerations of tragedy were inherent in the situation, and he made lavish use of them. It was not until dawn that he parted with Bettina, who was highly satisfied with the young prince's behavior.

She had told him repeatedly that, now that Fausta was in accord with him, he was no longer able to pass beneath the windows of her house unless he could enter it, and in that case there would be a signal. But Fabrizio, infatuated with Bettina and believing himself near the culmination of his campaign to conquer Fausta, could not force himself to stay in his village two leagues from Parma. The next evening, toward midnight, he came to Fausta's windows on horseback, and well accompanied, to sing a popular air for which he had composed different words. "Isn't this the way gallant lovers are supposed to act?" he said to himself.

Ever since Fausta had made known her desire for a rendezvous, his pursuit of her had seemed long and tiresome to him. "No, I don't love her," he thought as he sang rather badly beneath the windows of her house. "Bettina seems a hundred times more desirable to me, and she's the one I'd like to be with right now."

Having become bored, he was on his way back to his village when, five hundred paces or so from Fausta's house, a score of men flung themselves upon him; four of them seized the bridle of his horse while two of them grabbed his arms. Ludovico and Fabrizio's *bravi* were attacked, but managed to escape, firing their pistols. All this took place in an instant. Fifty lighted torches appeared in the street in the twinkling of an eye, as though by magic. The men were all well armed. Fabrizio had leapt off his horse, despite those who were holding him. He tried to break away, and even wounded a man who was gripping his arms with hands that were like vises; but he was astonished to hear this man say to him in a tone of great respect, "Your Highness will give me a pension for this wound, and that will be much better for me than falling into the crime of treason by drawing my sword against my prince."

"Ah, here's the punishment of my foolishness!" thought Fabrizio. "I'll have damned myself for a sin that didn't even seem attractive to me."

Scarcely had this little attempt at combat been ended when several lackeys in full livery appeared with a gilded sedan chair that was painted in a strange manner: it was one of those grotesque chairs used by masked revelers during the carnival. Six men with daggers in their hands asked His Highness to step into it, saying that the chilly night air might be bad for his voice. They all addressed him with an elaborate show of respect, and the word "prince" was repeated at every moment, almost in a shout. The procession set off. Fabrizio counted over fifty men carrying lighted torches in the street. It was about one o'clock in the morning. The people of the neighborhood had all come to their windows. The whole thing was carried out with a certain solemnity. "I was afraid of being stabbed by Count M——," thought Fabrizio, "but he's contented himself with mocking me: I didn't think he had such good taste. But does he really believe he's dealing with the prince? If he knows I'm only Fabrizio, look out for daggers!"

The fifty men carrying torches, and the twenty armed men, stopped for a long time beneath Fausta's windows, then went on to parade in front of the finest palaces in the city. Major-domos posted on either side of the sedan chair asked His Highness from time to time if he had any orders to give them. Fabrizio did not lose his head; by the light of the torches he saw that Ludovico and his men were following the procession as closely as possible. "Ludovico has only nine or ten men and doesn't dare to attack," he thought. From inside his sedan chair, he could see quitely clearly that the men who had been ordered to carry out this practical joke were armed to the teeth. He pretended to laugh with the major-domos assigned to attend him. After more than two hours of this triumphal march, he saw that they were going to pass the end of the street on which the Sanseverina palace stood.

As they were turning into the street that led to it, he quickly opened the door in the front of the sedan chair, leapt over one of the shafts and felled with his dagger one of the armed attendants who had thrust his torch in his face. Fabrizio himself was stabbed in the shoulder, and a second attendant burned his beard with a torch. Finally he reached Ludovico and shouted to him, "Kill! Kill anyone who's carrying a torch!" Ludovico used his sword to save his master from two men who were determined to pursue him. Fabrizio ran to the Sanseverina palace; out of curiosity, the porter had opened the little door, three feet high, that was cut into the big door, and was staring in bewilderment at all the torches. Fabrizio leapt inside and closed this miniature door behind him. He ran into the garden and escaped through a gate that opened onto a deserted street. An hour later, he was outside the city. At dawn he crossed the border of the State of Modena and reached safety.

That evening he entered Bologna. "A fine expedition!" he

199

said to himself. "I didn't even succeed in speaking to my beauty!" He hastened to write letters of apology to the count and the duchess, circumspect letters which, while depicting what was taking place in his heart, could give no information to an enemy. "I was in love with love," he wrote to the duchess. "I've done everything I could to experience it, but nature has apparently refused me a heart capable of love and melancholy; I can rise no higher than common pleasure...."

It would be impossible to describe the commotion this incident caused in Parma. Its mysteriousness stimulated curiosity; countless people had seen the torches and the sedan chair, but who was the man who had been abducted with every mark of respect? The next day, not one of the city's well-known personages was missing.

The common people who lived on the street where the prisoner had escaped maintained that they had seen a corpse. But in broad daylight, when they dared to leave their houses, they found no trace of the combat except a great deal of blood that had been shed on the pavement. Over twenty thousand inquisitive people came to examine the street during the day. Italian cities are accustomed to strange sights, but they always know the "why" and the "how." In this case, what amazed Parma was the fact that even a month later, when people had ceased to speak of nothing but the torch-light procession, no one, thanks to Count Mosca's prudence, had been able to guess the name of the rival who had tried to take Fausta away from Count M——. This jealous and vindictive lover had fled as soon as the procession began. By order of Count Mosca, Fausta was imprisoned in the citadel. The duchess laughed heartily over this little act of injustice which the count was forced to allow himself in order to baffle the curiosity of the prince, who might otherwise have managed to discover Fabrizio's identity.

At that time there was in Parma a learned man who had come from the North to write a history of the Middle Ages. He was in search of manuscripts in libraries, and the count had given him all possible authorizations. But the scholar proved to be irascible: he believed, for example, that everyone in Parma was trying to make fun of him. It is true that urchins sometimes followed him in the street because of the enormous head of bright red hair which he proudly displayed. He believed that at his inn he was charged exorbitant prices for everything, and he would not pay for the smallest trifle without first looking up its price in the travel book written by a Mrs. Starke, which has now gone into its twentieth edition because it indicates to the cautious Englishman the price of a turkey, an apple, a glass of milk, etc.

During the same evening when Fabrizio took his forced ride in the sedan chair, the red-maned scholar became furious at his inn and took out a pair of pocket pistols with which to avenge himself on the *cameriere* who was trying to charge him two soldi for a mediocre peach. He was arrested, for carrying pocket pistols is a great crime!

Since this irascible scholar was tall and thin, the next morning the count had the idea of passing him off in the eyes of the prince as the reckless man who had been the victim of a practical joke after trying to take Fausta away from Count M——. Carrying pocket pistols is punishable in Parma by three years at hard labor, but this penalty is never applied. After two weeks in prison, during which the scholar had seen only a lawyer who frightened him out of his wits with descriptions of the atrocious laws enacted by the timorous rulers of Parma against bearers of concealed weapons, another lawyer came to him and told him about the ride which Count M—— had inflicted on his unknown rival. "The police don't want to admit to the prince that they haven't been able to discover the identity of that rival: confess that you tried to win Fausta's favor, that fifty brigands captured you while you were singing under her window, and that they forced you to ride in a sedan chair for an hour without ever saying anything discourteous to you. There's nothing humiliating about such a confession, and you're only being asked to say a few words. As soon as you've gotten the police out of their difficulty by making your confession, they'll put you in a stagecoach, take you to the border and bid you good-by."

The scholar held out for a month; two or three times the prince was on the point of having him brought to the Ministry of the Interior and being present while he was questioned. But he had already stopped considering it when the historian, bored and exasperated, made up his mind to confess everything and was taken to the border. The prince remained convinced that Count M——'s rival had a forest of red hair.

Three days after his ride in the sedan chair, while Fabrizio, now hiding in Bologna, was planning with his faithful Ludovico to find some way of reaching Count M——, he learned that he too was hiding in a mountain village on the road to Florence. Count M—— had only three of his *buli* with him; the next day, as he was coming back from a stroll, he was captured by eight masked men who gave him to understand that they were police agents from Parma. He was blindfolded and taken to an inn two leagues further on in the mountains, where he was treated with great consideration and given a copious supper, including the finest Spanish and Italian wines.

"So I'm a prisoner of state?" he asked.

"Not at all!" politely replied Ludovico, who was still masked. "You've offended a private individual by having him carried around in a sedan chair. He wishes to fight a duel with you tomorrow morning. If you kill him, you'll find two good horses, money, and relays prepared for you along the road to Genoa."

"What's the name of this cutthroat?" asked the count angrily.

"His name is Bombace. You'll have your choice of weapons, and good, honorable seconds, but one of you must die!"

"Then this is a murder!" cried Count M——, frightened.

"God forbid! It's simply a duel to the death with a young man whom you had carried through the streets of Parma in the middle of the night, and who would continue to be dishonored if you remained alive. There isn't room for both of you on this earth, so try to kill him. There will be swords, pistols, sabers, all the weapons we were able to obtain in a few hours, because we've had to hurry. As you may know already, the Bologna police are very diligent, and they must not be allowed to prevent this duel, because it's necessary to the honor of the young man you've held up to ridicule."

"But if that young man is a prince—"

"He's a private individual like yourself, not nearly so rich as you are, in fact, but he wants a duel to the death, and he'll force you to fight, I warn you."

"I'm not afraid of anything in the world!" cried M——.

"That's what your adversary passionately desires," replied Ludovico. "Be prepared to defend your life early tomorrow morning: it will be attacked by a man who has good reason to be very angry, and he won't spare you. I repeat that you will have your choice of weapons. And make your will."

Toward six o'clock the next morning, breakfast was served to Count——, then a door of the room in which he was being kept was opened and he was asked to enter the courtyard of a country inn. This courtyard was surrounded by hedges and rather high walls, and its gates had been carefully closed.

In one corner, on a table which Count M—— was requested to approach, he found several bottles of wine and brandy, two pistols, two swords, two sabers, paper and ink.

A score of peasants were at the windows of the inn which overlooked the courtyard. Count M—— implored their pity: "They want to murder me!" he cried. "Save my life!"

"You're mistaken, or else you're trying to give a false impression!" Fabrizio shouted at him from the opposite corner of the courtyard, beside a table laden with weapons. He had taken off his coat, and his face was hidden by one of those wire masks which are used in fencing schools. "Please put on the wire mask that's beside you," he went on, "then walk toward me with either a sword or pistols: as you were told last night, you have your choice of weapons."

Count M—— raised endless objections and seemed extremely upset over having to fight a duel. As for Fabrizio, he was afraid the police might arrive, even though the inn was in the mountains, a good five leagues from Bologna. He finally began hurling the most outrageous insults at his adversary, until at last he had the satisfaction of making him angry. Count M—— picked up a sword and walked toward him. The duel began rather sluggishly.

A few minutes later it was interrupted by a great uproar. Our hero had clearly realized that he was throwing himself into an action which might become a subject of reproach, or at least of slanderous accusations, for the rest of his life. He had sent Ludovico into the countryside to recruit witnesses for him. Ludovico gave money to some strangers who were working in a nearby forest; they came running up, shouting, thinking it was a question of killing an enemy of the man who was paying them. When they reached the inn, Ludovico asked them to watch very carefully to see whether either of the two combatants acted treacherously by taking unfair advantage of the other.

The duel, interrupted for a moment by the bloodthirsty cries of the peasants, was slow in resuming. Fabrizio again insulted M——'s vanity. "Count," he shouted to him, "if a man is insolent, he must be brave! I realize it's a hard condition for you to accept, because you prefer to pay other men to be brave." M——, nettled once gain, cried out that he had attended the famous Battistini's fencing school in Naples for a long time, and that he was going to punish Fabrizio's insolence. Now that his anger had at last returned, he fought with fair determination; this, however, did not prevent Fabrizio from giving him a fine thrust in the chest which kept him in bed for several months. As he was giving first aid to the wounded man, Ludovico whispered in his ear,

"If you report this duel to the police, I'll have you stabbed in your bed."

Fabrizio fled to Florence. Since he had remained in hiding in Bologna, it was only in Florence that he received all the duchess's reproachful letters; she could not forgive him for having come to her concert without trying to speak to her. Fabrizio was delighted by Count Mosca's letters: they were filled with forthright friendship and noble sentiments. He gathered that the count had written to the authorities of Bologna in such a way as to clear him of any suspicions which might hang over his head with regard to the duel. The police acted with perfect justice: they noted that two foreigners, only one of whom, the wounded man (Count M——), was known, had fought with swords in front of more than thirty peasants and the village priest, who had come toward the end of the duel and made unsuccessful efforts to separate the two adversaries. Since the name of Giuseppe Bossi had not been mentioned, less than two months later Fabrizio ventured to return to Bologna, more firmly convinced than ever that he was doomed never to know the noble and intellectual aspect of love. He gave himself the pleasure of explaining this to the duchess at great length; he was weary of his lonely life and now passionately yearned for a return of those charming evenings he had spent with her and the count. He had not known the sweet delights of good company since then.

"I went through so much boredom with Fausta and the love I tried to arouse in myself," he wrote to the duchess, "that now, even if her whims were still favorable to me, I would not travel twenty leagues to hold her to her word. So there is no reason for you to be afraid, as you tell me you are, that I will go all the way to Paris, where she is now appearing for the first time, with enormous success. But I would travel any distance to spend one evening with you and the count, who is so good to his friends."

BOOK TWO

With its constant shouting, that republic would prevent us from enjoying the best of monarchies.

(*Chapter Twenty-Three*)

CHAPTER FOURTEEN

While Fabrizio was in pursuit of love in a village near Parma, Chief Justice Rassi, unaware that he was so close to him, continued to treat his case as though it were that of a liberal: he claimed to be unable to find any witnesses for the defense, or rather he intimidated them; and finally, after nearly a year of skillful work, on a certain Friday some two months after Fabrizio's last return to Bologna, the Marquise Raversi, overjoyed, stated publicly in her drawing room that the sentence which had been passed on young del Dongo only an hour before would be presented to the prince for his signature and approved by him. A few minutes later the duchess was informed of what her enemy had said.

"The count must be very badly served by his agents!" she thought. "Only this morning he believed that the sentence couldn't be passed within less than a week. Perhaps he wouldn't mind keeping my young vicar-general out of Parma. But," she added, humming a little tune, "we'll see him come back, and some day he'll be our archbishop."

She rang for her footman and said to him, "Have all the servants gather in the anteroom, even the cooks. Go to the Town-Major and get a permit for four post horses, and have them harnessed to my landau within half an hour." All the women of the household were set to work packing trunks, and the duchess hurriedly put on a traveling costume. This was all done without a word to the count; she was delighted at the thought of making fun of him a little.

"My friends," she said to the assembled servants, "I have just learned that my poor nephew is about to be condemned in his absence for having had the audacity to defend his life against an enraged lunatic; it was Giletti who tried to kill him. You have all been able to see for yourselves how gentle and inoffensive Fabrizio's character is. Justly indignant at this atrocious affront, I am going to Florence. I am leaving each one of you ten years' wages. If you are ever in distress, write to me, and as long as I have a single sequin left, there will be something for you."

The duchess meant exactly what she said, and at these last words the servants burst into tears; her own eyes were also wet. She added in a voice charged with emotion, "Pray for me, and for *Monsignore* Fabrizio del Dongo, chief vicar-general of the diocese, who will tomorrow be sentenced to prison, or, what would be less stupid, to death."

The servants' tears redoubled and gradually changed into cries that were almost seditious. The duchess got into her carriage and went to the prince's palace. Despite the unaccustomed hour, she requested an audience through General Fontana, the aide-de-camp on duty; she was not in full court dress, and this threw him into a profound stupor. As for the prince, he was not at all surprised, and still less annoyed, by her request for an audience. "We're about to see tears shed by lovely eyes!" he thought, rubbing his hands together. "She's come to ask for mercy. That proud beauty is going to humiliate herself at last! She was too unbearable with her little airs of independence! Her expressive eyes always seemed to say to me, whenever the slightest thing offended her, 'It would be much more pleasant to live in Naples or Milan than in your little town of Parma.' It's true that I don't rule Naples or Milan, but that great lady has still come to ask for something that depends on me alone, and which she's dying to obtain. I always thought that her nephew's coming here would give me an advantage over her, in one way or another."

While the prince was smiling at these thoughts and indulging in all these pleasant anticipations, he paced up and down his large study, at the door of which General Fontana had remained standing, as stiff as a soldier presenting arms. Seeing the prince's shining eyes, and recalling the duchess's traveling costume, he thought the monarchy was disintegrating. His amazement knew no bounds when he heard the prince say to him, "Ask the duchess to wait for a few minutes." The general executed his about-face like a soldier on the parade ground. The prince smiled again. "Fontana isn't accustomed," he thought, "to seeing that proud duchess kept waiting. His astonished face when he tells her she'll have to 'wait for a few minutes' will prepare the way for the touching tears that are going to be shed in this room."

Those few minutes were delightful for the prince; he paced back and forth with firm, steady steps; he *reigned*. "At this point," he thought, "I mustn't say anything that's not perfectly correct; whatever my feelings toward the duchess may be, I mustn't forget that she's one of the greatest ladies of my court. How did Louis XIV speak to his daughters the princesses when he had reason to be displeased with them?" And his eyes came to rest on the portrait of the great king.

The amusing part of it was that it never occurred to the prince to ask himself whether he would show mercy to Fabrizio or, if so, what form that mercy would take. Finally, after twenty minutes, the faithful Fontana reappeared at the door, but without saying anything. "Duchess Sanseverina may enter," cried the prince with a theatrical air. "The tears are about to begin," he thought, and, as though to prepare himself for such a spectacle, he took out his handkerchief.

Never before had the duchess been so vivacious and pretty: she seemed to be no more than twenty-five. When he saw her light, quick little steps scarcely touching the carpet, the poor aide-de-camp nearly lost his head altogether.

"I have many apologies to make to Your Serene Highness," said the duchess in her light, gay little voice. "I've taken the liberty of coming before you in a costume that's not exactly proper, but you've made me so accustomed to your kindness that I ventured to hope you would grant me your indulgence once again."

She spoke rather slowly, in order to give herself time to enjoy the expression on the prince's face; it was delightful, because of its profound astonishment and the traces of the regal airs which the position of his head and arms still accentuated. He had remained as though thunderstruck; from time to time he cried out in his shrill, agitated, almost inarticulate voice, "What! What!"

After paying him her compliments, the duchess, as though out of respect, left him ample time to reply, then added, "I venture to hope that Your Serene Highness will deign to forgive me for the unseemliness of my costume." But as she said this, her mocking eyes sparkled with such brilliance that the prince could not bear it. He looked up at the ceiling; with him, this was the final sign of the most extreme discomposure.

"What! What!" he said once again; then he had the good fortune to think of something more proper to say: "Have a seat, duchess." He drew a chair forward himself, and with a certain graciousness. She was not insensitive to this courtesy: she softened the boldness of her expression.

"What! What!" repeated the prince, figeting in his armchair as though unable to find a comfortable position.

"I'm going to take advantage of the cool night air to travel by post," said the duchess, "and since my absence may be rather long, I didn't want to leave your dominions without thanking you for all the kindness you've been gracious enough to show me for the past five years."

At these words the prince finally understood. He turned pale; he was the one man in the world who suffered most from finding himself mistaken in his expectations. Then he took on an air of grandeur quite worthy of the portrait of Louis XIV that hung before his eyes. "Good," thought the duchess, "now he's a man."

"And what is the reason for this sudden departure?" asked the prince in a rather firm tone.

"I've been planning to leave for a long time," replied the duchess, "and a little insult given to *Monsignore* del Dongo, who tomorrow will be sentenced either to death or to prison, has made me hasten my departure."

"And where are you going?"

"To Naples, I think." She stood up. "I now have only to take leave of you, Your Highness, and thank you very humbly for all your *past* kindness." She, too, spoke firmly, so much so that the prince saw clearly that everything would be over in a few seconds; he knew that, once her dramatic departure had taken place, no arrangement would be possible: she was not a woman to go back on her actions. He hurried after her.

"But you know very well, duchess," he said, taking her hand, "that I've always been fond of you, and that it was within your power to give my fondness another name. A murder has been committed, that's undeniable; I entrusted the investigation of the case to my best judges. . . ."

At these words, the duchess drew herself up to her full height. All semblance of respect and even of courtesy vanished in the twinkling of an eye: the outraged woman appeared clearly, an outraged woman addressing a man she knew to be insincere. It was with a look of violent anger and even of contempt that she said to the prince, stressing every word, "I am leaving Your Serene Highness's dominions forever, so that I may never again hear any mention of Chief Justice Rassi and the other infamous assassins who have condemned my nephew and so many others to death. If Your Serene Highness wishes to avoid injecting a note of bitterness into the last moments I am spending with a prince who is courteous and intelligent when he is not deceived, I humbly beg you not to remind me of those infamous judges who sell themselves for a thousand scudi or a decoration."

The admirable and, above all, genuine tone in which she spoke these words made the prince start in alarm; for an instant he was afraid his dignity might be compromised by a more direct accusation, but on the whole his feelings finally turned into pleasure: he admired the duchess. Everything about her at that moment rose to sublime beauty. "My God, but she's beautiful!" he thought. "Some things must be forgiven in such an extraordinary woman, who probably has no equal anywhere in Italy. . . . And with a little diplomacy it might not be impossible to make her my mistress some day. What a difference between a woman like her and the Marquise Balbi, who's nothing but an empty-headed doll, but still manages to steal at least three hundred thousand lire a year from my poor subjects! . . . But did I hear correctly?" he thought suddenly. "She said, 'condemned my nephew and so many others.'" Then anger rose above all else, and it was with a haughtiness worthy of his supreme rank that the prince said, after a silence, "And what must be done to keep the duchess from leaving?"

"Something of which you are incapable," she replied with bitter irony and undisguised contempt.

The prince was beside himself, but long practice in the business of being an absolute sovereign gave him the strength to resist his impulse. "I must have this woman," he thought, "I owe it to myself; and then I must make her die from contempt. . . . If she leaves this room, I'll never see her again." But, maddened with rage and hatred as he was at that moment, how could he think of something to say that would satisfy his self-esteem and, at the same time, induce the duchess not to leave his court immediately? "A gesture," he thought, "can't be repeated or held up to ridicule," and he placed himself between the duchess and the door. A short time later, he heard someone scratching on the door.

"Who's the damned fool," he cried, swearing at the top of his lungs, "who's come to inflict his idiotic presence on me?"

Poor General Fontana showed his pale and thoroughly bewildered face, then he mumbled, like a man in the throes of his death agony, "His Excellency Count Mosca requests the honor of an audience."

"Show him in!" shouted the prince, and as Mosca was bowing he said to him, "Well, here's Duchess Sanseverina, who says she's leaving Parma immediately to go and live in Naples, and as if that weren't bad enough, she's been making impertinent remarks to me!"

"What!" exclaimed Mosca, turning pale.

"Do you mean to say you didn't know she was planning to leave?"

"I had no idea of it! When I left her at six o'clock, she was cheerful and happy."

These words had an incredible effect on the prince. First he looked at Mosca, whose increasing pallor showed that he was speaking the truth and was not an accomplice to the duchess's impulsive decision. "In that case," he thought, "I'll lose her forever; pleasure and vengeance will vanish together. In Naples, she and her nephew Fabrizio will make epigrams about the great rage of the little Prince of Parma." Then he looked at the duchess. Anger and violent contempt were struggling for possession of her heart. Her eyes were now fixed on Count Mosca, and the delicate contours of her lovely lips expressed the bitterest disdain. Her whole face seemed to be saying, "Vile courtier!"

"So," thought the prince, after studying her, "I've lost that means of calling her back to Parma. It's still true that if she leaves this room at this moment she's lost to me. God only knows what she'll say about my judges in Naples. And with the intelligence and the divine power of persuasion that heaven has given her, she'll convince everyone. Thanks to her, I'll have the reputation of being a ridiculous tyrant who gets up every night to look under his bed. . . ." Then, in a skillful maneuver, as though intending to walk back and forth to diminish his agitation, the prince again placed himself in front of the door. The count was standing three paces to his right, pale, discomposed, and trembling so violently that he had to support himself on the back of the chair which the duchess had occupied at the beginning of the audience, and which the prince, in a moment of anger, had shoved away. The count was in love. "If she leaves, I'll follow her," he thought. "But will she want me to? That's the question."

Standing to the left of the prince with her arms folded and pressed against her chest, the duchess was looking at him with admirable impertinence; complete and profound pallor had replaced the vivid colors which had animated that sublime face only a short time before.

Unlike the two others, the prince had a red face and a worried expression. With his left hand he toyed convulsively with the cross attached to the Grand Cordon of his Order which he wore under his coat, while with his right hand he stroked his chin.

"What's to be done?" he said to Mosca, not knowing too well what he was doing, and carried along by his habit of consulting the count about everything.

"I really don't know, Your Serene Highness," replied the count with the air of a man about to breathe his last. He was scarcely able to pronounce the words of his answer. The tone of his voice gave the prince the first consolation his wounded pride had found since the beginning of the scene, and this little stroke of good fortune supplied him with a phrase which soothed his self-esteem.

"Well," he said, "I'm the most reasonable of the three of us. I'm willing to lay aside all consideration of my position in the world. I'm going to speak *as a friend*," and he added, with a fine condescending smile carefully imitated from the happy time of Louis XIV, "*as a friend speaking to friends.* Duchess, what must be done to make you forget your untimely decision?"

"I have no idea," replied the duchess with a deep sigh. "I have such a horror of Parma that I really have no idea." There was no intention of making an epigram in these words; it was obvious that sincerity itself had spoken through her lips.

The count turned sharply toward her: his courtier's soul was scandalized; then he gave the prince a supplicating look. With great dignity and self-possession, the prince let a few moments go by, then he said to the count, "I see that your charming friend is thoroughly overwrought. It's quite simple: she *adores* her nephew." He turned to the duchess and said, with a look of great gallantry and, at the same time, the expression one assumes when quoting a line from a play, "*What must one do to find favor in those lovely eyes?*"

The duchess had had time to reflect; slowly and firmly, as

though laying down an ultimatum, she answered, "You would have to write me a gracious letter, Your Highness, as you know so well how to do. You would say in it that, not being convinced of the guilt of Fabrizio del Dongo, the archbishop's chief vicar-general, you will not sign the sentence when it is presented to you, and that these unjust proceedings will have no consequence in the future."

"What do you mean, *unjust!*" cried the prince, reddening to the whites of his eyes and becoming angry again.

"That's not all!" retorted the duchess with Roman pride. "*This very evening*—and," she added, looking at the clock, "it's already a quarter past eleven—this very evening Your Serene Highness will send word to the Marquise Raversi that you advise her to go to the country to recover from the fatigue she must have suffered as the result of a certain trial she mentioned in her drawing room at the beginning of the evening."

The prince was pacing up and down the room like a man beside himself with rage.

"Has anyone ever seen such a woman before?" he cried. "She's showing disrespect for me!"

The duchess replied with perfect graciousness, "Never in my life have I had any thought of showing disrespect for Your Serene Highness. You've kindly condescended to say that you were speaking 'as a friend to friends.' I have no desire to remain in Parma," she added, looking at the count with the utmost contempt. This look decided the prince, who had till then been completely uncertain, even though her words might have seemed to announce a commitment; he cared nothing for words.

A few more remarks were exchanged, but finally Count Mosca was ordered to write the gracious letter requested by the duchess. He omitted the words, "These unjust proceedings will have no consequences in the future." "It's enough," he thought, "that the prince should not sign the sentence when it's presented to him." The prince thanked him with a glance as he signed the letter.

The count had made a serious error: the prince was tired and would have signed anything. He considered that he had played his cards well, and in his mind the whole scene was dominated by this idea: "If the duchess leaves, I'll find my court boring in less than a week." The count noticed that his master had changed the date to that of the following day. He looked at the clock: it was nearly midnight. He saw in this correction of the date nothing more than a fastidious desire to show proof of exactitude and efficient administration. As for the Marquise Raversi's exile, it caused no difficulty whatever: the prince took particular delight in exiling people.

"General Fontana!" he called, opening the door a little.

The general appeared with such an astonished and curious expression that the duchess and the count exchanged an amused glance, and this glance made peace between them.

"General Fontana," said the prince, "you will get into my carriage, which is waiting under the colonnade. You will go to the Marquise Raversi's house and have yourself announced to her; if she is in bed, you will specify that you have been sent by me, and when you are in her bedroom you will say these exact words, and no others: 'Marquise Raversi, His Serene Highness requests you to leave tomorrow morning, before eight o'clock, for your country house at Velleia. His Highness will notify you when you may return to Parma.'"

The prince's eyes sought those of the duchess, who, without thanking him as he expected, made an extremely respectful bow to him and walked swiftly out of the room.

"What a woman!" said the prince, turning to Count Mosca.

The count, overjoyed by the Marquise Raversi's exile, which would facilitate all his ministerial activities, spoke for a full half-hour with all the skill of a consummate courtier. He wanted to soothe the sovereign's self-esteem, and he did not take leave of him until he saw him thoroughly convinced that the anecdotal history of Louis XIV contained no finer page than the one he had just provided for his future historians.

When the duchess reached home she shut her door and gave orders that no one was to be admitted, not even the count. She wanted to be alone so that she could consider what idea she ought to form of the scene that had just taken place. She had acted impulsively, and for her own momentary pleasure; but no matter what action she might have let herself be swept into, she would have held to it firmly. She would not have blamed herself when she recovered her self-possession, and still less would she have repented: such was the character to which she owed the privilege of still being, at the age of thirty-six, the prettiest woman at court.

She was now thinking of what Parma could offer in the way of attractions, as though she had just returned from a long journey, so firmly had she believed, from nine o'clock till eleven, that she was about to leave Parma forever.

"The poor count cut an amusing figure when he learned of my departure in the prince's presence," she thought. "The fact is that he's a charming man with a rare heart! He'd have left his ministries to follow me.... But also, not once in five whole years has he been able to reproach me with any lack of consideration. How many women married before the altar could say as much to their lords and masters? I must admit that he's not at all self-important or smug. He arouses no desire to deceive him; with me, he always seems ashamed of his power.... He cut a comical figure in the presence of his lord and master; if he were here I'd kiss him. ... But not for anything in the world would I assume the task of amusing a minister who'd lost his portfolio. There's a malady which only death can cure ... and which brings on death. What a misfortune it would be to become a minister while still young! I must write to him: this is one of the things he ought to be clearly aware of before he quarrels with his prince.... But I'm forgetting my good servants."

The duchess rang. Her maidservants were still busy packing trunks. The carriage had been driven under the portico and was being loaded while all the servants who had no work to do stood around it with tears in their eyes. Cecchina, who on great occasions entered the duchess's bedroom alone, reported all these details to her.

"Tell them to come upstairs," said the duchess. A few moments later she went into the anteroom.

"I have been promised," she told her servants, "that the sentence passed on my nephew will not be signed by the sovereign." (This is the word used in Italy.) "I am deferring my departure. We'll see whether my enemies will have enough influence to have the decision changed."

After a short silence, the servants began shouting "Long live the duchess!" and wildly clapping their hands. The duchess, who had gone into the next room, reappeared like an actress taking a curtain call, bowed graciously to them and said, "My friends, I thank you." A word from her at that moment would have been enough to make them all march off to attack the palace. She beckoned to a postilion, a former smuggler who was devoted to her; he followed her.

"I want you to dress yourself as a prosperous peasant," she said to him, "and leave Parma as best you can. Rent a *sediola*, go to Bologna as quickly as possible and enter the city through the Florence gate, as though you were taking a pleasure drive. Cecchina will give you a package; deliver it to Fabrizio at the Pellegrino. He's in hiding there, and he goes by the name of Giuseppe Bossi. Don't give him away through carelessness. Pretend not to know him: my enemies may put spies on your trail. Fabrizio will send you back in a few hours or a few days, and it's especially on your way back that you must take extra precautions to avoid giving him away."

"Ah, the Marquise Raversi's men!" cried the postilion. "We're waiting for them, and they'll soon be exterminated if you want them to be."

"Some day, perhaps! But be sure, on your life, that you do nothing without my orders."

It was a copy of the prince's letter that the duchess wanted to send to Fabrizio, and she could not resist the pleasure of amusing him by adding a few words about the scene that had produced it; these few words lengthened into a ten-page letter. She sent for the postilion again.

"You can't leave," she told him, "until four o'clock, when the gates are opened."

"I was planning to go out through the main sewer; I'd be in water up to my chin, but I'd get through."

"No," said the duchess, "I won't expose one of my most faithful servants to the risk of catching a fever. Do you know anyone in the archbishop's household?"

"The second coachman is a friend of mine."

"Here's a letter for that saintly prelate. Slip quietly into his palace and have someone take you to his valet; I don't want the archbishop to be awakened. If he's already retired to his bedroom, spend the night in the palace, and, since he's in the habit of getting up at dawn, have yourself announced as my messenger at four o'clock tomorrow morning, ask the archbishop for his blessing, give him this package and take any letters he may give you for Bologna."

She sent the archbishop the original of the prince's letter. Since it concerned his chief vicar-general, she requested him to deposit it in the archives of his palace, where she hoped that her nephew's colleagues, the canons and other vicars-general, would be kind enough to take cognizance of it. All this was done under the seal of the utmost secrecy.

The duchess wrote to Archbishop Landriani with a familiarity which she felt sure would delight the worthy commoner. The signature alone took up three lines; the letter, a

215

very friendly one, was followed by these words: "Angelina-Cornelia-Isola Valserra del Dongo, Duchess Sanseverina."

"I don't think I've written so much," she said to herself, laughing, "since I signed my marriage contract with the poor duke! But such people can't be controlled without things like this; caricature passes for beauty in the eyes of the middle classes." She could not let the evening go by without yielding to the temptation to write the poor count a bantering letter. She formally announced to him, "for his guidance in his relations with crowned heads," that she did not feel capable of amusing a dismissed minister. "The prince frightens you," she wrote; "if you could no longer see him, would it then be my duty to frighten you?" She had this letter delivered to him at once.

As for the prince, at seven o'clock the next morning he sent for Count Zurla, Minister of the Interior. "Once again," he said to him, "give strict orders to all the podestas to arrest Fabrizio del Dongo. We've been informed that he may dare to reappear in our territory. Since he's now in Bologna, where he seems to be defying the actions of our law courts, post police officers who know him personally in the following places: in the villages along the road from Bologna to Parma, in the vicinity of Duchess Sanseverina's houses at Sacca and Castelnuovo, and around Count Mosca's country house. I venture to hope, count, that your great sagacity will enable you to prevent Count Mosca's penetrating eyes from giving him any knowledge of these orders from your sovereign. Understand this clear: I want Signor Fabrizio del Dongo arrested."

As soon as the Minister of the Interior was gone, Chief Justice Rassi came in through a secret door, bent double and bowing to the prince at every step. The scoundrel's face was a perfect picture: it did justice to all the infamy of his role, and while the quick, disorderly movements of his eyes betrayed his awareness of his merits, the arrogant, self-confident grimace of his lips showed that he knew how to fight against contempt.

Since this personage is going to have a rather great influence on Fabrizio's destiny, it may be well to say a few words about him here. He was tall and had handsome, shrewd eyes, but his face was severely pockmarked. As for intelligence, he had a great deal of it, and it was of the keenest kind. It was generally recognized that he had a thorough knowledge of law, but he distinguished himself chiefly by his resourcefulness. No matter how a case was presented to him, he could always quickly and easily find a solid legal basis for either a conviction or an acquittal. He was above all a master of the prosecutor's wiles.

This man, whose services to the Prince of Parma might have been envied by great monarchies, was known to have only one passion: to engage in intimate conversation with great personages and please them with buffooneries. It mattered little to him whether the powerful man laughed at what he said, or at him, or made revolting jokes about his wife: as long as he saw him laugh and was treated with familiarity, he was happy. Sometimes, not knowing how else to abuse the dignity of this great judge, the prince would give him a few kicks; if the kicks hurt him, he would begin to cry. But his instinct for buffoonery was so strong that he always preferred to be in the drawing room of a minister who jeered at him, rather than in his own drawing room, where he reigned despotically over all the black-robed gentlemen of Parma. Rassi had made a unique position for himself, in that it was impossible for the most insolent nobleman to humiliate him. His way of avenging the insults he endured all day long was to recount them to the prince, for he had acquired the privilege of saying anything to him. It is true that a well-applied, painful slap was often the only answer he received, but he never took any offense at that. The great judge's presence distracted the prince in his moments of bad humor: he could then entertain himself by abusing him outrageously. It can be seen that Rassi was almost a perfect man for life at court: he had neither honor nor resentment.

"There must be secrecy at all costs!" the prince shouted at him without greeting him, treating him with boorish contempt, despite his usual courtesy to everyone. "When is your sentence dated?"

"Yesterday morning, Your Serene Highness."

"How many judges signed it?"

"All five."

"And what is the penalty?"

"Twenty years in the fortress, as Your Serene Highness told me."

"A death sentence would have shocked people," said the prince, as though talking to himself. "It's a shame! What an effect it would have had on that woman! But he's a del Dongo, and that name is revered in Parma, because of the three almost successive archbishops. . . . You say twenty years?"

"Yes, Your Serene Highness," replied Chief Justice Rassi, still standing and bent double, "with, first of all, a public apology in front of Your Serene Highness's portrait, and, furthermore, a diet of bread and water every Friday and on the eve of every major holiday, 'since the criminal is notorious for his impiety.' That's for the future, and to ruin his career."

"Write this," said the prince: " 'His Serene Highness, having deigned to listen graciously to the most humble supplications of the Marquise del Dongo, mother of the guilty party, and Duchess Sanseverina, his aunt, who have pointed out to him that at the time of the crime their son and nephew was very young, and moreover led astray by a mad passion conceived for the wife of the unfortunte Giletti, has consented, despite the horror aroused by such a murder, to commute the sentence of Fabrizio del Dongo to twelve years in the fortress.' Give it to me to sign."

The prince signed the sentence and dated it the day before; then he handed it back to Rassi and said, "Write this immediately below my signature: 'Duchess Sanseverina having again thrown herself at His Highness's feet, he has granted permission for the criminal to have an hour of exercise every Thursday on the platform of the square tower commonly known as the Farnese Tower.' Sign that, and make sure you keep your mouth shut, no matter what you may hear anyone say in the city. You may tell Judge de Capitani, who voted for a sentence of two years and even made a speech in support of his ridiculous opinion, that I advise him to reread the laws and regulations. Once again: silence! Good night."

Chief Justice Rassi made three slow, deep bows which the prince did not watch.

This took place at seven o'clock in the morning. A few hours later, the news of the Marquise Raversi's exile spread through the city and its cafés. Everyone began talking at once about this great event. For a time, the marquise's exile drove from Parma that implacable enemy of small towns and small courts: boredom. General Fabio Conti, who had regarded himself as already a minister, claimed to have an attack of gout and did not leave his fortress for several days. The middle classes, and consequently the working classes also, concluded from what was happening that the prince had obviously decided to make *Monsignore* del Dongo the Archbishop of Parma. The shrewd politicians of the cafés went so far as to maintain that Father Landriani, the present archbishop, had been told to feign an illness and hand in his resignation; he would be given a large income from the tobacco tax, they were sure of it. This rumor reached the archbishop. It alarmed him greatly, and for several days his zeal for our hero was seriously paralyzed. Two months later, this fine piece of news appeared in the Paris newspapers, with the slight alteration that it was Count Mosca, nephew of Duchess Sanseverina, who was going to be made Archbishop of Parma.

In her country house at Velleia, the Marquise Raversi was furious. She was not one of those frail women who consider that they have taken vengeance when they have hurled abuse against their enemies. The day after her disgrace, Cavaliere Riscara and three other friends of hers presented themselves to the prince at her orders and asked permission to go and visit her at her country house. His Highness gave these gentlemen a gracious reception, and their arrival at Velleia was a great consolation to the marquise. Before the end of the second week, she had thirty people in her house, all those who were to be placed in office by a liberal ministry. She held a conference with the best informed of her friends every evening.

One evening, after having received many letters from Parma and Bologna during the day, she retired early. Her maid first brought into her bedroom her current lover, Count Baldi, an insignificant young man with a handsome face, and later Cavaliere Riscara, his predecessor. The latter was a little man, dark physically and morally, who had begun as a geometry teacher in the college for noblemen in Parma and now found himself a Knight of several Orders.

"I have the good habit," the marquise said to these two men, "of never destroying any papers, and it's a lucky thing for me now: here are nine letters written to me by Duchess Sanseverina on various occasions. You will both go to Genoa, and, among the convicts, there you will find an ex-notary named Burati, like the great Venetian poet . . . or perhaps it's Durati. Count Baldi, sit down at my desk and write what I'm going to dictate to you:

"'I am writing you this note because an idea has just occurred to me. I am going to my cottage near Castelnuovo: if you would like to come and spend twelve hours with me, I shall be very happy. After what has happened, it seems to me that there is no great danger; the clouds are clearing away. However, stop before you enter Castelnuovo. You will meet one of my servants on the road; they are all passionately devoted to you. You will, of course, keep the name of Bossi for this little journey. I have been told that you now wear a beard like a model Capuchin, and you have been seen in Parma only with a face befitting a vicar-general.' Do you understand, Riscara?"

"Perfectly. But the trip to Genoa is a useless luxury: I know a man in Parma who's not yet a convict, it's true, but who's sure to become one some day. He'll counterfeit the duchess's handwriting admirably."

At these words, Count Baldi opened his handsome eyes wide: only now had he begun to understand.

"If you know this worthy gentleman in Parma, whom you expect to see advance in the world," said the marquise to Riscara, "then he obviously knows you too, and his mistress, his confessor or his friend may be paid by the duchess to spy for her. I'd rather delay this little jest a few days and avoid exposing myself to any risk. Leave in two hours, like good little lambs, don't go to see a living soul in Genoa, and come back quickly."

Cavaliere Riscara hurried away, laughing. "It's time to pack up!" he said, talking through his nose like Punchinello and running in a burlesque manner. He wanted to leave Baldi alone with the marquise.

Five days later, Cavaliere Riscara brought her Count Baldi back to her with his skin rubbed raw: to save six leagues, he had been made to cross a mountain on muleback; he swore that he would never again let himself be talked into making a "long journey." He gave the marquise three copies of the letter she had dictated to him, and five or six other letters in the same handwriting, composed by Riscara, which might prove to be useful later on. One of these letters contained some delightful jokes about the prince's fears at night, and about the pitiful thinness of the Marquise Balbi, his mistress, who, it was said, left a mark like that of a pair of tongs on the cushion of an easy chair after she had sat on it for a moment. One would have sworn that all these letters had been written by Duchess Sanseverina's hand.

"I know, beyond all doubt," said the marquise, "that the young man closest to her heart, Fabrizio, is in Bologna or the immediate vicinity—"

"I'm too sick!" cried Count Baldi, interrupting her. "I beg

to be excused from that second journey, or at least to be allowed several days in which to recover my health."

"I'll plead your cause," said Riscara. He stood up and spoke softly to the marquise.

"All right, I agree," she replied, smiling. "Don't worry, you won't have to go," she said to Baldi with a rather disdainful air.

"Thank you!" he cried warmly.

Riscara went to Bologna alone in a post chaise. He had been there for scarcely two days when he saw Fabrizio and Marietta riding in a barouche together. "Well, well!" he said to himself. "Our future archbishop is apparently enjoying himself quite freely here! The duchess will have to be informed of this: she'll be delighted." He had no difficulty in following Fabrizio to find out where he lived.

The next morning, Fabrizio received the letter that had been manufactured in Genoa. He found it rather short, but suspected nothing. The thought of seeing the duchess and the count again made him wildly happy, and despite everything Ludovico could say, he took a post horse and galloped off. Without knowing it, he was followed at a short distance by Cavaliere Riscara, who, on arriving at the post before Castelnuovo, six leagues from Parma, had the pleasure of seeing a large crowd gathered in the square in front of the local jail: our hero had just been taken into it after being recognized at the post house, while changing horses, by two police officers who had been chosen and sent by Count Zurla.

Riscara's little eyes sparkled with joy. With exemplary patience, he verified everything that had just taken place in the little village, then sent a courier to the Marquise Raversi. After this, making his way though to see the picturesque church there, and then to look for a painting by Il Parmigiano which, he had been told, was to be found in that vicinity, he finally encountered the podesta of the village, who hastened to pay his respects to a Councilor of State. Riscara expressed surprise that the podesta, after being fortunate enough to apprehend a conspirator, had not immediately sent him to the citadel of Parma. "There is reason to fear," he said coldly, "that his many friends who were trying to find him two days ago, to facilitate his passage through His Serene Highness's territory, may run into the police. There were more than a dozen of those rebels, all on horseback."

"*Intelligenti pauca!*" exclaimed the podesta with a knowing look.

CHAPTER FIFTEEN

Two hours later, poor Fabrizio, handcuffed and attached with a long chain to the *sediola* in which he was forced to ride, set off for the citadel of Parma, escorted by eight constables. They had orders to bring with them all the other constables posted in the villages through which the procession would pass. The podesta himself accompanied this important prisoner. At about seven o'clock in the evening, the *sediola*, escorted by thirty constables and all the urchins in Parma, crossed the beautiful promenade, passed the house in which Fausta had lived a few months earlier, and finally drew up in front of the outer gate of the citadel just as General Fabio Conti and his daughter were about to come out. The governor's carriage stopped before reaching the drawbridge to make way for the *sediola* to which Fabrizio was chained. The general immediately shouted orders to close the gates of the citadel, and hurried to the office at the entrance to find out what was happening. He was not a little surprised when he recognized the prisoner, whose whole body had become stiff from being chained to the *sediola* during such a long journey. Four constables had taken him out and were now carrying him into the office. "So I now have in my power," thought the vainglorious governor, "that famous Fabrizio del Dongo, with whom the high society of Parma seems to have sworn to concern itself exclusively for the past year!"

The general had met him a score of times at court, in the duchess's palace and elsewhere, but he was careful not to show that he knew him: he would have been afraid of compromising himself.

"Draw up a detailed report," he said to the prison clerk, "of the delivery of the prisoner to me by the worthy podesta of Castelnuovo."

Barbone, the clerk, a terrifying man because of his martial appearance and the size of his beard, took on a more self-important air than usual: he could have passed for a German jailer. Thinking that it was chiefly Duchess Sanseverina who had prevented his master, the governor, from becoming Minister of War, he treated the prisoner with more than ordinary insolence. He addressed him as "*voi*," which in Italy is the form used in speaking to servants.

"I am a prelate of the Holy Roman Church," Fabrizio said to him firmly, "and a vicar-general of this diocese. My birth alone entitles me to respect."

"I know nothing about that!" the clerk retorted impertinently. "Prove what you say by showing me the documents that give you a right to those respectable titles!"

Fabrizio had no documents; he did not answer. General Fabio Conti, standing beside his clerk, watched him write without looking up at the prisoner, in order not to be obliged to say that he was really Fabrizio del Dongo.

Suddenly Clelia Conti, who was waiting in the carriage, heard a frightful uproar coming from the guardroom. In making an insolent and very long physical description of the prisoner, the clerk Barbone had ordered him to open his clothes so that he could verify the number and condition of the cuts he had received in his fight with Giletti.

"I can't," said Fabrizio, smiling bitterly. "I'm not in a position to obey your orders: my handcuffs make it impossible!"

"What!" cried the general with an innocent air. "The prisoner is handcuffed? Inside the fortress? That's against regulations! It requires a special order! Take off his handcuffs."

Fabrizio looked at him and thought, "Here's a fine Jesuit! For the past hour he's seen that these handcuffs were hurting me terribly, and now he pretends to be surprised!"

The handcuffs were taken off by the constables. They had just learned that he was Duchess Sanseverina's nephew, so they hastened to show him a honeyed politeness which contrasted with the clerk's rudeness. The latter seemed irritated by this; he said to Fabrizio, who was standing motionless, "Come on, hurry up! Show us the cuts poor Giletti gave you when you murdered him."

With one bound, Fabrizio rushed at the clerk and gave him such a violent slap, that it knocked him off his chair; he fell against the general's legs. The constables seized Fabrizio's arms. He again stood still. The general himself, and two constables who were beside him, quickly picked up the clerk, whose face was bleeding abundantly. Two other constables who had been standing further away ran over to close the door of the office, thinking the prisoner was trying to escape. The sergeant in command of them did not think that young del Dongo could make a very serious attempt to escape, since after all he was inside the citadel, but he nevertheless went over to the window to prevent any disorder, moved by professional instinct. The general's carriage had stopped just outside this open window, only two paces away. Clelia had drawn back into a corner, in order not to witness the sad scene that was taking place in the office. On hearing all this noise, she looked out.

"What's happening?" she said to the sergeant.

"It's young Fabrizio del Dongo, signorina: he just gave that insolent Barbone a fine slap in the face!"

"What! Is it Signor del Dongo they're putting in prison?"

"It certainly is," replied the sergeant. "It's because of the poor young man's noble birth that they're going through all that ceremony. I thought you knew, signorina."

Clelia continued to look out through the carriage window. When the constables surrounding the table stepped back a little, she saw the prisoner. "When I met him on the road to Lake Como," she said to herself, "who would have thought that I'd see him again for the first time in this sad situation? . . . He gave me his hand to help me into his mother's carriage. . . . He was already with the duchess! Had their love affair begun by then?"

The reader must be informed that, in the liberal party led by the Marquise Raversi and General Conti, everyone claimed to have no doubt about the amorous relations that were presumed to exist between Fabrizio and the duchess. Count Mosca, whom they all abhorred, was the butt of endless jokes because of his gullibility.

"So now he's a prisoner," thought Clelia, "and the prisoner of his enemies, too! Because, even if there are those who would like to think of Count Mosca as an angel, at the bottom of his heart he'll be delighted by this capture."

There was a loud burst of laughter from the guardroom.

"Jacopo," she said to the sergeant in a faltering voice, "tell me what's happening!"

"The general sternly asked the prisoner why he hit Barbone, and *Monsignore* Fabrizio answered calmly, 'He called me a murderer: have him show the documents that authorize him to give me that title.' And everyone laughed."

Barbone was replaced by a jailer who knew how to write. Clelia saw him come out, using his handkerchief to wipe away the blood that was streaming from his hideous face. "I'll kill that damned Fabrizio myself!" he said loudly. "I'll cheat the hangman. . ." etc., etc. He stopped between the general's carriage and the window of the office to look at Fabrizio, and his swearing redoubled.

"Get out of here," the sergeant said to him. "You should know better than to swear like that in front of the signorina!"

Barbone raised his head and looked inside the carriage. His eyes met Clelia's and a cry of horror escaped from her: never before had she seen such an atrocious expression from such close range. "He'll kill Fabrizio!" she thought. "I must tell Don Cesare." Don Cesare was her uncle, one of the most highly respected priests in Parma; General Conti, his brother, had obtained the post of treasurer and head chaplain of the prison for him.

The general got back into his carriage.

"Would you rather go home," he said to his daughter, "or wait for me, perhaps for a long time, in the courtyard of the palace? I must go and report all this to His Highness."

Fabrizio was just coming out of the office, escorted by three constables. They were taking him to the cell that had been assigned to him. Clelia was looking out of the carriage window and the prisoner was very close to her. At that moment she made this reply to her father's question: "I'll go with you." Hearing these words spoken so close to him, Fabrizio looked up and met the young girl's gaze. He was especially struck by the melancholy expression of her face. "How much more beautiful she's become," he thought, "since our meeting near Como! What a deeply thoughtful expression! . . . People are right to compare her with the duchess: what an angelic face!"

Barbone, the bleeding clerk, had not remained near the carriage without a reason. He made a gesture which stopped the three constables who were leading Fabrizio away, then walked around the carriage from the rear, came up to the general beside the door, and said to him, "Since the prisoner has committed an act of violence inside the citadel, shouldn't he be kept in handcuffs for three days, in accordance with Article 157 of the regulations?"

"Go to the devil!" cried the general. He was terribly upset over Fabrizio's arrest: he had to avoid driving either the duchess or Count Mosca to extremes, and furthermore, how would the count interpret the matter? The murder of a man like Giletti was actually a trifle: only intrigue had succeeded in making it into something important.

During this short dialogue, Fabrizio was superb as he stood among the constables. His proud, noble expression, his fine, delicate features, and the smile of contempt that hovered lightly on his lips, made a charming contrast with the coarse appearance of the constables surrounding him. But all this formed, so to speak, only the outer aspect of his expression; he was enraptured by Clelia's celestial beauty, and his eyes betrayed all his surprise. Profoundly pensive, she had not thought of withdrawing her head from the carriage window. He bowed to her with a half-smile of great respect, then, after a moment, said to her, "It seems to me, signorina, that once before, near a lake, I had the honor of meeting you in the presence of constables."

Clelia blushed and was so taken aback that she could think of nothing to reply. "How noble he looks among those coarse creatures!" she had been thinking when Fabrizio spoke to her. Her deep pity, bordering on a more tender emotion, deprived her of the presence of mind necessary to find any words at all. She became aware of her silence and blushed still more. Just then the bolts of the main gate of the citadel were drawn back violently: hadn't His Excellency's carriage been kept waiting for at least a minute? The noise was so loud beneath the arch that even if Clelia had found words in which to answer Fabrizio, he would not have been able to hear them.

As she was carried away by the horses, which broke into a gallop as soon as they crossed the drawbridge, Clelia said to herself, "He must have found me terribly ridiculous!" Then suddenly she added, "No, not only ridiculous: he must have thought I had a base soul, that I didn't answer his greeting because he's a prisoner and I'm the governor's daughter."

This idea drove her to despair, for in reality she had a lofty soul. "What makes my conduct thoroughly degrading," she thought, "is the fact that before, when we met for the first time, also 'in the presence of constables,' as he said, it was I who was a prisoner, and he helped me by getting me out of an awkward situation. . . . Yes, I have to admit it, my conduct was completely inexcusable: I was both rude and ungrateful. Poor young man! Now that he's in trouble, everyone will be ungrateful to him. And he said to me at the time, 'Will you remember my name in Parma?' How he must despise me now! It would have been so easy to say a polite word! Yes, I must admit that my conduct toward him was horrible. Before, if it hadn't been for the generous offer of his mother's carriage, I'd have had to walk in the dust with the constables, or, much worse, ride behind one of them on a horse. It was then my father who was under arrest, and I who was defenseless! Yes, my conduct was inexcusable. And how keenly a man like him must have felt it! What a contrast between his noble face and my conduct! What nobility! What serenity! How heroic he looked, surrounded by his vile enemies! I can understand the duchess's passion now: if he's like that in the midst of trying circumstances that may have horrible consequences, what must he be like when his heart is happy!"

The governor's carriage remained in the courtyard of the palace for over an hour and a half, and yet when he came down from his audience with the prince, Clelia did not feel that he had stayed too long.

"What is His Highness's will?" she asked.

"His lips said 'Prison!' and his eyes said 'Death!' "

"Death! Dear God!" cried Clelia.

"Quiet!" said the general irritably. "It was foolish of me to answer a child!"

Meanwhile, Fabrizio was climbing the three hundred and eighty steps that led to the Farnese Tower, a new prison built on the platform of the main tower at a tremendous height. Not once did he think, not clearly at least, of the great change that had just taken place in his fate. "What eyes!" he was saying to himself. "How many things they expressed! What profound pity! She seemed to be saying, 'Life is a web of misfortunes. Don't grieve too much over what's happening to you. Haven't we been placed in this world to be unhappy?' And how those lovely eyes remained fixed on me, even when the horses were moving so noisily through the arch!"

Fabrizio completely forgot to be unhappy.

Clelia went to several drawing rooms with her father. At the beginning of the evening, no one had yet heard the news of the arrest of the "great culprit," as the courtiers referred to the poor, rash young man two hours later.

It was noticed that evening that Clelia's face was more animated than usual. Now animation, the appearance of taking part in what was happening around her, was the main thing that was lacking in this beautiful girl. When her beauty was compared to that of the duchess, it was especially the impression she gave of not being moved by anything, of being above everything, that tipped the balance in her rival's favor. In England or France, countries of vanity, the opposite opinion would probably have prevailed. Clelia Conti was a young girl who was still a little too slender, and who might have been compared to the lovely figures of Guido Reni. We will not conceal the fact that, if one accepted the Greek standards of beauty, one might have objected that some of her features were too strongly marked: her lips, for example, filled with the most charming grace, were a little too thick.

The admirable singularity of this face, in which shone art-less grace and the celestial imprint of a noble soul, was that, although of the rarest and most singular beauty, it in no way resembled the heads of Greek statues. The duchess, on the other hand, had a little too much of the *recognized* beauty of the ideal, and her truly Lombard face recalled the voluptuous smiles and tender melancholy of Leonardo da Vinci's lovely paintings of Herodias. The duchess was vivacious, sparkling with mischievous wit, attaching herself passionately, if we may express it thus, to every subject which the flow of conversation brought before her mind's eye. To an equal degree, Clelia showed herself calm and slow to become aroused, whether out of contempt for what was around her, or out of nostalgia for some absent fancy. For a long time it had been thought that she would eventually become a nun. At the age of twenty she was seen to have a repugnance for going to balls; if she went to one with her father, it was only out of obedience, and to avoid acting contrary to the interests of his ambition.

"Heaven has given me the most beautiful and virtuous daughter in our sovereign's dominions," the vulgar-minded general repeated too often, "and yet it's impossible for me to put her to any use in the advancement of my career! My life is too isolated, I have no one but her in the world, and I urgently need a family to support me in society and give me access to certain drawing rooms where my merit, and especially my aptitude for ministerial office, would be established as an unassailable basis for all political discussion. But my beautiful, virtuous, pious daughter becomes cross whenever a young man who has a good position at court makes any attempt to win her favor! As soon as she's dismissed her suitor, her disposition becomes less somber and she seems almost cheerful, until another eligible man comes forward. The handsomest man at court, Count Baldi, presented himself and displeased her; he was succeeded by the richest man in His Highness's dominions, the Marquis Crescenzi, and she maintains that he would make her life miserable."

"There's no doubt about it," the general would say at other times, "my daughter's eyes are more beautiful than the duchess's, especially since, on rare occasions, they're capable of taking on a deeper expression; but when does anyone ever see that magnificent expression? Never in a drawing room where it might do her great honor, but in the carriage, alone with me, when she's let herself be overcome with pity, for example, by the misfortune of some hideous lout. I sometimes say to her, 'Keep some trace of that sublime look for the drawing rooms we'll appear in tonight,' but she never does anything of the sort: if she deigns to go into society with me, her pure, noble face shows only the rather haughty and discouraging expression of passive obedience."

As can be seen, the general spared no effort to find himself a suitable son-in-law, but what he said was true.

Courtiers, who have nothing to contemplate inside their souls, are attentive to everything around them. Those of Parma had observed that it was especially on days when Clelia could not tear herself away from her beloved daydreams, or pretend to take an interest in anything, that the duchess liked to try to draw her into conversation. Clelia had ash-blond hair that gently stood out against the delicate coloring of cheeks that were usually a little too pale. The shape of her forehead alone might have been enough to tell an attentive observer that her noble air, her demeanor so far above ordinary graces, sprang from a profound indifference to everything ordinary. It was the absence, not the impossibility of interest in anything. Since her father had become governor of the citadel, she had been happy, or at least free from sorrow, in her lofty apartment. The frightful number of steps that had to be climbed in order to reach the governor's residence, standing on the platform of the great tower, kept tiresome visitors away, and Clelia, for this physical reason, enjoyed the kind of freedom to be found in a convent; it was nearly the same happiness she had once expected to attain by becoming a nun. She was horrified at the very idea of placing her beloved solitude and her intimate thoughts at the disposal of a young man whom the title of husband would authorize to trouble her entire inner life. If she had not attained happiness by solitude, she had at least succeeded in avoiding sensations that would have been unbearably painful to her.

On the evening of the day when Fabrizio was taken to the fortress, the duchess met Clelia in the drawing room of the Minister of the Interior, Count Zurla. Everyone gathered around them; that evening, Clelia's beauty surpassed the duchess's. The expression of her eyes was so singular and profound that it was almost indiscreet; there was pity in her gaze, and also indignation and anger. The duchess's gaiety and sparkling ideas seemed to plunge Clelia into fits of sorrow that verged on horror. "How this poor woman will cry out and moan," she thought, "when she learns that her lover, that young man with such a great heart and such a noble face, has been thrown into prison! And those looks in the sovereign's eyes which condemn him to death! O absolute power, when will you cease to oppress Italy? O base, mercenary souls! And I'm the daughter of a jailer! And I did nothing to belie that noble character when I didn't deign to answer Fabrizio! And he was once my benefactor! What is he thinking about me at this moment, alone in his cell with his little lamp?" Revolted by this idea, Clelia glanced in horror at the magnificent illumination of the drawing rooms of the Minister of the Interior.

In the circle of courtiers who had gathered around the two reigning beauties, seeking to join in their conversation, people were saying, "Never before have they talked to each other with such animation, and at the same time such intimacy. The duchess is always trying to ward off the hatreds aroused by the Prime Minister; can it be that she's planning some great marriage for Clelia?" This conjecture was supported by something which the court had never seen before: Clelia's eyes had more fire, and even, if we may say so, more passion than those of the beautiful duchess.

For her part, the duchess was astonished, and, it may be said to her glory, delighted by the new charms she was discovering in the solitary young girl. She had been looking at her for an hour with a pleasure that is seldom felt at the sight of a rival. "What's happened to her?" she wondered. "She's never been so beautiful, or, one might say, so touching. Can it be that her heart has spoken? . . . But in that case, it's certainly an unhappy love; there's dark sorrow beneath that animation of hers. . . . But unhappy love keeps silent! Is she trying to bring back a faithless lover by shining in society?"

The duchess looked carefully at all the young men around them. Nowhere did she see an unusual expression: every face wore a look of more or less self-satisfied conceit. "There must be some miracle here," she thought, annoyed at being unable to fathom the mystery. "Where's Count Mosca, with all his shrewdness? No, I'm not mistaken: Clelia is looking at me attentively, as though I were the object of a completely new interest. Is it the result of some order given by her father, that vile courtier? I thought her young, noble heart was incapable of descending to mercenery matters. Does General Fabio Conti have some decisive request to make to the count?"

Toward ten o'clock, a friend of the duchess came up to her and whispered a few words in her ear. She turned extremely pale. Clelia took her hand and ventured to press it.

"I thank you, and I understand you now: you have a beautiful soul!" said the duchess with great effort; she scarcely had enough strength to utter these few words. She smiled repeatedly at the lady of the house, who rose to accompany her to the door of the last drawing room. This was an honor due only to a princess of the blood, and for the duchess it contrasted cruelly with her present position. She therefore smiled often at Countess Zurla, but despite extraordinary efforts she was not able to say a single word to her.

Clelia's eyes filled with tears as she watched the duchess pass through those drawing rooms in which the most distinguished members of society were gathered. "What will become of the poor woman when she's alone in her carriage?" she thought. "It would be indiscreet of me to offer to accompany her! I wouldn't dare. . . . And yet what a consolation it would be to the poor prisoner, sitting alone with his little lamp in some dreadful cell, if he knew he was loved that much! What frightful solitude he's been plunged into! And *we* are here in these brightly lighted drawing rooms! It's horrible! Is there any way of delivering a message to him? My God! That would be a betrayal of my father! His position is so precarious between the two parties! What will become of him if he exposes himself to the hatred of the duchess, who controls the will of the Prime Minister, who in turn controls three-quarters of all government affairs? On the other hand, the prince is constantly concerned with what takes place in the fortress, and he's very touchy on the subject; fear can make a man cruel. . . . In any case, Fabrizio" (Clelia no longer thought of him as Signor del Dongo) "is much more to be pitied! He stands to lose much more than a lucrative position! . . . And the duchess! . . . What a terrible passion love is! . . . And yet all those liars in society speak of it as though it were a source of happiness! Old women are pitied because they can no longer feel or inspire love! . . . I'll never forget what I've just seen: what a sudden change! How dull and lifeless the duchess's beautiful, radiant eyes became as soon as she heard the fatal words the Marquis N—— came to say to her! . . . Fabrizio must be truly worthy of love! . . ."

In the midst of these very serious reflections, which occupied her entire soul, the complimentary remarks that were still being made around her seemed even more disagreeable to her than usual. To escape from them, she walked to an open window that was half veiled by a taffeta curtain; she hoped that no one would be so bold as to follow her into her retreat. The window overlooked a little grove of orange trees that were planted directly in the ground, although it is true that they had to be protected by a roof in winter. She breathed in the fragrance of their blossoms with delight, and this pleasure seemed to restore a little calm to her soul. . . . "I found that he had a very noble air," she thought, "but to inspire such a passion in such a distinguished woman! . . . She can pride herself on having refused the prince's advances; she could have been the queen of his dominions if she'd wanted to. My father says that the prince's passion was so strong that he was willing to marry her if he ever became free to do so! . . . And her love for Fabrizio has lasted a long time, because it was at least five years ago that we met them near Lake Como! . . . Yes, it was five years ago," she said to herself after a moment of reflection. "I was struck by it even then, when so many things passed unnoticed before my childish eyes! How those two ladies seemed to admire Fabrizio!"

Clelia noticed with joy that none of the young men who had been speaking to her so eagerly had dared to come over to the balcony. One of them, the Marquis Crescenzi, had taken a few steps in that direction, then stopped at a gaming table. "If only I had a view of lovely orange trees like these from the little window of my apartment in the fortress, the only one that has any shade," she said to herself, "my thoughts would be less sad! But all I can see are the two huge stone blocks of the Farnese Tower! . . . Oh!" she exclaimed with a start, "perhaps that's where they've put him! I'm so eager to talk to Don Cesare! He'll be less stern than the general. My father surely won't tell me anything when we go home, but I'll find out everything from Don Cesare. . . . I have money; I might buy a few orange trees: if they were placed beneath the window of my aviary, they'd cut off my view of the great wall of the Farnese Tower. How much more odious it will be to me now that I know one of the people it hides from the light of day! . . .

"Yes, it was the third time I've seen him: once at court, during the princess's birthday ball; today, surrounded by three constables, while that horrible Barbone asked to have him handcuffed; and finally, near Lake Como . . . five years ago. He looked like such a young rascal then! How he stared at the constables, and what strange glances his mother and his aunt gave him! There was surely some secret that day, something private between them; at the time, I had the feeling that he, too, was afraid of the constables. . . ." Clelia shuddered. "But how ignorant I was! Even then, no doubt, the duchess had begun to take an interest in him. . . . How he made us laugh a little while later, when the ladies, in spite of their obvious concern, had grown a little accustomed to the presence of a stranger! . . . And today I didn't answer the words he spoke to me! . . . O ignorance and timidity, how often you resemble far more hateful things! And I'm like this when I'm over twenty! . . . I was right to think about the cloister; I'm really not made for anything but seclusion! 'A worthy daughter of a jailer!' he must have said to himself. He despises me, and as soon as he can write to the duchess he'll tell her about my lack of consideration, and she'll think I'm a terribly hypocritical girl, because after all, this evening I gave her reason to believe that I was filled with compassion for her sorrow."

Clelia heard someone coming toward her, apparently with the intention of standing beside her on the balcony. She felt annoyed, even though she had been reproaching herself; the musings from which she had been roused were not without a certain sweetness. "Here's an unwelcome visitor who's going to get a warm welcome!" she thought. She looked around with a disdainful expression and saw the timid face of the archbishop, who was approaching the balcony in almost imperceptible little movements. "That saintly man has no manners," she thought. "Why should he come to bother a poor girl like me? My tranquillity is all I possess." She greeted him with respect, but also with a certain haughtiness.

"Signorina," the prelate said to her, "have you heard the terrible news?"

Clelia's eyes had already taken on a quite different expression, but, following the instructions her father had repeated to her a hundred times, she replied with an air of ignorance which the language of her eyes openly contradicted: "I've heard nothing, monsignor."

"My chief vicar-general, poor Fabrizio del Dongo, who's no more guilty than I am of the death of that bandit Giletti, has been abducted from Bologna, where he was living under the assumed name of Giuseppe Bossi, and locked up in your citadel. He arrived there *chained* to the carriage that brought him. A jailer named Barbone, who was pardoned some time ago after murdering one of his brothers, tried to inflict a personal indignity on Fabrizio, but my young friend is not a man to tolerate an insult. He knocked his infamous adversary to the floor, whereupon they handcuffed him and put him in a cell twenty feet underground."

"No, he wasn't handcuffed."

"Ah! You know something!" exclaimed the archbishop. And the old man's features lost some of their profound discouragement. "But, first of all, someone may come to this balcony and interrupt us: would you be charitable enough to give this pastoral ring of mine to Don Cesare yourself?"

Clelia took the ring but did not know where to put it to avoid the risk of losing it.

"Put it on your thumb," said the archbishop, and he himself slipped it on. "Can I count on you to deliver it?"

"Yes, monsignor."

"Will you promise to keep secret what I'm about to tell you, even if you don't think it right to grant my request?"

"Of course, monsignor," replied Clelia, trembling when she saw the somber, serious look which the old man had suddenly assumed. "Our esteemed archbishop," she added, "would never give me orders unworthy of himself or of me."

"Tell Don Cesare that I commend my adopted son to him. I know that the policemen who arrested him didn't give him time to take his breviary, so I beg Don Cesare to let him have his own, and if your worthy uncle will send someone to my palace tomorrow, I'll replace the book he will have given to Fabrizio. I would also like Don Cesare to let Signor del Dongo have the ring now being worn on this pretty hand."

The archbishop was interrupted by General Fabio Conti, who came to take his daughter to his carriage. There was a brief conversation during which the prelate was not lacking in adroitness. Without making any mention of the newly arrived prisoner, he guided the conversation in such a way as to give himself the opportunity to utter certain moral and political maxims; for example: "There are moments of crisis in the life of a court which decide the fate of the greatest personages for a long time; it would be singularly imprudent to change into *personal hatred* the state of political disfavor which is often merely the result of opposed positions." Letting himself be carried away to some extent by his profound grief over Fabrizio's unexpected arrest, he went so far as to say that, while a man must certainly keep the positions he enjoys, there would be gratuitous rashness in incurring furious hatred by participating in certain things which are never forgotten.

When the general was in the carriage with his daughter, he said to her, "That might be called a threat. . . . Threats to a man like myself!" No more was said between them for the next twenty minutes.

On receiving the archbishop's pastoral ring, Clelia had

promised herself that she would speak to her father, when she was in the carriage, about the little service the prelate had asked of her. But after the word "threats," spoken with anger, she regarded it as certain that her father would intercept the message and the gift; she covered the ring with her left hand and pressed it passionately. During the entire trip from the Ministry of the Interior to the citadel, she wondered whether it would be criminal not to speak to her father. She was very pious and timorous, and her heart, usually so calm, was pounding with unaccustomed violence. But finally the "Who goes there?" of the sentry posted on the rampart above the gate rang out before she had found the right words to incline her father not to refuse, so great was her fear of a refusal! As she climbed the three hundred and sixty steps leading to the governor's residence, she was still unable to think of anything suitable.

She hastened to speak to her uncle. He scolded her and refused to become involved in anything.

CHAPTER SIXTEEN

"Think of it!" the general cried when he saw his brother Don Cesare. "The duchess is going to spend a hundred thousand scudi to make a fool of me and get her nephew out of prison!"

But, for the moment, we must leave Fabrizio in his cell at the top of the citadel of Parma; he is well guarded there, and we may find that he has changed a little when we return to him. First we shall concern ourselves with the court, where some extremely complicated intrigues, and especially the passions of an unhappy woman, are going to decide his fate. As he climbed the three hundred and ninety steps to his cell in the Farnese Tower, before the eyes of the governor, Fabrizio, who had so dreaded this moment, found that he had no time to think about his misfortunes.

When she came home from Count Zurla's house, the duchess motioned her servants to leave her; then, flinging herself fully dressed on her bed, she cried aloud, "Fabrizio's enemies have him in their power, and they may poison him because of me!" How can we depict the despair which, following this summing-up of the situation, took possession of a woman so little ruled by reason, so much a slave to the sensations of the moment, and, without admitting it to herself, so madly in love with the young prisoner? There were inarticulate cries, paroxysms of rage and convulsive movements, but not a single tear. She had sent her servants away because she had thought she would burst out sobbing as soon as she was alone; but tears, the first relief of great sorrow, were completely lacking in her. Her haughty soul was too thoroughly dominated by anger, indignation and awareness of her inferior position with regard to the prince.

"I'm so humiliated!" she kept exclaiming. "I've been outrageously insulted, and, much worse, Fabrizio's life has been placed in danger! Do they think I won't take vengeance? Not so fast, my prince! You may take my life from me, you have that power; but afterward I'll take yours! Alas, poor Fabrizio, what good will that do you? How different from the day when I made up my mind to leave Parma! And yet I thought I was unhappy then. . . . What blindness! I was about to break all the habits of a pleasant life. Alas, without knowing it, I was approaching an event that would decide my fate forever. If the count's base habits as an obsequious courtier hadn't led him to omit the words 'unjust proceedings' in the fatal letter which the prince's vanity granted to me, we'd have been saved. More by luck than by adroitness, I must confess, I'd touched his conceit on the subject of his beloved town of Parma. I threatened to leave then, I was free then! My God, I'm such a slave now!

"I'm now tied down in this foul cesspool, and Fabrizio is chained in the citadel, that citadel which has been the antechamber of death for so many distinguished prisoners! And I can no longer hold that tiger in check by the fear of seeing me leave his den! He's too intelligent not to realize that I'll never go away from the infamous tower to which my heart is chained. His wounded vanity may now suggest the wildest ideas to him, and their extraordinary cruelty would only stir up his prodigious conceit. If he renews his mawkish advances, if he says to me, 'Accept the homage of your slave, or Fabrizio will die,' well, there's the old story of Judith. . . . Yes, but if it would be only suicide for me, it would be murder for Fabrizio: the simple-minded successor, our crown prince, and that infamous hangman, Rassi, would have Fabrizio executed as my accomplice."

The duchess cried aloud; her wretched heart was tortured by the dilemma from which she could see no escape. Her distraught mind could not envisage any other possibility in the future. For ten minutes she was as agitated as a madwoman, then finally this horrible state was replaced for a short time by a sleep of exhaustion; life had been drained from her.

A few minutes later she awoke with a start and found herself sitting up on her bed; she had the idea that the prince was trying to cut off Fabrizio's head in her presence. How wildly she glanced around the room! When she had at last convinced herself that she had neither the prince nor Fabrizio before her eyes, she fell back on her bed and was on the verge of fainting. Her physical weakness was such that she felt unable to change her position. "Dear God, if only I could die!" she thought. "But how cowardly it would be of me to abandon Fabrizio in his misfortune! My mind is wandering. . . . I must return to reality, I must calmly take stock of the abominable situation I've almost deliberately plunged myself into. What fatal stupidity it was to come and live at the court of an absolute prince! A tyrant who knows all his victims! Their every glance strikes him as defiance to his power. Unfortunately, neither the count nor I realized it when I left Milan: I was thinking of the attractions of a pleasant court, something inferior, it's true, but something in the style of the happy days of Prince Eugene.

"From a distance no one has any idea of what it's like to live under the authority of a despot who knows all his subjects by sight. The outer form of despotism is the same as that of all other governments: there are judges, for example, but they're men like Rassi. The monster! He'd see nothing unusual in having his own father hanged, if the prince ordered him to do it. He'd call it his duty . . . How could I win over Rassi? I have no means of trying it, wretched woman that I am! What could I offer him? A hundred thousand lire, perhaps! And I've been told that the prince sent him a money box filled with ten thousand gold sequins after the first time that heaven showed its wrath against this miserable country to allowing him to escape from an attempt to stab him! Anyway, what sum could win him over? He has a soul of mud; after never seeing anything but contempt in the eyes of everyone around him, he now has the pleasure of seeing fear, and even respect. He may become Minister of Police—why not? If he does, three-quarters of the inhabitants of Parma will be his base courtiers and tremble before him as abjectly as he trembles before the prince.

"Since I can't flee this hateful place, I must make myself useful to Fabrizio here. But if I'm living alone and in despair, what can I do for him? Come, 'march, unhappy woman,' do your duty: go out into the world, pretend to be no longer thinking of Fabrizio . . . I must pretend to have forgotten you, my dear angel!"

At these words the duchess burst into tears; at last she was able to weep. After granting an hour to human weakness, she saw with some consolation that her thoughts were beginning to grow clearer. "If only I had a magic carpet," she said to herself, "I'd rescue Fabrizio from the citadel and take refuge with him in some happy place where we couldn't be pursued: Paris, for example. We'd live there at first on the twelve hundred lire a year which his father's business agent sends to me with such amusing regularity. I could certainly gather a hundred thousand lire from the débris of my fortune!" Her imagination passed in review, with moments of ineffable delight, all the details of the life she would lead three hundred leagues away from Parma. "There," she thought, "he could enter the army under an assumed name. With a place in one of the regiments of those gallant Frenchmen, young Valserra would make a reputation for himself and be happy at last."

These happy visions brought back her tears, but this time they were gentle. So happiness did exist somewhere! This state lasted a long time; the poor woman's mind rebelled against contemplating grim reality once again. Finally, when dawn was beginning to draw a white line across the tops of the trees in her garden, she made a violent effort: "In a few hours," she told herself, "I'll be on the battlefield; I'll have to be prepared to act, and if something irritating should happen, if the prince should take it into his head to say something to me about Fabrizio, I'm not sure of being able to keep all my self-control. I must therefore make definite plans without delay.

"If I'm declared a prisoner of state, Rassi will have everything in my house seized. On the first of this month, the count and I burned, as usual, all papers which the police might use to their advantage—and he's the Minister of Police, that's the amusing part of it! I have three rather valuable diamonds; Fulgenzio, my old boatman from Grianta, will leave tomorrow for Geneva, where he'll put them in a safe place. If Fabrizio should ever escape—dear God, be favorable to him!" she exclaimed, crossing herself, "the Marquis del Dongo's incredible baseness will make him decide that it's sinful to send money to a man who's being pursued by his lawful prince. But then Fabrizio will at least have my diamonds, and he'll be able to live.

"I must dismiss the count. . . . It would be impossible for me to be alone with him after what's happened. Poor man! He's not malicious, far from it: he's only weak. His commonplace soul can't rise to the level of ours. Poor Fabrizio! If only you could be here a little while, to take counsel with me about the dangers we both face!

"The count's meticulous prudence would hamper all my plans, and besides, I mustn't drag him into my ruin. . . . But why shouldn't that tyrant's vanity have me thrown into prison? I'll have conspired. . . . What could be easier to prove? If he sent me to his citadel, and if I could bribe someone to let me speak to Fabrizio, even for only an instant, with what courage we'd face death together! But let's forget such folly; Rassi would advise the prince to do away with me by poison: the sight of me riding through the streets in a cart might stir the sensibilities of his dear subjects. . . .

"Enough! I'm still romanticizing, although such fantasies are understandable in a woman whose real lot is so sad! The truth of the matter is that the prince won't send me to my death; but nothing could be easier than to put me in prison and keep me there. He'll have all sorts of incriminating papers hidden in some corner of my house, as was done to poor L——. Then a dozen false witnesses and three judges who won't have to be too corrupt, because there will be what they call 'conclusive evidence,' will be enough. I may be sentenced to death as a conspirator, and the prince, in his boundless mercy, considering the fact that I once had the honor of being admitted to his court, will commute my sentence to ten years in prison. But then, in order not to fall short of the violent nature which has made the Marquise Raversi and all my other enemies say so many idiotic things, I'll bravely poison myself, or so, at least, the public will be kind enough to believe. But I'm willing to bet that Rassi will come into my cell and gallantly hand me, on behalf of the prince, a little bottle of strychnine or laudanum.

"Yes, I must break openly with the count, because I don't want to drag him into my ruin. That would be ignoble of me—the poor man has loved me so sincerely! My foolishness was in believing that a genuine courtier had enough soul left to be capable of love. The prince will quite probably find some pretext for imprisoning me; he'll be afraid that I'll pervert public opinion with regard to Fabrizio. The count is full of honor; he'll immediately do something which the dullwitted oafs of the prince's court, in their profound amazement, will call an act of madness: he'll leave the court. I defied the prince's authority the night he wrote the letter for me, so I can expect the worst from his wounded vanity: does a man who was born a prince ever forget a feeling like the one I gave him that night? Furthermore, once the count has broken with me, he'll be in a better position to help Fabrizio. But my decision will drive him to despair. What if he should take vengeance? . . . No, that's an idea that would never occur to him. Unlike the prince, he doesn't have a fundamentally base nature. He may sign an infamous decree, groaning to himself, but he has a sense of honor. Besides, what reason will he have to take vengeance? I'll merely say to him after having loved him for five years without the slightest offense to his love, 'My dear count, I once had the happiness of loving you, but now that flame has died: I'm no longer in love with you. However, I know the depths of your heart; I still have great esteem for you, and you'll always be my best friend.' What answer can a gallant man make to such a declaration?

"I'll take a new lover, or at least society will think so. I'll say to that lover, 'After all, the prince was right to punish Fabrizio's rash act, but on his name-day our gracious sovereign will no doubt set him free.' Thus I'll gain six months. Prudence dictates that my new lover should be that corrupt judge, that infamous hangman, that Rassi. He'd feel ennobled, and I actually would give him entry into good society. But forgive me, dear Fabrizio: such an effort is beyond my power! That monster is still covered with the blood of D—— and Count P——! I'd faint with horror if he came near me, or rather I'd take a knife and plunge it into his black heart. Don't ask the impossible of me!

"Yes, above all I must forget Fabrizio! I must show no trace of anger against the prince, and recover my usual gaiety. It will seem all the more charming to those vile souls, first of all because I'll appear to be submitting to their sovereign with good grace, and secondly because, far from making fun of them, I'll be careful to make all their pretty little merits stand out. For example, I'll compliment Count Zurla on the beauty of the white feather in his hat, which he just had sent to him from Lyons, and which is his greatest delight.

"I must choose a lover from the Marquise Raversi's party. If the count goes, that will be the party in office, that's where the power will lie. One of the marquise's friends will be in command of the citadel, because Fabio Conti will become a minister. The prince is well-bred, intelligent and accustomed to the count's charming way of working; how will he be able to deal with that stupid ass, that king of fools who's devoted his whole life to the problem of whether His Highness's soldiers ought to wear seven buttons on their chests or nine? It's idiotic brutes like that who are very jealous of me, and that's why you're in danger, dear Fabrizio! It's idiotic brutes like that who are going to decide your fate and mine! So I mustn't let the count resign! He must stay in office, even if he has to suffer humiliations! He's always thought that handing in his resignation was the greatest sacrifice a Prime Minister could make, and each time his mirror tells him he's growing older, he offers me that sacrifice.

"I must therefore make a complete break with him, and allow a reconciliation only if that's the only way to prevent him from leaving. I'll make our parting as friendly as possible, of course, but after his obsequious omission of the words 'unjust proceedings' in the prince's letter, I feel that, in order not to hate him, I need to spend a few months without seeing him. On that decisive evening I had no need of his intelligence: all he had to do was write what I dictated. He had only to write those words *which I had won* by my strength of character, but his habits as a servile courtier prevailed. He told me the next day that he couldn't make his prince sign anything so absurd, that a full pardon was what I required. But with people like that, with those monsters of vanity and rancor known as the Farneses, one takes what one can get!"

At this thought, all the duchess's anger revived. "The prince has deceived me," she said to herself, "and with what baseness! That man has no excuse: he has intelligence, shrewdness and good judgment; there's nothing base about him except his passions. The count and I have noticed it a dozen times: his mind becomes vulgar only when he thinks someone has tried to insult him. Well, Fabrizio's crime has nothing to do with politics. It was an unimportant killing like a hundred others that are reported every year in the prince's happy dominions. The count swore to me that he'd gathered the most accurate information possible, and that Fabrizio was innocent. That Giletti wasn't without courage: finding himself only a few steps away from the border, he was suddenly tempted to get rid of a favored rival."

The duchess paused for a long time to consider whether it was possible to believe in Fabrizio's guilt. Not that she regarded it as a serious sin for a nobleman of her nephew's rank to put an end to the impertinence of an actor; but, in her despair, she was beginning to feel vaguely that she would be forced to fight to prove his innocence. "No," she thought finally, "here's one decisive proof: he's like poor Pietranera, he usually has weapons in all his pockets, but on that day he had only an old single-barreled gun—and even that was borrowed from one of the workmen.

"I hate the prince because he's deceived me, and deceived me in the most ignoble way. After signing a letter clearing Fabrizio, he had the poor boy abducted from Bologna and imprisoned. But that account will be settled."

Toward five o'clock in the morning, the duchess, exhausted by this long fit of despair, rang for her maids. They cried aloud when they saw her lying fully dressed on the bed, wearing her diamonds, white as the sheets, and with her eyes closed: she seemed to be lying in state after her death. They would have thought she was completely unconscious if they had not remembered that she had just rung for them. A few tears trickled down her lifeless cheeks from time to time. Her maids understood from a gesture she made that she wanted to be put to bed.

Twice that night, after leaving Count Zurla's house, Count Mosca had come to ask to see the duchess. Having been refused admittance both times, he wrote to her that he wanted her to advise him on a matter concerning himself: should he keep his post after the insult he had just received. "The young man is innocent," he wrote, "but even if he were guilty, should he have been arrested without informing me, his avowed protector?" The duchess did not see this letter until the following day.

The count had no virtue; we may even add that what the liberals understand by "virtue" (seeking the happiness of the greatest number) seemed to him nothing but a snare for the gullible. He believed himself obliged above all else to seek the happiness of Count Mosca della Rovere. But he was full of honor, and perfectly sincere when he spoke of resigning. He had never told a lie to the duchess. She paid no attention to his letter, however. She had made her decision, and it was a very painful one: to pretend to forget Fabrizio. After that effort, she was indifferent to everything else.

The next day at noon the count, who had called ten times at the Sanseverina palace, was finally admitted. He was appalled when he saw the duchess. "She looks forty!" he thought. "And yesterday she was so sparkling, so youthful! ... Everyone tells me that she looked just as young as Clelia

Conti during their long conversation last night, and that the duchess was much more attractive."

The duchess's voice and manner were as strange as her physical appearance. This manner, void of all passion, of all human interest, of all anger, made the count turn pale; it reminded him of the behavior of one of his friends who, a few months earlier, on the verge of death and having already received extreme unction, had wanted to talk to him.

After a few minutes, the duchess was able to speak: "Let us part, my dear count," she said in a faint but quite articulate voice which she did her best to make friendly. "We must! Heaven is my witness that my conduct toward you for the past five years has been irreproachable. You've given me a brilliant existence instead of the boredom that would have been my sad lot in the castle of Grianta; if it hadn't been for you, I'd have reached old age a few years earlier. As for me, my sole concern has been to try to help you find happiness. It's because I love you that I'm proposing this separation *à l'amiable*, as they say in France."

The count did not understand; she had to repeat her statement several times. He turned deathly pale, threw himself on his knees beside her bed and said everything that profound amazement, followed by the most intense despair, can inspire in an intelligent man who is passionately in love. He repeatedly offered to hand in his resignation and go with her to some retreat a thousand leagues away from Parma.

"How can you dare to speak of going away, when Fabrizio is here?" she finally cried out, half rising from her bed. But since she saw that Fabrizio's name had made a painful impression, she added after a short pause, gently squeezing the count's hand, "No, my friend, I won't tell you that I've loved you with that passion and rapture which, it seems to me, no one ever experiences after thirty—and I passed that age long ago. You've probably been told that I was in love with Fabrizio, because I know it was rumored in this spiteful court." (Her eyes flashed for the first time during this conversation when she spoke the word "spiteful.")

"I swear to you before God, and on Fabrizio's life, that never has the slightest thing occurred between him and me that could not have been decently witnessed by a third person. Neither will I tell you that I love him exactly as though I were his sister; I love him instinctively, so to speak. I love his courage, so simple and perfect that he can be said to be unaware of it himself. I remember that this kind of admiration began when he returned from Waterloo. He was still a child, despite his seventeen years; his great anxiety was to know whether he had been in the battle, and, if so, whether he could say that he had actually fought in it, even though he hadn't marched in any attack on an enemy battery or column. It was during the solemn discussion we had on this important subject that I first began to notice his perfect charm. His great soul revealed itself to me. What skillful lies a 'well-bred' young man would have told in his place! In short, if he's not happy, I can't be happy either. There's a statement that well describes the state of my heart; if it's not the truth, it's at least as much of it as I can see."

Encouraged by this tone of frankness and intimacy, the count tried to kiss her hand. She drew it back with a kind of horror. "The time for that is past," she said. "I'm a woman of thirty-seven, I'm on the threshold of old age. I already feel all its discouragement, and I may even be close to the grave. It's a terrible moment, from what people say, and yet it seems to me that I long for it. I feel the worst symptom of old age: my heart has been crushed by this horrible misfortune, and I can no longer love. I see in you, my dear count, only the shadow of someone who was once dear to me. I'll say more: it's gratitude alone that makes me talk to you this way."

"What will become of me?" the count said over and over. "I feel that I'm attached to you more passionately than in those early days when I used to see you at La Scala!"

"Shall I confess something to you, my dear friend? This talk of love bores me, and seems indecent to me. Come," she said, trying to smile, but in vain, "be brave! Be an intelligent man, a man of good judgment and resourcefulness in all emergencies. Be with me what you already are in the eyes of those who are indifferent to you: the ablest man and the greatest politician that Italy has produced for centuries."

The count stood up and paced back and forth for a few moments.

"It's impossible, my dear," he said at length. "I'm being torn by the most violent passion, and you ask me to consult my reason! I have no more reason now!"

"Please, let's not talk of passion," she said curtly. It was the first time, after two hours of conversation, that her voice had taken on any expression at all. The count, though in despair himself, tried to console her. "He's deceived me!" she cried, without making any reply to the reasons for hope which the count had brought forward. "He's deceived me in the most contemptible way!" and her deathly pallor ceased for

244

an instant. But the count noticed that, even in this moment of violent agitation, she still did not have the strength to raise her arms.

"Good God!" he thought. "Can it be possible that she's merely ill? But in that case it would be the beginning of some very serious illness." Filled with anxiety, he suggested calling in the famous Razori, the best physician in Parma and all of Italy.

"Do you want to give a stranger the pleasure of knowing the full depth of my despair? Is that the advice of a traitor or a friend?" And she looked at him with a strange expression in her eyes.

"It's all over," he thought in despair, "she has no more love for me! And worse still, she no longer even regards me as an ordinary man of honor."

"Let me tell you," he said eagerly, "that I've done everything I could to find out the details of the arrest that has driven us both to despair, but, oddly enough, I still know nothing positive. I've had the constables from the nearest station questioned: they saw the prisoner arrive by the road from Castelnuovo, and were ordered to follow the *sediola*. I immediately sent Bruno, whose zeal and devotion are well known to you, to go from station to station until he finds out where and how Fabrizio was arrested."

When she heard Fabrizio's name, the duchess was seized with a slight convulsion.

"Forgive me, my friend," she said to the count as soon as she was able to speak. "These facts interest me greatly. Give me all of them: I want to understand even the smallest details clearly."

"Well, first of all," said the count, trying to assume a somewhat lighter air in an effort to distract her a little, "I'm inclined to send a trustworthy messenger to Bruno to order him to go all the way to Bologna: that may be where they seized our young friend. When was his last letter dated?"

"Tuesday, five days ago."

"Had it been opened before you received it?"

"There was no trace of an opening. I must tell you that it's written on cheap paper; the address is in a woman's handwriting, and it bears the name of an old washerwoman who's related to my maid. The washerwoman thinks it's a question of a love affair, and Cecchina reimburses her for the delivery charges without telling her anything further."

The count, who had now taken on a thoroughly business-like tone, tried to discover, by discussing the matter with the duchess, on what day Fabrizio had been seized in Bologna. Only then did he realize, he who was ordinarily so perceptive, that this was the tone he should have adopted from the start. These details interested the wretched woman and seemed to distract her a little. If he had not been so much in love, this simple idea would have occurred to him as soon as he entered her bedroom. She told him to leave, so that he could send the new orders to the faithful Bruno without delay. When they touched briefly on the question of whether a sentence had been passed before the prince signed the letter addressed to the duchess, she rather eagerly seized the opportunity to say to the count, "I won't reproach you for omitting the words 'unjust proceedings' in the letter you wrote, and which he signed: you were in the grip of your courtier's instinct. Without realizing it, you let your master's interests take precedence over your friend's. You've placed your actions at my disposal, long ago; but it's not in your power to change your nature. You have great ability as a minister, but you also have the instincts of that profession. Your omission of the word 'unjust' has ruined me, but far be it from me to reproach you for it in any way; it was the fault of your instinct, not of your will."

"Remember," she went on, changing her tone, and with the most imperious air, "that I'm not too greatly upset by Fabrizio's arrest, that I've never had the slightest intention of leaving Parma, and that I'm filled with respect for the prince. That's what I want you to say, and this is what I want to say to you: since I plan to direct my conduct alone from now on, I want to part with you amicably, as a good friend of long standing. Consider me to be sixty years old; the young woman is dead in me. I can no longer exaggerate anything in the world, I can no longer love. But I'd be even more miserable than I am now if I should do anything to compromise your career. It may be part of my plan to give myself the appearance of having a young lover, and I wouldn't want to see you pained. I can swear to you by Fabrizio's happiness" (she paused for half a minute after these words) "that I have never once been unfaithful to you in the whole five years we have been together. That's a long time." She tried to smile; her pale cheeks quivered, but she was unable to part her lips. "I can even swear that I've never had either the intention or the desire to be unfaithful to you. With that clearly in mind, please leave me."

The count left the Sanseverina palace in despair; he could see that the duchess was determined to part with him, and he was more madly in love with her than ever. This is one of those things to which I am obliged to return often, because they are improbable outside of Italy. When he came home he sent at least six different people along the road to Castelnuovo and Bologna, and gave them letters.

"But that's not all," thought the unhappy count: "the prince may take it into his head to have the poor boy executed, to take vengeance for the way the duchess treated him the night he wrote that fatal letter. I felt that she was passing a limit that should never be passed, and it was to patch things up that I made the incredibly foolish mistake of omitting the words 'unjust proceedings,' the only ones that really bound the prince. But after all, are people like him ever bound by anything? . . . It was no doubt the greatest mistake I've ever made: I risked everything that makes life precious to me. I must now repair my blunder with skill and effort. But if it turns out that I can do nothing, even by sacrificing a little of my dignity, I'll leave the prince in the lurch; with his dreams of high politics, with his ideas of making himself the constitutional monarch of Lombardy, we'll see how he can replace me. . . . Fabio Conti is a fool, and Rassi's talent boils down to the ability to find a legal basis for hanging a man who's displeased those in power."

Once he had firmly resolved to resign from office if Fabrizio's punishment should go beyond ordinary confinement, the count said to himself, "If the duchess's rash defiance of the prince's vanity costs me my happiness, at least I'll still have my honor. . . . Now that I think of it, since I no longer care whether I keep my position or not, I can allow myself to do all sorts of things which, only this morning, would have seemed completely unthinkable to me. For example, I'll try everything that's humanly possible to arrange for Fabrizio's escape. . . . My God!" cried the count, breaking off abruptly and opening his eyes wide, as though at the sight of unexpected happiness. "The duchess said nothing to me about an escape—can it be that, for once in her life, she was insincere, and that her talk of parting with me was only an attempt to make me betray the prince? It's as good as done already!"

The count's eyes had regained their expression of ironic shrewdness. "That charming Rassi is paid by his master for those sentences which dishonor us all over Europe," he thought, "but he's not the kind of man to refuse payment from me for revealing his master's secrets. The brute has a mistress and a confessor, but his mistress is such a base creature that I mustn't speak to her: the next day she'd relate our

247

conversation to all the greengrocers' wives in the neighborhood." Revived by this glimmer of hope, the count was already on his way to the cathedral. Amazed by the lightness of his step, he smiled in spite of his grief. "This is what it's like to be no longer a minister!"

This cathedral, like many churches in Italy, serves as a passage from one street to another. The count saw one of the archbishop's vicars-general crossing the nave. "Since I've met you," he said to him, "please be kind enough to spare my gout the deadly strain of climbing up to see the archbishop. I'll be infinitely grateful to him if he will come down to the sacristy."

The archbishop was delighted by this message; he had countless things to tell the minister about Fabrizio. But the minister guessed that these things were nothing but empty words and would not listen to them.

"What kind of man is Dugnani, curate of San Paolo?"

"A small mind and a great ambition," replied the archbishop, "few scruples and extreme poverty, for we have our vices!"

"Good heavens, you depict character like Tacitus!" exclaimed the count. And he took his leave, laughing.

As soon as he reached the ministry he sent for Father Dugnani.

"You direct the conscience of my excellent friend, Chief Justice Rassi," he said to him. "Hasn't he anything to say to me?" And, without further words or ceremony, he dismissed him.

CHAPTER SEVENTEEN

The count regarded himself as already out of office. "Let's see now," he said to himself, "how many horses will we be able to have after my disgrace? For that's what my retirement will be called." He took stock of his fortune. He had entered the ministry with eighty thousand lire to his name. To his great surprise, he found that he now had no more than half a million. "Enough for an income of twenty thousand lire, at the most," he thought. "I must admit that I've been very foolish! There's not one middle-class citizen in Parma who doesn't believe I have an income of at least a hundred and fifty thousand, and on that subject the prince is as middle-class as anyone else. When they see me in poverty, they'll say I'm cleverly hiding my wealth. Well, by God, if I'm still a minister for three more months, that wealth will be doubled!"

He saw this idea as an opportunity for writing to the duchess, and he eagerly seized upon it. But to make her forgive him for writing to her, considering how things now stood between them, he filled his letter with figures and calculations. "The three of us," he wrote, "will have an income of only twenty thousand lire on which to live in Naples. Fabrizio and I will have one saddle-horse for both of us."

He had scarcely sent off his letter when Chief Justice Rassi was announced. He received him with a haughtiness that bordered on insolence.

"Tell me," he said to him, "why is it that, after capturing in Bologna a conspirator who was under my protection, and even planning to have his head cut off, you still have nothing to say to me? Do you at least know the name of my successor? Is it General Conti, or yourself?"

Rassi was thunderstruck. He was too little accustomed to the ways of good society to determine whether the count was speaking seriously or not. His face turned bright red and he mumbled a few words that were almost unintelligible. The count looked at him, enjoying his discomposure. But suddenly Rassi pulled himself together and cried out with perfect self-assurance and the air of Figaro caught red-handed by Almaviva: "I won't mince words with you, Your Excellency. What will you give me if I answer your questions as though you were my confessor?"

"The Cross of San Paolo" (this is the Order of Parma) "or money, if you can supply me with a good pretext for giving you some."

"I'd rather have the Cross of San Paolo, because it will make me a nobleman."

"What, my dear Chief Justice, you still have some respect for our poor nobility?"

"If I'd been born a nobleman," replied Rassi with all the impudence of his profession, "the relatives of the people I've hanged would hate me, but they wouldn't despise me."

"Very well, I'll save you from contempt," said the count. "Cure me of my ignorance. What do you intend to do with Fabrizio?"

"Well, the prince is in a terrible quandry. He's afraid that, bewitched by Armida's eyes—excuse my vivid language, I'm using his own words—he's afraid that, bewitched by the

249

lovely eyes which have also captivated him to some extent, you may leave him in the lurch, and there's no one like you for dealing with political matters in Lombardy. I'll even tell you," added Rassi, lowering his voice, "that there's a fine opportunity for you, one that's well worth the Cross of San Paolo you're going to give me. The prince would give you, as a reward from the State, a nice little estate worth six hundred thousand lire, which he would set aside from his own domains, or else a gratuity of three hundred thousand scudi, if you would agree not to concern yourself with Fabrizio del Dongo's fate, or at least not to talk to him about it except in public."

"I was expecting something better than that," said the count. "Not concerning myself with Fabrizio would mean breaking with the duchess."

"That's just what the prince said to me. The fact is that he's terribly angry at the duchess, just between you and me, and he's afraid that, to compensate yourself for your break with that charming lady, now that you're a widower you may ask him for the hand of his cousin, old Princess Isota, who's only fifty."

"He's guessed correctly!" cried the count. "Our master is the shrewdest man in Parma."

The grotesque idea of marrying this old princess had never entered the count's mind; nothing could have been less suited to a man who was bored to tears by court ceremonies.

He began tapping his snuffbox on the marble top of a little table near his chair. Rassi saw in this gesture of uncertainty the possibility of a fine windfall; his eyes sparkled.

"Please, Your Excellency," he said, "if you decide to accept either the estate or the cash gratuity, I beg you not to choose any other intermediary than myself. I'd do my best," he said, lowering his voice, "to increase the sum of money, or have a sizable forest added to the estate. If you would deign to use a little moderation and tact in speaking to the prince about that young brat who's been put in prison, it might be possible to make a duchy out of the land given to you as a token of the national gratitude. Allow me to repeat, Your Excellency: for the moment, the prince detests the duchess, but he's also in a quandry, so much so that I've sometimes thought there was some secret aspect of the matter which he didn't dare admit to me. There may be a gold mine here for both of us; I can sell you his most intimate secrets, and with perfect freedom, because everyone considers me your sworn enemy. He's furious with the duchess, but he also believes, like all of us, that you're the only man in the world who can bring about a successful conclusion to those secret negotiations concerning Milan. Will Your Excellency permit me to repeat the prince's words literally?" said Rassi, becoming excited. "The exact wording of a statement often gives it connotations that no paraphrase can capture, and you'll be able to see them more clearly than I do."

"You have my permission for everything," said the count, still absent-mindedly tapping the marble top of the table with his gold snuffbox, "and I'll be grateful."

"Give me transmissible letters-patent of nobility, independently of the Cross of San Paolo, and I'll be more than satisfied. Whenever I mention ennoblement to the prince, he answers me, 'Make a nobleman of a scoundrel like you? I'd have to close up shop the next day! No one in Parma would ever want to be ennobled after that!' To come back to the Milanese affair, the prince said to me, less than three days ago, 'That sly rogue is the only one who can follow the thread of our intrigues; if I dismiss him, or if he goes away with the duchess, I may as well give up all hope of ever becoming the beloved liberal leader of all Italy.'"

At these words, the count began to breathe freely again. "Fabrizio won't die," he thought.

Never before had Rassi been able to obtain an intimate conversation with the Prime Minister; he was beside himself with joy. He saw himself on the point of being able to discard the name of Rassi, which had become a synonym in Parma for everything base and vile: the common people gave the name to mad dogs, a number of soldiers had recently fought duels because one of the comrades had called them Rassi, and not a week went by without this unfortunate name being displayed in some outrageous sonnet. His son, an innocent young schoolboy of sixteen, was driven from cafés because of his name.

It was the burning memory of all these amenities of his position that led him to take a rash step.

"I have an estate which is called Riva," he said, drawing his chair closer to the count's. "I'd like to become Baron Riva."

"Why not?"

Rassi was wild with excitement. "Well, then, Your Excellency," he said, "I'll take the liberty of being indiscreet, of venturing to guess the object of your desires: you aspire to the hand of Princess Isota, and it's a noble ambition. Once you're a member of the family, you're safe from dismissal, you've got our man under your thumb. I won't hide from you that he's horrified at the thought of your marrying Princess Isota; but if your affairs were in the hands of someone skillful and *well paid*, there would be no reason to give up all hope of success."

"I, my dear baron, would have no hope of it; I disavow in advance anything you may say in my name. But on the day when that illustrious alliance finally fulfills my wishes and gives me that lofty position in the State, I'll give you three hundred thousand lire of my own money, or else I'll advise the prince to grant you some mark of favor which you yourself will prefer to that sum of money."

The reader has no doubt found this conversation too long, and yet we have spared him more than half of it. It went on for another two hours. Rassi was mad with joy when he left; the count had great hope of being able to save Fabrizio, and was more determined than ever to resign. He felt that his prestige needed to be renewed by the accession to power of men like Rassi and General Conti. He was keenly enjoying a possibility of taking vengeance on the prince which he was just beginning to envisage. "He may make the duchess leave," he cried, "but by God he'll have to give up all hope of becoming the constitutional monarch of Lombardy!" (This was a ridiculous delusion; the prince was an intelligent man, but he had dreamed of the idea so much that he had fallen madly in love with it.)

The count's joy knew no bounds as he hurried to tell the duchess about his conversation with the Chief Justice. He found her door closed to him; the porter hardly dared to confess to him that he had received this order from his mistress in person. The count sadly returned to the ministerial palace; the misfortune that had just befallen him completely eclipsed the joy that his conversation with the prince's confidant had given him. No longer having the heart to concern himself with anything, he was wandering sadly up and down his picture gallery when, a quarter of an hour later, he received a note worded as follows:

Since it is true, my dear and loyal friend, that we are now only friends, you must come to see me only three times a week. In two weeks we shall reduce those visits, always so dear to my heart, to two a month. If you want to please me, make this partial estrangement known publicly; if you want to give me back nearly all the love I once had for you, choose a new mistress for yourself.

As for me, I have great plans for distracting myself: I intend to go into society a great deal, and I may even find an intelligent man who will make me forget my misfortunes. As a friend, of course, you will always have first place in my heart, but I do not want it to be said that my conduct has been dictated by your wisdom, and above all I want it to be known that I have lost all influence over your decisions. In short, my dear count, rest assured that you will always be my dearest friend, but never anything else. Please give up all thought of a return to the past, it is all over now. You may count on my friendship forever.

This last blow was too much for the count's courage: he wrote a fine letter to the prince resigning from all his offices, and sent it to the duchess with a request to have it delivered to the palace. A short time later, his resignation was returned to him, torn into four pieces, and in one of the blank spaces of the paper the duchess had deigned to write, "*No, a thousand times no!*"

It would be difficult to describe the poor count's despair. "She's right, I agree," he kept saying to himself. "My omission of the words 'unjust proceedings' was a terrible disaster; it may cause Fabrizio's death, and his death will cause mine." Sick at heart, the count, who did not want to appear in the prince's palace until he was summoned there, wrote with his own hand the *motu proprio* which made Rassi a Knight of the Order of San Paolo and gave him transmissible nobility. He also wrote a half-page report explaining to the prince the reasons of state which made this measure advisable. He found a kind of melancholy joy in making a careful copy of each of these documents and sending them to the duchess.

He became lost in conjectures; he tried to guess what would be the future plan of action of the woman he loved. "She herself has no idea of what she'll do," he thought. "Only one thing is certain: nothing in the world could make her go back on a decision once she's announced it to me." His misery was further increased by the fact that he could not succeed in finding the duchess at fault. "She did me a gracious favor by loving me, and now she's stopped loving me after a mistake on my part that was involuntary, it's true, but which may have horrible consequences. I have no right to complain."

The next morning he learned that the duchess had begun appearing in society again: she had been seen the evening before in all the houses in which guests were being received.

What would he have done if he had encountered her in someone's drawing room? How should he speak to her? In what tone should he address her? And how could he avoid speaking to her?

The following day was a gloomy one: it was generally rumored that Fabrizio was going to be put to death. The whole town was deeply moved. It was also said that the prince, out of regard for Fabrizio's high birth, had been gracious enough to decide that he would be beheaded.

"It's I who am killing him," the count told himself. "I can never hope to see the duchess again." Despite this rather simple reasoning, he could not help calling at her house three times, although he went there on foot to avoid being noticed. In his despair, he even had the courage to write to her. He had sent for Rassi twice, but the Chief Justice had not appeared. "The scoundrel is betraying me," thought the count.

The next day, three great pieces of news agitated the high society of Parma, and even the middle classes. Fabrizio's execution was considered more certain than ever, and, as a strange complement to this news, it was reported, that the duchess did not seem to be too deeply upset. She apparently felt only mild regret over her young lover's approaching death; in any case, she was taking very skillful advantage of the pallor resulting from a rather serious indisposition into which she had fallen at the time of Fabrizio's arrest. From these details, middle-class citizens clearly recognized the hard-heartedness of a great lady of the court. Out of decency, however, and as a sacrifice to the shade of young Fabrizio, she had broken with Count Mosca. "What immorality!" cried the Jansenists of Parma. But already—it was incredible!—the duchess seemed disposed to listen to the gallantries of the handsomest young men at court. It had been observed, among other singular details, that she had been extremely gay in conversation with Count Baldi, the Marquise Raversi's present lover, and had joked with him a great deal about his frequent journeys to the castle of Velleia.

The lower middle class and the common people were indignant over Fabrizio's death sentence, which they attributed to Count Mosca's jealousy. The society of the court also devoted a great deal of attention to the count, but only to make fun of him, for the last of the three great pieces of news which we have announced was nothing less than that of the count's resignation. Everyone laughed at a ridiculous lover who, at the age of fifty-six, had sacrificed a magnificent position to his sorrow over being deserted by a heartless woman who had long since transferred her affections to a young man. Only the archbishop had the intelligence, or rather the heart, to realize that the count's honor forbade him to remain Prime Minister of a state whose ruler, without consulting him, was about to behead a young man who had been under his protection. The news of the count's resignation had the effect of curing General Fabio Conti of his gout, as we shall relate in due course, when we describe the way in which poor Fabrizio spent his time in the citadel while everyone in Parma was wondering about the hour of his execution.

The following day, the count again saw Bruno, the faithful agent he had sent to Bologna. He was deeply moved as soon as the man entered his office: the sight of him reminded him of the happy state in which he had been when he sent him to Bologna, almost in accord with the duchess. Bruno had just returned from Bologna. He had discovered nothing there; he had not been able to find Ludovico, whom the podesta of Castelnuovo had kept in his village jail.

"I'm going to send you back to Bologna," said the count. "The duchess will want the sad pleasure of knowing the details of Fabrizio's misfortune. Go to see the police sergeant in command of the station at Castelnuovo. But no!" he cried, interrupting himself. "Leave for Lombardy immediately, and distribute money to all our agents, lavishly. I want to get encouraging reports from all of them."

Having clearly understood the purpose of his mission, Bruno began writing out letters of credit. As the count was giving him his final instructions, he received a thoroughly false but well-written letter: it might have been taken for a letter sent by one friend to another to request a favor. The friend who had sent it was none other than the prince. Having heard of certain plans for retirement, he begged his friend Count Mosca to remain in office; he asked it of him in the name of "the dangers threatening the State," and ordered him to do it as his master. He added that, since the King of —— had placed two Cordons of his Order at his disposal, he was keeping one for himself and sending the other to his dear Count Mosca.

"That brute is the cause of my unhappiness!" the count exclaimed angrily in front of the dumbfounded Bruno. "He thinks he can win me over with the same hypocritical phrases we've so often concocted together to ensnare some poor fool or other!" He refused the Order that had been offered to him, and in his reply he wrote that the state of his health gave

255

him very little hope of being able to carry out the arduous duties of the ministry much longer. He was furious. A few moments later, Chief Justice Rassi was announced. He treated him like a dog.

"Well, I see that since I've made you a nobleman, you've begun to be insolent! Why didn't you come to thank me yesterday, as was your strict duty, you worthless scoundrel?"

Rassi was immune to insults: it was in this tone that the prince greeted him every day. But he wanted to be a baron, so he cleverly vindicated himself. Nothing could have been easier.

"The prince kept me glued to a desk all day yesterday: I couldn't leave the palace. His Highness made me copy, in my bad lawyer's handwriting, a pile of diplomatic papers so silly and long-winded that I really think his only aim was to hold me prisoner. When I was finally able to leave at five o'clock, dying of hunger, he ordered me to go straight home and stay there all night. And I saw two of his private spies, well known to me, strolling up and down my street till midnight. This morning, as soon as I was able, I ordered my carriage and drove to the door of the cathedral. I got out of the carriage very slowly, then hurried through the church, and here I am. At this moment, Your Excellency, you're the one man in the world I'm most passionately eager to please."

"And I'm not the least bit taken in by all those more or less well-fabricated stories, you impudent hypocrite! You refused to talk to me about Fabrizio day before yesterday; I respected your scruples and your oaths of secrecy, although, to a man like you, an oath is at best only a pretext. Today I want the truth: What's the meaning of these ridiculous rumors which claim that Fabrizio is going to be executed as the murderer of the actor Giletti?"

"No one can explain those rumors better than I, Your Excellency, because it was I myself who started them: the prince ordered me to do it. Now that I think of it, it may have been in order to keep me from telling you about it that he held me prisoner all day yesterday! He doesn't think I'm a fool, and he must have been certain that I'd bring my decoration to you and ask you to fasten it to my buttonhole."

"Stop making speeches and come to the point!" cried the count.

"The prince would no doubt be glad to have a death sentence against Signor del Dongo, but, as you probably know, he has only a sentence to twenty years in irons, which he himself commuted to twelve years in prison, with a diet of bread and water every Friday, and other religious practices."

"It was because I knew Fabrizio had been sentenced only to prison that I was alarmed by those rumors of an execution; I still remember Count Palanza's death, which you covered up so skillfully."

"That's when I should have been given my decoration!" cried Rassi, unabashed. "I should have struck while the iron was hot, while the prince was still eager for the count to die. I was a fool then, and it's because I'm now armed with that experience that I venture to advise you not to imitate me today." (This comparison seemed in the worst possible taste to the count, and he had to restrain himself from kicking Rassi.)

"First of all," Rassi went on, with the logic of a jurist and the perfect self-assurance of a man who cannot be offended by any insult, "the execution of the said del Dongo is out of the question: the prince wouldn't dare, times have changed a great deal! Furthermore, now that I'm a nobleman, and hope to become a baron through your aid, I wouldn't take a hand in it. As you know, the executioner can receive orders only from me, and I swear to you that Cavaliere Rassi will never issue such orders against Signor del Dongo."

"And you'll be acting wisely," said the count, eyeing him sternly.

"Let's make a distinction!" said Rassi, smiling. "I'm involved only in official deaths: if Signor del Dongo should die of a stomach-ache, don't attribute it to me! I don't know why, but the prince is terribly angry with Sanseverina." (Three days earlier, Rassi would have said "the duchess," but, like everyone else in Parma, he knew that she had broken with the Prime Minister.) The count was struck by the omission of her title in the mouth of such a man, and it is not difficult to imagine whether or not it pleased him. He gave Rassi a look of violent hatred, but then he thought, "My dearest angel, I can show you my love only by blind obedience to your orders!"

"I admit," he said to Rassi, "that I have no great interest in the duchess's various caprices; however, since she asked me to take charge of that young hothead Fabrizio, who should have stayed in Naples and not come here to complicate matters for us, I don't want him to be put to death while I'm in office, and I give you my word that you'll be a baron within a week after he leaves prison."

"In that case, Your Excellency, I won't be a baron until twelve years from now, because the prince is furious, and his hatred of the duchess is so violent that he tries to hide it."

"His Highness is too kind! Why does he need to hide his hatred, now that the duchess is no longer under the protection of his Prime Minister? However, I don't want to be accused of baseness, and especially not of jealousy: it was I who brought the duchess to Parma, and if Fabrizio dies in prison you won't be a baron, but you may be stabbed. But let's drop this trifle. The fact is that I've taken stock of my fortune, and I find that I scarcely have enough for an income of twenty thousand a year. With that in mind, I plan to hand in my humble resignation to the sovereign. I have some hope of being employed by the King of Naples: that great city will offer me all the distractions I need at this time, and which I can't find in a wretched village like Parma. I'll stay here only if you obtain Princess Isota's hand for me," and so on; the conversation went on endlessly in this direction.

When Rassi stood up to leave, the count said to him casually, "As you know, it's been said that Fabrizio betrayed me, in that he was one of the duchess's lovers. I don't accept that rumor, and, to belie it, I want you to have this purse delivered to him."

"But Your Excellency," said Rassi in alarm, looking at the purse, "that's an enormous sum, and the regulations—"

"It may seem enormous to *you*," said the count with an air of haughty disdain. "If a commoner like you sends money to a friend in prison, he thinks he's ruining himself if he gives him ten sequins. I'm determined that Fabrizio shall receive these ten thousand lire, and that no one at court shall know about it."

Rassi, frightened, tried to answer him, but the count impatiently shut the door in his face. "People like that," he said to himself, "acknowledge power only if it's cloaked in insolence." So saying, the great minister did something so ludicrous that it pains us to report it: he hurried to his desk, took out a miniature portrait of the duchess and covered it with passionate kisses. "Forgive me, my dearest angel," he cried, "for not throwing that swine out the window with my own hands after he dared to speak of you with a touch of familiarity! I acted with such great patience only in obedience to your orders, and he'll lose nothing by waiting!"

After a long conversation with the portrait, the count, who felt his heart dead within his breast, had the idea of a ridiculous action and carried it out with childish eagerness. He put on a coat with his décorations attached to it and went off to pay a visit to the old Princess Isota; never before in his life had he gone to see her except on New Year's Day. He found her surrounded by a number of dogs and decked out in all her finery, including even diamonds, as though she were about to make an appearance at court. When he expressed some fear of upsetting her plans, since she was evidently about to go out, Her Highness replied that a Princess of Parma owed it to herself to be always dressed in such a manner.

For the first time since his misfortune, the count felt a surge of gaiety. "I did well to come here," he thought, "and I must make my declaration this very day." The princess was delighted to receive a visit from a man who was so renowned for his wit, and was a Prime Minister besides; the poor spinster was not accustomed to such visitors. The count began with an adroit preamble on the subject of the vast distance which always separates an ordinary nobleman from the members of a reigning family.

"One must make a distinction," said the princess: "the daughter of a King of France, for example, has no hope of ever succeeding to the throne; but things are different in Parma. We Farneses must therefore always maintain a certain dignity in external matters, and I, a poor princess as you see me now, cannot say that it is absolutely impossible that you may some day be my Prime Minister."

The quaint unexpectedness of this idea gave the poor count a second moment of refreshing gaiety.

As he was leaving the residence of Princess Isota, who had blushed deeply on hearing him avow his passion for her, he encountered one of the palace attendants, who told him that the prince wanted to see him without delay.

"I'm ill," replied the count, delighted at the chance to be rude to his prince. "Ah, you drive me to desperation," he thought furiously, "and then you expect me to serve you! But there's one thing you must realize, my dear prince: in our time, having received power from Providence is no longer enough; it now requires great intelligence and a strong character to succeed in being a despot."

After dismissing the palace attendant, who was scandalized by the perfect health of this invalid, the count decided it would be amusing to call on the two men at court who had the most influence over General Fabio Conti. Above all, what made the count tremble, and robbed him of all his courage, was that the governor of the citadel was accused of having once gotten rid of a certain captain, a personal enemy of his, by the use of *acqua Toffana.**

The count knew that for the past week the duchess had been handing out incredible sums of money in an effort to establish secret communication with the citadel, but in his opinion there was little chance of success, for all eyes were still open too wide. We shall not relate to the reader all the attempts at bribery made by the unhappy woman. She was in despair, and she had the assistance of all sorts of thoroughly devoted agents, but there is perhaps only one task which is carried out perfectly in small, despotic courts, and that is the keeping of political prisoners. The only result achieved by the duchess's money was the dismissal from the citadel of nine or ten men of all ranks.

CHAPTER EIGHTEEN

Thus, despite their complete devotion to the prisoner, the duchess and the Prime Minister had been able to do very little for him. The prince was angry, and the court as well as the public took spiteful delight in Fabrizio's misfortune: he had been too fortunate before. The duchess's lavish distribution of gold had not enabled her to advance one step in her siege of the citadel. There was never a day when the Marquise Raversi or Cavaliere Riscara did not communicate some new report to General Fabio Conti. His weakness was carefully supported.

As we have already stated, on the day of his imprisonment Fabrizio was first taken to the governor's residence, an attractive building constructed in the eighteenth century from plans drawn up by Vanvitelli, who placed it a hundred and eighty feet above the ground, on the platform of the immense round tower. From the windows of this little palace, rising from the top of the enormous tower like a hump on a camel's back, Fabrizio had a view of the entire countryside and the Alps far off in the distance. Looking down at the foot of the citadel, he could follow the course of the Parma, a swift stream which turns to the right four leagues from the city and empties into the Po. Beyond the left bank of this stream, which forms a series of great white patches in the midst of

*A deadly poison.—L.B.

the green landscape, his delighted eyes distinctly saw each peak of the massive wall formed by the Alps across the northern end of Italy. These peaks, always covered with snow, even in August, which was the month in which Fabrizio was now looking at them, impart what might be called a nostalgic coolness to the sun-baked countryside. The eye can pick out their smallest details, and yet they are over thirty leagues away from the citadel of Parma. The vast view from the governor's attractive palace is cut off at one corner on the south by the Farnese Tower, in which a room was being hastily prepared for Fabrizio.

This second tower, as the reader may recall, was erected on the platform of the great tower in honor of a crown prince who, unlike Hippolitus, son of Theseus, had not repelled the advances of his young stepmother. The princess died within a few hours, and the prince's son did not regain his freedom until seventeen years later, when, on his father's death, he ascended the throne. The Farnese Tower, to which Fabrizio was taken after he had waited three-quarters of an hour, is very ugly on the outside. It rises fifty feet or so above the platform of the great tower and is adorned with a number of lightning rods.

The prince who, dissatisfied with his wife, built this prison which can be seen from all over the countryside, had the strange notion of trying to persuade his subjects that it had been there for many years before: it was for this reason that he imposed on it the name of the Farnese Tower. It was forbidden to speak of its construction, and yet from all parts of the city of Parma and the surrounding plains, everyone could clearly see the masons laying each one of the stones which compose the pentagonal edifice. In order to prove its great age, above the door, two feet wide and four feet high, which forms its entrance, there was a magnificent bas-relief depicting Alessandro Farnese, the famous general, forcing Henri IV to withdraw from Paris.

The first floor of this Farnese Tower, standing in such a conspicuous position, consists of a single room at least forty paces long, proportionately wide, and filled with extremely squat pillars, for this inordinately vast room is no more than fifteen feet high. It is occupied by the guards. In the center there is a staircase which winds around one of the pillars. It is a light little staircase made of filigreed iron, scarcely two feet wide.

Fabrizio climbed this staircase, which quivered beneath the weight of the jailers who were escorting him, until he came to the spacious rooms, over twenty feet high, which form a magnificent second floor. They had once been furnished with the greatest luxury for the young prince who spent the seventeen best years of his life in them. At one end of this apartment, the new prisoner was shown a chapel of the greatest splendor: its walls and vaulted ceiling are entirely covered with black marble. Pillars, also black and of the noblest proportions, stand in line along the black walls without touching them, and these walls are adorned with white marble skulls of colossal size, elegantly carved and placed above sets of crossbones.

"There's an invention of hatred unable to kill!" thought Fabrizio. "What a devilish idea to show it to me!"

Another light staircase of filigreed iron, also winding around a pillar, leads to the third floor of this prison, and it was in the rooms of this third floor, about fifteen feet high, that General Fabio Conti had been giving proof of his genius for the past year. First of all, under his direction, solid iron grilles had been placed over the windows of these rooms, which had once been occupied by the prince's servants. They are more than thirty feet above the flagstones that form the platform of the great round tower, and each of them has two windows. They are reached by means of a long corridor in the center of the building. In this narrow corridor, Fabrizio noticed three successive doors composed of enormous iron bars and rising all the way to the ceiling. It was the plans, cross-sections and elevations of all these fine inventions which had earned the general an interview with his master every week for two years. A conspirator placed in one of these rooms could not complain to public opinion that he was being treated in an inhuman manner, and yet he was unable to communicate with anyone in the world or make a movement without being heard. In each room, the general had placed heavy oak planks which formed a kind of bench three feet high, and this was his great invention, the one that gave him a claim to the Ministry of Police. On each bench he had placed a resonant wooden cell, ten feet high, which touched the wall only on the window side. A little corridor, four feet wide, ran along the three other sides, between the original walls of the prison, composed of enormous stone blocks, and the walls of the wooden cell, made of four thicknesses of walnut, oak and pine, firmly held together by iron bolts and countless nails.

Fabrizio was placed in one of these masterpieces of General Fabio Conti which had been constructed a year earlier. It had been given the fine name of "Passive Obedience." He ran over to the windows. The view through the bars was sublime. Only one little corner of the horizon was hidden, to the northwest, by the corniced roof of the governor's attractive residence, which was only three stories high; the bottom floor was occupied by the offices of the staff. Fabrizio's eyes were first drawn to one of the windows on the top floor, where he saw pretty cages containing a great number of birds of all kinds. He amused himself by listening to them sing, and watching them bid farewell to the last rays of the setting sun, while the jailers were bustling around him. This window with the bird cages was no more than twenty-five feet away from one of his own windows, and five or six feet below it, so that he looked down on the birds.

There was a moon that evening, and just as Fabrizio was entering his cell it was rising majestically above the horizon to the right, above the chain of the Alps in the direction of Treviso. It was only half-past eight. At the other end of the horizon, to the west, Monviso and the other Alpine peaks which run from Nice toward Mont Cenis and Turin were sharply outlined against the bright orange-red sunset. Without giving any thought to his misfortune, Fabrizio was moved and enraptured by this subline spectacle. "So Clelia Conti lives in this enchanting world!" he said to himself. "With her serious, pensive soul, she must enjoy this view more than anyone else. Here it's as though she were in the lonely mountains, a hundred leagues from Parma."

It was only after he had spent more than two hours at the window, admiring that horizon which spoke directly to his soul, and often also turning his eyes to the governor's attractive residence, that Fabrizio suddenly cried out, "But is this a prison? Is this what I've dreaded so intensely?" Instead of constantly seeing reasons for displeasure and bitterness, our hero let himself be spellbound by the charms of his prison.

His attention was abruptly recalled to reality by a frightful uproar: his wooden cell, rather like a cage and extremely resonant, was being violently shaken. The extraordinary noise was completed by shrill little cries and the barking of a dog. "What's happening?" wondered Fabrizio. "Can it be that I'm going to be able to escape so soon?" A moment later, he was laughing as perhaps no one else has ever laughed in a prison. By order of the general, the jailers had brought in an extremely vicious English dog which was used for guarding important prisoners and was to spend the night in the space so ingeniously contrived around Fabrizio's cage. The dog and a jailer were to sleep in the three-foot space between the original stone floor of the room and the wooden floor on which the prisoner could not take a step without being heard.

When Fabrizio had first entered the room known as "Passive Obedience," it had been occupied by a hundred enormous rats which had scurried off in all directions. The dog, a cross between a spaniel and an English fox terrier, was no beauty, but on the other hand he was extremely alert. He had been tied to the stone floor below the wooden room, but when he smelled the rats passing near him, he made such extraordinary efforts that he succeeded in slipping his head out of his collar: then came that admirable battle whose noise had roused Fabrizio from his happy revery. The rats that had been able to escape the dog's first onslaught took refuge in the wooden room. The dog came after them, up the six steps which led from the stone floor to Fabrizio's cage. Then began a much more frightful uproar; the room was shaken to its foundations. Fabrizio laughed like a madman, until tears came into his eyes. Grillo, the jailer, laughing with equal abandon, had closed the door. As the dog ran after the rats, he was not hampered by any furniture, for the room was completely bare; there was nothing to interfere with his leaps except an iron stove in one corner.

When the dog had triumphed over all his enemies, Fabrizio called him, patted him and succeeded in making friends with him. "If this dog ever sees me jumping over a wall," he thought, "he won't bark." But this clever plan was an affectation on his part: in his present state of mind, he found his happiness in playing with the dog. By some strange process on which he did not reflect, his heart was flooded with secret joy.

After running with the dog until he was out of breath, he said to the jailer, "What's your name?"

"Grillo, and I'm at Your Excellency's service for anything that's allowed by the regulations."

"Well then, my dear Grillo, a man named Giletti tried to murder me in the middle of a highway, I defended myself and killed him; I'd kill him again if I had it to do over, but nevertheless I want to lead a pleasant life while I'm your guest. Ask your superiors for permission to leave, then go to the Sanseverina palace and ask for some linen. In addition to that, I want you to buy me a large supply of *Nebiolo d'Asti*."

This is a rather good sparkling wine made in Piedmont, in Alfieri's native region. It is especially appreciated by the class of wine-lovers to which jailers belong. Nine or ten of these gentlemen were engaged in transferring to Fabrizio's wooden room several pieces of old and lavishly gilded furniture which they had taken from the prince's apartment on the second floor; they all reverently stored up in their minds the words that had been spoken with regard to the wine of Asti. Despite all their efforts, Fabrizio's installation for that night was pitiful; but he appeared to be upset by nothing except the lack of a bottle of good *Nebiolo*. "He seems like a nice young man," said the jailers as they left. "There's only one thing to hope for: that our officers will let money be sent in to him."

When he was alone and had somewhat recovered from all this commotion, "Is it possible that this is a prison?" thought Fabrizio, looking out at the immense horizon from Treviso to Monviso, the vast chain of the Alps, the snow-capped peaks, etc. "And it's my first night in prison, too! I can understand why Clelia Conti likes this airy solitude: it's a thousand leagues above the petty, malicious things that occupy our minds down there. If those birds below my window belong to her, I'll see her. . . . Will she blush when she sees me?" The prisoner was still debating this great question when he fell asleep at a very late hour of the night.

On the day following this night, the first one he had spent in prison, and during which he had never once became impatient, he was reduced to making conversation with Fox, the English dog. Grillo, the jailer, still gave him friendly looks, but a new order had made him mute, and he brought neither linen nor *Nebiolo*.

"Will I see Clelia?" Fabrizio asked himself when he woke up. "But are those birds hers?" The birds were beginning to chirp and sing, and at that height this was the only sound that came through the air. The vast silence which reigned up there gave Fabrizio a sensation of novelty and pleasure. He listened enraptured to the shrill, fitful little warblings with which his neighbors the birds were greeting the day. "If they belong to her," he thought, "she'll appear for a moment in that room down there below my window." And he gazed at the immense chain of the Alps, against the first tier of which the citadel of Parma seemed to rise like an outwork, his eyes kept returning to the magnificent lemonwood and mahogany cages which, adorned with gilded wires, stood in the middle of the bright room that served as an aviary. He later learned that this room was the only one on the top floor of the palace which had any shade between eleven o'clock and four, when it was protected from the sun by the Farnese Tower.

"How sad I'll be," he thought, "if, instead of the heavenly, pensive face I'm expecting, and which may blush a little if she sees me, I suddenly see the coarse face of some common chambermaid who's been sent to take care of the birds! But if I see Clelia, will she deign to notice me? I'll have to do something rash to attract her attention; my situation here ought to have some privileges; besides, we're both so alone here, so far from the world! I'm a prisoner—in other words, I'm what General Conti and the other vile rascals of his kind call one of their subordinates. But she has so much intelligence, or better, as the count says, so much heart, that, judging from what he's told me, she must despise her father's profession. That might account for her melancholy! A noble cause of sadness! But after all, I'm not exactly a stranger to her. She greeted me yesterday, and with such modest grace! I remember clearly that when we met near Como I said to her, 'Some day I'll go to see the beautiful pictures in Parma, and then will you be so kind as to remember this name: Fabrizio del Dongo?' Has she forgotten it? She was so young then!

"But I'm forgetting to be angry!" he suddenly said to himself in surprise, interrupting the course of his thoughts. "Could I be one of those men of great courage, of whom antiquity gave several examples to the world? Am I a hero without realizing it? Think of it: I was so afraid of prison, and yet now that I'm here I haven't even remembered to be sad! This is one case where it can certainly be said that the fear was a hundred times worse than the reality. I actually have to argue with myself to feel upset over my imprisonment, which, as Blanès said, may as easily last ten years as ten months! Can it be that the surprise of all these new surroundings has distracted me from the sorrow I ought to feel? Perhaps this cheerful humor, so involuntary and unreasonable, will suddenly cease; perhaps all at once I'll sink into the black despair I ought to be feeling now.

"In any case, it's amazing to be in prison and have to argue with myself to be sad! Yes, I must come back to my original supposition: perhaps I have a great character."

Fabrizio's musings were interrupted by the carpenter of the citadel, who had come to take measurements in order to make shutters for his windows: it was the first time the cell had been used, and the jailers had forgotten to complete it with this essential detail.

"So I'm going to be deprived of that sublime view!" thought Fabrizio, and he tried to feel sad about this privation.

"What!" he exclaimed suddenly, addressing the carpenter. "Does this mean that I'll no longer be able to see those pretty birds?"

"Ah, the signorina's birds, that she loves so much!" said the carpenter in a kindly tone. "They'll be hidden, cut off, blotted out, like everything else."

Speaking was as strictly prohibited for the carpenter as for the jailers, but he felt pity for the prisoner's youth. He told him that these enormous shutters, resting on the sills of the windows and slanting upward, were intended to give the prisoners a view of only the sky. "It's done for moral reasons," he said, "to help give the prisoners a feeling of wholesome sadness, and a desire to mend their ways. The general has also had the idea of taking the glass from their windows and replacing it with oiled paper."

Fabrizio was delighted with the epigrammatic turn of this conversation, which is extremely rare in Italy.

"I'd very much like to have a bird to cheer me up," he said. "I'm very fond of them. Buy me one from Signorina Clelia Conti's maid."

"What!" exclaimed the carpenter. "Do you know her? You say her name so easily."

"Who hasn't heard of that famous beauty? But I've had the honor of meeting her several times at court."

"The poor young lady is terribly bored here," said the carpenter. "She spends all her time down there with her birds. Just this morning she had some fine orange trees bought and placed at the door of the tower, just below your window. If it weren't for the cornice, you could see them."

This reply contained words that were very precious to Fabrizio; he found a tactful way of giving the carpenter some money.

"I'm breaking two regulations at once," the man said to him: "I'm talking to Your Excellency and I'm taking money. Day after tomorrow, when I come back to put up the shutters, I'll have a bird in my pocket. If I'm not alone, I'll pretend to let it escape from me. If possible, I'll even bring you a prayer book: it must be painful for you not to be able to recite your offices."

"So those birds do belong to her!" Fabrizio said to himself as soon as he was alone. "But in two days I'll no longer be able to see them!" At this thought, his eyes took on a look of sadness. But at last, to his inexpressible joy, after so much waiting and looking, toward noon Clelia came to take care of her birds. Fabrizio stood motionless and breathless, pressed up against the thick bars of his window. He noticed that she did not look up at him, but her movements were constrained, like those of someone aware of being watched. Even if she had wanted to, the poor girl could not have forgotten the faint smile she had seen on the prisoner's lips the day before, as the constables were leading him from the guardroom.

Although she was, to all appearances, carefully controlling all her actions, when she came near the window of the aviary she blushed quite noticeably. As he stood glued to the iron bars of his window, Fabrizio had the childish impulse to make a little noise by tapping on them with his hand, but then he was horrified at the mere thought of such an indelicate act. "It would serve me right if she sent her maid to take care of her birds for the next week." Such a discreet idea would never have occurred to him in Naples or Novara.

He followed her avidly with his eyes. "She'll surely leave without even deigning to cast a glance at this poor window," he thought, "even though it's almost exactly opposite her." But as she was coming back from the far end of the room, which Fabrizio, because of his more elevated position, could see quite clearly, she could not help glancing up at him as she walked, and this was enough to make him feel that he was authorized to bow to her. "Aren't we alone in the world here?" he thought, to give himself courage.

When she saw this bow, she stood still and lowered her eyes; then he saw her raise them again very slowly. Obviously making a great effort, she returned the prisoner's bow in the most solemn and distant manner, but she was unable to impose silence on her eyes: probably without her knowing it, they expressed for a moment the keenest pity. Fabrizio noticed that she blushed so deeply that the rosy tinge quickly spread to the top of her shoulders, from which the heat had forced her to remove a black lace shawl when she entered the aviary. The involuntary look with which he replied to her greeting redoubled her agitation. "How happy that poor woman would be," she said to herself, thinking of the duchess, "if she could see him only for an instant as I see him now!"

Fabrizio had some faint hope of saluting her again before she left, but, to avoid another exchange of courtesies, Clelia skillfully withdrew by degrees, from cage to cage, as though, in finishing, she had to take care of the birds nearest the door. She finally left. Fabrizio stood still, staring at the door through which she had just disappeared; he was a different man.

From then on, the sole object of his thoughts was to discover a way to go on seeing her, even after that horrible shutter had been placed in front of the window that overlooked the governor's residence.

On the previous evening, before going to bed, he had imposed on himself a long and tedious task of hiding most of the gold he had on him, in several of the rat holes which adorned his wooden cell. "Tonight I must hide my watch," he said to himself. "I've heard that with patience and a notched watch-spring it's possible to cut wood and even iron, so I'll be able to saw through that shutter."

The work of hiding his watch, which lasted a good two hours, did not seem long to him: he was thinking of various means to achieve his goal, and of what he knew how to do in the way of carpentry. "If I go about it right," he told himself, "I'll be able to cut out a section from the oak plank that will form the shutter, near the part resting on the window sill. I'll take that piece out and put it back when necessary. I'll give Grillo everything I have to make him willing not to notice my little trick."

All of Fabrizio's happiness now depended on the possibility of carrying out this plan, and he thought of nothing else. "If only I can manage to see her, I'll be happy. . . . But no, she must also see that I see her." All night long his head was filled with schemes of carpentry, and perhaps not once did he give any thought to the court of Parma, the prince's anger, etc. We must confess that neither did he give any thought to the grief with which the duchess was certainly overwhelmed.

He waited impatiently for the following day, but the carpenter did not return. He was apparently regarded in the prison as a liberal, and his superiors sent another carpenter in his place. This one was a grim-faced man who made no reply except a sinister grunt to all the pleasant remarks Fabrizio could think of to address to him.

Some of the duchess's many attempts to establish communication with Fabrizio had been discovered by the Marquise Raversi's many agents; through her, General Fabio Conti was daily warned, frightened and goaded by appeals to his vanity. Every eight hours, six soldiers of the guard were relieved by six others in the great room with the hundred pillars on the first floor. Furthermore, the governor posted a jailer to guard each of the three iron doors in the corridor, and poor Grillo, the only one who ever saw the prisoner, was allowed to leave the Farnese Tower only once a week, which irritated him greatly. He vented his ill-humor on Fabrizio, who was sensible enough to answer only with these words: "A good sup- ply of *Nebiolo d'Asti*, my friend." And he gave him money.

"We're forbidden to take even this, the thing that consoles us for all our troubles!" said Grillo indignantly, in a voice scarcely loud enough to be heard by the prisoner. "I ought to refuse, but I won't. Anyway, it's money wasted, because I can't tell you anything about anything. You must be terribly guilty—the whole citadel has been turned upside down be- cause of you. The duchess's clever maneuvers have already gotten three of us dismissed."

"Will the shutter be ready before noon?" This was the great question which made Fabrizio's heart pound all through that long morning. He counted the quarter-hours each time the clock of the citadel struck. Finally he heard it strike a quarter to twelve, and the shutter still had not come. Clelia reap- peared and began taking care of her birds. Cruel necessity had made Fabrizio's boldness take such great strides, and the danger of not seeing her again seemed to him so much more serious than anything else, that as he looked at her he dared to make a gesture of sawing through the shutter. It is true that as soon as she saw this gesture, so seditious in a prison, she bowed slightly and withdrew.

Fabrizio was thunderstruck. "Could she be so unreason- able," he wondered, "as to see ridiculous familiarity in a gesture dictated by the most serious necessity? I wanted to ask her to be kind enough in the future, when she's taking care of her birds, to cast an occasional glance at the window of my cell, even when she finds it covered by a big wooden shutter; I wanted to let her know that I'll do everything humanly possible to find some way to see her. My God! Can it be that she won't come tomorrow, because of that indis- creet gesture?"

This fear, which troubled Fabrizio's sleep, proved to be entirely justified: the next day, Clelia still had not appeared by three o'clock, when the work of placing the two big shutters over his windows was completed. The various pieces of the shutters had been hauled up from the platform of the great tower by means of ropes and pulleys attached from the outside to the iron bars of the windows. It is true that, hidden behind a blind in her room, Clelia had watched every move- ment of the workmen with anguish. She had clearly seen Fabrizio's frenzied anxiety, but she had still been able to keep the promise she had made to herself.

Clelia was a little sectarian of liberalism. In her childhood she had taken seriously all the liberal remarks she had heard in the society frequented by her father, who thought of nothing except making a good position for himself. From this she had begun to feel contempt and almost horror for the courtier's compliant character, hence her antipathy toward marriage. Since Fabrizio's arrival, she had been tormented by remorse. "My ignoble heart has begun to side with people who want to betray my father!" she thought. "He dared to make that gesture of sawing through a door! . . . But," she immediately added, heartbroken, "everyone in Parma is saying that he'll soon be dead! Tomorrow may be the fatal day! With the monsters who rule us, anything is possible! What gentleness, what heroic serenity in those eyes which are perhaps about to be closed forever! Dear God, what anguish the duchess must be feeling! They say she's in utter despair. If I were in her place, I'd go and stab the prince, like the heroic Charlotte Corday."

All through the third day of his imprisonment, Fabrizio was beside himself with rage, but only because he had not seen Clelia reappear. "Since she's angry at me anyway," he cried, "I should have told her I loved her," for he had arrived at this discovery. "No, it's not from greatness of soul that I'm giving no thought to imprisonment and belying Blanès prophecy; I can't claim that honor. In spite of myself I keep thinking of that look of sweet pity which Clelia gave me while the constables were leading me from the guardroom; that look has wiped out all my past life. Who would have thought I'd find such sweet eyes in such a place! And at the very moment when my sight had been sullied by the faces of Barbone and the general! Heaven appeared in the midst of those vile creatures. How can anyone help loving beauty, and trying to see it again? No, it's not from greatness of soul that I'm indifferent to all the little annoyances that my imprisonment inflicts on me."

Fabrizio's imagination, quickly passing over all possibilities, arrived at that of being set free. "The duchess's friendship will no doubt work miracles for me. If so, I'll give her only grudging thanks for my freedom, because this isn't the kind of place one returns to! Clelia and I move in different circles, so if I'm released from prison I'll almost never see her again! And after all, what harm does it do to be in prison? If Clelia would deign not to crush me with her anger, what else could I ask of heaven?"

On the evening of that day when he had not seen his pretty neighbor, he had an excellent idea: with the iron cross of the rosary given to all prisoners on their arrival, he began, successfully, to make a hole in the shutter. "This may be foolhardy," he said to himself before he began. "Didn't the carpenters say in my presence that the painters would come here tomorrow? What will they say if they find a hole in the shutter? But if I don't run that risk, I won't be able to see her tomorrow! Could I go a whole day without seeing her, through my own fault? And after she left me in anger?"

His rashness was rewarded, for after fifteen hours of work he saw Clelia, and, to crown his happiness, since she did not know he was watching her she stood staring at the shutter for a long time. He had ample opportunity to read all the signs of tender pity in her eyes. Toward the end of her stay, she even neglected to care for her birds, in order to spend whole minutes in motionless contemplation of the window. Her heart was deeply troubled; she was thinking of the duchess, whose extreme sorrow had aroused such pity in her, and yet she was beginning to hate her. She could not understand the profound melancholy that was taking possession of her, and she was angry with herself. Two or three times, Fabrizio's impatience nearly drove him to try to shake the shutter; it seemed to him that he would not be really happy until he could let Clelia know he was watching her. "But," he thought, "shy and reserved as she is, if she knew I could see her so easily she'd probably hide herself from my eyes."

He was much happier the next day (love can make happiness from such wretched trifles!): while she was gazing sadly at the shutter, he managed to push a piece of wire through the opening he had made with his iron cross, and he made signals to her which she obviously understood, at least in the sense that she knew he was trying to say, "I'm here and I can see you."

But he was unfortunate for several days afterward. He wanted to remove from the colossal shutter a section the size of his hand which he could replace at will, and which would enable him to see and be seen, to speak, by signals at least, of what was taking place in his heart. But he found that the noise of his extremely imperfect saw, which he had made by notching the spring of his watch with the cross, worried Grillo, who came to spend long hours in his cell. He thought he had noticed, however, that Clelia's severity diminished in proportion as the material difficulties of communication increased. He saw clearly that she no longer lowered her eyes and pretended to look at her birds when he tried to signal his presence to her by means of his little piece of wire. He had the pleasure of seeing that she never failed to appear in the aviary at the precise moment when the clock struck a quarter to twelve, and he was almost presumptuous enough to believe himself to be the cause of this scrupulous punctuality. Why? This idea does not seem reasonable, but love discerns nuances invisible to indifferent eyes, and draws endless conclusions from them.

For example, now that Clelia could no longer see the prisoner, she looked up at his window almost immediately each time she entered the aviary. This was during those sinister days when no one in Parma doubted that Fabrizio would soon be put to death. He alone knew nothing of it, but the horrible thought never left Clelia, so how could she reproach herself for her extreme interest in him? He was about to die! And for the cause of freedom! For it would have been too absurd to put a del Dongo to death for having plunged his sword into an itinerant actor. It was true, however, that the charming young man was attached to another woman! Clelia was profoundly unhappy, but without admitting to herself the precise nature of her interest in Fabrizio's fate. "If they put him to death," she thought, "I'll flee to a convent and never appear in court society again for the rest of my life! I'm horrified at the sight of those people! They're nothing but well-mannered murderers!"

On the eighth day of Fabrizio's imprisonment, she had great cause for shame. Absorbed in her sad thoughts, she was staring at the shutter that hid his window. He had not yet given her any sign of his presence. Suddenly he removed a small piece of the shutter, larger than a man's hand. He looked out at her with a joyous expression, and she saw his eyes greeting her. This unexpected trial was beyond her strength; she quickly turned around and began tending to her birds, but she was trembling so violently that she spilled the water she was trying to pour out for them, and her agitation was clearly apparent to Fabrizio. Unable to bear the situation any longer, she put an end to it by running away.

This was the happiest moment of Fabrizio's life, beyond all comparison. How vehemently he would have refused his freedom if it had been offered to him then!

The following day was the day of the duchess's great despair. Everyone in Parma regarded it as certain that Fabrizio's end was at hand. Clelia did not have the sad courage to show him a harshness that was not in her heart: she spent an hour and a half in the aviary, watched all his signals and often replied to him, at least by an expression of the keenest and most sincere interest. Now and then she would leave him for a few moments to hide her tears. Her feminine coquettishness made her keenly aware of the imperfection of the language they employed: if they had been able to speak to each other, in how many different ways would she have tried to discover the exact nature of his feelings for the duchess! Clelia was scarcely able to delude herself any longer: she felt hatred for Duchess Sanseverina.

One night Fabrizio began thinking somewhat seriously of his aunt. To his amazement, he hardly recognized her image in his mind. His memory of her had changed completely: she now seemed to be fifty years old.

"Good God!" he exclaimed with emotion. "How right I was not to tell her I loved her!" He had reached the point of being almost unable to understand why he had thought her so pretty. In this respect, his memory of Marietta had changed less noticeably; this was because he had never imagined that his soul had anything to do with his love for Marietta, whereas he had often believed that his whole soul belonged to the duchess. The Duchess of A—— and Marietta now gave him the impression of two young doves whose charm lay solely in their weakness and innocence, while the sublime image of Clelia Conti, having taken possession of his entire soul, went so far as to inspire him with terror. He felt all too clearly that the happiness of his whole life depended on her, and that it was within her power to make him the unhappiest of men. Each day he was mortally afraid that some caprice of her will, from which there was no appeal, might suddenly put an end to the strange, blissful life he led with her. In any case, she had filled the first two months of his imprisonment with joy. And twice a week, all through this period, General Fabio Conti said to the prince, "I can give you my word of honor, Your Highness, that the prisoner del Dongo never speaks to a living soul, and that he spends all his time either overwhelmed by the blackest despair, or else asleep."

Clelia came two or three times a day to see her birds, sometimes only for a few moments. If Fabrizio had not been so much in love with her, he would have seen clearly that she loved him, but he had terrible doubts about it. Clelia had had a piano placed in the aviary. As she struck the keys, so that the sound of the instrument would account for her presence there and occupy the attention of the sentries pacing back and forth beneath her windows, she would answer Fabrizio's questions with her eyes. There was one subject, however, on which she never made any reply, and she even ran away whenever he presented it too insistently: this happened each time his signals indicated certain feelings on his part which she could not fail to understand. On this point she was inflexible.

Thus, though tightly confined in a rather small cage, Fabrizio's life was fully occupied. It was entirely spent in seeking the solution of this important problem: "Does she love me?" The result of thousands of observations, constantly renewed but also constantly placed in doubt, was this: "All her voluntary gestures say no, but the involuntary movements of her eyes seem to confess that she's becoming fond of me."

Clelia fervently hoped to avoid a confession, and it was to ward off this danger that she angrily rejected a request which Fabrizio had made to her several times. The poverty of the resources employed by the poor prisoner ought, it would seem, to have aroused greater pity in her. He wanted to communicate with her by means of letters written on his hand with a piece of charcoal which he had been delighted to find in his stove. This device would have vastly increased their means of conversation, for it would have made possible the expression of precise ideas. His window was about twenty-five feet away from hers; it would have been too hazardous to speak to each other over the heads of the sentries pacing back and forth in front of the governor's residence. Fabrizio doubted that he was loved; if he had had any experience with love, he would no longer have had any doubts, but no woman had ever occupied his heart before. Furthermore, he had no suspicion of a secret which would have filled him with despair if he had known it: very serious consideration was being given to the possibility of a marriage between Clelia Conti and the Marquis Crescenzi, the richest man at court.

CHAPTER NINETEEN

General Fabio Conti's ambition, stimulated to the point of madness by the difficulties which had just arisen in Prime Minister Mosca's path, and which seemed to announce his downfall, had led him to make violent scenes with his daughter. He constantly and angrily repeated to her that she would ruin his career if she did not finally make up her mind to choose a husband. She was now past twenty and it was time to come to a decision. The cruel state of isolation in which her unreasonable obstinacy had placed him would have to come to an end, etc., etc.

At first, it was to escape from these frequent outbursts of temper that Clelia had taken refuge in the aviary. It could be reached only by means of a very awkward wooden staircase, and the governor's gout made it a serious obstacle for him.

For several weeks, Clelia's soul had been so agitated, and she herself was so uncertain as to what she ought to desire, that without exactly giving her word to her father, she had almost allowed herself to be committed. In one of his fits of anger, the general had shouted that he could easily send her to languish from boredom in the gloomiest convent in Parma, and that he would leave her there until she condescended to make a choice.

"You know that our whole family, though very ancient, has an income of less than six thousand lire, while the Marquis Crescenzi's fortune brings in over a hundred thousand scudi a year. Everyone at court agrees that he has a very gentle character; he's never given anyone cause for complaint; he's handsome, young, and in high favor with the prince: a woman would have to be raving mad to reject his advances! If this were your first refusal I might put up with it, but you've already refused five or six other matches, and the finest ones at court, like the little fool that you are! And tell me, what would become of you if I were retired at half-pay? What a triumph it would be for my enemies if I were seen living in some third-floor apartment, I who have so often been considered for the ministry! No, by heaven! My kindness has made me play the part of a gullible old graybeard long enough! You will give me some valid objection against that poor Marquis Crescenzi, who's kind enough to be in love with you, to be willing to marry you without a dowry and grant you a jointure of thirty thousand lire a year, which will at least be enough to pay for my lodging; you will talk to me sensibly, or, by heaven, you'll marry him two months from now!"

Clelia was struck by only one thing in this whole tirade: her father's threat to send her to a convent, and therefore away from the citadel, just when Fabrizio's life seemed to be hanging by a thread, for not a month passed in which the rumor of his approaching death did not again spread through the town and the court. No matter how she reasoned with herself, she could not bring herself to risk being separated from him at the very time when she was trembling for his life. This was to her the greatest evil; it was at least the most immediate.

Not that her heart felt any possibility of happiness, even if she were not sent away from Fabrizio: she believed him to be loved by the duchess, and her soul was torn by deadly jealousy. She was always thinking of the advantages of that woman who was so generally admired. The extreme reserve she had imposed on herself with regard to Fabrizio, the sign-language to which she had restricted him, her fear of falling into an act of indiscretion—everything seemed to combine to deprive her of all means of obtaining any enlightenment on the nature of his relationship with the duchess. Thus, every day she felt still more painfully the terrible unhappiness of having a rival in Fabrizio's heart, and every day she had less courage to face the danger of giving him an opportunity to tell her the whole truth about what was taking place in that heart. And yet how wonderful it would be to hear him confess his true feelings! What a joy it would be for her to clear away the horrible suspicions that were poisoning her life!

Fabrizio was fickle; in Naples he had had the reputation of changing his mistresses rather easily. Despite all the reserve imposed on a young unmarried lady, since becoming a canoness and beginning to go to court, Clelia, by listening attentively, though never asking questions, had come to know the reputation of each of the young men who had successively sought her hand in marriage. And Fabrizio was said to be more inconstant than any of them. He was in prison, he was bored, so he was paying court to the only woman he could speak to—what could be simpler? Indeed, what could be more *common*? And this was what grieved Clelia. Even if, by a complete revelation, she were to learn that he no longer loved the duchess, what confidence could she have in his words? Even if she were to believe in the sincerity of his statements, what confidence could she have in the duration of his feelings?

And finally, to fill her heart to overflowing with despair, was he not already far advanced in an ecclesiastical career? Was he not on the verge of binding himself with eternal vows? Were not the greatest dignities awaiting him in that kind of life? "If I still had the slightest glimmer of common sense," the unhappy Clelia told herself, "shouldn't I go away from here? Shouldn't I beg my father to shut me up in some faraway convent? And, to crown my misery, it's precisely the fear of being sent away from the citadel and shut up in a convent that governs all my conduct! It's that fear which obliges me to dissimulate, which forces me into the hideous and shameful lie of pretending to accept the Marquis Crescenzi's public attentions."

Clelia's character was profoundly reasonable; never before in her life had she had to reproach herself for a single ill-considered act, and yet her conduct in her present situation was the height of unreason—it is easy to imagine her suffering! It was all the more cruel because she did not delude herself: she was becoming attached to a man who was passionately loved by the most beautiful woman at court, a woman who was superior to her in so many ways! And even if he were free, he would still be incapable of a serious attachment, while she, as she felt only too well, would never have more than one attachment in her life.

And so it was with a heart torn by the most frightful remorse that Clelia came to the aviary every day. After she had been drawn there as though against her will, her anxiety would change its object and become less cruel, and her remorse would vanish for a time. Her heart would pound wildly as she watched for the moments when Fabrizio could open the little hatch he had made in the immense shutter which covered his window. Often the presence of the jailer Grillo in his cell would prevent him from conversing with her by signs.

At about eleven o'clock one night, Fabrizio heard some very strange noises in the citadel. At night, by leaning against the window and putting his head through the hatch, he was able to hear any fairly loud noise that was made on the great staircase, known as the "Three Hundred Steps," which led from the first courtyard inside the round tower to the stone platform on which had been built the governor's residence and the Farnese Tower in which Fabrizio was now imprisoned.

About halfway up, after a rise of a hundred and eighty steps, this staircase shifted from the south side of a vast courtyard to the north side; at this point there was a very light and narrow iron bridge, in the middle of which a guard was posted. He was relieved every six hours, and he had to stand aside to allow anyone to pass over the bridge he was guarding. This bridge was the only means of access to the governor's residence and the Farnese Tower, and two turns of a spring, to which the governor always carried the key, were enough to send the bridge hurtling into the courtyard more than three hundred feet below. Once this simple precaution had been taken, since there was no other staircase anywhere in the citadel, and since every night at midnight a sergeant brought the ropes of all the wells to a little room that could be entered only through the governor's bedroom, he was completely inaccessible in his residence, and it would have been equally impossible for anyone to reach the Farnese Tower. Fabrizio had clearly noticed this on the day he entered the citadel, and Grillo, who, like all jailers, loved to boast about his prison, had explained it to him several times, so he had little hope of being able to escape. However, he recalled one of Father Blanès' maxims: "The lover thinks more often of reaching his mistress than the husband thinks of guarding his wife, and the prisoner thinks more often of escaping than the jailer thinks of locking his door; therefore, no matter what the obstacles, the lover and the prisoner must succeed."

That night, Fabrizio distinctly heard a great number of men crossing the iron bridge, known as the "Slave's Bridge," because a Dalmatian slave had once succeeded in escaping by throwing the guard down into the courtyard.

"They're coming here to take someone away," thought Fabrizio. "Perhaps they're going to take me out and hang me. But there may be some disorder; I must be ready to make the most of it." He had taken his weapons and was already withdrawing his gold from some of its hiding places when he suddenly stopped short.

"Man is certainly an amusing animal!" he exclaimed. "What would an invisible spectator say if he were watching my preparations? Do I by any chance want to escape? What would happen to me the day after I returned to Parma? Wouldn't I do everything in my power to come back to Clelia? If there's any disorder, I'll take advantage of it to slip into the governor's residence: I may be able to speak to Clelia, and perhaps, using the disorder as my justification, I'll dare to kiss her hand. General Conti is extremely suspicious by nature, and equally vain: he has his residence guarded by five sentries, one at each corner of the building and a fifth at the entrance; but fortunately it's very dark tonight." Fabrizio stealthily walked over to see what Grillo and his dog were doing. The jailer was sound asleep in an ox-hide suspended from the ceiling by four ropes and surrounded by a coarse net. Fox, the dog, opened his eyes and quietly walked toward Fabrizio to rub up against him.

Our hero softly climbed back up the six steps which led to his wooden cell. The noise at the foot of the Farnese Tower, and precisely in front of his door, was becoming so loud that he thought Grillo might easily wake up. Armed with all his weapons and ready for action, Fabrizio was growing more convinced than ever that great adventures lay in store for him that night when suddenly he heard the beginning of the most beautiful symphony in the world: it was a serenade that was being played for either the general or his daughter. He burst into a fit of wild laughter. "And I was already thinking of wielding my dagger! As though a serenade weren't something infinitely more common than a revolt or an abduction requiring the presence of eighty people in a cell!" The music was excellent and seemed exquisite to Fabrizio, whose soul had had no distraction for so many weeks; it made him shed sweet tears. In his rapture, he addressed the most irresistible speeches to the fair Clelia.

But the next day, at noon, he found her in a mood of such dark melancholy, she was so pale, and he sometimes saw so much anger in the looks she gave him that he did not feel it would be permissible to question her about the serenade; he was afraid of being impolite.

Clelia had good reason to be sad: the serenade had been given for her by the Marquis Crescenzi, and so public an act was almost equivalent to an official announcement of their marriage. Until the day of the serenade, and until nine o'clock that evening, she had resisted bravely, but then she had had the weakness to yield when her father threatened to send her to a convent immediately.

"Oh! I'd never see him again!" she had said to herself, weeping. It was in vain that her reason had added, "I'd never again see the man who'll make me unhappy in every way, I'd never again see the duchess's lover, that fickle young man who had ten known mistresses in Naples and betrayed them all, that ambitious young man who, if he survives the sentence now hanging over his head, will take Holy Orders! It would be a crime for me ever to look at him again after he's left this citadel, and his natural inconstancy will spare me that temptation, for what am I to him? A pretext for being less bored during a few hours of each day he spends in prison."

In the midst of all this abuse, she suddenly recalled the way he had smiled when he looked at the constables who were surrounding him as he came out of the prison office, before going up to the Farnese Tower. Her eyes were flooded with tears. "What wouldn't I do for you, dear friend? You'll be my ruin, I know; such is my fate. I'm bringing on my own ruin in a terrible way tonight, by listening to this horrible serenade—but tomorrow, at noon, I'll see your eyes again!"

It was precisely on the morrow of this day when Clelia had made such great sacrifices for the young prisoner she loved with such devotion, it was on the morrow of this day when, seeing all his faults, she had sacrificed her life to him, that Fabrizio was driven to despair by her coldness. If, even using the extremely imperfect language of signs, he had done the slightest violence to her heart, she would probably not have been able to hold back her tears, and he would have obtained an avowal of everything she felt for him; but he lacked boldness, he was too mortally afraid of offending her: she might inflict too severe a punishment on him. In other words, Fabrizio had no experience of the kind of emotion aroused by the woman one loves; it was a sensation he had never felt before, even in its weakest form. After the day of the serenade, it took him a week to recover his usual footing of straightforward friendship with Clelia. The poor girl armed herself with severity, dying of fear that she might betray herself, and every day it seemed to Fabrizio that he was on worse terms with her than ever.

One day, when Fabrizio had been in prison for nearly three months without any communication from the outside, and yet without feeling unhappy, Grillo remained in his cell until very late in the morning. Fabrizio did not know how to get rid of him, and he was in despair. The clock had already struck half-past twelve before he was at last able to open the two little hatches, one foot high, which he had made in the fateful shutter.

Clelia was standing at the window of the aviary, her eyes fixed on Fabrizio's window; her drawn features expressed the most violent despair. As soon as she saw him, she motioned to him that all was lost. She rushed to her piano and, pretending to sing a recitative from the opera then in vogue, said to him in sentences interrupted by despair and the fear of being understood by the sentries beneath her window: "Thank God you're still alive! Barbone, the jailer whose insolence you punished the day you came here, disappeared from the citadel several days ago. He came back night before last, and since yesterday I've had reason to believe that he's trying to poison you. He prowls around the private kitchen of the palace, where your meals are prepared. I don't know anything for sure, but my maid believes that he shows his hideous face in the kitchen only with the aim of putting an end to your life. I was dying of anxiety when I didn't see you appear, I thought you were dead. Don't eat anything until further notice. I'll do everything possible to see that you receive a little chocolate. In any case, tonight at nine o'clock, if by the grace of heaven you have a piece of string, or if you can make a long ribbon from some of your linen, lower it from your window to the orange trees. I'll tie a rope to it, you'll pull it up to your cell, and by means of that rope I'll give you some bread and chocolate."

Fabrizio had kept, as though it were a treasure, the piece of charcoal he had found in the stove in his room. He hastened to take advantage of Clelia's emotion, and wrote on his hand a series of letters which spelled out these words: "I love you, and my life is precious to me only because I see you. Above all, send me some paper and a pencil."

As he had hoped, the extreme terror he could discern in her face prevented her from breaking off the conversation after the bold words, "I love you." She contented herself with showing great irritation. He was clever enough to add, "Because of the high wind that is blowing today, it is difficult for me to understand the information you are kind enough to give me in your singing. Your voice is covered by the sound of the piano. For example, what is this poison you have mentioned?"

At these words, her terror returned in full strength. She quickly began to trace large letters in ink on pages which she tore from a book, and Fabrizio was overjoyed to see that at last, after three months of effort, the means of communication he had so vainly solicited was now established. He was careful not to abandon the little ruse which had succeeded so well; he hoped to be able to write letters, so he constantly pretended not to understand the words that Clelia spelled out before his eyes.

She was obliged to leave the aviary and hurry back to her father. She dreaded above all that he might come there to look for her. His suspicious nature would not have been at all satisfied by the proximity of the aviary window to the shutter that masked the prisoner's window. A short time earlier, when Fabrizio's failure to appear was causing her such mortal anxiety, Clelia herself had had the idea that it might be possible to wrap a piece of paper around a small stone and throw it over the top of the shutter; if luck would have it that the jailer charged with guarding Fabrizio should happen not to be in his cell at that moment, it would be a reliable means of communication.

Our prisoner hastened to make a kind of ribbon from some of his linen, and that evening, shortly after nine o'clock, he distinctly heard a light tapping on one of the boxes containing the roots of the orange trees that stood beneath his window. He lowered the ribbon and it brought back a long, thin rope by means of which he drew up, first, a supply of chocolate, and then, to his ineffable delight, a roll of paper and a pencil. He lowered the rope again, but in vain: he received nothing more. Apparently the sentries had approached the orange trees. But he was intoxicated with joy. He hastened to write an endless letter to Clelia. As soon as it was finished, he tied it to one end of his rope and lowered it. For more than three-quarters of an hour he vainly waited for her to come and take it, and several times he drew it back to make changes in it. "If she doesn't see my letter tonight," he said to himself, "while she's still upset by her ideas of poison, tomorrow she may completely reject all thought of receiving a letter."

The fact is that Clelia had not been able to avoid going into town with her father. Fabrizio almost realized this when, at about half-past midnight, he heard the general's carriage return; he recognized the sound of the horses' hooves. How great was his joy when, a few minutes after hearing the general walk across the platform and the sentries present arms to him, he felt a movement in the rope that he had constantly kept wrapped around his arm! A heavy weight was being attached to it; then two little tugs on it gave him the signal to draw it up. He had difficulty in pulling the weight over a cornice which jutted far out beneath his window.

The object he had so much difficulty in pulling up was a decanter filled with water and wrapped in a shawl. It was with rapture that the poor young man, who had been living so long in such utter solitude, covered this shawl with kisses. But we must give up any attempt to depict his emotion when at last, after so many days of vain hope, he discovered a little note pinned to the shawl:

Drink nothing but water, eat nothing but chocolate. Tomorrow I will do everything in my power to get some bread to you. I will mark it on all sides with little crosses in ink. It is horrible to say, but it is necessary for you to know that Barbone may have been ordered to poison you. How could you not have realized that the subject dealt with in your penciled letter would surely displease me? I would therefore not write to you if it were not for the extreme danger which threatens us. I have just seen the duchess: she is in good health, and so is the count, but she has lost a great deal of weight. Do not write to me about that subject again. Do you want to make me angry?

It had taken a great effort on Clelia's part to write the third sentence from the end. Everyone in court society maintained that Duchess Sanseverina was becoming extremely friendly with the handsome Count Baldi, the Marquise Raversi's former lover. One thing was certain: he had broken in the most scandalous manner with the marquise, who had established him in society and been a mother to him for six years.

Clelia had been obliged to begin this hastily written note again, because the first draft gave some hint of the new love affair which the maliciousness of the public attributed to the duchess.

"How vile of me," she had exclaimed, "to say bad things to Fabrizio about the woman he loves!"

The next morning, long before daylight, Grillo came into Fabrizio's cell, set down a rather heavy package and disappeared without a word. This package contained a large loaf of bread marked on all sides with little crosses in ink. Fabrizio covered them with kisses; he was in love. Beside the bread was a roll of coins wrapped in many thicknesses of paper: it contained six thousand lire in sequins. Finally, he found a handsome, brand-new breviary. A hand he was beginning to know had written these words in one of the margins: "*Poison!* Beware of water, wine, everything; live on nothing but chocolate, and try to feed your untouched dinner to the dog. You must not appear to be suspicious, or the enemy will seek other means. In the name of God, do nothing foolish, and do not take this lightly!"

Fabrizio hastened to destroy these precious words, which might have compromised Clelia. He then picked up the breviary, tore out many of its pages and used them to make several alphabets, neatly tracing each letter in wine blackened with powdered charcoal. These alphabets were dry by a quarter to twelve, when Clelia appeared, standing two paces behind the aviary window. "The great thing now," he thought, "is to make her consent to use them." But fortunately it happened that she had many things to tell him about the attempt to poison him: a dog belonging to one of the maidservants had died after eating some food that was intended for Fabrizio. Far from objecting to the use of the alphabets, Clelia had prepared a magnificent one of her own, in ink. The conversation carried on by this means, a little awkward at first, lasted no less than an hour and a half, that is, during the entire time Clelia was able to remain in the aviary. Two or three times, when Fabrizio took the liberty of mentioning forbidden subjects, she made no reply, and turned away for a few minutes to tend to her birds.

Fabrizio had succeeded in making her promise that, along with the water she would send him that evening, she would also send him an alphabet written in ink, which would be much easier to see. He did not fail to write her a very long letter in which he was careful not to make any amorous remarks, at least not in a way that might offend her. This strategy was successful: his letter was accepted.

The next day, in their conversation by alphabets, Clelia did not reproach him. She informed him that the danger of poison was diminishing: Barbone had been attacked and nearly beaten to death by a group of men who were paying court to the girls who worked in the kitchen of the governor's residence, so he would probably never dare to enter the kitchen again. She confessed to Fabrizio that, for his sake, she had dared to steal a counterpoison from her father, and would send it to him. But it was still essential for him to reject immediately any food which tasted at all unusual.

Clelia had asked Don Cesare many questions without being able to discover the origin of the six thousand lire which Fabrizio had received. In any case, it was an excellent sign: his imprisonment was becoming less rigorous.

This episode of the poison furthered our prisoner's interests enormously, although he had never been able to obtain an avowal of anything resembling love. But he still had the happiness of living on intimate terms with Clelia. Every morning, and often in the afternoon, they had a long conversation with their alphabets. Every evening at nine o'clock, Clelia accepted a long letter, and sometimes answered it with a few words. She sent him newspapers and a few books. And finally, Grillo had been won over to the point where he was willing to bring Fabrizio bread and wine, which was given to him every day by Clelia's maid. From this, the jailer had concluded that the governor was not in accord with those who had instructed Barbone to poison the young *monsignore*, and he was glad, for a saying had arisen in the prison: "All you have to do is look *Monsignore* del Dongo in the face and he'll give you money."

Fabrizio had become very pale, for his health was suffering from his complete lack of exercise. Aside from this, however, he had never been so happy before. The tone of his conversations with Clelia was intimate, and sometimes quite gay. The only moments of her life that were not besieged by gloomy anticipations and remorse were those she spent conversing with him. One day she had the imprudence to say to him, "I admire your tact: since I'm the governor's daughter, you never speak to me of your desire to regain your freedom."

"That's because I have no such absurd idea," replied Fabrizio. "If I were back in Parma, how could I see you again? And life would be unbearable to me if I couldn't tell you all my thoughts. . . . No, not really all my thoughts, you won't allow that. Still, though, despite your unkindness, living without seeing you every day would be a much worse ordeal for me than my imprisonment! Never in my life have I been so happy! Isn't it amusing to find that happiness was waiting for me in a prison?"

"There are many things to be said on that subject," replied Clelia with an expression which abruptly became extremely serious and almost sinister.

"What!" he exclaimed in alarm. "Am I in danger of losing the tiny place I've been able to win in your heart, and which give me the only joy I have in the world?"

"Yes," she answered. "I have every reason to believe that you're not entirely honest with me, even though you're generally regarded as a man of honor. But I don't want to discuss that subject today."

This singular statement introduced a great deal of awkwardness into their conversation, and often they both had tears in their eyes.

Chief Justice Rassi was still eager to change his name; he was extremely tired of the one he had made for himself and wanted to become Baron Riva. Count Mosca, for his part, was working with all the skill at his command to strengthen this venal judge's passion for a barony, and at the same time he was trying to increase the prince's insane hope of becoming the constitutional monarch of Lombardy. These were the only means he could discover to delay Fabrizio's death.

The prince said to Rassi, "Two weeks of despair, then two weeks of hope: it's by a patient application of this treatment that we'll succeed in subduing that haughty woman's spirit; the wildest horses are broken in by just such an alternation between gentleness and severity. Apply the caustic firmly."

Consequently, every two weeks a new rumor of Fabrizio's approaching death arose in Parma. These reports always plunged the unhappy duchess into the depths of despair.

Faithful to her resolution not to drag the count into her ruin, she now saw him only twice a month; but she was punished for her cruelty to the poor man by the constantly recurring fits of black despair in which her life was spent. It was in vain that Count Mosca, overcoming the cruel jealousy aroused in him by the handsome Count Baldi's attentions, wrote to her when he could not see her, and passed on to her all the information he owed to the zeal of the future Baron Riva. To be capable of withstanding the frightful rumors about Fabrizio that were constantly in circulation, she would have had to spend all her time with a man of intelligence and heart like Mosca. Baldi was a nonentity; she was therefore left to her own thoughts, which made her life wretched, and the count could not succeed in communicating to her his reasons for hope.

By means of various rather ingenious pretexts, he had persuaded the prince to allow the transfer to a friendly castle in the very center of Lombardy, near Soronno, of all the records of the extremely complicated intrigues with which Ernesto-Ranuccio IV nourished his wildly insane hope of becoming the constitutional monarch of that beautiful country.

More than a score of these highly compromising documents were either in the prince's own handwriting or bore his signature, and if Fabrizio's life were seriously threatened, the count planned to inform His Highness that he was going to place them in the hands of a great power that could annihilate him with a single word.

Count Mosca felt that he could rely on the future Baron Riva; he feared only poison. Barbone's attempt had deeply alarmed him, so much so that he had decided to risk an action which might have appeared to be mad. One morning he came to the gate of the citadel and asked to see General Fabio Conti, who came down as far as the bastion above the gate. There, as they took a friendly stroll together, and after a little preface that was faintly sarcastic but still polite, the count did not hesitate to say to him, "If Fabrizio should die under suspicious circumstances, his death might be attributed to me. I'd be regarded as a jealous lover, and subjected to abominable ridicule. I'm determined not to accept that. And so, to clear myself, if he dies of illness, *I will kill you with my own hand*, you may count on it." General Fabio Conti made a magnificent reply and spoke of his courage, but the look the count had given him remained in his mind.

A few days later, as though he were working in concert

with the count, Chief Justice Rassi committed a rash act that was quite unusual for a man of his kind. The public contempt attached to his name, which had become a byword among the rabble, had been making him ill now that he had a fairly well-founded hope of being able to escape from it. He sent General Fabio Conti an official copy of the judgment sentencing Fabrizio to twelve years in the citadel. According to the law, this should have been done on the day following Fabrizio's arrival, but in Parma, where secret measures were commonplace, it was inconceivable that a judge should take such a step without an express order from the sovereign. For how was it possible to harbor the hope of redoubling the duchess's alarm and subduing her haughty spirit, as the prince had put it, once an official copy of the sentence had been issued by the Chancellery of Justice?

The day before General Fabio Conti received the official document from Chief Justice Rassi, he learned that the clerk Barbone had been given a thorough beating as he was returning to the citadel a little late. He concluded from this that there was no longer any question, in a certain quarter, of getting rid of Fabrizio. Having decided to move cautiously, he said nothing to the prince, during his next audience with him, about the official copy of the prisoner's sentence which had been transmitted to him, thereby saving Rassi from the immediate consequences of his folly.

Fortunately for the poor duchess's peace of mind, the count had discovered that Barbone's awkward attempt had been motivated by nothing but a desire for private vengeance, and he had caused the clerk to be given the warning we have already described.

Fabrizio was very pleasantly surprised when, after a hundred and thirty-five days of confinement in his narrow cage, the good chaplain, Don Cesare, came to him one Thursday to take him for a walk on top of the Farnese Tower. Fabrizio had not been there ten minutes before the fresh air made him faint. Don Cesare used this accident as a pretext for allowing him half an hour of exercise a day. This was a mistake: our hero's frequent exercise in the open air soon gave him back a strength which he misused.

There were several more serenades. The punctilious governor allowed them because they formed a bond between the Marquis Crescenzi and his daughter Clelia, whose character alarmed him: he felt vaguely that there was no point of contact between him and her, and he was always afraid of some impulsive act on her part. She might flee to a convent, and he would be disarmed. Furthermore, he was afraid that all that music, whose sounds might penetrate the deepest dungeons reserved for the blackest liberals, might contain signals. And the musicians themselves worried him; therefore, as soon as the serenade was over, they were locked up in great low-ceilinged rooms in the governor's residence which by day served as offices for the staff, and the doors were not opened until it was broad daylight the following morning. It was the governor himself who, standing on the "Slave's Bridge," had them searched in his presence and set them free, not without repeating to them several times that any one of them who had the audacity to attempt to deliver the slightest object or message to any prisoner would be hanged immediately. And they knew that, in his fear of losing favor, he would keep his word, so the Marquis Crescenzi was obliged to give triple pay to his musicians, who were greatly upset over having to spend the night in prison.

All that the duchess could obtain, and with great difficulty, from one of those timorous men was an agreement to deliver a letter to the governor. The letter was addressed to Fabrizio, and in it she lamented the misfortune which had prevented his friends outside from establishing any communication with him during the five months he had been in prison.

On entering the citadel, the bribed musician threw himself at General Fabio Conti's feet and confessed to him that a priest, whom he did not know, had insisted so strongly on his taking a letter addressed to Signor del Dongo that he had not dared to refuse, but that, faithful to his duty, he now hastened to place it in His Excellency's hands.

His Excellency was highly gratified: he knew the resources the duchess had at her disposal, and was greatly afraid of being outwitted. In his joy, he went to give the letter to the prince himself. His Highness was delighted.

"So the firmness of my administration has succeeded in avenging me! That haughty woman has been suffering for five months! But one of these days we're going to prepare a scaffold, and her wild imagination will be sure to convince her that it's for young del Dongo."

CHAPTER TWENTY

One night, toward one o'clock, Fabrizio, leaning against the window, had put his head through the opening he had made in the shutter and was gazing at the stars and the vast horizon that can be seen from the top of the Farnese Tower. As he cast his eyes over the countryside in the direction of Ferrara and the lower Po, he happened to notice an extremely small but rather bright light which seemed to be coming from the top of a tower. "That light must not be visible from the plain," he thought. "The thickness of the tower prevents it from being seen below. It must be a signal to some distant point." Suddenly he noticed that it was flashing at short intervals. "It's some girl talking to her lover in the next village." He counted nine successive flashes. "That's an I, since I is the ninth letter of the alphabet." After a pause, there were fourteen flashes. "That's an N." Then, after another pause, there was a single flash. "That's an A; the word is *Ina.*"

Imagine his joy and surprise when the successive flashes, separated by short pauses, finally spelled out these words: "*Ina pensa a te.*" (Obviously, "Gina is thinking of you.") He immediately replied by flashing his lamp through the opening in the shutter: "Fabrizio loves you."

The conversation continued till dawn. That night was the one hundred and seventy-third of his captivity, and he was told that signals had been sent to him every night for the past four months. But anyone might see and understand their signals, so that very night they began to establish a system of abbreviations: three short flashes indicated the duchess; four, the prince, two, Count Mosca; two short flashes followed by two long ones signified "escape." They agreed to use in the future the old alphabet *alla Monaca*, which, in order not to be read by indiscreet eyes, changes the usual number of each letter and gives it an arbitrary one. A, for example, is given the number ten, B the number three; in other words, three flashes of the lamp mean B, ten flashes mean A, and so on. A moment of darkness forms the separation between two words.

An appointment was made for the following night at one o'clock. On that night, the duchess came to the tower, which was a quarter of a league outside the town. Her eyes filled with tears when she saw the signals made by Fabrizio, whom she had so often believed to be dead. She told him herself, by flashes of the lamp, "I love you. Have courage, health, hope. Exercise in your cell. You will need the strength of your arms."

"I haven't seen him since Fausta's concert," she thought, "when he appeared at the door of my drawing room, dressed as a footman. Who could have said then what fate held in store for us!"

She had signals sent to him announcing that he would soon be set free, "thanks to the prince's kindness" (the signals might be intercepted), then she began sending affectionate messages to him herself; she could not tear herself away from him! Only the remonstrances of Ludovico, who, because he had been useful to Fabrizio, had become her factotum, finally induced her, when it was nearly daylight, to discontinue her signals, which might attract the attention of some spiteful observer.

The announcement, several times repeated, of his approaching release plunged Fabrizio into deep sadness. Clelia noticed it the next day and was rash enough to ask the cause of it.

"I find myself on the point of giving the duchess serious grounds for dissatisfaction."

"But what can she demand of her that you would refuse her?" exclaimed Clelia, overcome with curiosity.

"She wants me to leave the citadel," he replied, "and I will never consent to that."

Clelia was unable to answer; she looked at him and burst into tears. If he had been able to speak to her at close range, he might have been able to obtain an avowal of feelings whose uncertainty in his eyes often plunged him into profound discouragement. He felt keenly that, without Clelia's love, life had nothing to offer him except bitter sorrow or unbearable boredom. It seemed to him that it was no longer worth living only in order to return to the same pleasures that had interested him before he had come to know love, and, although suicide is not yet fashionable in Italy, he had thought of it as a last resource, if fate should separate him from Clelia.

The next day he received a long letter from her:

> You must, my friend, be told the truth: since you have been here, it has often been believed in Parma that your last day had come. It is true that you have been sentenced only to twelve years in prison, but it is un-

fortunately impossible to doubt that you are pursued by an all-powerful hatred, and I have trembled with fear a score of times that poison might put an end to your life. You must therefore seize any *possible* means of leaving the citadel. You can see that, for your sake, I am failing in my most sacred duties; judge the imminence of the danger by the things I am venturing to tell you, and which are so out of place on my lips. If it is absolutely necessary, if there is no other means of salvation, flee. Every moment you spend in this citadel may place your life in the greatest peril; remember that there is a faction at court whose plans have never been stopped by the prospect of crime. And have you not seen all the schemes of that faction constantly foiled by the superior skill of Count Mosca? But they have found a sure means of banishing him from Parma: the duchess's despair. And are they not only too sure to bring on that despair by the death of a young prisoner? This point alone, which is unanswerable, ought to make you judge your situation correctly.

You say that you are fond of me; consider, first of all, the insurmountable obstacles which stand in the way of any firm establishment of that feeling between us. We have met in our youth, we have held out a helping hand to each other in a period of misfortune, and fate has placed me in this harsh place to soften your sorrows, but I would reproach myself eternally if certain illusions, which are and always will be without justification, should incline you not to seize every possible opportunity of removing your life from such a terrible danger. My cruel imprudence in exchanging a few signs of friendship with you has robbed me of all peace of mind. If our childish games with alphabets should lead you to illusions which are so groundless, and which may be so disastrous for you, it would be futile for me to try to exonerate myself by recalling Barbone's attempt to poison you. I myself would have cast you into a more terrible and far more certain danger, through my efforts to save you from a momentary peril; and my imprudence will be forever unpardonable if it has given rise to feelings which make you reject the duchess's advice. See what you oblige me to repeat to you: Escape, I command you. . . .

This letter was very long; certain passages, such as the "I command you" which we have just quoted, gave moments of ecstatic hope to Fabrizio's love. It seemed to him that the underlying feelings in the letter were rather tender, even though the expressions were remarkably prudent. At other moments, he paid the penalty of his complete ignorance of this kind of warfare: he then saw merely friendship, or even nothing but the most common feeling of humanity, in this letter from Clelia.

However, nothing she told him made him alter his intentions for an instant. Even assuming that the perils she depicted were quite real, were a few momentary dangers too great a price to pay for the happiness of seeing her every day? What kind of life would he lead if he again took refuge in Bologna or Florence? For if he escaped from the citadel he would have to give up all hope of being allowed to live in Parma. And even if the prince should change his mind to the point of releasing him (which was extremely improbable, since for a powerful faction he had become a means of overthrowing Count Mosca), what kind of life would he lead in Parma, separated from Clelia by all the hatred which divided the two parties? Once or twice a month, perhaps, chance might place them in the same drawing room; but even then, what kind of conversation could he have with her? How could he ever regain that perfect intimacy which he now enjoyed for several hours a day? What would conversation in a drawing room be, compared to the conversation they now carried on with their alphabets? "And even if I have to buy this life of bliss, this unique chance of happiness, at the price of a few little dangers," he thought, "what harm is there in that? And wouldn't it give me still more happiness to have even a slight opportunity of proving my love to her?"

Fabrizio saw nothing in Clelia's letter but a chance to ask her to meet with him. This was the sole and constant object of all his desires; he had spoken to her only once, and only for an instant, on the day he entered the citadel, and over two hundred days had gone by since then.

An easy way of meeting with her presented itself. The excellent Don Cesare allowed Fabrizio half an hour of exercise on the terrace of the Farnese Tower every Thursday, but on the other days of the week this outing, which would have been visible to all the inhabitants of Parma and the vicinity, and might have seriously compromised the governor, did not take place until nightfall. The only means of access to the terrace of the Farnese Tower was the staircase inside the little belfry of the chapel decorated so ominously in black and white marble, as the reader may recall. Grillo always took Fabrizio to the chapel and unlocked the door of the belfry for him; he ought to have continued to do his duty by following him up the stairs, but since the evenings were beginning to be chilly, the jailer let him go up alone, locked the door of the belfry and went back to his room to warm himself. Now could not Clelia, accompanied by her maid, come to the black marble chapel some evening?

All of the long letter with which Fabrizio replied to Clelia's was calculated to obtain this meeting. And he confided to her with perfect sincerity, as though he were writing to someone else, all the reasons that had made him decide not to leave the citadel.

I would expose myself every day to the risk of a thousand deaths to have the happiness of speaking to you by means of our alphabets, which no longer stop us for an instant, and you want me to be foolish enough to exile myself to Parma, or perhaps Bologna, or even Florence! You want me to go away from you! I must tell you that such an effort would be impossible for me; it would be futile for me to give you my word, because I could not keep it.

The result of his request for a meeting with Clelia was an absence on her part which lasted no less than five days; for five days she came to the aviary only at times when she knew he was unable to make use of the little opening in the shutter. Fabrizio was in despair; he concluded from her absence that, despite certain glances which had made him conceive wild hopes, he had never inspired in her any feeling other than that of ordinary friendship. "If so," he thought, "what do I care about my life? If the prince wants to take it away from me, he'll be welcome; that's one more reason for not leaving the fortress." And it was with deep dejection and distaste that he replied every night to the signals of the little lamp. The duchess thought he had gone completely mad when she read these strange words on the record of the signals which Ludovico brought to her each morning: *I don't want to escape, I want to die here.*

During those five days, so painful for Fabrizio, Clelia was more unhappy than he. She was obsessed by this idea, so cruel for a noble soul: "My duty is to flee to some convent far from the citadel; when Fabrizio learns that I'm no longer here, and I'll see to it that he's told by Grillo and all the other jailers, he'll make up his mind to try to escape." But going to a convent would have meant giving up all hope of ever seeing Fabrizio again, and at a time when he was giving her such obvious proof that the feelings which once bound him to the duchess no longer existed! What more touching proof of love could a man give? After seven long months in prison, which had seriously affected his health, he was refusing to regain his freedom. A frivolous man, such as the courtiers' talk had depicted Fabrizio to Clelia, would have sacrificed a dozen mistresses in order to get out of the citadel one day sooner; and what would he not have done to get out of a prison in which poison might put an end to his life at any moment!

Clelia's courage failed her; she made the grave mistake of not fleeing to a convent, which would also have given her a natural means of breaking with the Marquis Crescenzi. Once she had made this mistake, how could she resist the young man, so charming, so sincere, so much in love, who was exposing his life to frightful dangers for the happiness of merely looking at her from one window to another? After five days of terrible inner conflict, mingled with moments of self-contempt, Clelia made up her mind to answer the letter in which Fabrizio had begged her to grant him the joy of speaking to her in the black marble chapel. She refused to meet him, it is true, and in rather harsh terms, but from that moment all peace of mind was lost to her. Her imagination constantly portrayed Fabrizio succumbing to poison, and she went up to the aviary seven or eight times a day, for she felt a passionate need to assure herself with her own eyes that he was still alive.

"If he stays in the fortress," she said to herself, "if he's exposed to all the horrible plots that the Raversi faction may be making against him with the object of driving Count Mosca away, it's solely because I was too cowardly to go to a convent! What excuse could he have for staying here if he were sure I'd gone away forever?"

Clelia, so timid and at the same time so proud, came to the point of risking a refusal on the part of the jailer Grillo, and, much worse, exposed herself to all the comments he might make about the singularity of her behavior. She descended to the humiliation of sending for him and telling him, in a faltering voice which betrayed her whole secret, that Fabrizio was going to regain his freedom within a few days, that Duchess Sanseverina was taking the most active measures to achieve this end, that it was often necessary to have an immediate reply from the prisoner to certain proposals that were being made, and that she urged him, Grillo, to allow Fabrizio to make an opening in the shutter that masked his window, in order that she might communicate to him by signs the information she received several times a day from Duchess Sanseverina.

Grillo smiled and assured her of his respect and obedience. She was deeply grateful to him for not saying anything more; it was obvious that he was fully aware of everything that had been happening for the past few months.

As soon as the jailer had left, Clelia made the signal by which she had agreed to call Fabrizio on important occasions. She told him everything she had just done. "You are determined to die by poison," she added. "I hope some day to have the courage to leave my father and flee to some faraway convent. That will be my obligation to you. I hope that you will then no longer reject any plans that may be proposed to you for getting you out of here. As long as you are here, I have moments of unreasoning horror. Never in my life have I contributed to anyone's misfortune, and yet it now seems to me that I am going to be the cause of your death. Such an idea about a perfect stranger would drive me to despair, so imagine what I feel when I tell myself that a friend, whose unreasonableness gives me serious cause for complaint, but whom I have been seeing every day for a long time, may be at that very moment in the throes of death. Sometimes I feel a need to learn from you yourself that you are alive.

"It was to escape from this terrible anguish that I have just lowered myself to the point of asking a favor of a subordinate who might have refused, and may still betray me. And it might be better for me if he did denounce me to my father, for I would immediately leave for a convent and cease to be the unwilling accomplice of your cruel madness. But believe me, this cannot go on much longer. You will obey the duchess's orders. Are you satisfied, my cruel friend? It is I who am begging you to betray my father! Call Grillo and give him a present."

Fabrizio was so much in love, and the simplest expression of Clelia's will plunged him into such fear, that even this strange message gave him no certainty of being loved. He called Grillo and paid him generously for his obligingness in the past. As for the future, he told him that for every day he allowed him to use the opening in the shutter, he would receive a sequin. Grillo was delighted with these terms.

"I'm going to talk frankly to you, *Monsignore*: would you be willing to eat your dinner cold every day? There's a simple way to avoid poison. But I must ask you to use the utmost discretion. A jailer must see everything and guess nothing," etc., etc. "Instead of one dog, I'll have several, and you yourself will feed them a sample of every dish you intend to eat. As for wine, I'll give you some of my own, and you'll touch only bottles from which I've drunk myself. But if you want to ruin me forever, Your Excellency, you have only to confide these details to someone, even to Signorina Clelia. Women are always women; if she should quarrel with you tomorrow, day after tomorrow, to take vengeance on you, she'd tell her father about the whole arrangement, and his greatest joy would be to have some reason for hanging a jailer. Next to Barbone, he's perhaps the most ruthless man in the fortress, and that's where the real danger of your position lies. He knows how to use poison, you can be sure of that, and he'd never forgive this idea of having three or four little dogs."

There was another serenade. Grillo now answered all of Fabrizio's questions. He was determined to be prudent, however, and not to betray Signorina Clelia, who, in his opinion, though about to marry the Marquis Crescenzi, the richest man in Parma, was nevertheless carrying on a love affair, so far as prison walls allowed, with the charming *Monsignore* del Dongo. He was answering Fabrizio's final questions about the serenade when he made the blunder of adding, "They say he'll marry her soon." It is easy to imagine the effect of this simple remark on Fabrizio. That night he answered the signals of the lamp only to announce that he was ill. When Clelia appeared in the aviary at ten o'clock the next morning, he asked her, with a ceremonious politeness that was quite new between them, why she had not told him frankly that she loved the Marquis Crescenzi and was about to marry him.

"Because none of that is true," she answered impatiently. The rest of her reply, however, was less straightforward. Fabrizio pointed this out to her and took advantage of the opportunity to renew his request for a meeting with her. Seeing that he questioned her sincerity, she granted his request almost immediately, at the same time pointing out to him that she would be dishonoring herself forever in Grillo's eyes.

That evening, when it was quite dark, she appeared, accompanied by her maid, in the black marble chapel. She stopped in the middle, beside the night light; her maid and Grillo withdrew thirty paces to the door. Clelia was trembling all over. She had prepared a fine speech; her goal was to avoid making a compromising confession, but the logic of passion is insistent: its deep interest in knowing the truth does not allow it to maintain forced circumspection, and at the same time its extreme devotion to the object of its love takes away all fear of giving offense. Fabrizio was at first dazzled by Clelia's beauty; for nearly eight months he had seen no one except jailers at close range. But the name of the Marquis Crescenzi brought back all his fury, which increased when he saw clearly that Clelia was answering with evasive caution. She herself realized that she was strengthening his suspicions instead of dissipating them. This feeling was too painful for her.

"Will you be happy," she said to him with a kind of anger, and with tears in her eyes, "to have made me disregard everything I owe to myself? Until the third of August last year, I'd never felt anything but aversion for the men who'd tried to please me. I had boundless and probably exaggerated contempt for the character of a courtier, and everyone who was happy at that court displeased me. On the other hand, I found exceptional qualities in a prisoner who was brought to this citadel on the third of August. I suffered, at first without realizing it, all the torments of jealousy. The charms of an attractive woman, and one whom I knew well, were like dagger-thrusts in my heart, because I believed, and still believe to some extent, that the prisoner was attached to her. The Marquis Crescenzi had asked for my hand in marriage, and her persecutions soon redoubled. He's very rich and we have no fortune. I was rejecting his advances with great freedom of mind when my father pronounced the fatal word 'convent.' I knew that if I left the citadel I could no longer watch over the life of the prisoner whose fate interested me. The greatest achievement of my precautions was that till then he had no inkling of the frightful dangers that were threatening his life. I'd promised myself never to betray either my father or my secret, but that woman of admirable energy, superior intelligence and inflexible will, who is still protecting the prisoner, offered him, or at least so I suppose, a means of escape. He rejected it and tried to persuade me that he was refusing to leave the citadel in order not to be separated from me.

"Then I made a great mistake. I struggled with myself for five days; I should have left the fortress immediately and gone to a convent: it would have been a simple way of breaking with the Marquis Crescenzi. I didn't have the courage to leave the fortress, and now I'm lost: I've become attached to a fickle man. I know how he behaved in Naples; what reason do I have to believe that his character has changed? Confined in a harsh prison, he's paid court to the only woman he could see; she's distracted him a little from his boredom. Since he could speak to her only with a certain difficulty, this amusement has taken on the false appearance of a passion. Having made a name for himself in the world by his courage, the prisoner imagines himself to be proving that his love is something more than a passing fancy by exposing himself to great danger in order to go on seeing the woman he believes he loves. But as soon as he's back in a great city, surrounded again by all the seductions of society, he'll become once again what he's always been: a man addicted to dissipation and amorous intrigue; and his poor prison companion will end her days in a convent, forgotten by that fickle man and consumed with eternal regret for having confessed her feelings to him."

This historic speech, of which we have given only the principal points, was, as can well be imagined, interrupted a score of times by Fabrizio. He was madly in love and therefore firmly convinced that he had never loved anyone before Clelia, and that it was his destiny to live only for her.

The reader can no doubt imagine the noble things he was saying when Clelia's maid came to tell her that the clock had just struck half-past eleven, and that the general might return at any moment. The parting was cruel.

"This may be the last time I'll ever seen you," Clelia said to him. "A measure which is obviously in the interest of the Raversi faction may provide you with a cruel way of proving that you're not inconstant." She then left him, choking with sobs and dying of shame at not being able to conceal them entirely from her maid and especially from Grillo. A second conversation would be possible only when the governor again announced that he was going to spend the evening in society. However, since Fabrizio's imprisonment and the interest it had aroused in the curious courtiers, he had judged it prudent to give himself an almost continuous attack of gout, so that his trips into Parma, governed by the demands of an adroit policy, were often not decided upon until the moment he got into his carriage.

After that evening in the marble chapel, Fabrizio's life was a series of transports of joy. Great obstacles, it is true, still seemed to stand in the way of his happiness, but in any case he had the supreme and almost unhoped-for joy of being loved by the divine creature who occupied all his thoughts.

On the third night after his meeting with Clelia, the signals from the lamp stopped early, at about midnight. Just as they ended, Fabrizio's head was almost broken by a large ball of lead which, having been thrown over the top of the shutter, crashed through the paper windowpane and fell into his cell.

This large ball was not nearly so heavy as its size seemed to indicate. Fabrizio easily succeeded in opening it and found a letter from the duchess inside. Through the archbishop, whose favor she had been carefully cultivating, she had won over a soldier in the garrison of the citadel. This man, highly skilled in the use of the sling, had either eluded or come to terms with the sentries posted at the door and each corner of the governor's residence.

> You must escape by means of ropes. I shudder as I give you this strange advice, and I have hesitated for over two months before communicating it to you, but the official outlook is growing darker every day, and we can expect the worst. By the way, begin signaling again with your lamp immediately, to show me that you have received this dangerous letter: send P, B and G in the *Monaca* code, that is, four, twelve and two. I will not breathe freely until I see that signal. I am now in the tower. You will be answered by N and O, seven and five. Once you have received this answer, send no more signals: give all your attention to understanding my letter.

Fabrizio hastened to send the prescribed signals, which were answered as promised; he then continued reading the letter:

> We can expect the worst: this is what I have been told by the three men in whom I have the greatest confidence, after making them swear on the Gospels to tell me the truth, however painful it might be to me. The first of these men threatened to stab the surgeon in Ferrara if he denounced you; the second one told you when you returned from Belgirate that it would have been more strictly prudent of you to have shot the servant who rode singing through the forest, leading a handsome though slightly lean horse; you do not know the third one: he is a highway robber, a friend of mine, a man of action if ever there was one, and as brave as you are, which is the main reason why I asked him to

tell me what you ought to do. All three of these men have told me, each without knowing that I had consulted the other two, that it is better for you to run the risk of breaking your neck than to spend eleven years and four months in constant fear of a poisoning which is quite probable.

For the next month, you must practice climbing up and down a knotted rope in your cell. Then, on a holiday when the garrison of the citadel has been given an extra ration of wine, you will make the great attempt. You will have three ropes of silk and hemp, as thick as a swan's quill. The first one will be eighty feet long and you will use it for descending the thirty-five feet from your window to the orange trees. The second one, three hundred feet long—and that is where the difficulty will lie, because of its weight—will take you to the bottom of the great tower, a drop of a hundred and eighty feet. You will use the third one, thirty feet long, for climbing down from the rampart. I spend all my time studying the great wall on the east, that is, on the side facing Ferrara: a crack caused by an earthquake has been filled in with a buttress which forms an inclined plane. My highway robber assures me that he would undertake to escape at that point without too much difficulty, and at a cost of nothing more than a few scratches, by sliding down the inclined plane formed by the buttress. The vertical distance is only twenty-eight feet to the very bottom. This is the side which is least well guarded.

All things considered, however, my highway robber, who has escaped from prison three times, and whom you would like if you knew him, although he detests people of your class; my highway robber, who is as agile and nimble as you, thinks that he would prefer to climb down the west side of the wall, exactly opposite the house once occupied by Fausta, which you know well. What would make him choose this side is the fact that the wall there, though inclined only slightly, is almost completely covered with bushes. There are twigs the size of your little finger which may well slash you if you are not careful, but which are also excellent to hold on to. Only this morning I was looking at this west side through an excellent telescope: the spot to choose is directly below a new stone which was placed in the balustrade two or three years ago. Just below this stone, you will find a bare space of about twenty feet: you must go very slowly there. (You must know how my heart quivers as I give you these terrible instructions, but courage consists in being able to choose the lesser evil, however horrible it may be.) After the bare space, you will come to eighty or ninety feet of very big bushes in which you will see birds fluttering, then a space of thirty feet in which there is nothing but grass, wallflowers and pellitories. Next, as you approach the ground, you will come to twenty feet of bushes, and finally, twenty-five or thirty feet of new plaster.

What would make me choose this side is that directly below the new stone in the balustrade is a wooden hut built by a soldier in his garden, and which the captain of engineers employed in the fortress is trying to force him to demolish. It is seventeen feet high and has a thatched roof which touches the great wall of the citadel. It is this roof which tempts me: in the frightful event of an accident, it would break your fall. When you reach that spot, you will be within the enclosure of the ramparts, which are rather carelessly guarded. If anyone should stop you, fire your pistols and defend yourself for a few minutes. Your friend from Ferrara and another brave man, the one I call the highway robber, will have ladders and will not hesitate to come to your rescue by climbing up the rather low rampart.

The rampart is only twenty-three feet high and slopes a great deal. I will be at the foot of this last wall with a good number of armed men.

I hope I will be able to send you five or six letters by the same channel as this one. I will repeat the same things in different terms, so that we will be in complete agreement. You can guess what I feel in my heart when I tell you that the man who thought you should have shot the servant—and who is, after all, the best of men, and is dying of remorse—believes that you will get by with nothing more than a broken arm. The highway robber, who has more experience in this kind of enterprise, thinks that if you come down very slowly, and, above all, without haste, your freedom will cost you only a few scratches. The great difficulty is to get ropes to you, and I have thought of nothing but that for the two weeks during which this great idea has taken up all my time.

I will not reply to your absurd statement, the only senseless thing you have ever said in your life: "I don't want to escape." The man who thought you should have shot the servant exclaimed that boredom had driven you mad. I will not hide from you the fact that we live in dread of a very imminent danger which may hasten the day of your escape. To announce this danger to you, the lamp will say several times in succession, "The castle is on fire." You will reply, "Are my books burned?"

This letter contained five or six more pages of details; it was written in microscopic letters on extremely thin paper.

"It's all excellent and very well planned," Fabrizio said to himself. "I owe eternal gratitude to the count and the duchess; they may think I'm afraid, but I won't escape. Has anyone ever fled from a place where he was blissfully happy, to plunge himself into a terrible exile in which everything would be lacking, even air to breathe? What would I do after I'd been in Florence for a month? I'd disguise myself, come back to this fortress and prowl around the gate, hoping to catch her eye for an instant!"

The next day, Fabrizio was frightened: he was at the window, toward eleven o'clock, looking at the magnificent landscape and waiting for the happy moment when he could see Clelia, when Grillo burst into his cell, out of breath.

"Hurry! Hurry, *Monsignore*! Jump into bed and pretend to be ill: three judges are on their way up here now! They're going to question you; think carefully before you answer, because they'll try to trip you up."

As he said these words, Grillo quickly closed the little hatch in the shutter, pushed Fabrizio onto his bed and threw two or three cloaks over him.

"Tell them you're in great pain and can't talk much, and be sure to make them repeat their questions, so you'll have time to think."

The three judges entered. "They're escaped convicts, not judges," thought Fabrizio when he saw their ignoble faces. They bowed gravely and occupied, without a word, the three chairs that were in the room.

"Signor Fabrizio del Dongo," said the eldest judge, "we are grieved by the sad mission which we have come to perform. We are here to announce to you the death of His Excellency the Marquis del Dongo, your father, Second Grand Major-domo of the Lombardo-Venetian Kingdom, Knight Grand Cross of the Orders of . . ." etc., etc. Fabrizio burst into tears; the judge continued: "The Marquise del Dongo, your mother, has imparted this news to you in a letter; but since, in addition to her account of the fact, she has made certain improper remarks, the court of justice, in a decree issued yesterday, has decided that only an extract of her letter will be communicated to you. The clerk of the court, Signor Bona, will now read you the extract."

When the clerk had finished reading, the judge came over to Fabrizio, who was still lying down, and pointed out to him the passages in his mother's letter, of which a copy had just been read to him. Fabrizio saw the words "unjust imprisonment" and "cruel punishment for a crime which is no crime at all." He then understood the reason for the judges' visit. In his contempt for those magistrates without integrity, he said nothing to them except this one sentence: "I am ill, gentlemen, and extremely weak, so please excuse me for not getting up."

When the judges had gone, he wept for a long time, but he said to himself, "Am I a hypocrite? I used to think I didn't love him at all."

On that day, and the days that followed, Clelia was very sad; she called him several times, but hardly had the courage to say a few words to him. On the morning of the fifth day after her meeting with him, she told him she would come to the black marble chapel that evening.

"I can say only a few words to you," she told him when she entered. She was trembling so violently that she had to lean on her maid. Then, after sending her back to the door of the chapel, she went on in a scarcely audible voice: "You must give me your word of honor that you will obey the duchess, that you will attempt to escape on the day she will set, and according to her instructions, or else tomorrow morning I will fleet to a convent, and I swear to you here that I will never speak another word to you as long as I live.

"Give me your promise," said Clelia with tears in her eyes, and as if beside herself with anguish, "or this is the last time we will ever speak to each other here. The life you're forcing me to lead is horrible: you're here because of me, and each day may be your last." At this point, she became so weak that she had to seek the support of a big armchair which had been placed long ago in the middle of the chapel for the use of the imprisoned prince; she was on the verge of fainting.

"What must I promise?" asked Fabrizio disconsolately.

"You know."

"I swear to plunge myself knowingly into horrible misery,

304

and to condemn myself to live far away from all that I love in the world."

"Make your promise more precise."

"I swear to obey the duchess, to escape whenever and however she wishes. And what will become of me when I'm no longer with you?"

"Swear to escape, no matter what may happen."

"What! Have you made up your mind to marry the Marquis Crescenzi as soon as I'm gone?"

"Good heavens! What kind of a heart do you think I have? ... But give me your word, or I'll never have another moment's peace of mind."

"Very well, I swear to escape from here whenever Duchess Sanseverina orders me to, and no matter what may happen between now and then."

Having obtained this oath, Clelia was so weak that she had to withdraw after thanking Fabrizio.

"Everything was ready for my departure tomorrow morning," she said to him, "if you had insisted on staying here. I would now have been seeing you for the last time in my life: I made that vow to the Madonna. Now, as soon as I can leave my room, I'll go and examine that terrible wall below the new stone in the balustrade."

The next day he found her so pale that it hurt him to look at her. She said to him from the window of the aviary, "Let's not delude ourselves, my dear friend: since there is sin in our friendship, I have no doubt that misfortune will come to us. You'll be discovered as you try to escape, and lost forever; or something even worse may happen. However, we must satisfy the demands of human prudence, which requires us to make every possible effort. In order to climb down the outside of the great tower, you'll need a strong rope more than two hundred feet long. Despite everything I've done since I learned of the duchess's plan, I've been able to get only ropes that form a length of barely fifty feet when tied together. By order of the governor, all ropes found in the fortress are burned, and the ropes are removed from the wells every evening; furthermore, they're so weak that they often break when pulling up their light weights. But pray God to forgive me, because I'm betraying my father, and working, unnatural daughter that I am, to inflict a deadly sorrow on him. Pray for me, and, if your life is saved, make a vow to consecrate every moment of it to the glory of God.

"Here's an idea that has occurred to me: in a week I'll leave the citadel to attend the wedding of one of the Marquis

Crescenzi's sisters. I'll come back at night, as is proper, but I'll do everything I can to return very late, and perhaps Barbone won't dare to examine me too closely. All the greatest ladies of the court will be at the wedding, including, no doubt, Duchess Sanseverina. In the name of God, arrange for one of those ladies to give me a tight bundle of rope, not too heavy, and compressed into as small a volume as possible. Even if I have to expose myself to a thousand deaths, I'll use any means, no matter how dangerous, to bring that bundle of rope into the citadel—in contempt, alas, of all my duties! If my father learns of it, I'll never see you again. But no matter what fate awaits me, I'll be happy within the bounds of a sisterly friendship if I can help to save you."

That very night, in their communication by lamps, Fabrizio told the duchess about this unique opportunity of having a sufficient quantity of rope brought into the citadel. But he begged her to keep it a secret even from the count, which seemed odd to her. "He's mad," she thought. "Prison has changed him; he's becoming panicky." The next day a lead ball, hurled by the slinger, brought the prisoner news of the greatest possible peril. The person who was undertaking to get the ropes to him, he was told, would be positively and literally saving his life. He hastened to convey this news to Clelia. The lead ball also brought him a precise plan of the west wall, along which he was to descend from the top of the great tower into the space between the bastions; from there, it would be fairly easy to escape, the ramparts being only twenty-three feet high and rather carelessly guarded. On the back of the plan was a magnificent sonnet, written in a small, delicate hand; in it, a noble soul exhorted Fabrizio to take flight, not to let his soul be debased and his body withered by the eleven years of captivity to which he was still condemned.

At this point an essential detail, and one which explains the duchess's courage in advising Fabrizio to attempt such a dangerous escape, obliges us to interrupt the story of this bold enterprise for a moment.

Like all parties which are not in power, the Raversi party was not very closely united. Cavaliere Riscara detested Chief Justice Rassi, whom he accused of having made him lose an important lawsuit in which he, Riscara, had actually been in the wrong. Through Riscara, the prince received an anonymous notification that an official copy of Fabrizio's sentence had been sent to the governor of the citadel. The Marquise Raversi, a skillful party leader, was angered by this treacherous move and immediately sent word of it to her friend the Chief Justice; she found it only natural that he should want to get something out of Count Mosca as long as he was in power. Rassi boldly went to the palace, feeling sure that he would get off with no more than a few kicks: the prince could not do without a skilled jurist, and Rassi had exiled, as being liberals, a judge and a lawyer who were the only men in Parma capable of taking his place.

The prince, beside himself with rage, overwhelmed him with insults and moved toward him to strike him.

"It was only a mistake on the part of a clerk," replied Rassi with the utmost coolness. "The act is prescribed by law, and should have been done the day after Signor del Dongo was confined in the citadel. The zealous clerk must have thought he'd overlooked it, and given me the accompanying letter to sign as a matter of course."

"Do you expect me to believe such clumsy lies?" the prince shouted furiously. "Why don't you admit that you've sold yourself to that scoundrel Mosca, and that that's why he gave you a decoration? But this time, by God, you won't get off with only a beating! I'll have you tried, I'll give you a dishonorable dismissal!"

"I defy you to have me tried!" replied Rassi with self-assurance, knowing that this was a sure way of calming the prince. "The law is on my side, and you have no second Rassi to find a way of getting around it. You won't dismiss me, because there are times when your nature is severe; you thirst for blood then, but at the same time you want to keep the esteem of all sensible Italians: that esteem is the *sine qua non* of your ambition. In short, you'll call on me again the next time your character makes you require an act of severity, and, as usual, I'll get you a strictly proper sentence, handed down by timid and fairly honest judges, which will satisfy your passions. Find another man in Parma as useful as I am!"

Having said this, Rassi fled. He had escaped with only five or six kicks and one hard blow with a ruler. On leaving the palace, he set off for his estate at Riva. He had some fear of being stabbed during the first surge of the prince's anger, but he did not doubt that within two weeks a courier would summon him back to the capital. While he was in the country, he spent his time arranging a safe method of communication with Count Mosca. He was madly in love with the title of baron, and he thought the prince placed too great a value on that once sublime thing, nobility, ever to confer it on him, whereas the count, very proud of his birth, respected only nobility proved by titles before the year 1400.

The Chief Justice had not been mistaken in his expectations: he had been on his estate for less than a week when one of the prince's friends, who had come there only by chance, advised him to return to Parma without delay. The prince laughed when he saw him, then took on a very serious air and told him to swear on the Gospels that he would keep secret what he was about to confide to him. Rassi swore solemnly, and the prince, his eyes flaming with hatred, cried out that he would never be the master of his own domain as long as Fabrizio del Dongo was alive.

"I can neither drive the duchess away nor tolerate her presence," he added. "Her glances defy me and spoil my whole life."

After letting the prince explain himself at great length, Rassi, pretending to be greatly perplexed, finally exclaimed, "Your Highness will be obeyed, naturally, but it's a terribly difficult matter! It's out of the question to condemn a del Dongo to death for the murder of a man like Giletti: it's already an amazing feat to have gotten twelve years in the citadel out of it. Furthermore, I suspect that the duchess has discovered three of the peasants who were working on the excavations at Sanguigna, and who were outside the trench when that bandit Giletti attacked del Dongo."

"And where are those witnesses?" asked the prince irritably.

"Hiding in Piedmont, I suppose. It would require a plot against Your Highness's life . . ."

"That has its dangers," said the prince. "It gives people ideas."

"But that's the whole of my official arsenal," said Rassi with feigned innocence.

"There's still poison."

"But who will give it? That imbecile Conti?"

"Well, from what I've heard, it wouldn't be his first attempt."

"He'd have to be made angry," said Rassi. "Besides, when he did away with the captain he was under thirty and in love, and he was infinitely less cowardly than he is nowadays. Reasons of state must certainly prevail over everything else, but, taken unawares like this, and at first sight, I can see no one to carry out the sovereign's orders except a clerk in the prison by the name of Barbone, whom Signor del Dongo knocked down on the day of his arrival there."

Once the prince had been put at ease, the conversation was

endless. He terminated it by granting his Chief Justice a month in which to act; Rassi had asked for two. The next day, he received a secret gift of a thousand sequins. He pondered matters for three days, and on the fourth he returned to his original line of reasoning, which seemed irrefutable to him: "First of all, only Count Mosca will have the courage to keep his word to me, because, in making me a baron, he won't be giving me anything he values. Secondly, by warning him I'll probably be saving myself from committing a crime for which I've been practically paid in advance. Thirdly, I'll be avenging the first humiliating blows received by Cavaliere Rassi." The following night, he reported his entire conversation with the prince to Count Mosca.

The count was secretly paying court to the duchess. It is true that he still saw her in her house only once or twice a month, but nearly every week, and whenever he was able to bring about an occasion for speaking of Fabrizio, the duchess, accompanied by Cecchina, came late in the evening to spend a few moments in the count's garden. She managed to deceive even her coachman, who was devoted to her: he believed her to be paying a visit to a nearby house.

One can imagine whether the count, having received the Chief Justice's terrible report, immediately gave the duchess the signal they had agreed upon. Although it was the middle of the night, she sent Cecchina to ask him to come to her house at once. The count, as delighted as any other man in love would have been by this semblance of intimacy, nevertheless hesitated to tell her everything: he was afraid she might be driven mad by grief.

However, after trying to find some roundabout way of breaking the sinister news to her, he finally told her everything; it was not in his power to keep a secret which she had asked him to tell her. In the past nine months her extreme sorrow had had a great influence on her ardent soul, and had strengthened it: she did not burst into sobs or lamentations.

On the following night she had the signal of great danger sent to Fabrizio: *The castle is on fire.* And he replied promptly: *Are my books burned?*

That same night, she was fortunate enough to have a letter conveyed to him in a lead ball. This was a week before the wedding of the Marquis Crescenzi's sister, during which the duchess committed an act of enormous imprudence, as we shall relate in due course.

CHAPTER TWENTY-ONE

Nearly a year before the period of her misfortune, the duchess had made a strange acquaintance. One day when she "had the moon" [was in a bad mood], as they say in Italy, she suddenly decided to go to her country house at Sacca, beyond Colorno, on a hill overlooking the Po. She took pleasure in beautifying this estate; she loved the vast forest which crowns the hill and touches the house, and she busied herself with having paths laid out through it in picturesque directions.

"You'll get yourself carried off by bandits, my fair duchess," the prince had said to her one day. "It's impossible that a forest in which you're known to walk should remain deserted." The prince had then cast a glance at the count, hoping to rouse his jealousy.

"I have no fear, Your Serene Highness," the duchess had replied innocently, "when I walk through my forest. I reassure myself with this thought: I've done no harm to anyone, so who could hate me?" This remark was considered audacious, for it recalled certain insults that had been uttered by the liberals of Parma, who were very insolent people.

On the day of the walk with which we are now concerned, the prince's words came back to the duchess's mind when she noticed that she was being followed through the forest at a distance by a very shabbily dressed man. After she had made an unexpected turn in the course of her walk, the stranger was so close to her that she was frightened. Her first impulse was to call her gamekeeper, whom she had left about a thousand paces behind, in the flower garden near the house. The stranger had time to come up to her and throw himself at her feet. He was young and extremely handsome, but wretchedly dressed; there were rents a foot long in his clothing, but the fire of an ardent soul glowed in his eyes.

"I've been sentenced to death, I'm a physician, my name is Ferrante Palla, I'm dying of hunger, and so are my five children."

The duchess had noticed that he was terribly thin; but his eyes were so handsome, and filled with such touching fervor, that they made it impossible to think of him as a criminal. "Palagi," she thought, "might have given eyes like those to

the Saint John in the Desert he just placed in the cathedral."
The idea of Saint John was suggested to her by Ferrante's
incredible thinness. She gave him the three sequins she had
in her purse and apologized for having so little to offer him,
explaining that she had just settled an account with her
gardener. Ferrante thanked her effusively.

"Alas," he said, "I once lived in cities and saw elegant
women, but ever since I got myself sentenced to death by
fulfilling my duties as a citizen, I've been living in the forest.
I was following you, not to ask you for charity or rob you,
but like a savage entranced by a vision of angelic beauty. It's
been so long since I last saw a pair of lovely white hands!"

"Please stand up," said the duchess, for he had remained
on his knees.

"Allow me to remain like this," said Ferrante. "This position
proves to me that I'm not now engaged in robbing, and that
calms me; for I may as well tell you that, since I can no
longer practice my profession, I make my living as a robber.
But at this moment I'm only an ordinary mortal worshiping
sublime beauty." The duchess realized that he was slightly
mad, but she was not afraid of him; she saw in his eyes that
he had a kind and ardent soul, and besides, she was not
repelled by unusual faces.

"I'm a physician, as I've already told you, and I had an
affair with the wife of the apothecary Sarasine, in Parma.
He caught us together and drove her from his house, along
with three children whom he rightly suspected of being mine,
not his. I've had two others since then. My five children and
their mother are living in abject poverty in a hut which I
built with my own hands, about a league from here, in the
forest. For I must keep away from the police, and the poor
woman refuses to part with me. I was sentenced to death,
and very unjustly. I was involved in a conspiracy. I hate the
prince, he's a tyrant. I didn't flee for lack of money. My
misfortunes are much greater, and I should have killed myself
long ago. I no longer love the poor woman who has given me
five children and ruined her life for me; I love another. But
if I kill myself, my five children and their mother will literally die of hunger." His voice had the ring of sincerity.

"But how do you live?" asked the duchess, moved to pity.

"The children's mother spins; the eldest girl is kept on a
farm owned by liberals, where she tends the sheep; as for
me, I rob travelers on the road between Piacenza and Genoa."

"How do you reconcile robbery with your liberal principles?"

311

"I keep a record of the people I rob, and if I ever have anything, I'll give them back the sums I've stolen. I feel that a Tribune of the People like myself is doing work which, by reason of its danger, is worth at least a hundred lire a month, so I'm careful not to take more than twelve hundred lire a year.... No, that's not true: I steal a small additional sum to pay the costs of having my works printed."

"What works?"

"*Will —— Ever Have a Chamber and a Budget?*"

"What!" exclaimed the duchess in amazement. "Is it you, sir, who are one of the greatest poets of our time, the famous Ferrante Palla?"

"Famous, perhaps, but certainly most unfortunate."

"And a man of your talent is forced to steal in order to live?"

"That may be the reason why I have some talent. So far, all our authors who have made a name for themselves have been paid by the government or the religion they wanted to undermine. But in my case, first of all I risk my life; and secondly, imagine the thoughts that agitate my mind when I go out to rob! 'Am I in the right?' I ask myself. 'Is the work of a Tribune of the People really worth a hundred lire a month?' I have two shirts, the coat I'm now wearing, a few poor weapons, and the certainty of ending my life at the end of a rope: I venture to believe that I'm disinterested. I'd be happy if it weren't for the fatal love which no longer allows me to find anything but unhappiness with the mother of my children. The ugliness of poverty is a burden to me: I like fine clothes, white hands..." He looked at the duchess's hands in such a way that she was seized with fear.

"Good-by," she said to him. "Is there anything I can do for you in Parma?"

"Give some thought now and then to this question: 'His task is to awaken men's hearts and prevent them from falling asleep in the false, completely material happiness which monarchies provide: is the service he renders to his fellow citizens worth a hundred lire a month?' It is my misfortune to be in love," he said very gently, "and for nearly two years my heart has been occupied by you alone, but until now I have seen you without frightening you." And he ran away with a prodigious speed which both astonished and reassured the duchess. "The police will have a hard time catching him!" she thought. "He really is mad!"

"He's mad," her servants told her. "We've known for a long time that the poor man was in love with you. Whenever you're here we see him wandering in the highest parts of the forest, and as soon as you're gone he always comes and sits in the places where you've stopped; he carefully picks up any flowers that may have fallen from your bouquet, and keeps them for a long time, stuck in his shabby hat."

"And you've never mentioned his follies to me," she said almost reproachfully.

"We were afraid you might tell Count Mosca, signora. Poor Ferrante is such a good man! He's never done anyone any harm, and because he loves our Napoleon he's been sentenced to death."

She said nothing to the count about her encounter, and since it was the first secret she had kept from him in four years, she had to stop short in the middle of a sentence a dozen times. She returned to Sacca with some gold, but Ferrante did not appear. She came back two weeks later: Ferrante, after having followed her for some time, skipping through the woods a hundred paces behind her, suddenly bore down on her with the swiftness of a hawk and fell to his knees as he had done the first time.

"Where were you two weeks ago?"

"In the mountains beyond Novi, robbing some mule-drivers on their way back from Milan after selling a load of oil."

"Take this purse."

Ferrante opened the purse, took out a sequin, kissed it and placed it inside his shirt, then returned the purse to her.

"You're a robber, and yet you're giving me back this purse!"

"Of course. I've made it a rule for myself that I must never have more than a hundred lire. The mother of my children now has eighty lire and I have twenty-five, so I have five lire more than I should, and if I were to be hanged at this moment I'd feel remorse. I took the sequin because it came from you, and I love you."

The tone of these words was perfect. "He's really in love," thought the duchess.

He seemed quite distraught that day. He said that there were people in Parma who owed him six hundred lire, and that if he had that sum he would repair his hut, in which his poor little children were always catching cold.

"I'll lend you the six hundred lire," said the duchess, overcome with pity.

"But then, since I'm a man in public office, wouldn't the opposition be able to slander me by saying that I'd sold myself?"

The duchess, deeply moved, offered to give him a hiding place in Parma if he would swear not to exercise his judicial functions there for the time being, and, above all, not to carry out any of the death sentences which, he said, he had privately passed.

"And if I'm hanged as a result of my rashness," he said gravely, "all those scoundrels, so harmful to the people, will go on living for many long years, and whose fault will it be? What will my father say when I meet him in heaven?"

The duchess talked to him for a long time about his little children, who might come down with some fatal illness because of the dampness; he finally accepted her offer of a hiding place in Parma.

During the single half-day he had spent in Parma after his marriage, Duke Sanseverina had shown the duchess a most unusual hiding place in the south corner of the palace that bears his name. The outer wall, which dates back from the Middle Ages, is eight feet thick. It has been hollowed out inside, forming a hiding place twenty feet high, but only two feet wide. Close beside it, one can admire the reservoir which is mentioned in all travel books, a famous work of the twelfth century, built during the siege of Parma by Emperor Sigismund, and later enclosed within the walls of the Sanseverina palace.

To enter this hiding place, one must move an enormous block of stone which turns on an iron pivot. The duchess was so deeply touched by Ferrante's madness, and by the fate of his children, for whom he stubbornly refused to accept any gift of value, that she allowed him to make use of this hiding place for a rather long time. She saw him again in the forest of Sacca a month later, and since he was a little calmer that day, he recited for her one of his sonnets, which seemed to her equal, if not superior, to any of the finest things that had been written in Italy for the past two centuries. Ferrante obtained several other meetings with her; but his love grew more ardent until it finally became importunate, and the duchess realized that it was following the natural course of any love which is given the possibility of conceiving a glimmer of hope. She sent him back into his forest and forbade him to speak to her; he obeyed immediately, with perfect good grace.

Things had reached this point when Fabrizio was arrested. Three days later, at nightfall, a Capuchin monk presented himself at the door of the Sanseverina palace and said that he had an important secret to communicate to the mistress of the house. She was so unhappy that she had him shown in: it was Ferrante. "A new iniquity is taking place here which ought to be looked into by the Tribune of the People," said Ferrante, mad with love. "On the other hand, acting as a private citizen, I have nothing to give Duchess Sanseverina except my life. I have come to place it at her disposal."

The duchess was deeply touched by this sincere devotion on the part of a robber and a madman. She spoke for a long time to the man who was regarded as the greatest poet of northern Italy, and wept a great deal. "Here's a man who understands my heart," she thought. He returned the next day, again at the hour of the *Ave Maria*, this time disguised as a servant in livery.

"I haven't left Parma; I've been told a horrible thing which my lips will not repeat, but here I am. You see before you not a court puppet, but a man!" He was on his knees as he spoke these words in a tone that gave them their full worth. "Yesterday I said to myself, 'She wept in my presence, so she's a little less unhappy!' "

"But think of the dangers that surround you: you'll be arrested in this city!"

"The Tribune of the People will say to you, 'Madam, what is life when duty calls?' The unhappy man, who has the sorrow of no longer feeling any passion for virtue now that he is consumed with love, will add, 'Duchess Sanseverina, Fabrizio, a great-hearted man, is perhaps about to perish: do not reject another great-hearted man who has come to offer himself to you! Here is a body of iron and a soul afraid of nothing in the world except displeasing you.' "

"If you speak to me of your feelings again, I will close my door to you forever."

The duchess had considered telling Ferrante that evening that she would grant a small income to his children, but she was afraid he might go right out and kill himself.

As soon as he was gone she said to herself, filled with gloomy forebodings, "I too may die, and may it please God that I shall, and soon, if I find a man worthy of the name, to whom I can commend my poor Fabrizio!"

An idea seized her mind; she took a sheet of paper and, using the few legal terms she knew, acknowledged in writing that she had received from Signor Ferrante Palla the sum of 25,000 lire, on the express condition that she would pay a life annuity of 1,500 lire to Signora Sarasine and her five children. "Furthermore," she added, "I hereby bequeath a life annuity of 300 lire to each of the five children, on condition that Ferrante Palla will give medical care to my nephew, Fabrizio del Dongo, and be a brother to him. I beg him to do so." She signed the document, foredated it by a year and put it away.

Ferrante returned two days later, at the time when the whole city was agitated by the rumor that Fabrizio was soon to be executed. Would the sad ceremony be carried out in the citadel or beneath the trees of the public promenade? A number of commoners strolled past the gate of the citadel that evening, to see if a scaffold was being erected; this spectacle had moved Ferrante. He found the duchess in tears and unable to speak. She greeted him with a gesture and pointed to a chair. Ferrante, disguised as a Capuchin monk that day, was superb: instead of sitting down, he knelt and prayed devoutly in an undertone. When the duchess seemed a little calmer, he stopped praying for an instant, without changing his position, and said, "Again he offers his life."

"Think what you're saying!" cried the duchess, and her eyes took on that haggard look which, after a fit of sobbing, announces that anger is winning out over sorrow.

"He offers you his life to place an obstacle in the way of Fabrizio's fate, or to avenge it."

"There are certain circumstances," replied the duchess, "in which I might accept the sacrifice of your life."

She looked at him with stern attention. A gleam of joy shone in his eyes; he quickly stood up and raised his arms to heaven. The duchess went off to get a sheet of paper hidden in the secret compartment of a big walnut cabinet. "Read this," she said to him. It was the deed of gift to his children, which we have already described.

Tears and sobs prevented Ferrante from reading it to the end; he fell to his knees.

"Give it back to me," said the duchess, and she burned the paper in the flame of a candle before his eyes. "My name must not appear if you are caught and executed—for your life is going to be in danger."

"It will be a joy to die in harming the tyrant, and a far greater joy to die for you. With that stated and clearly understood, please make no further mention of that trifling detail of money: I'd interpret it as an insulting doubt."

"If you're implicated in a crime, I may be implicated too," said the duchess, "and Fabrizio after me: it's for that reason, and not because I doubt your courage, that I demand that the man who is piercing my heart shall be poisoned, not killed in a violent attack. For the same reason, which is of great importance to me, I order you to do everything possible to save your own life."

"I'll carry out all your orders faithfully, promptly and carefully. I foresee that my vengeance will be mingled with yours, but even if it were otherwise, I would still obey you faithfully, promptly and carefully. I may not succeed, but I will use all my strength as a man."

"Your goal will be to poison Fabrizio's murderer."

"I've guessed that already, and during the twenty-seven months that I've been leading this wandering, abominable life, I've often thought of such an action on my own account."

"If I'm discovered and condemned as an accomplice," said the duchess proudly, "I don't want anyone to be able to accuse me of having led you astray. I order you to make no further attempt to see me before the time comes for our vengeance: you must not put him to death before I give you the signal. His death at this moment, for example, far from useful to me, would be harmful. His death will probably not have to take place until several months from now, but it will take place. I demand that he die by poison, and I would rather let him live than have him shot. For reasons I won't explain to you, I demand that your life be saved."

Ferrante was delighted by the tone of authority in which the duchess spoke to him; his eyes shone with profound joy. As we have said, he was terribly thin; but it could be seen that he had been extremely handsome in his early youth, and he believed that he was still what he had once been. "Am I mad," he thought, "or does the duchess really intend to make me the happiest of men some day, after I've given her that proof of my devotion? After all, why not? Am I not worth as much as that puppet Count Mosca, who hasn't been able to do anything for her in this emergency, not even arrange for Fabrizio's escape?"

"I may want him to die tomorrow," the duchess went on in the same tone of authority. "You know that big reservoir at one corner of the palace, near the hiding place you've sometimes occupied; there's a secret way of letting all its water run out into the street: that will be the signal for my vengeance. You'll see, if you're in Parma, or you'll hear, if you're in the forest, that the great reservoir of the Sanseverina palace has burst. Act immediately, but by poison, and above all, expose your life to as little danger as possible. Make sure no one ever finds out that I was involved."

"Words are useless," replied Ferrante with an enthusiasm he could scarcely restrain. "I've already decided on the means

317

I'll employ. That man's life has become even more odious to me than before, since I won't dare to see you again as long as he's alive. I'll wait for the signal of the reservoir flooding the street." He bowed abruptly and left. The duchess watched him walk away.

When he was in the next room she called him back.

"Ferrante, you sublime man!" she cried.

He came back, apparently impatient at being detained; his face was superb at that moment.

"What about your children?"

"Duchess, they will be richer than I; perhaps you will grant them a small income."

"Look," she said, handing him a large case made of olive wood, "here are all the diamonds I have left: they're worth fifty thousand lire."

"Oh, duchess! You humiliate me!" said Ferrante with a movement of horror; and his whole face changed completely.

"I won't see you again before the act has been carried out: I insist that you take them," said the duchess with a haughtiness that overwhelmed Ferrante. He put the case in his pocket and left.

When he had closed the door behind him, she called him back again. He came in looking uneasy. The duchess was standing in the middle of the drawing room; she threw herself in his arms. A moment later, he nearly fainted from happiness. She disengaged herself from his embrace and, with her eyes, told him to leave.

"There goes the only man who's understood me," she thought. "That's how Fabrizio would have acted if he had known my feelings."

There were two outstanding traits in the duchess's character: once she had willed something, she willed it forever, and she never reconsidered anything after she had made up her mind about it. In this connection, she would sometimes quote a saying of her first husband, the charming General Pietranera: "What insolence to myself! Why should I think myself more intelligent today than when I made that decision?"

From that moment onward, a kind of gaiety reappeared in her character. Before her fateful resolution, each time her mind had taken a step, each time she had discovered something new, she had been aware of her inferiority with regard to the prince, of her weakness and gullibility. The prince, in her opinion, had basely deceived her; and Count Mosca, as a result of his courtier's mentality, though innocently, had supported the prince. Once she had resolved to take vengeance, she had a feeling of strength, and each step taken by her mind gave her happiness. I am rather inclined to think that the immoral happiness which Italians derive from vengeance is due to the strength of their imagination; people of other countries do not, properly speaking, forgive: they forget.

The duchess did not see Palla again until Fabrizio's imprisonment was nearly ended. As the reader may have guessed, it was he who gave her the idea of escape. In the forest, two leagues from Sacca, there was a half-ruined medieval tower, more than a hundred feet high. Before speaking to her a second time about an escape, Ferrante asked her to send Ludovico and a few other reliable men to place a series of ladders against one side of this tower. In her presence, he climbed up the ladders and came down by means of an ordinary knotted rope; he repeated the experiment three times, then explained his idea again. A week later, Ludovico also tried descending from the old tower with a knotted rope. It was then that the duchess communicated the idea to Fabrizio.

During the last few days before the attempt, which might cause the prisoner's death, and in more ways than one, she never had a moment's peace unless Ferrante were by her side; his courage electrified her own. But it will be readily understood that she had to conceal this strange association from the count. She was not afraid that he would be shocked, but she would have been upset by his objections, which would have redoubled her anxiety. "What! Make an intimate advisor of a recognized madman who's under sentence of death? And," she added, speaking to herself, "a man who might later do such strange things!" Ferrante happened to be in her drawing room when the count came to tell her about the prince's conversation with Rassi, and when the count had left she had great difficulty in preventing Ferrante from going straight out to execute a frightful plan!

"I'm strong now," said this madman. "I no longer have any doubt about the legitimacy of the act!"

"But in the outburst of anger that would inevitably follow, Fabrizio would be put to death!"

"In that case, he'd be spared the danger of the escape; it's possible, even easy, but the young man lacks experience."

The wedding of the Marquis Crescenzi's sister was celebrated, and it was during the reception given on that occasion that the duchess met Clelia and was able to speak to her without arousing any suspicion in their fashionable observers. The duchess personally handed Clelia the bundle of ropes in the garden, where the two ladies had gone to get a breath of air. These ropes, carefully made of hemp and silk in equal proportions, and already knotted, were very thin and quite flexible. Ludovico had tested their strength; throughout their entire length they were capable of supporting a weight of eight hundred pounds without breaking. They had been compressed into several packets the size and shape of a quarto volume. Clelia took them and promised the duchess that everything humanly possible would be done to get them into the Farnese Tower.

"But I'm afraid of the timidity of your character; and besides," added the duchess politely, "what interest can you take in the fate of a stranger?"

"Signor del Dongo is in distress, *and I promise you that he will be saved by me!*"

But the duchess, counting very little on the presence of mind of a young girl of twenty, had taken other measures which she was careful not to mention to the governor's daughter. As was naturally to be expected, the governor was present at the reception given on the occasion of the wedding of the Marquis Crescenzi's sister. The duchess told herself that if she had someone give him a powerful narcotic it might be believed at first that he was having a stroke of apoplexy, and that then, instead of letting him be placed in his carriage to be taken back to the citadel, it might be possible, with a little adroitness, to win acceptance for the idea of using a litter which would happen to be in the house where the reception was being given. There, too, would be found a number of intelligent men, dressed as workmen employed for the reception, who, in the general confusion, would obligingly offer to carry the sick man back to his lofty residence. These men, under Ludovico's direction, had a rather large quantity of rope cleverly concealed beneath their clothes.

It can be seen that the duchess's mind had become really unbalanced since she had begun thinking seriously about Fabrizio's escape. The danger threatening her beloved nephew was too much for her soul, and, above all, it had lasted too long. Her excessive precautions nearly caused his escape to fail, as we shall see. Everything went off as she had planned, with this one difference, that the narcotic produced too strong an effect: everyone, including the physicians, believed that the general had had a stroke of apoplexy.

Fortunately Clelia, who was in despair, had no suspicion

of the duchess's criminal attempt. When the litter in which the general was lying half dead was carried into the citadel, the confusion was so great that Ludovico and his men were able to enter without difficulty; they were searched only as a matter of form when they reached the "Slave's Bridge." When they had carried the general to his bed, the servants took them to their quarters and entertained them very well. But after the meal, which did not end until shortly before morning, it was explained to them that a rule of the prison required them to be locked up for the rest of the night in the lower rooms of the governor's residence; in the morning, at daybreak, they would be released by the general's deputy.

Ludovico's men had managed to give him the ropes they were carrying, but he had great difficulty in catching Clelia's attention for a moment. Finally, as she was going from one room to another, he succeeded in making her see that he was setting down bundles of rope in a dark corner of one of the drawing rooms on the second floor. She was greatly astonished by this, and immediately conceived horrible suspicions.

"Who are you?" she said to Ludovico, and when he had given her an extremely ambiguous answer she went on: "I ought to have you arrested! You or your men have poisoned my father! Tell me at once what kind of poison you used, so that the doctor of the citadel can administer the proper remedies. Tell me at once, or you and your accomplices will never leave this citadel!"

"You're wrong to be alarmed, signorina," replied Ludovico with perfect grace and courtesy. "There's no poison involved: someone was rash enough to have the general given a dose of laudanum, and the servant ordered to carry out the crime apparently put a few drops too many in the glass. We'll regret it eternally, but you may be sure that, thanks to heaven, there is no danger of any kind: the governor should be treated as though he had taken an overdose of laudanum by mistake. But allow me to repeat that the servant ordered to commit the crime made no use of genuine poison, as Barbone did when he tried to poison *Monsignore* Fabrizio. There was no intention of avenging the danger to which *Monsignore* Fabrizio was exposed: that clumsy servant was given nothing but a small bottle containing laudanum, I give you my word, signorina! But if I were questioned officially, I'd naturally deny everything.

"Furthermore, if you speak to anyone, even the excellent Don Cesare, of laudanum and poison, Fabrizio will be killed by you. You will make all plans of escape forever impossible, and you know better than I that those who wish to poison him intend to use something more effective than laudanum. You also know that a certain person has granted only a month's delay for that crime, and that more than a week has gone by since the fatal order was received. Therefore, if you have me arrested, or if you merely say a word to Don Cesare or anyone else, you'll be delaying all our efforts by much more than a month, and I'll be right in saying that you've killed *Monsignore* Fabrizio yourself."

Clelia was horrified by Ludovico's strange tranquillity. "So here I am," she thought, "calmly talking with a man who's poisoned my father and addresses me with great courtesy! And it's love that has led me into all these crimes!"

Her remorse scarcely left her enough strength to speak; she said to Ludovico, "I'm going to lock you in this drawing room, then run to tell the doctor that my father has only been given a dose of laudanum. But good heavens, how am I going to say I discovered it? I'll come back afterward to release you."

She went as far as the door, then ran back and said, "But does Fabrizio know anything about the laudanum?"

"Certainly not, signorina! He'd never have consented to it! Besides, what good would it have done to tell him a useless secret? We're acting with the strictest caution. His life must be saved: someone whose will usually encounters no opposition has ordered that he be poisoned three weeks from now. And, to tell you everything, it's said that the task has been assigned to the terrible Chief Justice Rassi himself."

Clelia fled in terror. She had such confidence in Don Cesare's perfect integrity that, using a certain precaution, she dared to tell him that the general had been given laudanum and nothing else. Without answering, and without asking her any questions, Don Cesare hurried to the doctor.

Clelia returned to the drawing room in which she had locked Ludovico, intending to ply him with questions about the laudanum. She did not find him there: he had managed to escape. She saw a purse filled with sequins lying on a table, and a little box containing various kinds of poison. The sight of these poisons made her shudder. "How can I be sure," she thought, "that my father was given nothing but laudanum, and that the duchess hasn't tried to take vengeance for Barbone's attempt on Fabrizio's life? . . . Good heavens! Now I'm involved with my father's poisoners! And I'm letting them escape! And perhaps that man, under torture, might have confessed to something other than laudanum!" She fell

322

to her knees, burst into tears and prayed fervently to the Madonna.

Meanwhile the doctor of the citadel, greatly surprised by the information he had received from Don Cesare, according to which he was dealing with nothing but a dose of laudanum, administered the proper remedies. They soon put an end to the most alarming symptoms. The general regained his senses a little as day was beginning to break. His first act which showed that he had returned to consciousness was to hurl violent abuse at the colonel who was second in command of the citadel for having taken it upon himself to give a few thoroughly routine orders while the general was unconscious.

The general then flew into a rage against a kitchen maid who, in bringing him a bowl of broth, had ventured to utter the word "apoplexy."

"Am I old enough to have apoplexy?" he shouted. "Only my most rabid enemies could take pleasure in spreading such rumors! Besides, I haven't been bled, so how can even the most spiteful slanderers speak of apoplexy?"

Fabrizio, completely absorbed in preparations for his escape, could not imagine the cause of the strange noises that filled the citadel when the general was carried into it half dead. At first he had some idea that his sentence had been changed, and that they were coming to put him to death. Some time later, seeing that no one had come into his cell, he thought that Clelia had been betrayed, that, on her return to the fortress, the ropes she had probably been carrying had been taken away from her, and that all his plans of escape would be forever impossible. The next morning, at dawn, a man he had never seen before came into his cell and put down a basket of fruit without saying a word; the following letter was hidden beneath the fruit:

Filled with the keenest remorse over what has been done, not, thank heaven, with my consent, but as a result of an idea I had, I have made a vow to the Holy Virgin that if, through Her holy intercession, my father's life is saved, I will never refuse to obey any of his orders; I will marry the Marquis Crescenzi as soon as he requires me to do so, and I will never see you again. However, I consider it my duty to finish what has been begun. Next Sunday, on your return from Mass, to which you will be taken at my request (be sure to prepare your soul, for you may be killed in your difficult undertaking),

323

avoid going back to your cell as long as possible; you will find there what you will need for the undertaking. If you perish, my heart will be broken! Will you be able to accuse me of having contributed to your death? Has not the duchess herself told you several times that the Raversi faction is getting the upper hand? They want to bind the prince by an atrocity that will separate him forever from Count Mosca. The duchess has sworn to me, in tears, that escape is the last resource which still remains: you will perish if you do not attempt it. I can no longer look at you, for I have vowed not to, but if on Sunday, toward evening, you see me dressed entirely in black and standing at the usual window, that will be the signal: everything will be ready that night, so far as my feeble means allow. After eleven o'clock, perhaps not until midnight or one o'clock, a small lamp will appear in my window: that will be the decisive moment. Commend yourself to your patron saint, quickly put on the priest's habit with which you have been provided, and act.

Farewell, Fabrizio; I shall be praying, and shedding bitter tears, you may be sure, while you are running such grave risks. If you perish, I shall not survive you. Dear God, what am I saying? But if you succeed, I will never see you again. On Sunday, after Mass, you will find in your cell the money, poisons and ropes which have been sent to you by that formidable woman who loves you so passionately, and who has repeated to me three times that this decision had to be made. May God and the Holy Madonna preserve you!

Fabio Conti was a jailer who was always uneasy, always upset, always imagining the escape of one of his prisoners. He was loathed by everyone in the citadel, but since misfortune inspires the same resolutions in all men, the poor prisoners, even those who were chained in cells three feet high, three feet wide and eight feet long, in which they could neither sit nor stand, conceived the idea of having a *Te Deum* sung at their expense when they learned that the governor was out of danger. Two or three of those poor wretches composed sonnets in honor of Fabio Conti. How deeply misfortune had affected them! May whoever blames them be led by his destiny to spend a year in a cell three feet high, with eight ounces of bread a day, and fasting on Fridays.

Clelia, who never left her father's room except to go to the chapel to pray, said that the governor had decided that the rejoicings would not take place until Sunday. On the morning of that Sunday, Fabrizio attended the Mass and the *Te Deum*. In the evening there were fireworks, and, in the lower rooms of the palace, the soldiers were given a ration of wine that was four times the amount usually granted by the governor. Some unknown person had even sent several barrels of brandy, which the soldiers broke open. As they were getting drunk, they generously decided that the five soldiers posted as sentries around the governor's residence should not have to suffer because of their duty: as soon as they reached their sentry boxes, a trusty servant gave them wine, and those who took over from midnight till morning were also given brandy by someone whose identity remained unknown; furthermore, the bottle was always forgotten and left beside the sentry box (as was proven during the ensuing court-martial).

The disorder lasted longer than Clelia had expected. It was not until one o'clock that Fabrizio, who, more than a week earlier, had sawed through two bars of the window which did not face the aviary, began to take down the shutter. He was working almost directly over the heads of the sentries guarding the governor's residence, but they heard nothing. He had tied a few new knots in the long rope necessary for climbing down from that awesome height of a hundred and eighty feet. He coiled this rope over one shoulder. It hindered him greatly, for its bulk was enormous; the knots prevented it from forming a compact mass, and it stood out more than eighteen inches from his body. "Here's the great obstacle," he thought.

Having arranged this rope as best he could, he took the one with which he intended to descend the thirty-five feet that separated his window from the platform on which the governor's residence stood. But since, no matter how drunk the sentries might be, he still could not climb down directly over their heads, he went out, as we have said, through the second window of his cell, the one which overlooked the roof of a kind of vast guardroom.

Acting on some peculiar whim engen᷎ d by his weakened condition, as soon as General Fabio Conti could speak he had ordered two hundred soldiers brought into this old guardroom, which had not been used for the past hundred years. He said that, after having poisoned him, his enemies now planned to murder him in his bed, and these two hundred soldiers were to guard him. One may judge the effect of this unexpected precaution on Clelia's heart. The pious girl was fully aware of the extent to which she was betraying her father, who had already been nearly poisoned in the interest of the prisoner she loved. She almost saw in the unexpected arrival of those two hundred men a decree of Providence forbidding her to go any further in her efforts to set Fabrizio free.

But everyone in Parma was talking about the approaching death of the prisoner. This sad subject had been discussed even during the reception given on the occasion of Giulia Crescenzi's wedding. Since a man of Fabrizio's birth, and under the protection of the Prime Minister, had still not been released after spending nine months in prison for such a trifling matter as plunging his sword into an actor, there was surely some political issue involved in his case. And so, it was said, there was no use concerning oneself with him any longer: if it did not suit those in power to have him publicly executed, he would soon die of illness. A locksmith who had been called to General Fabio Conti's residence spoke of Fabrizio as though he were a prisoner who had long since been disposed of, and whose death was being kept secret for strategic reasons. This man's words decided Clelia.

CHAPTER TWENTY-TWO

During the day, Fabrizio was assailed by a number of serious and disagreeable reflections, but as he heard the clock striking the hours that were bringing him nearer to the moment of action he began feeling cheerful and alert. The duchess had written to him that the fresh air would have a strong and sudden effect on him, and that as soon as he was outside his cell he would find himself temporarily unable to go on; in that case, it would be better to run the risk of being recaptured than to fall from the top of a wall a hundred and eighty feet high. "If I have that misfortune," he thought, "I'll lie down against the parapet and sleep for an hour, then start again. Since I've given Clelia my word, I'd rather fall from the top of a rampart, no matter how high, than be constantly wondering about the taste of the bread I eat. What horrible pains a man must feel before the end, when he dies of poison! Fabio Conti won't bother his head with subtleties: he'll have me given some of the arsenic with which they kill rats in his citadel."

Toward midnight, one of those thick, white fogs in which the Po sometimes shrouds its banks spread first over the city, then over the esplanade and the bastions in the middle of which stands the great tower of the citadel. It seemed to Fabrizio that, from the parapet of the platform, it was no longer possible to see the little acacias surrounding the gardens that had been laid out by the soldiers at the foot of the hundred-and-eighty-foot wall. "That's excellent," he thought.

Shortly after the clock had struck half-past twelve, the signal of the little lamp appeared in the aviary window. Fabrizio was ready to act. He crossed himself, then tied to his bed the little rope intended to take him down the thirty-five feet that separated him from the platform on which the governor's residence stood. He climbed down without difficulty to the roof of the guardroom which had been occupied since the night before by the two hundred additional soldiers we have already mentioned. It was a quarter to one, but they were unfortunately still awake; as he cautiously crept across the roof of large curved tiles, Fabrizio heard them saying that the devil was on the roof and that they ought to try to shoot him. Several voices maintained that this was an extremely impious idea, others said that if a shot were fired without killing anything, the governor would put them all in prison for having uselessly alarmed the garrison.

The result of this fine discussion was that Fabrizio crossed the roof as swiftly as possible and made much more noise. When he climbed down his rope past the windows, which were fortunately four or five feet away from him because of the overhang of the roof, they were bristling with bayonets. Some people later claimed that Fabrizio, always impulsive, decided to play the part of the devil and threw the soldiers a handful of sequins. One thing is certain: he had scattered sequins over the floor of his cell, and also on the platform on his way from the Farnese Tower to the parapet, hoping that they would distract any soldiers who might come in pursuit of him.

Having reached the platform, where he was surrounded by sentries who normally called out an entire sentence—"All's well around my post!"—every quarter of an hour, he walked toward the western parapet and looked for the new stone.

What appears incredible, and might make one doubt the reality of Fabrizio's feat if its result had not been witnessed by an entire city, is that he was not seen and stopped by the sentries posted along the parapet. It is true that the fog we have mentioned was beginning to rise, and Fabrizio later said that when he was on the platform it seemed to be already halfway up the Farnese Tower. But this fog was not thick, and he could clearly see the sentries, some of whom were pacing back and forth. He added that, as if driven by some supernatural force, he boldly went over and stood between two sentries who were rather close to each other. He calmly unwound the long rope he had coiled around his body; it became tangled twice, and it took him a long time to untangle it and spread it out over the parapet. He could hear the soldiers talking all around him, and he was quite determined to stab the first one who moved toward him. "I wasn't at all worried," he said. "I felt as though I were performing some sort of ceremony."

When he had finally untangled his rope, he fastened it through a drainage hole in the parapet, climbed up on this parapet and prayed fervently; then, like a hero of the days of chivalry, he thought about Clelia for a moment. "How different I am," he said to himself, "from the fickle, libertine Fabrizio who entered this prison nine months ago!"

At last he began to descend that formidable height. He acted mechanically, he said, as though he were climbing down in broad daylight before the eyes of friends, to win a bet. About halfway down, he suddenly felt his arms lose their strength; he even believes that he let go of the rope for an instant, but quickly caught hold of it again. Perhaps, he said, he clutched the bushes as he slid past them, tearing his skin. Now and then he felt a terrible pain between his shoulders, so intense that it stopped his breathing. There was an extremely troublesome swaying motion: he constantly swung back and forth between the rope and the bushes. He was struck by several large birds which collided with him as they flew away after being awakened by him. The first few times this happened, he thought he had been caught by pursuers descending from the citadel in the same way as himself, and he prepared to defend himself. Finally he reached the base of the great tower without mishap, except for the fact that his hands were bleeding. He says that once he had made his way to the middle of the tower the slope it forms was of great help to him: he remained in contact with the wall, and the plants growing between the stones gave him useful support.

As he was coming down into the soldiers' gardens, he fell onto an acacia which, seen from above, seemed to be four or five feet high, but was actually fifteen or twenty. A drunken man who had been sleeping beneath it took him for a robber. When he fell from this tree, Fabrizio nearly dislocated his left arm. He began running toward the rampart, but, as he later said, his legs felt as though they were made of cotton; he had no strength left. Despite the danger, he sat down and drank a little of the brandy he had with him. He dozed off for a few minutes, so soundly that he no longer knew where he was; when he awoke, thinking himself in his cell, he could not understand why he saw trees.

Finally the terrible truth came back to him. He immediately walked to the rampart and climbed up on it by way of a large staircase. There was a soldier posted near it, but he was snoring in his sentry box. Fabrizio found a cannon lying in the grass and tied his third rope to it. It proved to be a little too short, and he fell into a muddy ditch in which there was about a foot of water.

As he was standing up and trying to get his bearings, he felt himself seized by two men; he was frightened for an instant, but he soon heard a voice saying softly in his ear, "Ah, *Monsignore! Monsignore!*" He realized vaguely that these were two of the duchess's men, then he fell into a dead faint. Some time later he felt himself being carried by men who were walking swiftly and silently; then they stopped, which caused him great anxiety. But he did not have the strength to speak or open his eyes. He felt someone embrace him tightly, and suddenly he recognized the fragrance of the duchess's clothes. This fragrance revived him; he opened his eyes and was able to utter the words, "Ah, dear friend!" Then he fainted again.

The faithful Bruno, with a squad of policemen devoted to the count, was stationed in reserve two hundred paces away. The count himself was hiding in a little house near the spot where the duchess had been waiting. He would not have hesitated, if necessary, to draw his sword, and a group of retired officers who were close friends of his were ready to do the same. He regarded himself as obliged to save Fabrizio, whose life seemed in great danger, and who would have been given a pardon signed by the prince if he, Mosca, had not been so foolish as to want to save the sovereign from signing his name to a foolish document.

Since midnight, the duchess, surrounded by men armed to the teeth, had been pacing to and fro in deep silence before the ramparts of the citadel. She could not stay in one place; she thought she would have to fight to save Fabrizio from the men who would be pursuing him. Her ardent imagination had led her to take a hundred precautions, too complicated to describe here, and all incredibly rash. It has been estimated that more than eighty men were on foot that night, expecting to fight for something extraordinary. Fortunately, Ferrante and Ludovico were in command of all those men, and the Minister of Police was not hostile. The count noticed that the duchess was betrayed by no one, and that no word of her plans had come to him in his capacity as a minister.

The duchess completely lost her head when she saw Fabrizio. She clasped him convulsively in her arms, then was overwhelmed with despair on seeing that she was covered with blood: it was blood from Fabrizio's hand. She thought he had been dangerously wounded. Aided by two of her men, she was taking off his coat to dress his wounds when Ludovico, who fortunately happened to be there, authoritatively placed her and Fabrizio in one of the little carriages that were hidden in a garden near the city gate, and they set off at full speed to cross the Po near Sacca. Ferrante, with a score of well-armed men, formed a rear guard, and he had sworn on his life that he would stop any pursuers who might appear. The count, alone and on foot, did not leave the vicinity of the citadel until two hours later, when he saw that there was still no one stirring. "Here I am, committing high treason!" he said to himself, overjoyed.

Ludovico had had the excellent idea of placing in one of the carriages a young surgeon who was attached to the duchess's household, and who was of much the same build as Fabrizio. "Flee in the direction of Bologna," he said to him. "Act foolishly, try to get yourself arrested, then give contradictory answers and finally admit that you're Fabrizio del Dongo. Do everything you can to gain time. Be clever in being foolish; you'll get off with a month in prison, and the duchess will give you fifty sequins."

"Does anyone think of money when he's serving the duchess?"

He set off and was arrested a few hours later, which delighted General Fabio Conti, and also Rassi, who had seen his barony vanishing at the same time as Fabrizio's danger.

The escape was not known in the citadel until about six o'clock in the morning, and it was ten o'clock before anyone dared to tell the prince about it. The duchess had been so well served that, despite Fabrizio's deep sleep, which she mistook for unconsciousness resulting from a serious wound, and therefore had the carriage stopped three times, she crossed the Po in a boat at four o'clock. Relays were waiting on the other bank. They traveled two leagues at great speed, then were delayed for over an hour while their passports were being examined. The duchess had all sorts of passports for herself and Fabrizio, but she was so distraught that she took it into her head to give two hundred lire to the clerk of the Austrian police, after which she took his hand and burst into tears. The clerk, greatly alarmed, began the examination all over again. They took the stagecoach, and the duchess paid so extravagantly that she aroused suspicion everywhere she went in that country where every foreigner is suspect. Once again, Ludovico came to her assistance: he said that the duchess was beside herself with grief because of the constant fever of young Count Mosca, son of the Prime Minister of Parma, whom she was taking to Pavia to be examined by the doctors there.

It was not until they were ten leagues beyond the Po that Fabrizio awoke completely. He had a dislocated shoulder and a great many scratches. The duchess was still behaving in such an extraordinary manner that the keeper of the village inn in which they had dinner thought he was dealing with a princess of the imperial blood, and was about to have her rendered the honors he considered to be her due when Ludovico told him that the princess would not fail to have him imprisoned if he ventured to have the bells rung.

Finally, toward six o'clock in the evening, they reached Piedmontese territory. Only then was Fabrizio in complete safety. He was taken to a little village off the main highway; his injured hands were treated and bandaged, and he slept for a few more hours.

It was in this village that the duchess committed an act which was not only horrible from the standpoint of morality, but was also fatal to her peace of mind for the rest of her life. A few weeks before Fabrizio's escape, on a day when everyone in Parma had gone to the gate of the citadel to try to see the scaffold that was being erected in the courtyard in his honor, she had shown Ludovico, now the factotum of her household, the secret mechanism by which one of the stones forming the bottom of the famous thirteenth-century reservoir of the Sanseverina palace, which we have already mentioned, could be removed from a small, well-hidden iron frame. While Fabrizio was sleeping in the *trattoria* of the little village, she sent for Ludovico; the looks she gave him were so strange that he thought she had gone mad.

"You no doubt expect me to give you a few thousand lire," she said to him. "Well, I'm not going to give you any money: I know you, you're a poet, and you'd soon squander it all.

331

Instead, I'm going to give you my little estate of La Ricciarda, a league from Casalmaggiore."

Ludovico threw himself at her feet, wild with joy, and protested in a tone of heartfelt sincerity that it was not to earn money that he had helped to save Fabrizio; he said that he had loved him with a special affection ever since he had once had the honor of driving him in the duchess's carriage when he was her third coachman. When Ludovico, who had a truly noble heart, felt that he had taken up enough of such a great lady's time, he took leave of her; but, with flashing eyes, she said to him, "Stay."

She paced the floor in silence, occasionally glancing at Ludovico with an incredible look in her eyes. Finally, seeing that her strange promenade showed no signs of ending, he decided he ought to speak to her.

"Signora, you've given me a gift so extravagant, so far above anything a poor man like myself could imagine, and, especially, so superior to the trifling services I've had the honor of rendering you, that my conscience won't allow me to keep your estate of La Ricciarda. I have the honor of giving you back your estate, and of begging you to grant me a pension of four hundred lire a year."

"How many times in your life," she said to him with somber pride, "have you ever heard of my giving up a plan once I've stated my intention of carrying it out?" Having said this, she went on pacing the floor for several minutes; then she stopped abruptly and cried out, "It's only by chance, and because he was able to charm that little girl, that Fabrizio's life has been saved! If he hadn't been charming, he'd have died. Can you deny that?" she said, moving toward Ludovico, her eyes aglow with somber fury. He stepped back a few paces, thinking her mad, which gave him serious misgivings about the ownership of the estate of La Ricciarda.

"Well," continued the duchess in the gentlest and most lighthearted tone imaginable, with a swift and total change of mood, "I want my good people of Sacca to have a day of wild gaiety that they'll remember for a long time. You'll go back to Sacca. Do you have any objection? Do you think you'll be running any risk?"

"Nothing to speak of, signora: none of the people of Sacca will ever say that I was in *Monsignore* Fabrizio's service. Besides, if I may venture to say so, signora, I'm dying to see *my* estate of La Ricciarda. It seems so odd to me to be a landowner!"

"I like your gaiety. The tenant of La Ricciarda owes me, I

believe, three or four years' rent; I'll make him a present of half of what he owes me and give the other half to you, on this condition: you will go to Sacca and say that day after tomorrow is the festival of one of my patron saints, and, on the evening of your arrival, you will have my house illuminated in the most splendid fashion. Spare neither money nor effort: remember that this is in honor of the greatest happiness in my life. I made preparations for this illumination a long time ago. For over three months I've been collecting in the cellars of my house everything that will be of use in this noble celebration. I've given the gardener all the fireworks necessary for a magnificent display: you will have them set off from the terrace overlooking the Po. I have eighty-nine big barrels of wine in my cellars: you will set up eighty-nine wine fountains in my park. If there's one bottle of wine still undrunk the next day, I'll say you don't love Fabrizio. When the wine fountains, the illumination and the fireworks are in full swing, you will discreetly slip away, because it's possible, and it's my hope, that in Parma all these fine things will be taken as an act of insolence."

"That's not only possible, it's certain. And it's also certain that Chief Justice Rassi, who signed *Monsignore* Fabrizio's death sentence, will be bursting with rage. In fact," Ludovico added timidly, "if you wanted to give more pleasure to your poor servant than by granting him half of the back rent on La Ricciarda, you'd allow me to play a little joke on that Rassi."

"You're a fine man!" cried the duchess gleefully. "But I absolutely forbid you to do anything to Rassi; I plan to have him publicly hanged, later on. As for you, try not to get yourself arrested at Sacca: everything would be spoiled if I lost you."

"Arrested, signora? Once I've said that I'm celebrating the festival of one of the duchess's patron saints, if the police send thirty constables to disturb anything, you can be sure that not one of them will still be on his horse by the time they've reached the red cross in the middle of the village. No, the people of Sacca don't let anyone step on their toes: they're all expert smugglers, and they worship you, signora."

"And finally," continued the duchess in a strangely casual tone, "if I give wine to my good people of Sacca, I want to flood the people of Parma. On the evening when my house is illuminated, take the best horse in my stable, ride to Parma as fast as you can and open the reservoir."

"Oh! What an excellent idea, signora!" cried Ludovico,

laughing like a madman. "Wine for the good people of Sacca, water for the miserable citizens of Parma who were so sure that *Monsignore* Fabrizio was going to be poisoned like poor L——."

Ludovico's jubilation was endless; the duchess benevolently watched his fits of unrestrained laughter. He kept repeating, "Wine for the people of Sacca, water for the people of Parma! You know better than I, signora, that when the reservoir was rashly opened twenty years ago, there was as much as a foot of water in several of the streets of Parma!"

"And water for the people of Parma!" replied the duchess, laughing. "The promenade in front of the citadel would have been filled with people if Fabrizio's head had been cut off. . . . Everyone calls him 'the great culprit.' . . . But, above all, do it carefully: I don't want a single living soul ever to know that the flood was started by you or ordered by me. Fabrizio, and even the count, must know nothing of this mad joke. . . . But I'm forgetting the poor people of Sacca: write a letter to my steward and I'll sign it as soon as you're finished. Tell him that for the festival of my patron saint he will distribute a hundred sequins to the poor people of Sacca, that he is to obey you in everything concerning the illumination, the fireworks and the wine, and that I want him to make sure there's not one full bottle left in my cellars the following day."

"Your steward will find only one difficulty, signora: in the five years that you've had the estate, you haven't left ten poor people in Sacca."

"*And water for the people of Parma!*" sang the duchess. "How will you carry out that joke?"

"My plans are all made: I'll leave Sacca at nine o'clock; at half-past ten, my horse will be at the 'Inn of the Three Block-heads,' on the road between Casalmaggiore and *my* estate of La Ricciarda; at eleven, I'll be in my room in the palace, and at a quarter past eleven there will be water for the people of Parma, and more than they want, to drink to the health of the great culprit. Ten minutes later, I'll leave the city by the Bologna road. As I pass by, I'll make a low bow to the citadel, which *Monsignore* Fabrizio's courage and your intelligence have just dishonored; then I'll take a cross-country path, which I know well, and make my entry into La Ricciarda."

Ludovico looked at the duchess and was frightened: she was staring intently at the bare wall six paces in front of her, and it must be admitted that the expression of her eyes was terrible. "Oh, my poor estate!" thought Ludovico. "The fact is that she's mad!" The duchess looked at him and guessed his thoughts.

"Ah, Signor Ludovico, the great poet, you want a written deed! Go get me a sheet of paper."

Ludovico did not wait to be told twice, and the duchess wrote with her own hand a long receipt, foredated by a year, in which she acknowledged having received from Ludovico San Micheli the sum of eighty thousand lire, and having given him as security her estate of La Ricciarda. If, at the end of twelve months, she had not repaid the eighty thousand lire, the estate was to become his property.

"It's a noble act," she thought, "to give a faithful servant nearly a third of what I have left for myself."

"Now," she said to Ludovico, "after the joke with the reservoir, I'll give you only two days to enjoy yourself at Casalmaggiore. To make the transfer valid, say that it's a matter which goes back more than a year. Rejoin me at Belgirate, and without the slightest delay. Fabrizio may go to England; if so, you'll go with him."

The duchess and Fabrizio reached Belgirate early the next morning.

They settled down in that enchanting village; but a deadly sorrow lay in store for the duchess on the shores of the beautiful lake there. Fabrizio had changed completely. From the first few moments when he was awakening, still rather lethargic, from the sleep into which he had fallen after his escape, she had noticed that something extraordinary was taking place inside him. The deep feeling which he made great efforts to conceal was a rather strange one; it was nothing less than this: he was in despair at being out of prison. He was careful not to admit this cause of his sadness, for it would have led to questions which he did not want to answer.

"What!" exclaimed the duchess in amazement. "When hunger forced you, to keep from fainting, to eat some of the hateful food prepared in the kitchen of the prison, weren't you horrified by the terrible feeling of having to wonder, 'Is there any unusual taste here? Am I now poisoning myself?'"

"I thought of death," replied Fabrizio, "as I suppose soldiers think of it: it was a possibility which I expected to avoid by my own skill."

What anxiety, what grief for the duchess! Her beloved Fabrizio, so exceptional, impetuous and original, was now,

335

before her eyes, a prey to profound reveries; he preferred solitude even to the pleasure of talking about everything, open-heartedly, with the best friend he had in the world. He was still kind, zealous and grateful to her, he would still have given his life for her; but his soul was elsewhere. They often glided four or five leagues over the surface of that divine lake in a boat without saying a word to each other. The conversation, the exchange of cold ideas which was now possible between them might have seemed pleasant to other people; but they, especially the duchess, remembered what their conversation had been like before they were separated by the fatal fight with Giletti. Fabrizio owed her an account of the nine months he had spent in a horrible prison, yet he had only brief and incomplete remarks to make about his stay there.

"This is what was bound to happen sooner or later," the duchess told herself with dark sadness. "Sorrow has aged me, or else he's really in love, and I hold only second place in his heart." Degraded and crushed by this greatest of all possible sorrows, she sometimes said to herself, "It seems to me that I'd now be less unhappy if it had been heaven's will that Ferrante should go completely mad, or lose his courage." Henceforth, this semi-regret poisoned her self-esteem. "I'm repenting of a decision after making it myself," she thought bitterly, "so I'm no longer a del Dongo! It's heaven's will: Fabrizio is in love, and what right have I to wish he weren't? Has one single word of real love ever been exchanged between us?"

This sensible idea robbed her of sleep, and she was a hundred times more unhappy in Belgirate than she had been in Parma, which showed that old age and its attendant weakening of character had come to her at the same time as the prospect of a glorious revenge. As for the woman who might be the cause of Fabrizio's strange reveries, it was scarcely possible to have any reasonable doubt: Clelia Conti, though normally an extremely dutiful daughter, had betrayed her father by consenting to make the garrison drunk, and Fabrizio never mentioned her! "But," thought the duchess, beating her breast in despair, "if the garrison hadn't been drunk, all my arrangements, all my careful efforts would have been useless, so it was she who saved him!"

It was only with extreme difficulty that the duchess was able to draw from Fabrizio any details of the events of that night, which, she said to herself, "would once have formed the subject of a constantly renewed conversation between us!

In those happy days, he would talk for hours on end, and with unfailing gaiety and zest, about any trifle I chose to mention."

Since they had to be prepared for anything, the duchess had found lodgings for Fabrizio in the port of Locarno, a Swiss town at the far end of Lake Maggiore. Every day she went there in her boat to meet him, and they spent long hours on the lake. Once when she decided to go up to his apartment, she found the walls of his bedroom covered with pictures of the city of Parma which he had ordered from Milan and even from Parma itself, a city he should have held in abhorrence. His little living room, converted into a studio, was littered with all the equipment of a painter in water colors, and she found him putting the finishing touches on a third picture of the Farnese Tower and the governor's residence.

"All you need to do now," she said to him resentfully, "is to paint a portrait from memory of that charming governor whose only wish was to poison you. And now that I think of it, you ought to write him a letter of apology for having taken the liberty of escaping and casting ridicule on his citadel."

The poor woman did not know how truly she had spoken: the first thing Fabrizio had done after reaching safety had been to write General Fabio Conti a letter that was perfectly polite and, in a sense, quite ridiculous. He asked his forgiveness for having escaped, citing as his excuse the fact that he had reason to believe that a certain subordinate in the prison had been ordered to poison him. It mattered little to him what he wrote: he hoped that Clelia would see his letter, and his cheeks were wet with tears as he wrote it. He ended it with a most amusing statement: he went so far as to say that, now that he had regained his freedom, he often missed his little room in the Farnese Tower. This was the principal idea in his letter, and he hoped that Clelia would understand it.

While he was still in the mood for writing, and again in the hope of being read by a certain person, he wrote a letter of thanks to Don Cesare, the kindly chaplain who had lent him some religious books. A few days later, he persuaded the owner of the small bookshop in Locarno to make a journey to Milan, where this bookseller, a friend of the famous bibliophile Reina, bought the most magnificent editions he could find of the works Don Cesare had lent to Fabrizio. The good chaplain received these books and a gracious letter in which

Fabrizio told him that, in moments of impatience for which a poor prisoner might perhaps be excused, he had covered the margins of the borrowed books with ridiculous notes. He therefore begged Don Cesare to replace them in his library by the volumes which, in his deep gratitude, he now took the liberty of presenting to him.

It was generous of Fabrizio to give the name of "notes" to the endless scribblings with which he had covered the margins of a folio edition of the works of Saint Jerome. In the hope that he might be able to send this book back to the good chaplain and exchange it for another, he had written in its margins a precise daily record of everything that had happened to him in prison; the great events were nothing less than ecstasies of "divine love" (the word "divine" took the place of another which he did not dare to write). Sometimes this divine love led the prisoner into deep despair; at other times, a voice that came to him through the air restored some hope to him and gave rise to transports of bliss. All this, fortunately, was written in prison ink made of wine, chocolate and soot, and Don Cesare had only glanced at it before putting the volume of Saint Jerome back on his shelves. If he had read what was written in the margins, he would have seen that one day the prisoner, thinking he had been poisoned, was congratulating himself on dying at a distance of less than forty paces from what he loved most in the world.

But eyes other than those of the good chaplain had read this page after Fabrizio's escape. The beautiful idea of dying near what one loves, expressed in a hundred different ways, was followed by a sonnet in which it was stated that the writer's soul, separated after excruciating torments from the body it had inhabited for twenty-three years, and driven by the instinct for happiness which is natural to all things once they have been given life, would not rise up to heaven to join the chorus of angels as soon as it was free, and if the awesome Judgment granted it pardon for its sins; but that, happier after death than during life, it would go only a short distance from the prison in which it had languished for so long, to be reunited with all that it had loved in the world. "And so," said the last line of the sonnet, "I shall have found my paradise on earth."

Although Fabrizio was never referred to in the citadel of Parma as anything but an infamous traitor who had violated his most sacred duties, Don Cesare was delighted by the sight of the fine books he had received from some unknown person; for Fabrizio had not written to him until a few days after sending them, for fear that his name might cause them to be indignantly refused. Don Cesare said nothing of this gift to his brother, who flew into a rage at the mere mention of Fabrizio's name; but since the prisoner's escape, he had resumed all his former intimacy with his charming niece, and, having once taught her a few words of Latin, he showed her the fine volumes he had received. Such had been Fabrizio's hope.

Clelia suddenly blushed deeply when she recognized his handwriting. Long, thin strips of yellow paper had been placed as bookmarks in various parts of one of the volumes. And since it is true to say that, in the midst of the sordid pecuniary interests and cold, colorless, commonplace thoughts that fill our lives, an action inspired by genuine passion rarely fails to produce its effect, so, as though a propitious deity were carefully leading her by the hand, Clelia, guided by this instinct, and by the thought of only one thing in the world, asked her uncle to compare his original volume of Saint Jerome with the one he had just received. How would it be possible to describe her rapture, bursting forth from the dark sadness into which Fabrizio's absence had plunged her, when she found in the margins of the original volume the sonnet we have mentioned, and the daily record of the love he had felt for her!

From the first day she knew that sonnet by heart; she would sing it as she leaned against her window sill, looking out at the window, now deserted, where she had so often seen a little opening appear in the shutter. This shutter had been taken down to be placed on a table in the courtroom as a piece of evidence in the ridiculous case which Rassi was preparing against Fabrizio, who was accused of the crime of having escaped, or, as the Chief Justice put it, laughing inwardly, "of having removed himself from the clemency of a magnanimous prince."

Each step that Clelia had taken was a source of keen remorse to her, and now that she was unhappy her remorse was all the keener. She tried to pacify her self-reproach to some extent by reminding herself of the vow never to see Fabrizio again which she had made to the Madonna when the general was nearly poisoned, and which she had renewed every day since then.

Her father had been made ill by Fabrizio's escape, and furthermore he had come close to losing his position when the prince, in his anger, had dismissed all the jailers of the

339

Farnese Tower and imprisoned them in the city jail. The general had been saved in part by the intercession of Count Mosca, who preferred to have him shut up at the top of his citadel rather than encounter him as an active and scheming rival in court circles.

It was during the two weeks of uncertainty with regard to the possible dismissal of General Fabio Conti, who was genuinely ill, that Clelia found the courage to carry out the sacrifice she had announced to Fabrizio. She had had the good sense to be ill on the day of general rejoicing which was also the day of the prisoner's escape, as the reader may recall; she was also ill the following day, and, in short, governed her conduct so well that, with the exception of the jailer Grillo, who had been specially assigned to guard Fabrizio, no one had any suspicion of her complicity, and Grillo remained silent.

But as soon as she no longer had any anxiety on that score, her righteous remorse began tormenting her more cruelly than ever. "What possible reason," she said to herself, "could lessen the guilt of a daughter who has betrayed her father?"

One evening, after a day spent almost entirely in the chapel, and in tears, she begged her uncle, Don Cesare, to go with her to see the general, whose outbursts of rage frightened her all the more because, no matter what was said to him, he always turned it into an occasion to curse Fabrizio, that vile traitor.

When she had come into her father's presence, she had the courage to say to him that her reason for having always refused to give her hand to the Marquis Crescenzi had been that she felt no inclination toward him, and that she was sure she would not find happiness in being married to him. At these words the general flew into another rage, and she had difficulty in making him listen to her again. She went on to say that if, attracted by the marquis' great wealth, her father felt it his duty to give her a strict order to marry him, she was ready to obey. The general was greatly astonished by this conclusion, which he had been so far from expecting; however, he finally rejoiced over it. "So," he said to his brother, "I won't be reduced to living in a third-floor apartment if I lose my position because of that scoundrel Fabrizio's ignoble act!"

Count Mosca did not fail to make a show of being deeply shocked by the escape of "that scoundrel Fabrizio," and on occasion he repeated the phrase invented by Rassi with regard to the base conduct of the prisoner, a very commonplace young man, incidentally, who had "removed himself from the prince's clemency." This clever phrase, appreciated in high society, made no impression on the common people. Left to their own good sense, though firmly convinced of Fabrizio's guilt, they admired the determination he had taken to climb down from such a great height. No one at court admired this courage.

As for the police, deeply humiliated by this setback, they had officially discovered that a band of twenty soldiers, bribed by the duchess, that horribly ungrateful woman whose name was never mentioned without a sigh, had given Fabrizio four ladders tied together, each one forty-five feet long; having let down a rope to which they tied these ladders, Fabrizio had had only the trivial merit of pulling them up to his cell. A few liberals known for their audacity, among them Dr. C——, an agent paid directly by the prince, endangered themselves by saying that this atrocious police force had been barbarous enough to order the shooting of eight of the wretched soldiers who had facilitated the escape of that ingrate Fabrizio. He was then blamed, even by the genuine liberals, for having caused the death of eight poor soldiers by his imprudence. It is thus that petty despotisms reduce the value of public opinion to nothing.*

CHAPTER TWENTY-THREE

In the midst of this general outburst of feeling against Fabrizio, only the Archbishop showed himself loyal to his young friend's cause. He dared to repeat, even at the princess's court, that maxim of jurisprudence according to which one ought, in any trial, to lend an unprejudiced ear to all arguments in defense of an absent party.

On the day after Fabrizio's escape, several people had received copies of a rather mediocre sonnet which celebrated this escape as one of the noblest acts of the century and compared Fabrizio to an angel coming down to earth with outspread wings. Two evenings later, everyone in Parma was repeating a sublime sonnet. It was Fabrizio's soliloquy as he slid down the rope, passing judgment on various incidents in his life. This sonnet gave him a higher rank in public opinion

* See page 432.

by reason of two magnificent lines; every connoisseur of poetry recognized the style of Ferrante Palla.

But at this point I ought to seek the aid of the epic style. Where can I find the colors in which to paint the torrents of indignation that suddenly overwhelmed all right-thinking hearts when the appalling insolence of the illumination of the duchess's house at Sacca became known? There was a unanimous outcry against her; even the genuine liberals felt that she had callously endangered the poor suspects being held in various prisons, and uselessly exasperated the sovereign. Count Mosca declared that there was only one thing left for her former friends to do, and that was to forget her. The chorus of execration was therefore complete; a stranger passing through the city would have been struck by the energy of public opinion. But in that country where people know how to appreciate the pleasure of vengeance, the illumination at Sacca, and the admirable feast given in the park to more than six thousand peasants, had an enormous success. Everyone in Parma repeated the story that the duchess had handed out a thousand sequins to her peasants; this explained the rather rough reception given to thirty constables whom the police had been foolish enough to send to the little village thirty-six hours after the sublime evening and the general drunkenness that had ensued. The constables, greeted with a hail of stones, had taken flight, and two of them, having fallen from their horses, had been thrown into the Po.

As for the bursting of the great reservoir of the Sanseverina palace, it had passed almost unnoticed; several streets had been flooded, but it had happened during the night, and by morning they had been no wetter than after a heavy rain. Ludovico had taken care to break the panes of one of the palace windows, thus providing an explanation for the entrance of thieves. A little ladder had even been found. Only Count Mosca recognized his friend's genius.

Fabrizio was fully determined to go back to Parma as soon as he could. He sent Ludovico to deliver a long letter to the archbishop. On his way back, when he came to the first village in Piedmont, San Nazzaro, to the west of Pavia, the faithful servant mailed a Latin epistle which the worthy prelate had written to his young protégé. We will add here a detail which, like a number of others, no doubt, will seem tedious in countries where there is no longer any need for precautions. The name of Fabrizio del Dongo was never written; all letters intended for him were addressed to Ludovico San Micheli, in Locarno, Switzerland, or in Belgirate,

Piedmont. The envelope was always made of coarse paper, the seal badly applied, the address almost illegible and sometimes supplemented with indications worthy of a cook. Each letter was dated from Naples, six days earlier than its actual date.

From the Piedmontese village of San Nazzaro, near Pavia, Ludovico returned to Parma with all possible speed: he had been charged with a mission to which Fabrizio attached the greatest importance. It was nothing less than to convey to Clelia Conti a silk handkerchief on which a sonnet by Petrarch had been printed. It is true that one word had been changed in this sonnet. Clelia found it on her table two days after she had received the thanks of the Marquis Crescenzi, who had declared himself to be the happiest of men, and there is no need to describe the impression made on her heart by this token of a still constant memory.

Ludovico had been instructed to procure all possible details of what was taking place in the citadel. It was he who told Fabrizio the sad news that the Marquis Crescenzi's marriage now seemed to be definitely settled; hardly a day went by without his giving some sort of celebration for Clelia inside the citadel. One decisive proof of the coming marriage was that the marquis, immensely rich and therefore extremely stingy, as is customary among the wealthy people of northern Italy, was making lavish preparations, even though he was marrying "a girl without a dowry." It is true that General Fabio Conti, whose vanity had been deeply offended by this phrase, the first one that had leapt into the minds of all his compatriots, had recently bought an estate for 300,000 lire, and, although he had nothing, he paid for it in cash, no doubt with money supplied by the marquis. The general had then declared that he was giving this estate to his daughter as her dowry.

But the fee for the registration of the deed, and all the other incidental expenses, came to more than 12,000 lire, which seemed a ridiculous waste of money to the marquis, an eminently logical man. For his part, he was having some tapestries made in Lyons. They had been splendidly designed, with harmonious colors well calculated to please the eye, by Pellagi, the celebrated painter of Bologna. These tapestries, each containing a segment of the coat of arms of the Crescenzi family, which, as everyone in the universe knows, is descended from the famous Crescentius, Consul of Rome in 985, were to adorn the seventeen salons which formed the ground floor of the marquis' palace. The tapestries, clocks and chandeliers sent to Parma cost more than 350,000 lire; the value of the new mirrors, added to those already in the house, amounted to 200,000 lire. With the exception of two salons whose decoration was a famous work of Parmigiano, the greatest painter of the region after the divine Correggio, all the rooms on the second and third floors were now occupied by the outstanding painters of Florence, Rome and Milan, who were adorning them with frescoes. Fogelberg, the great Swedish sculptor, Tenerani of Rome and Marchesi of Milan had been working for the past year on ten bas-reliefs depicting as many noble deeds of Crescentius, that truly great man. Most of the ceilings, painted in fresco, also presented some allusion to his life. There was general admiration of the ceiling on which Hayez, of Milan, had depicted Crescentius being received into the Elysian Fields by Francesco Sforza, Lorenzo the Magnificent, King Robert, Tribune Cola di Rienzi, Machiavelli, Dante and other great men of the Middle Ages. Admiration for these chosen souls is regarded as a kind of epigram against the men now in power.

All these magnificent details completely absorbed the attention of the nobility and middle classes of Parma, and pierced the heart of our hero when he read about them, described with artless admiration, in a long letter of more than twenty pages which Ludovico had dictated to a customs official at Casalmaggiore.

"And I'm so poor!" thought Fabrizio. "I have only an income of four thousand lire in all, and for all! It's really insolent of me to dare to be in love with Clelia Conti, for whom all these miracles are being performed."

One paragraph in Ludovico's long letter, but this one in his own crude handwriting, informed his master that one evening he had encountered Grillo, his former jailer, who was apparently now in hiding; he had been imprisoned, then released. Grillo had asked to be given a sequin, out of charity, and Ludovico had given him four in the duchess's name. The former jailers, twelve in all, who had recently been set free, were preparing to give a "knife-reception" (*trattamento di coltellate*) to the new jailers who had succeeded them, if they could ever manage to meet them outside the citadel. Grillo had said that there was a serenade in the fortress nearly every day, that Signorina Clelia was very pale and often ill, "and other things like that." As a result of this ridiculous phrase, Ludovico received an order by return mail to come back to Locarno. He did, and the details he gave in person were even more distressing to Fabrizio.

It is not difficult to imagine how charmingly he treated the poor duchess; he would have died a thousand deaths rather than utter the name of Clelia Conti in her presence. The duchess abhorred Parma; for Fabrizio, everything that reminded him of that city was both sublime and heartrending.

The duchess was less inclined than ever to forget her vengeance; she had been so happy before the incident of Giletti's death, and what a fate had now befallen her! She was living in expectation of a terrible event; she was careful to say nothing about it to Fabrizio, and yet when she had made her arrangement with Ferrante she had thought of the great joy she would some day give Fabrizio by telling him he was going to be avenged!

The reader can now form some idea of how pleasant their conversations were. A gloomy silence always reigned between them. To make their relations more agreeable, the duchess yielded to the temptation to play a trick on her excessively beloved nephew. The count wrote to her nearly every day; he apparently sent couriers, as in the days of their love affair, for his letters always bore the postmark of some small town in Switzerland. The poor man had to rack his brain to compose amusing letters and avoid speaking too openly of his love in them; she barely glanced over them. Alas, what does the faithfulness of an esteemed lover matter to a woman whose heart is pierced by the coldness of the man she prefers to him?

In the space of two months the duchess answered him only once, and that was to ask him to sound out the princess in order to learn whether, despite the insolence of the fireworks display, she would be glad to receive a letter from the duchess. The letter he was to present, if he saw fit, requested the position of Knight of Honor to the princess, which had recently become vacant, for the Marquis Crescenzi, and expressed the wish that it would be granted to him in consideration of his marriage. The duchess's letter was a masterpiece, filled with affectionate and perfectly expressed respect; in its courtly style not one word had been admitted whose consequences, even the most remote, might not be agreeable to the princess. And so the princess's reply was permeated with tender friendship tormented by the pains of absence:

Since your sudden departure, my son and I have not spent a single evening which has been even slightly enjoyable. Can it be, my dear duchess, that you no longer remember that it was you who made it possible for me

345

to have a consulting voice in the appointment of the officers of my household? Do you feel obliged to give me reasons for the marquis' appointment, as though the expression of your wish were not the best of reasons for me? The marquis will have his post, if my efforts are of any use; and there will always be a place, the foremost, in my heart for my charming duchess. My son uses exactly the same expressions, although they may be a little strong on the lips of a tall young man of twenty-one, and asks you for some specimens of minerals from the Orta Valley, near Belgirate. You may address your letters, which I hope will be frequent, to the count, who still hates you, and whom I like especially because of those feelings. The archbishop has also remained loyal to you. We all hope to see you again some day: remember that you must return. The Marquise Ghisleri, my Chief Lady in Waiting, is preparing to leave this world for a better one. The poor woman has caused me a great deal of sorrow, and she is displeasing me still more by departing so inopportunely; her illness makes me think of the name with which I would once have been so glad to replace hers, if I had been able to obtain such a sacrifice of independence on the part of that unique woman who, in fleeing from us, took with her all the joy of my little court, etc., etc.

It was therefore with the awareness of having done everything in her power to hasten the marriage which was filling Fabrizio with despair that the duchess saw him every day. Thus they would sometimes spend four or five hours together in her boat on the lake without saying a word to each other. On Fabrizio's side there was complete and perfect good will, but he was thinking of other things, and his artless, simple nature supplied him with nothing to say. The duchess saw this, and was tormented by it.

We have forgotten to mention in the proper place that the duchess had taken a house in Belgirate, a charming village which amply fulfills the promise of its name (the sight of a beautiful bend in the lake). From the French window of her drawing room, she could step into her boat. She had taken a quite ordinary one for which four rowers would have been enough; she engaged twelve, and made sure that there was a man from each of the villages in the vicinity of Belgirate. The third or fourth time she found herself in the middle of the lake with all these carefully chosen men, she ordered them to stop rowing, then said to them, "I regard you all as my friends, and I want to confide a secret to you. My nephew Fabrizio has escaped from prison, and some treacherous attempt may be made to recapture him, even though he's on your lake, which is a place of sanctuary. Keep your ears open and notify me of anything you may hear. I give you permission to enter my bedroom at any time, day or night."

The rowers responded enthusiastically; she knew how to make herself loved. But she did not believe there would be any attempt to recapture Fabrizio; her precautions were actually for herself, and she would never have thought of them before the fatal order to open the reservoir of the Sanseverina palace.

Her prudence had also led her to take an apartment for Fabrizio in the port of Locarno; every day either he came to see her or she went to see him in Switzerland. The pleasure they found in each other's company may be judged from the following detail: the Marquise del Dongo and her daughters came to see them twice, and they were glad to have these strangers present; for, regardless of family ties, we may apply the word "stranger" to a person who knows nothing of our most cherished interests, and whom we see only once a year.

The duchess was in Fabrizio's apartment in Locarno one evening with the marquise and her two daughters when the parish priest and the archpriest of the district came to pay their respects to these ladies. The archpriest, who had an interest in a business concern and kept abreast of all the latest news, suddenly announced, "The prince is dead!"

The duchess turned extremely pale; she scarcely had the courage to ask, "Have any details been given out?"

"No," replied the archpriest. "The report merely states the fact of his death, which is certain."

The duchess looked at Fabrizio. "I did that for him," she thought. "I'd have done things a thousand times worse, and here he is before me, indifferent and thinking of another woman!" It was beyond her strength to endure this horrible thought; she fainted. Everyone hurried to her assistance, but when she regained consciousness she noticed that Fabrizio was showing less concern than either of the two priests; he was daydreaming as usual.

"He's thinking of going back to Parma," she said to herself, "and perhaps of breaking off Clelia's marriage to the marquise; but I'll find a way to stop him."

Then, remembering the presence of the two priests, she

hastened to say, "He was a great prince, and one who was greatly slandered! This is a heavy loss to all of us!"

The priests took their leave, and the duchess, in order to be alone, announced that she was going to bed.

"Prudence no doubt requires that I should wait a month or two before going back to Parma," she thought, "but I feel that I'll never have that much patience; I'm suffering too much here. My heart can't bear the sight of Fabrizio's constant absorption, and his silence. Who would have thought I'd be bored while alone with him in a boat on this charming lake, and at a time when, to avenge him, I've done more than I can tell him! After such an experience, death means nothing. I'm now paying for the transports of happiness and childish joy I felt when he came to my palace in Parma after his stay in Naples. I had only to say a word and everything would have been settled, and perhaps, once he was bound to me, he would never have given a thought to that little Clelia; but that word was horribly repugnant to me. Now she's won out over me. What could be more natural? She's twenty, and I, careworn and ill, am twice her age! . . . I must die, I must put an end to this! A woman of forty means nothing to a man unless he has loved her in her youth.

"From now on, there's nothing left for me except the pleasures of vanity, and are they enough to make life worth living? All the more reason to go to Parma, and to amuse myself. If things take a certain turn, I'll be put to death. Well, what's wrong with that? I'll die a magnificent death, and just before the end, but only then, I'll say to Fabrizio, 'Ingrate! This is for you!' . . . Yes, Parma is the only place where I can find any occupation for what little life remains to me; I'll play the great lady there. How happy I'd be if I could still apprecite those honors which used to make the Marquise Raversi so miserable! In those days I could see my happiness only through the eyes of those who envied me. . . . My vanity has one consolation: with the exception of the count, perhaps, no one will ever guess the event that extinguished all life in my heart. I'll love Fabrizio, I'll devote myself to his interests, but he mustn't break off Clelia's marriage and finally marry her himself. No, that will not happen!"

The duchess had reached this point in her sad soliloquy when she heard a great noise in the house.

"Good," she said to herself, "they've come to arrest me! Ferrante must have been caught and made to confess. Well, so much the better! Now I'll have something to keep my mind

348

occupied: I'll fight with them for my life. But first of all, I mustn't let them take me."

Half-dressed, the duchess fled to the back of the garden: she was already thinking of climbing over a little wall and escaping into the open countryside. But then she saw some-one enter her bedroom. She recognized Bruno, the count's most trusted servant: he was alone with her maid. The duchess went up to the French window. Bruno was telling her maid about some injuries he had received. The duchess went inside. He nearly threw himself at her feet, and he begged her not to tell the count the absurd hour at which he had arrived.

"Immediately after the prince's death," he said, "the count gave orders to all post houses not to supply horses to any subject of the State of Parma, so I went all the way to the Po with our own horses. But as I was driving off the ferry, my carriage was overturned and broken to pieces, and I was bruised so badly that I couldn't ride a horse, as it was my duty to do."

"Well, it's now three o'clock in the morning," said the duchess: "I'll say you arrived at noon; be sure not to contra-dict me."

"I'm deeply grateful for your kindness."

Politics in a literary work is like a pistol shot in the middle of a concert: something crude, yet impossible to ignore.

We are about to speak of very ugly things which, for more than one reason, we would like to pass over in silence; but we are forced to deal with events which come within our prov-ince, since they take place in the hearts of our characters.

"But good heavens, how did the prince die?" said the duchess to Bruno.

"He was out shooting migratory birds in the marshes along the Po, two leagues from Sacca. He fell into a hole hidden by a clump of grass; he was sweating heavily and he caught a chill. They took him to an isolated house and he died there a few hours later. Some people say Signor Catena and Signor Borone died too, and that all three deaths were caused by the copper pots in the peasant's house they went to: the pots were covered with verdigris, and the whole party ate lunch there. But the hotheads, the Jacobins, who say whatever they like, are talking about a deliberate poisoning. All I know is that my friend Toto, a quartermaster in the palace guards, would have died if it hadn't been for the generous care of a peasant who seemed to know a lot about medicine and made him take some very strange remedies.

"But people have already stopped talking about the prince's death: the fact is that he was a cruel man. When I left, the common people were gathering to capture Chief Justice Rassi and kill him. They also wanted to go and set fire to the gates of the citadel, to try to let the prisoners escape, but it was said that Fabio Conti would fire his cannons. Others said the gunners of the citadel had poured water on their powder because they refused to massacre their fellow citizens.

"But there's something much more interesting: while the surgeon was tending to my poor arm at Sandolaro, a man who'd just come from Parma told us that the people had found Barbone, that famous clerk of the citadel, in the street: first they beat him, then they went off to hang him from a tree in the promenade nearest to the citadel. They were on their way to smash the fine statue of the prince that's in the palace gardens, but Count Mosca took a battalion of the palace guards, lined them up in front of the statue and had the people told that no one who came into the garden would go out alive. That frightened them away. But the strange part of it—and the man who'd just come from Parma, a former constable, repeated this to me several times—is that the count kicked General P——, commander of the palace guards, ripped off his epaulettes and had him taken out of the garden by two fusiliers."

"That's just like the count!" cried the duchess in a surge of joy which she would not have thought possible a few moments earlier. "He'll never allow anyone to insult our princess; and as for General P——, he always refused to serve the usurper, whereas the count, who was less squeamish about the matter, fought in all the Spanish campaigns, for which he's often been reproached at court."

The duchess had opened the count's letter, but she kept interrupting her reading of it to ask Bruno countless questions.

The letter was quite amusing; the count used the most lugubrious expressions, and yet the keenest joy broke out in every word; he avoided giving any details about the nature of the prince's death and finished his letter with these words:

> You will no doubt come back, my dear angel, but I advise you to wait a day or two for the courier whom the princess will send to you, I hope, today or tomorrow. Your return must be as glorious as your departure was bold. As for the great criminal who is with you, I expect to have him tried by twelve judges summoned from all over the State of Parma. But in order to have that

monster punished as he deserves, I must first be able to tear up the first sentence, if it exists.

The count had then reopened his letter:

Here is a very different matter: I have issued ammunition to the two battalions of the palace guards; I am going to fight and do my best to deserve the nickname of "Cruel" with which the liberals have honored me for so long. That old mummy, General P——, has dared to speak in the barracks of opening negotiations with the people, who are in a state of semi-revolt. I am writing this in the street: I am on my way to the palace, which no one will enter except over my dead body. Good-by! If I die, it will be in worshiping you in spite of everything, as I have lived. Do not forget to withdraw the 300,000 lire deposited in your name with D—— in Lyons. Here comes that poor devil Rassi, pale as death, and without his wig; you can't imagine what he looks like! The people are determined to hang him. That would be a great injustice: he deserves to be drawn and quartered. He took refuge in my house, and has now come running after me in the street. I'm not sure what I ought to do with him. . . . I don't want to take him to the prince's palace, because that would make a revolt break out there. F—— will see whether I love him: my first words to Rassi were, "I must have the sentence passed on Signor del Dongo, and any extra copies of it that you may have. And tell all those corrupt judges, who are the cause of this revolt, that I will have them all hanged, along with you, my dear friend, if they ever breathe a word about that sentence, which has never existed." In Fabrizio's name, I am sending a company of grenadiers to the archbishop. Good-by, my dear angel! My house will be burned, and I will lose the charming portraits I have of you. I am hurrying to the palace to throw out that infamous General P——, who is up to his old tricks: he is basely fawning on the people, just as he used to fawn on the late prince. All those generals are frightened to death; I think I'm going to have myself made commander in chief.

The duchess was malicious enough not to send someone to awaken Fabrizio; she felt for the count a surge of admiration which strongly resembled love. "All things considered," she thought, "I'll have to marry him." She immediately wrote a letter telling him so, and sent one of her men to deliver it to him. That night she had no time to be unhappy.

The next day, toward noon, she saw a boat manned by six rowers moving swiftly across the lake. She and Fabrizio soon recognized a man wearing the livery of the Prince of Parma; it was indeed one of his couriers, and before the boat reached shore he called out to the duchess, "The revolt has been quelled!" He gave her several letters from the count, an admirable letter from the princess, and a decree from Prince Ranuccio-Ernesto V, written on parchment, making her Duchess of San Giovanni and Chief Lady in Waiting to the princess dowager. The young prince, an expert on mineralogy, whom she regarded as an imbecile, had had enough intelligence to write her a short letter; but there was a suggestion of love at the end of it. It began thus:

> The count says that he is pleased with me. The fact is that I faced a few bullets at his side, and that my horse was hit. After seeing all the fuss that has been made over such a trifling matter, I am eager to take part in a real battle, but not against my own subjects. I owe everything to the count; all my generals, who have never been in battle, ran like rabbits: I believe two or three of them fled as far as Bologna. Since coming to power as the result of a great tragedy, I have signed no decree that has given me so much pleasure as the one which makes you my mother's Chief Lady in Waiting. She and I remembered that one day you admired the beautiful view from the villa of San Giovanni, which once belonged to Petrarch, or so it is said. My mother decided to give you that little estate, and I, not knowing what to give you, and not daring to offer you everything that rightfully belongs to you, have made you a duchess in my own domain; I do not know whether you are learned enough to know that Sanseverina is a Roman title. I have just given the Grand Cordon of my Order to our worthy archbishop, who has shown a firmness that is very rare in a man of seventy. You will not be angry with me for not having recalled all the ladies who were exiled. I have been told that from now on I must write the words "Your affectionate" before my signature; I regret being forced to make such lavish use of an assurance which is completely true only when I write to you.
>
> Your affectionate
> Ranuccio-Ernesto

Who would not have said, judging from this language, that the duchess was about to enjoy the highest favor? However, she found something quite strange in other letters from the count, which she received two hours later. He advised her, without explanation, to delay her return to Parma for a few days, and to write to the princess that she was seriously indisposed. She and Fabrizio nevertheless left for Parma immediately after dinner. Her goal, although she did not admit it to herself, was to hasten the Marquis Crescenzi's marriage. As for Fabrizio, he set off in a state of wild elation which seemed ridiculous to his aunt. He hoped to see Clelia again soon; he intended to take her away, or even abduct her, if he could find no other way of preventing her marriage.

The duchess and her nephew were extremely gay during the entire journey. At the last station before Parma, Fabrizio stopped briefly to change back into his ecclesiastical garments; he was usually dressed like a man in mourning. When he came into the duchess's room she said to him, "There's something mysterious in the count's letters, and I'm a little suspicious. I think it would be better for you to stay here a few hours. I'll send a messenger to you as soon as I've talked to that great minister." Fabrizio reluctantly yielded to this sensible advice.

The count's welcome to the duchess, whom he addressed as his wife, was accompanied by transports of joy worthy of a fifteen-year-old boy. For a long time he was unwilling to talk about politics, but when they finally returned to prosaic reason he said to her, "You were quite right to prevent Fabrizio from arriving officially: a reaction is in full swing here. Try to guess the name of the colleague the prince has given me as Minister of Justice! It's Rassi, my dear, Rassi, whom I treated like the vile wretch he is, on the day of our great commotion!

"By the way, let me warn you that everything that happened here has been suppressed. If you read our newspaper, you will learn that a clerk of the citadel by the name of Barbone has been killed by a fall from a carriage. As for the sixty-odd rascals I ordered to be shot when they attacked the statue of the prince in the palace gardens, they're in perfect health, but they're now traveling abroad. Count Zurla, the Minister of the Interior, personally went to the house of each one of those unfortunate heroes and gave fifteen sequins to his family or friends, along with an order to say that the deceased was away on a journey, and a very definite threat of imprisonment if they should let it be understood that he

353

had been killed. A man from my own Ministry of Foreign Affairs has been sent on a mission to the journalists of Milan and Turin to prevent them from mentioning the 'unfortunate incident'—that's the accepted expression—and he has orders to go on as far as Paris and London to publish in all the newspapers a semi-official denial of anything that may be said about our public disturbances. Another agent has been sent to Bologna and Florence. I've done nothing but shrug my shoulders.

"But the amusing part of it is that, at my age, I had a moment of fiery enthusiasm when I spoke to the soldiers of the palace guards and tore off the epaulettes of that contemptible General P——. During that moment I would have given my life for the prince without hesitation; I admit now that it would have been a very stupid way to end. Today the prince, kind young man though he is, would give a hundred scudi to have me die of an illness. He still doesn't dare to ask me to resign, but we speak to each other as seldom as possible, and I send him little written reports, as I used to do with the late prince after Fabrizio's imprisonment. Incidentally, I haven't torn up the sentence passed against him, for the very good reason that that scoundrel Rassi hasn't given it to me. So you were quite right to prevent Fabrizio from arriving here officially. The sentence is still in effect, and, although I don't think Rassi would dare to have your nephew arrested today, it's possible that two weeks from now he will. If Fabrizio is determined to return to Parma, have him come and stay with me."

"But what's the cause of all this?" cried the duchess in amazement.

"The prince has been persuaded that I'm behaving as though I were a dictator and a savior of the fatherland, that I want to lead him like a child, and that, still worse, in speaking of him I uttered the fatal words, 'that child.' The last accusation may be true: I was greatly excited that day. For example, I saw him as a great man because he wasn't too frightened in the midst of the first shots he'd ever heard in his life. He doesn't lack intelligence, and he conducts himself even better than his father. In short, I can't repeat it too often: he's basically honest and good, but his young, sincere heart is outraged whenever he's told of some unscrupulous trick, and he feels that anyone who even notices such things must have a very dark soul—remember the upbringing he's had!"

"You should have remembered that some day he would be

in power, Your Excellency, and you should therefore have appointed some intelligent man to be with him."

"First of all, we have the example of the Abbé de Condillac, who, after being appointed by my predecessor, the Marquis Felino, did nothing but make his pupil into the world's greatest fool. He took part in religious processions, but in 1796 he didn't know how to deal with Bonaparte, who would have tripled his domains. In the second place, I never expected to be Prime Minister for ten consecutive years. Now that I'm completely disillusioned, as I have been for the past month, I plan to amass a million lire, then leave this chaotic pigsty, which I've saved, to its own devices. If it hadn't been for me, Parma would have been a republic for two months, with the poet Ferrante Palla as its dictator."

This remark made the duchess blush. The count knew nothing.

"We're about to fall back into the usual eighteenth-century form of monarchy: the confessor and the mistress. At the bottom of his heart, the prince loves only mineralogy, and perhaps you, duchess. Since he came to power, his valet, whose brother I've just made a captain after nine months of service, has filled his head with the idea that he ought to be happier than anyone else because his profile is going to appear on coins. That brilliant idea has resulted in boredom.

"Now he must have an aide-de-camp to help remedy his boredom. Well, even if he were to offer me that famous million which we need in order to live well in Naples or Paris, I wouldn't want to be the remedy for His Highness's boredom and spend four or five hours with him every day. Besides, since I'm more intelligent than he is, within a month he'd regard me as a monster.

"The late prince was spiteful and envious, but he had been in battle and in command of troops, which gave him a certain firmness and dignity. It was obvious that he had the makings of a prince, and with him I could be a minister, good or bad. With this honest, candid and truly kind son of his, I'm forced to be a schemer. I now find myself the rival of the lowest women in the palace, and an inferior rival, too, because I'm sure to disregard all sorts of necessary details. For example, three days ago one of the women who place clean towels in the apartments every morning took it into her head to lose the key to one of the prince's English desks, whereupon His Highness refused to deal with any matter whose documents were inside that desk. For twenty lire, of course, he could have had the bottom removed from the

355

desk, or had it opened with a skeleton key, but Ranuccio-Ernesto V told me that would give the court locksmith bad habits.

"So far it's been absolutely impossible for him to maintain the same resolution for three days running. If he had been born Marquis So-and-So, with an adequate fortune, that young prince would have been one of the most reputable men at court, a kind of Louis XVI; but with that pious simplicity of his, how is he going to escape all the cunning traps that surround him? And so the drawing room of your enemy the Marquise Raversi is more powerful than ever. And it's been discovered there that I, who gave the order to fire on the people and was ready to kill three thousand men if necessary to prevent the desecration of the statue of the prince who was my master, am a rabid liberal, that I wanted to draw up a constitution, and a hundred other absurdities. With all this talk of a republic, the madmen here would prevent us from enjoying the best of monarchies. In short, duchess, you are the only member of the present liberal party, whose leadership my enemies impute to me, of whom the prince has not spoken in offensive terms. The archbishop, who is still a perfectly honorable man, is in deep disgrace for having spoken sensibly of what I did on 'the unfortunate day.'

"On the morning after that day, which wasn't yet called 'unfortunate,' when it was still true that the revolt had taken place, the prince told the archbishop he was going to make me a duke so that you wouldn't have to take an inferior title when you married me. I now think it's Rassi, whom I ennobled when he sold me the late prince's secrets, who's going to be promoted: to the rank of count. If so, it will make me look like a fool."

"And the poor prince will be spattered with mud."

"No doubt; but after all, he's on the throne, a position which makes ridicule vanish within two weeks. And so, my dear duchess, let's do as one does in the game of tricktrack: let's 'clear out.' "

"But we won't be very rich."

"Neither of us has any real need of luxury. If I have a horse and a seat in a box at the San Carlo in Naples, I'll be more than satisfied. It will never be the degree of luxury in which we live that will give us a position in society: it will be the pleasure which the intelligent people of the city may find in coming to your house for a cup of tea."

"But," said the duchess, "what would have happened on

the 'unfortunate day' if you'd remained aloof, as I hope you will in the future?"

"The troops would have fraternized with the people, there would have been three days of fire and slaughter (for it will take a hundred years to make a republic anything but an absurdity here), then two weeks of looting, until two or three regiments sent by some foreign power finally came in to restore order. Ferrante Palla was in the midst of the people, courageous and fanatical as usual; he no doubt had a dozen or so friends acting in concert with him, and Rassi will turn that into a superb conspiracy. One thing is certain: dressed in incredibly shabby clothes, he was distributing gold by the handful."

Amazed by all this news, the duchess hurried off to thank the princess.

When she entered the room, the tirewoman gave her the little gold key which is worn at the waist as an emblem of supreme authority in the part of the palace belonging to the princess. Clara Paolina quickly dismissed everyone present, and, once she was alone with her friend, persisted for some time in expressing herself only half clearly. The duchess did not understand too well what all this meant, and answered with a great deal of reserve. Finally the princess burst into tears, threw herself in the duchess's arms and cried out, "My unhappiness is going to begin all over again: my son will treat me worse than his father did!"

"I won't let that happen!" the duchess replied with feeling. "But first I must beg Your Serene Highness to deign to accept here the tribute of all my gratitude and deep respect."

"What do you mean?" cried the princess anxiously, fearing a resignation.

"I mean to request, Your Serene Highness, that whenever you allow me to go over to that Chinese porcelain figure on the mantelpiece and turn its head to the right, you will also allow me to call things by their true names."

"Is that all?" cried Clara Paolina, standing up and running over to turn the figure's head herself. "Speak to me with complete freedom, my dear Chief Lady in Waiting," she said in a charming tone.

"Your Highness, you have seen the situation quite clearly," said the duchess. "You and I are both in great danger. Fabrizio's sentence has not been revoked; therefore, as soon as there's a desire in certain quarters to get rid of me and insult you, he'll be imprisoned again. Our position is as bad as ever. As for myself, I'm going to marry the count, and we'll go to live in Naples or Paris. The latest blow of ingratitude that has been dealt to him has made him thoroughly disgusted with public affairs, and if it weren't for the interests of Your Serene Highness, I would advise him not to stay in this bedlam unless the prince gave him an enormous sum of money. Allow me to explain that the count, who had a hundred and thirty thousand lire when he took office, now has an income of no more than twenty thousand. For a long time I vainly urged him to think of his own fortune. During my absence he picked a quarrel with the prince's tax-farmers, who were dishonest, then replaced them with other dishonest men who have given him eight hundred thousand lire."

"What!" cried the princess in surprise. "Good heavens, I'm so sorry to hear that!"

"Shall I turn the figure's head to the left, Your Highness?" replied the duchess with great coolness.

"Good heavens, no!" said the princess. "But I'm sorry to hear that a man of the count's character should have thought of that kind of gain."

"If he hadn't committed that theft, he'd have been despised by all respectable people."

"Oh! Is it possible?"

"Your Highness," said the duchess, "except for my friend the Marquis Crescenzi, who has an income of three or four hundred thousand lire, everyone here steals. And how could it be otherwise in a place where gratitude for the greatest services lasts less than a month, and where money is therefore the only thing that's real and capable of withstanding disgrace? I'm going to take the liberty, Your Highness, of stating some terrible truths."

"You have my permission," said the princess with a deep sigh, "even though they are painfully unpleasant to me."

"Well then, Your Highness, your son the prince, a perfectly honorable man, may cause you much greater unhappiness than his father did. The late prince had at least an average amount of character; our present sovereign is never sure of wanting the same thing for three consecutive days. And so, in order to be sure of him, one must live with him constantly and never allow him to speak to anyone else. Since this truth is not difficult to discern, the new ultra-royalist party, led by those two clever people, Rassi and the Marquise Raversi, will try to give the prince a mistress. That mistress will have permission to make her own fortune and hand out a few minor posts, but she will be responsible to the party for keeping the prince's will steady.

"For my part, in order to be firmly established in Your Highness's court, I must have Rassi banished and reviled. Furthermore, I want Fabrizio to be tried by the most honest judges that can be found. If those gentlemen acknowledge, as I hope they will, that he is innocent, it will be quite natural to gratify the archbishop by making Fabrizio his coadjutor with the right of future succession. If I fail, the count and I will leave Parma; in that case, I will give Your Serene Highness this parting advice: you must never forgive Rassi, and you must never leave your good son's dominions. As long as you are near him, he will never do you any serious harm."

"I have followed your reasoning with all due attention," said the princess, smiling. "Am I to take it upon myself to provide a mistress for my son?"

"Not at all, Your Highness; but your first concern should be to make your drawing room the only one in which he enjoys himself."

The conversation was endless in this direction; the scales were falling from the eyes of the innocent and intelligent princess.

A messenger sent by the duchess told Fabrizio that he could enter the city, but that he would have to remain in hiding. He was barely noticed: disguised as a peasant, he spent his time in the wooden hut of a chestnut vendor opposite the gate of the citadel, beneath the trees of the public promenade.

CHAPTER TWENTY-FOUR

The duchess began organizing delightful evening parties in the palace, which had never seen so much gaiety before. Never had she been more charming than she was that winter, and yet she was living in the midst of the greatest dangers; but it is also true that no more than once or twice during that critical season did she think with any sadness about the extraordinary change that had come over Fabrizio.

The young prince came very early to each one of his mother's pleasant evening parties, and she would always say to him, "Go away and tend to your governing: I'm willing to bet that there are at least twenty reports on your desk waiting for a yes or a no, and I don't want everyone in

Europe to accuse me of making you a do-nothing king in order to rule in your place."

This advice had the disadvantage of always being offered at the most inopportune moments, that is, when the prince, having overcome his timidity, was taking part in some charade that amused him greatly. Twice a week there were parties in the country to which, on the pretext of winning the affection of the people for the new sovereign, the princess invited the prettiest women of the middle class. The duchess, who was the guiding spirit of that joyous court, hoped that these fair commoners, all mortally envious of the great success of the commoner Rassi, would tell the prince about one of that minister's countless scurrilous tricks. In addition to other childish ideas, the prince had that of maintaining a *moral* ministry.

Rassi had too much sense not to realize how dangerous these sparkling evenings at the princess's court, directed by his enemy, were to him. He had refused to give Count Mosca the perfectly legal sentence that had been passed against Fabrizio; either he or the duchess would therefore have to disappear from the court.

On the day of the popular uprising whose occurrence it was now good form to deny, money had been handed out to the people. Rassi had taken this as his point of departure; dressed more shabbily than usual, he went to the most squalid houses in the city and spent whole hours in serious conversation with their poor inhabitants. He was well rewarded for his efforts: after two weeks of this kind of life, he knew with certainty that Ferrante Palla had been the secret leader of the insurrection, and furthermore, that this man, who had been poor all his life, as befitted a great poet, had had eight or ten diamonds sold for him in Genoa.

Among others, there were five valuable stones which were actually worth more than 40,000 lire, but which, *ten days before the prince's death*, had been sold for 35,000 lire, because, it had been said, of an urgent need for money.

How can we describe the rapture of the Minister of Justice when he made this discovery? He saw clearly that he was being ridiculed every day at the court of the princess dowager, and several times, while talking business with him, the prince had laughed in his face with all the candor of youth. It must be admitted that Rassi had some singularly plebeian habits: for example, as soon as a discussion began to interest him, he would cross his legs and take one shoe in his hand; if his interest increased, he would spread his red cotton handkerchief over his leg, etc., etc. The prince had laughed heartily when one of the prettiest women of the middle class, knowing, incidentally, that she had very shapely legs, had jokingly imitated this elegant mannerism of the Minister of Justice.

Rassi requested a special audience with the prince and said to him, "Would you be willing, Your Highness, to give a hundred thousand lire to learn the exact nature of your august father's death? That sum would enable the authorities of justice to arrest the guilty parties, if there are any."

There could be no doubt of the prince's reply.

Some time later, Cecchina informed the duchess that she had been offered a large sum to allow a jeweler to examine her mistress's diamonds; she had indignantly refused. The duchess reprimanded her for her refusal, and a week later Cecchina had some diamonds to show. On the day set for their examination, Count Mosca had each jeweler in Parma carefully watched by two reliable men, and at midnight he came to tell the duchess that the inquisitive jeweler was none other than Rassi's brother. She was in a very gay mood that evening; she was in the palace, taking part in a *commedia dell'arte*, that is, a play in which the actors invent the dialogue as they go along, with an outline of the plot posted in the wings. Count Baldi, former friend of the Marquise Raversi, who was in the audience, was playing the part of the duchess's aspiring lover. The prince, the shyest man in Parma, but handsome and endowed with a tender heart, had been studying Count Baldi's part and wanted to play it in the second performance.

"I have very little time," the duchess said to Count Mosca. "I'm going to appear in the first scene of the second act. Let's go into the guardroom."

There, in the midst of a score of palace guards, all wide awake and keenly attentive to the conversation between the Prime Minister and the Chief Lady in Waiting, the duchess laughed and said to her lover, "You always scold me when I tell secrets unnecessarily. It's because of me that Ernesto V is now on the throne. I wanted to avenge Fabrizio, whom I loved much more then than I do today, although always quite innocently. I know you have little belief in that innocence, but it doesn't matter, since you love me in spite of my crimes. Well, here's a real crime for you: I gave all my diamonds to a very interesting madman by the name of Ferrante Palla, and even kissed him, to make him destroy the

361

man who wanted to have Fabrizio poisoned. Was there anything wrong in that?"

"Ah, so that's where Ferrante got the money for his uprising!" said the count, taken aback. "And you tell me all this in the guardroom!"

"It's because I'm in a hurry, and Rassi is now on the trail of the crime. It's quite true that I never said anything about an insurrection, because I abhor the Jacobins. Think it over and let me know your opinion after the play."

"I'll tell you right now that you must make the prince fall in love with you. . . . But without sacrificing your honor, of course!"

The duchess was called to make her entrance on stage; she hurried away.

A few days later, she received by post a long, ridiculous letter, signed with the name of a woman who had once been her maid. This woman asked to be employed at court, but the duchess had seen at a glance that it was neither her handwriting nor her style. When she opened the sheet to read the second page, a little miraculous picture of the Madonna, folded in a printed page from an old book, fell at her feet. After glancing at the picture, she read a few lines of the printed page. Her eyes shone, for she found these words on it:

The Tribune of the People has taken a hundred lire a month, and no more. With the rest, he tried to rekindle the sacred flame in hearts that had been frozen by selfishness. The fox is on my trail, and that is why I have not tried to see my beloved one last time. I said to myself, "She does not love the republic, she who is so superior to me in intelligence as well as in grace and beauty." Besides, how is it possible to establish a republic without republicans? In six months I shall be wandering on foot, microscope in hand, through the small towns of America: I shall learn whether I still ought to love the only rival you have in my heart. If you receive this letter, baroness, and if no profane eye has read it before you, have someone break one of the young ash trees that stand twenty paces away from the spot where I dared to speak to you for the first time. I will then have someone bury, beneath the big box tree in the garden which you once noticed during the days of my happiness, a box containing the things which are causing men of my opinions to be slandered. I would certainly not have written to you if the fox were not on my trail and might not eventually reach my angel. Look under the box tree in two weeks.

"Since he has a printing press at his disposal," thought the duchess, "we'll soon have a collection of sonnets. God only knows what name he'll give me in them!"

Her coquettishness led her to make a test: she claimed to be indisposed for a week, and the court had no more pleasant evenings. The princess, shocked by all the things her fear of her son had forced her to begin doing immediately after becoming a widow, went to spend this week in a convent adjoining the church in which the late prince was buried. This interruption of the evening parties left the prince with an enormous amount of leisure on his hands, and greatly decreased the favor enjoyed by the Minister of Justice. Ernesto V became aware of all the boredom that would descend on him if the duchess left the court, or merely ceased to fill it with joy. The evening parties began again, and the prince showed more and more interest in the *commedia dell'arte.* He planned to play a part himself, but did not dare to confess this ambition. One day, blushing deeply, he said to the duchess, "Why shouldn't I act too?"

"We're all at Your Highness's orders here. If you deign to give me the order, I'll have the plot of a play drawn up in which all your outstanding scenes will be with me, and since everyone is a little unsure of himself at first, if you'll watch me with a certain amount of attention I'll tell you what answers to give." Everything was arranged, and with infinite skill. The extremely shy prince was ashamed of being shy; the duchess's careful efforts to avoid making him suffer from this innate shyness made a deep impression on him.

On the night of his first appearance, the performance began half an hour earlier than usual. When the assembled company went into the theater from the drawing room it consisted only of nine or ten elderly women. These spectators did not overawe the prince, and besides, having been brought up in Munich on true monarchical principles, they always applauded. Using her authority as Chief Lady in Waiting, the duchess locked the door through which the common run of courtiers entered the theater. The prince, who had a literary mind and a handsome face, did quite well for himself in the first scenes; he intelligently repeated the lines which he read in the duchess's eyes, or which she indicated to him in an undertone. At a time when the few spectators were applauding with all their might, the duchess made a signal, the door of honor was opened, and the theater was quickly filled with all the pretty women of the court. Seeing that the prince was smiling graciously and appeared to be very happy, they all began to applaud; he blushed with happiness. He was playing the part of a man in love with the duchess. Far from having to suggest lines to him, she was soon obliged to urge him to shorten the scenes. He spoke of love with an enthusiasm that often embarrassed her, and his speeches went on for five minutes at a time.

The duchess was no longer the dazzling beauty she had been the year before: Fabrizio's imprisonment, and, still more, her stay on the shore of Lake Maggiore with him when he had grown morose and silent, had added ten years to the fair Gina's age. Her features had become accentuated; they showed more intelligence and less youthfulness. Except on rare occasions, they no longer had the sprightliness of youth; but on the stage, with the help of rouge and all the other aids which art supplies to actresses, she was still the prettiest woman at court. The prince's impassioned speeches put the courtiers on the alert; they all said to themselves that evening, "There's the Marquise Balbi of this new reign." The count was inwardly indignant.

When the play was over, the duchess said to the prince in front of the whole court, "You're too good an actor, Your Highness: everyone will say you're in love with a woman of thirty-eight, and that will prevent me from marrying the count. I won't perform with you again, Your Highness, unless you promise to speak to me as you would speak to a middle-aged woman, to the Marquise Raversi, for example."

The same play was repeated three times; the prince was wildly happy. But one evening he looked extremely worried. "Unless I'm mistaken," the duchess said to the princess, "Rassi is trying to play some trick on us. I would advise Your Highness to suggest a performance for tomorrow; the prince will act his part badly, and, in his despair, he'll tell you something."

The prince did indeed act his part very badly: the audience could scarcely hear him, and he no longer knew how to end his sentences. By the end of the first act he was nearly in tears. The duchess stood beside him, but she was cold and motionless. When he found himself alone with her for a moment in the backstage waiting room, he closed the door and said to her, "I'll never be able to get through the second and third acts. I absolutely refuse to go on being applauded out of politeness; the applause they've given me so far has cut me to the heart. Give me your advice: what should I do?"

"I'll go back on the stage, bow deeply to Her Highness, then to the audience, like a real theatrical manager, and announce that, since the actor who was playing the part of Lelio has suddenly become indisposed, the performance will be brought to a close with a few pieces of music. Count Rusca and young Ghisolfi will be delighted to show off their shrill, thin voices before such a distinguished gathering."

The prince took the duchess's hand and kissed it with rapture.

"If only you were a man!" he said to her. "You could give me some advice: Rassi has just placed on my desk a hundred and eighty-one depositions against the alleged murderers of my father. Besides the depositions, there's also a formal indictment over two hundred pages long. I have to read all that, and furthermore I've given my word to say nothing about it to the count. This is leading straight to some executions; already he wants me to have Ferrante Palla, that great poet whom I admire so much, abducted in France, near Antibes, where he's living under the name of Poncet."

"On the day when you have a liberal hanged, Rassi will be bound to the ministry by iron chains, and that's what he wants above all; but also, Your Highness, you will no longer be able to announce two hours in advance that you're going to leave the palace. I'll say nothing to the princess or the count about the cry of distress that has just escaped from you; but since, according to my oath, I must keep nothing secret from the princess, I would be glad if you would tell her the same things that you have just let slip while talking to me."

This idea diverted the sovereign's attention from his intense anguish over his failure as an actor.

"Very well, go and notify my mother. I'll see her in her main parlor."

The prince left the wings, walked through the drawing room adjacent to the theater, and sternly dismissed the chamberlain and the aide-de-camp who were following him. The princess hurriedly left the theater; when she reached the parlor, the duchess bowed deeply to her and her son and left them alone together. One may easily imagine the courtiers' agitation; it is such things which make court life so amusing. An hour later, the prince himself came to the door of the parlor and called in the duchess. The princess was in tears; her son's face was discomposed.

"Here," thought the duchess, "are two weak people in a

bad temper and looking for a pretext to become angry at someone." They both began talking at once to give her the details. She was very careful to answer in such a way as to put forward no ideas whatever. For two deadly hours the three actors in this tedious scene did not once step out of the roles we have indicated. The prince himself went to get the two enormous portfolios that Rassi had placed on his desk. When he walked out of his mother's parlor he found the entire court waiting for him. "Go away, leave me alone!" he shouted in an extremely impolite tone which they had never heard him use before. He did not want to be seen carrying the two portfolios himself: a prince must never carry anything. The courtiers vanished in the twinkling of an eye. When he came back, he saw no one except some footmen who were snuffing out the candles. He furiously ordered them to leave, then repeated the same order to poor Fontana, the aide-de-camp on duty that evening, who, in his zeal, had made the foolish mistake of staying behind.

"Everyone is doing his best to exasperate me tonight," he said irritably to the duchess when he returned to the parlor; he had a high regard for her intelligence, and he was furious with her for not having offered an opinion. As for her, she was determined to say nothing until she was asked for her opinion *quite explicitly*. At least another half-hour went by before the prince, who had a sense of his own dignity, finally made up his mind to say to her, "But you still haven't said anything, duchess."

"I'm here to serve the princess, and to forget very quickly what is said in front of me."

"Very well, then, duchess," said the prince, his face turning red, "I order you to give me your opinion."

"Crimes are punished in order to prevent their recurrence. Was the late prince poisoned? That's very doubtful. Was he poisoned by the Jacobins? That's what Rassi would very much like to prove, because he would then become a necessary instrument to Your Highness forever. In that case, Your Highness, whose reign is only beginning, can expect to spend a great many more evenings like this one. Most of your subjects say, and it's quite true, that you have a kindly disposition. As long as you haven't had some liberal hanged, you'll enjoy that reputation, and certainly no one will ever think of trying to poison you."

"Your conclusion is obvious!" cried the princess angrily. "You don't want my husband's murderers to be punished!"

"Then it must be because I'm bound to them by ties of tender friendship!"

The duchess saw in the prince's eyes that he believed her to be in league with his mother to dictate a line of conduct to him. The two women exchanged a quick succession of bitter retorts, after which the duchess protested that she would not say another word, and she was faithful to her resolution; but after a long discussion with his mother, the prince again ordered her to give her opinion.

"I swear to Your Highness that I will not!"

"Why, you're acting like a child!" exclaimed the prince.

"I beg you to speak, duchess," said the princess with an air of dignity.

"And I implore you to excuse me from doing so," replied the duchess. "But," she went on, addressing the prince, "you read French perfectly, Your Highness: to calm our agitated minds, would you read us one of La Fontaine's fables?"

The princess found the word "us" extremely insolent, but she looked both astonished and amused when her Chief Lady in Waiting, who had with great composure gone over to open the bookcase, came back with a volume of La Fontaine's *Fables*. She turned through the pages for a few moments, then handed it to the prince and said, "I beg Your Highness to read *all* of the fable."

Le Jardinier et son Seigneur

Un amateur de jardinage
Demi-bourgeois, demi-manant,
Possédait en certain village
Un jardin assez propre, et le clos attenant.
Il avait de plant vif fermé cette étendue:
Là croissaient à plaisir l'oseille et la laitue,
De quoi faire à Margot pour sa fête un bouquet,
Peu de jasmin d'Espagne et force serpolet.
Cette félicité par un lièvre troublée
Fit qu'au seigneur du bourg notre homme se plaignit.
Ce maudit animal vient prendre sa goulée
Soir et matin, dit-il, et des pièges se rit;
Les pierres, les bâtons y perdent leur crédit:
Il est sorcier, je crois.—Sorcier! je l'en défie,
Repartit le seigneur: fût-il diable, Miraut,
En dépit de ses tours, l'attrapera bientôt.
Je vous en défairai, bonhomme, sur ma vie.
—Et quand?—Et dès demain, sans tarder plus longtemps.

La partie ainsi faite, il vient avec ses gens.
—Çà, déjeunons, dit-il: vos poulets sont-ils tendres?
L'embarras des chasseurs succède au déjeuner.
Chacun s'anime et se prépare;
Les trompes et les cors font un tel tintamarre
Que le bonhomme est étonné.
Le pis fut que l'on mit en piteux équipage
Le pauvre potager. Adieu planches, carreaux;
Adieu chocorée et poireaux;
Adieu de quoi mettre au potage.
Le bonhomme disait: Ce sont là jeux de prince.
Mais on le laissait dire; et les chiens et les gens
Firent plus de dégats en une heure de temps
Que n'en auraient fait en cent ans
Tous les lièvres de la province.

Petits princes, videz vos débats entre vous;
De recourir aux rois vous seriez de grands fous.
Il ne les faut jamais engager dans vos guerres,
Ni les faire entrer sur vos terres.*

* A lover of gardening, half bourgeois, half peasant, owned, in a certain village, a well-kept garden and the field beside it. He had enclosed this land with a quickset hedge; there sorrel and lettuce grew in abundance, and, to make a bouquet for Margot on her name-day, a little Spanish jasmine and a great deal of wild thyme. When this felicity was troubled by a hare, our man went to complain to the lord of the town. "That cursed animal comes morning and evening to take a big mouthful," he said, "and he laughs at traps; sticks and stones are useless against him: I believe he is a wizard."—"A wizard! I defy him," replied the lord. "Even if he were a devil, my dog would soon catch him in spite of all his tricks. I'll rid you of him, my good man, I swear it on my life."—"When?"—"Tomorrow, without further delay." Having made this engagement, he arrived with his men. "Now then, let's have lunch," he said. "Are your chickens tender?" After lunch, the hunters began making preparations in boisterous confusion: the trumpets and horns made such an uproar that our man was stunned. And the worst of it was that the poor garden was reduced to a pitiful state. Farewell to plots and flower beds, farewell to chicory and leeks, farewell to all the things that make a soup. Our man said, "Such is the sport of princes," but no one heeded him; and the dogs and men did more damage in an hour than all the hares in the province would have done in a hundred years.

Princelings, settle your quarrels among yourselves; you would be fools to have recourse to kings. You must never involve them in your wars, or bring them into your dominions.

The reading of this fable was followed by a long silence. The prince paced the floor for a time after going over to the bookcase and putting the volume back in place.

"Well, duchess," said the princess, "will you deign to speak?"

"Certainly not—not unless His Highness makes me a minister. If I spoke here, I'd run the risk of losing my position as Chief Lady in Waiting."

There was another silence of at least a quarter of an hour. Finally the princess began thinking of the part played by Marie de Médicis, mother of Louis XIII (for several days the Chief Lady in Waiting had been having M. Bazin's excellent *History of Louis XIII* read aloud to his mistress). Though greatly annoyed, she reflected that the duchess might very well leave Parma, and that Rassi, of whom she was terribly afraid, might then imitate Richelieu and have her exiled by her son. At that moment, she would have given anything in the world to humiliate her Chief Lady in Waiting, but she could not. She stood up, went over to her with a somewhat exaggerated smile, took her hand and said, "Come, duchess, prove your friendship for me by speaking."

"Very well, a few words, but no more: Take all the papers assembled by that viper Rassi, burn them in the fireplace here, and never admit to him that they've been burned." She leaned close to the princess's ear and whispered in a familiar tone, "Rassi may be a Richelieu!"

"But those papers have cost me over eighty thousand lire, damn it!" cried the prince angrily.

"Prince," replied the duchess forcefully, "that's what it costs to employ lowborn scoundrels. Would to God that you might lose a million, and never give any credence to the vile rogues who kept your father from sleeping during the last six years of his reign!"

The word "lowborn" had greatly pleased the princess, who felt that the count and his mistress had too exclusive a regard for intelligence, which is always somewhat akin to Jacobinism.

During a short moment of profound silence, filled by the princess's reflections, the palace clock struck three. She stood up, bowed deeply to her son and said, "My health won't permit me to continue this discussion any longer. You ought never to have a *lowborn* minister; you'll never convince me that your Rassi hasn't stolen half the money he's made you spend on spying." She took two candles from the candlesticks and placed them in the fireplace in such a way as to keep them burning; then, coming back to her son, she said, "In my mind, La Fontaine's fable overrides my just desire to avenge my husband's death. Will Your Highness permit me to burn these documents?"

The prince remained motionless.

"He really has a stupid face," thought the duchess. "The count is right: the late prince wouldn't have kept us up till three o'clock in the morning before making up his mind."

Still standing, the princess continued: "That little lawyer would be very proud if he knew that his papers, filled with lies and arrange to serve his own advancement, had made the two greatest personages in Parma stay up all night."

The prince snatched up one of the portfolios like a madman and emptied all its contents into the fireplace. The mass of papers nearly smothered the two candles: the room became filled with smoke. Then the princess saw in her son's eyes that he was tempted to pick up a decanter and save those papers which had cost him eighty thousand lire.

"Open the window!" she cried angrily to the duchess, who hastened to obey. The papers all burst into flames at once; there was a great roar in the chimney and it was soon obvious that it had caught fire.

The prince had a petty soul with regard to anything involving money; he could already see his whole palace burning, and all the treasures in it destroyed. He ran over to the window and called the guards in a voice that had changed radically. When the soldiers had rushed wildly into the courtyard in response to his call, he returned to the fireplace, which was drawing air from the open window with a truly frightening noise. He became impatient, swore, walked around the room two or three times like a man completely beside himself, then finally ran out.

The princess and the duchess remained standing opposite each other and maintained a profound silence.

"Is there going to be more anger now?" wondered the duchess. "Well, I've already won my case." And she was preparing to be extremely impertinent in her replies when another thought flashed into her mind: she saw the second portfolio still intact. "No, my case is only half won!"

She said to the princess, rather coldly, "Does Your Highness order me to burn the rest of these papers?"

"And where will you burn them?" said the princess irritably.

"In the drawing room fireplace; if I throw them in one by one, there won't be any danger."

The duchess put the portfolio, bulging with papers, under

her arm, took a candle and went into the adjoining drawing room. She took time to make sure that this portfolio was the one containing the despositions, put five or six bundles of papers in her shawl, carefully burned the rest, then slipped away without taking leave of the princess.

"This is a fine piece of impertinence!" she said to herself, laughing. "But, with her affectations of being an inconsolable widow, she nearly made me lose my head on a scaffold."

When she heard the sound of the duchess's carriage, the princess was carried away with rage against her.

Despite the lateness of the hour, the duchess sent for the count; he had gone to the fire in the palace, but he soon appeared with the news that it was all over. "That little prince really showed a great deal of courage," he said, "and I complimented him on it effusively."

"Examine these depositions quickly, then let's burn them without delay."

The count read them and turned pale.

"They've come very near to the truth!" he exclaimed. "The investigation has been carried out with great skill. They're hot on the trail of Ferrante Palla, and we'll be in a tight spot if he confesses."

"But he won't!" cried the duchess. "He's a man of honor. Let's burn the papers!"

"Not yet. Allow me to write down the names of twelve or fifteen dangerous witnesses: I'll take the liberty of having them abducted if Rassi ever decides to try again."

"Let me remind Your Excellency that the prince has given his word not to say anything to his Minister of Justice about our nocturnal expedition."

"And he'll keep it, out of cowardice and fear of a scene."

"Now, my friend, this is a night which has greatly hastened our marriage; I wouldn't have wanted to bring you a criminal trial as my dowry, especially since it would have been for a crime that I was led to commit by my interest in another man."

The count was in love; he took her hand and cried out in protest with tears in his eyes.

"Before you go, give me some advice as to how I ought to behave with the princess. I'm utterly exhausted: I acted a part in the theater for an hour, then in her parlor for five hours."

"The insolence of your exit was enough vengeance for her harsh remarks, which were nothing but weakness. Adopt the same tone with her tomorrow as you did this morning; Rassi

371

is not yet in prison or in exile, and we haven't yet torn up Fabrizio's sentence.

"You were asking the princess to make a decision: that's always irritating to princesses, princes, and even Prime Ministers. After all, you're her Chief Lady in Waiting, in other words, her humble servant. By a reversal of feeling that's inevitable in people of weak character, three days from now Rassi will be in greater favor than ever. He'll try to have someone hanged: as long as he hasn't compromised the prince, he can't be sure of anything.

"A man was injured in the fire tonight, a tailor who showed really remarkable courage. Tomorrow I'm going to persuade the prince to pay a visit to that tailor. I'll be armed to the teeth and I'll keep a sharp lookout, although so far our young prince isn't hated. I want to accustom him to going out in the streets: it's a trick I'm going to play on Rassi, who will surely succeed me, and won't be able to permit such reckless actions. On the way back from our visit to the tailor, I'll take the prince past the statue of his father. He'll notice that stones have broken the Roman-style petticoat which the idiotic sculptor carved on it, and he'll have to be quite dull-witted not to make this remark without any prompting from me: 'That's what one gains from having Jacobins hanged,' to which I'll answer, 'You must hang either ten thousand or none at all; the massacre of Saint Bartholomew's Day destroyed the Protestants in France.'

"Tomorrow, my dear, before I go out with the prince, come to see him and say to him, 'Last night I performed the duties of a minister for you: I gave you advice, and in obeying your orders I incurred the princess's displeasure. You must pay me.' He'll expect a request for money and begin frowning. Leave him with that unpleasant idea as long as possible, then say to him, 'I beg Your Highness to order that Fabrizio be tried with a full hearing'—that means he must be present in person—'by the twelve most highly respected judges in Parma.' Then, without a moment's delay, give him a short decree and ask him to sign it. It will be written by your own lovely hand, but I'm going to dictate it to you. It will, of course, include a clause stating that the original sentence is annulled.

"There's one objection to that, although it probably won't occur to the prince if you keep things moving at a rapid pace. He may say to you, 'Fabrizio must allow himself to be imprisoned in the citadel.' If so, you'll answer, 'He'll allow himself to be confined in the city jail.' As you know, the city jail is completely under my control, so Fabrizio will be able to come and visit you every evening. If the prince says, 'No, his escape has stained the honor of my citadel, so, for the sake of form, I want him to go back to the same cell,' then you'll answer, 'No, because there he would be at the mercy of my enemy Rassi,' and, with one of those subtle feminine remarks of yours, you'll give him to understand that, in order to make Rassi relent, you might tell him about tonight's *auto-da-fé*. If he still insists, you'll announce that you're going to spend two weeks in your house at Sacca.

"You will send for Fabrizio and consult with him about this maneuver, which may lead him into prison. To anticipate every possibility, let me add that he'll be in danger during his imprisonment if Rassi should lose patience and have me poisoned. But that's quite unlikely; as you know, I've imported a French cook who's the gayest of men and likes to make puns, and puns are incompatible with murder. I've already told our friend Fabrizio that I've found all the witnesses to his noble and courageous act; it's clear that Giletti tried to murder him. I haven't told you about those witnesses till now because I wanted to give you a surprise, but that plan failed: the prince refused to sign. I've told our friend Fabrizio that I'd have him placed in a high ecclesiastical position, but that will be very hard for me to do if his enemies can point to an accusation of murder before the papal court.

"Do you realize, duchess, that if he isn't tried in the most solemn manner, the name of Giletti will be unpleasant to him for the rest of his life? Only a cowardly man would avoid a trial when he's sure of his innocence. Besides, even if Fabrizio were guilty, I'd have him acquitted. When I spoke to him, the young hothead wouldn't let me finish: he took the official directory and we picked out the most upright and learned judges; then, when we'd drawn up the list, we crossed off six names, intending to replace them with the names of six judges who were personal enemies of mine, but since we were able to find only two enemies, we filled out the list with the names of four scoundrels devoted to Rassi."

The duchess was greatly alarmed by the count's proposal, and not without cause, but she finally listened to reason and wrote out, at his dictation, the decree appointing the judges.

The count did not leave her until six o'clock in the morning. She tried to sleep, but in vain. At nine o'clock she had breakfast with Fabrizio, whom she found eager to stand trial; at ten o'clock she went to call on the princess and was told that Her Highness was not yet receiving any visitors; at eleven o'clock she saw the prince, who was holding his morning levee. He signed the decree without the slightest objection. She sent it to the count and went to bed.

It might be amusing to describe Rassi's fury when the count obliged him to countersign, in the prince's presence, the decree which His Highness had signed that morning; but events are pressing us to move on.

The count discussed the merit of each judge and offered to change the names. But the reader is perhaps a little tired of all these details of legal procedure and all these court intrigues. From all this we may draw the moral that any man who approaches a court jeopardizes his happiness, if he is happy, and, in any case, makes his future depend on the intrigues of a chambermaid.

On the other hand, in America, which is a republic, one must accept the endless boredom of currying favor with shopkeepers, and become as stupid as they are; and in America there is no opera.

When she got up that evening, the duchess was seized with keen anxiety: Fabrizio was nowhere to be found. Finally, toward midnight, she received a letter from him. Instead of surrendering himself to the city jail, where the count was in control, he had gone back to his old cell in the citadel, overjoyed to be living within a few feet of Clelia.

This was an act of enormous consequence: in the citadel, he was in greater danger of poison than ever. His folly drove the duchess to despair; she forgave the cause of it, his mad love for Clelia, because in a few days she was assuredly going to marry the rich Marquis Crescenzi, but it nevertheless restored all his former domination of her heart.

"That cursed paper I made the prince sign will be the cause of Fabrizio's death!" she thought. "Men are such fools, with their ideas of honor! As though one had to give any thought to honor under an absolute government, in a state where a man like Rassi is Minister of Justice! We should simply have accepted the pardon which the prince would have signed as readily as he signed the decree convening that special tribunal. After all, what does it matter if a man of Fabrizio's birth is more or less accused of killing an actor like Giletti with his sword?"

As soon as she received Fabrizio's letter, she hurried off to see the count, whom she found deathly pale.

"Good God, my dear, I'm unlucky in everything I try to do for that poor boy, and you're going to hold this against

374

me too! I can prove to you that I sent for the keeper of the city jail last night; your nephew would have been able to come to your house for tea. The terrible part of it is that neither you nor I can tell the prince that we're afraid of poison, and poison administered by Rassi: that suspicion would seem to him the height of immorality. However, if you demand it, I'm ready to go to see him in the palace; but I'm certain of what his answer will be. I'll say more: I offer you a means that I wouldn't use for myself. Since I've been in office here, I haven't had one single man put to death, and, as you know, I'm so foolish in that respect that sometimes, at nightfall, I still think of those two spies I rather casually ordered to be shot in Spain. Tell me, do you want me to get rid of Rassi for you? The danger in which he's placing Fabrizio is boundless; it gives him a sure way of making me get out of Parma."

This proposal pleased the duchess enormously, but she did not accept it.

"In our retirement beneath the beautiful sky of Naples," she said to the count, "I don't want you to have gloomy thoughts at night."

"But my dear, it seems to me that we have nothing but gloomy thoughts to choose from. What will become of you, or of me, for that matter, if Fabrizio dies of 'illness'?"

This idea gave new vigor to the discussion. The duchess finally ended it with these words: "Rassi owes his life to the fact that I love you more than I love Fabrizio; no, I don't want to poison every evening of the old age we're going to spend together."

She hurried to the fortress; General Fabio Conti was delighted to have to confront her with the strict terms of military law: "No one may enter a state prison without an order signed by the prince."

"But don't the Marquis Crescenzi and his musicians come to the citadel every day?"

"That's because I obtained an order from the prince for them."

The poor duchess did not know the full extent of her misfortune. General Fabio Conti had considered himself personally dishonored by Fabrizio's escape. When he saw him arrive at the citadel, he ought not to have admitted him, for he had received no order to that effect. "But," he had thought, "since heaven has sent him to me to restore my honor and save me from the ridicule that would have blighted my military career, I mustn't miss the opportunity. He'll no doubt be acquitted, so I have only a few days in which to take my vengeance."

CHAPTER TWENTY-FIVE

Our hero's arrival filled Clelia with despair: the poor girl, pious and honest with herself, could not escape the realization that there would never be any happiness for her apart from Fabrizio. But when her father had been nearly poisoned, she had vowed to the Madonna that she would offer him the sacrifice of marrying the Marquis Crescenzi. She had also vowed never to see Fabrizio again, and she was already in the grip of the most terrible remorse over the confession she had been driven to make in the letter she had written to him on the eve of his escape. How can we describe what took place in that forlorn heart when, as she was sadly watching her birds flutter about, occasionally raising her eyes from habit, and with tender emotion, to the window from which Fabrizio used to look at her, she suddenly saw him there again, greeting her with loving respect?

At first she thought that heaven had sent a vision to punish her, then her reason grasped the horrible truth. "They've recaptured him," she said to herself, "and he's lost!" She recalled the things that had been said in the fortress after his escape; the lowest jailers had considered themselves mortally insulted. She looked at Fabrizio, and, despite her efforts, her gaze fully revealed the passion that was driving her to despair.

"Do you believe," she seemed to be saying to him, "that I'll find happiness in the sumptuous palace that's being prepared for me? My father has told me over and over again that you're as poor as we are, but dear God, how gladly I'd share your poverty! But alas, we must never see each other again!"

Clelia did not have the strength to make use of her alphabets; as she looked at Fabrizio she began to feel faint and sank into a chair beside the window. Her head came to rest on the sill, and since she wanted to see him until the last moment, her face was turned toward him. He could see all her features clearly. When she opened her eyes a short time later, her first glance was at him. She saw tears in his eyes, but they were tears of extreme happiness: he had seen that absence had not made her forget him. For a time the poor young people remained as though spellbound by the sight of each other. Fabrizio dared to sing, as though accompanying himself on the guitar, a few improvised words which told her, "It was in order to see you again that I returned to prison. I'm going to be tried."

These words seemed to reawaken all of Clelia's virtue: she quickly stood up, hid her eyes and, by animated gestures, tried to convey to him that she must never see him again; she had promised this to the Madonna, and had looked at him only inadvertently. He dared once again to express his love. She fled in indignation, swearing to herself that she would never see him again, for such were the precise terms of her vow to the Madonna: *My eyes shall never see him again.* She had written it on a little piece of paper which her uncle, Don Cesare, had allowed her to burn on the altar during the offeratory, while he was saying Mass.

But, despite her vows, Fabrizio's presence in the Farnese Tower made her resume all her former ways. She had been spending most of her days alone in her room; now, as soon as she had recovered from the unexpected agitation into which the sight of Fabrizio had thrown her, she began moving all over the governor's residence, renewing acquaintance, so to speak, with all her friends in subordinate positions. A garrulous old woman who worked in the kitchen said to her mysteriously, "This time Signor Fabrizio won't get out of the citadel."

"He won't make the mistake of climbing down the walls again," said Clelia, "but he'll go out through the gate, if he's acquitted."

"I know what I'm talking about, and I'm telling you he'll leave this citadel feet first, and no other way."

Clelia turned extremely pale; the old woman noticed it and cut short her eloquence. She told herself it had been foolish of her to speak that way to the governor's daughter, whose duty would be to tell everyone that Fabrizio had died of illness. On her way up to her room, Clelia met the prison doctor, a timid but honest man, who told her with an air of great alarm that Fabrizio was seriously ill. She was scarcely able to stay on her feet. She looked everywhere for her uncle, good Don Cesare, and finally found him in the chapel, where he was praying fervently with a look of great distress on his face. The dinner bell rang. At table, the two brothers said nothing to each other until the end of the meal, when the general addressed a few extremely harsh words to his brother. The latter looked at the servants, who left the room.

"General," said Don Cesare to the governor, "I have the honor to inform you that I am leaving the citadel: I am going to hand in my resignation."

"Bravo! Bravissimo! To cast suspicion on me! . . . And would you please tell me your reason?"

"My conscience."

"Come, come! You're only an insignificant priest: you know nothing about honor!"

"Fabrizio is dead," thought Clelia. "They've poisoned him at dinner, or they'll do it tomorrow." She ran up to the aviary, resolved to sing a message to Fabrizio, accompanying herself on the piano. "I'll go to confession tomorrow," she told herself, "and I'll be forgiven for breaking my vow in order to save a man's life."

Imagine her consternation when, on reaching the aviary, she saw that the shutters on Fabrizio's windows had been replaced with planks attached to the iron bars! She frantically tried to warn him with a few words shouted rather than sung. There was no answer of any kind; the silence of death was already reigning in the Farnese Tower. "It's all over," she thought. She went downstairs, utterly distraught, then came back to take some small diamond earrings and what little money she had. She also took, in passing, the bread left over from dinner, which had been put away in a sideboard. "If he's still alive," she told herself, "it's my duty to save him."

She walked proudly toward the little door of the tower; it was open, but eight soldiers had just been posted in the pillared room on the first floor. She looked at them boldly. She intended to speak to the sergeant in command of them, but he was absent. She rushed up the little iron staircase that wound around one of the pillars. The soldiers looked at her in bewilderment, but, probably because of her lace shawl and her hat, they did not dare to say anything to her. There was no one on the second floor, but when she reached the third, at the entrance to the corridor which, as the reader may recall, was closed by three doors made of iron bars and led to Fabrizio's cell, she found a jailer whom she did not know. "He hasn't had dinner yet," he said to her with a frightened look on his face.

"I know that very well," she replied haughtily. He did not dare to stop her. Twenty paces further on, she found an old jailer with a very red face sitting on the first of the six wooden steps that led to Fabrizio's cell.

"Signorina," he said to her firmly, "do you have an order from the governor?"

"Don't you know who I am?"

Clelia was no longer her normal self, she was animated by a supernatural force. "I'm going to save my husband," she thought.

While the old jailer was protesting—"But my duty doesn't allow me. . ."—she ran up the six steps and threw herself against the door. There was an enormous key in the lock; it took all her strength to turn it. Just then the old jailer, half drunk, clutched the hem of her dress. She quickly slipped into the cell and shut the door, tearing her dress; then, since the jailer was pushing against the door, trying to come in after her, she secured it with a bolt that happened to be beneath her hand. She looked around the cell and saw Fabrizio sitting in front of a very small table on which his dinner had been placed. She ran to it, overturned it, seized Fabrizio's arm and said, "Have you eaten?"

He was enraptured by her intimate tone. In her agitation, she had forgotten her feminine reserve for the first time, and was now letting her love appear.

He had been about to begin that fatal meal; he took her in his arms and covered her with kisses. "My dinner was poisoned," he thought. "If I tell her I haven't touched it, religion will reassert its rights and she'll go away. But if she regards me as a dying man, I'll be able to make her stay with me. She wants to find a way of breaking off her hateful marriage, and chance has just offered us one: the jailers will gather outside the door and eventually break it open, then there will be such a scandal that the Marquis Crescenzi may be frightened into breaking off the marriage."

During the moment of silence occupied by these reflections, Fabrizio felt that Clelia was already trying to free herself from his embrace.

"I don't feel any pain yet," he said to her, "but soon it will overwhelm me and lay me at your feet; help me to die."

"Oh, my only friend, I'll die with you!" she said, and she clasped him in her arms, as though in a convulsive movement.

She was so beautiful, half dressed and in that state of extreme passion, that Fabrizio could not restrain an impulse that was almost beyond his will. He met with no resistance.

In that fervor of passion and generous emotion which follows extreme happiness, he thoughtlessly said to her, "The first moments of our happiness must not be sullied by a base lie: if it hadn't been for your courage, I'd now be either dead already or still writhing in horrible pain, but the fact is that

379

I was just about to begin my dinner when you came in; I haven't eaten any of it."

He elaborated on these horrible ideas in order to ward off the indignation he could already see in her eyes. She looked at him for a time, torn between two violent and contradictory feelings, then threw herself in his arms. They heard a loud noise in the corridor: the three iron doors were violently opened and closed, and voices were shouting.

"Oh, if only I had my weapons!" cried Fabrizio. "They made me hand them over before they'd let me in. They're no doubt coming to finish me off now! Good-by, my Clelia, I bless my death because it has been the cause of my happiness." Clelia kissed him and gave him a little dagger with an ivory handle and a blade not much longer than that of a pen-knife.

"Don't let them kill you," she said to him; "defend yourself to the last moment! My uncle is a man of courage and virtue: if he hears the noise, he'll save you. I'm going to talk to them." So saying, she ran to the door. "If you're not killed," she said with intense emotion, holding the bolt of the door and turning her head toward him, "let yourself die of hunger rather than touch any food that's given to you. Carry this bread with you at all times."

The noise was drawing nearer. Fabrizio seized her with both hands, pushed her away from the door, threw it open and rushed down the six wooden steps. He was still holding the little ivory-handled dagger, and he nearly thrust it into the vest of General Fontana, the prince's aide-de-camp, who hurriedly stepped back and cried out in alarm, "But I've come to save you, Signor del Dongo!"

Fabrizio went back up the six steps, called into the cell, "Fontana has come to save me," then returned to the general and calmly explained his conduct to him. He begged him at great length to forgive him for his first impulse of anger. "They were trying to poison me; the dinner that's now in my cell is poisoned. I had sense enough not to touch it, but I confess that I was outraged. When I heard you approaching, I thought they were coming to finish me off with daggers. . . . General, I demand that you give orders that no one is to enter my cell: the poison would be removed, and our good prince must know everything."

The general, extremely pale and thoroughly disconcerted, transmitted the orders indicated by Fabrizio to the picked group of jailers who were with him. These men, shamefaced at learning that the poison had been discovered, quickly went back downstairs; they hurried on ahead of the prince's aide-de-camp, ostensibly to leave the way clear for him on the narrow staircase, but actually in order to flee and disappear. To General Fontana's great surprise, Fabrizio lingered for a good quarter of an hour on the little iron staircase that wound around a pillar on the first floor: he wanted to give Clelia time to hide on the second floor.

It was the duchess who, after several wild attempts, had managed to have General Fontana sent to the citadel; she had succeeded only by chance. On leaving Count Mosca, who was as greatly alarmed as herself, she had hurried to the palace. The princess, who had a strong aversion to energetic action, which seemed vulgar to her, thought she had gone mad, and did not seem at all willing to take any unusual steps to help her. The duchess, beside herself with anxiety, wept bitterly and could only keep repeating, "But Your Highness, in a quarter of an hour Fabrizio will have died of poison!"

On seeing the princess's perfect composure, the duchess became mad with grief. She did not make this moral reflection, which would not have escaped a woman brought up in one of those northern religions which allow private judgment: "I was the first to use poison, so I shall perish by poison." In Italy, reflections of this kind in moments of passion seem boorish and inane, as a pun would seem in Paris under similar circumstances.

The duchess, in despair, ventured to go to the drawing room where she knew she would find the Marquis Crescenzi, who was in attendance that day. On her return to Parma, he had thanked her effusively for the post of Knight of Honor, to which, if it had not been for her, he could never have aspired. Protestations of unbounded devotion had not been lacking on his part. The duchess approached him with these words: "Fabrizio is now in the citadel, and Rassi is about to have him poisoned. I'm going to give you some chocolate and a bottle of water: put them in your pocket, go to the citadel and save my life by telling General Fabio Conti that you will break off your forthcoming marriage to his daughter if he doesn't allow you to give that water and chocolate to Fabrizio in person."

The marquis turned pale, and his face, far from being animated by these words, revealed the most fatuous embarrassment. He could not believe in the possibility of so frightful a crime in so moral a city as Parma, which was ruled by such a great prince, etc., etc. Furthermore, he uttered these platitudes very slowly. In short, the duchess found him to be a decent man, but extremely weak and unable to make up his mind to act. After a score of similar remarks, interrupted by her cries of impatience, he hit upon an excellent idea: the oath he had taken on becoming a Knight of Honor forbade him to become involved in any schemes against the government.

Who can imagine the duchess's anxiety and despair in her intense awareness that time was flying?

"But at least go to see the governor, tell him that I'll pursue Fabrizio's murderers as far as the depths of hell!"

Her desperation augmented her natural eloquence, but all this fiery emotion only frightened the marquis still more and redoubled his irresolution; at the end of an hour, he was even less disposed to act than he had been at the beginning.

The heartsick duchess, having reached the uttermost limits of despair, and knowing that the governor would certainly refuse nothing to such a rich prospective son-in-law, went so far as to throw herself at his feet. His cowardice now seemed to increase still more; her extraordinary act made him fear that he himself might be compromised without knowing it. But then an odd thing happened: the marquis, a good man at heart, was touched by the sight of such a beautiful woman, and especially a woman of such great power, weeping on her knees before him.

"I myself, so noble and so rich," he thought, "may some day be kneeling at the feet of some republican!" Tears came into his eyes, and it was finally agreed that the duchess, in her capacity as Chief Lady in Waiting, would take him to the princess and request permission for him to give Fabrizio a little basket whose contents he would claim not to know.

On the previous evening, before the duchess had learned of Fabrizio's mad decision to enter the citadel, a *commedia dell'arte* had been performed at court, and the prince, who always reserved the role of the duchess's lover for himself, had been so passionate in speaking to her of his love that he would have been ridiculous if, in Italy, a passionate man or a prince could ever be ridiculous!

The prince, very shy but always extremely serious about matters of love, met the duchess in one of the halls of the palace as she was taking the deeply perturbed Marquis Crescenzi to see the princess. He was so surprised and dazzled by the soul-stirring beauty imparted to her by her despair that, for the first time in his life, he showed strength of character. He dismissed the marquis with a gesture that was more than imperious and began making a formal declaration of love to the duchess. He had no doubt composed it long in advance, for it contained some rather sensible arguments:

"Since the properties of my rank forbid me to grant myself the supreme happiness of marrying you, I will swear to you by the Blessed Sacrament that I will never marry without your written permission. I realize that I shall be causing you to lose the hand of the Prime Minister, an intelligent and very charming man; but after all, he is fifty-six years old, and I am not yet twenty-two. I would consider it an insult to you, and one that would make me deserve your refusal, if I were to speak to you of advantages foreign to love; but everyone at my court who is preoccupied with money speaks with admiration of the proof of love which the count has given you in placing everything he possesses in your hands, and I would be only too glad to imitate him in that respect. You will make better use of my fortune than I could, and the annual sum turned over by my ministers to the Intendant General of my Crown will be completely at your disposal, so that it will be you, duchess, who will decide upon the sums I may spend each month."

The duchess found all these details extremely long: her heart was being tortured by the dangers to which Fabrizio was exposed.

"But Your Highness," she cried, "don't you know that Fabrizio is being poisoned in your citadel at this very moment? Save him! I believe everything you say."

She had made a thoroughly awkward blunder in expressing herself thus: at the mere mention of poison, all the spontaneity and good faith which the poor, moral-minded prince had brought into his conversation vanished in the twinkling of an eye. The duchess did not realize her mistake until it was too late to remedy it, and her despair increased, a thing she would have thought impossible. "If I hadn't spoken of poison," she thought, "I could have persuaded him to set Fabrizio free. Oh, my dear Fabrizio, I'm fated to pierce your heart by my stupidity!"

She had to spend a long time and employ a great deal of charm before she succeeded in making the prince return to his talk of passionate love, and even then he remained deeply shocked. It was his mind alone that spoke; his heart had been chilled, first by the idea of poison, then by this second idea, as disagreeable as the first one was frightful: "Poison is being used in my dominions, and I haven't been told about it!

Rassi wants to dishonor me in the eyes of Europe! And God only knows what I'll read next month in the Paris newspapers!"

Suddenly the shy young man's heart became silent; his mind had hit upon an idea: "You know how strongly I'm attached to you, dear duchess," he said. "I like to believe that your horrible ideas about poison are unfounded; they do make me reflect, however, and they almost make me forget for a moment the passion I feel for you, the only one I've ever felt in my life. I know I'm not very charming, I'm only a boy who's madly in love; but put me to the test anyway!"

He had become rather animated as he said this.

"Save Fabrizio and I'll believe anything you say!" replied the duchess. "I'm no doubt allowing myself to be carried away by the wild fears of a motherly heart, but I want you to send someone immediately to bring Fabrizio from the citadel, so that I can see him for myself. If he's still alive, you can send him straight from here to the city jail. He'll stay there for months on end, if you demand it, until his trial."

The duchess saw with despair that the prince, instead of promptly granting such a simple request, had become somber. His face was blushed; he looked at her, then lowered his eyes, and his cheeks turned pale. The idea of poison, inopportunely brought forward, had suggested to him an idea worthy of his father, or of Philip II; but he did not dare to express it.

"Duchess," he said to her at length, as though making a great effort, and in a tone that was far from gracious, "you despise me as a mere child, and, furthermore, as being without charm. Well, I'm going to tell you something that's horrible, but which has just been suggested to me by the deep and genuine passion I feel for you. If I had the slightest belief in your notion of poison, I would have acted already: my duty would have required it of me. But I see nothing in your request except an emotional whim, although it's possible, if you'll allow me to say so, that I don't see all its ramifications. You want me to act without consulting my ministers, when I've been reigning for barely three months! You're asking me to make a great exception to my usual way of acting, which, I confess, seems quite sensible to me. At this moment it is you, duchess, who are the absolute sovereign here; you have strengthened the hope that means everything to me, but an hour from now, when your imaginary fear of poison, your nightmare, has vanished, my presence will become unwelcome to you and you will dismiss me. I must therefore have an oath: swear to me, duchess, that if Fabrizio is restored to you safe and sound, I shall obtain from you, within three months' time, all the happiness my love can desire, that you will assure the happiness of my entire life by placing one hour of your own at my disposal, and that you will be wholly mine."

Just then the palace clock struck two. "Oh! It may be too late already!" she thought.

"I give you my word!" she cried, with a wild look in her eyes.

The prince immediately became a different man; he ran to the room occupied by his aides-de-camp, at the end of a gallery.

"General Fontana, ride to the citadel at full speed, go as quickly as you can to the cell in which Signor del Dongo is being kept, and bring him here to me. I must speak to him within twenty minutes, or fifteen, if possible."

"Oh, general," cried the duchess, who had followed the prince, "one minute may decide my life! A report, which is no doubt false, has made me fear that Fabrizio may be poisoned: as soon as you're within earshot, call out to him that he mustn't eat anything. If he's already begun his meal, make him vomit; tell him it was I who told you to do it, but use force if necessary. Tell him I'm following close behind you, and rest assured that I'll be indebted to you for the rest of my life."

"Duchess, my horse is already saddled, I'm considered to be a good rider, and I'm going to gallop at full speed: I'll reach the citadel eight minutes before you."

"And I ask you to grant me four of those eight minutes, duchess!" said the prince.

The aide-de-camp had already left; he was a man whose only merit was that he knew how to ride a horse. As soon as he had closed the door, the young prince, who again seemed to have some strength of character, seized the duchess's hand.

"Please come with me to the chapel," he said to her with passion. The duchess, dumbfounded for the first time in her life, followed him without a word. They walked swiftly along the entire length of the great gallery of the palace, the chapel being at the far end of it. On entering the chapel, the prince knelt, as much to the duchess as to the altar.

"Repeat your oath," he said to her passionately. "If you'd been kind, and if my unfortunate position as a prince hadn't

385

been a disadvantage to me, you'd have granted me out of pity for my love what you now owe to me because of your oath."

"If Fabrizio hasn't been poisoned, if I see him again, if he's still alive a week from now, and if you will make him Archbishop Landriani's coadjutor with the right of future succession, then my honor and my womanly dignity will be trampled underfoot and I will give myself to you."

"But *my dear*," said the prince, with a mixture of timid anxiety and tenderness that was quite amusing, "I'm afraid of some snare which I don't understand, and which might destroy my happiness: that would kill me. If the archbishop opposes me with one of those ecclesiastical arguments that can make an affair drag on for years on end, what will become of me? You can see that I'm acting in complete good faith; are you going to behave like a little Jesuit with me?"

"No: I tell you in good faith that if Fabrizio is saved, and if you do everything in your power to make him a coadjutor and a future archbishop, I will destroy my honor by giving myself to you. Will you promise to write 'Approved' on the margin of a request which the archbishop will present to you a week from now?"

"I'll sign a blank sheet of paper for you; reign over me and my dominions!" cried the prince, blushing with happiness and truly carried away. He demanded a second oath. He was so deeply moved that he forgot the shyness that was so natural to him, and there in the chapel of the palace, alone with the duchess, he murmured things to her which, had he said them three days earlier, would have changed her opinion of him. But the despair aroused in her by Fabrizio's danger had now given way to horror at the promise that had been wrung from her.

She was staggered by what she had just done. If she did not yet feel all the terrible bitterness of her promise, it was because her mind was entirely occupied with the question of whether General Fontana would be able to reach the citadel in time.

To spare herself the boyish prince's madly amorous speeches and turn the conversation to other matters, she praised a famous painting by Parmigiano which hung above the high altar of the chapel.

"Be so kind as to allow me to send it to you," said the prince.

"I accept," she replied, "but permit me to hurry off to meet Fabrizio now."

Looking utterly distraught, she told her coachman to make the horses gallop. On the bridge over the moat of the citadel, she met General Fontana and Fabrizio, who were coming out on foot.

"Have you eaten?"

"No, by a miracle."

The duchess threw her arms around Fabrizio's neck and fell into a faint which lasted for an hour and gave rise to fears first for her life, then for her reason.

General Fabio Conti had turned pale with anger at the sight of General Fontana, and he had been so slow in obeying the prince's orders that the aide-de-camp, who assumed that the duchess was going to occupy the position of reigning mistress, had finally lost his temper. The governor had intended to make Fabrizio's illness last for two or three days. "But now," he thought, "General Fontana, a man from the court, is going to find that insolent rascal writhing in the agony that will avenge me for his escape."

Fabio Conti, absorbed in thought, had stopped in the guardroom of the Farnese Tower and quickly sent the soldiers away; he did not want any witnesses to the scene that was about to take place. Five minutes later, he had been petrified with astonishment on hearing Fabrizio speak, and on seeing him, lively and alert, giving General Fontana a description of the prison. He had then disappeared.

Fabrizio showed himself to be a perfect gentleman in his interview with the prince. First of all, he did not want to act like a child who becomes frightened over nothing. When the prince kindly asked him how he felt, he replied, "Like a man who's dying of hunger, Your Serene Highness, since fortunately I've eaten neither lunch nor dinner." After having had the honor of thanking the prince, he requested permission to see the archbishop before going to the city jail. The prince had turned prodigiously pale when his childish mind was struck by the idea that the poison the duchess had told him about was not entirely a figment of her imagination. Absorbed in this cruel thought, he did not reply at first to Fabrizio's request to see the archbishop; then he felt obliged to make amends for his distraction with a great show of graciousness.

"Go out alone," he said to Fabrizio, "go through the streets of my capital unguarded. At ten or eleven o'clock, you will present yourself at the jail, where I hope you will not stay long."

On the morrow of this great day, the most remarkable day

of his life, the prince regarded himself as a little Napoleon; he had read that the great man had been well treated by several of the pretty women of his court. Now that he was a Napoleon in amorous intrigue, he recalled that he had also been a Napoleon under fire. He was still elated by the firmness of his conduct with the duchess. The awareness of having done something difficult made him a totally different man for two weeks: he became receptive to generous arguments, he showed a certain amount of character.

He began that day by burning the document which would have made Rassi a count. He dismissed General Fabio Conti and asked General Lange, his successor, to tell him the truth about the poison. Lange, a gallant Polish officer, frightened the jailers and told the prince that there had been a plan to poison Signor del Dongo's lunch, but that it would have been necessary to involve too many people in the secret; matters had been handled more successfully with regard to his dinner, however, and if it had not been for General Fontana's arrival, Signor del Dongo would have been lost. The prince was horror-stricken, but since he was really very much in love, it was a consolation for him to be able to say to himself, "It turns out that I actually did save Signor del Dongo's life, so the duchess won't dare not to keep the promise she made to me." Another idea occurred to him: "My duties are much more difficult than I thought; everyone agrees that the duchess has a brilliant mind, so in this case political considerations are in harmony with the wishes of my heart: it would be wonderful for me if she would consent to be my Prime Minister."

That evening the prince was so angry over the horrors he had discovered that he would not take part in the theatrical performance.

"I would be more than happy," he said to the duchess, "if you would rule my dominions as you rule my heart. First of all, let me tell you how I spent my day." He then gave her a detailed account of everything: the burning of the document that would have made Rossi a count, the appointment of Lange, his report on the attempted poisoning, etc. "I find that I have very little experience in the art of ruling. The count humiliates me with his jokes; he even jokes during meetings of the council, and in society he makes remarks whose truth you will dispute: he says that I'm only a child whom he can lead wherever he likes. In order to make Count Mosca's stories seem less plausible, I was persuaded to appoint that dangerous scoundrel Rassi as one of my ministers.

And General Conti still has such a high regard for Rassi's power that he's afraid to admit that it was either he or the Marquise Raversi who urged him to have your nephew murdered. I've a good mind simply to have General Fabio Conti tried by a court of law; the judges will find out whether or not he's guilty of attempted murder."

"But do you have any judges, Your Highness?"

"What!" exclaimed the prince, astonished.

"You have scholarly jurists who look quite solemn when they walk through the streets, but their judgments will always be controlled by the dominant faction of your court."

While the young prince, scandalized, was saying things which showed his candor much more than his sagacity, the duchess was thinking, "Would it really suit me to have Conti dishonored? No, of course not, because then his daughter's marriage to that honest, dull-witted Marquis Crescenzi would become impossible."

On this subject there was an endless discussion between the duchess and the prince. The prince was overwhelmed with admiration. In consideration of the marriage of Clelia Conti to the Marquis Crescenzi, but on that express condition, which he angrily stated to the ex-governor in person, he pardoned him for the attempted poisoning; however, following the duchess's advice, he exiled him until the time of his daughter's wedding. The duchess believed that she was no longer in love with Fabrizio, yet she still passionately wanted Clelia to marry the marquis; she hoped vaguely that Fabrizio's obsession would then gradually disappear.

The prince, carried away with happiness, wanted to give Rassi a dishonorable dismissal that very evening. The duchess said to him, laughing, "Do you know what Napoleon once said? 'A man who holds a high position, and who is watched by everyone, must never give in to violent impulses.' Besides, it's too late this evening; let's put off business matters till tomorrow."

She wanted to give herself time to consult the count. She gave him a precise account of the whole evening's conversation, except that she omitted the many allusions which the prince had made to a promise that was poisoning her life. She flattered herself that she would become so necessary to the prince that she could obtain an indefinite postponement by saying to him, "If you should have the barbarity to insist on subjecting me to that humiliation, for which I would never forgive you, I would leave your dominions the next day."

When she consulted him about Rassi's fate, the count took

a very philosophical attitude. Rassi and General Fabio Conti set off on a journey to Piedmont.

A singular difficulty arose in connection with Fabrizio's trial: the judges wanted to acquit him by acclamation in the first session. The count had to employ threats to make the trial last at least a week, and to make the judges take the trouble to listen to all the witnesses. "Those people are always the same," he thought.

On the day after his acquittal, Fabrizio del Dongo finally took over the post of vicar-general to the good Archbishop Landriani. That same day, the prince signed the dispatches necessary to obtain Fabrizio's appointment as coadjutor with the right of future succession, and less than two months later he was installed in that position.

Everyone complimented the duchess on her nephew's grave demeanor; the fact was that he was in despair. On the day after his deliverance, which was followed by General Fabio Conti's dismissal and exile, and the duchess's rise to high favor, Clelia had gone to stay with her aunt, Countess Contarini, a very rich and very old woman whose sole concern was the care of her health. It was now possible for Clelia to see Fabrizio, but if anyone had observed her present conduct, knowing what she had done before, he might have thought that her love for Fabrizio had ceased with his danger. Not only did he pass by Countess Contarini's house as often as decency would allow, but he had also succeeded, after endless difficulties, in renting a small apartment opposite its second-story windows. Once when Clelia had thoughtlessly gone to the window to watch a procession, she drew back instantly, as though terror-stricken: she had just seen Fabrizio, dressed in black, but like a very poor workman, looking at her from one of the windows of the dilapidated house across the street, whose panes were made of oiled paper, like those of his cell in the Farnese Tower. He would have liked to persuade himself that she was shunning him because of her father's disgrace, which public opinion attributed to the duchess, but he was too well aware of another cause of her avoidance, and nothing could distract him from his melancholy.

He had been unmoved by his acquittal, by his important office, the first one he had ever held, by his enviable position in society, and by the assiduous attentions lavished on him by all the ecclesiastics and devout laymen in the diocese. His charming apartment in the Sanseverina palace proved to be insufficient. To her great joy, the duchess was obliged to give him the entire third floor and two fine drawing rooms on the second floor, which were always filled with people waiting to curry favor with the young coadjutor. The clause giving him the right of future succession had produced an amazing effect: all the firm qualities of his character, which had once so greatly shocked the poor brainless courtiers, were now regarded as virtues.

It was a great lesson in philosophy for Fabrizio to find himself indifferent to all these honors, and much more unhappy in that magnificent apartment, with ten footmen wearing his livery, than he had been in his wooden cell in the Farnese Tower, surrounded by hideous jailers and constantly fearing for his life. His mother and his sister, Duchess V——, came to Parma to see him in his glory and were struck by his deep sadness. The Marquise del Dongo, now the least romantic of women, was so profoundly alarmed that she thought he must have been given some kind of slow poison while he was in the Farnese Tower. Despite her extreme discretion, she felt obliged to speak to him about this extraordinary sadness; he answered her only with tears.

A host of advantages, resulting from his exalted position, did nothing but irritate him. His brother, that vain soul cankered by the vilest kind of selfishness, wrote him an almost official letter of congratulation and enclosed a draft for 50,000 lire, to enable him, said the new marquis, to buy a carriage and horses worthy of his name. Fabrizio sent the money to his younger sister, who had made a bad marriage.

Count Mosca had had a fine Italian translation made of the genealogy of the Valserra del Dongo family, originally published in Latin by Fabrizio, Archbishop of Parma. He had it printed in a magnificent edition with the Latin text and the Italian translation on opposite pages. The engravings were reproduced in superb lithographs which had been made in Paris. At the duchess's request, a handsome portrait of Fabrizio had been placed opposite that of the old archbishop. This translation was published as having been done by Fabrizio during his first imprisonment. But everything had been extinguished in our hero, even the vanity that is so natural to man; he did not deign to read a single page of this work which had been attributed to him. His position in society made it obligatory for him to present a magnificently bound copy to the prince, who, feeling that he owed him some compensation for having almost died a painful death in the citadel, granted him the right of entry to his bed-chamber, a favor which confers the title of "Excellency."*

CHAPTER TWENTY-SIX

The only moments in which Fabrizio had some chance of emerging from his deep sadness were those he spent hiding behind the pane of glass with which he had replaced a square of oiled paper in the window of his apartment across the street from Countess Contarini's house, where, as we know, Clelia was now living. On the few occasions when he had seen her since leaving the citadel, he had been profoundly grieved by a striking change which seemed ominous to him. Since her lapse from virtue, her face had assumed a look of nobility and seriousness that was truly remarkable; she might have been taken for a woman of thirty. In this extraordinary change, Fabrizio saw the reflection of some firm resolution. "All day long," he thought, "she swears to herself that she'll be faithful to the vow she made to the Madonna, and never see me again."

Fabrizio guessed only part of Clelia's unhappiness: she knew that her father, now in deep disgrace, could not return to Parma and reappear at court (without which life was impossible for him) until the day of her marriage to the Marquis Crescenzi. She had written to him that she wanted to marry the marquis. The general was in Turin at the time, ill with grief. One effect of this great decision had been to add ten years to Clelia's age.

She was now well aware that Fabrizio had a window across the street from her aunt's house, but she had only once had the misfortune to look at him; as soon as she noticed a man with a face or a figure that resembled Fabrizio's in any way, she would immediately close her eyes. Her deep piety and her trust in the Madonna's aid were now her only resources. She had the sorrow of lacking respect for her father, her future husband's character seemed to her perfectly common-place and well adapted to the sentiments of high society, and finally, she adored a man whom she must never see again, and who yet had certain claims on her. It seemed to her that this combination of misfortunes constituted an utterly

* See page 432.

wretched fate, and we must admit that she was right. The best thing for her to do would have been to go and live two hundred leagues away from Parma after her marriage.

Fabrizio knew how profoundly modest she was, and how greatly displeased she was bound to be by any unusual act which might become a subject of gossip if it were discovered. Nevertheless, maddened by his extreme melancholy and her persistent refusal to look at him, he dared to bribe two servants employed by her aunt, Countess Contarini. Early one evening, Fabrizio, dressed in rural middle-class style, came to the door of the house, where one of the bribed servants was waiting for him; he announced himself as having just come from Turin with some letters for Clelia from her father. The servant delivered his message and showed him into an immense anteroom on the second floor. It was there that Fabrizio spent what was perhaps the most anxious quarter-hour of his life. If Clelia rejected him, he would lose all hope of ever having any peace of mind. "To put an end to the annoying duties imposed on me by my new dignity," he thought, "I'll rid the Church of a bad priest and take refuge in some Charterhouse* under an assumed name." At last the servant came in to announce that Signorina Clelia Conti was ready to receive him. Our hero's courage completely failed him; he nearly fainted from fear as he climbed the stairs to the third floor.

Clelia was sitting at the little table on which there was a single candle. As soon as she recognized Fabrizio beneath his disguise, she ran from him and hid at the far end of the room.

"This is how you care for my salvation!" she cried out to him, hiding her face in her hands. "You know very well that when my father was about to die of poison I vowed to the Madonna that I would never see you again! I've broken my vow only once, on the unhappiest day of my life, when I sincerely believed it was my duty to save you from death. I've already done a great deal by consenting to listen to you, on the basis of a strained and no doubt criminal interpretation of my vow."

Fabrizio was so astonished by this last sentence that it took him several seconds to rejoice over it. He had expected her to be violently angry and run away from him. He finally recovered his presence of mind and put out the candle. Although he believed he had understood her orders correctly,

* i.e., a Carthusian monastery.—L.B.

he trembled from head to foot as he walked to the far end of the room, where she had taken refuge behind a sofa. He did not know whether she would be offended or not if he kissed her hand; she was quivering with love, and threw herself in his arms.

"Dear Fabrizio," she said to him, "how slow you were in coming! I can talk to you only for an instant, because this is probably a great sin; when I promised never to see you again, I no doubt also meant to promise not to speak to you again. . . . But how could you persecute my poor father so cruelly for his idea of taking vengeance? After all, it was he who was first nearly poisoned to help you escape. Shouldn't you have done something for me after I risked my reputation so often to save you? And besides, you're now completely committed to Holy Orders: you couldn't marry me now even if I found some way to get rid of that odious marquis. And how could you dare to try to see me in broad daylight on the day of the procession, and make me commit a flagrant violation of my vow to the Madonna?"

Fabrizio clasped her in his arms, beside himself with amazement and happiness.

A conversation that had begun with so many things to be said on both sides could not fail to last a long time. Fabrizio told her the exact truth about her father's exile: the duchess had played no part in it whatever, for the good reason that she had never believed for an instant that the idea of poison had come from General Conti; she had always thought it to be a clever stratagem on the part of the Raversi faction, who were determined to drive out Count Mosca. This historical truth, developed at great length, made Clelia very happy; being obliged to hate someone closely connected with Fabrizio had been painful to her. She no longer regarded the duchess with a jealous eye.

The happiness created by this evening lasted only a few days.

The excellent Don Cesare returned from a journey to Turin, and, drawing courage from the perfect integrity of his heart, he ventured to go to see the duchess. After asking her to give him her word that she would not misuse the information he was about to confide to her, he confessed that his brother, misled by a false sense of honor, and believing that he had been insolently defied and forever disgraced in the eyes of the public, had felt obliged to take vengeance.

Don Cesare had not spoken for two minutes before he had won his case; his perfect virtue had touched the duchess, who was not accustomed to such a sight. He pleased her as a novelty.

"Hasten the marriage of the general's daughter to the Marquis Crescenzi," she said, "and I give you my word that I'll do everything in my power to have the general received as though he were returning from an ordinary journey. I'll invite him to dinner; are you satisfied? There will no doubt be some coolness at first, and he mustn't be in a hurry to ask to be reinstated as governor of the citadel. But, as you know, I have friendly feelings toward the marquis, and I won't hold a grudge against his father-in-law."

Armed with these words, Don Cesare went to tell his niece that she held in her hands the life of her father, who was sick with despair. For several months he had not appeared at any court.

Clelia decided to go to see her father. He was living in a village near Turin under an assumed name, for he had taken it into his head that the court of Parma had asked the court of Turin to extradite him so that he could be brought to trial. She found him ill and nearly out of his mind. That same evening she wrote Fabrizio a letter affirming their eternal separation. On receiving this letter, Fabrizio, who was developing a character exactly like that of his mistress, went into retreat at the monastery of Velleia, in the mountains ten leagues from Parma. Clelia wrote him a ten-page letter; she had once sworn to him that she would never marry the marquis without his permission, and she now asked him for it. Fabrizio granted it to her from the depths of his retreat at Velleia, in a letter filled with the purest friendship.

When she received this letter, whose tone of friendship, it must be admitted, irritated her, Clelia herself set the day of her wedding, whose attendant festivities added still greater luster to the splendor with which the court of Parma shone that winter.

Ranuccio-Ernesto V was a miser at heart, but he was also madly in love and hoped to establish the duchess permanently at his court, so he gave his mother a large sum of money and asked her to give entertainments with it. Her Chief Lady in Waiting made admirable use of this added wealth; the festivities in Parma that winter recalled the great days of the court of Milan and the charming Prince Eugene, Viceroy of Italy, whose kindness has left such a lasting memory.

The coadjutor's duties had called him back to Parma, but he announced that, for reasons of piety, he would continue his retreat in the small apartment which his protector, Archbishop Landriani, had forced him to take in his palace, and he went to shut himself up there, accompanied by a single servant. Thus he attended none of the brilliant festivities of the court; this earned him an immense reputation for saintliness in Parma and all over his future diocese.

One unexpected result of this retreat, to which Fabrizio was driven solely by his deep and hopeless melancholy, was that the good Archbishop Landriani, who had always loved him, and who had, in fact, been the first to have the idea of making him his coadjutor, began to feel somewhat jealous of him. The archbishop rightly considered himself obliged to go to all the court festivities, as is the custom in Italy. On these occasions he wore his ceremonial costume, which was nearly the same as the one he wore in the chancel of his cathedral. The hundreds of servants gathered in the pillared anteroom of the palace never failed to stand up and ask him for his blessing, which he was always willing to stop and bestow on them. It was during one of these moments of solemn silence that he heard a voice say, "Our archbishop goes to balls, and *Monsignore* del Dongo never leaves his room!"

That moment marked the end of the immense favor which Fabrizio had enjoyed in the archbishop's palace; but he was now able to stand on his own feet. His entire behavior, which had been inspired solely by the despair into which Clelia's forthcoming marriage had plunged him, was regarded as a manifestation of simple and sublime piety, and devout women were now reading, as a work of edification, the translation of the genealogy of his family, which was permeated with the most extravagant vanity. The booksellers of the city published a lithographed edition of his portrait; it was bought up in a few days, especially by people of the lower classes. The artist, in his ignorance, had embellished the portrait with some of the ornaments which ought to appear only on the portraits of bishops, and to which a coadjutor was not entitled. The archbishop saw one of these portraits, and his fury knew no bounds. He sent for Fabrizio and said some terribly harsh things to him, in terms which his emotion sometimes made extremely coarse.

As may be well imagined, it required no effort on Fabrizio's part to behave as Fénelon would have done in similar circumstances: he listened to the archbishop with the greatest possible humility and respect, and then, when the prelate had finished speaking, he told him the whole story of the translation of the genealogy which had been made during his first imprisonment, at Count Mosca's orders. It had been published for worldly ends, which he had always regarded as improper for a man of his calling. As for the portrait, he had had no more to do with the second edition than with the first, and when a bookseller had sent him twenty-four copies of it during his retreat in the archbishop's palace, he had sent his servant to buy a twenty-fifth, then, having learned by this means that the portrait was selling for thirty soldi, he had sent a hundred lire as payment for the twenty-four copies.

All these arguments, though set forth in the most reasonable tone by a man who had many other sorrows in his heart, stirred the archbishop's anger to the point of frenzy; he went so far as to accuse Fabrizio of hypocrisy.

"This is what lower-class men are like," thought Fabrizio, "even when they're intelligent!"

He had at that time a more serious cause for concern: his aunt was sending him letters in which she absolutely demanded that he return to his apartment in the Sanseverina palace, or that he at least come to see her from time to time. There, he would certainly hear talk of the splendid celebrations given by the Marquis Crescenzi in honor of his coming marriage, and he was not sure he would be able to endure this without making a spectacle of himself.

When the wedding ceremony took place, Fabrizio had already spent a whole week in complete silence, having ordered his servant, and all members of the palace staff with whom he had any dealings, not to say a word to him.

When Archbishop Landriani learned of this new affectation, he began sending for Fabrizio much oftener than usual and insisted on having long conversations with him; he even forced him to hold conferences with certain rural canons who claimed that the archbishop had violated their privileges. Fabrizio took all this with the perfect indifference of a man who has other things on his mind. "It would be better for me," he thought, "to become a Carthusian monk; I'd suffer less in the mountains of Velleia."

He went to see his aunt, and was unable to hold back his tears when he embraced her. She found him so changed, his eyes, made still larger by his extreme thinness, seemed to be bulging so far out of their sockets, and he looked so sickly and miserable dressed in the shabby black coat of an ordinary priest, that she, too, was unable to hold back her tears at this first meeting. But a moment later, when she told herself that all these changes in his appearance were caused by Clelia's marriage, her feelings were almost as violent as the archbishop's, though more skillfully controlled. She had the cruelty to speak to him at great length about certain striking details of the delightful celebrations given by the Marquis Crescenzi. Fabrizio did not answer, but his eyes closed a little, as though by a convulsive moement, and he turned paler than ever, which would have at first seemed impossible. In these moments of intense pain, his pallor took on a greenish hue.

Count Mosca came in; what he saw seemed incredible to him, and it completely cured him at last of all the jealousy which Fabrizio had never ceased to arouse in him. That clever man used the most tactful and ingenious turns of phrase in his efforts to restore to Fabrizio some interest in the things of this world. The count had always felt a great deal of esteem and considerable friendship for him; this friendship, no longer offset by jealousy, now became almost devoted. "Yes, he's paid dearly for his lofty position," he thought, recapitulating Fabrizio's misfortunes. On the pretext of showing him the painting by Parmigiano which the prince had sent to the duchess, he took Fabrizio aside and said to him, "Now then, my friend, let's talk to each other man to man. Is there anything I can do to help you? You needn't fear any questions on my part, but still, let me ask you whether money or power can be of any use to you. Speak, I'm at your orders; if you'd rather write, write to me."

Fabrizio embraced him affectionately and spoke to him about the painting.

"Your conduct is a masterpiece of skillful strategy," said the count, resuming the light tone of ordinary conversation. "You're preparing a very pleasant future for yourself: the prince respects you, the people worship you, and your shabby black coat gives Archbishop Landriani some bad nights. I have some experience in such matters, and I can swear to you that I wouldn't know what advice to give you to improve on what I see. You've reached perfection with your first step in society at the age of twenty-five. Everyone at court talks about you a great deal, and do you know to what you owe that distinction, which is unique at your age? To your shabby black coat. As you know, the duchess and I have at our disposal that old house which once belonged to Petrarch, on a lovely hill in the forest near the Po; it has occurred to me that if you ever get tired of all the petty and spiteful animosities aroused by envy, you could become the successor of Petrarch, whose fame would increase your own." The count was racking his brain to bring a smile to that austere face, but all his efforts were wasted. What made the change still more striking was that, until recently, if Fabrizio's face had any defect it was that of sometimes presenting an expression of sensual pleasure and gaiety at the wrong time.

The count did not let him leave without telling him that, despite the fact that he was still living in retreat, it might be considered an affectation if he did not appear at court on the following Saturday, which was the princess's birthday. This remark pierced Fabrizio's heart like a dagger. "Good God!" he thought. "Whatever made me come to this house?" He shuddered at the thought that he might encounter Clelia at court. This idea absorbed all others; he decided that his only chance would be to arrive at the palace just as the doors of the drawing rooms were being opened.

And so the name of *Monsignore* Fabrizio del Dongo was one of the first to be announced on the evening of the great celebration, and the princess received him with all possible honor. He kept his eyes on the clock, and as soon as it marked the twentieth minute of his presence he stood up to take his leave. Just then the prince came into his mother's drawing room. Having paid his respects to him for a few moments, Fabrizio was adroitly maneuvering himself toward the door when he was suddenly stopped by one of those trifling incidents of court life which the Chief Lady in Waiting knew so well how to arrange: the chamberlain in attendance came running up to him to tell him that he had been chosen to play whist with the prince. In Parma this was a signal honor, and one far above the coadjutor's rank in society. To play whist was a marked honor even for the archbishop. Fabrizio was cut to the heart when he heard the chamberlain's words, and although he had a deep-seated aversion to making any kind of scene in public, he was on the verge of announcing that he had been seized with a sudden spell of dizziness; but then he reflected that he would be exposed to questions and expressions of sympathy which would be even more intolerable to him than playing whist. He had a horror of speaking that evening.

Fortunately the Superior-General of the Franciscan Friars happened to be among the dignitaries who had come to pay their respects to the princess. This learned monk, a worthy emulator of Fontana and Duvoisin, had taken up a position in a far corner of the drawing room. Fabrizio stood in front of him in such a way that he could not see the door and began discussing theology with him. But he could not prevent his ears from hearing the announcement of the arrival of the

Marquis and Marquise Crescenzi. Against all his expectations, he felt a violent surge of anger.

"If," he thought, "I were Borso Valserra" (one of the generals of the first Sforza), "I'd go and stab that dull-witted marquis with this same little ivory-handled dagger given to me by Clelia on that happy day! I'd teach him to have the insolence to bring his wife into the same room with me!"

His expression changed so radically that the Superior-General said to him, "Do you feel unwell, Your Excellency?"

"I have a terrible headache . . . these lights hurt my eyes . . . I'm staying only because I've been chosen to play whist with the prince."

At these words, the Franciscan Superior-General, a man of middle-class origin, was so disconcerted that, not knowing what else to do, he began bowing to Fabrizio, who, being much more deeply troubled than the monk, began talking with strange volubility. He noticed that there was a profound silence behind him, then suddenly a violin bow was tapped against a music stand, a ritornel was played, and the famous Signora P—— sang that area by Cimarosa which was once so popular: "*Quelle pupille tenere!*"

Fabrizio held out for the first few bars, but soon his anger vanished and he felt a strong desire to burst into tears. "My God, what a ridiculous scene!" he thought. "And while I'm wearing this black coat, too!"

He decided it would be better to talk about himself: "When I fight against these violent headaches, as I'm doing this evening," he said to his companion, "they eventually result in fits of tears which, in view of my calling, might give rise to gossip; I therefore beg you, Your Illustrious Reverence, to allow me to shed tears as I look at you, and to pay no attention to them."

"Our Father Provincial at Cantazara suffers from the same affliction," said the Franciscan. And he began telling an endless story in an undertone.

The absurdity of this story, which led to a detailed account of the Father Provincial's evening meal, made Fabrizio smile, something that had not happened to him for a long time; but he soon stopped listening to the Franciscan. Signora P—— was singing, with divine talent, an aria by Pergolese (the princess liked old-fashioned music). There was a slight sound three paces away from Fabrizio; he looked around for the first time that evening. The chair that had just caused a floorboard to creak was occupied by Clelia, now the Marquise Crescenzi. Her eyes, filled with tears, squarely met Fabrizio's, which were hardly in better condition. She bowed her head. He looked at her for a few seconds longer, studying that head laden with diamonds; but his gaze expressed anger and disdain. Then, saying to himself, "*And my eyes will never look at you again,*" he turned back to his Franciscan and said to him, "My affliction is now becoming worse than ever."

And indeed he wept bitterly for more than half an hour. Fortunately a symphony by Mozart, horribly mangled, as is customary in Italy, came to his rescue and helped him to dry his tears.

He held firm and did not look around at the Marquise Crescenzi. Signora P—— sang again, and his soul, relieved by his tears, reached a state of perfect repose. Life then appeared to him in a different light. "Do I expect to be able to forget her entirely, right from the start?" he thought. "Would that be possible for me?" He arrived at this idea: "Can I ever be more miserable than I've been for the past two months? And if nothing can increase my anguish, why should I resist the pleasure of seeing her? She's forgotten her promises, she's fickle—aren't all women the same? But who could deny that she has a heavenly beauty? She has a look in her eyes that sends me into ecstatic raptures, whereas I have to force myself to look at other women who are considered to be among the most beautiful! Well, why not let myself be enraptured? It will at least give me a moment's respite."

Fabrizio had some knowledge of men, but no experience of the passions, otherwise he would have told himself that the momentary pleasure to which he was about to yield would nullify all the efforts he had been making for the past two months to forget Clelia.

The poor girl had come to the palace that evening only because her husband had forced her to do so, and she tried to leave after the first half-hour, saying that she was not feeling well. But the marquis told her that having his carriage brought out while many other carriages were still arriving would be a most unusual thing to do, and that it might even be interpreted as an indirect criticism of the princess's celebration.

"In my capacity as a Knight of Honor," he added, "I must remain in the drawing room, at the princess's orders, until everyone else has left. There may be, and no doubt will be, orders to be given to the servants—they're so careless! And would you like to have one of the princess's ordinary attendants usurp that honor?"

Clelia resigned herself; she had not seen Fabrizio, and she

still had hopes that he would not appear. But when the concert was about to begin and the princess gave permission for the ladies to be seated, Clelia, not at all alert to such things, let all the best seats near the princess be snatched away from her and was obliged to find a chair for herself at the back of the room, in the far corner where Fabrizio had taken refuge. When she reached her chair, the Superior-General's costume, an unusual sight in such a place, caught her eye, and at first she did not notice the thin man, wearing a simple black coat, to whom he was talking; but then a secret impulse made her look at this man more closely.

"Everyone else here," she thought, "is wearing either a uniform or a richly embroidered coat; who is that young man dressed so simply in black?" She was looking at him with profound attention when her chair was moved slightly by a lady on her way to take a seat. Fabrizio looked around; he had changed so much that she did not recognize him. At first she said to herself, "There's someone who looks like him, it must be his elder brother; but I thought he was only a few years older, and this man is about forty." Suddenly she recognized him by a movement of his lips.

"Poor boy, how he's suffered!" she thought; and she bowed her head because she was crushed by grief, not in order to be faithful to her vow. Her heart was flooded with pity; how far he had been from looking like this after nine months in prison; She did not look at him again; but, without exactly turning her eyes in his direction, she could see all his movements.

After the concert, she saw him walk over to the prince's card table, a few feet from the throne. She began breathing more freely now that he was no longer near her.

But the Marquis Crescenzi had deeply resented seeing his wife relegated to a seat so far from the throne; he had been busy all evening trying to persuade a lady seated three chairs away from the princess, and whose husband was under financial obligation to him, that she would do well to change places with the marquise. Since the poor woman resisted, as was only natural, he went off to find her debtor husband, who made her listen to the sad voice of reason, and at last the marquis had the pleasure of obtaining her consent to the exchange. He went to get his wife.

"You're always too modest," he said to her. "Why do you walk with your eyes lowered like that? People will take you for one of those middle-class women who are amazed to find themselves here, and whom everyone is amazed to see here.

It was just like that insane Chief Lady in Waiting to invite them! And people talk about checking the progress of Jacobinism! Remember that your husband holds the foremost male position in the princess's court, and that even if the republicans should succeed in doing away with the court and even with the nobility, your husband would still be the richest man in Parma. That's something you don't think about often enough."

The chair in which the marquis had the pleasure of seating his wife was only six paces away from the prince's card table. She could see Fabrizio only in profile, but she found him so emaciated, and he seemed to be so far above everything that might happen in this world—he who, before, would never let an incident pass without comment!—that she finally came to this terrible conclusion: Fabrizio had changed completely, he had forgotten her; his thinness had been caused by the severe fasts to which his piety subjected him. Clelia was confirmed in this sad idea by the conversation of everyone around her: they were all talking about the coadjutor and trying to discover the reason for the outstanding favor that had been bestowed on him—he, so young, had been given a seat at the prince's card table! They were amazed by the polite indifference and lofty air with which he threw down his cards, even when he was trumping one of His Highness's.

"Why, this is incredible!" exclaimed some of the old courtiers. "His aunt's favor has gone to his head. But, thank heaven, it won't last: our sovereign doesn't like people to give themselves little airs of superiority!" The duchess went up to the prince; the courtiers, who remained at a very respectful distance from the card table and could therefore overhear only a few stray words of the prince's conversation, noticed that Fabrizio blushed deeply. "His aunt must have lectured him about his haughty airs of indifference," they thought. Fabrizio had just heard Clelia's voice as she replied to the princess, who, in making her tour of the ballroom, had stopped to speak to the wife of her Knight of Honor. The time came when Fabrizio had to change his place at the card table; he then found himself directly facing Clelia, and he indulged several times in the pleasure of contemplating her. Feeling his gaze on her, the poor girl lost countenance completely. Several times she forgot what she owed to her vow: in her desire to discern what was taking place in Fabrizio's heart, she fixed her eyes on him.

When the prince's game ended, the ladies stood up to go into the supper room. There was some slight disorder. Fabrizio found himself quite close to Clelia; his resolution remained firm at first, but then he recognized the faint perfume she used on her clothes, and this sensation overthrew all the promises he had made to himself. He moved still closer to her, and murmured softly, as though speaking to himself, two lines from the sonnet by Petrarch which he had sent to her from Lake Maggiore, printed on a silk handkerchief: *"How happy I was when the world thought me unhappy, and now how different is my fate!"*

"No, he hasn't forgotten me!" thought Clelia, enraptured. "That noble heart is not inconstant!" And she dared to repeat to herself two other lines by Petrarch: *"No, you will never see me change, fair eyes that taught me to love."*

The princess withdrew immediately after supper; the prince followed her to her apartment and did not appear in the reception rooms. As soon as this became known, everyone began leaving at once. There was utter confusion in the anteroom; Clelia found herself near Fabrizio, and she was moved to pity by the profound misery she saw in his face. "Let's forget the past," she said to him. "Keep this as a token of *friendship*." So saying, she held her fan in such a way that he was able to take it.

Everything changed in Fabrizio's eyes: in an instant he was a different man. The next day he announced that his retreat was over and returned to occupy his magnificent apartment in the Sanseverina palace. The archbishop said, and believed, that the favor which the prince had shown to this new saint in inviting him to his card table had made him lose his head entirely; the duchess saw that he was in accord with Clelia.

This thought, which redoubled her unhappiness over the fatal promise she had made to the prince, decided her to go away for a time. Her whim aroused great amazement. What! How could she even think of leaving the court just when the favor she enjoyed seemed to be boundless. The count, perfectly happy since he had seen that there was no love between Fabrizio and the duchess, said to her, "This new prince is virtue personified, but I've referred to him as 'that child': will he ever forgive me? I see only one way of getting back into his good graces, and that's by absence. I'm going to display perfect amiability and respect for a time, then become ill and ask to be relieved of my duties. You'll allow me to do that, because Fabrizio's career is assured, but will you make me the immense sacrifice," he asked, laughing, "of exchanging the sublime title of duchess for a greatly inferior one? To

404

amuse myself, I'm going to leave all my affairs here in inextricable confusion. I used to have four or five good workers in my various ministries: I sent them into retirement two months ago for reading the French newpapers, and I've replaced them with incredible idiots.

"After our departure, the prince will find himself in such difficulties that, despite his horror of Rassi's character, I'm sure he'll be forced to recall him. As for me, I'm awaiting only an order from the tyrant who controls my fate; as soon as I receive it, I'll write an affectionate letter to my friend Rassi and tell him that I have every reason to hope that his merit will soon be appreciated at its true worth."*

CHAPTER TWENTY-SEVEN

This serious conversation took place on the day after Fabrizio's return to the Sanseverina palace. The duchess was still feeling the effects of the joy that shone forth in all of Fabrizio's actions. "So that pious little girl has deceived me!" she thought. "She couldn't resist her lover for even three months."

The certainty of a happy outcome had given the timorous young prince the courage to love. He got wind of the preparations for departure that were being made in the Sanseverina palace, and his French valet, who had little belief in the virtue of great ladies, fortified his courage with regard to the duchess. Ernesto V ventured to take a step which was severely condemned by the princess and all sensible people at court, and which the common people interpreted as a crowning confirmation of the amazing favor which the duchess now enjoyed: he went to see her at her house.

"You're leaving," he said to her in a serious tone which struck her as odious, "you're about to betray me and break your oath! And yet Fabrizio would now be dead if I'd delayed ten minutes in granting his pardon! You're going to leave me in misery, and if it hadn't been for your oath I would never have had the courage to love you as I do! Have you no honor?"

"Think about it carefully, Your Highness: in your whole life, has there ever been another period equal in happiness

* See page 432.

to the four months that have just gone by? Your glory as a sovereign, and, I venture to believe, your happiness as a charming man, have never risen to such heights before. Here's the agreement I propose to you: with your kind consent, I won't become your mistress for a fleeting moment, and by virtue of an oath extorted by fear, but I will devote my whole life to making you happy, I'll always be what I've been for the past four months, and perhaps love will eventually come to crown friendship. I wouldn't swear to the contrary."

"Well, then," said the prince, overjoyed, "take on another role, be even more than you have been: rule over me and my dominions, be my Prime Minister! I offer you a marriage such as the sad conventions of my rank allow; we have an example close at hand: the King of Naples has just married the Duchess of Partanna. I offer you all that I can: a marriage of the same kind. I'll add a prosaic political idea to show you that I'm no longer a child, and that I've thought of everything. I won't stress the condition I'm imposing on myself, that of being the last sovereign of my race, or the sorrow I'll feel when I see the great powers choose my successor during my lifetime; I bless those very real hardships because they give me one more means of proving my esteem and passion for you."

The duchess was not in doubt for an instant; the prince bored her and the count seemed perfectly charming to her: there was only one man in the world who could be preferred to him. Besides, she ruled the count, whereas the prince, dominated by the demands of his rank, would more or less have ruled her. And then he might become inconstant and take mistresses; in a few years, the difference between their ages would seem to give him a right to do so.

From the first moment, the prospect of boredom had settled everything in her mind; wishing to be gracious, however, she asked permission to think the matter over.

It would take too long to report here the almost affectionate turns of phrase and the infinitely charming terms in which she cloaked her refusal. The prince was angry; he saw all his happiness slipping away from him. What would become of him after the duchess had left his court? Furthermore, what a humiliation it was to be refused! "And what will my French valet say," he thought, "when I tell him about my defeat?"

The duchess artfully calmed the prince and gradually brought the discussion back to her original proposal.

"Your Highness, if you will be kind enough not to press for the fulfillment of a promise which is horrible to me, since it exposes me to self-contempt, I will spend the rest of my life at your court, and that court will always be what it has been this winter. All my time will be devoted to contributing to your happiness as a man, and to your glory as a sovereign. If you demand that I keep my promise, you will have blighted my entire life, and I will immediately leave your dominions forever. The day I lose my honor will also be the last day I will ever see you."

But the prince showed the obstinacy of all timorous people; moreover, his pride as a man and as a sovereign was stung by the refusal of his hand in marriage. He was thinking of all the difficulties he would have had to surmount in order to obtain acceptance of such a marriage, and which he had nevertheless been determined to overcome.

For three hours they both repeated the same arguments, often mingled with sharp words. "Are you trying to make me believe that you have no honor?" cried the prince. "If I'd hesitated this long on the day when General Fabio Conti was about to poison Fabrizio, you'd now be busy erecting a tomb for him in one of the churches in Parma!"

"Not in Parma: not in this city of poisoners!"

"Leave, then, duchess," retorted the prince angrily, "and take my contempt with you!"

As he was walking away, the duchess said to him softly, "Very well, come back at ten o'clock tonight, in the strictest incognito, and you'll make a fool's bargain. You'll see me for the last time, and I would have devoted my life to making you as happy as an absolute monarch can be in this age of Jacobins. And think of what your court will be like when I'm no longer there to force it out of its natural dullness and spitefulness."

"And you," said the prince, "are refusing the crown of Parma; more than that, in fact, because you wouldn't have been an ordinary princess, married for political reasons and unloved. My heart belongs entirely to you, and you would have been the absolute mistress of my actions and my government, forever."

"Yes, but your mother would have had a right to despise me as a vile schemer."

"Then I'd have sent her into exile with a pension!"

They exchanged cutting remarks for another three-quarters of an hour. The prince, who had a delicate soul, could not make up his mind either to exercise his right or let the duchess leave. He had been told that once the first victory had been won, no matter how, women always returned.

407

After having been ordered to leave by the indignant duchess, he dared to come back that night, trembling and thoroughly wretched, at three minutes to ten. At half-past ten the duchess got into her carriage and set off for Bologna. As soon as she was outside the prince's territory she wrote to the count:

> The sacrifice has been made. Do not ask me to be gay for the next month. I will never see Fabrizio again. I will wait for you in Bologna, and I will become Countess Mosca whenever you wish. I ask only one thing of you: never force me to return to the dominions I have just left, and always remember that, instead of an income of a hundred and fifty thousand lire, you are going to have thirty or forty thousand at most. The fools have all been watching you with open mouths, and you will be respected only insofar as you lower yourself to understand their petty ideas. You asked for it, George Dandin!*

Their wedding took place a week later at Perugia, in a church containing the tombs of the count's ancestors. The prince was in despair. He had sent three or four couriers to the duchess, and she had returned each one of his letters unopened. He had granted the count a magnificent pension, and awarded the Grand Cordon of his Order to Fabrizio.

"What I liked about our farewell," said the count to the new Countess Mosca della Rovere, "was that we parted the best of friends. He gave me a Spanish Grand Cordon and some diamonds worth at least as much as the Grand Cordon. He told me he'd make me a duke if it weren't for the fact that he wanted to keep that in reserve as a means of bringing you back to Parma. I have therefore been instructed to inform you—a fine mission for a husband!—that if you ever deign to return to Parma, even for only a month, I will be made a duke, under any name you choose, and you will have a fine estate."

The duchess refused this offer with a kind of horror.

After the scene which had taken place in the ballroom of the palace, and which had seemed rather decisive, Clelia appeared to have forgotten the love she seemed to have shared for a moment. The most violent remorse had taken

---

* A quotation from Molière's *George Dandin ou le Mari confondu.*—L.B.

possession of her virtuous and pious soul. Fabrizio realized this quite clearly, and despite all the hopes he tried to give himself, he sank into black melancholy. This time, however, his misery did not lead him into a retreat, as it had done at the time of Clelia's wedding.

The count had asked "his nephew" to keep him accurately informed of everything that took place at court, and Fabrizio, who was beginning to realize how much he owed to him, had promised himself he would perform this task with scrupulous care.

Like everyone else at court and in the city, Fabrizio did not doubt that his friend planned to return to the ministry, and with more power than he had ever had before. The count's predictions were soon verified: less than six weeks after his departure, Rassi was Prime Minister, Fabio Conti was Minister of War, and the prisons, which the count had nearly emptied, were filling up again. The prince felt that he was avenging himself on the duchess by placing these men in office; he was mad with love, and he particularly hated Count Mosca as his rival.

Fabrizio was being kept extremely busy. Archbishop Landriani, now seventy-two, had fallen into a state of great weakness and almost never left his palace, so his coadjutor had to perform nearly all his duties for him.

Clelia, overwhelmed with remorse and frightened by her confessor, had found an excellent way of keeping out of Fabrizio's sight: on the pretext of the approaching end of a first pregnancy, she had made herself a prisoner in her own house. But this house had a garden; Fabrizio managed to enter it, and in her favorite path he placed bouquets of flowers arranged in such a way as to convey a message, just as she had conveyed a message to him every evening during the last days of his imprisonment in the Farnese Tower.

Clelia was greatly upset by this attempt; her heart was dominated sometimes by remorse, sometimes by passion. For several months she did not allow herself to go into her garden; she even had qualms about glancing at it.

Fabrizio was beginning to think that he was going to be separated from her forever, and despair was beginning to take possession of his soul. The world in which he spent his time was painfully repugnant to him, and if he had not been inwardly convinced that the count would not find peace of mind until he was back in office, he would have gone into retreat in his little apartment in the archbishop's palace. It would have been pleasant for him to live alone with his thoughts, and never to hear a human voice again except in the performance of his duties.

"But," he thought, "no one can replace me in serving the interests of Count and Countess Mosca."

The prince continued to treat him with a respect which placed him in the foremost rank at court, and, to a large extent, he had earned this favor himself. His extreme reserve, which sprang from an indifference, bordering on disgust, to all the affectations and petty passions that fill the lives of men, had stung the young prince's vanity; he often said that Fabrizio was as intelligent as his aunt. The prince's artless soul had grasped half of a truth: that no one approached him in the same frame of mind as Fabrizio. Even the common run of courtiers could not fail to notice that the respect Fabrizio had won was quite different from what was usually accorded to a mere coadjutor, and that it surpassed even the respect which the prince showed for the archbishop. Fabrizio wrote to the count that if the prince ever had the intelligence to perceive the mess that had been made of his affairs by his ministers Rassi, Fabio Conti, Zurla and others of their caliber, he, Fabrizio, would no doubt be chosen to act as intermediary for a proposal which His Highness would make to the count, without, of course, too greatly humbling his pride. And he wrote the following to Countess Mosca:

•

If it were not for the fatal words "that child," applied by a man of genius to an august personage, that august personage would already have cried out, "Come back at once, and rid me of this rabble!" As of this moment, if the wife of the man of genius would deign to make an overture, no matter how slight, the count would be recalled with joy; but he will return on still more exalted terms if he will wait till the time is ripe. The princess's drawing rooms are now as full of boredom as anyone could wish. Rassi's absurdity is the only diversion there. Now that he is a count, he has become a maniac on the subject of nobility. Strict orders have been issued that anyone who cannot prove eight quarterings of nobility "shall no longer dare to present himself at the princess's evenings" (those are the exact words of the decree). All men who already have the right to enter the great gallery in the morning, and to wait along the sovereign's route when he goes to Mass, will continue to enjoy that privilege, but newcomers will have to prove eight quarterings of nobility. Whereupon it has been said that Rassi gives no quarter.

One may well imagine that such letters were not entrusted to the post. Countess Mosca replied from Naples:

> We have a concert every Thursday and an evening party every Sunday; our drawing rooms are always packed. The count is delighted with his excavations. He spends a thousand lire a month on them, and has just brought in some workmen from the Abruzzi Appenines who cost him only twenty-three soldi a day. You really ought to come and see us. This is at least the twentieth time, you ingrate, that I have sent you this summons.

Fabrizio had no intention of obeying her: even writing a letter every day to either her or the count seemed to him an almost unbearably irksome task. He will be forgiven when it is learned that he spent a whole year in this way, without ever being able to address a word to Clelia. All his attempts to establish some sort of communication with her had been rejected with horror. The habitual silence which, from boredom with life, he maintained at all times, except when he was at court or performing his duties, combined with the perfect moral purity of his conduct, had made him the object of such extraordinary veneration that he finally decided to follow the advice of his aunt, who had written to him:

> The prince has such great respect for you that you must expect to lose his favor before long; he will begin showing frequent signs of inattention, and the courtiers' horrible contempt will follow his. These petty despots, however honest they may be, are as fickle as fashion, and for the same reason: boredom. Only by preaching can you find the strength with which to oppose the sovereign's whims. You improvise so well in verse! Try to speak on religion for half an hour. You will utter heresies at first, but pay a learned and discreet theologian to attend your sermons and point out your mistakes; you will correct them the next day.

The kind of misery with which thwarted love fills the soul makes anything requiring attention and action become a terrible ordeal. But Fabrizio told himself that his influence with the common people, if he acquired any, might some day be useful to his aunt and the count, for whom his veneration was growing every day, in proportion as his worldly affairs taught him to know the maliciousness of mankind. He decided to preach, and his success, aided by his thinness and his shabby coat, was unparalleled. His listeners found in his sermons a tinge of deep sadness which, combined with his charming face and the stories of the high favor he enjoyed at court, conquered the hearts of all the women. They invented a tale about his having been one of the bravest captains in Napoleon's army. This absurd idea was soon regarded as an incontestable truth. Seats were reserved beforehand in the churches where he preached; poor people occupied them as early as five o'clock in the morning, with the object of selling them.

Fabrizio was so successful that he finally had an idea which changed everything within his heart: if only out of curiosity, Clelia might some day come to hear one of his sermons. Suddenly the spellbound public noticed that his talent was increasing: when he was deeply moved, he allowed himself to use images whose boldness would have made the most experienced orators shudder; sometimes, forgetting himself, he would have moments of impassioned inspiration, and the whole congregation would burst into tears. But it was in vain that his watchful eyes scanned all those faces turned toward the pulpit, seeking the one whose presence would have been such a great event for him.

"But if I ever have that good fortune," he thought, "I'll either faint or be at a total loss for words." To avoid this latter mishap, he composed a kind of tender and passionate prayer and kept it in his pulpit, on a stool; he planned to begin reading it if Clelia's presence should ever render him incapable of finding anything to say.

He learned one day, from those of the Marquis Crescenzi's servants whom he had bribed, that orders had been given to prepare the box of the Casa Crescenzi in the great theater for the following evening. The marquise had not appeared at any sort of performance for the past year, and it was a tenor who was then all the rage, and who filled the house every evening, that was about to make her depart from her habits. Fabrizio's first emotion was extreme joy. "At last I'll be able to see her for a whole evening!" he thought. "They say she's very pale." And he tried to imagine how that charming face would look, with its colors half effaced by inner conflicts.

His friend Ludovico, in consternation over what he called his master's madness, succeeded after a great deal of difficulty in obtaining a box in the third tier, almost directly over Clelia's. An idea occurred to Fabrizio: "I hope to give her the idea of coming to one of my sermons. I'll choose a very small church, so that I'll be able to see her clearly." He usually preached at three o'clock. On the morning of the day when the marquise was to go to the theater, he announced that, since he would be detained all day in the archbishop's palace by one of his official duties, he would preach that evening, contrary to his custom, at half-past eight, in the little church of Santa Maria della Visitazione, situated directly opposite one of the wings of the Crescenzi palace. Ludovico presented, on his behalf, an enormous number of candles to the nuns of the Order of the Visitation of Our Lady, with a request to illuminate their church brightly. He secured a whole company of grenadiers of the guard, and a sentry with a fixed bayonet was posted in front of each chapel, to prevent theft.

The sermon was not scheduled to begin until half-past eight, but the church was completely filled by two o'clock; one may imagine what an uproar there was in that normally quiet street dominated by the noble architecture of the Crescenzi palace. Fabrizio had announced that, in honor of Our Lady of Pity, he would preach on the subject of the pity which a generous soul ought to feel for anyone in distress, even if he is guilty.

Disguised with all possible care, Fabrizio went to his box in the theater just as the doors were being opened, and when there were still no lights. The performance began at eight o'clock, and a few minutes later he experienced a joy which cannot be conceived by anyone who has not felt it: he saw the door of the Crescenzi box open, and a moment later Clelia came into it; he had not seen her so clearly since the night when she had given him her fan. He thought he would choke with joy; he had such extraordinary sensations that he said to himself, "Perhaps I'm going to die! What a wonderful way to end this sad life! Perhaps I'm going to collapse in this box; the congregation in the church won't see me there tonight, and tomorrow they'll learn that their future archbishop has disgraced himself in a theater box—and while disguised as a servant in livery! Good-by to my whole reputation! But what do I care about my reputation?"

However, toward a quarter to nine Fabrizio forced himself to leave his box in the third tier and, with great difficulty, went on foot to the place where he was to take off his semi-livery and put on more suitable attire. He did not reach the Church of the Visitation until nine. He was in such a state of pallor and weakness that a rumor went through the church that the coadjutor would be unable to preach that evening. One may imagine the attentions lavished on him by the nuns from the grille of their inner visiting room, to which he had withdrawn. These ladies talked a great deal; he asked to be alone for a few moments, then hurried to his pulpit. One of his assistants had told him, toward three o'clock, that the church was entirely filled, but with people belonging to the lowest classes, who had apparently been attracted by the sight of the illumination. On entering the pulpit, Fabrizio was pleasantly surprised to find all the seats occupied by fashionable young people and extremely distinguished personages.

He began his sermon with a few words of apology which were received with suppressed cries of admiration. Then followed an impassioned description of the person in distress whom we ought to pity in order to pay due respect to Our Lady of Pity, who herself had suffered so much on earth. The orator was deeply moved; there were times when he was scarcely able to speak loudly enough to be heard in all parts of that little church. In the eyes of all the women and a large number of the men, he himself was the person in distress who ought to be pitied. A few minutes after the apology with which he had begun his sermon, it was noticed that he was not in his normal state: his sadness was felt to be more profound and wistful than usual. Once tears were seen his eyes; a sob burst forth from the entire congregation, so loudly that the sermon was interrupted.

This first interruption was followed by a dozen others: there were cries of admiration, outbursts of tears, and at every moment one could hear exclamations such as, "Ah, Holy Madonna!" or "Ah, dear God!" The emotion of that select assembly was so unanimous and so irresistible that no one was ashamed of crying aloud, and those who were carried away in this manner did not seem ridiculous to their neighbors.

During the intermission that is customary in the middle of a sermon, Fabrizio was told that the theater had been deserted; only one lady was still in her box: the Marquise Crescenzi. During this rest period, a loud clamor was suddenly heard in the church: the congregation was urging that a statue be erected to the coadjutor. The second part of his sermon was received with such excited and worldly enthusiasm, and outbursts of Christian contrition were so completely replaced by thoroughly secular cries of admiration, that when he was about to leave the pulpit he felt it his duty to address a mild reprimand to his listeners, whereupon they all walked out at once in a strangely stiff and formal manner. Then, when they were outside in the street, they began wildly applauding and shouting, *"Evviva del Dongo!"*

Fabrizio hurriedly glanced at his watch and ran over to a little barred window which lighted the narrow passage from the organ to the interior of the convent. Out of courtesy to the incredible and unprecedented crowd that filled the street, the porter of the Crescenzi palace had placed a dozen torches in those iron hands which project from the front walls of palaces built in the Middle Ages. Several minutes later, long before the shouting had ceased, the event which Fabrizio had been awaiting with such anxiety occurred: the Marquise Crescenzi's carriage, returning from the theater, appeared in the street. The coachman was forced to stop, and it was only at a very slow pace, and with much shouting to clear the way, that the carriage was able to reach the door.

Clelia had been touched by the sublime music, as are all unhappy hearts, but still more by the utter solitude of the performance, once she had learned the reason for it. In the middle of the second act, and while the admirable tenor was on stage, even the people in the orchestra seats had deserted the theater to try their luck at getting into the Church of the Visitation. When she found herself stopped by the crowd outside her door, she burst into tears. "I didn't make a bad choice!" she thought.

But, precisely because of this moment of tender emotion, she resisted the urging of the marquis and all the friends of the family, who could not understand why she did not go to hear such an amazing preacher. "Why, he's won out over the best tenor in Italy!" they said. "If I see him," she thought, "I'm lost!"

It was in vain that Fabrizio, whose talent seemed more brilliant every day, preached several more times in that same little church near the Crescenzi palace: he never saw Clelia, who finally even became annoyed at his presumption in coming to disturb her quiet street, after she had already driven him from her garden.

In glancing over the faces of the women listening to him, Fabrizio had some time ago begun to notice a dark and very pretty face with eyes that flashed fire. By the time he came to the ninth or tenth sentence of his sermon, those magnificent eyes were usually bathed in tears. When he was obliged to

415

say things that were long and boring to him, he was glad to rest his eyes on that face whose youthfulness pleased him. He learned that the girl's name was Annetta Marini, and that she was the only daughter and heiress of the richest cloth merchant in Parma, who had died a few months earlier.

Soon the name of this Annetta Marini, the cloth merchant's daughter, was on everyone's lips: she had fallen madly in love with Fabrizio. When the famous sermons began, arrangements had already been made for her marriage to Giacomo Rassi, eldest son of the Minister of Justice, who was not at all unattractive to her; but she had barely listened twice to *Monsignore* Fabrizio before she declared that she no longer wanted to get married, and when she was asked the reason for this abrupt change, she replied that it was unworthy of an honorable girl to marry one man when she was passionately in love with another. Her family tried, unsuccessfully at first, to find out who this other man might be.

But the burning tears which Annetta shed during the sermons put them on the track of the truth. When her mother and her uncles asked her if she loved *Monsignore* Fabrizio, she answered boldly that, since they had discovered the truth, she would not debase herself by lying. She added that, having no hope of ever marrying the man she adored, she wanted at least no longer to have her eyes offended by the sight of *Contino* Rassi's ridiculous face. Within two days, this ridicule cast on the son of a man who had earned the envy of the entire middle class was the topic of every conversation in Parma. Annetta Marini's answer seemed charming, and everyone repeated it. It was discussed in the Crescenzi palace as everywhere else.

Clelia was careful to make no mention of the subject in her drawing room, but she questioned her maid, and on the following Sunday, after attending Mass in the chapel of her palace, she took her maid with her in her carriage and went to attend a second Mass in Signorina Marini's parish church. She found all the elegant young men of the town assembled there, attracted by the same object; these gentlemen were standing near the door. Soon, from the great commotion among them, she gathered that Signorina Marini was entering the church. She found herself well placed to see her, and, despite her piety, she paid scarcely any attention to the Mass. She found in that middle-class beauty a certain air of self-assurance which, in her opinion, might have been appropriate, at most, in a woman who had been married for several years. Otherwise, she had a small, shapely figure, and her

416

eyes, as they say in Lombardy, seemed to make conversation with whatever they looked at. Clelia fled before the end of the Mass.

The next day the friends of the Crescenzi family, who always came to spend the evening with them, related a new anecdote about Annetta Marini's ridiculous behavior. Since her mother, fearing some act of madness on her part, left very little money at her disposal, Annetta had gone to offer a magnificent diamond ring, a present from her father, to the celebrated Hayez, who was then in Parma to decorate the drawing rooms of the Crescenzi palace, and asked him to paint a portrait of Signor del Dongo for her; but she wanted this portrait to show him dressed, not as a priest, but simply in black. And so, on the previous evening, little Annetta's mother had been greatly surprised, and still more scandalized, to find in her daughter's bedroom a magnificent portrait of Fabrizio del Dongo, set in the finest frame that had been gilded in Parma for the past twenty years.

CHAPTER TWENTY-EIGHT

Swept along by events, we have not had time to sketch a picture of the comical race of courtiers who abounded at the court of Parma, and who made extraordinary comments on the events we have related. In Parma, what made a little nobleman, possessing an income of three or four thousand lire, worthy of being present in black stockings at the prince's levees, was first of all never to have read Voltaire and Rousseau; this condition was not difficult to fulfill. Next, he had to know how to speak with deep concern about the sovereign's cold, or the latest case of minerals he had received from Saxony. If, after that, the nobleman never failed to attend Mass for a single day in the year, and if he could number two or three fat monks among his intimate friends, the prince would deign to speak to him once a year, two weeks before or two weeks after the first of January. This would give him high standing in his parish, and the tax collector would not dare to harass him too much if he was late in paying the annual sum of a hundred lire which was levied on his small estate.

Signor Gonzo was a poor devil of this sort. He was a man of very noble birth who, besides owning a little property, had obtained, through the Marquis Crescenzi's influence, a magnificent post which gave him eleven hundred and fifty lire a year. This man could have dined at home, but he had one passion: he was at ease and happy only when he was in the drawing room of some great personage who would say to him now and then, "Keep quiet, Gonzo, you're nothing but a fool." This judgment was dictated by resentment, for Gonzo was nearly always more intelligent than the great personage. He spoke quite charmingly on every subject, and furthermore he was always ready to change his opinion at a single grimace on the part of the master of the house. To tell the truth, although he was extremely adroit where his own interests were concerned, he had not one idea in his head, and if the prince did not happen to be suffering from a cold at the moment, he was sometimes at a loss when he entered a drawing room.

What had earned Gonzo a reputation in Parma was a magnificent cocked hat, adorned with a rather shabby black plume, which he wore even with his dress coat. But you should have seen the way he carried that plume, whether on his head or in his hand! There lay his talent and his self-importance. He would inquire about the health of the marquise's little dog with genuine anxiety, and if the Crescenzi palace had caught fire he would have risked his life to save one of those fine armchairs in gold brocade which for so many years had snagged his black silk breeches whenever he dared to sit down on one of them for a moment.

Seven or eight individuals of this species came into the Marquise Crescenzi's drawing room at seven o'clock every evening. As soon as they sat down, a footman magnificently attired in a pale yellow livery that was covered with silver braid, as was also the short red jacket which completed his splendor, would come to take the poor devils' hats and canes. He would be followed immediately by another servant bringing an infinitely small cup of coffee resting on a stand of silver filigree; and every half-hour a butler, wearing a sword and a magnificent French-style coat, would come in to offer ices.

Half an hour after the shabby little courtiers, five or six officers would arrive; they always talked loudly, with a very martial air, and they usually discussed the number and type of buttons which a soldier ought to wear on his coat to enable his commanding general to win victories. It would not have been prudent to quote a French newspaper in that drawing room, for even if the news had been extremely pleasant, such as, for example, the shooting of fifty liberals in Spain, the narrator would nevertheless have remained convicted of having read a French newspaper. The consummate achievement of all these people's skill was to obtain a increase of a hundred and fifty lire in their pensions every ten years. It is thus that a prince shares with his nobility the pleasure of reigning over the peasants and the middle classes.

The principal personage in the Crescenzi drawing room was unquestionably Cavaliere Foscarini; he was a perfectly honorable man, and had therefore spent some time in prison under every régime. He had been a member of that famous Chamber of Deputies in Milan which had rejected the registration law presented by Napoleon, a type of action that is rare in history. After having been the intimate friend of the marquis' mother for twenty years, Cavaliere Foscarini had continued to be the most influential man in the house. He always had some amusing story to tell, but nothing escaped his shrewdness, and the young marquise, who felt guilty at the bottom of her heart, trembled before him.

Since Gonzo had a real passion for this great nobleman, who said crude things to him and made him weep once or twice a year, his mania was to try to render him little services, and if he had not been paralyzed by the habits of extreme poverty, he might have succeeded occasionally, for he was not without a certain shrewdness, and a much greater amount of effrontery.

This Gonzo, such as we now know him, was rather contemptuous of the Marquise Crescenzi, for she had never spoken an impolite word to him in her life; but, after all, she was the wife of the famous Marquis Crescenzi, the princess's Knight of Honor, who said to him once or twice a month, "Keep quiet, Gonzo, you're a stupid fool."

Gonzo had noticed that anything that was said about little Annetta Marini momentarily roused the marquise from the state of dreamy indifference in which she usually remained until the clock struck eleven, when she would make tea and offer some to each man present, addressing him by name. Then, just before going up to her room, she would seem to become cheerful for a moment, and this was always the time chosen for reciting satirical sonnets to her.

Excellent ones are composed in Italy: it is the only kind of literature which still has a little life, for it is not subjected to official censorship. The courtiers of the Casa Crescenzi invariably prefaced their sonnets with these words: "Would the marquise be so kind as to allow the recital of a very bad sonnet in her presence?" And after the sonnet had made the company laugh, and had been repeated two or three times, one of the officers was sure to exclaim, "The Minister of Police ought to hang the authors of such infamous things!" In middle-class circles, on the other hand, these sonnets are greeted with the most open admiration, and copies of them are sold by lawyers' clerks.

From the kind of curiosity shown by the marquise, Gonzo concluded that she had heard too much praise of the beauty of little Annetta Marini, who furthermore had a fortune of a million lire, and that she was jealous of her. Since, with his constant smile and his complete effrontery toward anyone who was not noble, Gonzo was able to make his way into all circles, the next day he came into the marquise's drawing room carrying his plumed hat with a certain triumphant air which he usually displayed no more than once or twice a year, on those occasions when the prince had said to him, "Good-by, Gonzo."

After bowing respectfully to the marquise, Gonzo did not leave her, as was his custom, to go and sit down on the armchair that had just been brought out for him. He stood in the middle of the circle and cried out abruptly, "I've seen the portrait of *Monsignore* del Dongo!" Clelia was so taken aback that she had to lean on the arm of her chair; she tried to weather the storm, but she was soon forced to leave the room.

"You must admit, my poor Gonzo, that you're as tactless as anyone could be!" exclaimed one of the officers haughtily as he was finishing his fourth ice. "How can you not know that the coadjutor, who was one of the bravest colonels in Napoleon's army, once played an outrageous trick on the marquise's father by leaving the citadel, while General Conti was in command of it, as though he were walking out of the Steccata?" (The Steccata is the principal church in Parma.)

"It's true that I'm ignorant of many things, my dear captain, and I'm a poor imbecile who makes blunders all day long."

This reply, very much to the Italian taste, brought forth laughter at the elegant officer's expense. The marquise returned soon afterward; she had plucked up her courage, and she was not without some vague hope that she herself would be able to admire that portrait of Fabrizio, which was said to be excellent. She praised the talent of Hayez, who had painted it. Without knowing it, she smiled charmingly at Gonzo, who kept glancing slyly at the officer. Since all the other courtiers in the room were indulging in the same pleasure, the officer fled, not without conceiving a deadly hatred of Gonzo. The latter was triumphant, and as he was taking his leave at the end of the evening he was invited to dinner the following day.

"Here's another piece of news!" he cried the next day after dinner, when the servants had left the room. "Now our coadjutor has fallen in love with Annetta Marini!"

One may imagine the agitation aroused in Clelia's heart by this extraordinary statement. Even the marquis was disturbed.

"Gonzo, my friend, you're raving as usual! And you ought to show a little more reserve when you speak of a man who's had the honor of playing whist with His Highness eleven times!"

"Well, marquis," replied Gonzo with the crudeness of those of his species, "I can assure you that he'd also like to play games with little Annetta! But it's enough that these details displease you; they no longer exist for me, because above all I want to avoid offending my adorable marquis."

The marquis always withdrew to take a nap after dinner. He did without his nap that day, but Gonzo would rather have cut out his own tongue than add a single word about Annetta Marini, and he kept making prefatory remarks designed to give the marquis hope that he was going to return to the subject of her amorous adventures. Gonzo had to a superior degree that Italian wit which consists in gleefully withholding information which one's listener is eager to hear. The poor marquis, dying of curiosity, was obliged to make advances: he told Gonzo that he ate twice as much when he had the pleasure of dining with him. Gonzo did not understand, and began describing a magnificent gallery of pictures which the Marquise Balbi, the late prince's mistress, was collecting. "Good," thought the marquis, "at last he's coming to the portrait ordered by Annetta Marini!" But Gonzo was careful to do no such thing. The clock struck five, which greatly irritated the marquis, for it was his custom to get into his carriage at half-past five, after his nap, and drive to the Corso.

"Look what you're doing with your silly chatter!" he said rudely to Gonzo. "You're going to make me reach the Corso after the princess: I'm her Knight of Honor, and she may have some orders to give me! Come on, hurry! Tell me in a few words, if you can, what you've heard about the coadjutor's alleged love affair."

But Gonzo wanted to reserve this story for the marquise, who had invited him to dinner. He therefore gave a rapid,

421

sketchy version of it, and the marquis, half asleep, hurried off to take his nap. Gonzo adopted a totally different manner with the poor marquise. She had remained so young and guileless in her lofty position that she felt obliged to make amends for the rudeness with which the marquis had just spoken to him. Delighted by this success, he recovered all his eloquence and made it a pleasure, no less than a duty, to relate the story to her in endless detail.

Annetta Marini was paying as much as a sequin for each seat that was reserved for her at the sermons. She always came with two of her aunts and her father's former cashier. She had these seats held for her from the day before each sermon, and they were usually chosen almost directly in front of the pulpit, but slightly in the direction of the high altar, for she had noticed that the coadjutor often turned toward it. Now what the public had also noticed was that *not infrequently* the young preacher's expressive eyes would linger with pleasure on the strikingly beautiful young heiress; and apparently with attention, too, for as soon as he turned his eyes to her his sermon would become erudite: quotations would begin to abound in it, there were no more of those surges of emotion which spring from the heart, and the ladies, losing interest almost immediately, would begin looking at Annetta Marini and gossiping about her.

Clelia made Gonzo repeat these singular details three times to her. After the third time she became extremely thoughtful; she was calculating that it had been exactly fourteen months since she had last seen Fabrizio. "Would there be any great harm," she wondered, "in spending an hour in a church, not to see Fabrizio, but to hear a famous preacher? Besides, I'll sit far away from the pulpit, and I'll look at him only twice: once when I come in, and once at the end of the sermon. . . . No, I won't be going there to see Fabrizio, I'll be going to hear an amazing preacher!" In the midst of this reasoning she felt some remorse: her conduct had been so noble for the past fourteen months! "Well," she thought, to give herself a little peace of mind, "if the first woman who comes in this evening has been to hear *Monsignore* del Dongo preach, I'll go too; if not, I won't."

Once she had come to this decision, she overjoyed Gonzo by saying to him, "Try to find out when the coadjutor will preach next, and in what church. This evening, before you leave, I may ask you to do something for me."

As soon as Gonzo set off for the Corso, Clelia went out for a breath of fresh air in the garden of her palace. She did not trouble herself with the objection that she had not set foot in it for the past ten months. She was sprightly and animated, and the color had returned to her cheeks.

That evening, as each boring visitor entered the drawing room, her heart palpitated with emotion. At last Gonzo was announced, and he saw at a glance that he was going to be the indispensable man for a week. "The marquise is jealous of little Annetta," he thought. "What an excellent comedy it would make, with the marquise playing the leading role, Annetta the soubrette, and *Monsignore* del Dongo the lover! Two lire wouldn't be too much to pay for a ticket!" He was beside himself with joy; all evening he kept interrupting everyone and relating the most preposterous stories (for example, the one about the celebrated actress and the Marquis de Pequigny, which he had heard the day before from a French traveler).

As for the marquise, she could not sit still: she paced up and down the drawing room for a time, then went into an adjoining gallery in which the marquis allowed only pictures costing over twenty thousand lire. These pictures spoke to her so clearly that evening that they tired her heart with emotion. Finally she heard the double door opened; she hurried back into the drawing room: it was the Marquise Raversi! But as she spoke conventional words of greeting to her, Clelia felt her voice failing. The Marquise Raversi made her repeat this question twice, for she had not understood it at first: "What do you think of the famous preacher?"

"I used to regard him as a little schemer, a worthy nephew of the illustrious Countess Mosca, but the last time he preached—it was in the Church of the Visitation, by the way, just opposite your house—he was so sublime that all my hatred vanished, and I now consider him the most eloquent man I've ever heard."

"So you've attended one of his sermons?" asked Clelia, trembling with happiness.

"What? Weren't you listening to me?" said the marquise, laughing. "I wouldn't miss them for anything in the world! They say he's becoming consumptive, and that he'll soon stop preaching!"

As soon as the Marquise Raversi had left, Clelia called Gonzo into the gallery. "I've almost made up my mind," she said, "to hear that preacher whom everyone praises so highly. When will he preach next?"

"Three days from now, on Monday; and it almost seems

as though he's guessed your plans, because he's going to preach in the Church of the Visitation."

There was more to be said, but Clelia's voice had failed again; she walked around the gallery five or six times without adding another word. "She has vengeance on her mind," thought Gonzo. "How could anyone be so insolent as to escape from prison, especially when he has the honor of being guarded by a hero like General Fabio Conti?"

"But you'll have to hurry," he said with subtle irony. "He's consumptive, and I heard Dr. Bembo say he has less than a year to live. God is punishing him for having broken his ban by treacherously escaping from the citadel."

Clelia sat down on the couch in the gallery and motioned Gonzo to follow her example. A few moments later she handed him a little purse, in which she had already placed a few sequins, and said to him, "Have four seats reserved for me."

"Would it be permissible for poor Gonzo to slip into your entourage?"

"Of course; reserve five seats. . . . I have no desire to be near the pulpit, but I'd like to be able to see Signorina Marini, who's said to be so pretty."

Clelia was scarcely able to live through the three days that separated her from that famous Monday, the day of the sermon. Gonzo, for whom it was a great honor to be seen in public in the entourage of such a great lady, wore his French coat and his sword for the occasion. And that was not all: taking advantage of the nearness of the palace, he had a magnificent gilded armchair brought into the church for the marquise, which was considered the height of insolence by the middle-class members of the congregation. It can well be imagined how the poor marquise felt when she saw this chair, which had been placed directly in front of the pulpit. She was so embarrassed, trying to hide herself in a corner of the enormous armchair and keeping her eyes lowered, that she did not even have the courage to look at Annetta Marini, whom Gonzo pointed out to her with an effrontery that took her breath away. To that courtier, anyone not of noble birth was absolutely nothing.

Fabrizio appeared in the pulpit; he was so thin, so pale, so "wasted away," that Clelia's eyes instantly filled with tears. He said a few words, then stopped as though his voice had suddenly failed him; he vainly tried to begin a few sentences; he turned around and picked up a piece of paper with writing on it.

"My brethren," he said, "a soul in pain and quite worthy of all your pity urges you, through my voice, to pray for the end of his torments, which will cease only with his life."

He read the rest of the sheet of paper very slowly; but the expression of his voice was such that everyone, even Gonzo, was weeping before he had come to the middle of the prayer. "At least I won't be noticed," thought Clelia, bursting into tears.

As he read the words written on the paper, Fabrizio found two or three things to say about the unhappy man for whom he was soliciting the prayers of the congregation. Soon thoughts began thronging into his mind. While seeming to address the public, he spoke only to Clelia. He ended his sermon a little earlier than usual, because, despite all his efforts, he was becoming so overwhelmed by tears that he could no longer speak intelligibly. The best judges found this sermon strange, but at least equal in pathos to the famous sermon preached on the night of the great illumination. As for Clelia, no sooner had she heard the first ten lines of the prayer read by Fabrizio than she regarded it as a horrible crime to have been able to go fourteen months without seeing him. On returning home she went to bed so that she could think about him undisturbed, and early the next morning he received the following note:

I count on your honor. Hire four bodyguards whose discretion you can trust, and tonight, when the clock of the Steccata strikes midnight, come to a little door bearing the number 19, in the Strada San Paolo. Bear in mind that you may be attacked: do not come alone.

When he recognized that divine handwriting, Fabrizio fell to his knees and burst into tears. "At last," he cried, "after fourteen months and eight days! Farewell to preaching!"

It would take too long to describe all the various kinds of madness that took possession of the hearts of Fabrizio and Clelia that day. The little door indicated in the note was none other than that of the orangery of the Crescenzi palace, and Fabrizio found occasion to see it a dozen times in the course of the day. He armed himself, and a little before midnight, as he was walking past this door swiftly and alone, to his inexpressible joy he heard a familiar voice say to him very softly, "Come in here, friend of my heart."

He entered cautiously and found himself inside the orangery, but facing a heavily barred window three or four

425

feet above the ground. The darkness was intense; he had heard a sound from the window, and his hand was groping over the bars when he felt another hand slip between them, take hold of his and draw it to a pair of lips which kissed it.

"It's I," said a beloved voice. "I came here to tell you that I love you, and to ask if you will obey me."

It is not difficult to imagine his reply, his joy and his astonishment. After the first raptures, Clelia said to him, "As you know, I've made a vow to the Madonna never to see you again; that's why I've met you in this total darkness. I want you to know that if you should ever force me to look at you in broad daylight, everything will be over between us. But first of all, I want you to stop preaching in front of Annetta Marini, and don't think it was I who had the stupid idea of bringing an armchair into the House of God."

"My dearest angel, I'll never preach again in front of anyone: I began preaching only in the hope that some day I might see you."

"Don't say that—remember that *I* musn't see *you.*"

At this point, we ask permission to pass over a period of three years without saying a word about it.

At the time when we take up our story again, Count Mosca had long since returned to Parma as Prime Minister, and was more powerful than ever.

After those three years of divine happiness, Fabrizio's heart had a tender impulse which changed everything. Clelia had a charming two-year-old son named Sandrino, who was his mother's joy. He was always with her or on the Marquis Crescenzi's lap; Fabrizio, on the other hand, almost never saw him. He did not want him to become accustomed to loving another father. He conceived the plan of taking the boy away before his memories had become very distinct.

During the long hours of each day when Clelia could not be with her lover, she was consoled by Sandrino's presence; for we must admit something which will seem strange north of the Alps: despite her other failings, she had remained true to her vow. She had promised the Madonna, as the reader my recall, *never to see* Fabrizio; such were her exact words. She therefore met him only at night, and there were never any lights in the room.

But she met him every night, and the admirable part of it is that, in the midst of a court devoured by curiosity and boredom, Fabrizio's precautions had been so cleverly calculated that this *amicizia*, as they say in Lombardy, had never

426

been even suspected. Their love was too passionate to be without quarrels; Clelia was strongly inclined to jealousy, but their quarrels nearly always had another cause. If Fabrizio had taken advantage of a public ceremony to be in the same place with her and look at her, she would quickly leave on some pretext or other, and then she would banish him for a long time.

Everyone at the court of Parma was amazed that a woman so remarkable for her beauty and the loftiness of her mind had never been known to be involved in any intrigue; she aroused passions which inspired many extravagant acts, and often Fabrizio was also jealous.

The good Archbishop Landriani had long since died, and Fabrizio's piety, eloquence and exemplary morals had caused his predecessor to be forgotten. Fabrizio's elder brother had also died, and the entire family fortune had come into his possession. From that time onward, every year he had distributed among the curates and parish priests of his diocese the hundred and fifty thousand lire he received as his income from the Archbishopric of Parma.

It would be difficult to imagine a life more honored, more honorable and more useful than that which Fabrizio had made for himself before everything was upset by that unfortunate impulse of his heart.

"According to your vow, which I respect even though it's the greatest cause of unhappiness in my life, since you won't see me in daylight," he said to Clelia one night, "I'm forced to live constantly alone, with no other distraction than my work, and I don't even have enough work to do. In the midst of that sad, grim way of passing the long hours of each day, an idea has occurred to me which keeps tormenting me, and which I've been vainly struggling against for the past six months: my son won't love me; he never hears my name. He's being brought up amid the pleasant luxury of the Crescenzi palace, and he hardly knows me. On the few occasions when I see him, I think of his mother, because he reminds me of the heavenly beauty I can never see, and he must find that my face looks serious, which to children means gloomy."

"Well," said Clelia, "what's the point of this alarming speech you're making to me?"

"I want my son; I want him to live with me; I want to see him every day; I want him to become accustomed to loving me; I want to love him myself, freely. Since an unparalleled fate has deprived me of the happiness, enjoyed

427

by so many other loving hearts, of living with the woman I love, I want at least to have someone with me who will remind me of you, and replace you to some extent. All people and all worldly affairs are nothing but a burden to me in my enforced solitude; you know that ambition has been an empty word to me ever since I had the good fortune to be registered in prison by Barbone, and everything unrelated to feelings of the heart seems absurd to me in the melancholy that overwhelms me when I'm not with you."

It is easy to understand the sharp anguish with which her lover's sorrow filled poor Clelia's heart, and her sadness was all the deeper because she felt that, in a way, he was right. She went so far as to wonder whether she should not try to have her vow annulled. She could then receive Fabrizio during the day, like any other member of society, and her reputation for virtue was so well established that there would never be any gossip about her. She told herself that with a great deal of money she could succeed in having herself relieved of her vow; but she also felt that a worldly arrangement of that sort would not ease her conscience, and that an angry heaven might punish her for that new crime.

On the other hand, if she consented to yield to Fabrizio's thoroughly natural desire, if she tried to relieve the unhappiness of that loving heart she knew so well, and whose tranquillity was so seriously impaired by her strange vow, what chance would there be of abducting the only son of one of the greatest noblemen in Italy without having the true facts eventually discovered? The Marquis Crescenzi would spend enormous sums of money and take charge of the investigations himself, and sooner or later the abduction would become known. There was only one way to guard against this danger: the child would have to be sent far away, to Edinburgh, for example, or to Paris; but a mother's heart could never accept such a solution. The second plan which Fabrizio proposed was more reasonable, but in the eyes of that distraught mother it had something ominous about it, and seemed almost more horrible than the first. There would be a feigned illness, said Fabrizio; the child would apparently grow worse and worse until he finally died, while the Marquis Crescenzi was absent.

Clelia's repugnance, bordering on terror, caused a breach between them which could not last.

She maintained that they must not tempt God, that their beloved son was already the fruit of a crime, and that if they stirred up the divine anger any further, God would surely take the boy back to Himself. Fabrizio spoke of his singular destiny: "My love, and the position which chance has given me," he said, "force me to live in perpetual solitude. Unlike most of my colleagues, I can't enjoy the pleasures of intimate company, since you'll receive me only in darkness, which means that the part of my life which I can spend with you is reduced, so to speak, to a few instants."

Many tears were shed. Clelia fell ill; but she loved Fabrizio too much to go on refusing the terrible sacrifice he was asking of her. In appearance, Sandrino became ill; the marquis quickly sent for the most celebrated physicians, and Clelia was from then on confronted by a terrible difficulty which she had not foreseen: she had to prevent her beloved son from taking any of the remedies prescribed by the physicians; this was no easy matter.

The child, kept in bed longer than was good for his health, became genuinely ill. How could she tell the doctor the cause of this illness? Torn between two conflicting interests, both immeasurably dear to her, she was on the verge of losing her reason. Should she consent to an apparent cure, and thus sacrifice everything to be gained from that long and painful dissimulation? As for Fabrizio, he could neither give up his plan nor forgive himself for the violence he was doing to Clelia's heart. He had found a way to be admitted into the sick child's presence every night, and this had brought on another complication. Clelia always came to take care of her son, and Fabrizio was sometimes forced to see her by candlelight. This seemed to her poor sick heart a horrible sin, and one that portended Sandrino's death. It was in vain that the most celebrated casuists, consulted on the question of obedience to a vow when its consequences would obviously be harmful, had replied that the vow could not be regarded as having been broken in a sinful manner if the person bound by it failed to keep it, not for the sake of some vain pleasure of the senses, but in order to avoid an obvious evil. Clelia's despair was as great as ever, and Fabrizio could foresee the time when his fantastic idea would bring on her death as well as their son's.

He resorted to his close friend Count Mosca, who, seasoned old minister though he was, was deeply moved by this story of love, most of which had been unknown to him.

"I can promise you that the marquis will be gone for at least five or six days; just tell me when you want his absence to begin."

Two days later, as the marquis was riding back from one of his estates near Mantua, a band of brigands, apparently

429

paid to carry out some private vengeance, captured him, without mistreating him in any way, and placed him in a boat which traveled down the Po for three days, making the same trip which Fabrizio had made long before, after his famous fight with Giletti. On the fourth day, the brigands deposited the marquis on a deserted island in the river, after taking care to rob him thoroughly, leaving him with neither money nor any belongings of the slightest value. It took him two whole days to make his way back to his palace in Parma; he found it draped in black, and everyone inside it was over-whelmed with grief.

The abduction had been cleverly carried out, but it had dire consequences. Sandrino, secretly installed in a large and beautiful house where Clelia came to see him every day, died at the end of a few months. Clelia felt that a just punishment had fallen on her for having been unfaithful to her vow to the Madonna: she had seen Fabrizio so often by candlelight, and twice even in broad daylight, and always with such tender rapture, during Sandrino's illness! She survived her beloved son by only a few months, but she had the sweet consolation of dying in her lover's arms.

Fabrizio was too much in love, and too religious, to resort to suicide; he hoped to meet Clelia again in a better world, but he was too intelligent not to feel that he had a great deal to atone for.

A few days after Clelia's death, he signed documents allot-ting a pension of a thousand lire to each of his servants, and reserved an equal pension for himself. He gave some estates yielding an income of about a hundred thousand lire to Countess Mosca, a similar sum to the Marquise del Dongo, his mother, and what was left of his patrimony to one of his sisters who had made a bad marriage. On the following day, after sending to the proper authorities his resignation from his archbishopric and all the posts that had been successively bestowed on him by the favor of Ernesto V and the friend-ship of the Prime Minister, he retired to the Charterhouse of Parma, which stands in a forest near the Po, two leagues from Sacca.

Countess Mosca had strongly approved, at the time, of her husband's return to the ministry, but she still refused ever to set foot in the dominions of Ernesto V. She held her court at Vignano, a quarter of a league from Casalmaggiore, on the left bank of the Po and therefore in Austrian territory. There, in the magnificent palace which the count had built for her, she received all the high society of Parma on Thursdays, and her numerous friends every day. Fabrizio would not have let a day go by without coming to Vignano. The countess, in a word, combined all the appearances of happiness, but she lived only a short time after Fabrizio, whom she still adored, and who spent only a year in his Charterhouse.

The prisons of Parma were empty, the count was enormously rich, and Ernesto V was worshiped by his subjects, who compared his rule to that of the Grand Dukes of Tuscany.

TO THE HAPPY FEW

In the first edition of the *Charterhouse*, Stendhal amused himself by inserting cryptic footnotes at the ends of Chapters 3, 22, 25 and 26. His "code" consisted of abbreviations of Spanish, English, French and possibly Italian words. I am indebted to the scholarship of M. Henri Martineau for the interpretations which follow.

L.B.

* * * *

End of Chapter 3: "Para v. P. y E. x. 38"

= *Para vosotras Paquita y Eugenia, 15 décembre 1838.*
(Paquita and Eugenia de Montijo were two Spanish girls whom Stendhal knew in Paris.)

End of Chapter 22: "Tr. J.F.M. 31."

Two interpretations have been suggested:

   1) *Trieste, janvier, février, mars, 1831.*
   2) *Troubles, janvier, février, mars, 1831.*

End of Chapter 25: "4. 9. 38. 26. x. 38 fir. s. 6. f. last 26 m. 39. 3 Ri d. f. g. p. ha. s. so. p."

First line = *4 novembre 38 − 26 décembre 38; first sheet 6 février, last 26 mars 39.*

(Stendhal wrote the *Charterhouse* between Nov. 4 and Dec. 26, 1838, and corrected the printer's proofs between Feb. 6 and March 26, 1839. This note corrects his own false assertion, in the Foreword, that he wrote the book in 1830.)
To my knowledge, the second line has not yet been satisfactorily interpreted.

End of Chapter 26: "P y E in Olo"

= *Paquita y Eugenia in Oloron.*

(By the time Stendhal was correcting the proofs of the *Charterhouse*, Paquita and Eugenia de Montijo had left Paris and were staying briefly in Oloron, in southern France, before returning to Spain.)

BIBLIOGRAPHICAL NOTES

Autobiographical volumes in English translation:

The Life of Henri Brulard. Translated by Catherine Alison Phillips. New York: Knopf, 1925.

Memoirs of Egotism. Translated by Matthew Josephson. New York: Lear, 1949.

Private Diaries of Stendhal. Translated by Robert Sage. New York: Doubleday, 1954.

Substantial works of a biographical and/or critical nature include:

Adams, Robert M. *Stendhal: Notes on a Novelist.* New York: Noonday, 1959.

Clewes, Howard S. *Stendhal: An Introduction to the Novelist.* New York: Roy, 1951.

Green, F. C. *Stendhal.* New York: Macmillan, 1939.

Josephson, Matthew. *Stendhal, or the Pursuit of Happiness.* New York: Doubleday, 1946.

Levin, Harry. *Toward Stendhal.* New York: New Directions, 1945.

Martineau, Henri. *L'oeuvre de Stendhal.* Paris: Le Divan, 1945.

—*Le couer de Stendhal.* 2 vols. A survey of current scholarship.

Brief studies are included in the following:

Howe, Irving. "Stendhal: The Politics of Survival," in *Politics and the Novel.* New York: Horizon, 1957.

Krutch, Joseph W. *Five Masters.* Bloomington: Indiana, 1959.

Strachey, Lytton. *Books and Characters.* New York: Harcourt, 1922.

Zweig, Stefan. *Adepts in Self-Portraiture.* New York: Viking, 1929.

The illustration on the cover of this Bantam Classic was painted in water color and gouache by Sanford Kossin.

BANTAM CLASSICS

are chosen from the whole span
of living literature. They
comprise a balanced selection
of the best novels, poems, plays
and stories by writers whose
works and thoughts have made an
indelible impact on Western culture.